praise for Blackstrap Hawco

A *Globe and Mail* BEST BOOK
LONGLISTED FOR THE SCOTIABANK GILLER PRIZE
A *Quill and Quire* BEST BOOK OF THE YEAR
AN AMAZON.CA TOP TEN BOOK OF 2008

"Easily the best book of the year and an instant classic. Harvey's complex and riveting narrative [is] reminiscent of Faulkner's masterpiece *Absalom, Absalom!*. . . . There's—thankfully—not a snippet of faux sentimentality here. Harvey's writing is uncompromisingly blunt, brutal and honest."
—*Ottawa Xpress*

"Reminiscent of James Joyce's *Ulysses*. . . . A highly original novel told in a style akin to an impressionist painting." —*The Canada Post* (UK)

"There are moments that are literally awe-inspiring and writing so skilled it almost brought me to tears. . . . More ambitious than any Canadian novel in recent memory." —*The Vancouver Sun*

"Mesmerizing scenes worthy of a national epic. . . . Its meticulous construction and control contain a breadth of incident and characterization seen only in the most ambitious and imposing novels." —*The Globe and Mail*

"The Canadian equivalent of Gabriel García Márquez's epochal *One Hundred Years of Solitude*." —*Calgary Herald*

"Epic and masterful." —*January Magazine*

"Harvey does for Newfoundland what Faulkner did for the South. . . . A great writer. . . . Dirt-under-the-fingernails details rest alongside grandly conceived allegory, and the result is often thrilling."
—*Edmonton Journal*

Kenneth J. Harvey

Blackstrap Hawco

said to be about a Newfoundland family

Vintage Canada

VINTAGE CANADA EDITION, 2009

Copyright © 2008 Island Horse Productions Limited

Published in Canada by Vintage Canada, a division of Random House of Canada
Limited, Toronto, in 2009. Originally published in hardcover in Canada by Random
House Canada, a division of Random House of Canada Limited, Toronto, in 2008,
and simultaneously in the UK by Harvill Secker,
a division of Random House Group Limited. Distributed by Random House
of Canada Limited, Toronto.

Vintage Canada and colophon are registered trademarks of Random House of
Canada Limited.

www.randomhouse.ca

This book is a work of fiction. Names, characters, places, and incidents either are
the product of the author's imagination or are used fictitiously. Any resemblance to
actual persons, living or dead, events, or locales is entirely coincidental.

Grateful acknowledgment is made for permission to reprint
excerpts from the following copyrighted works:
'If You Could Read My Mind' by Gordon Lightfoot © 1969,
renewed 1997 Early Morning Music. Used by permission.
'Aunt Martha's Sheep' by Ellis Coles and Dick Nolan
© 1970 Ellis Coles. Used by permission.

Library and Archives Canada Cataloguing in Publication

Harvey, Kenneth J. (Kenneth Joseph), 1969–
Blackstrap Hawco / Kenneth J. Harvey.

ISBN 978-0-679-31430-1

I. Title.
PS8565.A6785B53 2009   C813'.54   C2008-905502-0

Text Design by SX Composing DTP, Rayleigh, Essex

Printed and bound in the United States of America

2 4 6 8 9 7 5 3 1

FOR

Joanne and Jennifer

This is a transcomposite narrative,
not an historical document,
nor a work of invention.

Book One

1886-1992

I n 1953, my great-grandfather, Jacob Hawco, faced death on the trapline. He was only three miles from his home in Bareneed, a small fishing community that eventually was resettled by the government of Joseph Smallwood in 1962, and then repopulated some time later.

My great-grandfather would sell his pelts to the merchant store in Bareneed. It was owned by Bowering Brothers. Jacob had met his future wife, Emily Duncan, my great-grandmother, in that store. Emily's father, Alan, who had fled Liverpool, England, for reasons that will later be revealed, had come to Bareneed to take over the store in 1926.

The story (below) of Jacob's peril on the trapline was told to me by Andrew Tuttle, who I recently discovered was my cousin and who now resides in Boston.

The story of my grandfather's birth was written down for me and is printed almost exactly as written, besides editorial corrections and tone alterations, by Pamela Critch (née Murphy), the great-great-granddaughter of the midwife in attendance.

The sections throughout this book featuring Blackstrap Hawco were originally in Book Two (Blackstrap's story from 1971 to 2007) and were moved to Book One in order to give cohesion to the collected diaries, interviews and journal entries that make up Book One of this narrative.

1953

Bareneed, Newfoundland

Blackstrap Hawco's father, Jacob, meets with wilderness injury prior to Blackstrap's birth

The rabbit was cleanly frozen, its glassy eyes depthless, its white fur vaguely speckled against the purity of snow. Crouching beside the rabbit, Jacob Hawco did not remove his mitts. His fingers were damp with sweat and might stick to the snare wire. He knew of the restrictions placed on using picture wire to snare rabbits, but he believed the decree was made by people who knew nothing of living off the land, of survival through one's own efforts. Ignorant people who insisted that their misunderstandings be forced upon everyone else, no matter what the cost. *Who're da real barbarians?* Jacob asked himself. *People never knowing people at all.*

The winter air was piercingly fresh to such a degree that it stung his skin. Yet there was not a breath of wind. Beyond the grove of spruce, birch and larch, the sun blazed against a field of white. Jacob stared toward the clearing, his breath rising to cloud the brilliant aura. He watched toward the luminous white while he loosened the snare loop from the groove cut into the rabbit's fur and throat. The white appeared to be shifting within itself, throbbing as though something startling might take form. He stared back down at the rabbit that appeared whiter with the glare burned into his eyes. He watched it laid out in both his hands. For a moment, he thought on the lightness of it, then lifted

4

the flap of the burlap satchel hanging from his shoulder, and dropped the rabbit in.

Turning and standing at once, he sensed his right boot breaking loose from its snowshoe, snapping a worn strap that needed tending, his boot plunging through the snow, toward the incline of a hidden burrow. He grabbed for a tree, snatched to hold, his mitts slipping along the thin bald limb. Instantly – before the pain was delivered – he knew of the damage he had caused himself, heard the bone snap, felt it through his entire body, the blare of the crack within the rush of noise resulting from one misdirected step.

Buckling onto the snow, he was vaguely aware – through the searing, deafening pain – of a fox scurrying out from the hole his foot had sunk into.

Sweet adorable Christ h'almighty, sweet mudder a' Christ, Jaysus, Jaysus, Jaysus. He cursed the pain, cursed himself, cursed his own stupidity to hold up strength. Face flinching with the immediacy of injury, he became aware of his arms sunk in the deep snow; the biting crystal cold at his wrists. *No way a' make'n it t'roo da woods now. No way. Stunned. How bloody, Christly stunned.* He raised his head to stare along the snow path, the blazing sun beyond the trees. He pulled his hands up out of the snow, struggled to lean on his side, used both hands to yank his boot from the hole, prop himself up on an elbow. The worst of the pain tore through him.

The misery he experienced when he rolled over was of inhuman cruelty. The sweat poured from his brow and cheeks, had no time to dot the snow before it froze onto his skin in sparkling salt crystals, yet sopped the hair beneath his woollen cap. He reached for a resilient branch of a bush sticking up through the snow, gathered a fistful, and hauled himself to a sitting position.

From where he sat, he stared at his leg. The blood on the snow. Not a great deal of it, a spray of flecks, although it could be pouring down, deeper into the soft snow, staining the ice-hard earth beneath. The wetness already frozen, stiffening the fabric of his trousers. The jagged bone broken through the skin and showing itself where its tip cut through his pants. Such violent damage from a simple fall. He knew he could not stand, would not even attempt it. There was no walking this way. Not with the buckle broken on his snowshoe. One foot sunk deep in the snow with each painful step, the other cradled on the surface by the snowshoe. Never could he walk like that.

A rustle of movement caught his eye. It pained to move his head, for now every part of him appeared connected directly to his leg. Clumps of accumulated snow quietly fell from the boughs of a nearby evergreen. Jacob watched the fox, favouring one front paw, show itself, out from around the trees. It stood there, studying him, raising its snout, sniffing the air.

Jacob searched around. Nothing to help him. No way of walking. He lay on his back, endured the chaos of misery as he rolled over onto his stomach. He would have to drag himself along the trapline, hoping his damaged leg would not freeze. He must keep off the ground. Preserve his body's warmth. Edge up a tree as he came across it. Stand for a while. Try to get ahead like that. Yet, ultimately, he would have to crawl most of the way. He thought of a fire, of returning to the tilt he had built a mile back in the woods. Heat would sustain him. The other way. He must turn the other way. Not toward the brilliant clearing at the edge of the grove, but deeper into the still, wintry woods. There he would find warmth.

No one was expecting him at home for days.

He was on the trapline, his leg broken. It was a pitiful situation, yet one that might be mastered. He grabbed for a bush, and, grimacing, edged himself ahead a few inches. He wished that Emily had allowed Jacob Jr. to come along. The boy would find his way out and return with help, but Jacob did not really need help. No, it was strangely funny in itself. He chuckled despite the agony, his humour boring into the pain. He would figure it all out. *Narry a problem. Narry a care in da world. Nut'n but clear roads ahead. I's at me leisure.* Jacob Jr. was in school learning from books of no good use to him, education at the insistence of Junior's educated mother. The boy should be here, in the woods, learning the truth of nature's doing.

T'ink, Jacob told himself. *Forget da foolishness 'n t'ink.* Already his neck muscles were beginning to strain from holding his head up off the snow. He reached for another bush, just barely out of reach, lurched for it, grabbed hold, struggled to pull his body ahead another few inches. He knew how reason alone would prevent him from becoming empty like the rabbit in his bag.

How to beat the odds?

How to survive?

He tried making plans, as a means of smothering the pain, yet his mind shifted on its own, to centre on the fine tale that would be salvaged from this stroke of misfortune. A glorious yarn worth telling. Emily loved an adventure story, the way Jacob kept her captivated by its telling, the glint in her eyes when she glanced up from her needlepoint, awaiting the next word while he reeled out the yarns about catastrophe at sea and the overcoming of great peril. Icebergs snapping in half nearby and spilling chunks of ice onto the deck up on the Labrador. Huge slabs of ice, big enough to punch holes in the wood, beating down around them, the vibrations knocking every man off his feet. Or men dying of unknown maladies on board and shoved away in crates piled high with pickling salt. Having to pass by the crate every day during his ocean-bound duties while they carried on their voyage. Muttering a few words in passing. A blessing. No turning back when there was a living to be earned. Not even death able to waylay a fishing voyage. Emily's favourite tales told with a bit of difference each time. This would amount to one of them. But the story would be of use to no one, would add up to nothing if it died in his head.

Pain was no story at all. It was nothing but an exclamation point. It came at him and he shut his eyes. Pain with its own varying, flickering shades of pink, red and white behind his eyelids.

Gradually, with his body relaxing from the clutch of torment, he grunted in near relief and reached ahead for another bush, snatched a handful of tangled branches and dragged himself forward. Squinting in mortal agony, he imagined Emily's eyes on him and drove the pain from his expression. He considered the way he would deliver the tale, sitting around the kitchen lantern at night, the amber glow on his face, Emily's smiling intent eyes carefully peeking at him as he explained with words and gesture, his hands making it whole again. And Jacob Jr. there, too. The boy wanting him to repeat the part about the fox. The part about the bone snapping. The terrible sound it made. The part about the trail he dragged himself along with the smear of red after him. The crackle of the woodstove behind Emily and Jacob Jr. The full warmth of his home with the wind howling beyond the windowpane, hurling snow pellets against the glass. He would live to smile at that.

Cringing out a chuckle, he grabbed another bush, yanked at it to feel it come loose in his hand. The entire bush up from the snow. Roots and all. A spray of dirt sprinkled along the snow. Grains of earth on his lips. He spat them away and strained a glance back to see the trail of his own blood smeared in the snow, exactly as he imagined. He snatched for another bush, wound the clump of branches around his mitt, dragged his body forward over the recesses of his snowshoe prints, the trail that had led him to his stroke of hard luck, the trail that he now retraced.

His thoughts on the fleeing fox. Had it been injured by his foot's intrusion into its burrow? He cast a glance off to the right, saw it trotting along, sitting when Jacob paused to dam his eyes shut and grind his teeth against a wicked flurry of pain. Other concerns niggled him through the breathless sweat of injury's noise that he heard and tasted like metal in his mouth each time he shifted.

The fox favoured its front paw as it trotted closer on three, sniffing at Jacob.

He thought ahead, the traps set, the fox. Steel jaws snapping shut to penetrate the fox's leg. It whimpered like a beagle barred out, sticking close. An omen, Jacob decided. *T'ink*, he told himself. *Dis'll be easy. Jus' git da right end'n fer da story.*

Emily.

How he grabbed for the branch and it snapped off in his hand. No, how the bush came up by the roots, snow flying back at him like a slap in the face. No, how the branch whipped back and lashed his face and he was blinded for minutes, not fully regaining his sight until . . . He would explain how movement slowed down, how the fox scurried from its hole, running off like a mutt, yapping, as Jacob toppled over into the soft snow, his arms sinking deep, trying to rise but impossible, impossible . . . No, how he passed out with the unbearable suffering and woke with his body gone numb, the side of his face pressed to the snow as though it were dead, nothing but meat. *Dat's all we be, Junior. Nut'n but da worst sort o' ugly meat widt da blessed life spilled outta us.* Barely a breath of life left in him, thinking of a way, and how he knew that he must set the leg himself with two pieces of wood, cleaved from a tree with his axe, and wait for it to mend. *Cleaved it meself, Emily, frum a larch tree pointed t'ward da east.* Drag himself over the trapline, checking the snares and traps he had set, careful not to set them off himself, collecting carcasses along the way, filling his satchel or dragging the carcasses at his side, pulling himself along, pulling the carcasses along, inch by inch. Him and his prized pelts, back to the safety of his tilt. *'N dere dey be, b'ys, right dere in dat sack. Nut'n to it.*

A dusting of snow sprinkled before his face. Looking up, he saw a lone crow shifting on a snow-covered bough and – despite his flinching pain – could not help but grin at the perfection of its deathly presence.

Blackstrap's mother, Emily, recalls the night her family fled Liverpool

The *Caribou* and the *Cabot* sailed between the straits of Conception Bay, carrying men from the iron ore mines on Bell Isle, back the ten or twelve miles to their home towns along the ragged-cliffed Newfoundland coast. Carbonear, Harbour Grace, Spaniard's Bay, Port de Grave, Bareneed. Good money was to be made on Bell Isle; the booming town was full of mainlanders, Americans and Canadians, shipped in with the knowledge required to exploit the resources and maintain the mines.

The men of Newfoundland, labourers renowned for their steadfast determination and selfless resilience, were put to work underground in the red tunnels of pillars and caves that slanted so deep into the earth that when they eventually levelled off they extended three miles out beneath the Atlantic Ocean. Submarine mines, the locals called them, holding an image of the sea above them while they toiled to displace the red iron ore rock. The weight of the sea suspended over their heads by God only knew how much earth. In the dead silence of the cavernous earth, Newfoundlanders toiled as muckers, spraggers, face-cleaners or blasters, while others were employed in the company office as clerks, or offloaded dynamite boats tied up at the wharf. The operation itself was overseen by people whose pristine voices were barren of accent, and knew nothing of the rolling Newfoundland dialect that speedily jumbled all words together as one.

Beyond the pastures of Bareneed, white with snow and gently sloping or rising to the north, south, east and west, Emily Hawco had a view of the craggy, steep-edged back of Bell Isle from her kitchen window. And beyond the island, that appeared as though it had been snapped off a larger chunk of land and set afloat, across the tickle, was the bay community of Portugal Cove. A further fifteen miles east along a narrow dirt road sat the city of St. John's, built on land that rose steeply from the harbour.

On clear evenings, tiny lights were visible as a pretty cluster on Bell Isle, and sometimes, when the wind travelled toward her across the three miles of water between Bareneed and Bell Isle, Emily was able to hear the alarms that sounded on the island when the shifts changed or when a fire was discovered. In the daytime, during the months of fitter weather when she tended to her garden or worked on the shore salting fish, she could see the small fishing dories anchored on the water or at the edge of the horizon that brought each craft in and out of definition.

The small, square house – in the kitchen window of which Emily sat watching the ocean – had no fence, the horses, goats or cow roaming where they chose in the spring, summer and fall.

The house was built on a slate rock foundation, its inner wooden planks eighteen inches wide and one inch thick, the pine timber cut in a local mill and of the exact sort employed to build boats. Inside, layers of wallpaper covered the wooden walls. Outside, narrow clapboarding had been nailed in place and painted a mustard yellow. Atop it all, a hip roof rose on a shallow pitch on four sides to a common meeting point.

The fire in the kitchen stove burned hot. There was a flush in Emily's cheeks as she gazed out over the water, discerned the movement of a distant boat heading toward Bell Isle. One of the ferries, the *Caribou* by the looks of it, was bringing men to work the mines.

There came a sound from overhead in Jacob's Uncle Ace's room. Something had fallen to the floor. Uncle Ace rarely left his room, never speaking since returning from his final journey to the ice during the seal hunt over twenty years ago. He merely sat on the edge of his bed and watched the floor. Hands joined on his lap, he appeared lost to the world, his presence in the house amounting to practically nil.

Snow began to drift straight down; large wet flakes beyond the pane. At the sight of snow, Emily began to fret for Jacob. She worried that a blizzard might rise, as it was wont to do. Grey skies sweeping in and with it, the blistering thrust of snow. Jacob trapped in the woods. Not able to find his way out. Freezing to death. It was the same inexplicable feeling she had experienced on occasions in the past when Jacob had been away, a peculiar sensation that her husband was not well, the feeling centred in her belly, seemingly in the baby that she carried and was due in another month. For the past three nights, she had been visited by dreams of Jacob talking to dead animals, holding them in his hands, stroking them and whispering in their ears as though to calm them and lull them back to life. She dreamed of an orb within her belly, floating in circles, made of something like glass but bendable, and Jacob centred there, slowly being covered in white. But she would not utter such thoughts to others in the community for fear of jinxing her husband.

Taking her hand from her cup of tea, she straightened her blue plaid bandanna atop her long, wavy black hair, then smoothed her apron over her pregnant belly just as a hard, tiny limb impressed itself beneath the fabric. An elbow or a foot. The baby shifting. It never ceased turning and kicking. This one wasn't like Jacob Junior at all, who had stayed inside her long after her due date. This one wanted out into the world.

Emily wondered if the baby might be a boy or girl. Another son, or a daughter? Ruminating on family, an image of her mother was brought to mind. When she thought of her mother, she pictured herself as a child. There was no other way of seeing it. Mentally skimming through her younger years, she became enthralled by the notion of how her privileged upbringing had come to an abrupt end and how different the lives of her children would be from hers.

Emily studied the floral spray design of her china cup. It held a similar pattern to the china used on her first journey by steamer, across the Atlantic. Liverpool to St. John's on the S.S. *Newfoundland*. She considered the side of the cup, thinking further back to that first night she had ever been up and out in the world so late, the stillness of the air and the bustle upon the docks back in Liverpool. The nostalgic pang for the city that she had not seen since childhood. A place that had taken on, through her clear and naive recollections, the qualities of a magical location that she had dreamed of for years after leaving.

She remembered shivering for the chill and for the powerful look of fear on her father's face. An image that time had been reluctant to purge from her memory. She and her mother waiting at the foot of the plank leading to the S.S. *Newfoundland* while her father spoke with two men in grey hats and dark overcoats, their voices growing sterner, rising toward argument. The men had tried to snatch hold of her father's arm, but he had pulled it free and backed away, raising his hands to them and motioning toward his family standing in wait, motioning specifically to Emily, it seemed.

'What's the matter?' Emily had asked.

'I don't know,' her mother had tersely responded, holding her fur collar against her throat, tightening her gloved grip on Emily's hand. A whiff of calf leather.

Her father's hat had been knocked away and he bent to pick it up, his eyes still fixed on the men, his overcoat falling open. One of the men made a move for him, but the other man held him back, seizing hold of his friend's arm.

Her father had backed off then, backed away until he was close to his wife and child. The two men remained where they were, watching with their hands in the pockets of their overcoats. One of the men snickered. The other made a motion at Emily, pointed his black-gloved finger at her face and cocked back his thumb. She had seen his cheeks round out and his lips pop open with a sound.

Her father had quickly returned to his wife and Emily, his breath hard. Sweat was sheening on his face in the dull spill from the on-deck lights above them, his eyes alert, darting toward the steamer.

'Onto the boat,' he said, practically shoving them ahead.

'Are they the police, Alan?' her mother had hurriedly enquired.

'No. Come on.' He made no motion to check back over his shoulder, yet Emily turned to see the two men in the long black overcoats and grey hats standing there, not moving, only following the family's climb up the plank with their steady eyes. One man had his hands in his pockets, the other had his readied at his sides.

'They know where we're going,' her mother gasped. 'Alan?'

'They were involved. They won't breathe a word.'

Years later, in Newfoundland, Emily's father would often make comments about the men who were watching them, the men who he claimed he was on the lookout for when he parked across the street on her tenth birthday, anticipating the men's arrival, and refusing to join the party. Emily had heard him pleading with her mother about the men who might come. He had to be on his toes, he insisted, vigilant. He had to make certain. For Emily's eleventh and twelfth birthdays, he stayed out of the house, as well. At first, Emily would go to the window, wishing him to come in, but eventually she accepted his behaviour as one of the many eccentricities that made him who he was. And then, one night before her thirteenth birthday, in a fit of panic after moving from St. John's to Bareneed to manage a merchant's affairs, Emily's father barred the door to their house and would not permit a single one of them to leave. They had remained inside for two days. 'Don't eat the food,' he warned, refusing to touch it. He had sniffed at the water, carefully tasting drops from his fingertip.

On the third day of their seclusion, Emily heard her mother giving instructions to the servant girl to send a telegram, while her father was tending to the fire in the sitting room, poking at the logs and shouting out names she did not recognize, threatening these names in a terrifying manner. Georgie and Willy. She remembered because the names reminded her of cartoon characters. Georgie and Willy, and what she would learn of them so many years later.

The warm smell of baking bread drew Emily back to the house in Bareneed, and soon touched Jacob Junior who raced down over the half-mile of sloping hill from where the small schoolhouse was positioned beside the church. Emily did not see him coming. She was watching toward the water, always staring toward the water. The water was the domain of men. The earth, the hold of women. Despite the memories of her childhood in England and then St. John's, and the emotions they summoned, she believed that she belonged in Bareneed, belonged in that house, on that piece of land with that varying, yet ultimately unchanging, view of the sea. She was not from there, but she would not feel at peace anywhere else other than in that house. This was her heart place.

Even though Jacob was on the trapline and not in his boat, Emily still took solace in the calming immensity of the ocean. Such a different life from her own early childhood, one she remembered with an aching she had no mind to return to, her mother gone now, a tender woman whose tenderness was needled until tragedy removed her, her father still living in the asylum, not knowing his name or having any idea of who he was, muttering the names of those in a faraway country. He refused to know her, no matter how many reassuring words she spoke in his presence. Denied it, going so far as to turn his face away when she stood before his eyes.

Emily believed her father was better off removed from his own mind as he was. She did not feel well thinking such bitter thoughts, understanding that those thoughts were more her mother's than her own, and that Emily must still love her father in some way, for there were special memories as well, delightful memories, yet she felt she would turn against herself, against her mother, if she admitted to this love of her father. A man who forbade her marriage to Jacob. *A man beneath you*, he had said from his room in the asylum, his eyes watching away. In a time when her father still knew who Emily was, although there were moments when he mistook her for her mother, dead many years by that time. *A man so far beneath you, Amanda.*

Watching the ocean, Emily felt the wintry lull of the water. She stood from the table, stepped close to the yellow enamel stove with its two higher warming compartments. Their silver handles required polishing. She would tend to it on Saturday night.

My own clean life now, she told herself, bending down to open the door a crack, her pregnant belly restricting her breath, so she was forced to breathe through her opened mouth. Jacob nothing like her father, thank God.

The bread was golden on top, moving toward a light shade of brown. A few more minutes.

Jacob's mother, Catherine, had taught Emily the traditional ways of baking, passed on a store of family recipes, and Emily was proud for having duplicated the process with such proficiency, for twinning the tastes she could make with those that Jacob recalled from his youth.

When Emily was a child, back in St. John's, before their ill-fated move to Bareneed, their servant girl, Jackie, would perform this chore, kneading the dough and then leaving it to rise in an enamel pan. Jackie would then pour Emily a glass of milk from the milk jug, the radio scratching out the tune 'Ain't She Sweet' and Jackie revealing the black pegs of her teeth to the young mistress of the house, the only one that Jackie would smile for, would share that intimacy with. And as Jackie went about her duties, Emily always felt, as did her mother, that such tasks should be carried out by oneself. Her mother had always been troubled by the notion of servants, of one person serving another. Even though it was a common occupation – one needed a number of servants to proficiently manage the stately Victorian houses of St. John's – she still could not help but feel that servant girls were being taken advantage of.

Her mother had stated her concern to her father, telling him that she pitied poor Jackie because of her predicament. She could imagine the horrible life she must be leading, with a fatherless child and a dearth of basic necessities in her life. But Jackie had seemed quite content following the birth of the child, seeming to soften in speech and action, to become even more caring, until the sickness plagued her.

'Imagine yourself in the shoes of that poor girl,' Emily's mother had commanded of her father. 'Use your imagination, for God's sake, Alan. Use your imagination!'

'Call it imagination, Amanda,' Alan had hastily replied, 'if you will, or merely the foolish thoughts of a wandering, unoccupied mind.'

Seated in her tapestry-covered high-back chair, her mother had been struck by silence, her eyes plainly displaying the wound. Her imagination, as always, attacked as an inept by-product of inactivity, of sloth, something that happens when other, more busy or eventful preoccupations did not trouble a person. It was one of the times Emily had hoped that her mother would reply angrily, would defend herself with as much vigour as required, shout, scream, if need be, but she had remained silent, accepting the decree, knowing then, it seemed, from that point forward that her husband was nothing like the man she had imagined.

Emily carefully shut the oven door and straightened, hearing the brisk excited sounds of Jacob Junior panting and kicking off his boots in the back porch.

The boy was beside her in an instant, looking up at his mother with a wide smile and holding a damp paper in both his hands.

'I got an A,' he said, beaming.

'That's wonderful, sweetheart. Come here and give me a kiss.' She bent as low as possible, again her breathing cut short by the pressure of the baby, and gave him a warm hug. 'I'm so proud of you, Junior.'

Stepping back, Junior glanced at his mother's belly – a constant source of intrigue for him – then turned, pulled his arms out of the worn sleeves of his coat and straightened them over the back of a chair. 'The teacher says I'm one of the best in class.'

'Wait till your father hears.'

'How many days now?'

Emily rested one hand on her belly, rubbed gently, almost without notice. 'Three or four more days,' she replied, trying to keep the worry from her tone. Turning, she bent to check on the bread. 'He'll be back before you know it.'

'I can't wait to tell him.' Junior yanked out a chair and sat at the table, anticipating the feast of what would soon be ready. Warm bread with melted butter and molasses. 'Hope he gets lots of fur.'

'You want the crust?'

Junior nodded hungrily. 'Yes, please.'

Emily smiled at her son's sweet manners, the proper quality of his speech, the way her son had taken after her in that respect. Mannerly. Refined. She felt another kick, of admonishment, she suspected, and was stilled by it, paused to place a hand on her belly.

'Is he kicking?'

'Yes.'

'Can I feel?' Junior was up out of his chair and had his hand on her belly in a flash. He kept his hand in place, his expression fixed as though he were listening. 'Cripes! I felt that.' His face beaming.

'Me, too.' She laid a hand on Junior's head, then turned away. 'Lots of butter and molasses?'

Junior nodded and licked his lips. 'Lord, I'm half starved, sure,' he said, impersonating his father.

Emily's smile widened, turned warmer. She had to look at him, to glance over his face, the reassuring presence of Jacob in him. 'The heat's stifling in here.'

'It's freezing out though.'

'I was listening to the radio.' Emily used her pot holder to open the door. The heat rushed against her face and she leaned back a moment before lifting out the bread pans, one at a time, setting them on the counter and smearing butter on top of the buns with a piece of wax paper. 'They had the names of some men back from Korea. Your friend Paddy's father was one of them . . .' Hesitating, she stumbled over an image of Paddy's father, Douglas, both legs gone. The community was talking about him in a hushed way, not himself anymore, not nearly himself since he came back from the fighting.

'Paddy's dad lost his legs,' Junior said outright. 'I saw him on the daybed in Paddy's house, lying there staring at the wall. White as a ghost, he was.'

'He's been through something horrible,' Emily informed Junior, her thoughts flashing through violent images of war, black and white pictures of cannons being fired, flares in darkness. The horror leading to what she had heard on the radio, news of atomic weapons, President Eisenhower warning that civilization was in jeopardy. By the sound of his voice, he truly meant it. The Big Three meeting so far away, but affecting the entire world right now. She would not explain any of that to her son. The threat of the entire world being blown to bits at the whim of a few men. Emily steadied herself, bracing her hands against the counter. She shut her eyes tightly, her thoughts on the baby. She breathed, drew her nerves to a calm, then straightened and turned.

'Junior?' She saw that he was staring at his paper on the table. He tried smoothing out his test, palms pressing to stretch each wrinkle, before he stood, lifted the paper and laid it neatly on the daybed across from the stove where his father liked to take a lie down after a good feed of salt beef and cabbage.

The sunlight spread low against the ground, steeping the woods in dim orange. Soon, it would be dark. A crow sounded high in a tree and Jacob Hawco listened as it lifted off, rustled a branch, then swept away, knocking a clump of snow down through the layered splay of branches. A soft sound as it landed atop the blanket of snow. The fire was warm enough. He gazed out at it through the opening of his spruce bough lean-to, saw the fox sleeping curled up beside the crackling flames, a strange sight that he now accepted as part of his predicament; the fox was there for a reason Jacob had not yet decided on.

He would not sleep much that night, waking every half-hour to the wind roaring beyond and above the trees where he was nestled, the wind swinging the carcasses back and forth where they were hung in the trees around him. They should have been hung further away from his lean-to, so as not to draw predators, but the damage done to his leg prevented him from keeping the carcasses at a distance. He needed them near him, to gather them with ease when the time to leave was upon him. Against his better judgement, he had even taken a few into the lean-to with him. Two white lynx with their grinning dead jaws. A pair of lovely pillows.

'Ye shud get out 'n see da world, b'y,' Jacob told the lynx. 'Quit fart'n 'round 'n try ta make a go of it.'

That night, he would wake to monitor the flames, ebbing and crackling. He would slide forward across the snow with a handful of dead branches that had been drying just out of reach of the flames.

Keep the fire going.

Nothing else of any value should the fire die. His right leg was stiff within the wooden splints he had skimmed down from a tree trunk with his axe. The tied cord had held as expected. He was not so damp now on his bed of evergreen boughs, not minding the wet that much. But he was unsteady despite the oaths he held up inside himself, uncertain if his flesh was freezing. His senses, resolutely under his command in fitter times, now confounded him.

Once he ate one of his tins of cold Irish stew, he felt noticeably better, less haggard and irritable. He wished for a cup of tea, but feared setting his small kettle in the fire. It might disturb the flames. Smother his confidence.

The first immobile day. It would take two more days without tea before he might decide that the fire was sturdy enough to accommodate the presence of metal. It was not safe, but soon it might become so.

I's get'n better, he insisted into the coldness, healing into stiffness, the orange sunlight beyond and through the trees deepening. Shadows pulling themselves across the snow like creatures dragging darkness along, spreading it before his eyes. The night was no less bothersome to him than the day. He was just meant to be more alert, for if something was lurking near, waiting to come for him and his carcasses, it would show itself in darkness, would snatch everything up in its jaws: Jacob, the carcasses and, even, the living fox. It would snatch even the omen up in its jaws and gallop away into a hole of its own making.

Jacob guffawed, chiding himself for pondering such dreary slop. Bleak thoughts laboured to make a man puny.

A rustle of movement ahead. The fox had awoken with a start, its sharp-featured head lifting to gaze directly at Jacob. It stared with glassy eyes for a moment as though deciding on something, before its jaws slowly opened, wider and wider as it yawned. Jacob tossed it the tin of Irish stew. The fox inclined its head forward to sniff at the tin, yet would not bother to nudge the scraps out of it, seeming in need of nothing, as it settled back, curled itself up and returned to sleep atop the freezing-cold snow.

From the darkening trees surrounding Jacob's wilderness den came the sound of a trap going off. Dead silence after that. The fox, with one eye open.

Isaac Tuttle, the coal merchant, witnesses Emily Hawco with adoration and humility

Isaac Tuttle delivered coal down into Bareneed once a month. He carried the coal on a horse-drawn cart and shovelled it into the bins or hatches of the houses in need. He first laboured at the top of the hill and worked his way lower into the pasture, filling orders along the way until he reached the last houses perched nearer the jagged cliffs. Payment was small and often – with the poorer families – non-existent. Regardless, Isaac kept a record of what he was owed, stating that one day, if the Lord be willing, the tides would turn and the people would make good on their debts.

''ard times, me friend,' he told the poor man or woman, trying to alleviate a bit of their hardship with a touch of cheer, trying not to make them feel small when they were already down on their luck. 'When t'ings pick up now, good buddy, ye c'n pay me wha'ch'ya owes. None ta worry udderwise.' Isaac Tuttle knew that there was little chance of the stricken making good on their debts, yet he had faith in the mercy of the Lord and prayed for better times for those unfortunate folk.

A number of the families still had debts written up in Isaac's father's book and his father had been dead going on ten years. The payment that he received from those with money was adequate to turn a profit, plus he ran the store in Cutland Junction, right next to the new railway station, and that was enough to make ends meet. It brought in the money needed to buy up the land all around the Junction and resell it to the businessmen townies coming out from St. John's in their chubby-looking, expensive cars to build their trouting cabins.

Emily heard the wheels of the cart creaking over the frozen earth. There had not been much snow and the cart made it easily down the path on its hard wheels. She heard the familiar snort of the horse, and was touched by shame and regret.

While placing the bread in the bread box, a tapping came at the back porch door, and Emily was given no time to steady herself before Isaac Tuttle stepped in, not waiting for a reply.

She considered ignoring him, yet thought that the height of ignorance. 'How you doing, Isaac?' she called in a level tone, trying to pretend her bad feelings away.

Isaac Tuttle banged the snow from his boots, then opened the kitchen door, humbly stuck his head in, took a peek at her, then immediately shifted his attention to the floor.

'Mighty fine 'eat 'n 'ere, me love,' he took an instant to say.

Emily waited for what she knew would come next.

20

'I'm 'ere widt da coal.'

'Yes, I know, Isaac.'

Isaac Tuttle nodded and squinted, his thick black eyebrows scrunching together. He nodded again. Glanced at her belly, glanced at the floor. ''Ere t'is. No need ta worry now.' He chuckled in a fit of nerves. 'Ye be warm fer da season.'

With her eyes not on him, Emily said out of habit or obligation: 'A cup of tea?'

'A cup 'a tea.' Isaac grinned at once, uncovering the brown stubs of his teeth. 'Yes, me duckie.' He pulled off his coal-smeared mittens, shirking off any feelings of unease that might have been lingering in the room. 'Dat'd be reet fine.'

'Don't mind your boots,' Emily said shortly. 'I'll be washing up the floor this afternoon.'

'No, now, I c'nt 'av dat.' He bent and tugged at the smutty laces, worked them loose, and pried off his boots. Standing in his floppy woollen socks, Isaac nodded obediently, watching Emily pump water into the kettle. He neatly laid his mittens on the oilcloth covering the kitchen table and took off his beaked salt and pepper cap, moving it around with his fingers.

'Skipper on da trapline?'

'Yes. The trapline.'

'Yays,' he said with an intake of breath, his eyes drawn, again and again, to her distended belly. 'I s'pected as much.'

Emily lifted off the stove's top damper and stoked the fire with the iron poker, then replaced the damper and slid the kettle into place. When she turned toward the table, she noticed that Isaac was blushing, her eyes having met his gaze of utter devotion. He shot a look toward the floor, moving his cap around in his hands, not yet having uncoiled the dirty grey scarf from his throat.

'Where Junior be at?'

The blush now spread across Emily's cheeks. 'He's doing his homework. Sit down, Isaac.' She motioned formally toward the chair.

'Yays.' He looked where she had pointed and inched uncertainly ahead, pulled out the chair, began to sit but then abruptly stood, waited for her to sit first, nodding nervously when she edged her chair out from the table and took a seat. Only then did Isaac quietly take his place across from her.

'Anudder young'n on da way.' He smiled and blushed a deeper red, nodded and peeked at her sideways before squinting fiercely, his big, vein-streaked nose twitching. A few moments later, he realized the comment had been a mistake. 'I seen Junior up on da hill, play'n widt da udder fellas. Young Paddy. 'Is fodder's 'ome frum d'war, ye knows all 'bout dat, I s'pose? Not a leg on 'im, da poor feller.'

'Yes, I know.'

'Both legs blown clear off. Not a leg ta call 'is own.' He held up two fingers, tutted and shook his head hard in bleak acknowledgement. 'Mighty shock'n stuff.' He stared at Emily's belly and winked, nodded nervously and grinned, 'God's bless'n.'

'Yes. God bless him.'

'Finest kind.' Isaac tipped his head, then stared at the ledge of the window beside him. He lifted his cap from where he was holding it under the table and laid it next to his mitts, arranging them carefully beside each other. When he stole a glance at Emily, he saw that she was gazing through the window, her face in profile, her pregnant beauty mesmerizing. It was only after she looked at him that he realized he had made a sound, that he had sighed or whimpered in wanting.

Emily watched him. It was a lovely look at first, but then her eyes, tracing the features of his impish face, filled with something grim, as though she might accuse him of some unfortunate deed.

Bowing his head, Isaac watched his grimy hands, the lines in his skin, the blackness arced beneath his fingernails. He gave a flinching shake of his head and tried scooping the black out from under one fingernail with another. Yet nothing could be removed as the black was more of a permanent stain.

'What, Isaac?'

He regarded her and his eyes were glazed with tears. Such beauty, he thought, bowing his head again, trying to scoop the dirt out. Thy neighbour's wife. Such treasure and beauty.

'Is something the matter?' she asked, knowing better, knowing full well, demanding this of him. No more than a child really. Is that why she had taken him in? Had allowed him. She stood to escape the thoughts that sent her plummeting back to a play of shadows in Liverpool.

'Naw sure.' He grinned at her, sniffing, and wiped his cheeks with the back of his hand, smearing the black. 'Dun't be so foolish. Dere's nut'n da matter. I were jus' delivering—'

'I *was* just delivering, Isaac. Was, not were.' Emily glanced at the kettle which had commenced steaming. She struggled to stand and Isaac leapt to his feet to help her, taking her hand and drawing her up with such a brisk and forceful pull that she was catapulted perfectly upright and had to catch her balance.

'Woo,' she said, steadying herself, gazing down at her feet. She then looked at Isaac to see that his eyes were on her hand, on the hand he had gripped. The black print of his fingers on her white skin.

There came a sound from overhead, something small hitting the bare floor, a pencil perhaps, dropping and rolling a little, and they both watched there.

'Junior,' Emily said, thinking, *He's always up there with Uncle Ace.*

'Yays.' Isaac gathered his hat and mitts, and squeezed them in his hands. Again, he grinned. 'I were delivering da coal . . . Best get ta it.'

'You're not staying for tea?' she chastised him.

Isaac shook his head, his expression sinking with remorse yet struggling to remain optimistic. 'Deliv'ries. C'nt 'av no un doin' widout.' He nodded resolutely. 'C'nt bear da t'ought 'o dat, 'specially da yungin's.' His eyes scrunched with a sheepish expression as though he might have admitted to something too delicate for words. He laughed to make it go away.

'You're sweet, Isaac,' she said mournfully. And she touched his cheek with the back of her smudged fingers, transferring the mark. First checking over her shoulder, she then faced Isaac again, leaning to kiss him on the lips. 'You're sweet,' a slow whisper.

Spirits restored, Isaac grinned, despite the tone in which the compliment was spoken. Again, he laughed, this time wetly, having to wipe at his chin for he had burst forth with joy. He nodded three times, a brisk succession stiff with formality. He barely raised his eyes to her, and uttered not another word before he left.

The weekend was filled with activity for Junior. Bazzing marbles with Paddy Murphy and Bren Coveyduck on the damp floor of Bren's barn, their fingers almost numb with the cold, the quartered meat from the recently slaughtered cow hanging above them, the smell of it only vaguely noticeable in the chilly air. He'd won two new unchipped whoppers. Skating down on the pond with Bren, barrel staves tied to their boots for blades, they'd shot an ice puck back and forth with the curved tree limbs they used for hockey sticks, the puck shrinking smaller and smaller until there was nothing left of it and they fell into argument about what bit of snow was actually in play. Trading comic books with Wince Drover, the fat man who worked in the general store and, subsequently, had access to all the comic books Junior wanted. And watching the parlour window be taken out of the Critch house. Junior had stood there with Paddy and Bren as the window trim was removed, piece by piece, and laid aside. Then the large window box had been edged out and carefully set down on the ground. Junior knew what was coming next. Waiting in silence by the Critch fence, he and the other boys had turned to stare up the lane, hearing the distant jangle of bells as they caught sight of the black, horse-drawn carriage with the coffin on board. Mister Myrden up front in black, reins in hand, not looking anywhere but straight ahead. Mist blasted from the horse's nostrils as it trod near. Silver bells jangled louder. The creak of the wheels over the hard earth sounded like death itself, impressing its trail toward them. The horse grew larger, towering over the boys, as it came to a halt a few feet before their frozen faces. Mister Myrden on the driver's bench watching them with numb interest.

Three of Old Missus Critch's sons had unloaded the coffin and fit it in through the hole in the house where two other men from Bareneed received it. One son had made a comment and another son had laughed, which made something shrink inside Junior. Then the sons had raised the parlour window and nudged it back into the hole, carefully realigned the window trimmings and nailed them in place, as though nothing had ever been opened up in that house.

Old Missus Critch had passed away. To Jacob Junior it seemed as if she had been old, sick, and dying for most of her life, yet she had often managed to call to him from her doorstep and, with trembling hand, offer him a peppermint knob from a dish, dipping her chin and grinning at the clump of pink and white that needed to be pried apart. "Av anudder,' she'd say. 'One fer yer mowt 'n one fer yer pocket.'

Dead old woman in a box. Gone. That's where she went when it was over, in a box, then into the ground. There would be a service, and all the children would have to go. No more peppermint knobs. No more porcelain dolls laid out on her doorstep to please and entice the Bareneed girls. Say a prayer for the soul of Old Missus Critch. Now, she's gone, the horrible witch. He'd imagined a girl skipping and singing that song.

It was Sunday after supper when Junior was in his room with his book of animals. He was thinking about the box and Old Missus Critch, the remembered taste of peppermint knobs in his mouth, while he tried reading about what a moose ate. He had just shifted his eyes over to the picture of a red fox when he heard his mother's cry. A startling sound he had never heard before. It was as though she were surprised and afraid at once, but slightly excited too. The moment after the sound, his mother called out to him. 'Junior.'

He was already on his feet and moving toward her room where she was standing by the bed staring down at the floor. A huge spill of water was darkly spread out over the wood. Junior looked to the jug on his mother's washstand. It was upright.

'Go get Missus Murphy.' Her voice was cut with concern. 'The baby.'

Junior did not know if he should be scared, but he was. Something was the matter with his mother, something like sudden sickness. At first, he hesitated, thinking that he or Uncle Ace might be able to help. He thought of his uncle, but knew that he hadn't been in the house for ages. Where is Uncle Ace? he now wondered. Where has he gone?

'Go,' said his mother, sweeping her long black hair back out of her face and looking at him, her forehead wrinkling. 'Hurry.'

He ran down over the stairs, his palm skimming the banister rail, took a turn and headed to the kitchen at the back of the house. In the back porch, he pulled on his boots but forgot his coat as he bolted out into the winter, the lash of the wind stinging his cheeks and hands, the snow gusting into his hair and caking there as he ran uphill toward the Murphy house. Looking back, already out of breath, he saw that he had not shut the door, light spilling out onto the snow, and spreading, then retracting as the door was violently pulled shut by the wind.

He passed the Critch house and saw the lamp on in the parlour, shadows moving behind there. Black and stretching tall and wide. Old Missus Critch rising up out of her box to chase after him through the blinding snow, wanting to tell him something the way she had always seemed to want to, after she gave him the peppermint knobs, her eyes watching his face in a sad strange way that spooked him. Even worse now that she was dead and after him, rising up from her sleep, the dish of peppermint knobs rattling in her hand as she bound across the snow to chew on his ankles.

He was clear of the Critch house, then passed the Coveyducks', a lamp burning in the kitchen window at the back, the stream of smoke pouring from the chimney bent and swept along by the hardness of the wind.

When he arrived at the Murphy house, he was completely out of breath and banging on the door in such a fit that Missus Murphy, Paddy's grandmother, not Paddy's mother, for Paddy's mother had perished in childbirth, answered with a look of alarm on her wrinkled face that might have been the exact face of Missus Critch in the dim light.

Stumbling back, Junior tried to speak, but could not squeak a word out. He struggled to swallow. 'It's Mom. Something the matter.' He glanced back over his shoulder, fearing for his mother's safety and dreading the claw-handed grasp of Old Missus Critch.

'Da baby?'

He shrugged. 'Don't know.'

'Run on 'ome ta be widt 'er. I'll be along da once.'

Junior turned and raced back down over the hill, into the pelting crystals, stumbling in the snow and falling, his hands sinking deep, the stinging frost at his wrists. He gazed up and over. The Critch house. Shadows in the lamplight. He looked back to see Old Missus Critch coming through the dusk in her shawl, a black bag in hand, not a dish of peppermint knobs. She was calling his name, screeching it out like a banshee. No, it was not the voice of the dead, but the howl of the wind. The black bag. Missus Murphy. He knew by the black bag, the one that babies were delivered in. The shawl blowing and rising as Missus Murphy braced herself against a blast of wind that blew her a little off course, bringing her arms out like feathery black wings for balance.

Junior pushed himself up and ran ahead, gasping, his heart hammering. He kept glancing back and was soon in the warmth of his house, his boots still on. 'Mom?'

A noise of pain sounded from upstairs.

Junior took the stairs two at a time, passing Uncle Ace somewhere along the way, the old man stood there as though watching toward the distance, his hair uncombed, his mouth crusted at the corners, his eyes like two entirely forgotten things. Junior charged into his parents' room to see his mother seated on the edge of the bed. The beating in his chest filled every inch of his body. The snow had already begun melting from his hair and was running down the back of his neck, the sensation making him flinch. He checked over his shoulder, fearing cold fingers upon him. Sweat and snow mingling as one. His mother's hands were now on her belly, her face seized with pain until the pain seemed to stop and her desperate, seeking eyes were questioning him.

'Where's Missus Murphy?' she asked, one hand reaching back on the bed as she began to lay down.

'She's coming,' he said to the sound of the back door banging shut downstairs.

Missus Murphy took her time rising up the stairs. Junior leaned over the banister and saw her, still covered in snow, lifting her legs one at a time and grunting, 'Me ol' knees're miserable dis eve.' Soon, she was there by his side. She brushed herself off and, with black bag in hand, a bag that seemed too small to hold a baby, she crossed into the room and shut the door.

Junior stood there, staring at the barred door, hearing the low calming words from Missus Murphy, hearing his mother's whimpers. He bent his head forward and shook the snow from his hair.

Soon, the door was yanked open, the fastness of the action urging Junior back a step.

'Dere's a kettle o' water on da stove. Bring 'er 'ere.' The door shut again. The monstrous, unbelievable sound of cloth being torn to shreds.

Junior raced downstairs to find the steaming kettle on the stove, snatched hold of its hot handle and carried it despite the pain burning into his palms, his legs stepping awkwardly as he lugged it ahead of himself up the stairs.

Outside his mother's door, he laid down the kettle, knocked and backed away. Again, the door was hauled open. Missus Murphy looked down at once, not even casting her eyes at Junior until she grabbed the kettle in hand and said: 'G'wan now,' tilting her head toward his bedroom at the back of the house. She then turned.

The door banged shut.

Junior looked at his palms, the red imprints of the kettle handle. There was not much to the pain now, but he felt it might get worse.

He remained on his feet, his shoulder against the wall. He waited, trying to hear beyond the door, but there was not much to be heard, only the occasional soothing comment from Missus Murphy, punctuated by the thrashing of snow against the house. This went on for quite some time. Junior felt himself slipping. Catching himself, he wondered if he might have been asleep. The house rocking with the punch of the winter wind. Dozing again, he saw Uncle Ace's smiling face and awoke with a start, stopping himself from sliding backwards.

A scream flinched his eyes to the door, a short scream, then a grunt and a whimpering. Wind pounded the walls and boomed in the floorboards. Soon, there was pleading and shouting, his mother in pain and need. He wondered what Missus Murphy was doing to her, what sort of torture.

'No, no, no,' from his mother. 'Ooohhhhh!'

'Now,' shouted Missus Murphy. 'Push da little bugger out.'

There was more screaming, almost savage, as the winter gale shoved harder, striking and striking . . .

Junior swiped tears from his eyes. He went nearer to the door, then backed away when another scream rose throughout the house, smothered by a rumble like thunder. He sobbed through his open mouth, not knowing what to do, his vision blurred with tears. His hand went out for the doorknob, then shot up to cover his ear.

'Mom?'

'Heave it outta ye, Maid. Heave it.'

There was much screeching and grunting as though his mother was being overtaken by something wicked, or was at war with Missus Murphy. The sounds continued for a long time, until Junior, weakened by his helplessness, slid down against the wall. Seated on the hallway runner, enduring the torment, he put his head on his knees and tried to block the sounds of human agony mingling with the throes of violent weather.

Then, his mother gone quiet.

Only words spoken in the distance. Barely heard words muttered from downstairs it seemed, but from who, from the lips of Uncle Ace?

He listened carefully, searching into the silence, a span of time that set him adrift within himself. He stood and pressed his ear to the door.

'Yays,' said Missus Murphy. 'Yays, tis a beauteous ball o' fluff.'

'Mom?' Junior lightly scratched at the door with his fingernails.

Not a sound from his mother now.

'MOM?'

'T'is just ta get da rest outta ye now.'

The sound of Missus Murphy talking to his mother calmed him, and he stood in silence for some time.

Finally, the door was flung open and Missus Murphy scowled at him. She was wiping her hands in a cloth smeared with red and pink, the lamplight directly behind her setting her hair aglow. 'Yer mudder's fit.' She stepped aside, and Junior could see that there was something in his mother's arms. His mother was watching it with a look of caution, her eyes barely open, strands of her long hair stuck to her face with sweat. She regarded Junior as he moved toward the bed, her face white and pink with heat, shining in the lamplight. He noticed blood on a clump of rags near his feet and his heart sped with fear. On the dresser, there was a flat chunk of what looked like bloody raw meat laid out on a piece of brown wrapping paper.

'Junior,' his mother whispered, the beginnings of a smile.

'Get me da bottle o' molasses in da kitchen,' commanded Missus Murphy.

Junior watched his mother. She nodded. Turning, he ran down the stairs, snatched the bottle and pounded his feet back up toward his mother's room, hoping that nothing might have changed too drastically in his brief absence.

Missus Murphy uncapped the bottle and scooped up a gleaming gob of black molasses on her finger, guiding it to the baby's mouth. "'E were born widt da white mowt. Dis'll cure 'im.'

Junior inched nearer until he could see the tiny hands and scrunched-up face that seemed to be the wrong colour. The molasses was leaking out the baby's mouth, staining the cheeks brownish-black. His mother carefully dabbed away the fluid with the edge of the cloth wrapped around the baby. Junior noticed the black bag open on the washstand. There were scissors and a bit of string inside. What did they have to do with making a baby? He could not prevent his eyes from turning toward the hideous slab of meat on the dresser.

'Tis a boy,' proclaimed Missus Murphy, recapping the molasses bottle. 'Just like ye.' Her hand came down on his shoulder, nudging him ahead. "Av a good gawk at dat. Tis wondrous ta 'av a'nudder blessed one.' She moved toward the dresser and gathered up the meat in the brown wrapper. When it was adequately secured, she left the room with it in both hands.

Junior checked the baby. It looked like a creature from another world.

'It's your brother,' said his mother. 'Your little brother.'

In wonder, Junior stared into his mother's face. She seemed weak but she was alive, despite the blood. This was all that mattered. The coming of the baby had not killed her.

In the kitchen, Missus Murphy opened the side door of the stove and gently set the wrapped afterbirth in the fire. She stood in waiting, with the orange flames wavering shadows across her face, listening to the crackles the afterbirth made while it burned, counting each crackle until the number reached ten. For a spell of seconds, there were no more and she feared for the baby, suspecting this might be the predetermined age of its demise. A tragedy to befall the Hawco household. But then the crackles recommenced. Missus Murphy counted through several similarly unusual pauses, until reaching the number 49. And even waited a while longer, as was customary. No other crackle sounded and so she shut the side door and made a mental note of the age, putting it away in her mind, beside the others of the babies born safely into her hands in Bareneed.

Paddy Murphy, while chopping wood, is frightened of the creature

It was Paddy Murphy who saw the creature limping through the snow, and who later told the story to every boy in Bareneed. Paddy Murphy who was splitting wood for the next morning, leaving the task until the last moments of light as he often did, his grandmother, gone off now to the Hawco house, having to pester him again and again to bring in the splits, his father not saying a word from where he was turned toward the wall on the kitchen daybed. His back to them, day and night. Not a single word. Refusing to eat even the offered spoonfuls of soup. Paddy's father soon to perish of misery through the conquering images stored in his head.

Paddy Murphy had heard a deep grunt leaning toward a growl, rising through the dusk. At first, stilled by fear, he hoped it might be the wind, for the wind was known to skim many a frightening sound from the trees, barns and houses. Paddy had merely raised his head, stayed expectantly hunched over the splitting log, not moving a muscle. He had stared up through the snow and spotted the approaching black figure.

At once, Paddy's mind darted through possible explanations for the creature. It might be a bear. Or what? What else might be that size and stood upright on its paws?

The dusk began to deepen, and the wind picked up, tearing the snow to a frenzy of misaligned bits, as the figure limped down over the hill, creeping from the direction of the church and graveyard, and dragging something horrible in its wake.

Paddy Murphy's heart sped a few beats, his breath vanishing as he heard a screech, and, darting a look overhead, saw the swoop of black like a smear in the deep grey sky circling through the blots of snow above the figure that was limping nearer now, making Paddy's skin prickle and the hairs at the back of his neck stand on end. He caught his breath, hoping that if he stayed perfectly still and upright, the creature would take no notice of him, would not snatch a whiff, would not rip him limb from limb in a splatter that remained red even in the dusk and on into the blinding dark.

A growl like a choking cough with each step. The ghoul advanced. Paddy's chest throbbed to his heartbeat as his eyes trailed after the creature. The sweat warming and chilling and creeping across his flesh. Ten more steps and it would pass right by the slats of Paddy's fence.

Paddy noticed that the axe had slipped out of his hand and fallen soundlessly into the snow. He should pick it up again, just in case, but he feared that his hand lacked the power to even grasp, let alone swing the axe should there be the need, and to bend forward now would leave him vulnerable where the creature might rush at him in a bolt of savage action, a deadly throat-gashing blur.

The black flying smear circled back toward the graveyard, following after itself, the fading caw of a crow through the muffle of snowfall. The blizzard rose to a sudden, ferocious push of wind, nudging Paddy who kept watching, his face raw from the pelt of snow that thickened to a bluster before his eyes. He was not able to stand steady as the figure limped by; it was dark and white at once, snow frozen in clumps all over it, a hint of copper-coloured fur wound up around its face. Bushy and full of snow crystals, the fur seemed to move on its own, unwind from the face as though to let it breathe, then wind back.

Growling, the creature passed no more than five feet in front of Paddy's face, and continued descending the hill, dragging its slaughter behind it, until it neared the Hawco house and stood outside, watching the light from an upstairs window.

Karen Hawco, Blackstrap Hawco's second wife (who later kept the Hawco name despite the hardships associated with it), underwent a great transformation in 1992. Although the changes were severe, she assured me that they were necessary. After leaving Newfoundland in 1993, she returned seven years later, to care for her brother, Glenn, who was stricken with MS. When I spoke with her, in her home in Port de Grave, she told me it was only after surviving her much-publicized near-murder that she was able to truly come to grips with the psychological problems that had plagued her from early childhood.

1992

Cutland Junction, Newfoundland

I

The hole in Isaac Tuttle's house

'E be a crooked ol' man like me.' Jacob Hawco shifts in his chair. Eyes more on Karen than Blackstrap. The words for her. 'Saucy as da black, Tuttle is, and da wors' sort o' Jew.' His old hands are scarred. Weatherbeaten. They grip the padded seat beneath him. Jerk it slightly forward. Closer to the steel table legs. 'I'm telling ya, he's rotten widt money. Miserable miser. 'E'd skin a louse fer a cent.' He taps one set of fingertips on the tabletop. In beat with his words. Like a tune playing in his head. Always. 'His father were a grand boat builder in 'is day, 'e could sneeze or spit a boat. 'E'd do dat when 'e weren't shovelling coal. His fadder's fadder were da bastard o' some missionary went sail'n up 'n down da coast a hundred year ago.' Jacob's clear blue eyes brighten. He tugs lightly on the bill of his baseball cap. Winks. Lifts his mug of tea with both hands. Cherubs painted on the mug. Brings the rim to his lips. A saucy boyish grin. He slurps with relish and wishes that his wife were there to chide him. If only it were possible. He slurps again. Her name?

33

He tries to remember. Slurps to summon it. Casts a look at Blackstrap's wife, Karen. That's not her name. His wife. His son's wife. But she has not noticed. Too busy loading the dishwasher. Not that she ever cared one way or the other. Ever. Not now, in these years. That woman. What was her name? He looks at the tabletop. Thinks hard on something. Then forgets. Nothing anyway to remember.

Blackstrap Hawco shuts the refrigerator door. Steps up to the table. His heavy boots against linoleum flooring. Hollow sounding underneath. He sets down his beer bottle. Rolls up the sleeves of his blue and black flannel jacket. Grabs the back of the padded chair. Pulls it out.

His father looks up.

'Heard it,' Blackstrap agrees in a gruff voice. Still standing.

Karen leans in front of him. Lifts his plate away. The canned carrots and peas. And a few strips of breaded chicken from a box in the freezer. Heated. Warmed. Untouched. Toss it in the trash.

'No doubting that,' he says. Catching the lovely smell of shampoo. And perfume off his wife. It makes him want to grab her backside. For the feel of it through cloth.

Without regarding Blackstrap, Karen turns. A glass and a plate. One in each hand.

Blackstrap pays no further mind to her. She seems nervous lately. Out of sorts. Worse and worse. What's to be nervous about? Everything she wants she's got. He sits across from his father and sets both elbows on the table. He joins his hands in front of his lips. 'Isaac Tuttle,' he remarks. No need for anything but a plain expression. Maybe he's holding back. Maybe not. That is how he looks. No longer certain.

''E's da one,' says the old man. Squinting, his bushy white eyebrows twitch. He points at his son's face. 'Ye knows. Ye jus dug dat well fer 'im back 'a Coombs Hill. It be years since I clapped eyes on 'im. Hidin' away in da woods like he do. Crazy as da loon.'

'Who?' asks Karen. She glances up from wiping out the microwave. Then the kitchen sink, around the rim. Scrub and scour. Any hint of bad news never fails to alarm her. Her nerves. They can't take the thought of it. Any sort of altercation. A plump woman with a soft attractive face. Long, thick, black hair. Her features say gentleness, except for the brown arcs under her eyes. They say: Worry and defeat. New-blue jeans hug wide hips. A pink T-shirt loosely hangs from her shoulders. Concealing large breasts that wobble at the slightest movement. Above a thick mid-section. When she speaks, the tip of her tongue pokes out, between upper and lower teeth. This makes her seem even gentler. Her softness. Her voice.

'Ye never 'erd tell 'a Isaac Tuttle?' Jacob gasps playfully. Turning more in his chair to catch a reaction.

'No,' she says, flatly.

Jacob shifts his attention. From Karen back to Blackstrap. Bewilderment in his eyes.

Blackstrap stares steadily at his father's face. Gives nothing away.

''E be da one who says 'e owns da land,' Jacob laughs. Shuts his eyes to laugh heartily. The humour surges right through him. His entirety. Until practically losing his breath. Breathing and wheezing. Bracing control. Calming with a sound like a sigh. And wiping at his eyes. 'Sweet . . . gentle Jaysus . . . Dis land.' His laughter quiets. He licks his lips. Gives his head a slow shake. He waits in silence before laughter bucks up again. Again, he shakes his head to rid himself of it. ''E sold da land ta da gover'ment fordy year ago, fer a few coppers, 'n 'e still t'inks 'e's Lard over ever'tin.'

Blackstrap Hawco regards his wife. One arm over the back of his chair. He thinks on the name: Isaac Tuttle. The man has surely turned crazy. Once a fit man. Once a decent, generous man. A friend to the family. But more a friend to his mother. A man who secured a job for Junior in the mines. On Bell Isle. Back before they were shut down. The mines where Junior perished.

Blackstrap frowns casually. Catches his sharp reflection in the toaster on the counter. Prematurely grey and white hair. Tinges of blonde still lingering in his bangs. Hard features. Unshaven. Tired but clear eyes. Like his father's. But his character nothing like his father's. Or maybe more. But no effortless laughter. No such ease from Blackstrap. What has been removed over the years. He watches his reflection lift the beer bottle. And take a steady drink. Done. He presses his lips together. Glances back at the table. Notices the rolling papers and pouch of tobacco. Reaches for them. Considers his father's face. The humour giving way there. More now that he is old. Content to laugh away matters. Not to bother with them. Not to fight. Dead soon enough, he often says. Or just to laugh, unknowing. His mind adrift.

'Isaac Tuttle.' Jacob widens his eyes.

'You mean our land,' Karen quickly says. She watches the old man. Then her husband. 'Is that what you're talking about?'

'Yays.' Jacob sputters. He tries but cannot contain the laughter. His chest rises and falls beneath navy, zip-up coveralls. 'Imagine dat!' He shifts in his chair. Sees that no one else is laughing. So his mood levels off. Watches Blackstrap's face with keen fatherly interest. Valuing his son's reaction because he has made him.

'Blacky?' asks Karen.

Blackstrap Hawco uses his fingers. Works the moist tobacco into a straight line in the paper. Increases the pressure. Tightly rolls the cigarette with stained fingertips. Dabs at the thin line of gum with his tongue. Then gives Karen a steady wink. He sticks the cigarette between his lips. Nods once, assuredly. 'Taken care of,' he says through the corner of his mouth. Pokes two fingers into the top pocket of his blue and black flannel jacket. Digs around for a pack of matches. Strikes a match head against the flint. Lifts the flame to the tip of his cigarette. Puffs twice. Fire blazing. He puffs it out. Through the cloud of smoke, he watches his wife.

Karen knows, by his faint crooked smile, he has a plan. No regard for the law. No concern for the consequences of his actions. The men do as they please out here. No regard for anything. A way of life. To evade the law. Her nerves crackle. Seem too near the underside of her skin. The surface. She looks toward the clock on the stove. Only fifteen minutes more and she can have a Valium.

Blackstrap winks at Jacob. Puffs on his cigarette. A generous intake, of smoke. A swig of beer.

He's crazy, Karen thinks. Just like his father. She hears both of them laugh. Jacob's easy laugh. Blackstrap's deep guttural soundings. Rumblings. How did I let myself be brought out here? Isolation. I thought it would be different. Interesting. Country living. It's cold. No one. Stagnation. Small communities around small communities. The names all foolish. Sounding wrong. And too bright. Too colourful for the simple people who live there in old or new houses. Others clustered together on black rock. The ocean down in nearby Bareneed. Cliffs and barrens and sparse scattered trees.

Blackstrap stands. Treads close by Karen's side. Not a hint of unease in them. Prepared for anything.

Karen leans back slightly. A delayed reaction. Meant to imply she was taken by surprise.

Blackstrap watches his wife's eyes. Not one moment longer than needed. 'What're ya thinking, woman?'

'What're you going to do?' she whispers.

Blackstrap says nothing.

He is happy, she tells herself. No, confident. Confident with his mean thoughts. But he is not a mean man. Not at all. He just acts that way. Why? She smells the sweet smoky scent. Burnt wood on him. The lingering stink of diesel from his backhoe.

Blackstrap glances over her features. Trying to fix the particulars to memory. Then, just like that, he turns away.

Karen watches him step off through the kitchen archway. She hears the front door opening. 'Careful,' she calls. But the sound is high and frightened. It barely wiggles free. She glances over. Blackstrap's father staring at her pink T-shirt. Then down further. His eyes linger along her thighs. He is forgetful lately. His mind just not the same. She thinks of turning away. But there is something pitiful about his attention. As if he is stuck somewhere. In memory. And she wrongly feels compassion. Because sometimes he does not know. Just does not know. Who he is. Where he is. Stop fooling yourself, she warns herself. Give it up. But the old man laughs away the idea of whatever he was thinking.

Emily is the single word in Jacob's mind. Emily being from St. John's. Just like this woman. This one in front of him. Could be Emily. A townie girl. Shaking his head. He sees the caring look on the woman's face. Stares at her eyes. Haunted. What is she frightened of? The same skin as his wife's. The white skin giving to the touch. He swallows hard. What was her name? Bravely offers a head-tilting wink. So old now. Never again. Emily, he is about to say. Wondering why she is that way now.

'I'm off den,' he says instead. Rapping his knuckles on the tabletop. Then rising from his chair. Walk away from it. What he does now. When he does not know. Walk away.

37

Karen nods. Returns to arranging plates. Glasses in the dishwasher. Listens until the old man is gone. Her thoughts on how much she hates doing dishes. Washing clothes. Vacuuming. Cleaning. The house. It never. The house. Never. Ends. Day in. Day out. The suffocating. Monotony. When does it get any better? She wants to know. Tears. In her eyes. When. Does life. Get easier?

The backhoe idles on the dark dirt road. Its headlights reaching high into the black ragged silhouette of spruce trees. Blackstrap Hawco sits in the earth-moving machine. Feeling the idling steel work its pulse through him. His legs and spine. His hand looks to be shivering against the glassy black knob. But he knows better. Switches off the engine. Kills the lights. Sits for a moment. In the silence. Watching into the black trees from his special height. Isaac Tuttle's house.

Climbing down the steel steps, he reaches the bottom. Feels his feet flat on the worn clay road. He takes a step through the still air. Pauses at once to hear something startled. Scrambling through the black dry brush. The clear sound to his right. An animal. Always there. Always moving in secret. Too big to be a rabbit. Too small to be a lynx. Must be a fox or a cat. By the amount of sound. Unseen. It stays that way.

Blackstrap glances up at the moon. The dull blue brightness on his face. He sees Tuttle's place ahead. Black rooftop at the edge of darkness. Imagines the well hole still fresh. Not yet rocked in. No plastic well-liner for Tuttle. Rocks. Slate. That's what he wanted. The way it used to be. The red ditch. Earth torn open. The gash running toward the new house. Where the pipe will be laid below the frost line. The wider, deeper hole where the flat-rock walls will be built. Like a chimney underground. He remembers the price he gave Tuttle. And the old man's angry blinking eyes behind thick-lensed glasses. His face reddening by the instant. 'Sure I owns da very land ye be settled on. I t'ought dis would be fer free on account o' yer mudder. Yer mudder, she be roll'n over in 'er grave if she could hear da words sprung frum yer mout'. Best of friends, we being. I gave 'er dat land. I gave it to 'er, when ye were 'ard up and ye yerself were but a pup. Ye dun't see me giv'n ye no bill fer dat parcel 'a land. I built da 'ouse fer ye, too. Didn't know dat, did ye? Now ye knows. Now ye knows da trute. I kept dat ta meself long 'nough. Yer mudder tol' yer crew dat it were built from money from 'er fadder. Da one in da insane asylum. T'weren't true. I built yer 'ouse when yer fadder were up on da Labrador. Lost in da woods sumw'er like 'e were wont ta do. Always lost sumw'er dat feller. I paid fer it.'

Saying such things to Blackstrap. It had been a sizeable mistake. Even Isaac Tuttle knew how wrong he was. Just as the words left him. His mind stuck on the notion. Give unto Caesar what is Caesar's. And give unto the Lord what is the Lord's.

Miserable old coot, Blackstrap tells himself. Using one of his father's phrases. One heard less and less in these worthless days. Standing in the dirt road, he lights a cigarette. Stares at the faint image. Listens to the quiet. Tuttle's new house under the moonlight. Liar. Tuttle likes houses. Tuttle has built quite a few. Built them. Then sold them. Blackstrap tells himself, Tuttle likes property. But he's a liar. Where is all his money? Strange for a religious man. But that's religion there. That's the church in a nutshell. Lick the altar rails. Pass the plate.

Taking a deep draw, Blackstrap pulls the smoke into his lungs. Glances back at his earth-moving machine. Heavy in the dimness. A capable presence. He exhales, the smoke discolouring the air. His eyes fixed on the shovel of his backhoe. Again, he checks the house. If he were a smiling man, he would do just that. But not him. With a slow inner nod, Blackstrap envisions it. How to issue his warning. This late at night. How to properly rouse Isaac Tuttle from his bed. From his sleep. To scare the living bejesus right out of him. To set things right.

Karen counts out the dollar bills in the porch. Then steps back into the house. Over to the dining room, just off the kitchen. The tin cash box. It rests on a long factory-made table. Brand new. One hundred and sixty-nine dollars at Woolco. She counts out correct change. Takes it from under the black tray. Counts it again to make certain. She forgets. Counts one more time. She brings back three twos. Hands them to Walt Coombs. Walt Coombs shows her his pink gums. Missing teeth. A few brown spikes. Rotting away. Sickening. Dirty. Dips his head three times. Gleeful. Creepy. Appreciation.

'T'anks, me duckie. T'anks.' A scary wide-open grin. The stuff of nightmares. One eye crossed. He picks up the beer cases. The ones Karen has handed over. Carefully backs out the front door. Turns to navigate the slant of concrete steps into the shadows.

'You're welcome,' Karen says, trying to be mannerly. Distracted by her fear of Walt Coombs. Despite what Blackstrap has said about him. Calling him a hard worker. With so many children. Everyone lost count of the number years ago. Looks after them all. A hard case. But looks after his children. She watches through the door. Walt loads the beer cases into his van. A thin man with a thin head sits in the passenger seat. Not saying a word. Just staring. Straight ahead. Stupid. Violent. Mindless. Who will they torture tonight? Kill? They might sit in the van. In the woods. Drink beer. Fling empties out into the trees. Laugh at the explosion. Man over nature. Something from English classes. School. Forget school. Those years ago. Bad years. Done with the beer. The two men with other thoughts. They might come back. Rape her. Like in that movie. The two of them. Laughing. Screaming. Kicking. Spitting. In their wreck of a van. Her trapped in the back. Pounding to get out. In the middle of the woods. Trees good for hiding things. The smell of fall rot like shit.

Karen shuts the door. Hard. Then opens it a crack. Her father-in-law has gone off into his shack next door. Set slightly back from their new bungalow. Its old narrow clapboard painted bubblegum pink. Hubcaps – dully gleaming under moonlight – litter the yard. She thinks of the months when she lived there. In the house that Blackstrap had lived in. Since resettlement. The 1960s. Being forced to move from Bareneed. A cost-saving government plan. She remembers how the old man used to tell her. How they took the house apart. In sections. Moved them here. A lie. She knows. She's heard different. About who really owns the house. The land. How the old man used to watch her. Like it was her fault. Even standing outside their bedroom door. She imagined him. Staring in. She had to get up and shut the door. In the middle of everything. Blackstrap grunting and falling away. She saw a show on fathers lusting after their daughter-in-laws. It was on television. And some of these women were even into it. Laughing about it. Big faces. Big mouths. Hair off in all directions. Her shoulders shudder. It was a blessing to get clear of living in his house. Before he did something. She doesn't trust the line of thought. The old men from out this way. Uncivilized and always thinking below their waists. Inbreeding for centuries. Mongrels in wheelchairs. Turned eyes. Sex with anything. Anything with a crack and a hair. What she heard in school. Old enough to bleed. Old enough to butcher. Close your legs, I can smell your last customer. Children. Where did they learn these things? Heads shaped wrong. Retarded. It meant nothing for men to try and have their way with their son's wives. That's probably what drove Blackstrap's first wife away. Patsy'd gone off. Pregnant. A small boy. Had a girl later. Three years ago. Karen knew her name. Patsy. Only because she'd been told the specifics by Mrs. Quinton. The woman at the corner store. Another woman at the post office. Talking. Telling. Always with news. Right or wrong. It didn't matter. Just say it. Tell it. Like it was fact. No one speaks of Patsy. Not even Blackstrap. He doesn't even mention his kids. Not a single word. Not their names. Not their ages. They don't call. Nothing. Karen tries to imagine his children. She doesn't want to have any. She'll have her tubes tied. Soon. She has an appointment in the hospital. St. John's. Won't tell Blackstrap. Can't tell him. No children. She could never look after them. Not properly. The way it was meant to be. Not like that. She wouldn't know how. And if she did she might hurt them. What would Blackstrap do? Leave her. And her children too. Hurt them. Like she was hurt. What sort of father would he be? Blackstrap. Not hers. Not him. Would he be mean? To his children. Ignore them. Beat them? Or take them everywhere with him. Always have them at his side. Him and the children. Against *her*. It was hard to imagine how he would behave. He was like his father. Spiteful. Silent. Stubborn. But Blackstrap was never one to show it. Like the old man. Blackstrap held it inside. Nuzzled it so silently close that it perished.

That period of living with Blackstrap's father. Karen had tried going for walks. Or locking herself in her bedroom. Pretending to read one of her thrillers. People living in fear. The paperbacks told her. Everything. Lock your door. She felt it. Perfectly. A page turner. Someone at the window. Something in the basement. Whenever she was left alone. With her book. With her father-in-law. Lock your door. The way he watched her. Her chest. When telling those stories from his past. Stories that involved Jacob's wife. Blackstrap's mother. Emily. The stories. They were all familiar to her. She'd heard them countless times from Blackstrap. When he got in a talking mood. Every few months a story would come out of him. While he nursed a beer bottle at the kitchen table. Karen tried to pretend interest. But she found herself drifting off. Eyes shifting out of focus. Going cross-eyed. Fitting in. Karen hadn't met Emily Hawco. But she had seen photographs. A real beauty. That old-fashioned sort. Delicate. Graceful. From a different age. Long black wavy hair. Like Karen's. And there was a resemblance. Too many stories. Karen listened to the tales. Over and over. Until she felt she might scream. That was the past. Get your head out of the past. And lock your door. Someone always watching. Wanting harm. Occasionally, though, she would get a laugh out of Jacob's biting sense of humour. But most times she just endured. Blocked him out. Thinking of more immediate thoughts. Grocery lists. Or recipes. New diet plans. Cutting down. Cutting back. Cut off. Gash. Clothes in the catalogue. What she could wear. And not wear. Shows she had seen on television. About AIDS. Infant killing. Sexual abuse. Fathers and daughters. Mothers and sons. It was sick. Ugly. Insane. She wanted more. And less. More of it. In her head. To be gone.

The noise of the rumbling muffler. Walt Coombs' van draws Karen's mind back to the calm. Sunday night. She shuts the front door. Sits in the green velour chair. Sits. Still. The smell of new carpet. Sits. Still. Plain in her nostrils. Everything freshly painted. Her face. Make-up. Fix her make-up. The smell of newness. Almost too strong. She sits still. Glances around. The sparse clean room. Not a stain on anything. Not a smudge. Not a speck of dust. And she is pleased. A little okay. Allows a little. Pleased with Blackstrap. He built the bungalow just like the one her mother owns. Back in St. John's. They even have the latest universal remote control. It works for their television. Twenty-four channels. And their video machine. She rents movies at least a few times a week. From the convenience store and take-out down in Brigus.

Leaning forward, she picks up the remote. From the glass-topped brass coffee table. Switches on television. Watches the opening sequence of a show. A helicopter shot of a city. And its building towers. Streets. Bold handsome people in suits and expensive evening gowns. She flicks the channel to a dog food commercial. Watches that. Food. A dish. A leather collar with studs. Head in a bowl. Eating. Eat, you bitch, eat. Then flicks the television off. She thinks of the dishes. They should be washed. Head in a bowl. And the phone calls she could make back to

St. John's. To talk with friends. She misses them. Nothing to do out here. Blackstrap gone most of the time. Working jobs. Hobbles, he calls them. With his backhoe. Or building cabins. Day and night. Putting up walls. Tearing things down. Or gone up in the country. To his own shack in Horsechops. Why the country? Why the woods? Don't they already live in the woods? Why deeper into the woods? Nothing but trees and animals and a pond with a boat. She misses her friends who would joke about this. Make fun of it. The way they live. Out here. The women all around here. All thinking alike. Always gossiping about stupid little things of no interest to her. Always displeased. And finding fault in everything. Blaming everyone for everything that goes wrong. In their lives. Everyone at fault. The schools. The mail. The telephone company. The council. The government. All to blame.

On clear moonbright nights like this. She often misses the city. Misses downtown. The lights. The cars. The memories flow into her head, effortlessly sweeping her up in the comfort of recollection. Easy and lovely and fluid to remember. The clubs with the men who used to buy her drinks and fall all over her. She misses that shy edge of control she had down to a science. She was always the quiet one in the group of girls, certain to get plenty of attention. The boys trying to get to her, teasing her. Not overweight like now. Maybe a little plump. Voluptuous in a way that was attractive. The boys thinking she was a virgin because virgins behaved that way. That's how she met Blackstrap. In the Sundance Saloon on George Street. He was standing there alone, leaning against a wooden post on the edge of the dance floor. Boldly watching women moving in beat to the pounding music. Then staring right at her. He'd watched her dancing with her girlfriends for half the night. Then bought her a beer. Delivered it to her, handed it over with an unsure nod. She had thanked him, and he had asked her name. He had asked so many things about her, so interested in what she had done, where she had come from, where she grew up.

Then he was leaving the bar. He wanted her to come along. She was reluctant to abandon her friends but he tempted her away, stepping off, staring back at her with dark challenging eyes. There was something dangerous about him. Something she had seen in no other man, but something more than danger. A sturdiness, but with obliging tenderness. She sensed it in the way he handed over her beer. A gracefulness that humanized his hard looks.

She followed him while her girlfriends said 'no, don't go, you don't know him,' or laughed and wished her luck. She and Blackstrap had ended up down on the harbour, walking along the long stretch of docks with Blackstrap pulling her onto one of the big boats, up the plank and then down the metal steps, stalking her around the deck, around the huge spools of thick cables and the slippery steel floor with the paint worn off. A wonderful, head-spinning adventure like nothing she had experienced. He had grabbed her while she laughed, and they had kissed up against the side of the boat. No sex, no feeling her up, just that contact, that kiss, slow and meaningful. His fingers on her cheek, his palm flat there, kissing like it meant everything. The way he looked in her eyes made her feel like he would protect her. Like he recognized her absolutely. Everything about her. And then he put her in a taxi, sent her home. Karen didn't see him until a few weeks later in a different bar. The Ship Inn. He was sitting alone, drinking a beer, and she left her friends to sit down with him, wondered why he was in St. John's again, knew where he was from, where he lived. Cutland Junction. An hour away by car. He said he was just looking. Looking for what, she wanted to know. He just watched her. Again, he asked more questions. Where her mother came from, where her father came from. Ireland or England. Her family. Way back. They came from somewhere. And brothers or sisters. This made her feel good. That he was interested, but she would not say much about her father. Mother. He saw why. He knew why. Her family, it had harmed her. He stopped asking. Her family was nothing to her. And too much to her. Both at the same time. Silence for a while as he stared off at a group of people laughing by the door. Then they talked, quietly, in the pub with the low lights. He asked for her phone number, and she gave it to him. He folded it into his pocket and winked at her.

'Nice talking,' he said, then stood and left.

Now. The difference. Now, there is a difference. In this room. This house. Alone. Blackstrap never dotes over her. He is kind. And considerate. But he often just takes what he is after. Yanking down her jeans. In the kitchen. And leaning her over the counter. Reaching forward to pull up her T-shirt. Pull her breasts from her bra. So they roll and press against the cool counter top. The quickness and thrust of him. Behind her. Is sometimes crazily arousing. Angry. Sad. Hurt. Excited. Ashamed. Behind shut eyes. Seeing other things. Hating. Him harder. Wishing. Him harder. In her. Harder. Bigger. In her. For once. She would like to lead him on. And just leave him standing without getting his. That kind of thrill. Emptiness. Nothing. Punishment. Every once in a while she has had to teach him. About arousing her. Placing his hands in tender places. Encouraging the gracefulness that she first saw in him. Not, now. When she cries. Because it can be good.

Thinking such thoughts. Memories of that first night, playfully then warmly kissing on the ship in the harbour arouses her, the steel and sea beneath her feet, she encourages the feeling to ward off the boredom.

Now. She feels heavy. Inside. Grey. Weightiness. She sighs. Forcing herself to think: Sex. Away from the perfectly clean living room. Freshly painted. Pushing Blackstrap away from her. Making him do exactly as she tells. Shoving his face into the places she likes best. Or worst. Her body grows warm and loose. That corner in her mind. Corner of tears where she stood. She will not face it. No one is home. She will not stand there. No one to harm her. The void of an empty house. She moves over. Sits on the couch. Closes her eyes. Pornographic images she has seen in rented movies. Nothing of the person. Where she gets it. Where it gets it. All those men. Lying down. She opens her legs. Her breasts too big. Cut them smaller. Tubes tied. Hospitalized self-mutilation. The way she used to do herself. Cut herself. The hospital now. It will do it for her. She has an appointment with the surgeon. Saw him once already. He took pictures from different angles. Drew lines. Showed her how it would happen. Stitches. Nipples moved. The doctor showed her more pictures. Bruised sliced breasts sewn back together. Less of them left. Less of her. Took more pictures of her breasts. Standing there with her shirt off. Her bra off. Open up and show him. The doctor. Soon. Only ten days more before they're off. Gone. Smaller. Not afraid of them. Men watching them. Always. Smaller. Hide to make her smaller. But not that small. Never that small again. So tiny. Hands rub the thick material. She imagines herself. Surgery. Jeans down along her thighs. Thinking. Following her thoughts. Her gut. Too flabby. Tummy tuck. Cut. Sucked out. Suck. They take her. Slice her. Suck it out. Stitch her up. The men. They make her. Bend her. Pull her. The men.

45

Operate. Suck. She bends her right knee. Raises her bottom. Forces her hand deeper. Internal. A hand inside searching. Lets her left leg drop off the couch. Open wider. You might feel a little pressure. Her face scrunching. Hurting nice. You're so young. Whose was it? The corner of tears. On her cheeks. Hurt me for being so . . . My body. Hurt. My body. Hurt *it*.

A sound startles her. Quickly she sits up straight. Pulls up her pants. Listens. Caught. Uncertain of a sound. An intruder. The mean excitement in her mind. Colour rising in her cheeks. She waits. Burning in her mouth. Then stands at once. Checks her pants. The closure. The button. A mistake. Caught imagining. No more sound. Not a knock at all. Who's out there?

She goes to the porch. Opens the door a crack. The thick woods around her. Lost in them. Trees. Inside. Blackstrap. Where is he? Hoping he will be home soon. The old man next door. She wipes her eyes. Smears make-up. Freshly painted. Looks at her watch. Relieved to see it's time for another pill. In the bathroom she locks the door. Takes her pill bottle from the drawer. From her cosmetic bag. Uncaps the bottle. She swallows one. Takes a little sip of water. A tiny sip. Tiny. Then takes another. Her face. She waits and stares. In the mirror. She has been crying in the mirror. She has been. That's her. That's me. She takes a breath. She has been.

Fixes her make-up. Fixes *it*.

II

And there he was . . . gone

Jacob Hawco stands in his front window. Watches the Christly RCMP car pull into his son's paved driveway. The vehicle rolls close to the tin garage door. He hears the car door shut. Sees the officer fitting on his foolish hat. Straightening it as he walks toward the long and then shorter flight of concrete stairs. Up to the door. Knuckles rapping. Canadian Mountie with no right here.

The old man watches. Grinds his teeth. Moves his jaw from side to side. He turns. Has to step around the clutter of old furniture. The tall cast iron floor lamps with lily-shaped glass shades and ornamental bases. Heavy wooden chairs. Tapestry worn threadbare. And old glass-doored oak and mahogany cabinets. He opens the door to the kitchen. Mere embers remain in the woodstove. He decides to leave it that way. Finding the heat to be almost unbearable. His back is troubling him. He lies down on the narrow day bed. Groaning in pain. And then relief. He stares at the window in the wall opposite him. A view of orange and yellow trees. Spotting the clot of evergreens that runs off for miles in all directions. Until the sharp-blue autumn sky stops them. Only the ragged line of their black-green peaks. He thinks of his son. Wonders where he could be. Missing for three days now. Gone where? With who? Or worse? Dead. Mother of mercy! Is Blackstrap dead? Junior gone. The little girl, too. All dead now?

Restlessly standing again with a groan. He returns to the front window. Stumbles over the edge of his wife's ship's chest. From the S.S. *Newfoundland*. His leg hurts. But he holds back the curse. Out of respect for Emily. He will not touch her things. Will not lift the lid. Will not let her spirit fill him again.

The RCMP car. Still parked where it should never be. Never. RCMP. The Canadian police in Newfoundland. A country once unto itself. The Dominion of Newfoundland. Before that bastard Joey Smallwood, that cheating, lying, fascist father of confederation, tore the lot of us from our blessed roots.

Less than half an hour later the officer appears again. Casually moves down the steps over there. He wears the same nothing expression as when he arrived. No character. Wishy-washy mainlander. Pissy-faced. Plainly regarding the ground as he walks toward his vehicle. Climbs in.

The cruiser backs out. Blackstrap's driveway. The only strip of pavement this side of Cutland Junction. Jacob taps on his window with his knuckles. To snag the officer's attention. To make a threat. He curses. And taps harder. But the cruiser is gone. Slowly rolling along the dirt road. The old man curses on Karen. Her who forced Blackstrap to have the driveway paved. He curses on her for always correcting the way they speak. He curses on her for being something they are not. And do not want to be. Ever. A townie trying to be proper. Trying to not sound like a Newfoundlander. Trying to kill off what it means to be a Newfoundlander.

Turning, he heads through the kitchen. Stomps out his back door. Trudges past the pile of seasoned stove wood. Rows of mismatched bricks stacked beside his red shed with its white trim. And makes his way forward, angling to his right. Across the fifteen feet of back lawn that separates their houses. His son's house built slightly ahead of his. So that it stands further up front. Karen wanted it that way. Wanted to hide what she called 'the shack.' Embarrassed by it. And all it contained.

On his way toward the bungalow's back door, he hears the screen door opening. And sees Karen sticking out her head.

'Hi,' she says.

'Dat mountie,' spits Jacob. Tossing one arm to the side. Pointing like the cop was just there.

'What?' she asks.

'Where's Blackstrap?'

'I don't know,' she says. Having to struggle to hold back tears.

'Mounties com'n 'round,' he says. Stepping backward from it. Like a bad stink.

'He did something to Isaac Tuttle.'

'Good on 'im.' Jacob drags a sleeve across his mouth. His eyes sudden with thought. Almost furious consideration for the consequences of his son's actions.

'Then he left.' Karen wipes at her eye. The butt of her palm smears warm that will not stop. Only worse. 'No one knows where. The police . . .'

'Goddam, Christ-awful Mounties,' Jacob rants. Bullied by the unwelcome presence of the woman's untouchable pain. Softening. A woman's tears. Crying like Emily. Weeping. The words come out of him, for Emily, to calm her: 'Don't worry 'bout Blackstrap, me love. You know better den dat. No need ta worry.' He smiles at her. And watches while she tries to smile. Maybe liking him through the tears. Wanting to move closer. To comfort her. But knowing she would pull away from his touch. Or fade. Dead as he suspects she is.

Isaac Tuttle at the kitchen table. Anxious to explain the deed to Constable Pope.

'I saw 'im hang'n 'round. Outside. Night.' Using his middle finger, Tuttle pokes his thick-lensed glasses up on his nose. The Lord shall smite thee with madness, and blindness, and astonishment of heart. Chews on his tongue. His eyes appear large. Wide. He stares directly at the officer. Thy sons and thy daughters shall be given unto another people. And there shall be no might in thine hand. 'Yays. Were a big moon. Ye knows da likes of dat. Huge moon. Hawco be just stand'n 'n stare'n down in da hole he made wit 'is backhoe. Big hole. Den he walk around,' Tuttle sweeps his arm in a wide loop. So that thou shalt be mad for the sight of thine eyes which thou shalt see. 'Da house look'n at ever'tin'. He see me stand'n in one of da windows so I moves 'way. Moves back. Back furder 'n furder.'

Constable Pope nods. Writes on his pad of paper. Occasionally, he flicks the page over. Glances at Mr. Tuttle to ask the clear meaning of a word. Or to say 'Yes' or 'Go on' before dipping his neatly combed brown-haired head down to continue writing. Quick scribbles to put it all together.

Isaac Tuttle whips up his hand. So that the man that is tender among you, his eyes shall be evil toward his brother, and toward the wife of his bosom. Shows the Mountie the gash in the shape of a circle. The gash from the branch that had scraped him. Deeply. When the bed was jammed against the tree trunk. High above the earth. The fruit of thy land, and all thy labours, shall a nation which thou knowest not eat up. Then he lifts his other hand. To furiously jab at the nose piece of his glasses.

'Yes, I see,' says Pope, patiently. Having been shown the wound already. Numerous times throughout the spell of Tuttle's statement.

'Ye saw, reet?'

'It's okay.'

'Tell us again. Tell me it.' And thy carcass shall be meat unto all fowls of the air.

'What?'

'Yer name, sir.'

'Cons'able Pope.'

Isaac Tuttle smiles. A big wet smile. And blinks. Cursed shalt thou be in the city. Licks his lips. And cursed shalt thou be in the field.

'Where ye frum, da way ye talk?' His wiry black eyebrows scrunching together. 'Kaybec?'

'Mo-ree'all.'

'Muntree'all?'

'Oui.'

Tuttle searches around the tabletop. Distracted. Cursed shalt be the fruit of thy body, and the fruit of thy land. Close to seventy years old. His hair remains coal black. Plastered to his head. Cursed shalt thou be when thou comest in, and cursed shalt thou be when thou goest out. But the stubble on his doughy misshapen face has gone grey.

'You say you move away from the window.'

'Yays, I did,' says Tuttle, newly shocked at the recollection. 'Yays x'actly dat.' Pointing his finger at the window above the kitchen sink. He shall lend to thee, and thou shalt not lend to him: he shall be the head, and thou shalt be the tail. But keeping his big eyes on the officer. 'Dat window. An' da last I saw of 'im until I hear da backhoe comin' up da road 'n den closer. Up da bank where da hole were dug fer me new well, 'n den.' His hairy hands begin to tremble. And it came to pass, when he heareth the words of this curse, that he bless himself in his heart. He places them against his knees. And presses down. 'Oh, me L'ard. He shuts his eyes. And that the whole land therefore is brimstone. His lids flinching. And ye have seen their abominations. 'Dun't know nut'n den till da back wall bust open, da backhoe coming troo.' He opens his eyes. Wide. Also every sickness, and every plague, which is not written. Wider through the thick lens. Them will the Lord bring upon thee, until thou be destroyed. Points toward the dining room wall patched up with wide bare planks of spruce. Tongue and groove. See, I have set before thee this day life and good, and death and evil. 'I ran fer da beddrum. Dun't know why. Sat on da bed, ran in dere. No, ran in dere'n sat on da bed. Lay down. I were staring. No, cross da wall at da picture o' da Sacred 'art 'a Jaysus 'n I get under da covers. Fever, shiver'n like I were touched by it. Yays, 'n I hear da engine, da grinding, da terrible sound. Fury com'n fer me, ta take me frum dis mortal 'ert.' Isaac Tuttle's head wavers. That ye shall surely perish, and that ye shall not prolong your days upon the land. He looks at the floor. Searches around. Moves his zip-up boots closer together. But if thine heart turn away, so that thou wilt not hear, but shalt be drawn away. His shoulders begin trembling. And then his sides sway slightly. Before his knees knock together. And thou shalt return and obey the voice. And his chair begins creeping backward along the floor. He manages to thrust it forward. And he said, I will hide my face from them. Bucking up and ahead. Then trembling backward again. Bucking forward. Of the Rock that begat thee thou art unmindful. Trembling back.

'Can I get you something?' asks Officer Pope. He thinks of throwing the man a rope. To pull him in. He thinks of someone going through the ice. But it is not tragic. Not life-threatening. In fact, it is peculiar. And he has to cough to hide his amusement.

Isaac Tuttle bends his elbows. And presses both fists together. They have moved me to jealousy with that which is not God. In front of his face. 'Da backhoe come crash'n tru 'n I were hide'n under da sheets 'n da noise were sum'n 'n I dun't know if 'e knew I were in dere or not. No, but den I felt meself lift'n off, tilt'n, 'n back'n out, da bed in da night air, rise'n, da gears shift'n, I's spin'n and then rush'n a'ed as somet'n' scraped into me hand. No, da devil's madness fer a while 'n I were settled up high, levelled off, 'n da backhoe were gone. I were settled 'n da backhoe were gone. I were settled . . .' Tuttle lowers his fists. My doctrine shall drop as the rain. Opens his eyes. My speech shall distill as the dew. Seeing who sits in front of him. He is the Rock, his work is perfect. He is startled. 'A bunch 'a noise,' he whispers tightly, 'like da end. 'N when I pawed me way out from under da sheets I seen where I be. In a tree, up high, dat big dogberry tree, da bed crooked 'n swaying like da sea beneat' me so's I hadda clutch da mattress. Out in da back 'n it be pitch. Black 'a night 'n I could see da back red lights o' da dozer going down da road like two devil eyes 'n dat Blackstrap Hawco. Hawco. In da driver's seat. Dat's da last I saw o' 'im. I din't do nut'n ta 'im. No. Like people say. I n'ver touched 'im. N'ver took no shot at 'im.' Tuttle raises his hand. To show the circle-shaped wound. For a fire is kindled in mine anger. What was left. How he was marked by it. And shall burn unto the lowest hell.

'And you see him not again?' asks Constable Pope. Carefully looking down at his pad. The small space left beneath the words. 'Right, yes?'

'N'ver. 'E gone. Off. Ye ask me it's dat wife a 'is. She be mak'n eyes. Yes and widt ever'un all da time.' Tuttle grins plainly. Like it means nothing now. For they are a nation void of counsel. Chews on his fat tongue. Neither is there any understanding in them. Jabs at his glasses. The sword without, and terror within. Lets his tongue come out to slowly creep along his lips. Were it not that I feared the wrath of the enemy. Before chewing it back into place. 'She one a dem Townie womb'n. She want more den da good L'ard can provide from nature. No fear or belief in da good L'ard. 'N she affer 'im fer nut'n but ever'tin. Maybe she done away wid 'im. Poison'd 'im or somet'n.'

'You know there were bloods found outside your house. Drops and drops lead down the road.'

'Wha'? I can't hear ye. Deaf as a doornail in dis ear.' Tuttle taps that ear. Leans to the other side. And in that mighty hand, and in all the great terror. He stares with big eyes. In all the signs and the wonders. Shoves his glasses up on his nose. And the Lord shewed him. Silent to it.

'Do you own a firearm, sir? There were bloods found.'

Isaac Tuttle stares. Thy shoes shall be iron and brass. Shifts his eyes to the mark. The sign. The Wound. To me belongeth vengeance, and recompense; their foot shall slide in due time. 'Me own blood.'

'I'm going to have to ask you answer the question.'

'Wha' question?'

'Do you own a firearm?'

'Naw.'

'You are certain?'

'Yays. Me own blood out dere where I climbed down frum da dogberry 'n tore up me trousers 'n me leg and went ta 'av a look.'

Constable Pope writes on his pad. Turns the page. Writes more. Then he shuts it. Stands. Hat on the table. He puts it on his head. Looks at Isaac Tuttle. Then turns for the door as if not wanting to hear another word. Pausing, he glances briefly back. 'Thank you, Mr. Tuttle. I will write up the statements here. You come by to sign tomorrow.'

'Is awright,' he says, nodding. But he does not stand. He simply watches the officer leave. Door shuts. Boom. Safe again. He looks up at the ceiling, mumbling, 'No, no, no, yes,' and stands to move into his bedroom. Where he walks close to the pedestal in the corner. The suckling also with the grey hairs. Reads aloud from the good book, Matthew 5:37: 'Let wha' ye say be simply "Yes" or "No"; anyt'in more den dis comes from evil. No or yes,' he says. Ashamed of himself for speaking so many words. For their rock is not our Rock. Nothing right. Always too many words since Emily's death. For their vine is of the vine of Sodom. His mind torn to word shreds. The teeth of beasts upon them. His head. Their grapes are grapes of gall. Blackstrap. To do such a thing to him. Of all people. He smacks his forehead with his knuckles. They shall be burnt with hunger. He would put out his eyes if he had the courage. Which did eat the fat of sacrifice. Put out his own eyes to live in utter blackness. Is not this laid up in store with me? To face the loss of her. And seal up among my treasures. Stood still, blind and seeing.

III

Come back home

'If you see him, tell him to call,' Karen says into the receiver. She nibbles on her bottom lip. Chews on a piece of skin. A sob catching in her throat. Why has Blackstrap? Why has he left her? What has she done? 'The police were here.' Her chest shudders. Making her aware of the weight of her body. She presses one arm against her chest. To steady her flesh. Her shoulders hurt from the heft of her breasts. They ache all the time. Even worse now with her period coming. The straps of her bra cutting into her shoulders. Two deep grooves in her flesh that will not go away. She knows a friend who had that done. Made them smaller. Moved the nipples. You couldn't have children. Not after that. She doesn't want children. Never. She thinks of vegetables. Carrots. And lettuce. Diet food. A rat nibbling in her mouth.

  'You come stay with me,' says the man's voice. Reasonable on the other end. 'Come back home. I've got a spare room. I'll even drive out and get you if you want.'

'No.'

'Yes.'

'No, I can't, Glenn.' She remembers them. The three of them as children. Her brothers always with her. Taking care of her. Her parents. Hating them.

'What's going to happen to you out there, alone, in the middle of nowhere with lunatics everywhere? Crazy baymen. I went to school with crazy baymen. They used to bus them in.'

'No.' She begins crying. 'They're not baymen.' Wiping at her eyes. Dragging her mascara toward her temples. Imagining her face. How horrible she must look. Her eyes too small. 'I can't.' She pulls the long cord away from the wall phone. Winds it around her hand. Turns in the kitchen archway. To stare into the living room. Thinks of straightening things up. Of vacuuming. Of dusting. The shelves lined with her ceramic angel collection. Thinks of eating. Of throwing up. Another pill. Don't throw up. The pill. Valium. Birth control. Vitamins.

'I have to go, now, Glenn.'

'You call me if anything happens. Anything. I'll be here. I'm just watching a movie.'

Karen leans to glance ahead at the window. Only the road and the trees rising up from the valley. And across the distant highway. She cannot see. She knew where she was coming. She knew what it would be like. Didn't she? In hiding.

'Karen?'

'Yes.' Her voice barely squeaks out.

'Karen, you hear me?'

'Okay,' she says, sadly.

'Just call.'

'Okay.' She hesitates. Him always looking after her. Then asks: 'How are Mom and Dad?'

Silence.

Quiet.

Keeping quiet.

In their heads.

'I don't know.'

'Okay, bye.' Karen presses the disconnection button. Slowly resets the receiver. Her stomach grumbles. She steps to the refrigerator. She does not want carrots. Or lettuce. She wants chocolate. Ice-cream. And chocolate sauce. Butterscotch sauce. Whipped cream. Cherries. The sweetness in her throat. Her head deep in it. Turning to glimpse the kitchen window. She sees a face. A horrid face. Smeared with red and black. The face disappears. Then there is the sound of someone trying to enter. Through the back door. *Is it locked?* she asks herself. No one really there, is it? Lock your door. *No, not locked!* Gasping, she slams the refrigerator door. Bottles jingle inside. The face again. She rushes for the wall phone. Lifts the receiver. Her finger trembling. Her fear finally. The dial tone. The electronic beep of each punched number. Spaced too much. Too close.

The back door flung open.

The connection ringing.

Footsteps hammering across the floor. A man's bulky presence. Charging up behind. Out of sight. Muttering something. Reciting words. And her scream. Brought upon itself. Shrill. Alert. Coming to her from somewhere else. Deep inside. She drops the receiver.

A hand over her mouth. A grunt in her ear. All of it like before. Years ago. When she was smaller. Bigger now. More of her tininess.

'Emily.'

Sadly, most of the people in this book are now dead. Shab Reardon is no exception. And most might say: Good riddance. Saved numerous times from death, Shab seemed indestructible, and the very facts of his demise continue to change, depending on who you talk to. Some say he was killed by a man named Spoke Cummings in a small open boat while struggling over a shotgun to blast birds from the sky. Others say he was beaten to death by his foster daughter who disappeared some time following Shab's own disappearance and was later discovered in a mental institution in Alberta. Shab's foster son maintains that Shab was killed by a stranger, a man who didn't like the explicit propositions that Shab was directing toward him. Shab's foster son claims that he was there and witnessed the entire episode. Whether this is believable or not is anyone's guess, because the boy was known to be the worst sort of liar.

1962

wabana/bell isle

dear mom

'luh, i'll fuk'n level ya,' shab reardon bellowed, his greyish-white hair combed neatly with the grease of brylcreem, his stout face that of a handsome, charismatic man gone bad from drink and a heritage of brutality, a guttural howl in the name of some forefather's forefather, down the line of ramshackle midnight terror suffered by their children and their children and theirs, usually a quiet, meek soul, a man who drank and brooded alone for hours, watching where his hands were set against the table, meant to be left alone while studying his glass and thinking on self-shaped shadows, until he chuckled away the foolish darkness made golden now, worked himself up from his solitary table in the back of dick's lounge, buoyed by drink and reclaimed rage like a fortifying punch in the arm, buddy buddy this violence, a friend to him, a friend to a friend, shoving his six-foot-five mountain of a body to its feet and, with a riotous declaration, slapping his own table aside, all eyes on him, knowing he might murder every single person in the bar in a fit of blind rage, and not suffer the slightest scratch in return, not a blessed mark, 'i'll flatten ya, flatter den piss on a plate,' slamming his fist so hard against the bar the entire building shook on its foundation, even the stray handful of men out talking close to the island's dock turned their heads in the midst of conversation, knowing that a racket must be underway in the one-storey rectangular building, and casually returning to take in the bloody carnage,

grabbing the nearest man by the sides of his head, a man near dead from drink and wobbling out a string of meaningless words, shab thrust his forehead between the man's eyes, the body crippling back and hitting a table, glasses and bottles exploding like death-trap carnival merriment, before collapsing entirely, dropping with a boom, the music from the jukebox: wolverton mountain, where they warn you not to go,

jacob hawco junior stepping in from the parking lot was forced to turn sideways to avoid the recoiling body, his shift ending, he entered with the others, unwashed in overalls, red iron ore dust caked to their skin, fingernails caked with dirt like dried blood, impossible to scrub clean, jacob junior looked down at the man on the floor and then at shab who gave him a wink and a manly, everything's-right-as-rain nod, then raised both meaty fists above his head and roared pain-laughter as other men, men of a similar profoundly ragged distinction, roared as well, roared and cheered and, in a liberating rampage of mashed memory release, commenced beating the daylights out of one another,

the arriving men, wishing for a few beers and a bit of reasonable conversation, gathered around the bar, shouting out orders, paying little mind to shab and the others, knowing that it would all end in time, the energy expended, wound down and half-hearted forgiving, bruised and bloody chummy, until others reached similar breaking points, brought there by the thought of one family name fighting another, bad dealings from one to the other, or the theft of one woman, bad blood boiling in beer and rum a few hours further on and on, the violence as common a sight in dick's as the pool tables, tables and chairs, and jukebox,

'what're you drinking, man?' the canadian, norman park, asked junior, pulling a wad of bills from his pocket, norman, labelled a canadian, even though newfoundland had been suckle-squeezed into canada, an after-thought of an island afloat and tagged onto the vast largely uninhabited country since 1949, always the canadian, mainlander, come-from-away, newfoundlanders still newfoundlanders, only newfoundlanders, always newfoundlanders, only newfoundlanders knew newfound-landers, no matter who claimed them as theirs, 'that's what i like, always paid in the green stuff,' grinning to show perfect teeth made that way by canada, he spread the bills before his thin face and – with head thrown back – laughed like a snaky madman, all pleasure to him, nothing but, a fast car, engine taken apart and put back together in a morning, as simple as that, no one thought nothing of knowing what they knew,

'india,' junior agreed, glancing back at the man on the floor, jimmy linegar, who now stirred and slid one leg over the other before rolling onto his side, crippled child, son, father, there he lay, ten children at home in rags and filthy with lice, a hut in shacktown, one and the same, he had made himself almost everyone who had ever suffered, he suffered for them, suffered through them,

'two india,' norman called to the bartender, elbows on the bar, eyeing his young friend, eyes slit with the humour that kept him moving, always forward, toward the sign marked: give up on anything, laugh it off, 'you look freaked,' he checked junior, checked the body on the floor, saw that jimmy linegar was rising on two wobbly arms, two streaks of blood smeared from two nostrils, two eyes staring straight toward wide-opened nothing, picture perfect,

junior smiled his boyishness brighter, an ever-expanding smile that often came early but showed signs of uncertainty, in his mind, his mind always what he was, never much of a body, always a mind, even down in the clay-dirt grave of a mine, more mind watching the ragged, etched walls, more mind wondering on oxygen, than body doing, but to help others, not himself, without word, stepping ahead to offer jimmy linegar a hand from the littered floor, broken bits of glass sprayed here and there, cigarette butts soaked through, then guiding jimmy back to the bar where jimmy settled and, paying not the slightest bit of attention to his bloody nose nor the state of his nicked and cut fingers, raised one shaky-blur of a hand for another beer, called out to make certain he was seen, for he was near blind to himself and secretly wished for feathery wings and the stunning end in which to wear them, amen, he was saying, garbled as it was and making itself heard as 'beer',

norman turned to the sound of beer bottles pulled from the cooler, uncapped, clunked down before him, the end of the shift, the chubby brown bottles on the bar, the bartender's tattooed hands that held cards all night, liked playing poker at one end of the bar until he'd won everything, watches and wallets and wives, he paid the bartender and left the change, a gift that meant more than its face value,

'thanks,' junior took hold of the beer, tilting it at norman, feeling how the bottle was only vaguely cool, he took a drink, the unchilled sting of ale going down, 'not cold,' a glance at jimmy linegar counting coins out on the bar with the concentration of a shell-shocked surgeon,

norman shrugged, made a clicking sound with his tongue, broke out his big handsome grin, with two dimples framing white teeth, 'settle for what you can get,' nothing touched him,

'right,' junior took another drink, stared off across the club, the wooden tables and chairs and workers sitting, some with women in high-neck terri-cloth halters or sleeveless pullovers, long skirts, with polka dots, or plaid slacks, laughing-kissing-arguing, picture perfect, oh, where was his camera, back at his room, frame that, eyes that saw only portraits and snippets, captured, he always thought of everything in the past tense, including himself most of all, junior hawco was a, junior hawco felt that, junior hawco believed in, black and white pictures, he didn't care much for colour,

norman's eyes watched junior's, 'you getting any sleep, man,'

junior's smile broad, not a clue how to explain how he could not sleep, how he had no time for sleep, rather be awake in that alert sense of sleeplessness that made even the most common objects astonishing,

'you don't sleep, right, too fucking groovy in the head,' norman's fingers fluttering by the sides of his head, eyes cast around, witness to a brilliant wash of psychedelic colours, 'you're too groovy in the head,'

junior laughing at the canadian's words, like an animal in a cartoon, a loud noise catching his attention, he turned to see shab reardon with the fire axe from its case, swinging it over his head, then down, a few women screaming while wood splintered, a table fell away in ragged halves and glasses smashed, in a surprisingly gentle way, as they slid onto the floor,

59

everyone stood back, out of range, an expectant mumbling from the men, the jukebox now with connie francis' voice, speaking lamentful words about not hurting her, please don't make her cry, for love was life's greatest joy,

'far fucking out,' norman said, a low frisbee-caught whistle, watching the action,

junior ran curved fingers along the stubby neck of his bottle, looked at norman's lips that just then sang along, his eyes moving away when norman returned his gaze from the commotion,

'you hear about shab's rat,' asked the canadian,

'what rat,'

'the fucking rat he feeds, got him branded and everything, his initials branded on the rat with wire, the rat died,'

'i never heard,'

'not listening then,'

junior smiling,

'took him years down there to get the rat to take the food, came right up to him eventually, he loved the rat, you know that bag stuffed with grass, the one shab catches a nap on,'

junior nodded,

'nish said he saw the rat sleeping there, on the pillow, right by shab's head, both of them snoozing away, he saved the rat from the guys that had him wired with a blasting cap, the rats they put in the water down there, then hit the charge, sparks and a fried rat, you seen that,'

junior nodded,

more madness noise behind them, so they turned to witness what might collect them together,

'crazy, man, that big gorilla's outta control, magilla gorilla,' he glanced at junior's bottle, 'finished that one,'

'no,' his smile spiked with nerves, junior shrugged barely, to himself, not at the question, he picked at the beer label with both thumbnails, he wanted quiet, always, a candle in a small clean room, the idea with the action only slower, 'what happened to the rat,'

'crawled off into an engine, that's what they say, no one saw it, but then the engine caught up and there was a smell,'

junior trembled a nervous laugh, took a drink,

'you should get some sleep, man, shit,'

junior nodded, 'okay,' heard shab's roar, thinking, *sleep a dog's jaws, snatching away my eyes, yelping with the hotness of them against its tongue as it runs*, he peeked at norman's pants, the red dust on cloth, feared the mines, the depth of a ceaseless burial, but desired nothing more than to be down, underground, within the stifling, comforting hold of earth, fear that he lived for,

'HEY,' shab roared up beside junior, threw his huge arm around the young man's shoulders, towered above him, 'how's she go'n, me old trout,' he twisted his head around, shouting out over the crowd, 'junior's da fucking best 'a all you shit-maggots put ta'gedder,' he raised his hand that still held the axe, and with his free hand jabbed one thick leathery finger toward the side of junior's head, 'da fucking best, give'm a beer, give'm two,' slapped junior on the back, stared at the canadian, narrowed his eyes,

norman took a slow drink from his bottle,

'wha' da fuck are you,'

norman thought maybe to say: a rat,

'where you from, buddy,'

'toronto,' norman answered at once,

'fuh'k dat place, shithole widt flash'n lights,'

'sure, fuck that place, you bet,' norman raised his bottle in salute, took a drink, easy as that,

shab stared, 'ahright fer now,' spoken through his teeth, 'ahright, yer almost funny, buddy,' again slapping junior's back and trudging off, gripping the axe handle with both hands up close to the blade and sweeping his eyes around for anyone who dared poke a look at him,

norman shook his head, turned toward the bar, slouching, leaned both elbows there, 'serious downer, junior jones,'

junior studied norman's back, narrow shoulders, gently laid a hand there, 'don't worry about him,' he said,

norman laughed at impossibility, took a drink, 'to rats everywhere,'

'shhh,' a smiling look over his shoulder, 'not so loud,' then the announcement, 'my round,' sensing the alcohol displace fatigue, smarter, brighter, he felt almost right to himself, again glanced over his shoulder for norman's sake, saw that shab was pacified by a few of his buddies, now sitting at a table, leaned back in his chair throne, as the men talked to him, reasoned with him, king shab stared, listening, nodding like every word they spoke was pure reason that rallied to extend the kingdom,

junior thought through the night ahead, women would come to him as they always did, how he would make excuses, patiently regarding the side of norman's face, wondered if he should try something with him tonight, heart speeding at the mere thought of action, sometimes afraid he would not have the power to stop himself from leaning closer, then closer still, the man's lips, his rough stubbly face, eye to eye, sensing aftershave, the presence of the canadian, his foreign and perfect lush heat, naked by candlelight, a pen to paper, poetry, anatomy, the lines of a torso in near darkness,

he thinks he loves the man, feels love, imagines love, and from love finds his mind alight with images of his family he would write down this way:

the sun on the grass drew a smell that was both sweet and earthy, blackstrap watched his father work, putting in posts that he drove deep into the ground with the maul, his mother, emily, hanging wash on the line and there were the shapes of fabric and colours that stirred languidly in the slightest gesture of a breeze,

jacob hawco paused to wipe the sweat from his brow, his bare arm already glistening with sweat and his tanned back sheened, making the patches of black hair seem blacker,

'you hungry, blacky,' emily asked, fitting a clothes pin over the line and the shoulder of his father's white sunday shirt that made blackstrap think of church tomorrow,

'no, i'm helping,'

'okay, then,' she clipped the final item onto the line, her new sleeveless blue blouse with yellow daisies, then turned and paused to stare toward bell isle, as she often did, considering junior, blackstrap suspected, then raised the basket under her arm, swept some hair away from her face, and stepped in the open back door,

blackstrap stared at the island, too, wondering about the adventures his brother must be having so far down into the earth, the shafts going down only so far and then curving out, taking the men beneath the water, this thought suited blackstrap, he liked to ponder it, once when they had sailed over on the caribou to visit portugal cove, blackstrap had asked his father to hold him high above the ship's railing so he could stare down into the rolling blue, trying to catch a glimpse of junior and the other workers, working beneath the water, the height had felt right, hanging over the water, he wasn't scared, he had said 'let go,' but his father had not heard him above the hum of the ship's engine,

'i'll hammer it now,' blackstrap said as if it were simply meant to be, no question, no argument, nine years old and big for his age, he moved in beside his father and placed one hand on the wooden handle,

jacob looked down at the boy's hand,

'how old ye be now,'

'you know,'

''n why'd i know,'

''cause it were me birt'day last week,' blackstrap professed, 'and yer me fadder, yer supposed ta know,'

jacob laughed and released hold of the maul, he stared up at the sky, his chest rising and falling to the vigorous beating of his heart, he blew out breath, then made a sound and sat on the warm grass, drawing his knees up and wiping the sweat from his brows with the butt of his palm, 'give't a try den, g'wan, i'll rest me weary bones, dun't strain yerself, now,'

blackstrap swung the maul above his head, slamming it down against the post top, dead on,

jacob shook his head, glancing out across the land that sloped away from their house, toward the headland where the gulls brought their bones to pick over, and the flat presence of bell isle beyond, thinking of junior and how he was doing, expecting a visit soon, he listened to the radio coming from the open window, the news, iron ore company of canada officially announcing the opening of their project at labrador city, jacob thought of the mines on bell isle closing down, a two-week shutdown of the last surviving mine, number three, the one that junior worked in, a visit home, there was news of something called telstar that orbited space on that very day, its pioneering mission to bring the world a new voice, ears and eyes,

the newsman said: 'in triumphant baptism tuesday night, telstar sent television pictures spanning the atlantic to france and england,'

63

jacob looked toward the sky, and further word, something about a
blast over the nevada desert, the news broadcast, never a good thing,
what came at a man new,

blackstrap swung the maul, lifted it above his head and grunted,
pulling down with his arms and shoulders and back,

jacob turned his gaze to the water and the sunlight catching on the
small crests that barely rose, he considered the rumours he had heard
about premier smallwood moving the people from the small
communities to larger ones, idiocy, he felt sick to his stomach for the
fight that he knew would prove futile against government thought, he
licked the sweat from above his top lip and stood, turning to see that
blackstrap had driven the post knee-level into the ground,

'sweet christ, me son,' he snatched the maul handle in mid swing,
yanked it cleanly from his son's hands, 'wha're ya do'n,' he demanded,
'how'm i gunna get dat back out,' intently watching the young boy, stood
there without a drop of sweat on his face, his breath not the slightest bit
strained, the boy staring at jacob, nothing short of offended at being
interrupted, his hand out for the maul, wanting it back, wiggling his
fingers, tipping his head, so that jacob burst out laughing,

junior hawco raced through the pitch black field, running blind, not
knowing what he might strike, any moment, a wall of darkness stopping
dead somewhere, laughing all the way, free and shouting in drunken
merriment, singing his father's songs in excess, his voice nothing like
that, his arms out at his sides, until finding the end, not as humorous but
more solid than ever imagined, smacking into something hard and
steady, and realizing, as the air punched out of him and he flew back
with feet rising up for the plummet, by the slight rustling sound and
snort of breath coming through his blindness, that a horse had turned
its head to look at the inconsequential speck of weight that had slammed
against its side, the sky a starless, moonless excess of black that wanted
to swell inside him, he felt not a pang, not a rock beneath, only grass, but
the smell of dung, cow or horse nearby, no, cow, by the sweeter smell of
it, he took time standing, carefully, one hand to the moist ground, dazed,
the dim stray lights from houses in the distance, touched his nose, the
echo of sound from the collision in his ears now ebbing, he stood on

unsteady legs, sensed the heat, the horse, the muted glimmer of eye, the odour of hair, the sniff of soft, wide nostrils, the idea of a creature posed in darkness, blending so perfectly, solid, without worry, faith in such objects not easily moved, his namesake, mother and father, brother blackstrap, a horse, who loves you now, he loves everyone, this horse,

hands on the warm bulk, junior blindly inched toward the head, feeling its body, its thick neck, its long impressive head shifting slightly, restrained force, knowing what it might do, could do, the horse knowing itself, better than anything, felt its lips, tough and so tender at once, pried his fingers past the soft lips to cup his hand against the teeth, at once, feeling unbearable sorrow, the horse shifted its legs backward, *afraid of me*, junior thought, *my touch, everyone*,

'shhh, don't be afraid,' he whispered, calling up a recollection of worn-out, crippled horses stood before a ragged hole in a cliff at the back of the island, two-hundred-foot-deep crevice with ledges along the way down for smacking hard against, the crack they called it, a shotgun raised toward the horse, people often gathered to watch as the old horses, with a bang through their heads, went over, dropping onto their sides and tumbling with a kick or two or three, over the grassy lip, into the brownish-black gap of merciless rock, the crack, where garbage and excess of refuse was tossed down, too, at night, on his walks, junior visited to aim a flashlight down at rotting carcasses of horses, young boys' voices coming up behind, paying little attention to him, with flashlights and twelve-gauges, they shone lights down into the crack, shouting for an echo then blowing holes in the sides of the meaty horses as a dark greyish wash of rats streamed out both ends, a feast of creation cut short in the crack,

a pretty trick, junior thought, *i wasn't made for this*, he rubbed the side of the horse's face, scratched the short smooth hair along the bridge of its nose, even though he pretended familiarity with the dark fields, his head was rattled, he vowed to stick to the roads from there on, safer, except for the barking dogs and the stray body of a drunk miner to stumble over,

'you weren't made for this either,' junior whispered, 'were you,' smiled in the darkness and the horse shifted its head, nudging his arm so that he almost tripped backward again, 'hey,' his grin felt wonderful, in the darkness, as if it might be aglow, *the power*, he thought, for all to see, his grin from hundreds of feet above the dark field, marvelling at the texture of the horse's nostrils, then startled as something touched his back, nudged him hard, from behind, his breath jammed by the thought of another seeing him there, expecting a voice, what are you doing, who are you, he spun around, hoping against hope, for norman, his friend, or shab reardon, following him, sniffing, coaxing, wondering who he was, norman, another horse, not the might of his friend shab reardon, in the dark, shab not so calm, not so silent, but a horse regardless, then another horse at his side, and another, sniffing, expecting, what did he have for them, what had he brought to them,

shab reardon found the door unlocked, stumbled quickly through it, booze shuffling a feet–brain mismatch, slamming into the staircase post, a thunderous crack, it hurt more than him, then tilting off into the wall to his right, one hand up to save himself, someone had tipped the floor, he stayed on his feet, knowing better than to fall, to fall meant black end end end, grumbling toward action, he shoved himself away and tripped over a stray boot, grumbling more, searching for what it was, a boot, a cat, a lump, staggering down the hallway, his eyes raised without knowing, seeing ahead now, practically no difference, he stood in a doorway, braced a hand against the casing to either side, eyes staring straight, unseeing from the momentum of his stride, all a blur, leaving himself, re-entering himself, his body must be steadied, then his vision, the kitchen, he coughed loudly, wondering where in christ's name he was,

'fack'n khhhh,' he said, disgruntled, head drooped to his chest, with a quick shove, he hurled himself around, trudged back up the hallway, toward the shut door on the right, maybe a bedroom, maybe gertie sprawled out there, waiting for him, one hand slid against the door, harder now, pressing, he rattled the knob with the other, it turned and the door flung open against his weight, he fell inward, striking the table below the knee, the heavy glass ashtray thudding onto the floor, then his body hitting an orchestra of noise, music that suited him, good for a laugh, that sound, booming, the piano the key to everything, the jumbled musical sound he soon recognized to be something other than the catastrophic score of his actions,

gertie didn't own a piano, he cursed, ferociously, stomped his boot against the rug, savagely dissatisfied by how the rug had muffled the racket he was intent on making, he shoved himself toward the parlour doorway, catching hold of the banister that led upstairs and holding it with one hand, an anchor that secured him against the gale blowing out through his eyes, swirling around to dizzy him, he swivelled toward the stairway, clung to the banister before it had the chance to bend away, he did not see old missus babb standing in the shadows at the top of the stairs, in her night coat, whispering, 'our father, who art in heaven, hallowed be thy . . .' missus babb praying to saint jude, the saint of lost causes, as shab attempted a step, lifting one foot, he slammed sideways into the wall and fell backward onto his side, goddamn stairs, he always hated, the rise in his ribs, the rise and the flat, the rise and the flat, how was he supposed to know, how they worked, level was bad enough, he managed a barking laugh while getting up, reaching out for the banister, a man set perilously adrift at sea, his fingers needy as he grunted, he pulled himself to his feet and shakily navigated a succession of two impossibly difficult stairs, up, level, up, before missus babb screamed and shab flew backward, imagining an attack of birds, his heavy body crashed so soundly onto the floor that missus babb heard the china rattling in the dining room cabinet, saw the unlit light fixture sway above the staircase, thinking it might snap from its wire, one hand to her mouth,

mumbling, shab wrestled with himself until near the open doorway, he raised himself to his feet then smashed into the door framing, whacking his head with such force that he was dazed for seconds, perfectly still, wondering about an old orange cat he had as a boy, a moment later, he mumbled something resembling 'oh,' yet was not quite that, a sound as plain and clear as any word spoken by a sober man, but unknown, then shab lurched forward through the doorway, into the blackness, compelled to do so only by his feet, but not really wanting any part of it, gertie and her big tits, he'd find them, fucking titties, he grabbed at his crotch and laughed, wavering blindly across the yard, one like the other, all the same, they should suffer, he howled at the moon that was up there somewhere, meaning to pull it down from the smothering sky,

there was a fire across the flat expanse of bell isle, the crescendoing wail, the siren-like whistle from the mines alerting everyone, people stood vigil in windows or out in yards, searching the flames in the night, the height, the distance, the speculation, they soon discovered, this fire was far from junior hawco, where he stood behind his window, spotting the flames off toward the section of the island they called the green, they called shacktown, flickering lowly, colours shifting, orange, red, seemingly so small, he lifted his hand to use the space between thumb and forefinger to measure the size of the blaze, took a slow toke from the jay pinched between his other fingers,

a few inches, he thought of the fire, *what harm could possibly come of it, too much time before flames reached there*, he would step on them,

turning away, he stared at his work clothes on the floor in the dim bedroom, left there, covered in red dust, add water, what have you got, he chuckled, stood naked and looked down at his body, took another toke, his long toes, the hair on his legs, taut stomach, as if to determine the nature of his penis, he tapped the tip with his finger, then wet two fingertips and doused the flame on the tip of the jay, out, no damage done, he sniffed his fingers, the resin, he loved that smell, a tantalizing aroma,

'trouble there,' he whispered, exhaling smoke, eyes heavier, buzz-thinking on the middle-aged man in the old raglan who, day in, day out, stood beside the monument in town square, his face a question mark of trepidation, his voice insistent, 'trouble dere,' while he pointed out spaces in the sky, 'trouble dere,' carefully moving his finger, tracing out what he saw as no one else, 'trouble dere,' stuck in the scene where he had witnessed his friend's head sliced off in the mines, years ago, his friend (junior names him buddy) standing in the tram car, coming up from underground and the other men pulling buddy down, knowing better, the danger, their concern too late, buddy's body headless, head bouncing high then dropping, landing with a sloppy thud in trouble dere's lap, its helmet still on, the lamp shining up, buddy's eyes blinking, maybe still seeing, all his friends, the vibration of the car opening

68

buddy's lips, junior imagined, lips about to say something, but, finally, buddy's face nothing other than perplexed, so much for buddy, trouble dere for sure, trouble dere forever, it would not let you forget, why did it not let you forget,

junior found himself, standing too still, his body, what was it, really, ugly thoughts like these, they were with him, then gone, he was real and in them, then not, they reminded him of writing to his mother, back in bareneed, she liked the stories he sent her, sitting on the edge of the bed, he laid the snuffed jay on the night table, next to the white paper, leaning, he clicked on the small lamp, aware of the soft amber light cast against his flesh, speculatively touching the back of his right hand with the fingers of his left, the vein,

how come i can see everything, except my face and my asshole, he smiled to himself, a good smile that he felt might help him, *something to that, question number 3,567 to ask god,*

lifting the pen from the night table, he pressed its tip against the top sheet of paper beside the lamp, his hand holding a pen, that was all he saw of himself, that was the portrait now, he took his camera from the bed beside him, aimed with one hand, at his hand holding the pen, an awkward attempt to focus and press the shutter button, the picture might be blurred, the shutter speed slow in this light, he laid the camera down,

he wrote: question 3,568 – why are men so horribly afraid of loving other men, tempted to add: mom, but refrained, tempted to add: how stupid to even ask, but refrained, and moved the sheet aside to write a letter:

Dear Mom:
    There is a woman here afflicted by such poverty that she wheels a cart around town picking up bits of coal that have fallen from the coal delivery trucks. Her name is Sadie and I see her every day as though this is the only thing she was made for; my eyes to see.
    There is a man who shovels coal for Missus Neary, a man named Jimmy who is so sorry and humble you could do nothing other than love him like a brother, for he is broken-down and in need of affection. He reminds me of Isaac Tuttle. Missus Neary

gives him two dollars and a mug of pot liquor for his labours. Done with his mug, Jimmy nods and nods, backing toward the door, where he steps out into the night and returns to his ten children and the memory of his wife dead from cancer, and sits up all night staring into his own head and the damage he has fixed on. Loneliness. Yet he loves his children more than anything that might deter him from living. They are the only things that, once thought of, make him smile perfectly.

There is a man where you order coal, over on Compressor Hill, who has a hole where his nose once was and two narrow lidless slits for eyes. To blink he must scrunch up his face so the underside of his skin cleans his eyes. When his hand slides forward to accept your money, you see that there are only flesh-true stumps for fingers. His lips appear hard, and next to the opening where his nose once was there is a twisted clump of skin where the fit and educated physicians worked with their tools to give him some sort of nose. A nose that is as monstrous as any damage that could have been exacted. I do not know his name. It is only the face I remember.

You'll be glad to know that in my room, there is a font of holy water hanging from the wall,

junior stopped writing to glance at the font, then his eyes returned to the letter, the words, his handwriting, ink from his brain, he crumpled it all into a ball and tossed it toward the shut panelled door, began another letter:

dear mom:
how are you, i am fine.

invention, make believe, he laughed and wiped at his lips, he had overdone the laugh, not intended, he rose from the bed and retrieved the crumpled letter, deciding he might send it along after all, smoothing out the wrinkles, gently lifting the paper in both hands and bringing it to his eyes, studying the texture, its porous nature, he thought of trees, of being deceived, told himself that he must flee bell isle after his next pay cheque, number three mine shutting down soon, for two weeks, number four shut down for good back in january, he will return only for another month or so, one of the fortunate one thousand miners retained by dosco, while six hundred and twelve others got the axe, including norman, the canadian, gone now, junior would return at the end of july, work enough time to save money for a trip to toronto or boston, he reasoned with himself, this was not running away, it was, in fact, a necessity, to travel afar in search of men more like himself, not belonging here, an instinct,

better dope on the mainland, too, he smiled, then thought of his father, his younger brother, blackstrap, the rock, younger but already as big as him, blackstrap would never leave, not his father and brother, they would never leave, not newfoundland, not the rugged island afloat in the atlantic and battered ceaselessly, never ever leave, because they thought they belonged, that sentiment was them, survivors of ill weather and economic woe, they were made of that, built from it, and like the people at dick's they would fight each other to prove it, to crack the face of ill weather and economic woe, but where were they from really, all of them, england, ireland, why did they think they belonged in a place that they settled for, left one place and came to another, to hold on to that new place with pride and vigour, not where they were from, really, and his mother, she did not belong there, why, why did she remain,

junior fell back against his bed, his thoughts exhausting, he raised the camera above him in both hands, aimed it at his face, how in-focus was he, he had no idea, stared into the lens, his faint, curved reflection, pressed the shutter button regardless, sat up again, laid down the camera, too aware of his actions now, too, too aware, lifted the jay between his lips, fell back again, flicked the match to light it, sat up, fell back again, he wondered about the fire outside and shab reardon who lived on the green, his mind returning to shab, drawn there like an animal, the fire burning, here and there, he puffed:

gertie ryan knew it would prove futile to try and move, a few moments beyond the thrusting, pounding point, when she felt she could not draw another breath into her pneumonia-scarred lungs, shab reardon rolled off, to the side, dead asleep and snoring instantly, gertie was cold now and wheezing, naked with shab's semen trickling chillingly along her backside, she crawled over him and set her twisted feet on the floor, wiped herself with the back of her skirt and stood, hobbled toward the doorway where two children stood, silently, watching her,

'gwan ta bed outtuv it,' she said, her raspy throat scratchier now with thirst, the boy and girl hesitated, expressionless, remained where they were, only turning slightly to watch their mother sway unsteadily into the kitchen, their eyes pristinely dim with shadows, moving on legs bent by a childhood scrape with polio, she disappeared into the doorway so that the children could not see what their mother was doing, the doorway at the wrong angle and they could not see in, they heard the clink of a glass from the kitchen, a curse, then swallowing and a begrudgingly satisfied grunt, a moment later, they heard the front door open, two men talking and laughing noisily as they stomped in, the children stayed where they were, hungry, no food in the house, the older of the two, the girl, looking down at the boy, listening for his thoughts,

gertie laughed a wheeze for the men, she argued over liquor and payment,

'geev't first,' she said, her voice strained, shoving at something, a man laughed and there was the sound of grabbing, the sound of stumbling and dishes rattling, a pause as coins mutely clinked off each other then were slapped down on the counter, 'now den,' said one of the men, the sounds of different faster laughter from deep in the throat,

'i wants me turn,' a man's high-pitched voice, 'hurry up, b'y da fuh'k, jeeze i'm gunna bust wid you hoggin' dat cunny,'

'sum fak'n loose,' said a huskier, snorting voice, 'drive a truck up dere wid a scoop on da front,'

the sound of a wooden box, an empty dynamite crate from the mines, kicked across the kitchen, metal legs creaking and scraping, jolting and jolting, along the floor, the sound of playful rhythm, tittering and movement that attracted the children who shuffled away from the bedroom, first peeking a look at each other, then peeking a look in at where shab reardon snored and barked threats from his sleep, toward the light that spilt from the kitchen, the children leaned there in the doorway, their mother's naked legs, feet on the floor, their mother bent over the kitchen table, their mother's arms lifting a bottle to their mother's mouth, the men with their overalls covered in red dust, down around their ankles, their hands and faces red with iron ore, their bodies white as flour, pale, untouched, winking over at the boy and girl as they took turns for fifty cents, the huskier one watching the girl more closely, while he worked away at the mother, his head filling with ideas that his pay could easily make real, the girl frowning, knowing too soon, but stunned by this, the boy's eyes reflecting,

the huskier man pulled out and turned toward the girl, the other man stepped near the girl, his grimy hand out to the girl, his face smiling up close to the girl, his breath on the girl, 'giv's a smile, me duckie,' their mother's arm lifting the bottle, their mother's mouth laughing outloud, laughing ha-ha to forget,

Uncle Ace Hawco, my great-great-great-uncle, was revered in Bareneed. Not only had he been on the same sealing expedition that supposedly claimed his brother at the age of twenty-six, but he was said to have suffered a miserable death on the ice and come back to life. Throughout his years, after returning to Bareneed, most had no idea if he was living or dead. Not a morsel of bread or a drop of water passed between his lips. His sister-in-law, Catherine, claimed that what had returned to Bareneed was, in fact, the bare remnants of Uncle Ace, nothing other than a spirit lost even to itself.

1926

I

St. John's, Newfoundland

Bloody decks

Blackstrap's Great-Uncle Ace sails for the seal slaughter

A crowd, hailing from every large and small settlement around the island, poured into St. John's in early March to see the sealing boats off at the harbour. The sight of such jubilant crowds, men in brim hats and long, woollen overcoats or in ragged caps and threadbare suit jackets, women from lowly and refined walks of life, energetic boys with dogs and shy girls in their pretty coats, swarming on the dock always confounded Ace Hawco. He saw no cause for celebration, no true reward in strength in numbers nor in the whiff of coming slaughter. It was less of a victor's sport and more of an abomination. There was a perfect dreadfulness to all of it, a terribly oppressive sense of desperation that forced him to draw deep breaths for fear of losing his breath entirely and vanishing in a smothering rain of bloody black. The slaughter on the ice loomed large in his head. The bone-splintering clubbing and brisk whisper of the slicing.

The men surrounding him were not men at all, but beasts set upon beasts. Slit-eyed and deformed by savagery. And he was nothing if not one of them.

To most, the boisterous clamour of genuine well-wishers, be it however unseemly to Ace, was a welcome-enough beginning to a voyage soon to be filled with vigorous labour and countless hardships. Hundreds of men, with their family members and friends, travelled in from the outports, arriving by train, horse-drawn sleigh or dog team, or on foot, walking for fifty or a hundred miles through the cruel bite of March air, to seek out a berth aboard one of the sealing vessels. The others were on hand to wish their loved ones a prosperous and safe hunt, a struggle with life and death itself that would, in the end – if the coin toss landed life-side-up – see each man earning ten or twenty dollars for their troubles. Yet it was not purely for the money that they descended upon St. John's in such numbers. It was for the adventure of the voyage, linking their minds and hearts through generations, and permitting the young – through slaughter – to amass the age-defining stories, until they were able to give recital. The hunt was not merely for seals, but for a victory to be won from the daring challenge to their sister ships of the fleet. Who might return with the greatest number of pelts in their hold and claim the title: Highliner of the Season.

A deep-voiced group of sealers sang songs from the decks, and waved their hats, others climbed up into the ratlines and swept their arms through the air, while yet others, like Ace, remained coldly silent, thinking ahead to the freezing, perilous journey, the leaping from pan to pan of brilliant ice far up north to club the young whitecoats that lay still, crying like babies and spilling tears while their soft skulls were bashed open and their hides sculped clear of their carcasses.

The crews of the three sealing vessels tied up at the dock, the *Ranger*, *Eagle* and *Terra Nova*, hollered as the *Terra Nova*'s lines were tossed off and the vessel commenced drifting. Horns from the *Eagle* and *Ranger* bellowed in good-luck exclamation. And the crews, numbering near one hundred and eighty aboard each vessel, stood on freezing decks in their shirtsleeves or threadbare sweaters, jackets and caps, and roared and cheered, 'Ta da fat.'

In response, the onshore well-wishers, crowded together in high spirits, called out, over and over: 'Bloody decks!'

As the weighty hull of the *Terra Nova* floated away from the dock, Uncle Ace located his sister-in-law, Catherine Hawco, and his nephew, Jacob, in the crowd. The five-year-old boy, up in his mother's arms, was waving vigorously and with devotion. The boy smiling. The sight of them poured sickness into Uncle Ace's heart. The boy who had no memory of how his father, Francis, had sailed out on a similar voyage, four springs ago, to be lost on the ice when a storm blustered over the men, grey in the distance, at first, and then nothing but grey and whiteness like a blinding living thing hissing in from all points on the compass at once. White beneath the men's feet, white above their heads and before their faces, white to all sides. The ferocious, merciless gale battering them for two full days without cease, obliterating the existence of anything with definition, even their own bodies gradually turning white. Nothing but snow for fifty miles, north, south, east and west, and the men in the midst of it all, wandering blindly in circles, for there was no centre, no point of reference, the ship not far from them, trapped in the ice and waiting out the storm. The captain knowing that there was nothing to do but sit tight. In the vast cloud of snow, as large and desolate as an unoccupied country, his ship was a miniature of tiny wooden sticks, his men a gathering of dots regrettably built from human bones. All white and frozen atop an eternity of water that moved freely beneath ice.

Days later, what was thought to be Francis' body was discovered frozen, a mere hundred feet from the ship, clutching hold of one of his nephews, young Nathan Hawco. Flesh made into opaque glass. Both bodies bonded together by cold and death and love, and carried to the steamer by three living men where the solid mass was hauled up over the side by winch, loaded like a statue to be transported yet never erected. Buried, instead, in the sheltering earth. Other crew members were discovered living in a state of such torment that they were obliged to have limbs removed and discarded in the track of their broken sanity. Others were never found, their bodies slabs of eternal white, floating off in eerie exile, to be walked upon by arctic fox or polar bear, or, perhaps, in time, to be chewed warm again.

The frozen bodies had been unloaded on the docks in St. John's where women screeched and bawled to see their sons and husbands returned to them in such a hideous state of mortality. Living sons and daughters huddled near, straining to recognize a fatherly face, but recognizing nothing of the sort, only a man's misshapen features, expressions unseen in the daily routine of a warm house, a man's twisted body, bones dislodged by the fluid's freezing mass, a man's frozen, unseeing eyes reflecting theirs only.

Uncle Ace had helped load the bodies onto carriages that were directed, through the sunny streets, to the King Edward Hospital. Once there and unloaded, the frozen carcasses were immersed in bathtubs filled with steaming water. Only then, when thawed, did the remains become familiar to the living, re-form into figures resembling the merely dead. With each thawed body, the air in the hospital grew colder to the point where all present could witness their breath hanging before them in clouds, as though the souls of the unfortunates, now unsealed from their veils of ice, were wafting from the floating bodies in trails of cold vapour. Uncle Ace had been expected to visit the hospital in order to identify his brother, Francis, one of the chunks of frozen white that he had unloaded from the ship, now laid out, the body warmed, yet remaining crooked in a pose of anguish and tremulous fear, the harrowing expression on its face as unmovable as fifty-foot-thick ice. There lay what was thought to be his brother, but not his brother, only a kindred death mirrored in sentiment. It was himself if anyone at all. His twin. An omen of sorts before the body took on yet other features, unrecognizable as any living man, yet assumed to be the one in need of claiming. Bright blue opened eyes and blonde hair with traces of grey where there had never been. A man much like the two of them, yet not. While others claimed the body to belong to Francis Hawco, Ace wondered where his brother might be now? Liberated from this profound closeness to self.

Francis' boy, Jacob, was barely one year old when he lost his father, and Uncle Ace was quick to lend his sister-in-law, Catherine, a hand, to help out in whatever way possible, and, in so doing, spending such time in his brother's place and marvelling over the pallor of the grieving woman, had become much like the boy's father, the only father Jacob had ever known.

As the *Terra Nova* drifted further from the dock, Uncle Ace considered shouting out one of the customary farewells to Catherine and Jacob: 'Keep a watch out fer me spirit.' But he could not summon the nerve nor the will to hurl the words from his body. Instead, he simply stared moodily as the shore slipped away, as the tremulous, unbalanced water opened up between him and sure footing. At first, he hummed under his breath, then whispered a farewell dirge:

> Down came 'is old-aged fadder
> A-wiping off 'is eyes,
> 'N cried out broken-'earted,
> 'Where did ye leave me child?'
>
> 'E cried out broken-'earted,
> 'Where did ye leave me child?
> Fer 'is tender mudder I be sure
> Will screech and now run wild.'
>
> Oh dun't lament, ye parents,
> Da losing o' yer son,
> A proper prayer be offered up
> Fer 'im dat now be gone.
>
> Likewise men 'n cabin b'ys,
> Men, women, 'n each child,
> A proper prayer fer Uncle Ace,
> May 'e rest in peace a'while.

II

Liverpool, England

The single bullet

*Blackstrap's grandmother, Amanda, learns of their
imminent departure from Liverpool*

Alan Duncan glanced up from his newspaper to see his wife Amanda
lounging in her favourite wingback chair, reading the copy of O. Henry's
Heart of the West she had purchased at that cluttered shop on Bold
Street, and had been dipping into for days now. Her expression
exhibited concern for the characters that lived for her on the pages. *Lost
in her book*, Alan told himself. *She has absolutely no idea of the mess we're in.
Silly woman with her inane preoccupations.* It was only a matter of weeks,
perhaps days, before they must flee, his heart twinging at the thought of
poor little Emily and what might become of her. He had attempted to
set things right, to pay the price, but his finances had been drained by
the blackmailers and money was of little concern to these people in the
higher echelons. For them, there were other aphrodisiacs more potent
than pounds.

Amanda and Emily would be better off without him. After all, he had
brought it upon them, hadn't he, his association with this league of fine
gentlemen. No, *he* would be better off without *them*. Why a family
anyway? Why the claustrophobia of that sort of life? But then who
would look after Emily? It was anything but her fault. He regretted
deeply the idea of leaving his belongings behind. This sense of impending loss commanded an intense appreciation of all that surrounded him.
He studied the bookcases neatly set into two walls, the hard-edged
sheen of crafted mahogany and – upright on the shelves – the dark
leather-bound historical volumes and gilt-edged collections of verse. His

eyes took in the polished mahogany furniture, the regal portrait of his mother and father. Two as one, their stern, gloomy stare filled with an admonishing ponderance that seemed to prophesy his ultimate failure. Under such a weighty, collective gaze, how could their only son be anything other than what he was? *Be prepared*, their eyes seemed to chastise. *You will fail because all of this came easily to you. You lack the common sense of a self-made man.*

Miffed, Alan's glance turned quicker. It skimmed over the fine rugs, the scarlet tapestry-upholstered divan. He rattled the paper without knowing. Even the house itself would be confiscated or burned to the ground, hopefully not with them in it.

The sharp-sounding horn of a Rover Nine beyond the window drew Amanda's eyes from her book. She glanced briefly to the lace curtains with a grace that affected Alan in the saddest manner. She was a lady, after all, with a pedigree from the finest merchant stock (this she never mentioned, of course, she wasn't that sort, yet it was always implied), and what was he? The car horn had commanded Alan to his feet and set off a sharp cramp in his stomach where he laid his fingertips. Thinking of the Milk of Magnesia in the bathroom cabinet, he feared that downing the entire bottle would offer not the slightest modicum of relief.

Amanda's eyes followed him as he crossed the room. At the window, he cautiously lifted back the edge of the drapes to peek out. No glint of a sinister car parked on the street. Alan regarded his wife. She had returned to her book. He had not told her yet of the disgrace, or even harm, that might be brought upon his family. There was only distance between them, a wall of tension he had been consciously building to make the hardship of telling – if need be – less painful.

Through the soft light from the dimmed, teardrop chandelier overhead, Amanda looked at him, smiling vaguely, yet not without concern. A blessed beauty, she was.

'How is your book?' he asked.

'O. Henry must be quite a man.' She admired the book cover in her lap, then laid it on the ornate-edged side table. 'So touching.' Studying the floral spray cup and saucer resting beside the book, she decided that the tea must be cold by now and so shifted her attention toward her husband, noticing the peculiar expression on his face, the manner with which he was regarding her, in an almost sickly fashion, as though the mere sight of her was slowly turning him.

'Is something the matter?' she asked, having sensed, over the past few weeks – by the late visitors and the frequent extended telephone calls – that something was not quite right with Alan's business affairs.

'No, nothing,' he assured her, returning to his chair, to sit and raise the newspaper to conceal his face. He folded over the page of the broadsheet, holding it up higher. Not a peek at her. A sheet of blurred words that could tell him nothing. His eyes would not focus. Instead, he ruminated on ways of laying out the truth. When? It must be now. Now or never. Rustling the newspaper, he lowered it and was bothered to see that his wife was leaving the room.

'Where are you going?' he demanded, as though his wife might be attempting to elude his sudden push for courage.

Amanda turned slowly from the door, cup and saucer neatly balanced in hand, and smartly looked at him. 'And who do you think you're addressing?'

'Why don't you let one of the servants remove that?' He nodded toward her burden of cup and saucer.

'I have no problem with it,' she said, her face hardened by his words.

'Take advantage of them now. You might not have them forever.' He felt compelled to look away from the baldness of this revelation.

Amanda was watching him, still in silence, an exhausted sense of anticipation making her believe that anything he had to say could not possibly be as awful as the tension fastened between them for the past month. She longed for a spell of relief. Why wouldn't he, why couldn't he simply say what was troubling him?

'I have to leave here,' he revealed, 'very soon.'

'Oh, Alan,' she exhaled, sunkenly disappointed, shaking her slight, ebony-haired head. 'What have you done this time?'

'Not one wrong thing, I assure you. I am not the problem.'

'Then how many wrong things?'

Alan laughed with a bitterness that seemed to scar his lungs. 'Wonderful you can hold to your sense of humour.'

'What must we do without now?' Returning from the door, she reset the cup and saucer on the table and patiently stood beside her chair.

'It is not simply a question of what we will have to do without.'

'What do you mean?' Worriedly, she touched the armrest of the divan, then slowly sat down on the very edge of it.

'I just told you, I'll have to leave here.'

'You've said that before.' Amanda cast her eyes at the rug, then raised them to stare at her husband with a new look, one that implied how truly saddened she was by her ill fortune of ever having set eyes on him. This weak man. This spineless failure. If it were not for Emily, she would have left ages ago.

'Where will you go?' she asked, thinking, *Fleeing, running away, like a criminal.*

'I haven't decided exactly.'

'Then where do you *think* you are going? And what about us?'

'A place called Newfoundland.'

'Oh, dear God.' She took a breath as though the wind had been knocked out of her, her hand coming up to clutch the low arm of the divan as she sank back. There had been a recent article in the *Liverpool Echo* written by Lord Beaver who had vividly documented the hardships of life in Newfoundland, the pitiful squalor and rampant disease that were pervasive throughout that colonial outpost. A moment later, after collecting her wits, she managed, 'Is it that bad, you have to go so far?'

'It's probably best . . . if you come as well.' Alan shamefully kept his eyes fixed on his paper, then challenged her with a stare, his trim handsome face the product of generations of particular British breeding. A softness in his features, as though an essential element had not only been neglected to be bred into him, but – rather – had been bred out.

'Us.'

'They could arrest me,' he told her.

Amanda held her tongue, retreated into silence for a count of moments, then sighed a whisper, 'Poor, poor Emily.'

'Stop with that nonsense,' Alan snapped. 'This will be for Emily's sake. Don't you think I feel bad enough?'

'Oh, yes, you must feel terrible. Poor darling.'

Alan glared at her, a ruckus of thoughts noisily batting around in his head. He did not deserve this. He shouldn't stand for it. Not from her. Not from his own wife.

'You never learn, do you. You just never learn.'

'Learn what?'

At a loss for words, she stood and strode for the door, needing to see Emily, wanting to hold her because the holding of her husband would impart nothing. He was as insubstantial as a ghost. She would simply slip through him.

'I have to leave in a matter of days,' he said, quietly.

'I?'

'Yes.' He knew that they were meant to come too. After all, this was about Emily; she was the one who required protection, but he felt it best to start out with the idea of him leaving. That would be less of a blow.

'And what becomes of us? You said that we should go as well. Just then. What have you done?'

'Nothing.'

'Enough to see us in danger?'

'No, of course not.'

'You're lying. It's you. Always you and your nonsense. Whatever nonsense you've wrapped yourself up in.'

Outraged, Alan watched his wife, not knowing how to reply, then deciding to get it done with. 'Only a few ship's trunks each.'

'You knew this all along. I can see that.' Amanda made a noise of suppressed rage, as though she were grappling with the urge to murder him with her bare hands, and stomped from the room. She rushed as best she could, the skirt of her jade crêpe smock limiting her stride, out into the small front foyer, her heels clipping along the veined marble, moving up the carpeted stairs and across the long portrait-and-landscape-hung hallway toward Emily's room. The door was shut. Inside, the air remained comfortable from the embers lingering in the fireplace. Amanda moved to the sleigh bed and looked down on the sleeping seven-year-old, her black hair spread out against the pillow, a God-given innocence beaming from her face in the moonlight through the window.

Amanda had no greater need than to hold her, to hug her daughter tightly, but that would wake the child, perhaps startle her. It would amount to little more than a selfish act. And so Amanda remained standing, stilled by thought. She glanced toward the heavy drawn curtains that were open a crack and wondered of the voyage across the Atlantic. A new land. A backward place inhabited by drunken Irishmen. She could not help but cry, stifling her sudden sobs. She stopped herself and regained composure, bracing herself with the thought: *One of us must be strong, if only for you, sweetheart.*

Taking one last aching look at her daughter, Amanda saw that the quilts were without need of straightening and so kissed Emily lightly on the cheek and turned away to see the dark impression of Alan stood in the doorway, the newspaper hanging from his left hand, his right hand holding something fitted into his mouth.

There was a moment of silence that Alan held, as if clamped between his teeth like the hardness of steel, before his finger nudged, pulling the trigger. There came the clicking sound of the pin striking an empty chamber. With theatrical sadness, he slipped the short barrel from his mouth and cast his eyes away, toward the deep red and grey hallway runner.

'If this would make you happier,' he said.

Pathetic, Amanda thought, aware that Alan did not own bullets, wishing for an arm steady and wilful enough to punch him in the mouth. She hastened from the room, elbowing Alan out of her way, while she carefully shut Emily's door, then quietly moved toward one of the guest rooms, where she crossed the threshold and locked the panelled door. Another clicking sound, seemingly characterizing a similar emptiness that now lingered throughout the house.

Alan stood before his daughter's shut door, studying the panels, the dark varnished wood. He thought of the servants in the lower back rooms and the mess they would have been obligated to clean up should the revolver have fired the single bullet he had spun in its chamber. A servant's last chore in his employ, to scrub bits of his brain from the walls of his father's house. A fitting final duty.

III

Off Cape Bonavista, the Atlantic Ocean

Brilliant sparklings of red in the sun

Uncle Ace loses his mind

The ship creaked in the black ocean darkness, heading NNW. The harsh scraping sounds of ice prying against the iron-sheathed bow trembled through the bunk Uncle Ace lay awake in. Beneath him, the boat shuddered to the thunderous splitting of ice, as lines of cracks sprouted and zig-zagged off over the moonlit, silvery ice fields like veins reaching out for miles into the magnificently treacherous unknowable.

The men to all sides of Uncle Ace in the black hole snored within their wooden bunks, many of them having consumed a near lethal amount of rum on shore, enough to blot out the first night's journey. A few men stayed up into the wee hours, sitting awake at the table, talking, laughing, smoking and spitting, the shadows grotesquely shifting on their faces as the overhead lantern listlessly inclined back and forth.

Other men lay in their bunks, breath misting from their mouths, eyes glistening in the faint light, each one of them a clear distance from sleep, their minds blanched awake by imaginings of the icefields spreading out into darkness, praying for a bounty of seals that would crown them the most profitable ship, needing the money for the bare necessities, yet always clinging to the hope for a pittance more than the merchants were ever willing to let slip from their coffers.

Uncle Ace's young bunkmate, Billy Gilbert from Buchans, lay still behind him, the heat of the young fellow's body flush against his back. The boy was sleeping, his breath even and untroubled. No worries in the golden glow, the easy infallibility of youth. With both men crammed in the narrow bunk, it was only the wooden lip that prevented Uncle Ace from tumbling out onto the coal-strewn, slush-muddy floor.

Directly across from Uncle Ace, there was movement in the empty bunk previously claimed by two men from Port de Grave still gathered at the table. Something had shifted beneath the grey greasy quilt, nudged the wrinkles and creases. In time, the shifting travelled the length of the covering, then ceased as the weighty vermin crawled free and slunk onto the floor.

Uncle Ace pondered death. He faced, as often was the case, his own death, ruminated on climbing the ladder from the black hole and stepping onto the snowy deck where he might throw himself overboard, his body crashing through ice and into the mute, suffocating embrace of black water. It would not be wet. It would not be cold. It would be peacefully pleasant, and he would be gone. In his fishing dory in the summer, his thoughts often pulled him that way, his eyes fixed on the surface of the magnetic sea. With its deeply gaping enormity, it instilled in him a feeling that his presence upon it made him less and less, reducing him to nothing. The immeasurable weight and breadth of the watery sea cancelled his birth, withdrew his eyes and, in so doing, made him absolutely invisible to himself.

Despite the cold, he began to sweat and his heart sped. The tingling that never failed to work deeper and broader, like the waking of something sleeping, poured its ugliness through him so that he feared he was being driven out of his own body and mind by a barely containable and uncustomarily savage form of derangement. He threw his legs over the edge of the bunk, sat up, then, in a fit of unrest, stood. A few faces turned from over toward the table. Men Uncle Ace did not recognize. They watched with dull, dumb interest, barely interest at all, more of the nothing that he felt himself becoming. One man crouched near the useless stove fire, a slice of bread toasting on the point of his knife. The man coughed from the smoke. The boat timbers groaned steadily. Overhead, the lantern swung. Shadows shifted and stretched, then inclined the other way, smearing the contours of the men's faces that returned to their stories, to their cigarettes, to their chawing and spitting, to their dim, masking laughter that shielded them from every blow the world would or could deliver.

Uncle Ace stood there, his eyes unfocused. As though to reel himself in, he thought of home, of his garden back in Bareneed. He imagined green grass. Meadows. The calm ocean that appeared less malevolent beneath a sunny sky. He imagined tilting his face back and having the sun warm him. Clouds sweeping in. The chill. The greyness. The death of all things living. Weeds to crowd out the healthy. The endless plucking. The crows pecking at what came up. His garden would need planting when he returned, and the roof of his own house required patching, a leak in the upstairs bedroom, the room that was once his mother's and father's, another leak in the room where he and Francis and their twin sisters, who had perished at the age of seven, had slept in a narrow bed. Water dripping into his parents' house. Weeds sprouting. No one living in that house now, not since the death of his own wife, Alice, and their son, Peter. Tuberculosis. Coughing and coughing and wilting smaller. Weeds. Yet he kept up the maintenance whenever his meagre earnings allowed. A struggle to deal with it, to shift his despairing bones in gestures of simple action, keeping his parents' house in good repair for his nephew, Jacob, who might need it in the years to come. Hope against hope. A wife and a family for him. Children that might expire horribly as Uncle Ace had seen his sisters do. Weeds plucked out so that the garden might grow. Brothers and sisters from families throughout Bareneed wasting away from unknown maladies, nothing to do to prevent it, to stop the end of the little ones. Disease and malnourishment. And pluck them out. Different times now. Different times when not nearly so many children were stricken. The goat and sheep that needed feeding. Catherine would see to them. A devout woman who could manage the daily chores of any man, splitting and salting fish, toiling in the garden, baking, scrubbing the house from floor to rafter, and still finding time to traipse up the valley to church for morning and night service.

The thought of Catherine polished the blackness in him. Recalling her eyes, he felt the heavy pull of her superstition. The ancient complexity of her beliefs. The language of her hands that blessed herself upon rising and retiring, before a meal and at the mention of a stricken soul. The wood that he cut for her, a pleasure in that action, cleaving it, a crackling fire to drive off the niggling, persistent cold that coursed through him even in summer, but not enough wood to do her, for she was always cold and liked the fire blazing. If need be, she would cut more wood for the stove, carrying the splits in the pouch of her apron. A capable woman. Brought up right by Ace's parents after he and Francis had found her that day in the woods. Uncle Ace had always been fond of Catherine, and had been pleased when Francis married her. He had even been happy for them, a fleeting gesture that feathered the dust from his heart. Feathered pink then freshly wilting black against him. Death. Francis and Catherine had been content, like two love-birds.

The soles of Ace's boots trembled, a tin cup rattled against the table and was silenced by a quick palm, as ice was split and tossed aside in giant slabs that piled up to either side of the vessel. Ace came back to his dreary self, the glimmer dimming from his eyes as they glanced toward the ladder that would take him up from tweendecks. Again, he imagined rising to the deck, if only to peer down at the edges of the ice slabs, gleaming greenish-blue under the too-near moonlight. The beauty of that and the dark tug of the gluttonous abyss beneath.

A laugh rose from the table where a thin, eager-faced man in a brown sweater hawked and spat. A shadow trod down the ladder and approached the others, murmured: 'Da glass be fallin'.' Eyes searched from one to the other. A nod barely made here and there. The barometer dropping, an Atlantic storm galing through the minds of each man, blinding him with silence.

The greenwood and oak hulk of the *Terra Nova* tilted starboard, then back, levelling and smoothly dipping toward port-side. The lantern swung in accord. Shadows skimmed one way, skulked to utter stillness, then stretched blackness the other way, bending definition. Uncle Ace stood with his back to the black wooden hull, his palms and forehead damp with sweat, while he stared at the filth and breathed in the petulant stench of men. He glanced down and saw the eyes of his young bunkmate, Billy Gilbert, now curiously watching up, the young man in for a taste of it. Uncle Ace gave no word, nor notice. He regarded the men and found his thoughts, one by one, moving him along latitudes he feared in himself. He stood there for a stretch of time he could not measure. The men paid him no mind, accepting what they had heard of him as truth, for every man knew, or had learned from another, that Ace Hawco was mad.

*

88

They came upon the seals at dawn, passing the larger dangerous hood seals, some of them over ten feet long, barking savagely up at the boat and baring their sharp teeth. Passing alongside the hoods, the men knew the main herd was close at hand. They aimed their rifles across the railing and shot each hood silent, before they, as sentinels, were able to slip into the water thus signalling the others of the urgency to flee. Better that they were dead, and worrylessly still.

As the final hood was bullet-punched to sleep, an ear-crackling cheer rose up from the men on deck who were moving barrows of rock ballast under command, carrying shovelfuls of glowing coals to make fires elsewhere, or sharpening their sculping knives on a makeshift grindstone. One man flung handfuls of salt on the stairs and rails to melt the glitter, while the bulk of the others crowded the rails.

'First in da fat,' one black-toothed man winked at Uncle Ace. He rubbed his bare, scarred hands together and nudged two others who were gathered near, passing a smoke amongst them. 'We be inta da swiles soon.'

The boat laboured on, quivering while it carved its course, snapping the fresh ice and tilting it aside, languid slab upon slab rising.

Uncle Ace stared out over the icefields that radiated so white beneath the March sun that the ice appeared to be made of light itself, nothing but beaming white that gave the impression the vessel was suspended by the aura, held magically above it, only the sound of the thunderous crunching convincing him that they were, in fact, moving through something solid, breaking the white radiance to pieces so that they might sail through it.

A shout issued from the barrelman high above the ratlines, 'Swiles!'

Uncle Ace looked into the sky, then back at the ice. Up ahead, specks of grey and black, bugs against snow, became evident, and then the delayed notice of specks of tainted whiteness. Baby seals, their whitecoats vaguely yellowish.

Another roar of shouts and fighting cheers.

The *Terra Nova* dropped anchor, its chain rattling, and the labouring grind of the engines was silenced. There came a shout from Captain Kane: 'Starburd over. G'wan, me sons,' as the men cheered again, gathered ropes, gaffs and belts and hurriedly stepped down ladders nailed to the sides of the vessel.

With gaffs in hand, the men trod carefully, testing and leaping toward the harder whiteness in the centre of the ice pans, the blinding thrust of the sun against crystal white making them squint to assure themselves of the crammed edges, the boundaries that would tilt and open, exposing the pull of the black water beneath.

Captain Kane watched from the bridge, warm in his enclosure. He gazed out at the panoramic view beyond his window, delighted by the steamer's nearness to the herd, not needing to send his men off miles in search of seals, not yet anyway. Through the bridge glass, he saw a hundred and twenty of his men, grey, brown and black dots spreading out along variously patterned trails, then the smaller specks that were the seals: dogs, bitches and pups. The cowardly dogs deserted the pack at once, lumbering and hunching away until slipping into the water to save their lives, the bitches holding steady a while longer, but soon fleeing, too, into the ocean where they swam deep, then resurfaced, their eyes and nostrils poked above the water, watching toward the hunters and pups.

Soon, only a few large hood seals remained, and the hundreds of harp whitecoats left unguarded to stare up with huge brown-black eyes, unknowing, as the gaffs swished down to smash their soft skulls to splinters, the crimson sparklings of red in the sun, flaring blasts of sprinkles, holding Captain Kane's attention. Gush after gush as a hundred and twenty gaffs came down, and from the whitecoats the slow seeping of vividly glorious red across white.

The men progressed with ease, rolling over the thrashing seals and gashing them open where they lay, sculping to cut away the hides and front flippers in a few swift, economical strokes, leaving the carcasses as a meal for other predators. Each man gouging holes in the hides to thread their towing ropes through, pulling the steaming hides behind them, the white, red-drenched fur against the ice, the fat exposed and jiggling. The men fanned out and forward far beneath Captain Kane as the brilliance of the white ice was slowly replaced by more brilliant and heartening blazes of red.

'Mighty fine patch, as they say,' the captain told his second hand, Wil Critch, a grisly-faced man with two wide, mismatched eyes.

'We be da highliner dis year, Cap'n,' Critch enthused, drawing a celebratory cigarette from his packet of Gems, a luxury soon to be exhausted.

'A fit year,' Captain Kane barked assuredly and noticed ahead and twenty degrees starboard, the sealing ship *Ranger* passing far off, slowly heading further north, soon to cut across their path. He bit down on his cigarette holder and glanced toward the fields, bolstered by the stillness of the air outside, not a breath of wind. The seal herds might scatter at the mere scent of smoke. But it was a bright sunny day and the young seals would not move. They feared sunburn from going in and out of the water on sunny days, a sunburn that could scorch them so badly a man could pop his finger through their hides. It was their lazy fate to give themselves up to slaughter, rather than stir an inch in the mollifying sun.

'Take over,' the captain told Critch, pulling on his long fur coat and donning his fur hat while puffing on his cigarette holder.

The second hand shifted in without comment as the captain strode toward the starboard bridge door and pulled it open, feeling the sharp northern air sting his face, stiffening the hairs in his nostrils. At once, he heard the steady progression of fleshy whacks. Meaty popping sounds that rose above the icefields, and were slightly out of rhythm with the actual movements of the gaffs coming down, for the sound took a moment to travel. Standing on the deck, with hands firmly gripping the rail, Captain Kane called to his men, 'Yes, boys. Yes.' He stared up at the blue sky. Not a sign of a storm, yet the barometer had been dropping steadily since the previous evening. The glass did not lie.

A few of the men closer to the ship turned toward the harsh, good-humoured sound of the captain's voice, raising their arms in agreement, knowing, by the plentitude of hides, the bounty of their good fortune.

Captain Kane glanced east, monitoring the *Ranger* as she laboured forward, no more ahead than she was when he last took notice. The captain knew she was sailing toward the bulk of the pack positioned further north. At the rate the *Ranger* was travelling, his men could get to it sooner on foot.

Down on the ice, the sealers continued clubbing and skinning, avoiding the old dog hoods who could bite a man's arm or leg off. The occasional threatening beast, too sluggish to haul its six-hundred-pound hulk to the safety of open water, was done away with as a menace. One man whacked at the dog hood's back, distracting it, while the other jammed his gaff down its throat. The hide was not worth so much as the whitecoats', yet they skinned it regardless, for every penny counted, then wiped the blood from the blades in their sleeves, hands dripping red, their faces marked as they scratched their unshaved cheeks. A number of black and white turrs and wild ducks landed in the near distance, catching the scent and hopping closer to peck at the remains.

Done with skinning the ten-foot dog, the men stood, leaning on their gaffs, and watched the seal, bloody and exposed, inch away from them. They chuckled in unison, for the humour was indisputable. The beast, not yet dead, quivered as it hunched off, groaning and lumbering its internal smear toward the edge of the ice pan, where it pushed itself into the open water, and, flipperless, writhed its body to swim away.

In time, not a seal was left living, and the men, stooped forward, dragged the pelts toward the ship, the copious trails winding and stretching long and red. And, as they neared the vessel, the joyous cry of Captain Kane resounded out over the icefields: 'Come ashore, boys. You've done good this morning.'

The pelts were winched aboard and the men scaled the side of the vessel, hooking their gaffs on the railing and, with partially numb fingers and hands, pulling themselves up and over. In celebration, the men were given black tea, boiled from chunks of iceberg carried back to ship, the ice covered in fat and blood from their hands, a few of them offered condensed milk in their tea, the first time in their lives they had ever tasted such a luxury. Along with their tea, they were handed clumps of hard tack that they snapped bits off and worked to a doughy pulp in their mouths. Drenched in the brilliant colour of fresh slaughter, and warming themselves around the ondeck fires, they enthused over the wealth of pelts and thanked the Lord for such plentitude and blessings.

Invigorated and done with their mug up, the men were given instructions to move north, as Captain Kane had spotted more seals in his spyglass. The vessel would remain anchored where it was, not risking further journey ahead, the ice too resilient to chance damage to the hull with another push forward.

The men stood and waited, lingering a few more moments, a number of them staring into the sky, others glancing around, north to south, the mood of celebration crushed. There were no shouts or cheers when they went over the second time, for whispered word of the barometer's continued drop was passed around. Nevertheless, the sealers were made to journey out, deeper into the icefields to master the seals before other steamers in the fleet gained a chance to reach them.

The men jumped the ice pans without comment, occasionally glancing back to see that the ship had grown smaller, and smaller again. The sky blue overhead, the sun so intense that they all feared snow blindness in the coming night.

'Glarious day,' muttered Jesse Knee, the master watch responsible for Uncle Ace's party of men.

Not a single man gave reply.

Uncle Ace kept to himself, despite the dogging insistence of his bunkmate, Billy Gilbert from Buchans, who followed after Ace like a stray mongrel, hoping that the veteran of the slaughter might keep him out of harm's way.

At first, the snow was not visible, the flakes minuscule pellets that stung the skin, the sky not nearly grey. With clubs raised, a number of men stared toward the clouds, while others were bent on ignoring the downfall, refusing to believe that it was anything more than a sprinkle. Regardless, all men worked faster, keeping pace with the others, not speaking a word for fear of reprisal. Then, finally, as the bite of snow began to harm the face, and the wind purred toward a howl, the mutterings of discontent were sounded.

'Keep at 'er, b'ys,' instructed the master watch, Jesse Knee. 'Finish up widt dis patch o' swiles, den 'ead 'er back.'

'Da wedder be stained widt da nip o' violence,' Uncle Ace said to young Billy Gilbert who was hunched over, slicing open a bitch; blood and milk gushed free to pool against the ice and bejewel the accumulating snow. Billy gave no reply, but simply cast his eyes up to the grey sky as a wild duck swooped in to settle beside them and drink up the milk.

The men paid heed to the master watch, skinning and peeking to see Jesse Knee staring back toward the *Terra Nova*, still able to make out a fleck of brown. When the vessel was no longer a fleck, and merely a dot in memory, the master watch gave the order to rope the seals and make a run for it.

At once, the men secured their hides and trudged along the ice, ropes over their shoulders and wound around their arms and hands, bent forward with the weight of the steaming hides pulled behind them, the snow freezing in their beards and eyebrows, melting to run down into their eyes and along their cheeks. Freezing again. Melting. The crystals in their eyelashes clustering. Behind each man, a red trail wavered that was gradually masked by white.

Uncle Ace passed through a group of sealers paused to aid a man who had broken through a breathing hole punched by one of the seals. The sealers helped the sorry soul, pulling him out with the hooks of their gaffs, while he sputtered and trembled, but was soon warmed, as his clothes became frozen stiff, entombing him.

Jesse Knee gripped his compass from his pocket, and spied the needle that pointed east. No bob to it. He banged it against his leg. The needle stuck. The snow thickening, biting and nipping at the men's already-raw faces while they trudged ahead, drifting east and, eventually, further north without their knowing.

In time, as the fear and gnawing cold spiked their minds, the men argued about direction, some pointing one way and claiming it to be the correct direction, others professing the opposite. Fewer and fewer words were spoken as each man became enshrouded in white. Ice hung from their beards. Snow crusted on their jackets, pants and mitts. Icicles drooped from their running nostrils. The temperature dropped to a punishing, unbearable degree of feeling. Numbness soon set in, damaging limbs, so that some could not manage to raise one foot in front of the other. They collapsed.

Jesse Knee ordered the sealers under his watch to remain as one, but the men, barely able to see their hands when outreached before them, broke off into groups of family and friends, as the snow turned heavier again and lent the white wilderness the look of desolate eternity in all directions. The wind howled its way into their heads, so that each of them heard the exact animal-killing sound.

In time, as the grey began to deepen, the men discarded their hides, and – dropping to their knees – paused to slice open the stray seals they found living along the way. Shoving their hands into the warmth of blood and grease, and keeping them there, wishing feeling back into their fingers, while the still-living seals barked or screeched. Life tingling to such an excruciating degree that they raised their hands and smeared their faces with blood and grease. Revelling in their warm bath, they cupped the blood in their palms and poured it over their jackets and pants, over their boots and caps, and scrambled to sculp other hides so that they might shut their eyes against the brutal white and feel the sweet washing ease of warmth.

Through the snow that had mounted to a wretched blast of white, the red men trudged on paths utterly unknown to them, lost in the stinging, freezing wasteland, and pausing along the way to replenish their crimson colour from head to toe. One man removed his shirt to feel the full heat of blood, others stripped naked, dipping their clothes inside the open seals, soaking the fabric through and through, then redressing in the sopping warmth.

Watching the march of bloody men through a moment's lull of wind, Uncle Ace felt his mind tremor. Halting, he let the rope drop from his shoulder and stood erect, relieved in a peculiar way to witness the red men silently drifting ahead, out of sight, out of reach. The white was more fitting if it became absolute again. Uncle Ace noticed one of the red men hesitantly inclining back toward him. Red bootprints in the snow. At first, the features – painted as they were – were astonishingly unfamiliar.

Young Billy Gilbert shielded his face from the wind, which now thrust fiercely at Uncle Ace's back. The young man waved his red hand toward Uncle Ace, encouraging him and shouting unheard words.

Uncle Ace beheld the single red man who came nearer and pulled at Uncle Ace's arm. But Ace was immovable, as though his will was frozen stiff. The young, red man spoke more words.

Uncle Ace stared with eyes that held nothing, until Billy stumbled off, weeping tears that cleared trails through the clumps of frozen snow and blood on his cheeks, and glanced back twice before he, once again, was shrouded by white.

Uncle Ace heard the calls and movements of the red men distancing themselves from his reach. It was a trick just to stand still, to watch the red be covered in white, the white banking up around his boots and legs. Nothing to it, that feeling of being surrounded by softness and imminent enclosure as the wind ripped at his face.

How long could he stand there on his weakened, exhausted legs?

In time, out from the white, there came a soundless ruffling in the wind, a swaying akin to the flapping of a grey flag darkening toward the blackest smudge in Ace's mind. At first, he thought it might be a murder of crows, grouped together and flying as one. Yet within the squall of calamity's trickery, the black soon faded to grey again as it neared, a figure approached, at first grey, then darker grey, then brownish-red and white and upon him. A man with eyebrows and lashes frozen white. The man ventured right up to Uncle Ace then turned to point into the white.

'Me house,' the man insisted. 'It be t'roo dere. Come in fer a mug o' tea.' Assuredly, the man nodded and regarded Uncle Ace. 'A fine mug o' tea, so's ye c'n collect yerself. Warm ye right up.' Then the man turned and stumbled off into the white, so that he was a darker grey, flapping, fluttering, then a lighter grey, before being buried upright and moving in the bleached wall of oblivion.

At once, there came a calling, muddled in the wind. An alert shout that could not be comprehended, until it neared and was flatly made out: 'Da ship.' The shout, joyous in its exclamation, drifted closer, its source bodiless. Then it was in front of him, remaining unseen, 'Da ship is comin'.' The shout was repeated and kept on, fading, so that Uncle Ace never did catch sight of who might be revelling in celebration. Again, the wind filled his ears.

Uncle Ace noticed another figure darken the air near him, becoming grey but pausing before it might gain further definition. A mere shade of itself. Gradually, the figure leaned and braced both hands against the ice. Some time later, inclined as though in pose, it sank down further, resting on its side until flat to the ice. Slowly, with a careful sweeping gesture of its arm, it drew snow toward its face, gathered a mound up higher, patting the muffling snow tighter and higher up over its head until the figure remained still. Never moved again.

With his eyes on the ice, Uncle Ace now saw a mound nearer him, a mound of white through which there were patches of brown here and there. Soon, the wind-borne snow covered over each hint of brown, and the mound itself disappeared into the immuring plain of white.

Uncle Ace turned to his left, facing east, he suspected, yet could never know for certain, facing west, facing away, facing toward, to catch a blurry glimpse of motion, drifting across the ice a few feet away. He listened with frozen ears. No sound of movement, only the wind carrying snow. A small white dog trotting by. No, they had no dog on board. The bushy tail. An arctic fox. Could it be? Not by its tread. A cat covered in clumps of white, its fur unseen. A mascot lost from one of the sealing vessels. It simply walked by, its gait changing to convince him, that it was, in fact, a fox. Wasn't it? *If so, it knows where it be off to*, thought Uncle Ace. It lived in this, lived through weather ten times worse, as did the seals who had escaped into the water, with their nostrils poked up through their breathing holes. Half fish, half animal. Oxygen always there. No matter what.

A place not fit for men.

Through the harsh wind that blew mercilessly against the right side of his head, deafening his right ear, then his left as he turned fully around, Uncle Ace searched for the source of a sound he had heard behind him, a sound that he took to be the movements of a man, or a troupe of men, lost and coming up behind him after having circled around in crippling confusion.

Facing the direction he thought they might have come from, yet might have been the direction they were meant to travel toward, he saw no man, only the vague appearance of a five-foot-long dog seal, facing him through the scattered blow of the blizzard and hovering above the ice. At first, the dog was whole and growling, writhing while it bared its sharp teeth, its growl as resonant and steady as the wind itself, its huge black eyes watching him as the top of its head disappeared and blood gushed down through its fur to run and splatter into a scarlet pool against the ice. Piece by piece, the now silenced seal was torn to shreds in mid-air as blood and chunks of meat flew loose.

Uncle Ace stood in wonder, judging this seemingly impossible sight as a sign of his dissipating mortality. Awe-struck, he took a heavy step forward, as the blowing snow made the vision flicker, appear and disappear, before his eyes. There was a terrifying mystery there, one that Uncle Ace wished, and, perhaps, feared, to discover the true meaning of. This vision was speaking to him, to the numbness of his freezing flesh.

Through the snow, bits of seal continued vanishing, as though swallowed by invisible jaws. A chunk of seal, attached to the tail, dropped to the ice and soon levitated again, the remaining sections of it vanishing in two ragged strokes.

It was not until Uncle Ace was practically upon the final mutilated piece of seal, jerking about in mid-air, as though alive itself, his numb fingers reaching out to intuit the realness of it, that he searched toward the sky to see two gleaming eyes, watching down at him. The eyes were black and a foot above his head. The final piece of seal was taken in. And all was calm for a moment, as though in a conclusive fit of devouring, the world had ceased to be. Then the noise in Uncle Ace's head mounted once more, filled by the screeching howl of wind and his own words: *Always sum't'n ta trouble a man.*

Two bloody paws held still in the air. Hunters' eyes remained trained on each other through the faithless storm. Once invisible jaws roared open to expose pink and black. Teeth unseen. Sheets of snow were flung between them as seconds passed, ticked on immeasurably, gusting toward a blank stretch of minutes, before the wind reared again, growling with a punishing fury as yet unheard, and the killing blow was struck.

The journal belonging to Ace's brother, Francis Hawco, was discovered on a nameless stretch of shore by archaeologists from Memorial University. It was found wrapped in linen inside the remnants of an old shack, believed to have been the home of Francis Hawco, long thought to have perished on the ice while sealing. Fortunately, a copy had been made of the journal by Bill Riche, the young archaeologist who was part of the team that discovered it.

1971-1972

(*December 24, 1971*)

Emily was alone in the dark, sinking and remembering, while the bed seeped through her. Waves of relief lapping over, her heartbeat languidly surging, ebbing to the pull of the pills like the tide commanding her invisible blood. It was near the end. She heard voices, muddled through the walls. Male voices. She did not know who they were. She did not remember. They were talking about a woman. Possibly her. Planning her rescue. How would they save her? Who would they have to save first, in order to save her? Her children. Junior. Ruth. But then laughter. Why would they be laughing so heartlessly? And loud accordion music. The song then slowed to one of lament, sung for her, about her. The fear she tasted was of an unknown variety, without anxiety, without sweat. Her skin so dry. Stuffed with stones and tossed into the water. Sinking as she was, she joined the others, as a memory to wash up on a far-off shore, to disembark and start again.

Jacob was mortally saddened to hear the mummers' last tune. They had been trying to get free of the Hawco house for hours, many more kitchens to visit before Christmas Eve was done, but Jacob had been filling their glasses with rum and handing out bottles of beer from two cases tucked away under the table. Again and again, he tried to cajole them into staying.

'One more tune, b'ys.' He even stood from his chair and waved his arms for the return of the men and women whose identities remained concealed behind veils and masks, and beneath three or four layers of clothes. 'Come on, cripes.' He knew that after their departure, there would be nothing but suffocating loneliness left in the room. Now that he had a good load of beer in him he couldn't be left alone. What would be the point? No one sitting with him, drinking and breathing in that boozy state. Fascinated by the overlooked details of a life. Intrigued by talk. Where would the easy laughter come from?

The mummers edged away and were working their boots back on. There was much discussion and joking, the sound of it amplified in the hollow of the back porch.

Jacob tugged on one of the mummers' shoulders, a man dressed like a woman with a huge brassiere on over his coat, and a fiddle tucked under his arm. 'One more tune, b'y, wha's yer hurry? Don't be so measly. Christ, it ain't even daylight yet.'

'Yays,' said the mummer, chuckling and giving Jacob's arm a friendly squeeze. 'Love ta, Jacob, me old buddy, but we're due over ta Zack Pottle's.'

The mummers spilled out the back door, laughing and steadying themselves in the dark yard. A few patches of snow set aglow from the kitchen light. The air crisp. Not a breath of wind.

Jacob checked the sky, then pointed in declaration. A shooting star. 'Look, b'ys. It's Santy Claus.'

The mummers glanced up and searched around to see nothing but a multitude of stars. A few pointed while others smacked hands away in disbelief, 'G'wan. Dere's no Santy up dere,' said one. 'I sees him,' said another. 'Dere! Dere! Hello, Santy Claus.' Then they headed on, laughing and waving and singing. One of them tripped over himself and the others pulled him to his feet.

'None of dat, now,' one chided the fallen. Another tut-tutted and they all burst into laughter, then stray bits of song, their voices blending.

Jacob heard them make their way down to their car. Car doors opened and shut, the engine started. Laughter crammed inside, muffled by metal. The squeal of a loose fan belt. The rumble of a rusted muffler. Gone, they were. Gone in a God-awful, soul-gutting way.

Jacob stood on the back step in his stocking feet and listened. He stared past the shed toward the dark line of evergreens. He threatened to head into those woods, stride into those trees and not come out. Never. His true home, after all. It always was. Leave it all behind. The house. Emily. Blackstrap. Be lost. Fifty-three years old. He couldn't believe that he was meant to live this long. It's all right though. There's nothing the matter with it. Finest kind. Flawless. He chuckled. Pull through anything. Wouldn't want to be dead. This blessed life is none too shabby a thing.

Taking a breath, Jacob swayed a little, beset upon by heart-sodden longing. He trod back into the kitchen, the room newly emptied of people whose presences he still believed in. He stared at the floor, thought of having another beer. Naw. A waste now with no one here. Time to pack it in. He glanced toward the kitchen doorway and thought of Emily alone in her room. She went to bed a while ago. Dead to the world by now. It might have been hours. He could use her company. He could go in there and try for a bit of fun, but Emily wouldn't have any of it. He could go in there and sit on the edge of the bed, watch her face sleeping. Grin like a boy at the sight of that. How much did he love her? Too bloody much. He loved her too bloody much for his own good. All those years together. From where Emily worked in the merchant's shop to here. Jacob's mind wandered down the lane and into Cutland Junction where it stopped at Rosalyn Shears' place. Husband dead with a heart attack just last year. Alone. Childless, and she liked a beer. She liked a laugh too. Sexy the way she gladly laughed.

Enough of that. Don't be stunned. He shook his head.

And where's Blackstrap? Probably off with Agnes Bishop. Sweet girl, that one. Christ, to do it all over again. A young woman. No, he wouldn't have any of that. He wouldn't let his half-snapped head take him back to it. Dun't be wishing yer life away. No regrets. He wiped his sleeve across his mouth and glanced at the clock on the stove: 12.15. Into Christmas Day. He stared down at the floor again, gave his head a little shake. Wondered who he was, stood there. Forgot who he was for a second.

Funny, it was. The way everything worked out. Not a worry in the world unless you let the worry take you. What could possibly be so bad? Nothing. It would all work itself out. No need dwelling on the troubles to come. Nonsense. Another beer. Why not? He grabbed up the bottle opener and popped the cap off another, tilted it back.

'Nut'n da matter widt it,' he said, looking around the smoky kitchen.

The chairs still pulled out and at odd angles. The table cluttered with empty bottles and glasses. A few overflowing ashtrays.

Gone. What remained was all. Gloom. Frig it.

What's on television, he wondered, his thoughts brightening. He went out into the living room and clicked on the screen, stood there looking at a woman opening a tin of cat food.

'Dat looks delicious,' he said, licking his lips.

Not a bad-looking woman. Done up too much, though, and too skinny. He clicked the dial to the other channel. A black and white movie. A Santy Claus in a department store in New York City. By the looks of it and the sound of the music, it was going to be a heartbreaker.

Jacob collapsed into his chair and watched the little girl sitting on Santa's lap. She asked a question that was supposed to bring tears to Jacob's eyes. Did a good job of it. That little voice with the way it was sad-talking. The little girl reminded him of something. The department store reminded him of something. The clothes reminded him of something. Years ago. It all reminded him of something. It reminded him of other times, other places, other people. Reminded him of a feeling that was near to being his, was once his, but never really was, not quite.

He heard a door shut and turned to see down the hallway. A little girl in bare feet. No, Emily coming out of the bathroom. A big girl. A woman. Only the sight of her back as she went into the kitchen, her long dark hair out over her nightgown. The sight charged a shiver through him, rattled his shoulders. He watched the screen again. It was not her he saw. Just a memory.

Sometime later he heard another door click shut and looked that way. No one in the hallway. Emily back in bed. Asleep, or staring. Blank space. Alone. Deserted. No one there at all. He almost nodded off.

The television was interesting for a while. The little girl on the screen needed convincing. He was all for it. For making her happy. That little girl. She was so cute. What was he just thinking. He caught himself in a nod. His little girl. Ruth. Gone now. Not on the screen anymore. And then it all blurred away. And he saw the little girl. 'Daddy,' said Ruth, arms held out for him to pick her up. Another dream of Ruth. 'Has Santy Claus come yet?'

'Naw yet, but I saw 'im, sweet'eart. 'E were up in da sky.'

The grooved oval rings of her fingerprints. Her body dropped into water. The rings expanding. Every line on her skin, hooked and released. In water was where she found them. Ruth. Junior. In water. It was the sinking that took you. That was all of them, Emily thought. The sinking through mattress and board and dirt to the rivulets of water that flowed to sea. The soul disassembled in the stream. And there was the piece of boat board. The piece of the wreckage of the ship they thought was safe to sail upon. Their faces before her. That was all of them. They were dead. No, I am dead. They were better off without me. Two of them, only two of them. Is that all I had? Where is Blackstrap? Have I killed him, too? Something had happened. Something was happening. It was all of them now. In salt water, tears were nothing out of the ordinary.

Jacob shifted in his seat. He had slipped off to sleep and woken with a start, choking on a snore, and trying to clutch hold of a dream.

The test pattern was up on the screen, a low steady beep. An emergency sound. He stood and switched off the television. There was a bit of a recollection he was clinging on to but drew further away from him as he tried to face it.

There was something the matter. If it was in the space around him or in his head he was not certain. There were times when he looked at an object and had to think for a moment to name it. Times when he held something in his hand and wondered what it was. That sure as Christ couldn't be normal. He wondered if it might have to do with getting older. Remembering a name he had known all his life became a struggle. It was at times like these when he thought of Ruth and of Junior. They became others around him. They became part of the confusion. The stoppage. The damming. The cutting off. He imagined them in his house. Imagined their lives. Imagined their children. He allowed himself the wondering pain of that for a few moments and then he shut it off. He barred them away, his dead daughter and his dead son. He barred them out.

Standing where he was, he noticed the coloured lights blurred in his eyes. He focused. Green, yellow, red and blue. Big bulbs glowing. Tinsel hanging and sparkling. Presents wrapped and placed under the lower spruce boughs. Christmas. He went over to the tree and tested the needles. Not dry yet. He thought of a commercial he saw earlier that day for a doll that you could feed with a bottle. A doll that drank and peed. He could not remember her face. He tried and then she came to him. Ruth. Always around Christmas time. The gathered family. Arms held out and up to be lifted. She would be fourteen or fifteen years old. Fifteen. And Junior would be twenty-nine. Jacob's firstborn, delivered in 1943.

Blackstrap.

No sense dwelling on all that. He reached down and pulled out the plug for the Christmas tree lights. Presents there in the shadows. Coloured wrapping. Santa Clauses, snowmen and angels.

(*May, 1972*)

'Well, I guess ye'll be off den,' said Jacob, pressing his hands against the kitchen table and rising to his feet. 'It were a pleasure meeting you, dough. I must say. Nice of ye ta make da journey frum Sin-Jon's ta bring us me fadder's diary. Christ, if dat ain't da queerest sort o' mystery, wha? Who'd a t'ought such a t'ing were possible?'

Jacob winked and glanced over to see Blackstrap stood leaning in the kitchen doorway. His nineteen-year-old son not saying a word. Not one for talking. Less and less as he got older.

Bill Riche slowly rose from his chair. He had long hair and wire-rimmed glasses, and didn't seem to understand what was going on. Confounded, he looked at his woollen shoulder bag on the floor.

Jacob glanced down, only noticing that purse now. He could see a tape recorder in there and a microphone with the thin black cord wrapped around it. An empty man's story-stealing instrument.

'I was going to ask a few questions about—'

'Now, dere's no point ta ask'n questions 'bout sum't'n we knows nut'n 'bout.' Jacob laughed and shifted another quick look at Blackstrap. 'Nice 'o ye ta drop by widt da news, dough.' He patted Bill Riche on the shoulder, helping him along. ''N t'anks fer dat journal. Dere might be a bit of interest'n stuff in dat, fer sure. Da wife likes ta read.'

'Well, I was hoping to take the journal—'

Jacob slapped Bill Riche on the back, this time a little harder than before so that the wind was almost knocked out of him. 'Dun't be so foolish now. G'way widt ya.'

Hearing a sound of movement, Jacob turned to see Blackstrap step from the kitchen doorway and head for the door that led to the back porch. Blackstrap opened it and went out. A second later, he passed by the kitchen window, no doubt going to move the pickup truck so that Bill Riche might drive away in his yellow VW Bug. The sooner, the better.

In a fuss of confusion, Bill Riche bent to gather his woollen purse. Hurriedly, he hooked it over his shoulder as Jacob edged him toward the door.

'When can I come back then?' Riche asked in desperation.

The sound of the young feller's voice was beginning to irk Jacob. He thought of grabbing him by the scruff of his neck and heaving him through the doorway. A stranger in a man's house, thinking he had some right to be there with his busybody questions.

'Why not give us a call. Dat'd be lovely.' Jacob had Bill Riche in the back porch now, his hand on the young feller's arm, guiding him out.

'When?'

'Any old time ye likes, b'y. Give us a call. By da way, how ye plan on voting in the election?' The back door opened and out they went.

'I don't usually vote, as a protest.'

'Ah, good fer ye.' Not a speck of sense in his head, Jacob thought. The poor lost soul. 'Back ta Sin-Jon's widt ye den. Where ye can 'av a nice long think about it all.' Like a wet noodle, Jacob told himself, dat shit-soft townie.

'Mom?'

'Yes,' said Emily, groggily. 'Who's out there, Blacky?'

'A fellow from the university.' Blackstrap always tried his best to speak plainly when around his mother. She had heard him talking on the telephone and around his friends, in the dialect more like his father's. She recalled telling him how Junior used to speak, with a pure voice, perfect grammar, his words always clear. She was proud of that. But, now, she wondered if she had done the right thing, comparing the two of them.

'Why's he here?'

'He found a diary.'

'What?' she asked quietly and moved a little in her bed.

'A diary.'

'From who?' Emily shifted more, leaned up hopefully on one elbow, as though willing to come awake. 'Who wrote it?'

'This guy says it belonged to Dad's father.'

'What?' She squinted at him, unable to get a clear view in the dim room. The drapes were pulled, masking the daylight. Morning or night, the drapes remained the same. 'Come in. I can't understand what you're saying.'

Blackstrap stepped across the threshold. She heard him taking a breath, pausing. With the fresh air flowing in from the hallway, she got the sense of the smell in her room. Dust and medication. Menthol. A sourness.

'From when?' she asked, almost with regret. 'You have it?'

'Yes.' He held it up. 'It says he lived off shipwrecks. He didn't freeze on the ice at all. He survived.'

'Let me see it.' Her hand came out from under the covers.

'It's old.'

'Here,' she said, her fingers stretching toward it, her face not so much worried now as interested. She leaned her body a little. 'Let me see.' She reached for the light on her night table. Her thumb and forefinger slowly turned the switch stem until it clicked. Low, yellow light filled the room. It took a while to sit up and arrange the pillows right behind her. She still felt weak, the strength gone out of her since the overdose.

In her hand, she held the journal, knowing that it had been found, saved, knowing that it had endured. There was a warmth in the leather, a subtleness. The pages were delicate. She turned them and studied the words, written in ink by a nib. Already, for reasons unknown to her, there were tears in her eyes. It was too much for her to take. The words of a life in her hands. She blinked and tears flooded loose, streaming down her cheeks. She sniffed and wiped at her nose. Soon, she was sobbing uncontrollably. She shook her head, trying to dam the tears. In her eyes, the words were a mess, although she could still make out the flow of the script. It was beautiful. Words from the hand of a dead man who lived off of shipwrecks. Her chest bucked with greater sobs, her hands trembled. Wondering why she was reacting that way, she took a breath and laid the diary on her lap, reached for a tissue. Blackstrap was there for her, taking the tissue from the box and handing it over.

'That's okay,' she said, her mouth a grimace while she wiped at her eyes. She looked up at Blackstrap. What was he seeing of her? 'It's okay.' She balled up the tissue in her fist and regarded the journal. 'Don't worry.' Her hand over the page. Her sobs became shorter. She held them in and they rocked her body until she opened her mouth and shut her eyes, shut the book cover and placed her palms against it. What did she want to see? She wondered. What did she want to see in her head? There was nothing, only blackness. She would not imagine. But then she saw the dead man stood on that desolate coast. The masts of submerged ships poking out from the water. Hundreds of them practically blocking the view of him.

A minute later, to the sound of Blackstrap's voice, 'Mom,' she opened her eyes and saw him.

'It's okay,' she said. 'I'm just going to read this.'

Blackstrap stood in wait.

'Thanks for bringing it to me.'

Blackstrap nodded. 'You want anything?'

She shook her head, carefully opened the book to its front endpapers. Written there in script: The Marooned Adventures of Francis Hawco Who Will Perish on This Day or, Perhaps, the Next.

Emily heard the click of her door shutting, then she turned the page:

The month of May, 1919.

It is my assumption that one day this diary might be found. I am remiss to report that I have had to cleave off my left hand and three of the toes on my right foot. Fire irons were utilized to staunch the flow of blood. The operation would not have been possible had I not witnessed a similar procedure aboard the SS *Newfoundland* three years prior, for that procedure had been burned into my memory, as though by those very fire irons. How I managed to remain conscious is a mystery. There was a great quantity of perspiration and pain like a bodily fit or seizure. During the amputation, I found myself speaking as though to another person. 'You'll be fine, yes,' I said. 'The pain will only be pain. Endurable.' The toes I did first, tiny little fobs with barely a bone in them, knowing that the hand would be a greater chore, one that would leave me with fever. It is only now, three weeks after the ordeal, that I have resurfaced from the hallucinations, from under the scowls and leers of the faces that have come to visit me in my delirium, to question my very existence and how I found myself upon this watery land which appears to be a living museum to shipwrecks.

The ice is large in my memory, a vast field of white like unconsciousness itself, looming and plaguing my sense of self. Lost as I was in my hunt for seals, I recall losing sensation in my limbs. The ice chill working its way through my toes, feet and shins. My arms like stubs, for that was all that seemed to remain of warm, blood-flowing flesh when I felt a shuddering in the ice beneath my feet and suspected it might be a whale about to smash through the ice at any moment. I shifted in various directions, all the while surveying the ice for signs of cracking. Finally, I stared in the direction I assumed to be east and saw, through the grey blizzard, the masts of a ship. A ship that was not under steam. A ship that was silent and languidly moving as though adrift. At first, I believed it to be a trick played upon me by the weariness in my head. I assumed that I was so near to perishing that whatever I witnessed now would be mere fabrication, a peek into the world of all possibility where I was soon to exist eternally.

How I made my way toward the steamer is unknown to me. I had no sensation in my legs and so the drift forward was just that, a hovering and nearing until I could discern the fullness of the ship. It darkened morosely and became distinct. The large pans of ice that the bow was cutting through were loose enough to be penetrated. The ice was piled to either side of the vessel in ridges. As I came alongside it and drifted sideways to follow its gradual movement, I peeked to my right to see that – beyond a final ice ridge – open water was worrisomely ahead. Intuitively, I scrambled toward the ridge, trying to climb and grip the edges of the ice pans that had been tossed into small hills by the cut of the vessel, yet my hands were useless and I could manage nothing. The bow of the vessel was now in open water and the hull would soon pass. I tried shouting, but there were no men present on the deck. This realization struck me and I almost lost my feeble grip and gave up, tumbled toward the pans six feet beneath me. Not a man on deck. A cursed ship.

Casting aside the shudder of superstition, I leaned into the ice and attempted to roll to the top of the ridge. I had lost sensation in my hands and so my fingers were entirely useless, unable to grip. I pushed with what muscle remained in my legs and hopped upward, bending at the waist and rolling onto the top of the ridge. The vessel was scraping against the ice and I practically lost my footing. If I did not jump at that exact moment the ship would be beyond, and my chances of escape forever lost. Yet I knew that if I threw myself toward the vessel, I would be unable to grip hold of any stick of wood. It would have to be a descent onto my side. The rear of the vessel was close. I threw myself and struck the railing and plummeted, not landing as anticipated. Regardless, I had made it. Winded, I remained on my back for several moments and stared up at the masts, then I shifted my eyes along the deck. Where were the hands? Not a soul was present. I could not help but wonder if I – by delivering myself here – had saved myself or rather thrust my being into an even more perilous situation. What plague had taken this ship? What ambush awaited me?

(September)

The television screen showed masked men in tracksuits. One of them was holding a machine gun out a window. It was not a clear picture, which made the image even more frightening.

The announcer said: 'Five Arab terrorists, dressed in track sweat suits to disguise themselves as athletes, had climbed the fence surrounding the Olympic Village. The men have been identified as belonging to a PLO faction called Black September. Their demands: Israel must release two hundred Arab prisoners. The terrorists have also demanded that they be given safe passage out of Germany. Otherwise, they claim that the nine Israeli hostages will be killed.'

'Savages,' Jacob muttered. 'Worse den dose black Protestants.' A few seconds later, he recalled that he was a Catholic and was shaken by the realization that he had forgotten, that he was looking at the situation as an outsider.

He reached for his bottle of beer. Taking a drink, his eyes went to the living room window. He could see the sky. Stars. A clear summer night. A nice night for a run in his pickup, to check up on the community, but his favourite program was coming on in a few minutes, right after the late world news. He looked at the side table by his chair and saw the plate of supper sent down from Rosalyn Shears. Cod tongues and fries made in a cooker. A good shake of salt over the works. He was a little parched. He finished off his beer and set the bottle at rest. The news was almost done. He got up for another beer, went to the fridge in the kitchen, took out a bottle and popped the cap off with the opener. Satisfied, he returned to his chair and noticed his stomach. He held it with both hands, squeezing. 'A bit of a gut on me,' he said. 'Right prosperous, I am.'

Emily Hawco saw the flicker on her way from her bedroom to the bathroom. She shut the door and stood before the mirror, tried to avoid her eyes, the too-familiar outline of her face. The sound of the television was indistinct, although the occasional word came through. She heard a clang, metal against metal, and looked out the bathroom window at the front yard. Blackstrap had a light run out by extension cord and was under a car, its front wheels up on a ramp. Emily wondered about stability. She imagined what might happen if the ramp gave way or the car slipped its gear and reversed. What might be crushed in Blackstrap?

There were three other cars lined up on the road. All of them in need of repair.

Emily watched Blackstrap slide out from under the front of the car. He stood and stared at the shut bonnet. He did not move for a while but he was breathing heavily. There was mist coming from his nostrils. He scratched his forehead, scratched the back of his head. Then stared off across the dark land.

Her son. The most complicated man she had ever known. Filled with the need to prove himself. But to who? And why?

The journal she had been reading, written by Francis Hawco, contained many facts she did not know, facts that Jacob and Blackstrap did not know. Secrets. But how sane was Francis Hawco? How much damage was done to him out in the icy wilderness and then alone all those years? How believable were his stories? How true? And why didn't he leave? Why did he continue to stay on that shore when he might have left at any time? Been rescued by the ships that passed, the ships that knew he was there. The ships he traded shipwrecked goods with. Why did he remain there in that shack, living through his days and nights to bury the dead who washed ashore?

Reading the words had elicited such peculiar feelings in her. It were as though the voice she had been hearing was a combination of Blackstrap's and Junior's. Both of her boys. Francis alone with himself on that shore. Exiled. Like Junior, the fact that he was so different, and Blackstrap alone, too, always alone, never belonging, never wanting to belong, but believing he belonged to this shelterless place. Believing that the most important thing was to be a Newfoundlander, against all the odds.

And where was the voice of Ruth? Where was she? Why was it that Emily could not hear her daughter, see her daughter? What had been left of her? What was Ruth's voice? The voice she never had. The words she never learned. A language of deformation and disorder. That was all. Screeches, shrieks and bellows. Louder and quieter. Louder and quieter, until Emily understood each one, each inflection, but never that they were leading to death, speaking of death.

Her fault. The pills. The pills she had taken to help deal with the pain of Junior's death. She turned away from the guilt that stormed her, inclined her head as though to evade it. Her eyes on the toilet. The shut lid. The water beneath. The pills poisoned Ruth in her womb. Poisoned and reshaped her. Leaked disfigurement into the embryo's veins. Altered the perfect baby. Twisted the perfect baby. A twisted child. But what of her soul? Wasn't that exactly as it should have been?

The shut lid of the toilet. The water beneath it. Why had she felt the need to drown Ruth? When bath time should have been a playful time. Why was the urge so powerful? Why did she need to fight it? Was it instinct? A sick child. Kill the sick child. Emily felt a spell of weakness and touched the wall, then sat on the shut toilet lid. She watched her feet, imagined her toes missing. The need to cut them off because they had been rendered useless by the cold, by nature. She heard the clanging of a hammer. Blackstrap back under the vehicle.

Standing, she had a drink of water from a small paper cup. She continued avoiding her reflection, knowing that she looked a fright. A pill was what she needed. Codeine. Just to help her through this wavering state of being. To steady herself inside. To generate a balance that was almost bearable.

The hallway seemed darker when she left the bathroom, the flicker from the television brighter. She caught sight of someone swimming. Up and down above and below the water's surface. The sound from the television: 'Despite the tragedy that has threatened to cancel this event, or, perhaps, in defiance of this tragedy, US swimmer Mark Spitz has become the first athlete in the history of these games to win seven Olympic gold medals.'

A win and then a cut to gunfire. A body she knew nothing about. Dead on the screen. Guns at a sporting event. The reporter's voice, proud, it seemed: 'And yet the summer Olympics have resumed in Munich, Germany, even after the massacre.'

Emily went into her bedroom and shut the door, pressed it shut with both hands to make certain. Then she climbed into bed and lifted the journal from the night table. She opened it to where she had left off:

A shipwreck last night off Goat Head. I was nudged awake by the booming noise of it running aground. There was little that could be discerned through the fog. Yet the voices carried, echoing forlornly through the grey. Scraps of worried words high in the sky and seeming to crowd me, issuing from all directions. I rowed out in the fog, to see what might be salvaged of the crew. But there was not a sign of a single living person when I neared the wreckage. I counted two bodies afloat, having no idea that I was upon them until they struck the bow of my boat. Others might reach me by morning, wash up on shore. To date, I have buried twenty-three men and one woman. There is a graveyard stretching far behind my tilt. A field of wooden crosses where the dead rise – one by one – to speak with me. Having risen from their burial ground, they enter my shelter to recite their tales. So much to learn by simply listening. By accepting them for what they have to say. In this manner, they are never dead. The more I listen, the more substantial they become, until, at last, they are, through me, living again. Having achieved this feat, they then offer gratitude and wander off, content to be what they have made of themselves. No one knowing the better.

Yet the one woman who I have buried refuses to speak her story. She lingers at my table and mutely watches me. Her choked heart will not permit her to relate her testimony of woe. It would seem her preference is to remain dead to the world. How might I convince her to speak herself alive?

The journal rested on the seat between Emily and Blackstrap. They were heading east from Cutland Junction to St. John's, an hour's run, to visit the Avalon Mall.

Emily watched out her window, the spruce trees flashing by for miles. Forests of evergreens and then barrens dotted by huge boulders. She remembered what she had read about the ice age. A book on Newfoundland. Millions of years ago the continents had divided. A part of Newfoundland had taken shape from one ancient continent. Another section of the island from another ancient continent. The people who once occupied this island. The Maritime Archaic Indians. The Paleoeskimos. The Dorsets. The Real Indians. The Beothuk. It was all she could do to focus, to hold on to these facts that kept her from tumbling. History. Why was it that she had settled here? What made her discover such contentment and familiarity in this oppressive landscape?

She looked at Blackstrap. He watched through the windshield. Why was she afraid of him? What was it? His loneliness? The loneliness she created in him. What did he need? Nothing. Like one of those massive boulders on the barrens. No one capable of ever moving him, single-handedly.

The trees pressed nearer the highway. Clots of evergreens lined both sides, then receded to open up wide, deep stretches of desolate barrens with boulders spotted here and there. Groups of small ponds dotted the landscape and then disappeared as the evergreens re-formed, rising in low hills in the distance as the land ascended and fell, always lumpy and ceaselessly bleak. She imagined the earth covered in white. A group of lost men in ancient ice-crusted garbs, pushing on through a blinding blizzard, toward her.

Watching the land sweep by, she felt sorrowfully not a part of it, as though she were a ghost mourning her own translucence. How to become a part of the land. Only to survive it or have it destroy her. She recalled the woman in Francis Hawco's journal. The dead woman. The ghost who never spoke herself alive. Sometimes it was better to not speak oneself alive. It was best to remain dead. The dead could not be damaged. The dead became their own selves and no one else's. To pass the story on meant to keep oneself alive, to engender the darkness. Regardless, Emily continued rereading the journal, hoping that the woman might speak on the third or fourth reading, might tell Francis Hawco what it was that had led to her death. To know the cause might draw an antidote to mind, for there was always hope for a cure from misery, if one could only divine the root.

Not one word from her, so that, in her wondering state, Emily believed that she might have been able to furnish the woman's words. She imagined that the woman spoke, but not until the absolute end, the decisive entry, seemingly not by the hand of Francis Hawco, but penned by a feminine hand that had survived him. Emily's hand writing the closing sentence in the journal, finally, from the shipwrecked woman:

'Why is every thing made for the living?'

'Why is every object and moment the exclusive currency of the living?'

'Why are the living assumed to be the essential and substantial ones?'

'Why do the living never truly see the dead for what they are?'

Blackstrap walked down the wide corridor of the Avalon Mall with his mother at his side. There were bunches of children and teenagers around, making themselves known, joking with each other or trying to look dangerous. School finished for the summer. Alice Cooper's 'School's Out' sounded in Blackstrap's head. It was on the radio when they parked in the lot. Alice. A woman's name for a man. He'd seen Alice Cooper on television. Done up with make-up and dressed in flashy woman's clothing. A queer sight to behold. But if Alice Cooper wanted to make a spectacle of himself then that was his business. Nothing to do with Blackstrap. He still liked the music. Men in woman's clothing. It called to mind the time Junior dressed Blackstrap up as a little girl. Blackstrap must have been five or six and Junior fifteen. They both were dressed up and standing in front of the mirror. That reflection. One short boy, one tall boy. The memory gave him a sickly feeling in his gut that came up from his testicles, as though his testicles had been tapped. Emily had thought it funny, her two sons in her clothes, but Jacob had grumbled and considered it no laughing matter. His mother laughing. His mother playing with them. His mother out in the yard hanging laundry. His mother out in the vegetable garden pulling weeds. Junior would be twenty-nine. Every now and then, Blackstrap found himself figuring Junior's age and wondering what his older brother might be doing now. Where he would be living. What they might do together. The three of them, Blackstrap, Junior and their father. The three of them together in a boat or in the woods.

Blackstrap understood why his father stayed away from St. John's. On Blackstrap's way in Kenmount Road, their pickup truck was almost struck twice by cars pulling out of the car dealerships that lined both sides of the road. The noses of the cars edging out into traffic, edging further out, so they could almost be clipped. The mall parking lot was even worse than the roads. Cars trying to find a place to park, racing to swerve into an open space. It was like a feeding frenzy. And the inside corridors of the mall were like the roads, too. Everyone moving in directions that were confusing. Everyone trying to find a place.

Up ahead, a woman with long sandy-blonde hair was looking down at a pair of boots on display. Agnes. His heart sped. Agnes deciding it was the wrong thing to do, to be away. She had decided to return where she belonged. Agnes turned fully around and Blackstrap saw more of her face. It was not Agnes. The woman looked nothing like her. Agnes was gone. Entirely gone. On the mainland, in university, as good as dead.

Coming back to himself, Blackstrap noticed that his mother was not by his side. He stopped and glanced toward the main doors, saw her paused there, looking at a map in a large case. Her wavy black hair was cut shoulder-length. She was wearing a grey, black and white long coat with a white fake-fur collar. He went back to her.

'The bookstore,' she said, trailing her finger down over the front of the glass and reading the names of the stores in a flat voice.

Blackstrap looked around, trying to appear not interested.

'I don't know,' his mother whispered. 'Classics, I think. Yes. Classics Bookstore.' She said the number 24. Then studied the map.

Blackstrap stepped up to the map displayed inside the case.

'You are here,' said his mother, putting one finger on a red 'X.' 'Eighteen. Twenty-one. Twenty-four.' She set a finger from her other hand on the box with the number 24 in it.

Blackstrap measured the distance between his mother's fingers, the angle sloping from one to the other. He stared up the wide corridor.

'Here,' he said, tilting his head in what he knew was the right direction. He stepped away and his mother followed after him. While he slowed for her to catch up, he thought of taking her arm, helping her, but she was not old like that. Not old like some of the women he saw in the mall. The people here were making him feel angry. He did not know any of them and they were ignoring him. They didn't even notice each other. Ignore everyone, like they were the only ones who existed.

The tiled flooring began to slant upward. They passed a jewellery store with lots of glass cases, a clothes store with plenty of racks, and found Classics Bookstore across from Fred's Records that had music playing from inside. He glanced in and saw two young guys behind the cash register laughing at something. He knew the name of the place because he'd heard ads on the radio and been in there before to buy a few albums.

Blackstrap led his mother into the small bookstore across the way. She stood in front of one of the display shelves, regarding the books. Not knowing what to do. There were a large number of books beneath a poster of a man in a suit with a red rose in his lapel. The man had his hair slicked back and was holding a cat. Venetian blinds shut behind him. He looked dangerous. Blackstrap checked the cover. There were strings hanging down and attached to the big black letters that made up the name of the book. It was like someone was trying to turn the words into a puppet. He shifted his step a little, looked at another big display of books. Blood-red letters on black.

A tall, young woman behind the cash register was watching him. He noticed this when he turned. His mother cautiously wandered through an aisle of books.

'Can I help you?' said the woman from the counter.

Blackstrap said nothing in return, thinking.

The woman smiled then nodded at the books with the blood-red letters. 'Have you read *The Exorcist?*'

He shook his head. 'My mother's looking for a book,' he said, using the voice that he felt might best suit the woman.

'What sort of book?' The young woman came out from behind the counter, closed the little door that clicked shut.

Blackstrap shrugged. He checked to see where his mother was, then quickly followed after her, went right up to her side.

'What sort of book you want?' he asked.

His mother straightened her head from the tilt it was on from trying to read the names of the books in a row.

'What?'

'Wha' sort of book?' He glanced at the woman who was coming toward them. Blackstrap stepped back, out of the way, hands in the pockets of his jeans, to let the woman get near his mother.

'Can I help you?' she asked.

'I don't know,' his mother said, in a way that made him feel like she had just woken up to find herself there. 'I'm looking for journals, I guess.'

'Blank?'

'No, written in, from ships.'

'Maybe our war section.'

'War? No, not war. No, actually. Books about shipwrecks. Maybe.'

'Local?'

'Pardon me?'

'Of local interest?'

His mother stared at the woman, her face not recognizing what was being asked.

'About Newfoundland?'

'Yes, Newfoundland.'

The young woman pressed her lips together in a smile. 'That'd be our "Local Interest" section. This way, over here.' The woman directed them to a few shelves toward the back. 'You might find something here.'

His mother scanned the shelves.

'Newfie Jokes,' she whispered, her fingers reaching out to shift one of the booklets aside. A number of them were arranged on the top shelf, a series by the looks of the similar covers with different colours. The covers with drawings of one fat fisherman and one skinny one. Both of them with stunned faces. His mother picked one up and opened it, read quietly, with a careful interest, like it was a book that contained secrets: 'An old-timer Newfoundland fisherman was working on a wharf when a tourist from the mainland came along and asked: "Do you have any sons to help with your work?" The fisherman gave it a brief bit of consideration and then replied, "Yes, sir, I have two living and one in Toronto."'

His mother didn't even smile at the joke. She started reading another but gave up and laid the book back.

On the lower shelf, she found a cookbook with Newfoundland recipes. None of this seemed to interest her. In fact, it seemed to frighten her by the look on her face.

She wandered off, slowly checking other shelves, stopping to put her hand against a shelf and wait. At the end of one long aisle, she reached for a book, took it in her hands.

'It's about the Antarctic,' she said to Blackstrap, her voice almost hopeful. 'Ice. A man named Shackleton.'

Blackstrap nodded, not wanting any part of it. There was nothing in this store for him. He felt nervous, edgy, like he had a hangover. He wanted to leave. The lights were too bright, blaring above his head.

His mother read a bit of the book and her eyes turned wet. 'Exactly,' she said. 'Yes, this one.' She took it to the counter and opened her purse to pay. Blackstrap waited outside the store until his mother came up to him with the bag in her hand. 'I'll take that,' he said, reaching for it.

'No,' said his mother. 'You don't need to.' She watched straight ahead, walked in a strange way, like something might make her tip, might make her fall if she was not careful.

Blackstrap retraced his steps, remembering the map, and found the door where they first entered. When he got outside, into the fresh air, a weight left him and he breathed easier.

'Is that what you were after?' he asked, nodding toward her bag.

'Yes, thanks,' said his mother, facing the hundreds of vehicles before her, then looking at him with a serious expression. 'I don't know what I'd do without you, Blackstrap. I really don't. I think I'd die.'

(October)

There was a knock on the door. Emily had heard a car pulling up in front of her house, and had risen to peek out the living room window. A grey-haired man in a suit, with a leather satchel under his arm, was walking up the beachrock path. She assumed that it had something to do with the upcoming election. Jacob's part in it as regional co-ordinator for the Tories, his new preoccupation getting Joey Smallwood booted out of government, or it could have been one of the candidates coming around to seek her support. She avoided answering the front door. Whoever knocked at the front door was a stranger. Friends always entered through the door at the back of the house.

Regardless, the man would not stop knocking. Emily laid down the book about the polar explorer and moved toward the hallway. Before reaching the hallway, she paused to peek around the corner where she could see down to the front door. Through the top window in the door, the man was staring in, his eyes directly on her. She faltered back, as though punched, but then stepped ahead creating an awkward movement that made her feel guilty of something. In an attempt to cover up the mistake, she hurried her pace to the door and opened it.

The man had a paper in his hand.

'Is Jacob Hawco at home?'

'No, I'm sorry.'

'I have papers for him. You can sign for them.' He took a pen from his pocket, clicked down the tip. 'Your name is?'

'Emily.'

'Emily Hawco?'

'Yes.'

He eyed her for a moment, as though to make certain she was who she said she was. Then he wrote something on a piece of paper. 'Sign here.' He handed her the pen. At once, she signed. The man watched her hand, his eyes moving to her face. When Emily was finished, the man took the pen from her fingers. But he did not hand over the paper as expected. 'Can I see some ID, please?'

'ID?'

'Driver's licence would do.'

'I don't have a driver's licence.'

'Birth certificate.'

Emily watched the paper in the man's hands. The words at the top read: *Supreme Court of Newfoundland.* She hadn't noticed this before. Her head gave a little shake.

'Are you refusing to show identification?' the man asked.

'What?'

'Are you refusing to show identification?'

'I don't . . .'

The man ticked something on his sheet and handed over the paper. It was a legal document. Emily took it in both her hands and read the words: PLAINTIFF: Memorial University. DEFENDANT: Jacob Hawco. She heard a car door slam and looked up to see the man drive away.

Baffled, with the legal document in hand, she edged back into the house and shut the door. The Statement of Claim was about the journal. Words typed there described the origins of the journal, where it was found and who had written it. Emily took the piece of paper into her room and stood there. She had no idea what to do, fear radiating from that document into her heart.

Bending down, she lifted the edge of the mattress and slid the papers in deep. She then went back out to the living room and took up the journal, where it lay beside the book on the explorer, and returned to her bedroom. She pulled back the bed covers and climbed in, covering herself, where she remained, staring at the ceiling and clutching the journal to her breast, dreading that what she had done was so wrong. The man had been angry with her. She should have shown him what he wanted. Her birth certificate. She had done the wrong thing. She was now going to get into trouble with the courts, with the law. She might go to jail. She shut her eyes. And, worse still, they were going to take the journal away from her.

(December)

An RCMP cruiser arrived with a yellow VW Bug trailing behind it. Jacob Hawco saw it from where he stood in the living room window. He heard the whine of a snowmobile. Blackstrap coming through the forest trail, crossing the tracks and cutting through the trees at the back of the house. Engine shut off. Blackstrap off it and walking away before it was even fully stopped. That's how he always did it.

Jacob watched the officer being trailed by the spineless little shit from the university. The two men stepped across his lawn and approached his door. A solid knock sounded.

Sighing, Jacob went to answer it.

'Jacob Hawco?'

Jacob nodded at the RCMP officer.

'A judgement has been made in your absence. You are ordered by the Supreme Court of Newfoundland to give over possession of the journal of Francis Hawco.'

'Wha'?' Jacob shook his head. 'Journal?'

Jacob searched beyond the officer to see Blackstrap coming up the rear. The two men heard him arriving and turned to see who it might be.

'Hey,' said the young fellow, smiling like everything was okay.

Blackstrap glared as if to knock him down. He moved beside the officer and shoved by the young fellow who made an unexpected sound. Banging snow from his boots, he then entered the house, turned and took up position behind his father.

'Dey've come 'bout some journal?' Jacob squinted and shrugged. Shook his head. Confounded. 'Ye know anyt'ing 'bout a journal?' He said the word 'journal' like it was something new to his mouth.

'Don't know nothin' about that,' said Blackstrap.

'You both were here,' said the young fellow, pointing toward the kitchen. 'We sat at the table. Remember?'

Blackstrap and Jacob plainly, wordlessly looked at the young fellow.

'Are you refusing to produce the journal?' asked the RCMP officer.

'Don't 'av a clue wha' yer on about.'

'You are instructed to turn over the journal within ten days or risk arrest for failing to obey the orders of the crown.'

'Whose crown be dat?' asked Jacob.

The officer gave nothing in reply. He handed over the paper, and turned away and left. The young fellow from the university trailed after the officer until reaching the lane, where they separated and climbed into their cars. The young fellow glanced back at Blackstrap and Jacob as if he was afraid or sorry. Hard to tell the difference in a face like that.

Jacob watched the cars drive off. 'Friggin' Mounties.' He spun around and cast his eyes across Blackstrap's face, then down at the paper. 'Wha's ta be done?'

In silence, Blackstrap watched the yellow VW Bug as it curved up the road and disappeared around the evergreens. He moved ahead of his father, closer to the door's threshold. He felt his father's hand on his arm.

'None of dat now,' Jacob said, drawing Blackstrap back into the house. 'He ain't wort' it.'

'I know what happens,' Emily said, holding her coat to her throat.

The barely visible orange flames rose out of the rusty barrel. Jacob stood in the waver of heat, the snow brilliant white behind him. He glanced over his shoulder to see Blackstrap leaned in the doorway of the shed.

Emily held out the journal.

Jacob took it and raised a long stick to shove down the length of the book's spine, the point prying between the homemade page stitchings. He held it over the fire and lowered it, watching the pages ignite, then glancing at Emily whose face had gone as white as a ghost's.

The pages burned easily. Jacob caught a scent of the leather heating up. Hide. It reminded him of a hundred memories of skinning animals, of cooking animals with a bit of hide still on. The scent of the paper burning was distinct. The roar and crackle of fire gave way to the greater roar of the train nearing the junction. They all remained still while the train passed. Jacob studied the flames until they had blackened the pages all the way back to the spine. Then he lifted it out and dropped it on the ground, kicked a pile of snow to hiss on top of it.

At once, Emily bent there carefully brushing the snow aside, uncovering what had been buried. Bits of black came away in white. The pages burnt through. Shreds of words had endured the flames, but what remained of the ragged edges of paper were black and deep brown.

Regardless, Emily turned the charred pages with her white, bloodless hands. 'I know what happens,' she said, reading through the ruins while filling in those vanished words.

On the specified date in the court order, the RCMP cruiser pulled up Hawco Lane, with the yellow VW trailing after it like a toy.

In unison, the officer and the young fellow approached the door of the Hawco residence.

When the journal was requested, Jacob said: 'Yes, b'y, we did come across dat after all.' He gave a friendly wink and went into the house. A few moments later, he returned, wagging the charred journal in his hands.

'Had a spell of bad luck, it did,' he said, nodding at the scorched remnants. 'It were filled widt such lively tales dat it leapt right inta da stove one day. Full of spirit dat journal. Cripes, I never saw da like of it 'fore!'

Although Emily Hawco, my great-grandmother, was never truly accepted in Bareneed (anyone coming to Bareneed from another place was referred to as an 'immigrant' even if they lived there for the remainder of their life), she often had women visitors from the community who came to see what sort of gossip might be taken away. The women would tell one another of the fancy place settings and elaborate tables of food that were laid out, claiming that she thought she was so 'high and mighty' and 'butter wouldn't melt in her mouth.' Being the daughter of a merchant only made matters worse.

1953

Cutland Junction

The perfect skin of these women

The rumble in the earth rattled the cups and saucers and set the windows in Isaac Tuttle's house shimmying with a duller rattle.

Glancing out his back window, across the thirty feet of frosty land toward the narrow-gauge track, Isaac sighted the matt blackness of the train moving steadily along, his eyes trained on the windows of the passenger compartments and the faces of the men and women, some in profile, others studying the land and houses as the train slowed toward the station. The bold, iron authenticity of the locomotive never failed to impress him. A machine of unbendable presence.

Scanning the windows and passengers, Isaac's imagination conjured thoughts of the hundreds of different lives that moved through the Junction on their way east to St. John's. People from Canada, or America, even Europeans occasionally arrived, if only for a few brief minutes, in Cutland Junction, venturing from Nova Scotia where the train was driven onto the ship, the nine-hour voyage across the Cabot Strait, then docking on the west coast of Newfoundland, in Port aux Basque. Years ago, Isaac had worked in the truck-to-truck transfer shed over on the west coast, changing the wheels beneath the boxcars from standard gauge to the narrow-gauge truck that suited the tracks running across the island.

Working in the railway yard as a young man in his twenties, he had lived a miser's life while marvelling at the people, the clothes they wore, the men in tan or blue double-breasted suits, so smart looking, and the gracefulness of the women in their fancy hats and coats, soft gloves on their fine slim fingers. Not a smudge of dirt on either one of them. They were clean. Blessed.

It was from this air of wealth that Isaac had come to realize the money that could be made, the money that was rolling across the one-thousand-mile stretch of island wilderness and ready to be picked up at every stop if there were only something of worth to offer.

Near the time of his revelation, he had received a cable from the priest; the message clear and exact: 'Your Father Gravely Ill. Return Home A Necessity.' And so Isaac had left the west coast, headed east on a twenty-four-hour train ride, back to his home town, Cutland Junction, where he tended to his father, who was coughing and spitting up black, and unable to rise from his bed without collapsing in exhaustion. At once, Isaac took over his father's coal delivery business from his father's brother, Tommy, who was partial to drink, kept no records of delivery, squandered the coal payments, and even missed delivery dates, so that there were people, mostly the poor and ill-fated, who were near perishing from the cold.

Isaac set the business right, delivered in a dependable fashion, so that he was praised for his efforts by the good people of Cutland Junction and Bareneed who had cursed his uncle Tommy for the drunkard's slack ways. Isaac even paid his father's brother a small amount to keep him in liquor and, more importantly, out of his path, while he set up shop from the wages he had hoarded on the west coast. And in this store that he had hired a man to build, he set aside the window space and a full corner to display the latest fashions that he shipped in from London, New York and Paris. A coat, shirt or skirt expertly stitched together from a fine fabric made the travellers seem so beyond these woods, so sophisticated and of a mysterious elegance that produced in him a longing for the possibilities of their lives.

The fashions drew refined ladies and gentlemen to his store during their station stop in Cutland Junction. The conductor forced to wait so frequently that the fifteen-minute stopover was eventually written into the schedule by the Newfoundland Railway Corporation.

Isaac's store was an oddity; the passengers disbelieved that the dresses and suits displayed in the shop window of Isaac Tuttle's General Store could be found there in the middle of nowhere. In disbelief, they would glance over their shoulders to face the dense wilderness, the snow-covered boughs of the evergreens, that carried on eastward for eighty miles until reaching a city built in the hollow bowl of a harbour that skirted the Atlantic Ocean. St. John's. A place of near civility where the fish trade prospered in the hands of a few families of merchants.

The passengers bought the garments in Isaac Tuttle's General Store as souvenirs to which a colourful story was attached. It intrigued the ladies to no end. They whispered about which friend or relative they might tell on their return home, how this one or that one would never believe such a thing, while they glanced back at Isaac Tuttle behind the counter, the imprint of the comb's rake grooved in his slicked hair, his collar yellowed and of a period passed, his blackened hands joined behind his back, a shelf of holy pictures and icons displayed on the wall above him, his big eyes fixed on them, his grin pointed sheepishly sharp. They could not help but wonder what this man could be made of. Why did he import these fashions and yet dress in worn garments of such threadbare nature himself? All of them wondering how or why this was possible, while Isaac studied the perfect skin of these women, savoured the foreign clarity of their speech, bathed in the scent of their bottled perfumes tinged by the heat of their bodies. He had listened in on conversations at the station in Port aux Basque, found delight in the way these sacred women spoke. Hearing the exchange between two passing women, he would smile to himself, almost giggle at the way they were so utterly different from the men and women of Cutland Junction. They trod like angels, drifting about his shop, setting gloved fingertips to an item, touching to determine if an object might be meant for them.

Emily spoke in the same manner, but still with a trace of a British intonation in how she shaped her words. Isaac adored her, secretly, unbearably. When he was with her, he felt the way Frank Sinatra sang.

He imagined tilting a fedora down over his eyes, drawing on a cigarette and taking Emily's hand, stepping out with her to all the extraordinary places he read about in movie magazines. Nightclubs and restaurants. He'd seen pictures of movie stars gazing into the cameras while dining at a noted ritzy establishment. Holding such images in his head, he saved his money so that he might buy the train fare to New York. Two tickets. One for him and one for Emily. One day Emily would be his. If only she had married him instead of Jacob Hawco. Emily's new baby had just been born. He flushed at the idea, recollecting the intimate moments they had spent together months ago, and wondering if it had been real at all. If Emily had actually taken him in that way. It gave him a splitting headache to think of it. If their union had been real, then why was Emily now acting so distant toward him? She should leave Jacob. She should admit her love of him. They should elope. If Jacob only knew the truth when he looked at that baby.

Regardless, the baby offered a fine excuse for paying a visit. It was ten days since its birth so it would be Emily's Sitting-Up Day. The Groaning Cake and other dainty fare would be laid out on the table. And a crowd of mostly women would be down for a visit, but he could hazard a visit himself. He might duck his head in without being given much notice to peek a look at Emily. The new baby in her arms. The baby that should be his.

Jacob was back from the trapline, made out to be some sort of hero for a broken leg he had been foolish enough to achieve while in the woods. Probably broke it himself, on purpose, so he could limp back acting all full of himself after fixing it up. Just like him to behave that way, even if he did almost freeze to death. The bragging bugger. That was the tenth or twelfth time he'd almost perished in the woods or drowned out on the sea. Why wouldn't he just get it done and over with? Rather than being looked upon as a hero, why didn't people just tag him for what he truly was: stunned?

Isaac tutted chastisingly and blessed himself for thinking such thoughts, faithfully muttered a prayer for the Lord's forgiveness, then decided it might be appropriate to bring Jacob a pack of Player's Navy Cut from the shop in honour of his salvation. And a holy card of the Blessed Virgin for Emily. No doubt, Junior might like a comic book.

What did he have for the baby? Perhaps it would be best to bring two packages of cigarettes. Good idea to keep on Jacob's good side, so Isaac could continue coming around. And maybe, with a little coaxing, Jacob would tell Isaac the story. Not that Isaac cared to have his ear bent by outlandish tales strung together by a man's reckless pride. But he would listen for the sake of being in Emily's presence and to watch what those tales did to the face of his eternally beloved.

Bareneed

Saint Blackstrap of Bareneed

(Sitting-Up Day)

'We could name'm after yer fadder,' Jacob suggested, limping theatrically toward the stove to set the kettle on the damper. 'Alan.'

The kitchen was crowded with people from the community, mostly women come to view the baby and to praise Emily for having the sturdy health and constitution that permitted her to survive the ordeal. Missus Murphy, the midwife, took the honoured spot at the table, next to Emily, while the remaining seat was reserved for Jacob's Uncle Ace, who sat there not uttering a word, merely staring from one face to another, and listening as though perplexed by the possibility of speech. No one ever spoke of the terrible experience out on the sealing icefields thirty years ago that had delivered suffering of such ferociousness it had snatched away Uncle Ace's voice forever. The story that silenced a man was best left to itself.

Emily looked over at Jacob, not knowing how to react, uncertain if Jacob had suggested the name 'Alan' out of sincerity or as a slap in the face to her father, the man who had forbidden their marriage.

Jacob patted the Groaning Cake he had baked for Emily, testing for heat, then picked a stray raisin off the edge of it, chewed it up, savouring the taste of the half-burnt raisin. He then worked the lever on the pump, gushing out a glass of water. Without regarding Emily again, he drank it back in one confident swallow. 'I'm right t'irsty. Don't know why.'

A few in the room laughed as they often did at Jacob's comment, for most things Jacob said seemed tinged with humour. It was not necessarily the meaning of the spoken words, but rather the larger-than-life lilt of his tone that drew people toward laughter, as though he were goading them on and they were pleased to ceaselessly acknowledge his bravado.

'It's all that salt meat you love to eat,' Emily informed him, just as she did every time he was curious about his thirst. A few laughed outright, while others sipped from their cups of tea. Two young girls, Mildred Bishop and Nadine Newell, from further up the hill stood by Emily, one at each shoulder, making faces and sounds, trying to coax a smile out of the baby, all to no avail. The newborn merely watched the girls with a flat expression bordering on distaste.

In the corner, young Billy Coombs, a man of twenty or twenty-five (no one knew for certain as he was frozen in the grips of childhood), with a round belly and bloated face, stood back against the wall, his dull eyes slowly watching the people, his mouth open in a pose of nonsensical comment as his tongue came out every now and again to smear his bloated lips.

Aunt Minnie was seated in a chair by the hall doorway with her accordion at ready on her lap. She had taken off her coat but left her woollen hat perched high on her head. She nodded and winked at the occasional stray comment, happy as a lark to simply observe the people mill about, her white chin whiskers twitching occasionally while she clicked her slipping dentures back in place and waited on a time when she might be instructed to start playing.

Emily smiled down at the baby, its steady eyes curiously staring up at her.

'Yays, you're right dere,' Jacob considered. 'The salt would make me t'irsty.'

A few grins, a handful of chuckles, an amused wink here and there, and a head-tilting nod of agreement from Aunt Minnie. 'T'irsty,' she repeated. 'Would be 'bout right.'

Looking toward Jacob, Emily saw that he was standing above her, plainly staring down at the baby, then over at the wooden cradle on the floor toward the daybed. She suspected that he thought she might be spoiling the infant, having him up in her arms all the time.

Jacob's fingertips tapped out a tune on the tabletop and he hummed along. He ended up the tapping and humming with a few words, his voice high and like velvet: 'Mussels in the corrr-ner,' then glanced over at Aunt Minnie who nodded and pulled out her dentures to store safely away in her pocket, so as to protect them from flying from her mouth when the merriment prevailed. Grinning a toothless grin, she leaned a little forward, jerked her arms into action as the accordion squeezed out three sharp uneven notes, then swept into a steady flurry of memory-tunes, her elbows bobbing.

With eyes on Aunt Minnie, Jacob's boots drummed the floor as a gust of wind rose at his back. People had started clapping. Jacob turned to see Junior coming into the room, the boy's school slate tucked under his arm, his bottle of water stuck out of his pocket and some papers in his other hand. His cheeks and nose were rosy.

'Close dat door, Junior,' barked Jacob. 'Enough ta freeze da arse off ya.'

Junior stepped in and turned, hand on the tarnished brass knob, he pulled shut the door with a bang that was barely heard above the music, clapping and hooting.

Junior brought the sheet of paper to his father and poked it at him.

'Wha's dis, me son?'

'Bears,' Junior shouted proudly. 'See, that's you and Mom and me and the small one there's the baby.' He pointed with his finger, glanced brightly up at his father's face. 'We're learning about polar bears.'

'Dat's mighty fine, Junior,' Jacob said, laying the drawing on the table without further comment and limping toward the kettle which jetted a flow of steam toward the ceiling.

Emily regarded Junior, then Jacob, knowing that in his heart of hearts he had no time for schooling, and believed that Jacob Junior should be out in the boat or on the trapline like his Uncle Ace was at the age of ten, schooling robbing the boy of his bloodline.

'Come over, sweetheart.' Emily smiled, drawing Junior near. The boy leaned back against her, his elbow on her leg, and stared at the drawing on the table. Emily made an extra effort to admire its qualities, until the baby began wailing.

'That's just perfect,' Emily said to Junior. 'You can see the white.'

'I coloured it. White and yellow too. Bren's cat is white but he looks yellow in the snow.'

'Shhh,' said Emily, rocking the baby.

A wrinkled, blue-veined hand slowly reached forward, its fingers resting on the drawing a few moments before Uncle Ace inched it toward him across the table. He stared down at the polar bears, his eyes steady and serious, then he turned his head to consider Junior, his white brow scrunched together with worry and curiosity.

Junior watched Uncle Ace, waiting for some sort of sign, but Uncle Ace merely returned his perplexed eyes to the drawing and continued studying it. He raised one trembling finger and set it against the biggest bear. 'Tt,' he said, but no one was listening. 'Tt.'

At the sound of Uncle Ace's voice, the baby ceased crying.

Junior nodded at the old man and gave him a smile.

'Tt,' Uncle Ace kept on, his tongue between his teeth. Then he shut his eyes, as though in sleep, and frowned.

Junior glanced at the baby's head, the light fine hair. The eyes that stared with serious wonder.

'He's some small,' Junior said, feeling proud that Uncle Ace, a man who rarely paid much mind to anything put before him, had taken such an interest in his drawing. The notice invigorated him. 'His fingers are right tiny.'

'We were just trying to name him.'

One of the girls, Mildred Bishop, the eldest of the two and the one who would be helping with the baby in the coming months, reached to take up the infant, while Emily carefully allowed the transfer.

The accordion music came to a halt and Aunt Minnie sat still again, grinning and nodding at the bits of applause, then sheepishly eyeing the Groaning Cake on the counter while fishing her dentures from her pocket.

Young Billy Coombs made a whelping sound, like the cry of a seal. The sound was ignored by all, save for Uncle Ace whose eyes opened on the picture of the bears then moved to Billy's face.

'How about Butch?' asked Junior.

'I don't know about Butch,' said Emily.

Jacob laid a cup down in front of Emily. She smiled briefly in thanks and lifted the tea, sensing the rising heat against her lips and lightly blowing to cool it. A cup was then set down before Missus Murphy who said: 'T'ank ye,' and glanced over the plates of cakes and biscuits, baked by the visiting women and laid out on the table. She reached and took a lemon square, transferred it slowly to her plate so as not to spill crumbs everywhere.

Emily noticed Uncle Ace, who was watching her with eyes full of emotion she could make no sense of. He now held the drawing in both hands and at a distance from his face.

The baby commenced crying and Mildred Bishop went about trying to calm him, but to no avail. Her attempts only added vigour to the baby's protests. Flustered, she handed him back to Emily and he ceased wailing at once.

'He'll get used to you,' Emily said.

Quiet as a dove, the baby stared up at Emily's face.

'How 'bout Weepy?' Jacob offered.

There was much laughter. Aunt Minnie even let loose with one long cackle that ended in a wink, a tilt of her head, and a delighted smacking of gums, her dentures set at ready on her lap.

'Don't be so heartless,' someone said in the room. A woman's voice.

Jacob watched a crow through the window. He imagined it to be the same one that had followed him from the woods. He searched the treeline for the fox that had slept beside the stove in the kitchen on the first night of his return, then had fled the next morning, scampering over the wooden floor and out the back door, as though suddenly brought to realization. Despite its escape, it might be lingering near for a scrap of food, but there was no sign of it. Jacob gave a quiet laugh, then glanced at Uncle Ace who was now watching the crow.

'How about Molasses?' said Junior.

'Yays,' said Aunt Minnie, nodding winsomely. 'T'is a good 'n. Yays. Lovely name.'

The women smiled at Junior, admiring his good looks and charm, just like his father in that respect, the boy constantly fawned over by the women of Bareneed. A little gentleman. A strong hand mussed up his hair. It was his father.

'Blackstrap molasses,' said Jacob, swallowing a healthy mouthful of rum, his blue eyes gleaming with wicked humour.

'Blackstrap!' said Junior, playing to the crowd. 'Now that's a name to reckon with.'

Laughter rose from the gathered numbers, the glint in each eye speaking volumes: Like father, like son.

'Mighty fine,' said someone.

'Yays,' said Aunt Minnie, chuckling and blinking fiercely. 'Yays. Hee, hee.'

Emily and Jacob laughed outright at Junior's statement, Jacob leaning forward to lay a hand on his son's small shoulder, then returning his attention to the window where another large black bird suddenly swooped down onto his snow-covered garden. Two for joy.

Emily sipped her tea, studied her husband. For countless nights, she had been up with the baby, and hardly had a wink of sleep, so her perception was near immaculate. Pristine. As such, the mere sight of her husband was beginning to irritate her. She noticed the sloppy manner in which he wore his shirt, the stubble on his face, the lines running from the corners of his eyes, his wind-tanned leathery skin, the careful way he considered her words, as if he cared too dearly about what she had to say, yet pretended not to, listened attentively then dismissed her words, only to ponder them in the hours to come and hesitantly, quietly, admit to their truth.

'Go comb your hair,' Emily said, her tone harsher than intended.

Pinning Emily with a look that cast a darkness over his face, Jacob stood rigid. 'I'm not one'a'yer children, womb'n,' he grumbled. 'Watch yer bobber.'

'Blackstrap,' Junior quickly repeated, up on his tiptoes, aiming to avoid argument.

'No,' said Emily, ignoring Jacob and the eyes that were hotly trained on her, realizing she had made a mistake and wanting out of it. 'It must be a saint's name. Joseph . . .'

'Like with Jesus,' exclaimed Junior, further encouraged to have the conversation back on track.

'Thomas . . . Alphonsus,' Emily said to Junior. 'Or Francis, after your father's father.'

Jacob continued glaring at Emily, unwilling to let his ire wane.

'Blackstrap it is,' he said shortly, limping toward the back porch. 'Saint Blackstrap of Bareneed,' he muttered under his breath, then whistled a sharp steady tune while he pulled on his cap and mittens, then was out the door, yanking it closed with a bang.

The room went silent, uncomfortably still, until Junior asked, 'Was Dad serious?'

'About what?'

Then young Billy Coombs yelped, clapped his palms together once. He said a word that sounded like: Pufuct.

'Blackstrap?'

'No, Junior,' Emily said. 'The priest won't baptize him that.' Gazing down at the baby cradled in her arms, she leaned forward and kissed the top of his head, paying no mind to Jacob, unwilling to let him sink her spirits on her Sitting-Up Day. Just as her lips touched the baby, he bawled out, his tiny mouth quivering.

A bit of conversation had started up again. Jack Tobin, whose manner was scarcely bruised by any sort of ill will or altercation, raised his fiddle from between his legs and stroked a few notes, then caressed a quiet ballad from his instrument, the notes so sweet that they calmed Emily's heart, and shushed the baby. When the ballad sank to bittersweet lament and ended on that note, the baby began to cry again.

'Oh, you're such a fussy bugger,' Emily said, tentatively trying the name, 'Alphonsus.' She smiled and tickled the baby's cheek, but he jerked his head away. Just a reflex, she thought. Quietly on her tongue, 'Alphonsus.' The baby's cry rose toward a screech.

'Shhh, Blackstrap,' said Junior, pushing in by his mother's side. The baby fell silent, its big eyes enthralled by Junior's image.

What a queer name, Emily thought, but it seemed to suit him. Her father, Alan, would abhor it for its coarseness.

'Blackstrap,' she said, louder this time as though testing the strength of it.

'Blackstrap,' repeated one woman speculatively, the sound echoed like a hiccup by young Billy Coombs, who slid his back nearer along the wall.

'Yeah,' Junior called out, startling the baby whose arms jerked away from his sides, his cry razoring the air.

134

This brought on a few titters of laughter and a few sighs of pity for the little one's upset, then the passing of stray comments back and forth that coaxed a bit more liveliness into the room. Caught up in the levity, the fiddler now broke loose with a heart-jigging sweep of reels. Jack Tobin's foot pounding the kitchen floor while Aunt Minnie joined in.

Emily diligently shushed the baby.

'Sorry,' Junior half shouted.

A chill entered the room and Junior turned to see what he thought might be his father returning, but was, in fact, Isaac Tuttle stood in the back doorway, looking straight at Junior's mother, his face as red as a boiled beet.

'Come in,' Emily called out, tipping her head in welcome.

Isaac grinned sheepishly, then edged his way in, carefully shut the door. He winked at Junior and grinned some more while fishing a black-smudged comic book from his pocket, then handed it over. Without acknowledging Junior's awestruck 'Thank you,' Isaac commenced unloading his pockets and laying the seemingly endless string of gifts on the kitchen counter.

While the gifts were being set in order, a knock came on the door. Still clutching the comic book, Junior hurried over, brushing past Isaac Tuttle to pull it open. Stood there was Stanley Barnes, the fifteen-year-old who delivered messages for his mother, Ada, the telegraph operator up across from the church. He held his hand out to Junior. In it was a message.

'It's fer yer mudder,' said Stanley, as every face in the room turned inquisitive. 'From da Mental in S'int Jahns.'

During collecting stories for this book, I have always been attracted to Isaac Tuttle and his peculiar way of life and view of things. In fact, after reading many of his journal scribblings, I felt that I was almost able to think like him, when in a certain state of mind. As might be imagined, many of the scenes involving him are of my own arrangement, but taken from the spirit of his writing. I hope that I have done him justice. Mixing speculation with fact often worries an author. Then again, approximations of your own design are sometimes all you really know of a person.

1992

Cutland Junction

I

Observances

10.40 a.m., September 16. Constable Pope drives along the west side of Coombs Hill. Pulls his police cruiser over. Parks on the side of the dirt road. Fifteen feet ahead, a backhoe. Pope has already verified the owner's name. Blackstrap Hawco: Age 37. Medium height. Blonde hair with patches of grey. Blue eyes. No recognizable scars. The backhoe was there yesterday. Exact same place. Constable Pope decides to take another look. There is no need to bother fitting on his hat. No one around to impress with formality. He steps from the car. The quietude is immediate. Captivating. Pope stands amid the wilderness. Trying to ignore the silence. He looks up at the sky. Immense. If he were a different man, a man he sometimes sees himself as, he might smile at the pure autumn blue. But he does not. The sun is on his face. Not a sound of a bug. The temperature: 73 degrees. He listens for three seconds. Then heads toward the machine. Six feet behind the backhoe. He hears a sound indicating movement in the bushes. He stops. Perfectly still. Stares into the woods toward west. Nothing in his field of vision.

There are no trails close by. Pope has already investigated the possibility. Cupping his hands around his mouth, he calls, 'Hawco.' The sound rolls across the valley. The sound rises up along the evergreen backside of Coombs Hill. And higher. Into the sky he will not check again.

Turning, Constable Pope scans across the forest. Calls for what he decides will be the final time. Listening, he hears a distant sound. What he takes for a woman's scream. The pitch is shrill. Needles through the wilderness. It might be the sound of a hawk, Pope thinks. But remains unconvinced. The human quality of sound easily identified. Precise. Karen Hawco comes to mind. His visit with her concerning her husband's disappearance. The first time he laid eyes on her. He was struck speechless. Struck dumb. He wonders why the strong attraction. No great beauty. Plump with black hair. He prefers blondes. Wonders if she might remind him of someone. But she does not. What is it about the woman? His mind veers away from her image. Once again, he considers the source of the sound. If it were a bird, it would be large. Again, he hears the cry, muddled as if from behind glass. Rising over the hill. Then down through the density of spruce. Sound carrying the incredible distances it takes to reach one other person. Pope guesses a mile and a half away. Maybe nearer. Karen Hawco. He thinks of making a radio call. Reporting the sound. But what might it really be? An argument in a house? A woman screaming in frustration. Shouting at her children. Not Karen Hawco. He is only thinking of her. Pre-occupied with the recollection of her face. He feels it though. Feels her.

'Hawco,' he calls. And the woman-like scream sounds again. It might be a crow. Or a bird capable of mimicry. Responding to his own outburst. Are those birds native to Newfoundland? He cannot recall. No knowledge of the wilderness. At this point, he steps toward the backhoe. Grabs the cold rail. And climbs up one step. Then grips the parallel rail with his other hand. Takes another step. At that height, he can see into the compartment. Ripped black seat with the stuffing worn dirty grey. Taped with silver duct tape. A dusty green baseball cap. A greasy rag of red and black flannel tied around one of the long black shifts. No sign of recent activity. The interior is exactly as it was when he checked yesterday.

Constable Pope turns. Gazes out over the land. With his weight shifted, he must tighten his grip on the rail. He is aware of his boots against the narrow steel steps. He notices the autumn colours. Mingled amongst the spruce. No movement that he can see. Nothing that might indicate the presence of a man. The presence of a body. He eases up on his focus. Takes in the entirety of the scene. The brash, heart-tightening beauty of the immense view. The land reminds him of Mount Royal. The park in Montreal. But no open space. More desolate with its black-green stunted trees. Kept from reaching mainland heights by the brief summer season. The harsh, punishing winter winds. The salty mist from the ocean. And the rocky barren soil. A more natural uncultivated beauty. The land purified through some sort of rugged aching.

Climbing back down, Constable Pope glances back to check the cruiser. The sun is warmer than he assumed it should be. In this part of the country. Since transferring to Newfoundland, two months ago, he has been ceaselessly surprised. Newfoundland was supposed to be freezing all the time. Nothing but snow. People living in igloos. The people a big joke. Newfies. He finds them more dangerous than charming. Liars and thieves. Half-honest gangsters. Always after something for nothing.

Static from his radio. A call coming through. He forgets the landscape, the colours. The cries of large self-governed birds. He strides for his vehicle. Pulls open the door. Sits in. Leans across the seat. Snatches hold of the mouthpiece. Speaks. Someone responds. Relaying information. He inspects the dashboard. Glimpses up at the sky. Stares into the trees. The meshing of limbs. Dense furry evergreens speckled with orange and yellow leaves. The stench of rot. He recalls the odour from his times in the woods as a boy. Back to school. The nip in the air. The rot underfoot. A piece of clothing in the woods.

The view blurs. The dispatcher gives mores details. He puts it all together while he listens. His eyes fixed on the seat. His own composition. Sketchy details. A break and entry four kilometers further down the same dirt road. Deeper into cottage country. No, not cottage country. But cabin country. That's what the Newfies call their summer places.

Families from St. John's filling their cottages with valuable toys. The impoverished local Newfs envying so many expensive gadgets. Here in the woods. Such wealth. For profit or revenge, the locals find communal joy in robbing the townies blind.

Karen cannot gather the strength. Cannot pull up her jeans. Bunched down around her ankles. Cover herself. On her back. It doesn't matter now. Air on her calves. Thighs. Wet. Spot. Dot. Trickle. Drip. On the kitchen floor. Fluid warmed. Now chilling outside. Not hers. But from inside. Her head languidly dips left. A television program. Something like this once. A survivor. She thought the woman might be angry. But wasn't. Like it was natural. Supposed to happen. Expected. Where is anger? Hate? Eyes transfixed. By the silver refrigerator vent. Dust in grey clumps. Where is anger? It didn't happen. Not angry. Dead. Silently. She shifts her gaze. Along the floor. The stove drawer. A chip out of the almond enamel. In the left corner. The infraction an emotionless observation. A speck gouged.

Chipped.

Enamel.

Fingernails.

Gouged.

Out of her.

Her T-shirt torn down the centre. Hangs away. Fabric like skin split open. From the centre of her chest. Bra still fastened in the back. Yanked up. Away from her. White breasts. Weight loosely resting. Against the sides of her arms. Loose. Flesh. Flat to the floor. She feels so. Nothing. Only so. So is what she feels. In her body. Next week. Lop them off.

Observances, she thinks. A word. Lodged in her mind. A marble stuck in wet clay. *Observances*. She cannot cry. That was taken. Her voice shrunken. So small she cannot possibly. Speak. The refrigerator clicks on. Flinching. Something whirring. Then the ringing. Of the telephone. Flinching. That cracks inside. Like eggshells. Not dead, she thinks. Eggshells cracked but nothing born. Blankly looks up at the telephone. So high above her. Looming. Unseen before. From this angle. Vision like weight. Presses down on her. She might be scared. If there was hatred. Her skin is cold. Things so high. Above her. She had never suspected how cold. The floor could actually be. Blank against her back. The feeling spreading. Into her spine. Her legs. She concentrates on holding it. In one place. Just there. Between her legs. Just there. Push. It out. Dot. Trickle. Stream. Gasp. Bear down. Her nipples. Body. Deeper than body. This freezing urge. Hatred. Hatched.

Her heavy arms. Lifted. She folds them. Across her breasts. Blinks at the ceiling. The flat glass shade. With the bulb not on. Behind it. The aluminium back door opens. Footsteps in the floorboards. Bootsteps. Against her back. Vibrating. In her. Through her.

'Dear Jaysus,' a voice says. Nearer now. Standing over her. She sees that it is the old man. Tries covering herself. Turns her face. Away. Realizes her mouth is. Open. A rat hiding in there. Curled up. Like a baby sob. She bursts out. Crying. So is an infant. A rat shrieking. The bugs and rodents infesting every hole. Scurry across her. House. Home. House. Another man. Making it all too real. Blimp.

Her hand rises. Her bare flesh moving. To cry. She covers herself. Tries her voice. So small, 'goaway.' Only the size of a frozen pea. But it works. When she clicks it loose. Smearing beneath. Her dry tongue. Through the parchness of her throat. The wetness of her sobs. What will eat. And drink. In her. Discontinuity – 'help.' Hatched and crushed. Insects. Trickling out of her. She retches. The old man steps back. She retches again. Vomits. Into her hair.

Jacob Hawco's breath turns heavier, hotter, in his throat. His eyes shift for the window. Stare out into the back yard. He squints at the buzzing in his ears. Trying to decipher what might be bearing down on him. His weathered hand starts for the door frame. She has fallen. Emily. He goes to help her up. But it is too late. She is already dead. Emily has fallen. It was that sound that did it. The cry of the baby she heard. Emily. He knows who has done this. The wind. No, a man. He was witness to the van that came, that carried the man, the man that wanted, the man that owned. Fleeing like the wind. The living drift.

Jacob will not trouble the woman. Who was it he thought was Emily? Who? A blanket will help. But he takes heed of the woman's violent moans. She gasps for air. Is Emily dying? He goes to her. Kneels. Looks into her face. Which face? Whose? A pain flits in his left eye, a slicing sharpness cuts through his brain. A razor over notched feelings. His wrinkled eyelids jam shut. Flinching, he jerks violently to one side. Time not being right for him. What year was it, he wonders. Is it. Him on the floor. Three feet from Emily. His son's daughter. Emily, is it? Ruth. His left arm out to her. If it is his arm. He sees it. But not for what it is. Reaching out. Fingers creeping. Then. He cannot. Remember.

A thing.

Karen turns. Her head to see. The old man. His eyes. Vacant. White. Eye to eye. Him. Her. Watching. Her. So is what? So is her.

II

Two missing weeks

Blackstrap Hawco charges the dozer ahead. Shovelling a mound of freshly unearthed rust-coloured clay down over the bank. Where the trees grow off into miles of distance. The smell of earth and sod. The roll of large rocks and chainsawed stumps. Torn clear with their tangle of roots. The machine roars back and forth. Heaping up soil until the space is clear. Level. Nothing but rich flat earth on the lot where he'll build Vardy's cabin. Him and Paddy. A week and a half's work.

Leaving the engine idling, he climbs down. And steps backwards. Regards what he has accomplished. Sees the scope broaden with each step in reverse. Beyond the lot, the grey and beige boulders spotting the barrens. And further off. Sharp rocks jutting out of low purplish hills. A line of stunted spruce beyond. Landscape unyielding inside him. He stops. Then returns. Leans against the side of the vibrating steel, its pulse working through his body.

Rolling a cigarette, he notices his boots are caked with mud. Bangs them against the steel. Then strikes a match to the cigarette. Cups his hands around the flame. Tilts his head forward. His unshaven cheeks sucking in.

The smoke drawn deep into his lungs. Then streaming to blow out the match. Thinks of the Soiree dance later that night. The people setting up for it on his way over. Thinks of Karen. She wouldn't go with him. Never out anywhere with him. He hears her laugh. The raunchy laugh new to her. The way she was when he returned. His father ill. He turns his head from the thought. Eyes on the land. Karen's laugh. Like she had something to do with it. A crackle shot through both of them. He sees her smoking. The store-bought cigarettes in the red package. He pictures her name on his arm. The new tattoo he had cut into his skin on a tear in St. John's. The first time he'd been there in a year or more. Having to return to Cutland Junction. To face the changes. Just like that. His father struck down. His wife not herself.

It was one of Karen's brothers, Tuffy, who told Blackstrap. Everyone was looking for him. When he stopped by Tuffy's apartment. After the third day of drinking. Have a wash and get the news. Blackstrap had called home. Heard Karen's strange nervous voice. Loud and laughing and cursing over the phone. And he'd known then that something terrible had happened. His wife no longer quiet. Refined. He thought maybe she was drunk. But it was different from drunk. Wilder. With a skittish wind in her voice that clattered through her.

Blackstrap pulls off his blue and black flannel jacket. Yanks up his sleeve. Turns his left arm to look at the skin. Her name, KAREN. Beneath an outline of a naked lady with dark wavy hair like Karen's. Long like Karen's used to be. Before she cut it off. Blackstrap had even made the fat man with the crew cut dot a few freckles in place along her throat. He couldn't do them along the back of her neck and shoulders. The way they actually were. Because the tattoo was only front-on. Blackstrap had argued with drunken logic. That the freckles could be put on the back of his arm. But the man said it would cost extra. Like doing another tattoo. And Blackstrap had demanded that it be done. Threatened to destroy the cramped tattoo shop on Water Street West. Step out from behind the divider. Rip the samples off the walls. The fat man had stood. Pointed his thick arm toward the door. Roaring, 'Get the fuck outta my shop,' pudgy fingers held out. 'Money first.'

Blackstrap grumbles his wife's name. Holds the cigarette between his lips. Squints away the smoke. Sweeps down his sleeve. Shoves his arms back into his jacket.

He climbs up on the dozer. Shuts it off. Pockets the key. Wanders away. Leaves the machine for Batten to pick up on the flat bed. Walks out toward the site opening where his backhoe is parked. He climbs up. Starts it. Backs out.

Rattling and bumping over the dirt road, he soon hits the pavement. Where it begins alongside of Coombs Hill. Running down into the valley. Past Wilf's New Place. Through the random display of shacks and bungalows. Passing cars with drivers that wink or honk. And up over the road where he takes a right. The pavement turning to dirt again. Down the grade of the road. Sees his new beige bungalow at his left. High on its concrete foundation. His father's old low bubblegum pink house beside his own.

Blackstrap spots the tiny figure he knows is Karen. Walking down the front concrete steps. Moving across the drive and into the old man's wooden front door. The old man suddenly struck down. A stroke. The doctor told Blackstrap when he visited his father in Carbonear Hospital. The old man not talking. Not seeing anymore. Blindness like any illness. Not something taken away but something added. And Karen tending to him. Caring for Jacob in a way she never did. For anyone before.

Karen wipes the old man's lips. A cloth warm in her hand. The moist smear pressing down. To clean away the crusted scum. She stares at his face. Sees that he is not. Concerned with her. His eyes fixed. On the ceiling. While the muscles in his face. Tic against her touch. Unshaven cheeks. Tendons stretched in his neck.

Leaning close to his left ear. She whispers, 'Don't you ever. Tell. Don't you dare, old man,' then straightens. Nervously sucking in. Her bottom lip. Studying him for reaction. She dips the cloth. Into the blue plastic bowl. Then twists it out. Wrings it out. Wipes along his chin. With one hand. The other flicking back. The sheet that covers his naked greyish skin. She sees. That he has soiled the sheets. The smell pooling water. In her eyes. In her mouth. She leans near. Grabs his head. With both hands. Presses lips to his eyes. Licks his open eyes. And groans. Grinds against him. To get in. Then lowers her aim. Shoving her tongue. Deep into his soundless throat. Teeth hard against teeth.

Retching, rising, she rubs the cloth lower. Along his thighs. Over his grey penis. Tears of disgust. Dead. Like it was made that way. To stiffen and crack. In two. She rubs. Warming. The blood. Through it. A memory growing. Grey to pink. Dead alive. Drops the cloth and pulls. And pulls. And pulls. Alive. Predator from the sky. Spying down. A glance toward the doorway. No one. Then dives. The stench. The body. Ugliness. Lower. Faithlessness. Lower. Loveliness. Lower. And loathing. Her breathing. Hard. Her stabbing laugh. The retching tears. With lips around. What cannot be helped. The love of father. Coming alive in her mouth.

The old man. Open mouth. Whimpers low.

She spits in the pan. Rinses her hands. Wipes the tears from her eyes. A drag of her sleeve. Mascara smeared whorishly. Rinses the cloth. The water turning muddy brown. A string of semen suspended in waste. Father and daughter. Floating there.

Patiently she cleans. The old man's scrawny flesh. After everything. Her chore. Washes his chest. Gently. His stomach. Her gaze set on his face. His blank eyes. Staring toward the ceiling. Seem to taunt. Not a word out of him. Since that day. He found her. On the floor and fell. Beside her. As one. The memory cutting low. Between Karen's legs. Turning her stomach. To paste. Her knees trembling. Erratically. Cold. To fall back. Through all those years. If only to tumble. And have arms catch her.

After trading the backhoe for his father's pickup, Blackstrap pulls in behind the string of parked cars. He can hear the band playing before he steps out and shuts his door. It's already dark. The night is clear. The weather good. He knows that the dance will go on late. He scans the cars on his way to the fire hall, recognizing a few of the vehicles. He passes a chip truck parked near the hall. A short line of people stood at the window. Men half drunk already. The usual ones who started earlier in the day. Wobbly limbs. They'll be gone home soon, causing all sorts of mischief. Then, maybe, back at the dance again later.

The dance is set up in the middle of the street. Between the post office and the fire hall. Tables and chairs arranged under two blue and white canopies. Coloured lights hung on strings. A stage up against the front of the hall. A three-man band stood on it. Guitar. Bass. Drums. The singer talking between songs. Offering the next song up to someone back from Toronto. The event roped in with orange plastic snow fencing.

Blackstrap pays his five dollars and they give him a blue Soiree button. The volunteer firemen running the show. Some of them have their black baseball caps or windbreakers on with the fireman logo stitched with gold thread. He wouldn't mind having one of those, but he never had it in him to join the firemen. He could never stand being a part of a group like that. Even if it was a good group.

He puts his button in his pocket and walks on. At his left, people are seated at tables underneath the night shade of a canopy. A bit of light in there coming from the stage. A few heads turn to look at him. The others keep watching the band. One old woman clapping her hands to the music.

Off to his right, the door to the hall is opened. He wanders in there. No tables set up yet for tomorrow's turkey dinner. The space wide open. Hollow under bootstep. He walks toward the cubbyhole window in the back. Waits a few minutes for the ones in front of him to be served. Then buys a handful of beer tickets. He gets a few nods and hellos as he moves on, past the washrooms where the women are already lined up, and on toward another door.

Out in the room where the fire trucks are usually parked. A long bar is set up along the back. A few upright coolers with glass doors for beer and a table with bottles on it. The garage doors are open. A view of the stackable tables arranged on the other side of the stage under another canopy. And an open section of dance floor pavement.

Blackstrap orders his beer from one of the volunteer firemen. A man with a hairlip and crew cut who's quick to serve. There isn't much of a crowd yet. That won't happen for a few hours. By the time he gets five or six beers in him, there'll be a crowd around him. Not even something he notices. The crowd just there from out of nowhere.

He wanders toward the front of the hall. He takes a drink of beer while watching people dancing. Young and old dancing alike under the stars. Not much difference in the style. Even with the slow songs. People he sees behind windshields or passing by in stores all year. Just people going about their business. Only a comment or two passed back and forth. Here now. Celebrating being from Cutland Junction. He looks around for Paddy. Blackstrap was going to pick him up. Get a dozen beers for the car and have a few before arriving. But Paddy wasn't home. His mother said so over the phone. She didn't know where he was. 'On da loose somewhere,' was what she'd said. 'Up ta no good gallyvanting 'round, right like himself.'

Blackstrap takes another drink and notices a woman stood close by. She's thin and has some sort of handmade cap on her head. There's a tiny knapsack or purse on her back. Straps over both shoulders. Shorts that are almost pants and a sleeveless T-shirt that shows off her muscles. Blackstrap has seen her riding a bicycle around Cutland Junction a while ago. He's even seen her down in Bareneed. Riding over the grass near the cliffs and water. Stopping to eat something from a baggie. Nibbling like a squirrel. Blackstrap keeps his eyes on her to see what she's all about. Soon, a tall man comes up to her. He has delicate glasses on his face and is watching around like he's never been anywhere in his life. He has his hands in his pockets and checks the woman's face. He stands there waiting for her to say something.

The band finishes their song and the woman's voice comes loud. 'That's just the way it is around here,' she's saying to the man.

Up on stage, the singer mentions something about taking a break. Then the musicians lay down their instruments and check around to make sure everything's in order.

A few others from the area go over to the woman with the homemade cap. They start talking quickly, trying to find out all the news. With the band stopped, Blackstrap can hear bits and pieces of what's being said.

'Eighteen years,' says the woman when someone asks her how long she's been away. 'Yer in T'ronto, right?' says one of the women. The ex-Newfoundlander nods. Someone asks her what she's doing up along. And the woman says she works for an advertising agency. One of the women says, 'Like Chelsey in *Da Young 'n da Restless?*' The ex-Newfoundlander nods and looks at the man. The smile she gives is like a secret that everyone else can't stand to be around. Then her eyes are on the ground. Like she thinks herself so special.

Blackstrap's heard about her. He knows her name from people talking over the years. Her first time home since she left. Blackstrap wonders how you can stay away. How you can come from a place and not fit in anymore. Like you were created somewhere else to start with. How you can come from a place and then make fun of it. Because that's what the woman is doing. She's making a mockery of everyone around her. Just by the way she's standing there. By the way she's dressed. By the way she looks at the man. Like they're the only two in it together. And everyone else is just there for a laugh.

Blackstrap shifts his thoughts away. No sense wasting good energy on the likes of them. He thinks back to the trouble with Tuttle. The bed up in the trees. A pretty picture. He imagines beds up in trees everywhere. That's where a good lot of people belong. He drains his third beer and notices he has a bit of an appetite. He is still stood in the spot he likes, watching out over the dance area that's deserted with the band stopped. He checks over his shoulder. The crowd has thickened behind him. A few men give him winks or tilts of their heads. He tilts his head in return. Then he goes out and orders one of the moose sausages being cooked on a black barbecue. He watches the young one behind the short table putting it on a bun for him. She's back from the university in St. John's, studying to be a teacher. The university that Smallwood built. His mother always praised the idea of that. Education. He tries thinking of anything important people might ever learn from a book. But nothing comes to mind. He takes the sausage and pays the young one. It's soft and tasty when he bites into it. A bit of spice to the meat. Tender as anything. One doesn't do much for him, so he orders another.

'Some skin around tonight, wha'?'

Blackstrap turns to see Paddy stood beside him. Grinning that sharp grin of his. Paddy tips his chin toward one young woman with a fancy perm.

'You wanna moose sausage?'

Paddy looks at what's in Blackstrap's hand.

'Naw, can't eat on an empty stomach. You knows dat, b'y.'

'Get ya a beer den.' He chews and swallows. Done, he wipes the paper napkin over his lips and bunches it up, tosses it in the green garbage bucket.

Paddy nods, his face beaming while he scans another young woman. A group of three of them all close together at a table. Paddy's got his good shirt on, the beige cowboy shirt his brother sent him from Calgary. Bought at the Stampede up there. And his hair's combed nicely.

'Jeez.' Paddy shakes his head and grins some more. 'Dere's no end to da tail 'round here.'

Blackstrap checks the stage because the band has just started in again. He watches the people get up right away to dance. Couples he has seen all his life. He knows most of them by name. He knows where they live. Who their parents or children are. Their grandchildren. Their grandparents. He thinks it is one of the finest things he has ever seen. All of these people together. From Bareneed and Cupids and Brigus gathered for a party in the road. The first of its kind for the area. Something done right for a change. Worth the effort.

'Ya never see people like this,' Blackstrap says to Paddy, leaning near and raising his voice. Paddy says nothing in reply. His head just bobs a little to the music. 'All year ya go around and see people in cars. But nothing like this. Get'n ta see everyone.' He is proud of it in some way. Delighted by it.

The band is playing an old Dick Nolan song, 'Aunt Martha's Sheep.' A favourite of the crowd. Everyone's up dancing or clapping their hands. The story of the boys from Carmenville who stole Aunt Martha's sheep. And the Mountie who comes to investigate after smelling the meat cooking. The boys invite him in and give the Mountie a bunch of lies about cooking a bit of moose.

The lead singer sings on while the dancers clap their hands:

He said thanks a lot and he sat right down and I gave him a piece
    of the sheep.
This is the finest piece of moose I knows I ever eat.
About two o'clock in the morning he bid us all good-day,
If we get any clues on the sheep, sir, we'll phone you right away.

He said thanks a lot, you're a darn fine bunch, and your promise I
    know you'll keep.
And if everyone was as good as you she wouldn't have lost her
    sheep.
After he left we had the piece we had in the oven to roast,

We might have stole the sheep, boys, but the Mountie ate the most.

It takes Blackstrap a while to get to the bar. The crowd is wall-to-wall now. An oldtimer is watching up at Blackstrap when he orders two beers. The oldtimer is half the size of Blackstrap and has a silver cane. His thin hair greased back and big glasses on his face.

'Mr Hawco,' says the oldtimer, raising his beer.

Blackstrap raises his. Then the other. The one for Paddy.

'Wha're ye up ta dis even'n?'

'Having a beer.'

The oldtimer laughs and gives him a big smile. ''N how's skipper dese days?'

'A'right.'

'I haven't seen 'im 'round in a dog's age.'

Blackstrap is elbowed and turns to see who did it. If there was any intention behind the poke. But he can't see any eyes locked on him. So he looks back at the oldtimer.

'We'll be hearing more from you,' says the oldtimer. 'Jacob Hawco's young fellow.' He puts out his hand and Blackstrap shakes it. 'Big boots ta fill. Livin' up ta dat Hawco name of yers.'

Blackstrap nods. 'Have a good one.' He heads off and the music gets louder as he steps outside. The band playing 'Bad Moon Rising' by CCR. He finds Paddy near a group of young women. He's wobbling a bit and watching them. But they're not watching him. Blackstrap hands him his beer.

'Dey won't dance widt me,' says Paddy, his voice straining above the music.

'Wouldn't blame 'em, not one frig'n bit.'

Paddy takes a drink from the bottle. 'Some friend you turn'n outta be.' Paddy laughs outright. And the girls peek a look at Blackstrap. One of them eyeing him up and down. The wife of one of the firefighters. She's thin and has long black hair. A bit of a curl in it. But it looks greasy. One or two of her teeth are rotten when she smiles. There's something about her though. She's raunchy. Sexy. Always shagging around with someone.

'Wha'd'ya at, Blacky?' she says.

He shakes his head. Tries to ignore her by staring out over the crowd.

'Where's yer woman to?'

'Home sewing.'

A few of the women giggle.

'Home frig'n herself,' Paddy shouts out.

The women make shocked expressions, then laugh. One of them commenting that it sounds like a good idea and she should be home at that herself.

Blackstrap wouldn't give either of them the time of day. He wanders off. Karen never wants to go anywhere around the community. She likes the look of the place, but not the people. In hiding is how he thinks of her, with a few beers in him. She reminds him of an animal in a burrow. He finishes off his beer and goes for another.

With a beer in each hand, he steps out and returns to watching the couples dancing. Drinking, he feels a need for more food in his stomach. The beer's starting to do things to his head. Make him think in a way that's not usually the way he sees the world.

He hands a beer to Paddy, who's finally got a woman up dancing, and leaves the dance area for the chip truck. There's three people in the line-up ahead of him. So it gives him time to watch the young pretty woman serving in the order window. She's got a cute chubby face and short blonde hair. When she takes an order or hands one out, she leans forward with her arms on the ledge and her extra-white breasts round up from her low-cut T-shirt. It makes him even hungrier and happier. He stands there watching people ordering and being handed their trays of fries. When he gets to the window, he says what he wants without checking the red letters on the order board.

'Large fry.' He gives her a small smile.

'Gravy?' she asks.

'No.'

'Anything to drink?'

He shakes his head, thinking he should say more. But he's suddenly angry for some reason. He looks over his shoulder. Other people in the line-up, laughing and talking. With his head turned, he can hear the music clearly. The singer: 'Sunday Morning Coming Down.' He knows the tune, but can't remember if it's by Johnny Cash or Kristofferson.

When he turns back, the young blonde names the price. He digs in his pocket. She's already watching his eyes when he hands the money over. Her lips are full and seem soft just by the looks of them. Her manner is good-natured. It doesn't seem like she's been sad a day in her life, but she's not stupid either. Blackstrap can tell. She's bright, sharp as a tack. It's in her eyes. She leans out and gives him his change. The touch of her fingers against his palm.

Up this close, he can't help but watch her moving around inside the chip truck. Talking to the people shaking the wire baskets of fries, rubbing her bare arms. And then she lays his order on the ledge, seeming extra interested in his eyes, but then shy, looking past his shoulder. He takes his order and turns away. He's frowning while he sprinkles on lots of salt and malt vinegar and squirts on blobs of ketchup everywhere. Walking off, he shakes his head, can't stand himself. He should have said something to her. He won't look back to see if she's looking. He won't even do that. He wanders off toward the pickup, leans with his back against the driver's door and eats the fries. He's thinking of his mother for some reason and his head goes dead. An emptiness. A faint ringing in his ears. A swell. The rain and the sea a black throb. He finishes the fries and tosses the smeared tray into the grass. Getting into the pickup, he sits there thinking about the woman in the chip truck. Perfect. What would she ever have to do with him?

He's watching ahead through the windshield. The beer taking him the wrong way now. He needs more or less of it. He doesn't notice the woman leaning near his window. A tapping on the glass and he turns to see the fireman's wife. Hands in the back pockets of her jeans. Slowly, he rolls down the window halfway.

'What're ya do'n?'

'Leaving.'

'Dat sounds right like you.'

He stares through the windshield again. He starts the engine.

'Go'n home ta yer woman.'

He refuses to look at her.

'She won't be 'round here much longer. The likes of her.' The thin woman straightens, folds her arms against her chest, watching him. 'Where's Patsy to now? Hooked up widt some udder feller?'

His eyes on the chip truck. Every now and then he can see the blonde head leaning out. He has never felt as sad in his life. But he does not know why. What might have happened to him? Nothing.

He notices the fireman's wife on her way back to the dance.

He turns the wheel and pulls out, drives away, takes a right after the chip truck, following the orange detour sign around back, up along the narrow old roads that were once cart paths, long before the main one was laid.

The bible slams gunshot shut. And had turned their rivers into blood; and their floods that they could not drink. Tuttle's eyes obscured behind tight lids. Lips muttering: Then said I, O my Lord, what *are* these? And the angel that talked with me said unto me, I will shew thee what these *be*. His eyes bolt open. Wide eyes through thick lenses. And I besought thy disciples to cast him out; and they could not. He chews his tongue and scampers from the bedroom. Blasphemous visions nipping at his heels. Quickly, he spews two Hail Marys. Offers them up but blotches the thread. O Lord, I beseech thee, let now thine ear be attentive to the prayer of thy servant. The Blessed Virgin fallen over. On the floor of Hawco's house. Robe flung above her waist. Yellow aura seeping. The porcelain crack he'd made in her. And he commanded the most mighty men that *were* his army to bind Shadrach, Meshach, and Abed-nego, *and* to cast *them* into the burning fiery furnace.

Chewing his tongue, Isaac shuffles to one side of the small living room. Erected there. A shrine to the Blessed Virgin. Thy words have upholden him that was falling, and thou hast strengthened the feeble knees. Emily Hawco's face in place of Mary's. Isaac peeks through the corners of his eyes. Let the day perish, wherein I was born, and the night *in which* it was said, There is a man child conceived. The face of Blackstrap Hawco's wife. Plastered in place of Mary's. On all the holy statues. Screaming a silent, frenzied blur. Behold, thou *art* fair, my beloved, yea, pleasant: also our bed *is* green.

Isaac Tuttle. The watcher. The romantic. The moralist. Storms from the room. No longer his home. His body. Madly shuffles for the door to throw it open. Races with clipped frantic steps up his dirt drive. Onto the narrow potholed road and across. For the sons of Athaliah, that wicked woman, had broken up the house of God; and also all the dedicated things of the house of the Lord did they bestow upon Baalim. Turning to question his house. No longer his. A building like any other. Quiet. Unoccupied. He drops. Lands awkwardly on his knees. Falling back. Into low branches that enmesh him. The soft earth cushioning. As he catches himself. His balance. Forward. The Lord of hosts hath sworn by himself, *saying*, Surely I will fill thee with men, as with caterpillars; and they shall lift up a shout against thee. Reaching out. Rocking. Through the brittle branches. Fingers dig among dry dirt and gravel. Catching beneath his fingernails snatching hold of a small thin rock. Seemingly oval. A wafer. And holding it tightly between his palms. Warming it with meaning before shoving it into his mouth. I have done judgement and justice: leave me not to mine oppressors.

Mumbling, 'Da body 'a Christ.' Working to swallow the rigid-edged shape. 'Amen.' Rock pressing dents into his throat's soft lining. Gouging like a meal gone down wrong. O how love I thy law! It *is* my meditation all the day. He reaches again. Grips a jagged-edged grey rock. Never had he meant to do what was done. I will never forget thy precepts: for with them thou hast quickened me. No. Yes, he had. I opened my mouth, and panted: for I longed for thy commandments.

'Emlee,' cries Isaac. Trying to convince who? He had gone to face Blackstrap. To preach scripture and provoke a confession. For they have not served thee in their kingdom, and in thy greatness that thou gavest them, and in the large and fat land which thou gavest before them, neither turned they from their wicked works. What perverted his holy obligation? And turned his words black with action. With lust. For the city woman. Unchaste and filthy. Less a woman. From the towers and wheels. A denatured spirit. Hear now this, O foolish people, and without understanding; which have eyes, and see not; which have ears and hear not. An urban sprawl of pagans. Fashion versus God.

He hears, *Cheap property, brought 'ere by Hawco. And I'll take dat instead.*

So that all which fell that day of Benjamin were twenty and five thousand men that drew the sword; all these *were* men of valour. Oh, the pleasure. To eat of the unpure. While he hiccupped thickly in his chest. And squeezed her flesh. In his fists. I sleep, but my heart waketh: *it is* the voice of my beloved that knocketh, *saying*, Open to me, my sister, my love, my dove, my undefiled: for my head is filled with dew, *and* my locks with the drops of the night.

'Emlee.' Without hearing. While he madly thrusts. Break the woman and all else lays beneath her dirt. Who *is* she *that* looketh forth as the morning, fair as the moon, clear as the sun, *and* terrible as *an army* with banners? And she had wept lavational tears. Enraptured by the spirit. Those banners against the sky. Of his long perished loved one. Emily whimpering, humbled by the propriety of her salvation. The breathless hammering in Isaac's heart. While he watched. Dumbfounded. Until the woman stopped. Grunting. Seeming to be struck gentle and calm. When it shall hail, coming down on the forest; and the city shall be low in a low place. She stared right through him. Catching the light in his soul. Filled by the luminosity of the Holy Spirit. While his spine prickled with the million-fingertipped patter of angels. Homilizing with a voice resounding, Worthy is the lamb that was slain to receive power, and riches, and wisdom, and strength, and honour, and glory, and blessing. She had laughed then like a howl. Under a battery of stones. In defilement.

A sharp stone lifted. Isaac Tuttle stares above his head. At the dust of angels weaving through autumn branches. Their nakedness. And the startlingly white spread of their wings. Thrust open in a fluff of seed. To remain afloat. Opening their cupped palms. To show him their tongues in the pools of their hands. Wriggling. And in those days shall men seek death, and shall not find it; and shall desire to die, and death shall flee from them. Isaac Tuttle pulls hold of his tongue. Shuts his crying eyes to press with force. Carves down the centre length. Gouging his fleshy fob, back and forth. Forking at the thick base. One woe is past; *and*, behold, there come more hereafter. As his mouth with the warm seep. And is soon awash with blood. The tip waggingly split. Take *it*, and eat it up; and it shall make thy belly bitter, but it shall be in thy mouth sweet as honey. Two woes.

Feeling wicked in this wretched shivering. Joyously stammering. Unspeakably lovely. The angels. A golden flurry of fluttering rolls his eyes inward to see.

In the grip of rapture's provocation, Isaac Tuttle swoons.

Karen lifts her coffee cup. Quick eyes watching Blackstrap. Over the rim. Slurping. Then lowering the mug. Tomorrow. The doctor. The clinic. She takes a full wet draw. From her cigarette. Her head adrift. With the buzz. The scent of sickness. On her body. The old man. She thinks, *Both of us*. Not be washed off. To the doctor where it is safe. The hospital. Sterility. Suck out. The baby. Cut off. The breasts that ache more now. Growing larger. For the suckling. Sucking. The hospital. Sucking. Where it is safe. Where she is the suckling. She laughs. Once. Abruptly. Swallows. Another mouthful of smoke. Pregnant. She thinks. Pregnant. Smoke it. Out.

Turning from the sink, from staring out into the back yard where the shed door lies open, Blackstrap glances at Karen. He has just drunk a glass of water and his lips are wet. He wipes the sleeve of his sweater across his mouth and stares at his wife's face. He thinks of calling Paddy, setting things up for tomorrow. Two-by-fours and two-by-sixes for the concrete footing.

'Show me the tattoo again,' Karen says snidely. 'Blacky.'

Blackstrap says nothing, merely shakes his head. He looks at her in a distanced way. The fit all wrong, with her no longer in her place. He notices the telephone on the wall. And five pounds of three-inch nails. Never forget the nails. No electricity on the cabin site. The lumber to be sawed by hand. Or maybe with the chainsaw that Paddy likes to use, to sharpen, to worry over, like he's the only one to know anything about it.

'I need to see it,' she says. Nods. As her voice rises. Standing. From her chair. It scrapes. Along the flooring.

Blackstrap's muscles flinch against this outburst, but he remains steady. His mud-caked boots on the floor. He wants to make that call. Before Paddy starts drinking and forgets about the morning.

Rushing to him, Karen shoves up the sleeve of his sweater. The flat blue-black outline evident. Her name. And the naked feet. The crotch. The belly. The breasts. The shoulders. The neck. The head. The hair.

And the blank face that looks nothing. Like her. Blank. Blind resemblance. A smutty feeling. That clings to her. Like the dullness of the ink.

'Yes,' she says. Leaning. To gently kiss. The tattoo. Pressing her lips to her own. Name.

Blackstrap touches Karen's thick black hair. He watches her face and thinks of a trapped animal, stuck there and loose at once. Twisting one way, then the other to yank clear.

She stares. Hungrily up at him. Her smile wide. Greedy want. She strokes his arm. Snatches for his crotch. Jabs her palm there. Wisps of smoke rise. From the table.

'Yes,' she says. Gritting teeth.

Blackstrap notices Karen's cigarette burning in the ashtray. He thinks of the burning of the land, smoke rising above evergreens, and the backhoe idling out front, and the blackened trees that must be moved for a cabin lot. Burnt instead of chainsawed. One way of doing it. The sooty touch of the stumps like pencil lead. Another one behind Coombs Hill. Townies moving out in droves. Blackstrap worries about his father. He smells the sickness of his father off Karen.

'My turn,' says Karen. Raising her head to bite. His stubbly cheek. Pressing against him. Biting harder. Her teeth. Groaning a throat laugh.

Blackstrap shoves her back toward the table where she crashes into a chair. The telephone dings. He should call Paddy. His wife nothing but an irritant, a woman in his way of getting the job done.

Off balance, Karen drops. Onto the seat. Her eyes averting Blackstrap's. While she nervously reaches. For her cigarette. In the ashtray. 'My turn,' she whispers, accusingly. Taking a long harsh draw. Then knocking the ash off. The cigarette gone hot. And soft. She darts a peek at Blackstrap. Sees how he has placed his fingers. Against the tattoo. As if holding a bandage in place. Stopping something vital. From leaking out.

Blackstrap gives her no further consideration. He yanks his sleeve down with his eyes turned from her, masking the mark, makes the call to Paddy. No answer. Then leaves the house in a fit of not knowing.

*

156

Jacob tries to tell himself what he sees. He cannot hear and speak at once. Inside himself with his mouth and ears. Eyes on the ceiling. Junior Hawco stuck there like a bug. Face pressed sideways. A flash gone off. Frozen white. Is this winter? Palms and soles stuck. Jagged limbs bent at angles to the ceiling. Why there now? And a girl. Another flash. A picture in a book. A little girl huddled near. Face in a locket. Eyes green and leaking. Junior's eyes turned twisted to see. Straining at that angle. At that time. At that place. Afloat. And pinned. Where else would he be found? My father. Losing everything but not me. The dead. Never losing the dead. Losing your mind. But never the dead. The dead more than mind. I saw what was done. You bring me back in body to look this way. Says Junior. Your head wrong. I cannot fit here. I was soul. I was so much soul. And nothing but body now in your unblessed world. The girl giggles. Foam from her lips. I am not friendly, she says. I am friendly. See. Her voice tiny. I am not me, Daddy. Not anymore. Not me. Jagged teeth sharpened from biting on stone. Out from under the earth. Now that you are not. Giggle. Gag. Sprinkles of dirt into his open eyes. Her tongue dirt-brown. They cough, and sprinkle him, oh, how they cough, his dead children.

Suitcase packed. Karen leaves. Her brother, Glenn, has come for her in the car. She does not turn to see the house. Goodbye. The car pulls away. Crosses where the train tracks used to be. Glenn says nothing. Knows better.

They drive through the community. Down the valley. Up along the dirt road that joins to the highway. The long black road stretching straight ahead. Forest black. Ominous. To all sides. A moon above them. Clear dark sky with a hint of blue. Light on the edges and treetops. Almost pretty. Ghost trees. Not themselves.

Glenn switches on the radio. A commercial for fast food. A song about love.

Karen watches. Through the windshield. She feels calm with her brother. A ride in a vehicle. With him. The lull. Not a word spoken. Still, she cannot look at him. Her brother beside her. What they have been through. Together. To help each other. Her head drifts. Toward the window. Her eyes shut. She sleeps.

The car on the highway. Headlights through darkness. Leaving the land behind.

Glenn's eyes on the road. His hand on her inner thigh. While she sleeps.

Blackstrap parks the backhoe outside Wilf's New Place. This new place much like the place Wilf opened first. Only now it is a larger square room built onto the side of his house. A yellow clapboard dwelling with a cola sign over the second door. Set down where the road slopes deeply. Then rises before curving off into the woods toward the secluded penitentiary. Wilf bought a pool table at a government auction in St. John's. Centred it atop a sheet of grey panelling laid in the middle of the new room. Men and women slept on the green felt in the afternoon hours. When they drank so much under-the-counter beer and black rum. They could no longer stand. Legs and arms hung over the grooved chrome edges. Twisting off in all directions.

The bodies of a man and a woman rest there now. While Wilf blinks from behind the aspinite counter at the back of the room. His hand on the ledge. He nods with his head on a permanent tilt close to his shoulder. The tail of his green and grey plaid shirt hangs out around his waist. He nods again and turns, dragging one leg, shuffling over to the big cooler. Opening the long glass door, he pops the caps off two colas. So the young boys could mix the black rum to make sure it will be sweet. And not sting to such a wicked degree.

'Whiskey,' says Blackstrap, wondering on the quiet. All eyes on him. He was thought to meet Paddy here. Work to be done. But no sign of him at home either.

Wilf pours from the bottle.

Leo, a skinny stick of a man, nodding and drinking. Not saying a word. Beer bottle up. Beer bottle down. Gord stood there beside Leo, smearing the laughing tears from his eyes with his pudgy oil-stained hand. He has been laughing at something, and is still chuckling. While he sips from the beer bottle some moonshine has been poured into. His face is small and his rounded cheeks burn red. When he smiles to show two rows of badly chipped teeth from chewing the caps off bottletops. Whenever a bottle needs opening, Gord always quick to snatch it away.

Impatiently bending the cap off with his teeth. While watching the person as if to say, 'Dere's no trick ta dis. Ya jus' gotta 'av balls.' Breathing heavily, he moves his wide body to take a look around the room.

Leo lays his long arm around Gord's shoulders. Catching sight of Blackstrap, he senses the humour slipping off. He coughs and straightens up, weakly shaking his head and giving a merry sigh. Leo turns to the counter again to face Wilf's white oval head. Tilted to the side and bent close to his shoulder. His greyish-brown beard brushes against the front of his shirt. As he stiffly tosses a bag of cheezies to a boy leaning against the pool table.

Blackstrap sips his whiskey. The smell of it full in his nostrils when he swallows. Looks toward the opening that leads into Wilf's house. The curtain hanging there, separating the rooms, has fallen loose. And he sees the small brown couch low to the floor. And the colourful crocheted quilt thrown over it. The woodstove in the centre of the room. With a black-bottomed kettle resting on top. And a small square of carpet under the wooden box that is a coffee table. An orange and grey cat slowly leaps onto the box. Curls up to sleep.

A grumble rises from the pool table. A man wearing a dark blue baseball cap twists and tosses in his sleep. As if to fight off a commotion before rolling dangerously close to the edge. Half of his body dangles for a moment. Before all of him slips over. Dropping and crashing onto the floor. Bottles and windows rattle. And the floor shakes violently. Before the vibrations settle disagreeably. Like an explosion has been set off close to Wilf's New Place.

Two oldtimers sitting at a small round table by the door stare glumly at where the body has fallen. The body that now gets up without knowing what happened. The man stumbles toward a table. Sits. Stares at his feet. One of the oldtimers looks at the other. Their faces remaining unchanged. They each take a drink. One of beer. The other of rum.

Blackstrap finishes his whiskey. The place still. In silence. He orders another. No ice. No mix. His hand up to stop Wilf from adding anything to water the taste.

Then, finally, hours later, when noise comes again. From the others drinking. Arguing. Explaining. Sound building from where it was tucked away in each man.

'I was through yer place a few day ago.' Leo still not looking at him. Nervous but wanting to say what was on his mind. Brave with the booze in him. 'On da Sunday fer a case.'

Blackstrap swallows the whiskey, nods for another. Shows the glass. Raises it so Wilf can pour. Eyes around the room moving from Blackstrap to Leo. Wilf's head tilted at that angle from a car crash. Something broken that never killed him. That should have. A man lives with anything. 'Yeah,' says Blackstrap as an afterthought.

'You had company.'

Leo leaves it at that. The stutter of a smile. Rotten teeth showing for a second. Gord takes a sideways step in the other direction. Away. Not close to any of that. Not a part of it. He even mutters something resembling those words. Elbow skimming along the bar.

Blackstrap drinks another whiskey. Heat rising in him. He glances around at the faces that know. The secret. No tongue ever held quiet. No movement ever going unreported in a community battered by loss. Everything gained back this way.

They might not be looking right at him. But they all know. Gord with his head turned to be left out. Staring toward the opening to Wilf's house. His back to them. Staying that way he becomes suspicious in Blackstrap's mind.

What kind of company? Karen seeing someone else. That would explain the change. Another man. Another time. Another place. Gord.

Wilf says nothing. Usually can't stop talking, stuttering out words. But says nothing now. Pours another whiskey to get through it. A tremble that won't let a word out of his mouth.

It takes a few more hours. A grudge thickening his blood. Whiskey thickening his thoughts into shapes full and dark. And all his. Only his. Made that way by him.

But he is told when leaving with the noise of late-night laughter. Pounding through the walls. Not about him. But he cannot help believing that every sound is. Stood outside in the crisp night air looking up at his backhoe. Then the sky. The stars as bright as he can ever remember. The brilliance of those closer. And the dust of others too far away.

Waiting for Gord. Waiting for Leo. He can wait.

In time the door opens. And Leo shows himself. His face unknowing in its merriment. Blackstrap stood there seeing him. Rushes from where he's leaned on the backhoe. Storms forward and hits Leo. Knocks him back and down. Then bends and kneels and hits him again. One action. And another. Leo's head thudding against clapboard. Bouncing.

'Who was it?' Blackstrap spits.

'Isaac,' says Leo, knowing right away what is being asked. Drunk but holding to what matters. Blood on his mouth. On his tongue where he bit it. 'Tuttle.' Blood on his chin. Dribbling. Blood flickering onto the dark moist night ground where he is hit again.

Blackstrap not nearly himself stopping. Snorts to taunt himself. Who knew what in him? Takes a moment to watch Leo's face. His fist held back. Spring-rock loaded. Hit him again? Hit him once more for saying? For knowing. Kill him for knowing. But instead flicks his grip from Leo's coat and rises. Turns. Knowing it would come to pass. Had to. Sick in every bone. He starts off on foot. Isaac Tuttle. A menace for too many years. A rustling in the trees nearby. Something Blackstrap takes for an animal.

Patrick Lambly, although not yet bearing the Hawco name, was the beginning of the Hawco story in Newfoundland. The passenger list from the steamer Venus *that departed the port of Limerick had him listed (right below Abigail Labody, spinster) as a labourer. During my research in Ireland, I discovered various facts about Patrick's father and mother and paternal and maternal grandparents, but to list those facts here would mean to clutter things up. If the reader is interested, these documents might be found in the hall of records in the parish of Rathjordan in County Limerick. Enough to say, his people were decent folks, not the rogues and criminals that I expected (and, maybe, even hoped) they might be.*

1886

Limerick, Ireland

Patrick Lambly and Rose Cavanagh's journey to Talamh an Éisc

It was those early memories of his mother's wilting starvation and his lame father's indenture to a landowner (by whom he was neglectfully worked to death) that drove Patrick Lambly, under the cover of night, from his beloved county of Limerick toward the broad horizon of the sea. The road that he travelled was known to him, each step measured against memory, for he had taken this path in darkness on many occasions with the exact similar threat of his departure, only to find diversion in the Ragged Death, his holdall hoisted up onto the bar while a good laugh was had about the utter foolhardiness of undertaking such a leaving, and plans were yarned together to no definite end.

It would be different this night. With the cries of his children worsening, day by day, he would not turn back. This night, unlike the others, he had taken no time to gather a few articles in a holdall, for he feared waking his wife, Siobin, or the ill baby, Claire, and two-year-old,

Angus. It was enough to simply creep from the door unnoticed. The rusty hinges painstakingly creaking like a perishing creature's cry.

On past nights, in the Ragged Death, he had sold all articles that might be gathered in a holdall to further his drinking. A pittance had been received for each article, with Patrick settling for the two-pence price of a pint for anything he might hold in his possession. The good that could be sifted from his worth was measured in increments of nil. He understood and denied this while he recited words in his head:

> The lanky hank of a she in the inn over there
> Nearly killed me for asking the loan of a glass of beer:
> May the devil grip the whey-faced slut by the hair,
> And beat bad manners out of her skin for a year.
>
> If I asked her master he'd give me a cask a day;
> But she, with the beer at hand, not a gill would arrange!
> May she marry a ghost and bear him a kitten, and may
> The High King of Glory permit her to get the mange

and pondered dipping into the Ragged Death for a pint or two to fortify him for his journey down over the hills toward the harbour. Christ, what good was such thirst to a man, the satiating of which would not extend his longevity, would it, but rather drive him deeper into a madder thirst or hunger for something otherwise which was entirely unagreeable. Yet seemingly agreeable, quite agreeable and ascending perfection, at the time.

Regardless, his shoulders inclined toward the Ragged Death, while his feet steered him steadily ahead. A peek in the window was all he desired. There they stood at the bar, the lads most known to him. The two Tommys. O'Neary and Shea. Christopher Kearney. Philip Foley. There was golden laughter, golden warmth within, all of it pouring freely over a man, to comfort him as he stumbled toward his most dire need or end. His fingers went up to the muddy pane and his fingernail picked at the dirt, clearing a better view of them all. Oh, it was succulent splendour. The view alone and the imagined fragrance of brew.

It would all be different once he had crossed the ocean and arrived upon the shores of Talamh an Éisc. Once his transport had been repaid, his indenture to a merchant worked off, he would have the required currency to return and provide his wife and children with a bounty. Men from Limerick went off on similar journeys in the spring, only to return in the winter to warm and deserved welcomes. David O'Mara and Tommy Cavanagh were regulars on the journey, Tommy having sent for his wife and children just this past month. It was with them that he must now add his number. Away from cursed Ireland. He would not shed a tear should he never set foot on its damnable soil again.

Tasting the thirst in his mouth, he argued his will one way then the other. His view through the window took a turn toward unpleasant as the wench came into view. Despicable, she was, Christly despicable and whorish, for denying a man like himself a bit of leeway. The sooner he got away, the better for all. Never to have to set eyes on that wretched female again. She with her heavy bosoms and enchanting brown eyes. She with her fragile hands and floury skin. She with her devil's tongue entwining his in dreams of the past nights. All that was required of him was to expend the initial effort, to step beyond the Ragged Death, no matter how enticing might seem its enclosure. How difficult could that possibly be, just this one time, to step beyond, to let his shadow fall over the doorway in passing, rather than have that very door be flung open and have the welcoming voices of his mates come out to meet him? In truth, it would be all grim talk of the damnable current state of affairs and the need to pour a shine over it. Let his shadow fall over the door in passing. But the weakness that leaned him nearer the windowpane soon had his nose squashed up against it in an abundantly unbecoming fashion.

'Here,' said Patrick. 'Yes.' As though he might be recollecting a cherished memory, a celebration of Christmas or harvest. 'Yes.' A story or two to be taken away at the end of the evening. If it were not for the slut, he might manage a decent bit of credit.

A burst of laughter from within as pints were drawn from casks and raised to lips warmed by conversation. A glowing palace amid the dark and desolate rubble of this village.

Patrick straightened and took a look back from whence he had come. There were no lights in the direction where he took his shack to be.

Christ, was there ever a more miserable father and husband? he wondered. He could weep from the feeling of physical uselessness, from the spiritual undoing of self-recrimination. The parcel of land that had once been his, upon which now he was merely a tenant, had become a worthless clod of dirt that would take no seed, as though it might have been poisoned by his own worthless sweat or the poems he spoke to it late in the evening, only the earth ever seeming to listen.

With a heart-heavy sigh, he turned his head to survey the path beyond the Ragged Death. Without the holdall, he would have nothing to sell, except, of course, the holdall itself. Straightening with a start from his dipped position toward the window, he felt a surge of optimism. Yes, why hadn't the idea crossed his mind on the previous nights where he had, again and again, planned his heroic departure, following a lambasting from his wife that he should go, that he should help them, for God's sake, that he should not let his daughter and son starve in their infancy?

He might sell the holdall.

On newly spirited feet, he trod back along the path he had taken from his house, hearing his own good-natured voice engaged in spirited song:

> *Here is the crab tree,*
> *Firm and erect,*
> *In spite of the thin soil,*
> *In spite of neglect.*
> *The twisted root grapples*
> *For sap with the rock,*
> *And draws the hard juice*
> *To the succulent top*

while he wandered back on this very path, night after night, from the Ragged Death. With thoughts of that vile barmaid swimming lewdly in his head and – underfoot – the earth sprouting from the seeds of his intentions.

The dark shack up ahead.

In silence, he approached it and, with the discreetness of a mouse and the gentleness of a lamb, delicately opened the creaking door just enough to slip his sideways body through and face the threatening stillness within. His wife and daughter and son were sleeping in the bed, under the thin, moth-eaten blanket that a sewing needle could no longer mend, his wife clutching the holdall to her sleeping breast.

Where Rose's Ronan is lost to sickness aboard

Missus Rose Cavanagh and her two children, eight-year-old Elizabeth and six-year-old Ronan, had been fetched from County Limerick by her husband, Tommy Cavanagh. There had been little reluctance on her part to make away from the scurrilous misery of Ireland and join her husband in Talamh an Éisc. The only hint of reluctance was centred on the shameful expansion of her belly, an admission that she was with child, despite the fact that Tommy had been abroad in Talamh an Éisc for a time approaching three years, and one year without a visit home.

On that violent and punishing five-week voyage across the Atlantic, she had lost her only son. Even though it was stated that provisions had been made for a doctor to be on board, the doctor was inebriated on most accounts and could not be roused on others. A dearth of care was provided for the ailing Ronan. However, in a rare moment of sobriety, between waking and his regulation rum breakfast, the doctor had been reluctantly brought to the boy and had, upon sighting the pustules, in a fit of nerves and red-faced coughing, and with an eagerness to seek steadiness and escape, briskly pronounced, in a quavering voice, that the boy had come down with smallpox. Yes, smallpox, he repeated louder, grandly sweeping one arm back through the air, for the doctor, in his spare time, had devoted himself to the studies of an amateur thespian. With a lick of his lips and a rub of his bristly face, the doctor had then backed from the room, as though he were witnessing a horror of astonishing and unheard of proportion that had befallen the confines of the ship, and turned to flee in terror. A performance that did not fail to move the ship's populace, for the doctor's verdict had sent a general surge of panic throughout the bulk of the passengers and had, rather than drive men and women away from the young boy, drawn persons to him in hopes of catching a mild case of the disease that would see them clear of being struck down by the more severe sort.

A number of frantic passengers stripped the boy of his clothes and blankets while – in a tremor of delirium and in the dim sway of lamplight – the child muttered a weak sing-song that resembled a nursery rhyme:

> *on rock,*
> *on sea,*
> *not you,*
> *just me,*
> *we sail,*
> *we wait,*
> *we fail . . .*

and his mother, Rose, clutched the talisman bag she had worn around her neck with the dust of the boy's dried umbilical cord inside mingled with the hairs she had removed from his head.

No mercy in action as the passengers fought to wrap themselves in the dying boy's articles:

> *on rock,*
> *on sea,*
> *not you,*
> *just me,*
> *we sail,*
> *we wait,*
> *we fail*

while others attempted to extract the boy's virus by wiping a cloth over the sores then cut themselves with blades or jagged bits of tin and rubbed the soiled cloth over their wounds. It was rumoured that this was a way of escaping the illness. Word had spread quickly of this practical remedy, yet, unbeknownst to the excited practitioners, in most cases it simply brought on a severe form of the disease that suffocated the victim.

Perhaps the most bizarre practice initiated by a few of the crew members, who had witnessed the undertaking in far-off lands, was the collecting of scabs from the boy's pustules that were dried and ground into powder. The powder was then inhaled in hopes of bringing on an inoculate's invincibility. This nightmarish behaviour was carried out in the presence of the afflicted boy, the sound of snorting and sniffing from a bench toward the dim corner. The passengers caring nothing for the pregnant Rose Cavanagh's sobbing protests while they hovered over Ronan's ruined body like ghouls in the shadow-pulling lamplight.

Yet when the boy died, having not survived the ordeal and thus being of no use as a preventative measure to the others, the passengers refused to sanction the standard procedure of packing the body in a crate of salt until docking; the boy was doused in vinegar and stuffed in a crate by one of the ship men, Cuz O'Malley, a tongueless one-eyed layabout who did as instructed and intuited these instructions – as was his primal training – by the mere pointing of a finger.

And, so, the boy's death became the sole piece of gossip that pre-occupied all on board. That and the waiting on the others to perish became the gamble of prattle. It took no time for the pustules to spring from the newly sick, and the men – those still healthy and wishing to remain so – ambushed each infected male and briskly tossed them overboard, while the women were locked away together with their children to perish in the most dreadful and pitiful manner among themselves, in their own filth and within a cacophony of moans and wails and screeches that were rocked in the belly of the steady unrelenting ship. Any word uttered against this procedure – by husband or wife or child – would see the protester forever spied upon and shunned to the point of utter mistrust.

With the dead boy still on board, the healthy passengers – meant to land on foreign shores and not have themselves perish like the child – decided they should rid the ship of the boy. If ever there was a befitting representative of bad luck, the boy was it. A dead boy stuffed away in the bowels of the ship like a dead heart, the smothered scream of its beat propelling them forward across the black sea. Ill fortune at the very core. It was agreed wholeheartedly that the boy must be disposed of. Some insisted that the box be set ablaze and then released into the sea, the fire required to burn off the distemper so it would not trail after the ship in its wake. A man from Cork insisted that the salt of the sea would punish any distemper out of existence. That would be suitable. Either way, the crate containing the boy was taken into possession of the crew and was stored upright, in a shallow room which contained nothing but contaminants and the natterings of rats that seemed to thrive in the void. Cuz O'Malley, the sole seaman who passed through this oily, rumbling corridor, would catch the splintering sounds of gnawing and the low fresh moaning of what might have been taken for a child, yet he would refuse to investigate. The ghost of that boy would be equally as contagious as the living person that breathed out poison, and if the vermin were feeding off the ghost then so much the better, for the ghost would be consumed and no longer of a haunting bother.

While the gossip spread, Missus Cavanagh and her daughter, Elizabeth, were loathed, until the time when the passengers might be certain that no sickness dwelled within them. The accusations and fits of recrimination continued to increase in volume and intensity, as each new passenger was stricken and ambushed, until a fortnight after the boy's death, the crate was retrieved from the contaminated void by Cuz O'Malley, and dragged to the deck where it lay with the crowd around it, convinced that death was not severe enough a punishment and wishing further harm upon the boy.

Within a ragged hole chewed clear through the side of the crate, a slim pale hand was evident, as was the flicker of a moan that could only be prompted by the imaginings of night terrors. A few, who still believed that the boy might be of a saving value, knelt before the crate and pressed hands, cheeks and lips to the crate; one such person was the boy's mother, although her intentions were contrary, as were those of the boy's sister, Elizabeth, who shuddered and sobbed and backed clear of the crowd until striking the railing with the inky blackness below, sweeping by in smooth persistence. And with each palm or face that neared the crate, the impish graceful mutter sounded from within the box so that all became frightened out of their wits and sang for the crate's ejection.

Beneath the moonlight, the passengers kept their distance yet gathered, nearer, then further, compelled to watch while Cuz dragged the crate to the very centre of the deck and arranged the ropes through the pulleys before being fitted around the crate. Done with the rigging, Cuz hurriedly poured lamp oil over the crate and motioned with a blunt toss of his arm to the winchman. When the crate was eye-level on its ascent under the full strain of the winch, Cuz stepped back and pressed a flaming torch to it. The spreading blue and orange blaze enshrouded the crate and burned into the sky. The eyes of the passengers watched and saw nothing but a searing wash of red and orange wavering through the night and then, as was expected, the terminating plummet, and a sweep of blackness as all went still. The wind died down and there was not a sound, save for the low whimperings of a little boy that never changed in urgency nor pitch.

There was a clamorous racket in Patrick Lambly's ears as he came to himself within a hollow darkness throbbing to all sides of him. He found that he was sealed in somewhere, then tipping, so that he clutched on to the sides of where he had been laid out only to find that there were no sides, only what he assumed to be a greasy wooden floor. He rolled a little before pressing against a form that might be another man. In the clutch of panic, he sat upright in an attempt to fix his whereabouts.

His ears, sharpened by the skin-shaving prickle of fear, discerned the creaking of timbers. A soul-wobbling waver spread from his centre and he suspected he might be sick to his stomach by the smothering thought that he was adrift. No turning back. How he made it aboard a ship was unknown to him. The last he recalled was an argument with his wife that rose in volume until it crescendoed with the rattling screech of the baby. He had been pulling to get the holdall, threatening to leave, 'Yes, yes,' his wife's voice had been insisting, 'go, that's wha' I've been saying ta ye fer months on end.' And he had been struggling with the holdall, as though he were at war with it.

Despite his wife's insistence that he go, the cursed woman would not release her grip from where it was hugging the holdall. In his struggle, Patrick had felt as though he were both taking the case from her and trying to give it back at the identical time.

Presently, he reached out at his sides and patted the space around him in search of his holdall. Gone, or lost out there in the breathable darkness.

At once, as his senses returned to the throb of his current predicament, there was a thickening of the notion that the direction in which he, or rather the vessel, was travelling was an utter mystery to him. Had he been shanghaied? This agitating uncertainty graduated to unease and, subsequently, prompted the waver to spread and gush into his throat. Unwittingly, he choked and turned to vomit, while hoping he had not struck anyone with the abundance of his spew.

There came a groan of protest and hands clutching and hurling him sideways into the air. Patrick's head rammed against a timber and he collapsed in a pile, his legs buckled beneath him. When his fingers searched the back of his head, he found a warm trickle there. Was there blood on his fingertips? He could glean no view of it in the absence of light, and gave out a cry, which provoked titters from a few of the dark forms. Gripes were passed about concerning the condition of the sorry sort who had managed to so litter the vessel floor. Murderous grumblings that, would there have been even the dimmest of light, might have graduated to action. Patrick barely heard them, for his mind seemed to be evaporating. The top of his head floating off while his senses turned to vapour one at a time.

Faintly, he sniffed at his fingers, then touched them to his lips, smearing the fluid there. Tasting the copper, the sweetness and metallic linger, he was not long evaporating completely and dropping away to the floorboards with a thud that drew speculative mutters from the horde.

Yet no one had bothered to investigate, for Patrick Lambly, in his initial inebriated state of unconsciousness, had already had his pockets rifled through, and like most on the ship carried nothing of worth, not even a knife that might help prevent a man from being robbed of the absolute nothing in his possession.

When the overhead hatch was finally opened, light gave Patrick a revelation of the huddle that he was hunched amongst. There were both men and women crammed into the hollow of the ship, some in bunks, others at rest wherever space might allow. Throughout the night, there had been the noise of snoring and grumbling and hawking and spitting and coupling whether agreed to or otherwise in the blackness that belonged to no one and so possessed not a single limitation in behaviour or intent.

It was enough to catch a breath of fresh air and be relieved of the warm mingling of bodily stenches. Hunched over like the others, for the lowness of the ceiling prevented any other posture, Patrick shifted toward the hatch, and waited his turn to climb the ladder, his head rising into a view of blue that strained his eyes. How far to where they were going? There was nothing but blue in every direction that the people who had been hidden away between decks now looked at with silent wonder, the vastness of the sea utterly confounding.

Patrick was on deck no more than a few moments, staring at the watery expansiveness with a look of loss and regret, when he was told to report to the galley. Puzzled and feeling sickly, he quietly began to explain that he was a passenger.

'Ye c'n see dat I dun't give a fack,' said the shipman, who possessed a short thick body, hair braided to his shoulders and a scar across both his lips. 'Get yer fawsty boggy arse below.' The seaman made a stamp of his boot, blinked his eyes fiercely and sliced his arm through the air in a gesture of intended injury.

Patrick went in the direction the seaman had pointed. Stepping down the greasy stairs he was careful to hold the one rail that went only so far before it had been broken off. In fact, the walls encasing the steep stairway were missing planks here and there, showing the inner darkness of the ship.

The heat from the iron stoves met him and worsened as he descended. Before he reached the galley floor, sweat was already glistening on his face, expanding a few smudges of grime toward his temples.

The faces at work barely gave him notice, and he stood wondering what he was meant to do before a fat, hairy arm swept toward him and pointed to an unoccupied space beside a tall, broad man. There were planks on the counter, seemingly the ones torn from the walls of the ship and the men were carving objects from the wood. Where he had expected to be engaged in the preparation of food, he found that he was carving long spokes from the hardwood.

He followed the lead of the tall man with the shaved head beside him, while giving consideration to whether or not a word might be appropriate. He glanced down the line and saw men's hands doing the same as his.

An hour later, he had not spoken, but his thirst had become naggingly evident. The heat had drained him and he worried more and more for a drink, the dearth of alcohol in his body shading every aspect of his existence with a dire pallor.

The man at the head of the line was drinking from a bottle. He was talking in a language Patrick could make no sense of. It was not Irish or English but some other. The man handed the bottle to other men toward the head of the line yet no one would drink from it. Patrick thought he would swallow its entire contents if only he were offered. He looked up at the big man at his side who was looking down at him and then turned his head to regard the man at the head of the line.

The big man went back to his business. After finishing off the spoke he was carving, the man said: 'Portugee.'

Patrick nodded when the big man turned his eyes on him.

'What're ye?' asked the man.

'Éireannach mé.'

'Hailing frum where?'

'Limerick.'

The big man considered this, 'Alright den.'

They continued work until there came a break and the big man tilted his head toward Patrick, indicating that he follow in mute secrecy.

The man took the ladder in three strides, holding on to nothing and seemingly shooting through the hatch hole. Patrick followed after him. On deck, he trailed after the big man who strode with steadfast purpose until he reached the Portugee who had been below at the head of the table. Without slowing his stride he grabbed hold of the Portugee and hurled him overboard. Patrick glanced around to see that there was no man in sight. He checked toward the crow's nest. No one at watch.

The big man now had the Portugee's bottle in his hand. He wiped the top of it with his open palm, as large as both of Patrick's.

'Swig?' asked the man, thrusting the bottle toward Patrick, who felt instant relief as tears flooded mercifully into his eyes. He took hold of the bottle and drank. It was like red wine only sweeter, thicker. 'I wun't be cutting up nar more facking widgets.'

Patrick continued drinking, sucking the sweet bliss into his guts in a manner that made the big man smile, showing his perfect teeth. Teeth so white Patrick could not believe it.

With a laugh, the big man snatched the bottle from Patrick and finished off its contents. He then pulled back his top lip and smacked the lip of the bottle off his front teeth. The glass broke and fell. He took a bite from the bottle, chewing it up. 'Nut'n but sand is all.' The big man grinned. 'Nar'tn like da likes a ye 'n me. Made 'a da cut 'a rock.' He flung the remnants of the broken bottle overboard and held out both arms, showing off the blots of tattoos and the scars. 'Nar a bone ev'r injured, unbreakable I were tol' by t'ree physicians I've fell up against in me life. Unfacking breakable.'

Patrick raised a newly steady finger to point at his own forehead. 'Same's up here, wha's tucked away in me t'ick skull.'

A moment passed before the big man, finally catching the intent of the joke, laughed in sudden complicity: 'Yays, dat's da facking spirit,' said he. 'T'is only da t'ought 'a harm dat brings it upon yer sarry soul.'

Tommy Cavanagh stood upon the Harbour Grace dock and, with scarcely known pleasure, feasted his eyes upon his wife, Rose, and daughter, Elizabeth, making their presence evident on the gangplank. No greater treasure might have been laid before him. In the three years that he had been under servitude in Newfoundland, shipped there for pickpocketing, and sentenced to two years or transport (he had chosen the latter, which included the branding of his right hand) to Talamh an Éisc, he had managed to store away a sum large enough to build his own two-room tilt and thus get clear of the windowless fishermen's cabin where the men were stacked in bunks occupied for sleep alone. Of the four pounds required for Rose, Ronan and Elizabeth's transport, he had managed to pay an initial fee of one pound. The remaining monies due for their transport would set him in the debt of Master Lawton, who would deduct the amount, if any remained after supplies had been accounted for, from Tommy's catch in the fall. Humble as was Tommy's nature, he was not the sort to utter the slightest protest against his extended indenture. The arrival of his family was a blessing from the Lord. The punt Tommy worked on with three other men remained profitable to Master Lawton, if not entirely to the fishermen, yet, as such, there was no need to fear for the future.

As Tommy's anxious eyes continued with their search – curious as to know why Ronan might be lagging behind, and soon puzzled by the cumbersome walk of his beloved wife – he found only the sad defeat in Rose's face as validation of the vanishing. It came over him as a wave of confusion that tattered toward ravishing misunderstanding, and broke clear on the barren earth of bewildering dread. This intuition concerning the death of Ronan, and the growing conspicuousness of his wife's extended girth, punched a hole through his head. His features slackened and his joyfully expectant posture deflated to a stoop.

'Dere's nut'n left o' 'im,' Rose said, her teary eyes searching back toward the ship, as though, only now in reaching the steadfast reality of land, the absoluteness of the truth became substantial.

With cap in hand, and heart overcome by the greater weakness of pain over anger, Tommy remained apart from Rose and Elizabeth, for his expectations, sweetly built from years of toil, had been blackly soured. There he stood on the dock, clinging to hope, his head tilting to see beyond those disembarking for a view of a smaller person who might have strayed, until all passengers and crew had departed and the servants, sent by their masters, had settled accounts with the ship's master for the fees owing upon delivery of the labourers or passengers.

Tommy watched while what was thought to be the final occupant, Captain Jones, a retired officer from the Queen's Royal Navy, trod from the deck toward him.

The captain, upon sighting Rose's burning stare and then shifting his eyes to Tommy, showed no sign of faltering confidence. In fact, he seemed bolstered by what he was now destined to face, and hurried his step toward Tommy.

Once before Tommy, the captain professed: 'Your son was a carrier. If it were not for his removal from my vessel, he might have infected the lot. Good thing that occurrence was stalled, for our sakes, as well as yours.' With this, Captain Jones tapped Tommy's chest with the white gloves he held in his hand and studied the fisherman's face with puckered lips. With eyes lowered, Tommy made a motion to speak, yet could find no spirit in him to challenge this educated man. The captain, immune to the ire of Rose's stare, then turned abruptly to be greeted by his own wife and children, whom he embraced openly and with fondness.

Again, Tommy's eyes searched the abandoned vessel. All were gone, he thought. Was it true? All had left the ship. It might as well have carried not a single soul. But, no. While Rose and Elizabeth stood in silence and in wait, and the din of the departing carried on behind him, Tommy noticed movement upon the deck. A lone, diminutive form nearing the gangway. A figure that limped as though injured and watched toward his feet. A boy. Ronan.

Cuz O'Malley.

Rose had seen no sign of the mute man since that night when he had set blaze to her son's body, twenty-two days into the journey. He lumbered along, watching toward the planks of the wharf, as though lost in disgruntled thought, until he was stood directly before Tommy. Head bowed and body stinking of filth, Cuz cautiously put out both hands and held them near Tommy's shirt. There were two fingers missing on his right hand and a thumb severed from his left. The scarred and calloused fingers stirred, as though in want of touch, the grimy cuffs of his ill-fitted shirt extending near his knuckles. The two fingers and blunt thumb on Cuz's right hand slid nearer to rest on Tommy's shirtfront where the fingers tremored and patted, until Cuz raised his one eye and his grotesque frown was the entirety of his lower face and his sappy eye stared hungrily and yet with a savage peacefulness that brought tears to Tommy's eyes, for there was communion there in disgust.

With the sound of Rose growling low in her throat, Tommy wept openly, while his wife set her injurious stare on Cuz O'Malley until the cripple snatched hold of Elizabeth's hand and tried to walk off with her. Elizabeth, making a cry, leaned away and yanked her hand free, finding in her palm a folded note upon which was drawn a portrait of her brother, Ronan, the boy's face active in the telling of some urgent truth.

Cuz backed away and limped off to meet no one and go nowhere expected.

Alone as three, Tommy, Rose and Elizabeth Cavanagh studied the drawing, then pressed nearer and held on for dear life as they wept together for the return of one. Between them, a hard rounded belly felt by the two.

Done clutching on to each other for the sake of mercy, forgiveness and misery, Tommy, Rose and Elizabeth separated, never to find such familial closeness again. In silence and despondency, they wandered toward the lone sea chest left on the wharf and carried it to the small open boat that would transport them from Harbour Grace to Bareneed.

Tommy sat toward the helm, drawing the oars back and forth with great strokes, while he stared away at the sea and the coast, then watched his living daughter, wondering why.

The land passed beside them, giant ragged cliffs with stunted spruce trees tucked into nooks and crannies. Tufts of grass sprouted here and there from dirt, bringing Ireland to Rose's mind. Here, however, the landscape appeared more medieval, desolate and scorched than that of her native home, which, under the troubled gaze of her husband and with the fresh gouge in her heart, she now wished she had never departed. Goats leaned to remain upright on the steep incline of a cliff, their hard hooves slipping with each nudge of movement, yet none of them plummeted into the ocean as Rose expected. She sat with the sea chest before her, her eyes set on the box that held all left of home. In addition to her own items of clothing, there were the one spare suit of clothing that Ronan had owned and the single dress belonging to Elizabeth. A dress that had been tailored by Elizabeth's grandmother, dead two years ago from a malignant madness that left her clawing the walls, the dress prepared for a crossing-over that the grandmother had years ago foretold.

The deep blue ocean was without ripple as the open boat sailed across its surface.

Tommy Cavanagh watched his daughter while he stroked the oars. His gaze held there, avoiding his wife's presence like the plague.

'*Daid?*' asked Elizabeth in a voice tamed by Irish. 'Why're ye staring at me face?'

Tommy gave no answer in reply, wondering on the sound of his daughter's words, spoken in the language of his homeland, a sound more foreign and unsavoury now transplanted here. He kept rowing and staring as long as his eyes could endure, a trick to pull away for the explanation or comfort or damage that might be recognized in that young face.

'What're ye staring at?' Elizabeth put in again, to which no reply was given, which made the child's intolerable obviousness of her own existence more explicit. Rose, hearing the child's voice rising up from the slat beside her, gave an enquiring look in that direction. Her eyes remained there, unable to help herself.

Adrift, thought Tommy. *Bheith ar fuaidreamh.*

Elizabeth looked from her mother to her father. '*A Thiarna!*' said she. 'What in da name o' God are ye staring at?'

Tommy Cavanagh rowed, the bow of the boat aimed toward the looming headland in the distance, behind which lay a small cove where the shacks of Bareneed were cheerlessly cloistered.

The quarters arranged for Rose and Elizabeth were Tommy's own, two rooms with an open stone hearth and hole cut in the ceiling for the ventilation of smoke. The beds were two heaps of swamp grass, rotted rags and boughs arranged in the far corners. Of this, or any other matter, Tommy never spoke. He merely met eyes with Elizabeth and nodded toward the beds which reeked of human offence.

The other room in the tilt was occupied by four small children, the second eldest being a girl of six who spoke not a word. There was no sign of a mother. The children were without clothes and picked and scratched at each other ceaselessly.

Tommy made no mention of them. Those children. He would leave them to themselves as he had for weeks, since the death of those who loved over them. Not so much an impoverished, pitiable presence now, as an infestation. His blood in none of them.

Rose had just unpacked her belongings from her chest and prepared the necessities of privacy, setting down on a narrow ledge fastened to the wall her soap and a comb she had saved from her mother, when the naked children were upon the two articles and made off with them, grunting and shivering and screaming as they chewed off bits of the soap, dropping the bar every few feet and leaving a trail of crumbs that the youngest ones squatted over and picked up between two tiny fingers to stare at and then gobble down. As a snatching and squawking group, they moved toward and through the door before climbing into a small rotted boat outside another shack, its boards greyed by age to the point of black.

Tommy walked to the doorway and paused, as though thinking on something he might have forgotten or wished to have said, yet would not turn to face the room one final time. He put his cap on his head and strolled down over the valley toward the sea where there was work to be tended to, and then up over the headland where his small form could be seen climbing, grasping at bushes and newly sprouted spruce and rocks before reaching the top, where he stood, and then knelt on one knee, staring out, northeast, to sea.

The naked children returned without the soap or comb and were upon Rose at once, pushing her in through the doorway, touching her belly and pressing their faces there, listening or kissing or patting the mound. They squealed and bounced at the thought of something hidden from them, the youngest, barely able to walk, opening and shutting his hand over and over, and sucking on his bottom lip while making 'ma, ma, ma' noises, while yet another bent and shoved her head up Rose's skirts.

Although she tried to accommodate them, Rose soon grew weary of their attention. Only one of them, the eldest, a boy, kept absolutely away from her. He was struck by some bone-twisting affliction that had not had its entire way with him. He leaned against the inside wall, picking at the moss that had been poked into the seams, his eyes searching elsewhere. His manner brought Rose's mother to mind. Occasionally, the boy watched her with a sideways leer that was both menacing and horribly needful. In the boy's growing expression of delight, Rose saw that his teeth were cracked and chipped so that he came to possess a monstrous smirk. Of course, she had seen this sort of child before, the wrongdoing of families too closely linked by blood to have that blood run purely away from itself. The boy took an interest in Elizabeth and went to her and clung on. Elizabeth tried to edge away from him, yet there was no doing so. He yelped and made a hissing sound like one of the cats that roamed freely in and out of the shack, so that Rose was forced to drive the twisted boy from the room.

That night, the naked children slept with Rose, but soon, one by one, made their way over to Elizabeth who shied away from them, finding them frightening with their eyes watching her in the dark, and their fingers twirling her hair and mouths sucking on the strands. The eldest boy did not return, making Elizabeth thankful for that small mercy, at least, while Rose, awake as well, worried for her life with Tommy, who had not yet returned.

Elizabeth, unable to endure the children's persistent pawing, slid away, over to the straw, where she settled alongside her mother and kept watch over the huddle in the other corner. She wished for her home and her friends, until sleep easily took her, as it was wont to do with children, and the naked children returned to her long after midnight, doing what they chose with her in her sleep, until they had satisfied their curiosity and gravitated toward the bigger female body, Rose.

The next morning, while Rose was rising, carefully freeing herself from the gaggle of sleeping children, so as not to wake them and take the brunt of their ceaseless demands, a knock sounded on the door and a man in a suit, vest and wide-brimmed hat appeared in the opening. The man identified himself as '*Máistir* Lawton,' yet that appeared to be the full extent of his Irish. Rose expected no such visit and, so, was startled to see the man stood so vividly at the edge of the room.

'Unfortunate news, I'm afraid,' said the master. 'Your husband has been drowned. Fishermen discovered his body this morn.' The master pointed off toward the water. 'It was from the headland that he plummeted to his death.'

Rose caught little of the meaning of the merchant's speech. He spoke in English, which she was worried to understand, and had avoided learning back in Limerick, despite Elizabeth's insistence and knowledge of it. It was only the word 'husband' that made the sentiment carry through. She nodded and cast a glance at Elizabeth, who was not awake and might know the implication of the words.

'You understand?'

Rose gave consideration to the master's face. She said: 'I can't catch yer meaning,' in her own dialect, which was unintelligible to the master.

The master spoke again, his tone prompting her to give a simple nod, for this seemed the desired response.

With this, the master took an expressionless look around the room, and turned to leave the misery to the miserable.

Rose remained stood in the shack, ruminating on what had been said about Tommy.

In time, the woman from the nearest shack, whose name was Minnie, came to tell Rose the news. It was as anticipated and feared, for what might be expected of the trouble she had brought with her, the baby in her womb that she now cursed for causing such piteous and insufferable woe?

The bishop at sea, and a visit to Bareneed

(from the journals of Bishop Flax)

The Newfoundland Church ship was put into commission this year on the 20th of April, and on that evening was dispatched to Bareneed, in Conception Bay, for duties performed on behalf of the *Society for the Propagation of the Gospel in Foreign Parts*, under which society I have had the honour to be a missionary in British North America nearly ten years.

It was under great difficulties that I had kept even the slightest diary of my journey; my ink would frequently be drunk by unbaptized children, in spite of all my precautions; my supply of paper was always necessarily scanty, and it occasionally altogether failed me, in districts where it would have been as reasonable to have expected a gas-lamp for my convenience at night, as a sheet of letter-paper by day. Had it not been for some boxes of paper, which had been dispersed along the shore from different wrecks, I might have failed entirely in procuring this convenience in some places where my application was successful.

The notes which I succeeded in keeping, under all these disadvantages, were, moreover, very slight; they were intended merely to furnish me with brief particulars of dates and journeys, and duties performed.

The evening of the 20th of April, we bore against a head-wind through the night, and by dawn managed to reach Brigus, south of Bareneed in Conception Bay.

Here we saw the wreck of the *Royal Nigger*, a fine vessel of the Messrs. Newman's, which had run ashore at this place on her way to St. John's, about Christmas last, and which, I regret to say, the people, instead of protecting as they might have done for its owners, had been unprincipled enough to plunder and break up.

A great many gulls were upon a bulk on the shore, which we learned to be the remnants of a beached whale, the occasion of which drew from memory the day I toured the whaling establishment of Messrs. Hunt and Newman at Swanger's Cove. The machine with which the fat of the whale is cut into small pieces for the boiler, reminded me of a similar machine which I have seen used by sausage-makers in England. The refuse pieces of the whale, which are left in the boiler, after the oil is extracted, furnish, I am informed, all the fuel which is required for heating the coppers. This recalls to my recollection the fact that the early settlers on this island used to make fires with piles of the carcasses of fat penguins, a bird which used then to be very common, but is now extinct, or has left the island. They were most cruelly treated while they abounded in the island, being often plucked for their feathers and then turned loose to perish, or burnt in piles as above described.

On our arrival at Bareneed, the people, being upon their fishing-ground outside, had seen us go into their harbour, so they returned, on so unusual an event as the entrance of a strange boat to their harbour. In this place, so plentiful is the fish all the year round, that the women and children cut holes in the salt-water ice, and catch great quantities of cod-fish all through the winter.

Upon shore, I soon learned that one of those scourges of this coast, a floating grog-shop, under the name of a 'trading-vessel,' had been sojourning in Bareneed, last week, and had kept 'all hands,' during the time of its stay, in a state of intoxication: and it was likely, now that they had not a stick to burn, or a fish for the kettle; and, as this floating nuisance had only left the place the day before, it was not unlikely that the fumes of the intoxicating poisons thus supplied, had not yet evaporated.

Every hole and corner in the tilt which I first visited, that was not taken up by the human inmates, being occupied by pigs, ducks, fowls, sheep, or dogs, I was glad to find a more roomy and a cleaner retreat in another tilt; here, though, the door did not close by at least a foot, to prevent the inconvenience of smoke, which is almost universal in these houses where the cooking is done on an open stone hearth with only a hole in the roof for ventilation.

I sat upon a chest and listened to the poor widower, who was my host, speak of his deceased wife with deep affection: the anxiety, too, which he showed to bring up his children well by catechizing them, and hearing them repeat their prayers before they retired to the single bed which served for the entire family of eight, was very creditable.

Although these services, which I begged my presence might not be permitted to interrupt, were mixed with much which I deem error, yet I could not but wish that many a careless Protestant could have seen this pious Romanist, and been led to imitate so praiseworthy an attention to the religious interests of his children.

The settlers at Bareneed are chiefly of Irish extraction. I heard in the evening, that of three Englishmen who had been for years settled among them, one alone, a native of Greenwich, had not turned to the Romish faith. I went, therefore, to visit him in the morning. At his tilt, over a pond or lake, about two miles from the harbour, which sat alone, I found he was from home. He had heard the preceding evening of the arrival in the settlement of a clergyman, and attempted to cross the harbour after dark in a state of inebriation to have some conversation with me; had capsized his canoe, and had in consequence of his wet condition, slept at the tilt in the harbour, which I had passed at day-break. I returned thither, and found him at the house of J. D. of Arundel, one of the Englishmen who had turned Papist. The man requiring reformation informed me that his fondness for spirits had kept him thus poor, and he could trace to this source all his lapses, and all his misfortunes.

By the light of a piece of ignited seal's fat, placed in a scallop shell, which served for the lamp of our humble sanctuary in the woods, he assured me in our conversation that he had forsworn the further use of spirits. I made acquaintance here, for the first time, with a decoction of the tops of the spruce branches, to which I afterwards became much accustomed, as a substitute for tea, and which, from experience, I can pronounce to be very salutary and bracing, though not so palatable, as the beverage supplied by the Honourable East India Company.

In conversation, I told him of a strength greater than his own; this I entreated him to implore. He was much affected by a prayer in which I proposed he should join me in his tilt: he kept a standing posture when I commenced, but the poor fellow soon sank upon his knees, and before the conclusion of my prayer on his behalf, he was weeping like a child. It will give some idea of the prevailing use of spirits in this island, and of the consequent discouragement which the minister is doomed to experience, if I mention that notwithstanding all which I had said against the use of this intoxicating stimulant, in all which he had heartily acquiesced, and bringing the test of his own melancholy experience, had declared voluntarily, that he had left it off, he yet offered to myself, on my rising from my knees, what is called 'a morning,' from a little keg, which he drew from under his straw bed; and, on my reminding him, when about to help himself, that he had engaged to break off this habit, he excused himself by saying he had made a reservation for the use of the remaining contents of that keg. I was reminded of Jeremiah xiii. 23. I promised the poor fellow a prayer-book, which he was most anxious to possess.

We were put across the Harbour arm, back to Bareneed where I finally assembled two dozen people in the Shea household, baptized three children, and churched one woman, and was much pleased with their simple manner of singing.

As not one in this settlement could read, I was requested to read a letter containing intelligence of the most interesting kind, of which the family had been in ignorance, although they had had it by them for weeks. In many similar settlements, I was engaged in writing letters for the people to relatives who had been settled, some ten, some twenty years, in other parts of the island, and with whom they had been unable to hold any communication since their original settlement in the country, or, at least, since their dispersion.

A cock crowing during the preceding night was said, by a woman in one of the fishermen's tilts, to portend rain: I found the next day, as I subsequently did on many other occasions during my present trip, that this augury was quite correct. The woman, a new arrival from Ireland with the name Rose Cavanagh, was only weeks before made a widow by what was openly spoken of as the suicide of her husband. The suffering woman was unfortunate enough to not only have experienced this loss, but also to have found herself in the cursed condition of pregnancy with bastard child. Despite these trespasses, we were not dissuaded from ensuring that the Saviour provided for her and delivered the required spiritual sustenance.

In my visits to the different tilts, I was, again, much shocked at the poverty of the people, which was greater here than any which I had ever witnessed in Newfoundland. Some married females in one house were literally almost in a state of nudity; their manifest want of cleanliness, however, made it seem probable – as I was afterwards informed was the case – that part of their poverty might be traced to mismanagement. It must be most distressing to any merchant, or other settler, who is himself raised above poverty, and is possessed of human feeling, to live in a place where the improvidence of the people makes them so wretchedly dependent, for a greater part of the year, as the people are in this settlement.

While I was arranging these notes to send to England, I have heard of the decease of one of the wretched females mentioned above. I held service in Mr. Shea's house in her name which was attended by thirty-two.

One tilt was visited by me in this settlement, the dimensions of which were only twelve feet by ten, and I found living in it a man and his wife – the master and mistress of the house – two married daughters with their husbands and children, amounting, in all, to fifteen souls!

I found a fine old widow lady here who has forty grandchildren living: her feelings had been severely tried at the death of her husband, to whom she had been many years allied, and was fondly attached. She had, in early youth, been a Protestant, but from conviction had renounced the errors of that faith, and attached herself to the church of her husband. On her making the anxious enquiry of her husband on his death-bed, 'Whether he would like to turn?' he, affixing a very different meaning to her affectionate enquiry, than that which merely implied his being turned in his bed, begged that the poor woman would go out of his sight, and not disturb his last moments, adding 'that he had occasionally before doubted the sincerity of her professed conversion, but he had rather have cherished the delusion to the last, than have been thus cruelly undeceived at such a moment!'

While in the settlement, I endeavoured to remove here, and in other places along the coast, an unfavourable impression which some of the ignorant had conceived, and some mischievous and interested traders had encouraged, respecting a supply of seed potatoes, which, during the last year, had been sent by the colonial government, for gratuitous distribution among the distressed inhabitants of this and the other bays of the island.

The potatoes sent did not suffice for the supply of all who needed them, and those which respectable merchants imported for sale, or transported from St. John, and sold from their own stores, were alleged to be part of the gratuitous supply furnished by Government. However, delicate investigation of the matter with Master Lawton gave little remedy.

Master Lawton, while exceeding all bounds of gentle and generous hospitality, preferred an exchange of anecdotes regarding the area.

Here he went into details of the helpless states of intoxication preferred by the inhabitants over sensible diversions. Women, and among them positively girls of fourteen, may be seen, under the plea of its helping them in their work, habitually taking their 'morning' of raw spirits before breakfast.

'I have seen this dram repeated a second time before a seven o'clock breakfast,' said Master Lawton. 'The same, the girls among the rest, also smoke tobacco in short pipes, blackened with constant use, like what the Irish here call "dudees," all day long. The instant they drop into a neighbour's house and are seated by the fire, there is a shuffling of the clothes, and the pipe, already partly filled, is drawn from the side pocket, and applied to the ashes for lighting.'

As is often the case, once conversation turns to heated gossip, our talk degenerated further, with complaints of the habitual conversation of the people and its disgusting character; profanity is the dialect, decency and delicacy are the rare exceptions.

'Children swear at their parents, and frequently strike them,' said Master Lawton, raising his eyebrows, then offering me accommodation in one of his better rooms, which I was obliged to accept considering his fine standing.

In darkness, while smoking a cigarette offered by Ferrol, who was off playing cards with the crew, Patrick took notice of the lantern lights adrift in the distance. The lights, while interesting to watch, held little meaning. The shouts passed from one man to another from the rear of him barely registered, as they were not uncommon, although rarer in the night. He smoked his cigarette, his body slipping gradually to the left, registering a sudden change in compass direction. He glanced down into the black water, a gleam barely discernible as the moon was locked behind clouds. The shouting rose in volume and then stopped.

The steamer's engine gave out, its vibration dying beneath his boots.

Done with his cigarette, Patrick flicked it over the rail and turned to check what might be the matter. The scene before him was a cloak of pitch black, as every lantern on board had been extinguished. He gazed up toward the captain's deck to discover not one light aglow within. In time, he felt a presence before him, a sniff and the flutter of movement further left. As the moon freed itself from a billowed edge of black cloud, members of the crew were revealed positioned before him, silently still as though they had perished on their feet and were stood as mere monuments to their truer selves.

The eyes in every face were fixed on the distant lights, barely a breath issuing from the collection of mouths, their flesh beneath the dim moonlight bluish-white and unbecoming.

At once, all heads turned in the direction of the cabins as a boisterous noise was heard. A man clearing his throat and stomping onto the deck. Who other than Ferrol? Patrick suspected.

A few of the men shook their heads in censure and one foolish fellow even placed his finger to his lips to shush Ferrol.

'Wha's dis?'

The men pointed toward the distant lights. A young man, a mate of no more than seventeen, whispered: 'It's a four-masted privateering schooner.'

A four-master, thought Patrick. Did such a thing exist? And

privateering? Why would such a ship be so far north? The ship they were sailing on was a steamer, not a trading vessel.

'Americans,' the young man, in a censured hiss of a voice, announced.

The previous day, Patrick had heard the same young mate bragging that he possessed an authentic mate's licence, a requirement that had recently been introduced under an appendage to outdated naval law. There had been an argument between the young man and an older man from Dublin who laughed off the thought of licensing, the elder tormenting the younger with volleys of rough wisdom. The young man went on to explain, with the utmost precision and in a gratingly insistent voice, other forthcoming changes to naval laws. It was a miraculous show of restraint on the part of the seamen that the young man hadn't been hurled overboard, an action that would, doubtlessly, yet occur.

'Dere,' said Ferrol, nodding his bald head in a stabbing gesture, and stomping ahead. It was only the railing that prevented him from venturing further, for he seemed set on treading straight to the ship, regardless of the daunting stretch of water that separated the vessels. Ferrol laughed derisively and looked back at the men. 'Facking idjiots!' he roared in a voice quarried from stone and reverberating through the ship to echo up into the heavens.

A few low curses were uttered, in hopes of silencing Ferrol, while the men cringed and stiffened further.

'No onlookers,' shouted Ferrol, pointing toward the women and children who had come up from below. 'Back ta tweendecks,' he demanded with a thrust of his arm. Not moving fast enough for Ferrol's liking, they were hurried along by a roar of 'Now.' With the racket of Ferrol's bellow thundering in their heads, they could not have scurried off faster. 'Turn dis facking vessel t'ward dem Amurican bassards.'

'Da rudder's snapped,' said one man. 'On da attempt ta navigate off course.'

Ferrol faced the lights that were approaching and Patrick saw, despite the dearth of moonlight, the gleam of mad pleasure in Ferrol's eyes and the bone-gnawing grin spread on his lips. 'Dey'll be abreast us soon 'nough,' he said with dark cheer, and spun, treading directly toward the captain's bridge, while slapping mates away as he bounded up the stairs. Arriving to protests from all present on the bridge, he slammed the captain into a wall. 'Light da facking lanterns,' he called back to Patrick, who, like most of the men now crammed in the doorway, had followed after Ferrol, and whose presence Ferrol somehow sightlessly discerned. 'Da rest o' ye rat fackers offa me bridge.' With one meaty hand, Ferrol seized hold of the wheel and made to spin it, only to find it jammed.

The *Venus*' captain, a long disgraced British naval officer, kept quiet and slunk from the bridge, muttering something about mutiny that made Ferrol burst with laughter in such an outrageous and extravagant manner that he was forced to drag his sleeve across his chin to make away with the spittle. Checking through the glass, Ferrol said, 'Dey 'av arms. Break out da weapons.'

Weapons, thought Patrick, where were their weapons? The other men seemed equally confused, nattering at each other in a way that insinuated their desire not only to avoid fighting but to seek ample hiding space. Few of them ever imagining such a ruckus was possible.

Ferrol, seeming to possess familiarity with the exact location of all stores on board, appointed Patrick as captain, stood him at the snagged wheel, and went off to break the rifles from the cupboards. He tossed the weapons from one man to another, with instructions to blast the American dogs from the sea, for what was an American anyway, Ferrol decreed, 'but a facking British bassard widt his cack ferever clapped in da muff 'a some'n else's missus.'

The men, each with a lifetime's experience with rifles, took hold of these ones as though they had never laid eyes nor set hands upon such astonishing contraptions before. They held them inappropriately and let the barrels point inertly toward their boots.

Ferrol, catching sight of this limp behaviour, went about fiercely slapping men and engaging in the worst sort of name-calling.

In time, as the four-master drifted within rifle range, gunfire was recklessly and half-heartedly exchanged, with several members of the crew succumbing to injury. The steamer, unprepared for such confrontations, was out of munitions in a short time.

'Fer facking Ireland,' Ferrol was roaring while the American ship pulled starboard. With his rifle of no further use to him, he flung it into the sky and commenced picking up barrels and hurling them at crew members of the rival vessel, crushing a few to death, as snapping of bones and splintering of skulls rose from the deck. The American crew members, confused by the seeming rain of barrels, discontinued their gunfire to dodge the barrels. Other Irishmen, attempting to lift barrels and mirror Ferrol's actions, were still straining under the weight of their first attempt, when the *Venus* was boarded, the well-armed American crew neatly advancing.

Ferrol, giving up on his arsenal of barrels, charged toward the rifles that were aimed at him and snatched hold of them, only to be shot twice, yet he kept on, until struck by a rifle butt that knocked him backward into a crate of dry provisions, where he lay felled and bleeding.

'Where are you bound for?' one of the American crew demanded, his English pristine and noble. No one was willing to answer until the young man, the one with the licence, who, no doubt, was most informed on the laws of the sea and the necessities of speaking truth to prospective tormentors, revealed: '*Talamh an Éisc.*'

'Ah, Newfoundland,' said the American officer with a laugh and a look to his fellow shipmates, who laughed openly and grinned at the contagion of the joke. 'The leper colony to the north of us. You'll have a blessed time there. Plenty of fish. We are most grateful for all that has been done for us by the dog-eating Irish fishmongers, yet it remains a backward place where the Irish, as ever, mingle their seed amongst their own children.'

This accusation stirred a noise from the distance as Ferrol, as though catching a whiff of the comment, groggily came to life.

The American officer, only giving the groans minimal attention, continued in a tone of self-cherish, with his worldly words: 'We have our troubles with the Irish in America. Drunken felons. We've been sent to deliver a message. That message being this.' He turned and fired his pistol into the face of a woman, who having heard the commotion had been chosen to seek out its source and report back to those who had once been safely locked away. Her face exploded in a mash of red as her legs jerked beneath her and kept jerking in accordance with the shrieking of her daughter of seven years, until those legs were horizontal and pointedly still. The child, who had sneaked along to be in what she believed to be the safety of her mother's presence, continued shrieking and was promptly shot, the shriek gone dead, the small body landing against Ferrol, the child's blood gushing warmly into his eyes which were now opening to see this changed world.

'Kill a few of them,' instructed the officer. 'And remember our creed: Seed spilled in an Irish whore contaminates the spirit of England. If you must indulge, take the verifiably fruitless route up the rear.'

The baby came without effort in the moments before dawn, the labour brief, as though Rose's body, having endured the birth of its previous two offshoots, had become familiar with the process and abandoned the struggle. Rose named the girl Catherine, after her mother. She was a quiet, fair-haired baby, with the deep-set, suspicious eyes of Peter Proudfoot, the British landowner who had made a regular ritual of his midnight visits with Rose back in Limerick.

On the day following her birth, the baby slept through most of the hours, waking only to nurse and to stare at the visiting bishop who entered Rose's shack to baptize the infant, the second such ritual he had undertaken that afternoon on his enduring schedule of holy rites. The bishop spoke perfect Irish, which consoled Rose, although the baptismal ritual itself was recited in the sacred undertones of Latin.

The baptism could not have come too soon, for on the second day, just as Rose had envisioned in the dream she had awoken from, the baby had disappeared from its wooden-crate cradle. One of the Bareneed women, Emily Bishop, claimed that the black-cloaked wind, the messenger for the fairies, had been witnessed making away with the newborn. Women from the shacks assured Rose that the baby would eventually find its way back, although they could not attest to the condition in which the infant would be returned. The women suspected something grotesque would be discovered in the cradle in due time, a creature with a gnarled face and lumpy forehead, and so took greater interest in the tilt and its residents, wanting to be the first to manage a peek at the horrible changeling.

Rose took solace in the fact that the infant had, at least, been baptized, so that if any harm should come to her, Heaven would welcome little Catherine into its glorious realm. Rose prayed to St. Jude for Catherine's safety, with a compassion and desperation possible only from a mother, reciting rosary after rosary to the Blessed Virgin, and was further comforted by the appearance of the bishop at her door, joining her in prayer, while the naked children darted about the room, all silenced by the authoritative stare of the bishop, save for the eldest boy who shrieked with a raving wildness and fled.

Bishop Flax had insisted that Rose visit the graveyard alongside the Catholic church at the head of the valley where, in the presence of two old ladies in black shawls who had stood in vigil, he recited a deeply felt prayer over the grave of Tommy Cavanagh, whose rock-battered and water-soaked body was buried in a pine box six feet under.

'Take comfort in the end,' the bishop soothingly intoned. 'There is goodness to be had from all of this. You have been chosen, singled out to suffer in the name of the Lord, you will bear the burden. As Jesus struggled beneath affliction, the ghastly weight of his cross, so you, too, will be burdened by this mortal pain. Accept it and allow the Lord to enter your heart, where your pain and his pain might mingle in holy reverie.'

Bishop Flax had then brought Rose aboard his vessel to counsel her. The loss of a baby, the death of a husband. A woman from another land, so lost, so vulnerable and in want of soothing. Much to the bishop's surprise, there was an intoxicating loveliness about the woman, the way her filthy hair could still seem elegant, and the smell of her in passing – despite the fact that she was not of a position to afford scented aromas – was soul-loving, her body exuding its own natural fragrance that was sublime.

A table was set in the galley. Silver cutlery from Willowbank was laid out around rose-bordered china from the House of Palermo in Italy. The baptismal gift of a succulent lamb from one of the residents in shacktown had been cooked and was roasted and steaming in the centre of the table, its tender, skinned head intact. Scalloped potatoes had been prepared from the local offerings of potatoes and cream, provisions from the nearly bare cellars and cupboards of the locals who willingly made this offering to a man of God.

'I am accustomed to more humble meals than this, believe me. My travels tend to afford me victuals of the more austere sort, those shared with the fisherfolk and farmers. This is a treat. A blessing. Please,' said the bishop. 'Eat.'

Rose looked at the food with an ailing expression.

'You have no appetite?' he asked, pouring wine into his silver goblet.

'No,' was all Rose could manage.

The bishop kept his eyes on her throughout the meal, chewing and drinking and wondering. 'This wine is very pleasant. Made from blueberries, I hear.'

Rose kept her eyes lowered to her plate. In time, she lifted the weighty fork and poked at her cut of lamb that had been sliced from the centre, her stomach shrinking protectively around the thought of it.

The bishop was wiping his whiskers as he stood and placed the napkin on the table. He stepped toward Rose and sat in a chair which he pulled up by her side. 'You must eat, to keep your strength.' He delicately took the fork from her and raised the knife, slicing away a piece of the most tender lamb toward the bone of the chop. 'Here.' He lifted the fork to her lips and was thrilled at the sight of them parting to accept nourishment. 'Yes, please, eat.' Again, he cut another piece. 'Drink.' He offered her the goblet, his own goblet, which he rose from his chair to retrieve. 'Good for the blood,' he said, the final word sending a waft of warmness into Rose's face. She drank as instructed, then allowed the bishop to feed her a forkful of creamy potatoes. He continued doing so, commenting on her lost baby and the rumours he heard from the women in Bareneed.

'The baby was not your husband's. Is there truth to this, my child?'

Rose nodded in mortal embarrassment.

'Better that it has been removed then. Here . . . eat.' He fed her more meat. 'You must keep up strength. The turmoil of what you have endured strives on hunger. It would be no blessed fasting, yours.'

The bishop spoke more of the bastard child, his words becoming barbed with severity, until his guest's plate was perfectly cleaned.

Once done, the bishop stood, watching Rose, whose eyelids fluttered slightly, her throat contracting. Expecting a reaction of this sort, the bishop turned for the ash bin near the door and held it out for her. Rose's face inclined forward as she held her hair away from her cheeks. It was an intimacy the bishop could not bear, watching this woman vomit, spit, choke and, subsequently, moan.

When Rose was done with her expulsion, the bishop dabbed her lips dry with the napkin provided, and, again, took his seat beside her.

'This only confirms the menace,' the bishop assured her, watching Rose's left shoulder, so that Rose suspected a fleck of something from her mouth might be there. The bishop's fingers reached to brush it away. Inadvertently, his fingers slipped the dress down, enough to catch the hint of cleavage where the voluptuous curves of her weighty, milk-laden breasts began. He took a moment to stare there, before Rose fixed her garment. Then the bishop studied Rose's face, whose eyes were filled with sickness and inexplicable wonder.

This man, she was thinking, this man. *Diabhalta Easpag.* Further sickness in the pit of her stomach.

'Your spirit has been disburdened. Not so laden now.' The bishop gave a brief smile then, again, slipped the dress from her shoulder, lowering it further until the heft of her curves became pronounced and the dark arc of her right nipple showed itself. 'Stand,' the bishop instructed, rising while holding out his open palms. Rose complied, setting her hand on the edge of the thick table to steady herself.

Nearer to her now, taking in her fragrance and the creamy white pallor of her skin, enthralled by how the green veins were so pronounced in her breasts, the bishop edged the material down further and set his fingertips to her left nipple, a quiver coursing through him that stuttered in his moist breath. Searching Rose's eyes, as though testing for objection, he thought one word: physiology, then lowered his mouth to the nipple and sucked, his mouth steadily contracting and releasing. He drank plentifully, his actions turning vigorous while his hands squeezed her breast more energetically, pumping the milk into his throat.

When the bishop was done, he wiped at his lips, watching Rose's face which was turned in profile, and passed passive comment, 'There is no greater person than a mother.' Then he crooked his head to sup from the other breast. 'There is no purer joy than milk from a woman. Udders no different from a cow's, yet sacred, the balance, the heft, not profane, yet the spirit.' Quizzically, he searched Rose's eyes, as though she were a perfect stranger to him, not of his world, then fed upon her again.

Rose watched toward the door, cringing through the ordeal and wishing it would only come to an end. Another man. One like any other.

She feared that God might strike them both dead. Tears pooled in her eyes, for now it seemed that the Lord himself, rather than being removed from the lewd proceedings, was savaging her. She wept at the thought that came into her mind and could not be vanquished, only made more sacrilegious as the bishop continued.

Done with his feasting, the bishop lost no time wiping the milk from his moustache. At once, he turned Rose around and led her nearer the corner. There, he bent her forward and raised her skirts, leaning to the side to ensure that her udders were hanging in a pendulous fashion. Again, he lowered his mouth, licking and sucking between the warm mound from which creation had recently sprung. As suspected, the smell of her was ambrosial, the heat invigorating and inciting. He worked with dedication until his entire face was soaked and gleaming. Standing, he quickly freed himself from his garments before freely taking her from behind.

Rose felt nothing. At that point, her eyes went dead. It was not her sight that was obliterated, but her willingness to see, her mouth, her nose, her face withdrawn to a place where she herself might never be found. She became a shadow masked by greater shadows. It was only her ears that experienced sensation. The grunting thrust from the bishop's throat and, hopefully, disturbingly, the far-off cry of a baby on the ship. The bishop, too, must have heard, for he paused long enough to let silence fall over the room. And there it was, singular, exact, fragile, the cry of a baby, her baby, Catherine.

The ship afloat on the dark water. Anchored off shore. Beneath a bright, round moon. A single baby's cry hovering over the bay.

The bishop returned to his rhythmic jabbing, the music of tiny voices playing through his mind. He rammed Rose forward again and again, while panic and hope filled Rose's heart.

The bishop muttered words that Rose could not discern, yet, once repeated, became clearer, 'What do you hear?'

Rose said nothing, her mouth plugged black, while her ears strained to hear and her eyes searched the wall before her, as though seeking a hole that might deliver her nearer the sound.

'Tell me, *striapach*.'

She would not say it. Could not for him.

'Beyond these walls, within the bowels of this ship, we keep those born wicked. *Striapach.* We know. The newest sing the loudest. That bastard baby of yours, I know. Where there are flames there is salvation.' And with that his momentum intensified until Rose felt she might be injured by the widening and lengthening of his plunge. She braced a hand against the wall, her sweaty palm slipping in distress. 'What is it? Tell me, now. Tell me.'

'A baby,' Rose whispered, her throat thick with a sob, tears warming her eyes back to life. 'My *babai.*'

'Yes,' he said, the pitch of his voice crescendoing. 'Have another that will never know you.' And he pounded her violently, as though to murder not her body, but the thought of her, and stopped, holding himself still, yet straining, his essence stretching away from its centre, into her aching, contracting womb.

The Duncans settled well with the society of merchants in St. John's, maintaining a lifestyle much similar to the one they were accustomed to prior to being disgraced back in Liverpool. Uncle Ace Hawco, on his return from the sealing grounds, took action against the merchant, Mr. Bowering, in a way that was talked about for decades after the fact and even immortalized in the memoir of William Coaker, founder of the Fishermen's Protective Union, who cited Ace Hawco for his exemplary bravery.

1926

St. John's, Newfoundland
& Bareneed

The Duncans settle in

'Shall I save the Daily Dot Puzzle?' Amanda called up the stairway that inclined toward the second storey, the pitch of her voice and the chandelier light muted by dark polished wooden walls. Glancing down at the newspaper in hand, she considered Mutt and Jeff, then Snoodles, smiling mildly. Eyes still lingering. 'Emily?'

'Yes,' the sound of the young girl's voice hollering out in frustration from the labour of a strenuous task. 'I'm changing my clothes, Mummy.'

'Alright. I'll hold it for you.' Amanda turned for the parlour doorway, directly across from the foot of the stairs, and entered the room. She sat on the low-back green velvet divan. Resting one hand on the carved armrest, her fingers traced the wooden grooves while she thought of Emily and the extra attention she was directing toward her daughter lately. She was attempting to cope. Again, last night, Alan did not return home, but telephoned to say he would be in meetings at the Newfoundland Hotel all evening. Try as she might to avoid dwelling on it, she could not help but imagine the specifics of those meetings.

Fading back to the present, Amanda studied the advertisements for the movies, noting the new John Barrymore picture show. A sea picture. Alan would certainly be willing to see that one. The man of adventure. The dashing John Barrymore fleeing England under the cover of night. Now, there would be a movie truly worth seeing. John Barrymore shuddering and snivelling with fear. Checking further down the page, she sighted an advertisement for the new electric ranges. *The Electric Age is here*. She wondered what this might mean. Reading quietly, 'Before the rush begins have your electric range installed.' She thought it might be a novel idea and made a mental note to ask Alan if it would be within their means to purchase one. They seemed to have an abundance of money lately, contrary to what she expected when fleeing Liverpool. They had settled in a much grander home with an expansive back yard and lovely mature maple trees that cast down wonderful shadows in the summer sunlight.

Presently, she wondered how Alan would react to her request for the range. He would probably just brush it off with some cynical remark about new corrupt devices before carrying on about his latest golf game at Baly Haly Country Club or with a story from one of the prominent city merchants.

To ensure the purchase of the electric range, it would mean catching Alan at the pinnacle of guilt. He was such a despicable man at times. She invested no faith nor trust in his judgement and resolutely believed he would fail again. Alan failed consistently and miserably in business, until learning a few of the merchant tricks and catching on with regards to the proper way to cheat the local fishermen out of their bounteous catches. Hearing him talk with the other merchants, bragging about taking advantage of the inbred stupidity of the lowly locals – mostly Irishmen, boghoppers as he called them – gave her a sickly feeling, a soul-embracing nudge of disgust at her husband's malicious stab at self-esteem. She was in no way proud of him. No respect for him. Yet leaving would mean what? How would she support herself? The arrangement was fine as it stood, but she longed for a true lover. A man who spoke of matters of the heart and head. Valentino. A film of his was the coming attraction.

Amanda drew a mental picture of the houses along Circular Road, the stately three-storey Victorian structures owned by prominent businessmen, doctors and judges. The Crosbies. The Hickmans. The Bairds. The Jobs. The Woodfords. All with elaborate front drives, an entry and an exit. Alan must have stolen quite a substantial sum of money from the people back in Liverpool to afford this sort of luxury. While she found the thought distasteful, it intrigued her in a peculiar way, for the thoughts of misappropriated opulence surrounding them. It was almost possible to forgive her husband, ignore him, focus on playing up his smart points, for the sake of her family, so that Emily might continue to belong to the proper circle of friends.

Amanda had been invited to tea with the Hickmans on the following Tuesday, and each of the children in the area had responded favourably to invitations to Emily's tenth birthday party. There was a ceaseless string of invitations to tea parties or bridge games. If she accepted every overture she would never be at home. And there was work with the various committees that sent clothes and blankets to the outports. Several of her new friends, wives of prominent merchants, seemed to be working themselves to death on behalf of the poor outport people. They had the whole top floor of the Newfoundland Hotel donated to their use plus a large packing and storage room in the basement. They also were working in concert with the rugged Nonia nurses who single-handedly tended to huge areas of outports, as there were no doctors available. One of the latest projects Amanda was involved in was packaging and shipping seeds to the Nonia nurses who were helping people dig and set gardens around their houses so they could, at least, grow a crop of vegetables. Presently, beriberi was a plague on the island. And just last month there had been the fire at Mt. Cashel Orphanage. They were raising money for the reconstruction. It was such a deserving project. The priests there were absolute miracle workers, so devoted and saintly.

'How's this, Mum?' Emily stood prettily at the edge of the room. Turning in a circle, she then gracefully bowed, holding the edges of her new blue velvet dress, the collar trimmed with cream lace.

'Oh, absolutely beautiful, darling.' Amanda laid the paper to one side and gestured with her hands. 'Come here. Let me see.'

When the child stepped nearer, Amanda fussed with the dress, straightening it along her daughter's waist. Then she observed Emily, her eyes filled with worship, yet not without the vagueness of a wound. 'Ten years old tomorrow.' She bit her bottom lip. 'You can see the woman in your face already.'

'My first real party dress.' Emily spun around, her black curls rising and then settling on her shoulders when she halted.

'I was just reading that *Rin Tin Tin* is playing at the Nickel Theatre.'

'This dress is too smart for that place.'

'Then maybe *Biff, Bing, Bang.*'

'Is that theatre?' she asked grandly.

'Umm, not really. Well, I guess.' Amanda blinked at the advertisement. 'Twenty-five big numbers in their sensational overseas review.'

'I'll just save it for parties.'

'And *The Sea Beast* is playing. Your father likes John—'

Her words were cut short by the sound of the front door opening. Both Emily and Amanda turned their heads to see Alan returning. According to his attire, he had come from a golf game, his cap and baggy trousers making him the picture of provincial fashion. He stepped into the parlour doorway, his face showing off the highlights of an afternoon's sunning. He smiled at them in a way that betrayed time spent in the lounge. Amanda's expression fell, but Emily's remained bright as she proudly spun around for him.

'Let me see,' Alan said, tipping back his hat and stepping nearer. Bending to her, a smell of perfume and alcohol wafted into the space between him and his wife.

'You're absolutely beautiful,' Alan told his daughter, setting his hands on her shoulders. 'I've brought you something.' He reached into his pocket and extracted a wooden hair clasp, the wood deep and polished.

'Thank you.' Emily took it from him, holding it in her hands.

With his eyes on the clasp, Alan reached forward and pulled a long hair from within its teeth. It took a while and he offhandedly put the hair in his pocket. 'One of mine must have got caught in it when I was trying it on.' He made a clown's mouth with his lips and kissed her wetly on the cheek. 'No truer beauty than you.'

The flowery haze of perfume that clung to her husband wilted Amanda's attempt at a smile, filling her with contempt.

'Isn't she just perfect?' Alan said, addressing his wife, his booze-soft afternoon eyes sighting her sickened expression, and his face gradually mirrored his wife's displeasure. As was characteristic of his position in such matters, he recovered quickly. Sniffed and seemed to think ahead of other possibilities.

Taking this for the sign of admission Amanda had come to recognize, she rose to her feet, glaring at him. *Everything shows so easily in his face*, she silently raged, scolding herself for not having known him, truly known him before accepting his proposal of marriage. Her father had warned her. Her father had seen Alan for what he truly was.

'How was your golf game?' she asked spitefully, before marching from the room.

'Excellent,' Alan called out, as though to the entire house, following her step with his eyes from where he remained crouched beside his daughter, his tanned hands weakening on Emily's shoulders.

'Mummy?'

Amanda hurried toward the broad stairway and up the carpeted steps, away from Alan, his failures and betrayals, away from his deception, his smirking sense of courage that always faltered on his lips and in the face of the slightest adversity. It was forever more about himself. Him and his wants, his strength in drink, his weakness.

Emily shifted her gaze to her father, her eyes filled more with uncertainty than the previous giving pleasure of love. She leaned away from him, recognizing the smell on his breath. The trouble smell. Sweet and ugly at once.

'Are you off to a party?' Alan asked hopefully.

'No,' Emily flatly replied, her eyes on the hair clasp.

Another hair there, Alan noticed, yet refused to remove it. 'Then why the dress?' At once, Alan's tone adopted a hint of aggravation, things not going his way from the moment he entered the room. The mood against him. The two women in his family against him, always against him, despite the fact that he had saved them from ruination. Saved the little girl from a life of wretchedness. He considered storming from the house to rejoin his boisterous friends at the club, some of them with their young sons and daughters who he often played games with out on the grounds. High from the effects of afternoon cocktails, he had left Baly

Haly early to be with his family, but his family had soured his mood. He realized that he was staring at his daughter. At the moment of his realization, she rushed off after her mother.

Alan rose from his crouch, stood for a moment in the empty parlour, then headed for the front door. Hand on the porch doorknob, he paused to look back at the staircase, to where Emily was racing away from him. Such a grand staircase, the banister carved exquisitely.

Show 'im wha' feel'n means

The *Terra Nova* sailed into St. John's harbour with the hides and fat of 22,529 seals in its belly, and the bodies of eighteen dead laid out frozen on its deck. It had been a prosperous year for those who never perished, with each surviving crew member receiving the unexpectedly great sum of $107.12.

A murmur briskly mounted toward a cheer that went up from the waiting crowd as the vessel cleared the north side of the cliff-framed narrows and edged into view. The crowd had heard in advance the news of prosperity, the information wired ahead. The *Terra Nova* would be the highliner after all, under the capable hands of the legendary Captain Abram Kane.

Positioned on the harbourfront, among the crowds shouting their welcome, the illustrious president of Bowering Brothers himself stood in fur coat and with a great prosperous smile that widened as the ship neared the dock, and the lines were tossed down to the men who secured them around the wooden gumps.

At once, the sealers strode down the gangway as they glanced out over the crowd, some of them smiling, accepting the warmness of the welcome, while others carefully held the rope railing to either side of them, and watched flatly, with ruined eyes. Only a semblance of themselves.

With feet firmly on land, the men wandered off, as though to claim shelter from those who might be seeking them, or meet loved ones – wives and children – who expressed their delight with hugs and kisses, and anxiously put forth questions regarding the details of the journey.

The joyous clamour built and remained vibrant with much celebration, until the noise slowly began to diminish. One by one, heads turned to see what had silenced their neighbour. A hush, like a string of crystal ice forming over water, wove itself through the crowd. On the gangway, a grotesque grey slab of cargo, then another, was being carried toward the dock, one man at the head, another at the feet. The crowd spread away, making a path to allow the bodies to be loaded onto the waiting carriages. The crowd watched in respectful silence, a woman squeezing a husband's hand, a child hugging tight to a father's ragged jacket as the bodies were carefully slid aboard the carriages. Even the gulls seemed to have vacated the sky and the water cease lapping at the dock.

When the last of the ice-twisted dead had been taken off ship, a lone man appeared at the top of the gangway, a man with a look that saw, yet knew of little beyond the flash of movement, the colours, the bodies, the noise. The bandage wound around his chest was evident through the rips in the front of his shirt that fluttered in the bite of March gusts.

It was passed around among the crowd, by the men who had been aboard, that that man, Uncle Ace Hawco, had survived because his blood had frozen. The cold had been so fierce that the wound had sealed itself in an icy web over a pool of red that you could later poke your finger through. The blood beneath it. Freezing deeper, closer, thickening the clot. Yet what had brought him such an injury had remained a mystery. These words spoken back and forth and changed and rearranged and added to and taken from, while Uncle Ace Hawco listlessly trod down that gangway with a look of misunderstanding, as though the crowd were a new curiosity to him.

Catherine pressed through the mob that began parting to make way for Ace, even though he was still on the gangway, while eight-year-old Jacob trailed after his mother, watching up at the faces.

Hesitantly, Uncle Ace made his way down the plank, until he stood level upon the dock. He stared at the smiling woman, Catherine, who came to face him, then down at the boy, Jacob. Two of them near enough to touch. The dead were there before him. To think of them urged their eyes open from pitiful darkness. A single thought and the perished were granted vision through his eyes, could witness life around him, but if he thought of the dead hour after hour, they would infuse him with their own being and his life would be driven out to be glutted entirely by their presence. Could these dead get any nearer than where they stood? Were they capable of touching? And then they did touch him. Hands on his arms. The way he stared prevented Catherine's and Jacob's truer affection from bounding forth. Uncle Ace gazed around, while Catherine noticed the slashes in his shirt and the stained bandage beneath it. His breath clouded thicker in the nippy air as he searched the dock, seeming to recognize one of the men, a man in a long fur coat and bowler hat.

Without word, Uncle Ace stepped away from Catherine and Jacob, evenly advanced toward Mister Bowering, staring at the man who had regained his good humour a few moments after the unloading of the dead. Ace checked over his shoulder to see the frozen men blindly trailing after his footsteps through the slushy snow, while he pressed through the jostle of bodies surrounding him. He then watched ahead, sighting Bowering who jovially raised up on his tiptoes to scan the vessel's deck, piled high with pelts, the hollow of the ship overflowing with fur and fat.

Surveying the man's fine overcoat, crisp shirt and tie, and shining bowler hat, Uncle Ace said: *I know ye, dead man.*

'What was that?' Bowering enquired, thinking that the sealer might have spoken, but uncertain, as words were not discernible through the celebratory gestures being bestowed upon him by his fellow businessmen: Harry Job, Peter Baird and Alan Duncan.

Drifting forward, Uncle Ace neared the man and carefully extended his leathery thumbless right hand, which the president grasped automatically, with vigour, happy to be mingling with a few of the sealers who had brought him such good fortune. Bowering's smile turned triumphant, brimming with professional delight and a hint of amusement at being approached by one of the rugged baymen. He turned toward the crowd and raised his other arm as a raucous cheer went up and photograph bulbs flashed, washing out the dead men who surrounded Bowering. *Show 'im wha' feel'n means*, they said, their fingers searching through Bowering's pockets, warming their fingertips in his eyes and in his mouth. All unknown to Bowering, evident only through the faint agitation he had begun to experience. He tried his best not to show offence at the smell of the sealer, the stench of fat and blood caked and crusted onto his clothing, his bushy moustache and beard sparkling with frost, his hard deep eyes staring in a lost way that now registered concern in Bowering's mind.

Show 'im wha' feel'n means ta lose.

Mister Bowering turned toward the photographers, toward the cameras that had captured him in this congenial pose, and Uncle Ace with his blank stare. Merchant and sealer joined together in a gesture of camaraderie. Again Bowering smiled into the camera, but the new smile was strained as the hand clutching his continued to tighten. A bulb flashed and Bowering felt the hat flying from his head, not having witnessed Uncle Ace raising his scarred, grubby hand to slap it off, but thinking that the hat had been dislodged by the swell of the shifting crowd.

Carve da skin from 'is nose.

While Bowering bent uncertainly to retrieve his hat, Uncle Ace raked his fingers through his own greasy hair, then lowered his hand, mussing up Bowering's slicked-back hair in a way that guaranteed a few of the lice, his flourishing friends, would be transferred.

Straightening, Bowering stared at the man grimly, smoothing back his hair with his stiff fingers, then checked the palm of his hand.

Uncle Ace leaned toward Bowering's ear and whispered: *I seen ye done up in yer white hide. T'were glorious.*

The president of Bowering Brothers could not make out the words that barely rose from the hollow of Uncle Ace's mouth as a grunting stutter. Regardless, he offered a hesitant smile, thinking that the man had put forth a statement of appreciation and congratulations.

Da holes o' 'is skin leak sweat. See.

Again, Uncle Ace grasped Mister Bowering's hand, squeezing and shaking it mechanically, fiercely with both of his, the crowd cheering as other men pressed nearer. Music punctured the air as the welcome band was signalled to strike up again.

Uncle Ace glared at Mister Bowering's smiling lips, lashing his hand up and down, until Bowering appeared worried that his flapping arm might be torn from its socket, and other associates from Bowering Brothers closed in on the scene, sensing that something was out of sorts. But before the men could gather closer, Uncle Ace, while muttering: *T'is da suck o' da sea where ye finds yer true treasure*, hauled Bowering toward the bow of the boat, shoving aside the crowds, and – still clamped on to Bowering's hand – whirled to the side, lifting the dapper man from his feet and flinging him into the frigid Atlantic.

A shocked sideways descent through space and then a mighty splash as the president of Bowering Brothers landed on his back and was followed in by four frozen dead men who leapt after him, the first two grabbing hold of his wrists, while the remaining two gripped his ankles. With a terrified, air-gulping shout and flailing of deadened limbs, Bowering sank like a sack of stones.

A crowd of sealers had fallen in behind Ace Hawco, buffering him from the Bowering Brothers' men. No one willing to claim they witnessed the deed, no one willing to rush to the rescue, only one of Mister Bowering's anxious henchmen, Alan Duncan, pushing his way through, leaning over the edge of the high wharf, witlessly attempting to reach Bowering so far below, so witless in fact that one of the other sealers was obliged to raise the heel of his hobnailed boot and deliver a solid blow to the man's rump, driving him into the harbour, as well, for all of his foolish loyalty. And in after him freely went more of the frozen dead men.

Lord over them all

Haymarket Square bustled with cars and horse-drawn carriages. A streetcar rumbled along Duckworth Street, its image reflected in the windows of the rows of shops joined together in architectural prosperity.

'I don't like the new uniforms,' Emily said, staring at the ticket taker. 'The blue was much nicer than grey. They turn my stomach.'

'Don't be so bloody rude,' her father said bluntly, unwilling to meet eyes with the obviously miffed ticket taker. Alan Duncan's head was sodden from a late night. Suffering the menace of such a punishing physical state, he regretted having promised to take Emily along with him the previous evening.

Emily knelt up on her seat, staring at her father's face, his eyes looking away. He was on his way to see Mister Bowering, the man who her father always spoke of with such pleasure. She had heard as much from arguments between her mother and father, where her father never failed to put Mister Bowering 'up on a pedestal,' as her mother said. Whatever that meant. Twisting, she stared back at the other people, studying their hard faces and their drab clothes. Jackie, their servant, had the same kind of sharp hard face. A lot of the people did in St. John's. They were of 'low breeding,' a term used by her father, which also meant they were 'Catlicks.' She wanted to call out, 'Kiss me arse,' to all of them, one of her favourite expressions she'd heard in the schoolyard.

'Why are we riding the streetcar with these people?' She turned to study her father's profile, his longish nose and tight small lips, his eyes set back in his head, his hair thinning along his forehead. Impulsively, she gave him a peck on the cheek.

'Turn around in your seat,' he said, giving her face and attire a brisk look over.

Emily sighed as she plunked down.

Alan Duncan stared at his daughter, as though wondering what the child might mean to him. 'I thought you would appreciate a ride on the streetcars. You always seem to be talking about them. The people on them. Well, here we are. With the riff-raff.'

'I like to watch them go by. That doesn't mean I fancy riding them.'

Alan faced the front of the car, distracted, his eyes catching on the merchant stalls through the windows as they approached Haymarket Square.

'I have a meeting.'

'I know, with Mister Bowering, your hero. Is that why we're taking the streetcar? We have our own car, you know.' The clang of the streetcar bell overrode her words. She repeated, 'Car.'

Alan sighed and stood, taking hold of his daughter's hand. 'Come along. It was for an adventure. Something to take away as a memory.' Stepping down from the streetcar, Alan led his daughter among the crowds of farmers and fishermen peddling their wares. The vegetables looked fresh, with dirt still clinging to the carrot and potato. The fish, too, appeared wholesome, although there was no shortage of blue-arsed flies swirling and settling.

'You enjoy this hustle and bustle?' Alan asked. Clearing his throat, he tried playing the part of concerned, reasonable parent. He glanced down at his daughter with an overconfident fatherly smile.

Emily nodded without looking at him, her eyes busy taking in all the sights. The women appealed to her most, the dresses and pretty hats that she studied, wondering how they might look on her or her mother. She stopped by a tall horse and gazed up at him.

'Holy moley,' she exclaimed, enthralled by the massive thickness of the horse's neck, the restrained power of its bulk, all supported by such skinny legs. 'Can we get a horse, Daddy?'

'If you're a good little girl, I'll look into it. We'll have to find the proper stables. God only knows if such things exist here.'

Emily wandered along, only vaguely attuned to the pull of her father's progression. Moving into the shadowed entranceway of a low brick building, Emily stared back at the sight of another little girl of her age, dressed in dull clothes, a dirtiness about her, the girl coughing and coughing, having to stop in her tracks. TB, Emily thought. Never play with the TB children. A constant warning from her mother.

The door shut and there was silence. At once, the sickly smell of fresh paint mingled potently with an odour of dampness and rot. The stairs were narrow and Emily held the dark wooden banister, trailing behind her father who had now, much to Emily's relief, released hold of her hand.

'Come along,' he said.

Emily refused to increase her pace, intently watching her hand skim along the smooth banister.

On the third flight of stairs, her legs became leaden and she called out, 'Daddy, please carry me.' Her father trod back down over the stairs and swooped her up, hurrying up each step in a way that both pleased and frightened her. She regarded the side of her father's face. He was sweating and a patch of his sandy-blonde hair was glossily plastered to his temple beneath the brim of his felt hat.

At the top landing, he plopped her down on her feet and straightened his jacket. Through an opened doorway, an unoccupied desk sat in an outer office, papers stacked in three neat piles. Emily counted them and made note of it, playing games such as this, so she could tell her mother, 'There were three stacks of paper on the desk,' and her mother would be impressed and proud of the keen observances of her daughter.

'Can I come in, too?' Emily had been to many meetings like this and had always been made to busy herself in the outer offices. There was never anyone sitting at those desks, it being a Saturday or Sunday. The answer was usually a solid 'no.'

'Busy yourself out here. Leaf through the magazines. Pretend you're my personal secretary.' Her father offered a smile that meant something else and tapped on the inner door, the frosted glass rattling in a way that made Emily wish to hear it smash. The pretty sound it would make jingling to the floor.

A voice came from behind the door, 'Come in.'

Her father did not check her again. He did, however, leave the door slightly open. Moving closer and to the side, Emily could see Mister Bowering rising from his chair, giving a merry salute and then a handshake before both of them took their seats.

'Nice to see you, Alan.'

'Nice to see you, too, Mister Bowering.'

'How's your family?'

'Fine.'

Emily sat, waiting for mention of her name, reference to the fact that she was waiting in the outer room, but her father didn't offer anything, making her feel abandoned, and so she frowned.

'Well,' Mister Bowering laughed mildly. 'Have you given further consideration to my offer?'

'Yes, I have indeed. Over the past few days, I've weighed it out.'

'And?'

'And . . . I'm really not certain we're prepared to make that move . . . as much as we appreciate the offer.'

'Ah, that's unfortunate.' There was pause, and when he spoke again, Mister Bowering's voice seemed to have been altered. 'How can I convince you, Alan?'

'I'm not certain how.'

Mister Bowering sighed. 'I can't leave that incompetent in charge out there much longer. He's given far too much credit. I need someone with restraint, a strong man who won't buckle under the demands of those . . . fishermen.'

'Yes, I understand.'

'I must have an answer today. I've already informed Seaward of his removal.'

'The positive points are quite obvious, but the negative aspects continue to pester me.'

'Which are?'

'The isolation.'

'Bareneed is no more remote than any other place. Keep in mind the position you'll have there. You'll be lord over everything. Seaward has turned soft on me. Coaker has a bee in everyone's bonnet now. The Fishermen's Union. I need an associate with no fear of that.' Mister Bowering laughed outright, the laugh like a fat hole punched in the air. 'And why should we fear it? The Union's a joke. It won't last. We're dealing with that.'

'The sealers and fishermen are behind him. I don't want to get caught up in any of that, particularly in a small community. It might turn stormy, sentiments, I mean.'

Emily had edged closer to the crack in the door and peered in. What was Bareneed? she wondered. Moving? Were they moving? Was it back to England? She saw her father's friend winking at her father.

'Those sealers are like stray dogs,' said Mister Bowering. 'They're everywhere. You can always get a shipload of them. Anytime. They consider it some sort of perverse rite of passage. Back in New York we have to shanghai men to get them to work under the same conditions, but here. Not a problem. They're Newfoundlanders.' Mister Bowering made a fist and raised it triumphantly in the air. 'Mongrel Irishmen, hooray!'

Alan Duncan chuckled under his breath.

Emily liked the sound of her father's laughter, not hearing it often enough. Grinning, she thought she might giggle and so backed away from the door. She stared at the wall across from her, her mind now preoccupied with the possible complications of moving. She was just beginning to form friendships here. A move would disrupt everything, unless it was back to England where she might rejoin her old friends, Pratty and Bridget. She was becoming impatient, wanted to leave, to question her father about the move. Plus it was a sunny day outside, despite the nip in the air. She wanted to be out in it, to have another look

210

at that big horse. She sighed and stared at the framed pictures of ships on the walls, imagined herself as a captain, sailing to the sealing grounds, laying out a nice supper for the sealers, making certain they had warm cozy beds to sleep in. All to displease her father.

Bowering opened the top drawer in his desk and took out a photograph. 'Have you seen the house you'll be living in?' There was a two-storey white house on the rise of a hill overlooking a clutter of black shacks near the water. He took out another photograph of a store with a sign out front: Bowering Brothers.

'Remember, Alan, we are not in Newfoundland to buy fish but to sell goods.'

Alan said nothing, yet his face betrayed concern.

'You suddenly look like you've come down with a conscience. After what went on back in England. What? You think I didn't hear the details? Word travels fast among merchants, hey? Small tight family of friends. Don't worry, I've said nothing. Trust me.'

At the mention of England, Emily listened more closely, moving to peek in the door, immediately catching sight of her father turned in his chair, staring back at her, his face drained of colour as though he had seen a ghost. She flinched against his horrified gaze.

'Go,' he said quietly, slouched to the side. Then, slowly straightening with his hands on the armrests, he cleared his throat and called weakly, 'I'm almost through, Emily. Have a look at some of those magazines out there.'

She heard her name from Mister Bowering's lips, 'Emily. What a pretty name.'

'Thank you,' Emily muttered saucily and spun away.

'Is she the one?' Mister Bowering asked.

But her father said nothing in return.

'So, are you in?'

'Lord over them all, eh?' said Alan, trying to adopt a stronger demeanour, to not sound as small and low-voiced, not as wounded and frail.

'Exactly . . . Look, I'm willing to toss in more of the Conception Bay area. Brigus. Port de Grave, along with Bareneed. A percentage of revenues.'

There was a moment of reflection. 'Well, that's promising.' Alan laughed outright, on his way to regaining his previous vigour.

'Yes, it is.'

'Yes.' Alan nodded. 'Alright then.'

Mister Bowering guffawed and reached forward to shake Alan's hand. 'We'll get together in the coming days to sort out the specifics. How things are run out there, etcetera. There are several families heavily in my debt. I'll mention that now, and one such family specifically, the Hawcos. You'll see to that?'

'Yes, of course.' Alan watched Mister Bowering. 'Hawcos?'

Mister Bowering remained silent. He took a moment to light a cigar from the ashtray. 'Ace Hawco, one of the sealers.'

'The one on the dock?'

Mister Bowering nodded. 'I believe he was responsible for your little dip, as well.'

'I heard you sent a constable for him?'

'No. I felt we'd be better able to deal with him.'

'I see,' said Alan, his voice tinged with a hint of confusion.

'There are others, of course,' he put in, waving the comment away with a dismissive gesture used to clear the cigar smoke from before his face. 'But I'll need certain debts repaid briskly. You might be required to confiscate houses. Can you manage that sort of thing?'

'Ah . . . yes, of course.'

'Splendid. Cigar?'

Bareneed, thought Emily, huffing to herself. She did not like the sounds of it. What sorts of people would be living in a place like that?

A place where the living might exist

Once treated at the infirmary, released home to Bareneed, and deloused with Blackard's Lotion, Uncle Ace sat in the lamplight of a March's early evening.

Catherine, who was mending the sole pair of Jacob's pants, which were worn down the backside, glanced up at her brother-in-law to see what might be in his mind. Watching him, she often wished for his twin, for Francis, for there were differences between the two, something she never thought possible upon first sighting them in the woods those thirty years ago. A mirror image, she had thought. A trick of the light. Yet, no, they could never be one and the same, their dispositions entirely different.

Uncle Ace watched Catherine as though disbelieving in his own presence in that house. A cup of tea rested near his fingertips. He looked down and seemed to wonder what might be in the cup. An unstable surface. Men so tiny and adrift their calls held no resonance, their raised limbs like thistles, barely evident. Across the steamy ice, they were hauling a structure with the aid of ropes. A house, a dwelling. There was a surface in the mug, yet there was something beneath it. Beneath the sea, beneath the earth, there was a boy digging a tunnel, digging through red rock, digging his way to a deeper death that no one would ever understand.

'Wise fer ya ta stay clear 'a da seal hunt from here on in.' Catherine took a glimpse of Ace, before dipping her eyes back to her sewing. 'After dat foolishness ye got on widt. Flinging Mister Bow'ring inta da water. T'anks be ta Jaysus he were saved in da end.' She began to smile but bit down on her lip and tutted crossly, three times, casting off her amusement with a shake of her head. 'Saints preserve us.'

Uncle Ace regarded the woman who had taken him from the place where he had stepped off the boat. The bodies had been offloaded before him, yet they had followed him here. What was he expected to do with them? One was stood near his chair, staring at him with his frost-blackened fingers extended in fright. The other was flush to the stove, rubbing his hands together. *Christ, dere's no warmth ta be had*, cursed the man, setting his gloved hand directly on the iron of the stove and keeping it there, to no avail. *Da crackling wood gives af frost sparks*. And what of the others? The ones who he remembered yet could not recognize. The ones who now stared out through his eyes?

'Mister Bow'ring'll be right aboard ye next year,' Catherine said with a nod, drawing the threaded needle high while she moved a peppermint knob around in her mouth, sucking quietly, then shifting it from one cheek to the other. 'Ta point ye out. T'is a wonder he never sent da Rangers after ye.'

Uncle Ace turned his head to see a boy glide across the threshold of the room. Not a bit frozen. Not a tinge of marble-green to his face. The boy was living, a lovely, vaguely pink hue.

'How come we only got da one 'a me here?' Jacob asked outright.

With eyes fixed on Jacob, Catherine bit through the thread, then stabbed the needle in the fancy pin cushion with the face of the King of England embroidered on it that Uncle Ace had brought her from St. John's as a gift last season.

'Only one made like ye.' Catherine nodded reasonably. ''N dun't be so saucy widt yer mout'.'

Uncle Ace cast his eyes into his mug. His body. Not his house.

'No,' Jacob said, adamantly shaking his head while tossing a bit of something into the ash can. 'Da Butlers up da hill got fifteen chil'ren. Every'n got lots. How come I got no brudders or sisters?'

Uncle Ace glanced out the window, where a young man stood, stiff as a rail, staring in. *Have ye seen me mudder?* he screeched out, as though the calm of the winter night were deafening. *I promised ta be home 'n 'av no harm come ta me.*

Catherine studied her needlework, moved the peppermint knob from one cheek to the other and swallowed the taste. Sighing, she smoothed out the seam on her lap, checking over the job with a gentle survey of her fingertips. Done, she lowered the lamplight a tad.

'Yer father died before his day,' Catherine said, matter-of-factly, yet with a hint of sad tolerance.

Uncle Ace shifted his eyes from the young man outside the window to the woman. The woman who was warm, too, a pinkness in her cheeks. The truly dead. The warm boy beside her. Younger. Deader. Why were these two warm? he wondered, while all the others were eaten by cold?

'Ye knows dat,' Catherine continued. 'He died in 'is health.'

'But why we got no more chil'ren?'

'None more like ye were found in da cabbage patch. 'Nuf o' dat now,' she chastised.

Jacob boldly stared at Uncle Ace, interested in the man's eyes, then shifted his attention to his uncle's shirt where the rips in the front had been stitched over by Catherine's fine handiwork.

'Wha' happened ta yer chest?' Jacob asked.

'Jacob,' Catherine warned. 'Now, I tol' ye 'bout ask'n dat. Off ta bed, g'wan widt ye.'

'He wun't answer, sure. Ya got ta keep ask'n. When's 'e ever gonna answer?'

Uncle Ace stared down at his chest. Cautiously, he set his fingertips to the centre, pressed them there, tapped, the tinkle of ice, then moved them back, lifted them through the air until they were raised to his face. He studied the deep sheen on his fingertips, then turned them toward the boy, to answer. He wiped his fingertips in his own face, sensing the warmth. That was what kept him alive. Wasn't it? The warmth of his own blood. Or was it the spillage of tears? At once, he rose from his chair, pulled on his coat, took his hammer from the back porch and went out the door.

Catherine sat still, as though something had left her, never to be returned. She felt a shudder in her that struck with such a resounding blow she was forced to shut her eyes for stability's sake. *Sum'n walk'n o'er me grave*, she told herself.

'Where's he gone off to'? asked Jacob.

Catherine opened her eyes to look at her son then shifted them to the slop bucket in the corner of the room.

'Where's 'e gone?'

'Jacob, fer Christ's sake, can ye shut yer gob fer once.'

Soon, there came the sound of hammering.

'He's build'n sumtin',' said Jacob, moving behind the chair Uncle Ace had been seated in, to stare out the window.

Catherine stood and leaned near the window. From her position, she could see Uncle Ace's shack and his kitchen window. Here was the man, swinging back his hammer, pounding holes in the walls.

'Wha's he fix'n over dere?' asked Jacob.

Ace continued pounding, then reached into those holes to yank loose the boards and haul them out. Once a large enough hole had been opened up, Uncle Ace stood still, facing it. There came a bellow as his head was thrown back, his mouth held wide. The sound rattled the windowpane against which Catherine's fingertips were pressed. One long string of gibberish that continued for minutes, slowing toward the end, so that words gradually became evident. What had been flooding from Uncle Ace's mouth in an unbroken, alphabetized torrent were names.

In the days that followed, Uncle Ace was joined by men in the community willing to help demolish his shack. The men took care in removing the boards for they had no idea what Ace might use the wood for. From a number of salvaged planks, Uncle Ace built a long, low box that everyone took to be a casket.

With the remaining wood, he commenced putting up what the men standing by came to realize was the shell for a new shack. Almost the same, but different from the one he had taken apart.

When he and the men were done, when the final nail had been driven, Uncle Ace stepped out and took Jacob from the group of dead boys that lingered near, amid the sparse sticks of furniture that had been removed and awaited reshelter, and walked him into the house.

In the kitchen, Ace pointed to a spot in the centre of the floor. With his uncle's coaxing, Jacob moved toward the spot, not knowing what might be wanted of him, and stood positioned in the middle of the room. Through the window, he could see his mother in the kitchen window of his family home. She was watching him, nodding to herself.

Uncle Ace fixed his stare on the boy, then surveyed the clear interior. No one dead in this newly built thing. No one laying claim to it.

Here was a place where the living boy might exist, without fear of harrowing intrusion.

Amanda writes home

Amanda took it as her obligation to write letters to Annie Gull whenever possible, keeping her apprised of their situation as it developed. Even though Amanda was not certain if Annie could read or if she was even living back in Liverpool, she forwarded the letters to the address Annie had given her on the girl's only visit to Amanda's home. On that visit, Annie had asked for one look at the treasure that Amanda was keeping, and then pledged never to return.

The only proof Amanda had that the letters were reaching their destination was that they were not returned to her.

Amanda knew more of Alan's dealings back home than he realized, for Annie had explained what had happened with her brothers and the men who associated with them. However, Annie had been sworn to not betray the whole truth, stating that her life would be placed in jeopardy should she break that promise. In the interest of her family's preservation, Amanda had chosen to sublimate this knowledge, pledging to shelter Emily through whatever means available to her.

Dear Annie:

Sunday. Emily got us up early & we got breakfast quickly, & Alan – in top hat and frock coat – drove us up to Cabot Tower and we found a lovely corner among the rocks where we could sit & paint the view. Emily is quite talented with colours and has a fine eye. We got down just in time for church – a lunch party & Government House, & then out again to the south side of the harbour, where we had never been before. We had to leave the car & walk over & under fishermen's flakes & along wooden ways along the rocks with the sea roaring in and out of the coves below – & then up a long wooden way to the lighthouse where we found several parties of friends sunning themselves on the grass among the rocks. It is a beautiful spot; you get the sweep of the bay to 'Spear Head' & the Gibraltar that is our Signal Hill with Cabot Tower – a great rock with magnificent old red sandstone cliffs. And the sea so blue & the harbour water at our feet such clear deep green. The south hill is almost as fine a rock as Signal Hill – they both rise sheer 500 ft. from the sea. We had tea at the lighthouse, & the lighthouse keeper rose from bed to show Emily his treasures. His great-grandfather and grandfather & father had all been keepers of this lighthouse in turn. His wife, such a lovely woman of about 35, is granddaughter of the old Captain Kane, who brought home his 1,000,000th seal this year. Captain Sheppard allowed Emily to sound the foghorn 3 times. It must have been startling to hear the foghorn on that brilliantly clear day. It is such a melancholy old cow – a minor tone. 'Stay clear,' Emily called out toward the sea. 'Be careful, poor fishermen.' The 'poor fishermen' something she must have heard from me in my conversations.

I have learned that there are so many tiny communities scattered along the coast – fisherfolk whose ancestors settled just here or there because there was enough fishing for perhaps one or two families. And many of the villages, & towns even, are so inaccessible – they can only be reached by sea. There are poor creatures living in shacks without doors & without any heating in the bitter winter cold. All over the island, the poor people are in a desperate case. Women stay in bed till 1 o'c. because there is nothing to get up for. In other places the people never go to bed because they have no blankets, so they huddle together round whatever fire they have.

The population is a problem. The Roman Catholics teach, I am told, that an R.C. who produces 7 little R.C.s is certain of his ticket to Heaven. Children swarm, quite irrespective of whether there are the means of subsistence.

The merchants here have put nothing they could help back into the land; they have taken their fortunes abroad – spent their money in England where they send their children to boarding schools.

Last night, we had such a dainty dinner, so simple: soup, a wonderful fish jelly (green), a dish of cod tongues done in a white sauce, & vegetables & fresh green peas sent with it, & a trifle.

We have been having some impressive dinner parties – important people first, with a few unimportants to lighten the weight. People here are very friendly and easy to entertain.

After the particular dinner mentioned above, there was conversation and I, perhaps pig-headedly, brought up the topic of merchants sending their children away to schools in England, a practice I have always felt was sorry in some way, to which in reply one of the merchants said: 'Can you blame us? Who would choose to educate their children in an island where there is no education to be compared with what they can get in Canada or England?' And another, more sullen merchant glowered: 'We chose the life for ourselves. There's no reason why we should condemn our children to it.'

'We're none of us Newfoundlanders,' remarked one of the wives, 'so we can say what we like' – and there was a pause. I gather I was expected to welcome an opportunity to unburden myself. I did not.

Yours, Amanda Duncan

ps: By the bye, should you decide to forward a reply, don't forget to address us St. John's, Newfoundland. There is a St. John in Nova Scotia or New Brunswick, so don't leave out the Newfoundland.

The disintegration of my great-grandfather's mind has always been a mystery to me and everyone who knew him. It was peculiar because according to the pathologist's report Jacob Hawco did not suffer from Alzheimer's disease, as suspected in the 1990s. It was a peculiar thing to read Emily's journals, listening to her describe coming back from the dead of depression, coming alive, while Jacob slowly began to fade into oblivion.

1974‑1977

(*April*, 1974)

The three bookshelves that had hung on Emily's bedroom wall for years had been replaced. Jacob had measured the space and built a floor-to-ceiling bookshelf that fitted into the exact area on Emily's side of the bed. Gradually, the new shelves became more and more crowded, as Emily saw her way deeper into the frozen wilderness that each book's author appeared to covet.

Emily had arranged with the bookstore in St. John's to have her books shipped by mail. On her last visit to the bookstore, she had seen how the woman who worked there had looked up the books in giant volumes like encyclopaedias with all the listings for all published books. Emily called the store on the telephone and then sent them the money by mail. If there was a space in time before she finished one book and the next one arrived, she read one of the old books, having little memory of most of them. Once she had been away from a book for a while, the particulars of it vanished, bit by bit, as did the harsh particulars of her own memories.

She read continuously. If she sat at the kitchen table having tea, a book was laid out in front of her. A book rested open on the counter when she was making soup, her eyes going to it as though it were a recipe.

Those were the things for the dead, she said to herself, making cookies for Ruth. Making salt beef and cabbage for Junior. The living eat, but it was all made for the dead. That made the dead content. She left the baked goods on the plate and watched them. In time, they disappeared.

The burning of the journal had done her heart good. She could not understand why. She had expected that it would make her miserable, return her to her former state where she existed in pools of shadowy lead where the slightest movement or word was a muted violation of her bound inner self. Each thought a ten-ton dead thing to be extracted from the centre of her being and dragged clear of her.

It was on the icefields now where she saw herself, on a trail with an Arctic explorer, the men perishing from starvation, but the silver tea service that had been taken along still transported through the blizzard. The clink of the silver tea service in someone's sack. This was hope to her. What was so attractive about this vision, so fortifying? Go into the blinding white wilderness and carry your etiquette with you as a reminder of civility, humanity. This was hope to her. A man frozen to death in the snow, a man set upon and eaten by other men, with his silver tea service by his side. To her mind, there was nothing as astonishingly beautiful as that.

Beyond the kitchen window, the snow was coming down in big flakes, not fat flakes but ones that were delicate and thinly constructed. Emily watched them fall slow and straight, neatly separated in the air as they descended, as though spaced intentionally, they landed on Junior's sleeves and seemed made of feathers mixed with a material lighter than cotton. In minutes, the snow began to thicken, the flakes seemingly growing larger, wetter, turning fuller in body. The snow then thinned and faded, becoming almost invisible before disappearing entirely.

Emily baked a cherry cake with plenty of cherries and sliced it open. The red dots full and split. Eat, she would tell herself, not touching it, and the cake would be eaten. Slice by slice, it would vanish. Only crumbs left on the plate that she would squat with her thumb and bring to her mouth as though they were a sacrament.

(June, 1974)

Jacob saw the news on television. Three fish plants, including the one down in Bareneed, would be closing at the end of August. The rumour had been around for a while, but the TV had made it so. The reporter said that a few years ago the cod catch had been the highest ever: 810,000 tonnes off the northeast coast. Foreign vessels accounted for 85 per cent of the catch. Federal fisheries minister Jack Davis up in Ottawa said it was time to support continental control. He said that foreign over-fishing was why inshore fishermen were catching only half of what they were in the 1950s. This news made Jacob grumble and curse. He slapped at the armrest of his chair and leaned forward, muttering a threat. The Atlantic fishery workforce should be cut back by 25,000 people. The time had come for the federal government to stop subsidizing capital investment in the fishery. What to do about those workers? Those fishermen. Relocation and re-employment of unemployed fishermen should begin immediately.

Jacob sprang to his feet. 'Like Christ!'

Those were the recommendations, said the reporter. But, yesterday, the proposals were rejected by cabinet.

'Good fer cabinet,' said Jacob, giving a solid nod. 'Dey won't drive us out. More friggin' relocation. Blast dose fuh'k'n foreigners outta da water. If I were a younger man. Blackstrap?' he called, looking around the living room, listening, wondering where Blackstrap might be. He assumed everyone was in the house with him, but who was in the house? He had no idea.

The Bareneed fish plant was the only employment opportunity breathing a bit of life into Jacob's hometown community. Three-quarters of the houses around there were filled up with welfare people now. An utter shame. And, soon, the other quarter of houses would be sheltering the unemployed too. The fish plant resting there at the base of the massive headland. Boats coming and going. Trucks hauling fish in and out. The bit of remaining life in the processing of fish that were shipped off to foreigners.

Where would they sell their measly catch now? They could bring it to Port de Grave but that plant, as far as he had heard, was already operating at capacity. Twenty-four hours a day. They wouldn't be wanting more fish there. Where was the Fishermen's Union when they were needed? Useless. Probably down in Florida lolling on the beach and sucking up fruity drinks. A bunch of mouthpieces that needed a good swift boot in the arse.

It was all looking grim. Money was getting scarce. Sell the boat, if he could find a buyer, and be done with it. There was already a glut of boats for sale on the market, plus hundreds of doreys hauled up on shore with grass growing up around them from sitting idle for years. Every now and then, someone burned their boat to make a point, but it was old news now. Another boat on fire. It barely drew a crowd anymore, except for a few juvenile-delinquent pyromaniacs.

Jacob snickered at the TV and went over to watch out the window, toward the trees. He listened for the train. What time was it? His eyes were drawn back to the TV screen and his thoughts were dissolved by the theme song for *Gilligan's Island*. The rush of canned laughter providing even better distraction. And there she was: Ginger. Wasn't she something. What a dress! Christ, b'y, now dat's funny. And dat Mr. Howell. A friggin' riot. Acting all uppity when he were stranded in da worst sort o' backward place with nothing, not even a pot ta piss in.

Jacob went back to his chair and sat, staring at the screen and smiling, grinning, laughing.

(August, 1974)

'Richard Nixon, battered by controversy over the Watergate break-ins, has announced he is stepping down as president of the United States. The president's resignation is seen by many as a move to avoid an impeachment trial and possible removal from office. Mr. Nixon has been charged by the House Judiciary Committee with "high crimes and misdemeanours."

'The president informed the American people of his resignation in a television broadcast from the White House.

'Initially, Mr. Nixon maintained that it was his duty to complete his term of office despite the Watergate charges relating to the 1972 break-in at the offices of the Democratic National Committee.

'"In the past days, however, it has become evident that I no longer have a strong enough political base in the Congress to justify continuing that effort."

'Adding to the initial scandal, was the uncovering of tape recordings that confirmed the president attempted to manipulate the police investigation into the Watergate crimes.

'Mr. Nixon will be succeeded by US Vice-President Gerald Ford. Mr. Ford will be sworn in as the 38th president tomorrow.

'"As president I must put the interests of America first."'

(September, 1974)

Jacob looked out the kitchen window. The vegetable garden. Time to pick the crop and store it away in the root cellar. The summer had not been good. Fog and grey skies. The crop had failed to reach its potential size. He thought of the supermarket. Why, he wondered. Go to the supermarket. Give up on the land. Too much labour for nothing. Maybe he could get Emily to give him a hand. That was usually her chore, tending the garden. She had been at it a bit, which was good. Nice to see her back in the garden, getting out and about more, but most times her head was stuck in a book about those frozen dead fellows. He would sometimes joke about her marrying one of them. 'Dat's who ye should've married. They wouldn't be any bodder if ye kept 'em on ice.'

'I did marry one,' Emily would say in reply. And Jacob would always take that as a compliment.

And where was Blackstrap? Off in the woods cutting wood?

'Emily?'

No reply.

Maybe they both went off somewhere and he forgot where.

Out in the garden, he bent and pulled up a row of carrots, tossed them in an empty 40-gallon salt-beef bucket. At the end of one row, he straightened and turned to look back. Crows overhead. One of them sounding. One for sadness. He searched around for another to make a pair, found it. Two for mirth. A seagull that looked like a crow. What was the difference between black and white? He thought he might solve a mystery. Black was black and white was white. This made him feel better, until he noticed the row of holes. He stared. A hole in the ground. It struck him. There was time to stare now. To stare and wonder. Not when he was younger. There was no rest. He looked toward the barn. No animals. He thought he heard mooing. But that couldn't be so. No hay. He thought of the shore and the split fish laid out on flakes to dry. The hay laid out in another spot up the shore, the spot used by his family for generations, ever since his grandfather,

Patrick Hawco, came over from . . . County Clare, was it? No, that was someone else. It began with an 'L.' Christ, he shook his head. Forget it. Patrick was his name. He had drowned trying to rescue sailors off the shore. Foreigners. Portugee. In a punt. Out in a storm. Who in dere right friggin' mind would ever launch a punt in a storm?

He could get into his pickup and drive to the grocery store in Bay Roberts. Standing there, with the calm autumn all around him, he heard it. To his surprise, the surge. The ocean, just there. Toward his left. Through the trees. A beach. He turned in expectation, but it was not the ocean. He faced a forest. Not the ocean, but the sound of the wind rising in the evergreens. Then he heard the rumble of an outboard motor. A boat returning to shore. No, the school bus in the distance. Children getting off, their noises as they ran and called out to one another. Where was the train? Its schedule must have been cut back. It came before the school bus. It hadn't today. Had there been an accident? Then he remembered that the schedule had, in fact, changed. How long ago?

The carrots were almost picked. The turnips were next to be done. He left the rows of potatoes for last because they numbered the most.

There came the whirring of a chainsaw from somewhere far off. Wood cut up for winter.

He was thinking: Burn the boat. Wood for winter. He stared in through the kitchen window. From his position, he had a view of the living room. The television still on. Images flashing. He turned to stare up at the sun and kept his eyes fixed there until the sky washed out white.

He looked back to the garden. A patch of green where the grass had grown over.

Emily suspected that Jacob would soon lose his boat. That might not be such a bad thing, because she feared for his return each time he left shore. However, presently, it was not the dangers of the sea that concerned her, but the dangerous state of her husband's mind.

Emily was aware that Blackstrap had not taken in as much money at the seal hunt as last year because of the protesters. The market had been cut back in Europe. A wave of anti-seal-hunt sentiment sweeping various countries. People thinking purely with their hearts, while every other sort of animal was slaughtered without word of protest, and children died of starvation by the minute.

She could go to work at the fish plant in Port de Grave. They were always looking for workers on the line. Most men wouldn't work there. Jacob wouldn't either. Fish plant work was for women and young men. Blackstrap was off in the woods cutting firewood. There was a great demand for firewood that time of year. But firewood money was not as regular as a paycheque from the fish plant. Blackstrap refused to work in the fish plant as well. He had for one summer when he was sixteen and had come home stinking of fish, like the old days, the way everyone used to stink of fish. He was surly for most of the summer, having to take off his rubber boots, apron and hairnet, and strip off his clothes out back before coming into the house. The rubber gloves he was meant to wear ate away at his hands until his skin looked like it had been burned. It took months for them to lose their pinkness and for all the skin to peel clean. Emily had tried to tend to them, but Blackstrap would have no part of it. He hadn't complained about it either. And he wouldn't put the cream on his hands. Her hand cream. He wouldn't have anything to do with that. Nothing to soothe him. Nothing to help heal. Blackstrap would rather be fixing cars or hauling wood. Not standing over a belt separating the male and female capelin, the noise so loud around him that shouted words could not be made out.

Work. The thought of it drew the leaden density back into her being. She raised her book. Reading in the daytime was beginning to feel more like a luxury than a medicinal necessity. Keeping herself away from her family. Locking herself away behind a door. Why did it feel as though it was something that *had* to be done? Something linked to her very existence? Jacob in front of his TV. Some days, forgetting that he was supposed to fish. Blackstrap out to keep it all together. Poor soul. He knew what mattered.

Emily focused on the words. The exploration party in the Antarctic had eaten one of the Manchurian ponies used for pulling the sleighs. The pony had a name, Penny, and used to be fawned over by the men. It did not matter now. Familiarity. Friendship. There was only one thing they were now prospecting from the snow and ice: hope.

They would all soon die. Each and every one of them. Frozen into that icy terrain that most believed was best left unexplored. Not her. She would go there in an instant. It was what she woke thinking each morning. A plain of white in her head. A storm closing in. Bracing herself as it blew in grey from the far distance. She would plan it. She would save what little money she could scrape together. Yes, she would get a job if need be. She would tread freely into that blinding white gale to find endurance – instead of crippling fear – in the prospect of loss.

Jacob lifted his mug of tea. There was something about that grandfather on *The Waltons* that made him want to be his friend, invite him over for a good feed. The grandfather on *The Waltons* would appreciate a Newfoundland cook-up, a plate piled high with chicken and salt beef and pease pudding and dressing and vegetables with the whole works slathered over with steaming-hot gravy. None of that Swanson TV dinner, although he was growing fond of the whipped potatoes if you put a little extra butter on them; he particularly liked the potato crust on top, and the little apple cobbler wasn't bad either. Not enough of it though to truly satisfy a hungry man.

Another swallow of tea. Jacob glanced at the clock on the wall. What came on after *The Waltons*? He wished that *The Waltons* would just keep running, one show after another. If there was only a way of doing that. He liked that family, liked being with them. He could watch them all day. He would give them a hand, if he could. Work day and night for them. Watch day and night. Working with them. Helping them. They could use a hand every now and then. They were in hard straits, but they always stuck together. That's the way a family was supposed to be.

(July, 1975)
Emily had finished scrubbing the kitchen floor and washing the dishes. Now, she clipped one of Blackstrap's plaid shirts to the clothes line. The wheels squeaked as she pulled the bottom line toward her so that the shirt moved out toward the shed. The sun was behind her, warming her hair. As the day progressed, the sun would shift along the side of the house and eventually, toward evening, hang in the sky over the shed where it would set into the trees and spill orange in through the windows at the back of the house.

While clipping a pair of trousers on the line, Emily caught sight of a flash of vivid blue. A blue jay had landed on a nearby spruce. It screeched and hopped around, swaying the boughs. Blue jays always intrigued her because they were a bird she used to think never existed in Newfoundland. The first time she had seen one, last year, she had asked Jacob whether it was native to the island. He had answered by saying that the birds had always been around, as long as he could remember, even when he was a boy down in Bareneed.

Emily wondered why she couldn't remember ever seeing one until then. The bird was large, almost as big as a crow. They were definitely new to the area. Why now? she wondered. Why have they come? She noticed the bird's size and height, as though she might be reading of the bird in one of her books, the way every sort of landscape and living thing was described in detail. Her mind locked on a field of white snow, a bamboo pole with a black flag at the top, the marker for a depot of provisions left out in the expanse of snow by explorers as they made their way into unexplored terrain. Too warm here, where she lived. Too hot.

She reached into her laundry basket and took up a pair of Blackstrap's underwear, pinned them on the line. She wondered if he had a new girlfriend now. There was that young one, Agnes Bishop, who went away, back for a spell of time there a while ago. How long ago was that? A month? A year? Blackstrap was not one to talk about his life. And when Jacob ribbed him about who his latest girlfriend was, Blackstrap said nothing in reply and seemed to stiffen as though protecting himself. He spent practically no time in the house. Emily knew how he felt penned in, always the need to be outside since he was a boy, to be doing something with his hands. Still, what Blackstrap did with his spare time was an utter mystery to her.

'Come 'ere, I tells ya da news,' Jacob called out as Blackstrap entered the house. 'Dat fisheries minister, Romeo what's his name, LeBlank or something, were in Sin John's. Did ya hear what he was on about?'

'No.' Blackstrap stood in the living room doorway. He wiped at his mouth with the side of his hand and looked back from where he had come. Then he turned and moved down the hallway and into his room.

'Da most sensible bit of news I heard frum da federal gover'ment in years,' Jacob continued, raising his voice. 'Dey're setting a two-hundred-mile limit fer dose foreign trawlers ta keep dem bastards clear of our cod. Coming inta effect in January. Keep dem dat far away frum us. Two hundred mile. Not nearly far enough. Bloody friggers.'

Jacob kept watching toward the hallway, saw Blackstrap come out of his room with a pair of jeans in his hands. Blackstrap moved into the kitchen so that Jacob had to raise his voice even more:

'Not far 'nough, I says. Kick dere arses right ta da udder side of da ocean is wha' dey should do. Da Portugee and da Spaniards, dey deserves a good smack in da gob. Jus' cause dey were 'ere a hundred year ago dey figure dey can stick around 'n suck da fish out from under us.'

Blackstrap reappeared in the hallway with a sports bag in hand, the one he used for his ice skates. Distracted, he went back into his bedroom. It looked like he was going skating. But it was summer the last time Jacob noticed.

'If dere were a shred of decency in da world, someone would blast dose friggin' pirates clear outta da friggin', God-forsaken water.'

Again, Blackstrap came out of his bedroom and stopped, glanced at the door to his mother's bedroom. It was shut.

'Where ye off ta?'

'Nowhere.' Blackstrap turned away and left the house, the back door shutting after him. In a moment, his car started and drove away, the sound of the engine fading.

(November, 1975)

With Christmas just around the corner, Emily applied for a job at several places. She was hired at the gas station chain in Port de Grave. Each afternoon, Jacob drove her there in silence and let her out. He was dead set against the whole idea of it, but he wouldn't take unemployment insurance like the other fishermen did, like he was entitled to. So many weeks of work, so many weeks of handouts from the federal government. He wouldn't have anything to do with being what he called 'a government poverty case,' even if it was only for part of the year. Call it whatever program name you liked, Emily knew that Jacob felt it was still an admission of defeat, and the mark of a lesser man made that way by charity. Years ago, there would've been no need for Emily to work, no need for unemployment insurance. Everyone got by just fine. A hand-to-mouth existence occasionally, but none of the more complicated pressures that existed today. People not having enough money to pay their mortgage or make their car payments. Those things being taken away from people, and rightly so, Jacob insisted. If you couldn't afford it, why buy it? So someone else could own it for you and you lived in it or drove around in it as a second-class citizen, as a boarder. Interest tacked on top of interest until the price doubled or tripled. What sort of fool would get caught up in that swindling racket?

Thank God they owned their own house. A true blessing there. And Jacob's boat was entirely his own, despite the fact that he didn't make as much money from his catch as he used to. He hadn't told Emily as much. He was not one to talk about money, but she knew by the little signs. He no longer boasted about the size of his catch. No longer seemed to have the prosperous energy he once possessed. Even a few years ago, Jacob would have found work doing anything, welding, repairing machinery or driving a plough. But lately, he was more and more forgetful. Emily even worried about him driving his pickup. She had thought of mentioning that he should go to the doctor, but he wouldn't have anything to do with doctors or hospitals. Emily feared that something might be going wrong with his mind. She didn't believe that he would become violent like those people she heard about on TV, but she was concerned about his inability to function. Then again, there were times she feared him. Certain times, at night, when she despaired.

If Blackstrap hadn't gone away, Emily might have felt more secure, might have asked him to have a talk with Jacob, to try to reason with him about seeing a doctor. But Blackstrap had been gone since July. Away. Working in Halifax. She could not talk with Jacob any longer. Away. All of her children away. Jacob talked constantly about TV shows and tragic news from the United States. The way he looked at her when he explained the killings and disasters brought out something in his face that never existed before. He seemed desperate to tell her, even though she had explained to him that she did not want to hear. That sort of news made the grey creep back in like a water stain moving from the outer edge of paper toward the centre to turn the paper into slate.

The envelopes that arrived from Blackstrap contained crisp twenty-dollar bills. The envelopes were addressed to Mr. Jacob Hawco, Cutland Junction, Newfoundland. The writing appeared to be feminine and Emily wondered who might be addressing the envelopes for Blackstrap. Jacob brought the envelopes home from the post office. Even though they were addressed to him, he handed them over to her, as though he wouldn't have anything to do with the money, as though it belonged to her. She being the woman. Blackstrap in Halifax, after that young Agnes Bishop, chasing her there. The money Emily's fault.

Emily looked out the window of the gas station and saw a car pull up to the pumps. She found it sad watching the cars be filled, the need to keep going, to travel. She wished they still had their horse. Cars scared her. Two young people from Cutland Junction were recently killed on the highway. She barely knew them. They were boyfriend and girlfriend. Teenagers in high school. She had gone to the funeral home and looked at them. It had been a mistake. She had watched the mothers weeping near the open caskets, being comforted by family and friends. She would not go near them. She merely stood and stared and then she left, her head wavering with a giddiness that, rather than filling her with mortal sadness, made her feel relieved.

She had walked home through Cutland Junction, aware of the breath in her nostrils, aware of her eyes seeing the stillness, aware of the way her skin felt the night air . . . A car had come up behind her and slowed. The window rolled down. It was Isaac Tuttle. Did she need a ride, he asked. No, she had said. I'm fine. Isaac had nodded a few times while keeping his eyes on her face, then slowly rolled up his window and headed off. She had watched the car drive away and was made stony by her recollection of them together. How long ago was that? And what had come of it? A horrible sickness at her centre. She would not allow herself to think of it. It always led to one person. Blackstrap.

(*January, 1977*)

'Let's do it,' said Gary Gilmore. Famous last words. Stick a cigarette in his mouth.

Gary Gilmore was blindfolded. The firing squad took aim. Gary Gilmore died. The way he fell was perfectly believable. It was a re-enactment for TV. An actor named Gary Gilmore played Gary

Gilmore. The resemblance was remarkable. The image was made unsteady to look like it was taken by someone who wasn't supposed to be there. Secret footage captured by a camera under a coat. But the actor didn't really die. When the camera was shut off, the actor got up and went home. Believe it, anyway. Like it happened. Some of it was real. Some of it was not.

People talked about the real thing. Witnesses who were allowed to watch. Given permission. Assigned seats. It was almost funny, one man said. Jacob didn't know who the man was because Jacob had just switched the channel on, from a laugh track to this. First man executed in the United States since 1967. There were opinions as to why that happened. For. Against. Why murder at all?

Jacob almost laughed. Foolishness. Fools, the whole lot of 'em. 'Fools,' he said aloud, then switched the channel. Americans. Archie Bunker. The Jews. The Black People. The Spics. That was funny, too. Someone else's problem. But why was it sad sometimes? Why did Archie Bunker look so sad sometimes?

Jacob flicked the channel back. Gilmore deserved it, anyway. Most people seemed to think so. He was meant to die. If only they had shown the real thing. It might have been all the more believable. It might have made Jacob almost care.

(March, 1977)

Pictures in newspapers and magazines of Brigitte Bardot. She was glamorous. Gorgeous. Foreign. Blonde hair. Puffy lips. She was not old yet. But she was getting there. Soon, she would be nobody. Brigitte Bardot hugged the baby seal. Her hands were positioned just so. A ring on her finger, a gold bracelet on her wrist. Fingernails painted. Her expression of soft concern was something she recalled from a director who once helped her feel that way. A director who fucked her into feeling that way when she was younger. That was the look she remembered. She summoned. Snap the picture. Know how to manipulate, said the director, naked in a room with a glass of bourbon in his hand. The words in her head. Know how to move the audience. The baby seal was pure pure pure white and had big sad sad sad black eyes. Who would kill such a thing? Who would be so heartless? Not an adolescent. If we were all ungrown. Cuddly and fluffy. Not a child who just knew that these things were wrong. A child who hated her parents for eating meat. How could you?! Cannibals! The baby seal. Please, save the baby seal. Not a child, really, though. Answer me that. Why did things have to die? Little things. Why?

Brigitte Bardot lay down on the ice with the baby seal. She pulled the baby seal closer. She felt the warmth of the baby seal. It was alive. Poor baby. Alive. Look, everyone, see, it was alive because of me. So real. If it were not dead. If I were not god. If nothing ever had to die. Ever. If only the baby seal were hers. Why? Brigitte Bardot felt it to be so. Felt it deep inside. The way the director did. Deep inside. This living thing. She once was. This baby seal she once was. She was acting for a cause. The baby seal was stuffed, wasn't it? Maybe only a rumour, but a real baby seal would have bitten a chunk right out of the fading beauty of Brigitte Bardot's face.

When Emily turned the channel, the voice said: 'Bank of America announced today that all of its credit cards will now bear the name VISA.' She turned off the TV and went to bed.

Outside, icicles hung halfway to the ground from the eaves. Water dripped from them. It was mild outside. Had been mild. Emily was planning her trip to the pole. She was saving money under her mattress. Money they could have used elsewhere, but she needed. The thick snow on the roof had melted underneath, then frozen to ice. Now, when the ice melted it broke away and slid from the roof, rumbled and crashed to the ground outside. Huge ice chunks there in the morning when Emily went out to investigate. Soon, it would be spring. She had to leave before then.

(*April*, 1977)
Annie Hall, the way the thoughts came up on the bottom of the screen, the things that the two characters were actually thinking, not what they were saying, but what they were thinking. It was really funny. Commercial? No, something someone said to someone else about the movie. It was not a TV commercial. It was something someone heard from someone. It was explained to Jacob. He did not understand. No thoughts coming up at the bottom of the screen because what they were saying was what they were actually thinking. That's what happened when you talked.

(May, 1977)

'Killing for the sake of killing,' a commentator commented.

'David Berkowitz (aka "Son of Sam") pleaded guilty to shooting six people with a forty-four-caliber gun. He was known as Berkowitz, the name of his adoptive parents, although his given name was David Falco. His birth mother was named Betty Broder and was raised in a poor Jewish family. Tony Falco, an Italian-American Catholic, was Berkowitz's birth father.'

'He will be remembered.'

'Whatever his name was,' said a comedian, years later.

(June, 1977)

'I'm Your Boogie Man That's The Way I Like It Keep It Comin' Love Get Down Tonight Shake Shake Shake Shake Your Booty'

(July, 1977)

Today, twelve Hanafi Moslems were convicted in Washington on hostage charges.

Today, Mohammed al-Zahaby, an Egyptian minister, was murdered.

Today, the USSR secretly carried out an underground nuclear test.

(August, 1977)

Thousands of TRS-80 computers, sold by Radio Shack, were ordered immediately upon the device's introduction. In a press release, issued by Karl Marx, a renowned Mexican luddite, who had absolutely nothing to do with the machine's invention nor sale, the TRS-80 was denounced as a typewriter with a TV screen. 'It is the end of the beginning,' said Marx (or so he was wrongly quoted as having said).

(September, 1977)

At the 29th Emmy Awards, the *Mary Tyler Moore Show*, Carroll O'Conner and Bea Arthur were the big winners. TV's Rhoda got divorced. Steven Biko, a South African white neo-Nazi student leader, died laughing while in police custody. General Motors introduced the first US diesel automobile, the Oldsmobile 88. Cheryl Ladd replaced Farrah Fawcett on *Charlie's Angels*.

(October, 1977)

Indira Gandhi was arrested for jaywalking. Bing Crosby, singer/actor (*Going My Way*), died of an apparent drug overdose at the tender age of twenty-four. Reggie Jackson hit thirty-four thousand consecutive homers, tying the series record of the fellow who had a chocolate bar named after him.

(November, 1977)

President Carter raised minimum wages of $2.30 to $113.35 an hour, effective January 1, 1978. The country prospers for a week. Then collapses. Guy Lombardo, orchestra leader ('Auld Lang Syne'), assassinated by twenty-seven hits of acid in Houston at seventy-five. Wings release 'Mull of Kintyre' and 'Paul is Dead,' prompting everyone to agree that, yes, Paul is dead. President Jimmy Carter welcomed the Shah of Iran and his band, the Payolas. Egyptian President Sadat formally accepted an invitation to visit the fashionable eastside disco Israel. *Jesus Christ Superstar* opened at Longacre Theater, New York City, for one performance before seven nuns set themselves ablaze in protest, cancelling all future shows and a planned major motion picture. Andrew Lloyd Webber and Tim Rice were executed before firing squad, while everyone thought: Hey, isn't that Gary Gilmore and the actor who played him?

(December, 1977)

Saturday Night Fever, starring John Travolta, premiered in Bangladesh. The New York Society for the Preservation of American Entertainment in Starving Nations bought 300 movie tickets for 300 dead children who, according to their publicists, 'weren't up to the event' and sent their regrets. Thirty-six died as a grain elevator at the Continental Grain Company plant exploded, struck by a stray Apollo spacecraft. France performed a nuclear test at Mururoa Island. To the relief of all civilized nations, the test results came back negative. Charlie Chaplin, actor (*Modern Times*), died in Switzerland of apparent sadness. He was eighty-eight. Ted Bundy, serial killer (*Many Young Women*) escaped from jail in Colorado, later found at a video games arcade, venting. Human rights activists issued a statement praising Mr. Bundy for at least trying.

The vast number of photographs taken by Junior Hawco are collected in the Newfoundland archives in The Rooms, having been donated by his brother, Blackstrap, shortly before his incarceration. From viewing them, I was able to recreate various scenes from Junior's life. The photographs have been studied by a local gallery owner, Emma Butler, and have been judged to be of an original and highly professional nature. At the time of writing this, Ms. Butler had chosen thirteen photographs to be enlarged and exhibited at her gallery.

1962

I

in the midst of life we are in death

'do you believe in life after death, mr. hawco,' junior laughing purely to himself, two fingertips sprinkling grass into a rolling paper beneath the dim illumination of a lamp that flickered through light stolen from heaven, energy run rampant, radiating too intensely among the living who never can quite see themselves in that light, it was late at night, he could not sleep, why ever would he sleep, never again, he tried, lay down and shut his eyes, saw only the mirror of before, too freaky to stay that way, sitting up again, with nimble movements of denial, dipping into flakes and picking out a seed, tossing the seed away, unneeded, it landed with a crash, seeds so weighty no longer growing a life, he raised his camera from the bedside table to focus, the seed barely visible in the viewfinder, in and out of blur, like a sleepy eye awakening to practically seeing, and pressed the shutter when sharp and exact,

he was trying not to think, death, no seeds needed, then why all the noise, again, the flicker of a light, neon, houselights, tvs, streetlamps, a camera flash, all of it draining the stars, never bright again, his eyes awash, a photo of himself in time, taken with a background he thought to be,

'no belief in life after death means no belief in myself,'

'says who,'

'me, wasn't it,' a quick peek over his shoulder, in search of a culprit, 'just then,'

'why won't you,'

'what,'

'face up to your own death,'

'i don't like the face, painted one way, sure, it can be touched up a bit, but there's no masking it, as they say, life's just death with a wish up its ass,'

'as who say,'

'as me say,'

a twin on the bed, speaking quietly as he rolled the joint, he thought it might have been another mirror, as in shutting his eyes, such abundance of reflection, 'we've come from a long line of hardy sea-going characters, haven't we, wrinkled bun faces, with much folksy flavour steeped darkly in an ale and rum brew of superstition, all "buddy" this and "how's she going" that and "not a bad day out dere t'day" this and "what're ya at" that, vernacular never fitting from our mouth, no, not mouths, under isolated lamplight, of course, and the persistent click of capturing, again, you, with the camera,'

'not so us though, not so ever us,'

'we're progressive, we can see that about ourselves, dope in hand and all, we don't sound anything like a toothless, gum-smacking, winking, fiddling newfie, particularly now that we're dead, our voice paralleled with our true own, there's no more pretending, no need to fog up the slang to fit in around the house, but we miss them, don't we, we want to be a part of them, so desperately, those outport, outpost people, isolated as they rightly are in sadness and despondency, no lesser or greater than any ruined martyr's life,' licking the thin gum line of the rolling paper to seal it all in,

'it's all in pretending who you are, i had *nothing* to do with it, born talking this way, inside my head on the outside, not a word ever clipped by dialect, my mother was from britain, she taught me right proper, but this voice was always mine, absent in its purity,'

'proper way to lord over everyone, and an accent there, too, only different,' 'hey, i love my mother,'

'hey, not me, not really,'

'frig off then,' slipping the joint between his lips, he let it hang, a macho stance, winked at his twin, tipped up his chin, 'how's it going, sweetheart,'

'you know, i always adored you,'

'screw off, faggot,'

'hey, you're the faggot, i'm just along for the ride,'

'tut, tut, tut, book time with a psychiatrist, he'll read to you, one theory after another guaranteed to get resluts,'

'i never met a shrink who couldn't provoke himself to think, always with questions that i didn't want an answer to,'

'questions like, where you from anyway,'

'i was hooked from a dna pool three universes over, us queers always snatch their twin in their final breaths, each gasp a pluck in the pool until the final snagging inhale, and up we come,'

'says who,'

'says you, us, we,'

junior chuckling, lifting matches from the night table, sparking one, the warm orange glow assaulting his eyes, a flash going off, he blew out the flame with the corner of his mouth, shook the match a few slow times, then cracked it before dropping it onto the table, the flicker of a light, someone stealing, living, trying not to be frightened of the dark, a child's scared face illuminated in bed, fingers clutching the bedcovers, then darkness to confirm suspicions, and sunlight, smiling into breakfast,

'who would've thought such a meal as this, free dope a fringe benefit of being so succinctly mortalized, ceaseless reaping of a heavenly state, that higher slice of consciousness without effort or concentration, cheers, as they say in some far-off land i can almost remember, the single gene on which the woes of england and ireland are chemically interwoven not bred into me, to look at it now in its bordered meaninglessness,'

the smoke deeply into his lungs, he held it there, studying the joint, the ragged burning tip, its fat centre and narrow ends,

'yum,' squeezing out the word while holding smoke in his lungs, he licked at his lips, then exhaled, watching the thin, smoky wisp stream from his body to clarify itself, 'so, misters hawco, or is it mister hawcos, this death stone that we're on, it sucks us deeper to the core, aren't we even just a little bit scared, hippy man, not so much of a lark now, to know yourself this dearly and alone with only me,'

'yes, very much so, thank you,' he fell back onto the bed, a quiet screaming sound as through tumbling from a skyscraper, flailing arms, kicking legs, then, at rest, staring at the ceiling, hearing the fading racket of his actions, now too calm, too still, another draw and clamping out the words with the smoke still in his lungs, and the camera raised, his curved reflection in the lens, the memory of its capture enough, 'it's true though, you can't stop thinking of your family, like some kind of rugged ragged dark cartoon that's pulling you back there, a magnet in my chest, back to that house on a cliff by the sea . . . dive from the edge,'

shutter clicking, eyes shut, junior exhaled, coming up from under water, smoke gushing from his lungs,

'they're quite a bunch of characters,'

'and we love them, right,'

'oh, yes, deeply and eternally, they're my family, and there's never any end to that,'

'but we don't fit in, never did, the proverbial black sheep, cute pink faggot skin beneath our overly friendly fleece,'

'but i have blonde hair,'

'once a rump rider, dreary dearie, always a rump rider,'

'now that i've finally got over the chore of living, shouldn't i be normalized and chasing women, why aren't i homo-perfectus, dreaming of linda sue's lovely lacy bonnet and cleverly concealed cans,'

junior laughing outright, sitting up, eyelids heavy, eyes puffed slits, smiling with sturdy impenetrable resolve, the air smelling of mothballs, it brought him to his feet and led him to the closet, inside there were clothes stored away, coats and dresses and hat boxes on the floor, the addictive odour of mothballs, he couldn't get enough of them, leaning his head in, sniffing, whispers from within, not only him sniffing, but others, unseen, sniffing through their possessions, turning, he studied the room in awe, was he really dead, he wondered, the tingle not going through him, the fear of the thought absent, the room not such a bad place, if this was where he was to live for all eternity, he hadn't tried the knob yet, he had found himself back here, his last place of rest, of sleeping,

missus neary had done the room up nicely with doilies and statues of the virgin mary, and a portrait of the lord with a cross made of palm leaves tucked into the frame, and not to forget the crucifix above the bed, junior glanced there, threw his hands up to cover his face, hissed manically, laughed it off, made scratching motions with his fingernails, where was god now, hello, hello, a bad joke, a rotten joke, a sickly feeling that brought tears to his eyes, why the tears, and the regret, please, forgive me, jesus, desperate for a moment, he expected someone to stomp into the room and slap him across the face, maybe a cross nun in a black and white habit, a priest with a strap, a female angel with a machine gun chomping on a cigar, buck up, laddy, er i'll blow ya ta kingdom come, either intrusive body welcomed, he found himself deserving, his eyes settling on the only photograph he ever cared enough about to have enlarged, the black and white he took years ago in bareneed, tacked there beneath the crucifix, a man on his knees with sticks for support, and children gathered around him to watch and listen,

'crucifixion,'

in reverence, he thought of norman, the canadian, arousal still buried deep in his pants, who would have figured, what would happen if he masturbated, frozen in climax, jaw agape, would he shoot a stream of feathers, poof, poof, poof and poooooooofffff, ta-da, poofter, the godly canadian had given him the marijuana, they had smoked together, shared similar thoughts, but junior hadn't dared to cross the line, to touch his friend, that was what they were, friends, junior convinced himself, don't ruin it, although having now passed on, he could undoubtedly overpower norman, take him in his sleep, junior wondered if he might be able to travel across countries at will, if he might be a succubus or . . . what was the male equivalent of a succubus, a vampire, was that in the same league, he hadn't watched enough horror movies to piece it all together, there was an upside to this after all, this damnable deadness, it was not the heart that stopped, each chamber still opening and shutting to let in the let out, but the body that went like forgetfulness, there was something to norman's mannerisms that implied he leaned that way as well, although it might just have been close friendship, he should know the difference, those mothballs, hell, they were good, he turned to pull in another whiff, noticed toward the bottom of the closet, dead moths, he bent and looked closer, the vein-like wing designs, glowingly transparent, not moths, but flakes of skin, his skin, he rose and shut the door, what door, and the skin fluttered to rise, always enter and leave by the same door, otherwise, bad luck,

'we're just so gosh-darn confused,' another draw, the narrow end of the joint pinched between fingernails, he licked two fingertips on his other hand and smothered the flame, staring down at his bare feet, his long toes with fair hair, the veins and concealed joints, they began to bother him, make him squeamish, he covered one foot with the other, then decided to pull his socks on, why the body still with him, he didn't like his, never did, why not simply his essence, golden and floating with a choir hitting a magical combination of sustained high notes, tugging at what might have been thought of as the soul,

how feeble his imagination now in recollection,

'what's the matter, junior,' whose voice now, not his own, a woman's,

'junior,'

'that's not my dead name,' said he or his twin, 'what's my dead name, call me by my dead name, expliticus, i have grown too vivid, no longer junior to what,'

a gentle knocking on his door, he froze where he was sitting, concerned now, looking for his twin, face to face, they stared, the presence of another man, just like him, what would people think, two of them alone in a room, identical, both sets of eyes on the camera casing, how much film left, how many shots, the proper settings for exposure to let the light in,

'yes,' called out perhaps too loudly, he could not tell, the meekest sound bursting out of him,

'hello,' missus neary's whispering voice, younger, childlike, 'hello,'

'yes,' he coughed lightly, clearing his throat, was she dead, too, in what manner, or did she, living, know how to converse with the dead, perhaps there was no difference to her, junior waved his twin toward the closet, 'hide,'

'oh, come on, the closet, of all places,'

'get,'

'there seems ta be a waft of smoke coming from yer room,' a caring soft statement, not meddling, but concerned kindness, child no longer ungrown, the voice maturing with worry,

'only a candle, missus neary,' he lit a match, coughing to cover the sound, then brought the flame to the wick of a holy, baptismal candle, 'just a second,' he wanted to see her face, her lovely face, perhaps younger than he remembered, by the sounds of what was spoken behind the door, he fanned the lingering smoke from the air, then checked to see his twin safely concealed,

opening the door,

amazed when his eyes locked with hers, enthralled by the startling beauty of sight alone, they were pale blue and gorgeous, her face old and truly magnificent, such sweet-smelling, benevolent antiquity in her powdered skin, such simple good humour evident there, a candle in her wrinkled hand, even though there was electricity in the house, the light against her lined face imbuing the image with softness, the sentiment mingling with the scent of fragrant powders, the scent reminding him of his grandmother catherine, who she obligingly became, in her other hand a small clear vial of holy water, she leaned to the side, tossing a sprinkle into the room, the candle flame flickering, the bulb's filament quivering the same, the light beyond the window in darkness, lightning,

'too much light down dere,' she said, 'dimming da t'rob o' da sacred heart,'

'i was watching the fire,' junior said, accustomed to his grandmother's antics with holy water,

one night, during a wind storm, he had opened his door only to recoil back from the shock of holy water sprinkled in his face, his grandmother wandering the house, reciting a prayer while tossing water against the doors and into the rooms,

now, he wondered in whose house he was living,

his grandmother, eyes on his face, a son he could be to her, once removed, smiling quietly, her eyes blackening, draining, 'yes, da whistle were sounding, it woke me,' eyes blacker still, 'fire a'ways awakens me,'

'i believe it's out now,' mouth so dry, confounded, 'the fire,'

his grandmother noticed and mistook it as a need for sleep, 'it's started in raining,' droplets shimmering in her pupils, he glanced toward the window, having not heard, now hearing the gush beyond the pane,

'it's pour'n buckets, get some rest, me love, ya need it after saving dat man, rest be da cure o' ye,'

'i hope so,' regarding her again, her face that would never leave him, he assured himself, tears streaming down his face, there but not, never to be again, licking them from his lips, her lips,

missus neary remained, stood in front of him, wanting or capturing the unspoken, a voice, her dead face a mysterious history he would never know nor understand, she not present at all, him neither, the shiver he never felt, the tears not his,

he wanted to say, tell me, and that was all it took, at once he knew everything there was of her, millions of tiny images pulsing through time, of feeling, of small and large objects changing,

each a birth,

a finger on a petal,

'ye have such a lovely complexion,' spoke missus neary,

junior bursting out with laughter, wiping at his mouth, then at his eyes, 'thanks, sorry, i wasn't expecting that, thanks, really,'

'have ye got enough blankets in dere ta keep yerself warm,'

'yeah,' a quick glance back, 'i'm fine,'

'i'm poisoned with dis weather,' she said, 'it bodders me poor ol' knees,'

'it's not nice at all,'

gently a smile, and junior's heart gracefully relieved, his grandmother again, her features showing through the flicker, the complete opposite of harrowing,

'sleep tight,' she said, 'don't let da bedbugs bite,' and she turned to fling holy water in her path, carefully drifting off in her slippers, down the corridor toward the rows of rooms to all sides of her, a boarder sleeping in each wrought-iron bed, missus neary compelled, one foot in front of the other, only because she believed it probable,

junior's eyes with the image of her disappearance into the shadows that she called into, then he closed the door, stood in silence, marvelling at the endearing quality of this life, in this dark house, on this dark land, while the rain poured beyond the window, tears from the sky where he thought the glass pane his face, the cellar his feet, and the siren had been shut down, as the fire was now extinguished,

shab reardon woke to the sound of his own roar cut in half, tossing in the bedsheets, the slosh in his brain, chemistry a dreadful mix from birth, made to die by his mother, drunk all her life, his fist slamming the wall, knocking flakes of plaster down onto his greasy hair, the reverberating boom, a punch always preferred, from the moment of waking, waking the orphan girl, nil, ten years old, her eyes fluttering open, muscles tensing as she flinched a dreadful stare toward the doorway, gertie, asleep beside her on the mattress, a four-year-old boy, none, son of gertie's dead cousin, dreaming on the floor in a broken-railed crib salvaged from the crack,

nil knew what-was-called-her-mother wouldn't wake, her arm still hurting from three nights ago, she wanted to visit the surgery where it would be fixed, her mother refusing, too many bruises, too many scrapes and scars, mended breaks and snaps, grabbed at her arm and bent it one way, then the other, scowling and muttering, nut'n da matter, shut up widt dat nonsense, or ye'll get da back of me hand, ya liddle nuisance, but it still hurt, it ached and the pain was a knife going in every time she moved, she rolled toward her mother, her arm dead almost, not wanting to watch the door, believing if shab saw her back-on he might think she was sleeping, holding on to what-was-called-her-mother, holding on as she was pried away, not yet, her grip never strong enough,

listening, peeking a look over her shoulder, the doorway dark, she blinked and breathed, the knobby knot of a man in her black remem-berings, cuddled closer to what-was-called-her-mother, the smell off her, a blend of scent she knew might mean love, the bottom of nil's nightdress cold against her legs, the sheet damp beneath her, she had peed the bed again, reached down and touched her nightdress, felt that it was wet, squeezed it, what-was-called-her-mother would be mad, she would be smacked, she would be forced to kneel, to clean, to show her tongue, to hide her face in her hands, while words kept coming, she dared not look over her shoulder although she heard the breathing knobby knot of a bulk, tightened her muscles, held on, if only her hands bigger, cursed by childhood, the breath and the footsteps toward the bed and the yanking, stinging pull of her hair that shocked tears to her eyes and stole strength from her limbs in the flesh of panic, she let go, what-was-called-her-mother did not wake, but she thought she saw her turning, groggily checking over her shoulder as nil was dragged off the edge of the bed, hard across the floor, knowing better than to kick, only hurt her feet, her neck at that bent angle, it would not stop anything, kicking and screaming, she thought she heard a hacking laugh from what-was-called-her-mother's bed,

mommy,

where are you,

my mommy,

mine,

the knobby knot with her in the room where it happened, the door shut in daylight, knelt on the floor, her mouth shaped, pinned against the bed with one big stump, leg, knee, arm,

'stay,' threatened using one hand to swipe the nightdress over her thin hips, heavy arm sliding along her chest, across her throat, lifted her against the mattress edge, light as a feather-doll, pressed down hard while working calloused fingers along her underwear's elastic leg hole, fingertips rough and rubbing too hard, pinching in the catch of flesh between her legs, three fingers forced deep, digging and twisting,

hurts, nil thought,

nil crying,

nil nothing not, *hurts, hurts, stings like fire, dead be the light gone from me, paled in the shadow of men be the larger always,*

nil sobbing, *the darker, the nightmare,*

i be zero carrying a curse in a candy-flavoured beaded purse, forever, fucked, if i
i
i only knew the word, fuuuuuucked,

nil knowing not knowing like razor blades dragged vertically across the left eye, then the right, eyes oozing toward understanding,

cunt, he said, not a word, not a word to anyone, in the mouth of a peep-squeak girl who sings it away, hums in a see-sawing melody, those words not nice, uhn-uhn,

now hers to hold and hide from others,

shab smacked her bottom, sore arm behind her back, swiped down his underwear,

245

nil felt the fob of flesh probing, searching blindly, jabbing until it broke the hole and the first stinging entry, then burning and tearing into nothing as everything widened and surged upward, a body within her body rising to break loose, the pain, that entire body climbing up her spine, one hand around front, over her shrieking mouth,

i am the death of humanity, thought nil,

nil cried, *i am the death of humanity, i am the death of humanity*, opened mouth into the grey pillow, if only the words the feeling spoke, skin against skin, a red-black shadow in the corner of her eyes, gertie biting her lips, nervously smoking a cigarette, fire outside the windows, she stepped hesitantly toward the bed, took a draw, handed shab the cigarette, fidgeting and giggling for the years she knew of this taught her, of what she stood in, where she crawled from, what was done to her in the name of other dark nights, surviving to show how to survive, how easy now the knowing of what he would do to her, the brutal thrill, to it, it, it, knowing where he would put it, one step back, an explosion of excitement tingling in her blood, reversing, back but forward, ahead into the black-red wound, her legs atremble as she settled in the doorway, the watcher, her large eyes staring, fixed on the struggle, the nightdress-hiked-higher punishment, in a bedroom, in a house built by a father gone, the muffled shreds of screeching that she should almost stop, and more explosions, as shab broke the foster girl from someone/somewhere else, broke nil with a savagery that made none of it livingly real, her foster son, none, not a part of this, sleeping in his rattling crib, dreaming of cowboys and indians, not dead yet, not yet in that hell, a dynamite explosion on the island, ripping through half of them, nil, gertie, shab, missus neary, but not yet none, the dreaming boy, tossed from the wreckage, up into a tree, balanced in the highest limbs, hell raging beneath none, what he would live from this point on, a boy, soon a man, with two words in his cock, his muscles,

fucking destroy,

taught, said nil
taught, said gertie
taught, said shab

II

dust

the woods smelled dank from the previous night's rain, blackstrap's
boots glistened with moisture from the clumps of grass and moss he
trudged through, the shotgun heavy, broken open the way it was made
no difference, it was how blackstrap's father told him to carry the
shotgun, hand on the barrel, stock pushed up into his armpit, he was
looking for crows, black and big and worthless, his eyes sharp into the
shadows of limbs and trunks and down along the tangle of grass and
thick roots that made the ground troublesome to tread through, his
pockets stuffed with hard bread for fairies, just in case, so they wouldn't
carry him off, his mother insisting, putting the bread in his pockets, her
son not believing, laughing off the idea while doing just that,

crows ate their garden, plucked out the carrots and flew away with
them, dug up the potatoes, ate whatever they could steal in the clutch of
their sleek black beaks, gathered together and made early morning noise,
one squawk passed from bird to bird, treetop to treetop, until the entire
sky echoed in an uproar at daybreak,

further in, he came upon his favourite spot, an area with the softest,
brightest green grass and ferns he had ever seen, reaching down,
brushing his fingers along the grass, the shaded luxury, the trees high
above him, the sense of enclosure, he stood, breathing the sweetness of
damp grass, he dug a shell from his pocket, slid it into the chamber
where it fitted exactly, butting the metal end with his palm to make
certain, snugly set, he snapped shut the dull steel, cradled the heavy
straightness of it in both his hands, held it like a small animal, far above,
he heard a cry that startled him, a cry unlike a bird's, he aimed overhead,
but found nothing, staring down the barrel, aiming, it and his eye, the
trees towering away from him, maybe the whistle he sometimes heard
from bell isle, sound blowing this way when the wind carried it, but this
too loud and remaining fully inside him, startling him toward fright, his

nine-year-old heart skipped a beat, gasping, he checked toward the shadows of ferns, something darker had moved there, an animal, the height and bulk of a person, blackstrap stopped, needing to breathe, aware of that, sweat rising at his temples, his brother smiling behind the dusty sunlight sifting vertically through the criss-cross design of limbs, tilting back his head, his brother's white jaw easing open to speak, pink dust spilling from his mouth, over his chin, a mound like an hourglass on the earth, a dull thud against the grass, against blackstrap's feet, looking down, fearing he had lost a limb, dropping off in trance, he saw the shotgun, fallen from his hands, he looked toward the ferns again, where he came to escape, to hide from his father's demands, nothing there, only the sound of his heart stampeding in his chest, like a wild animal cut loose and thrashing through the brush, broken, lame, his brother's gentle laugh, coolness against his face and hands, against his armpits and crotch, a cool breeze and then a moose without antlers, a cow, its glassy eyes watching him, carefully, he reached with one hand, squatting for the shotgun, hoping the moose would not break the stillness, sway in turning and stride crashing through the trees, snapping branches while it bolted away,

blackstrap's fingers touched metal, then higher, wood, the stock, he peeked at the ground, both small hands reaching, his eyes floating higher, rising to see the moose, the statue, he remained crouched and took each moment as a full measure to raise the shotgun, the barrel hole pointed at the moose, aiming for where his father told him, the place where the heart pumped, just there, one eye shut, a hazy blur inching on the barrel, he focused to see a spider, brown legs and a lighter brown spot on its back, the spot inside a light brown circle, he remembered the bigger ones he had shot with his homemade slingshot, cut from the Y of a branch, sling made from rubber salvaged from the nearby dump he picked through,

blackstrap had watched the bigger spider walk along a length of clapboard on the shed, then pulled back the rock, pinched between the rubber, and let it go, dead aim, the spider splattered into a beige blob, the stone ricocheting off,

'why'd you do that,' junior had asked, snatching away the slingshot,

blackstrap with eyes on the stopped thing smeared on the shed wall, 'how would you like it if someone squashed you,'

'who,'

one eye shut, staring down the length of the barrel, he refocused on the moose, found where his father told him to shoot and there came a cry, a call, a shout, that might have been an explosion but sounded like a voice heard when waking, almost recognized, a flinch from the moose, a realization as its body thought to move, and he pulled the trigger, a sharp blast in his face and right ear ringing, thrown backwards, landing, he saw up, the treetops, the blue sky high above him, his shoulder aching as though punched, he scraped his hand on a rock trying to sit quickly, to make certain the moose was not charging toward him in a blur of hoof hammering to trample,

the moose gone,

without knowing, in fright, in action, blackstrap picked up the shotgun and stood, moved nearer, trembling from the shock of the blast that still rattled in his body, on his feet, he caught sight of the brown bulk in the grass, bigger now that it was on its side, he cautiously trod toward it, expecting it to kick back up, those legs a mystery, raise its head and struggle in reverse, but it did not whip itself into movement,

dead as a doornail,

crouching again to watch, close but not beside it, the warm shotgun resting on his lap, a rug was what it looked like, a lumpy rug, still squat down, he shifted nearer, in a duck walk through the grass and bushes and buried acorns sprouting spruce, fir, pine, until beside it, he reached out to touch the long hairs, the warmth of fur, warmer than the shotgun, thought of lying down beside it and resting his head on its heat, like he had done with his dog, he felt sleepy, the strange hairs on the fur, long and rough, what sort of animal, not a pet, bigger, to blast into oblivion, the bulk of the body beneath the fur, bigger than a man, his first moose, something to show his father, he turned and searched back through the woods, his father proud of this, he thought of the hunting knife strapped to his belt, the one that had belonged to his great-grandfather, patrick hawco, passed on to junior, who didn't want it, claimed by blackstrap instead, and wondered about cutting away the hide, what was meant to be done, the necessary next step, but decided to leave it as it was until his father saw, so they could skin it together, he rose, his feet turning to run for home, seeing the calf stood in the distance, a smaller animal, the size of a little horse, a pony, his body stopping just like that, knowing in newer silence, waiting for the stillness to give up,

but the stillness did not, it kept them locked together in fright, in comparison, two same-sized creatures magnetized by the woods,

both heartbeats pumping faster than was meant,

it was blackstrap who finally shifted, reaching for a shell from his pocket, and the calf turned in automatic fright to crash deeper into the wilderness, smashing into trees and stunning itself, motionless on its hooves, facing away,

blackstrap tossed the empty shell out, slid the new one in, snapped shut the shotgun, and took steady aim, blasting the calf over,

there, ahead of where the calf had fallen, an escape path into the green, the kicking of its hooves on a sideways angle, but no movement down that path where it might have never been seen again,

jacob remembered helping his uncle ace spread the black nets over the grass, uncle ace, working silently with the concentration of a man seemingly slowed by paralysis, would mend nets further down by the inlet where the boats were tied up, a different location from where jacob now threaded the line, piecing the torn net back together, he called over to charlie coffin, a comment about uncle ace and what the oldtimer would think of the whole scene now, if he were still living,

'naw bloody much,' charlie coffin called back, sitting on a rock, with hands braced on knees, puffing out his cheeks and smoking a home-rolled cigarette, he lifted his workgreen cap and scratched at his generously bald spot, then tugged it back on, frowning and solidly tilting his head to punctuate the point, his thoughts on his old friend, ace, how they used to play together as boys, high up on the headland, into the sky, overlooking the sea, the green pastures and the pocket of shacks, a million years ago, still a young man in a wrinkled skin suit, living not so much for now, but for then and the utter waste of it,

'naw bloody much's right,' jacob agreed with a solid nod and a laugh, threading the line, mending the torn net that kept him from going out in the boat, 'you 'ear from junior da week,' asked charlie, picking a ladybug from his green pants and letting it walk over his palm and the back of his hand to spread its luck,

'da missus got a letter, yeah,'

'dey're clos'n down da mines over on da isle,'

jacob breathed in, 'yeah,' pulled a length of thread through the hole,

'won't be long 'fore da whole christly mess be closed up, mark me words,'

jacob muttering, 'all shagged up,' he sensed a flash in the sky, drew his eyes to the heavens and heard the cry that pained him, as if stitches had been torn from a gut wound, he checked charlie coffin, but his friend's eyes were contemplating the ground, seeming not to have heard a sound,

he stared toward bell isle, studying the water, imagining the mines three miles out under conception bay, junior down there digging beneath land and water,

quickly looking to his right, up the long sloping pasture, he saw emily in the front yard, shading her eyes with one hand while she stared toward the sky, jacob's white sunday shirt hung damply from her hand, her pregnant belly not showing yet, she had been putting out the wash and something had drawn her from the back, led her toward the front of the house, standing before one of the tall front windows, a white cross dividing the four panes,

jacob felt the gape of distance turn to a feeling of unbearable closeness,

'you hear dat,' jacob asked, almost with fright, casting a look toward the rocky headland covered in clots of grass, stunted spruce and narrow loose dirt paths, the headland lifting before him, blocking a full view of bell isle, as though the rumble had come from the mass of rock,

"ear wha',' asked charlie coffin,

jacob stood from where he was knelt at work, his knees aching, his fingers gone stone cold, something opening up in him, a dark boundless rushing, leaving him unburdened, he tossed the net from his fingers, striding up the bank, toward his wife who – without thought or explanation – handed jacob his sunday shirt and turned, stumbling toward the front door, the door they never entered in avoidance of bad luck, stricken, she tripped in over the threshold, her hands braced in the door frame to steady herself,

III

when junior was tom, before he was dead

a faint lopping of water against the steel hull, the hum of the engine, the ocean dark and blue, and gulls following in the ferry's wake, hanging in the pale worry-free sky,

junior had climbed up one of the steel ladders, escaping the exhaust stink from the parked, idling cars to stand on a white metal ledge with the sea air on his face and in his hair, elbows on the railing, watching back at the reddish cliffs of bell isle, their rocky, jagged height shadowed ominous, once named wabana, the abnaki indian name for 'place where the sun first shines,' junior remembered the canadian, norman park, telling him that, never had he heard it before, he tossed out pieces of bread from his sandwich, an excursion lunch packed by missus neary, the gulls diving for the offerings, plucking the crusts from the water and hanging off to the side, waiting for further movement from him, norman park gone, this same deck, two weeks ago, this same railing where shab reardon broke leo jackman's arm, snapped it over the rail, then tossed leo jackman overboard, leo fooling around with shab's wife, gertie, everyone, in fact, shagging around with her, the orange life preserver flung to leo, junior had done that with shab standing right beside him, shab not minding, he just wanted leo hurt, not dead,

there was a lull as the boat cut its engine, coasted in a soundless way that pleased junior, he held his breath, until the steel jarred against the rubber tires secured to the dock, nudging its way in, lines tossed out, he remembered his father and blackstrap, fishing, coming ashore, junior waiting on the wharf, to hear what they would tell him about being on the water, always a humorous story of triumph or near tragedy, told with serious intakes of breath, his father, the instigator, blackstrap often with a bit of a cocky smile, now, with guilt at their memory and at the thought of where he was venturing, men after all, his father and his brother, men, unlike him, the reason and the need, junior waited for the steel ramp to be lowered, the cars directed out into portugal cove, a friendly toot from an occasional horn, he waved but would not accept the rides other workers offered him into st. john's, he walked past the cars, wanting no one to know where he was staying, and headed for a taxi, climbing in, he said: the holiday inn, the cabbie clicked over the meter arm and the ticking ensued, that frequently attracted junior's attention, as if he might not have enough money to pay, even though his pocket was filled with fifty-dollar bills, always a fear of some sort, of never measuring up,

passing between the towering bookends of rock blasted open to make way for the road, junior observed the water that cascaded down the rock at his right, running off and under the road, everything downhill, finally, everything coursing back, to spill into the sea, life like that, but maybe not his, spilling back to nothing, now clear of the rock, away from the sea, he took in the old, square houses with their fenced yards and small barns, the road winding up and away for several miles, then more water, the flat expanse of windsor lake, and the forested hills beyond its shores, soon a sign for the airport that stirred in him a longing for permanent departure, beyond that, farmland, then more houses, down the incline of a steep road where they stopped at traffic lights, beyond and to their left, the hotel, the beginning of the city,

pulling up to the enclosed entranceway, the cabbie flicked off the meter arm, leaned slightly to the side and matter-of-factly announced the price, junior paid and climbed out, small suitcase in hand, one of his mother's suitcases, solidly built with solid brass clasps, it had belonged to his mother's mother, amanda, dead from tb, a woman who wanted better for his mother, that was often the argument, british, refined, his father despised the woman, suitcase in hand, he stepped along the enclosed concrete passageway with its wide red carpet and in through the double doors, he set his suitcase on the floor, uncertain if he should interrupt the desk clerk who was involved in writing something down, not noticing junior, not paying attention, until junior coughed and the clerk raised his finger, held the finger in the air while he finished his work,

moments later, the clerk looked up, offering a closed-lip smile, 'yes?'

'i'd like a room, please?' junior asked, conscious of his age, his youth, wondering if he required some sort of identification, as he sometimes did when visiting the bars downtown, he had been in here before with his father and mother, while his mother shopped and called on her father in the lunatic asylum, junior's father sitting in a hotel lobby chair, grumbling about money wasted,

the clerk lifted a card and placed a pen diagonally across the lines to be filled out,

junior wrote what came to mind, had fun with it,

'will you be paying by credit card,'

'cash,' junior said,

'we require one piece of identification,'

junior, suddenly troubled, 'driver's licence okay,' the clerk would see his name, the difference, who he really was,

'yes,' the clerk said, 'that will do,'

junior placed the licence on the counter, looked toward the glass doors, in case he needed to dash off, the clerk never even checked it,

'that's fine,'

junior waited for further instruction, nothing came, he assumed that was it, a key in his hand, a key on an orange plastic fob, he turned away and stepped across the lobby, through the double doors, into the long dimly lit corridor, junior read the numbers on the doors until he found his room, fit the key into the lock, thought and then felt what a wonderful sense of freedom these places offer, inside, he took a moment to smell the air, then set his bag on the bed and clicked on the television, two beds, he observed, everything clean, thrilled by the prospects of what he would discover here, pulled open the drapes and looked out over the swimming pool and the small pond beyond it, more water, he undressed in front of the tall windows, this bold sense of revelation, regarded his reflection, with thoughts of who might be in the other rooms, the lives, what were they doing, where they had come from, he put his clothes back on, and left his room, making certain he had the key in his pocket before closing the door,

he wandered into the lobby, bought a newspaper and sat on one of the couches, read about how the british legislature had urged for mercy killings of babies born deformed and limbless, victims of a drug called thalidomide taken by their mothers during pregnancy, the queen mother's visit to canada, a photograph, that gloved hand of hers, waving, the preordained curve of her fingers, a meeting of the atlantic premiers, junior looked at the individual photographs, smallwood, the man his father hated, smallwood, robichaud, stanfield and shaw, he read about a bell isle man who had drowned in port arthur, ontario, a name he did not know, and saw that actor billy gray, who portrayed the teenage son on father knows best, received a six-month sentence for possession of marijuana, what would norman park think of that, a laugh and a half, norman, he had norman's address in toronto, maybe that's where junior would go, what would norman think, be happy to see him, be suspicious, standing in a doorway, the two of them facing one another,

junior glanced up from his reading to watch the men who passed before him, those who met his eyes did so with the fleeting interest of the business-minded, his presence of no true use to them, he read on about a blast over the nevada desert, an h-bomb type device, in the mightiest blast yet fired in the united states, sent a shower of rock and sand soaring spectacularly thousands of feet over the nevada desert, *spectacularly*, junior thought, glancing up to see another man pass, a man whose eyes lingered on his, woman's eyes in a man's face, they both knew in an instant, junior read on, a flash brilliantly visible fifty-five miles away at 10.00 p.m., *brilliantly*, junior thought, licking his lips, and glancing up to see that the man was now seated across from him, he read 'a wallop equal to 100,000 tons of tnt,' *wallop*, junior smiled to himself, 'it rose to perhaps 7,000 feet, looking to observers like a giant chrysanthemum bloom,' junior looked up at the man, *bloom*, seeing the man's gentle smile that warmed his lips, so that he rose and followed after the man, down the corridor, the man's room in a different wing, the man unlocking his door, leaving it open, junior checked over his shoulder before stepping in, inside the man's room, the man talked, standing by the window, asked junior his name, where he was from, junior said his name was tom, the man said his name was fred, tom and fred drank beer, the man talked about news, the biggest stories, then became nervous, more confident, less confident, the man named fred moved closer to tom, at first, fred was gentle, calm, smooth hands, but then he kissed roughly, unshaven, it hurt tom's face, his hands grabbed, pulled too hard, it was fast then, all of it, when it was tom's turn, he gagged, fred moved quicker with his hips, as though fred thought tom might change his mind, as though fred wanted to get it over with, something that had to be done,

when the energy had been exasperated, when junior was no longer tom, but himself, he could not help but cry, changed as he was, he could not help it, the tears poured out, why, the man who remained fred held him in his arms, they lay together on one of the man's beds, not the bed the man would be sleeping in, until the man stood and told junior that he was very good, a nice body, young, and junior smiled away the tears, shook his head at his foolishness, and sat up, secretively wiped at his eyes, the man a little older, always older than him, his back against the headboard, admiring the way the man walked about the room, stark naked, smoking a cigarette and talking, at first calmly, then more nervous, junior wishing he had his camera, but the man would never allow a picture, captured like this, the man came back to the bed and stood there, as junior began to feel a little better, telling junior he had an appointment, he was late, he looked at his watch, junior saw the wedding ring that wasn't there before, the man had plans and he was late, fred had plans, and that junior must leave now, must go, must leave now, be gone, out of there, fred even pointed to the door, his voice unrecognizable,

junior quickly dressed, thinking, why in this room, why like this, and he left, not another word, back to his room where he picked up his camera, went outside the hotel in the fresh air, he stared back in the direction from where he had come, raised the camera, pressed the shutter, captured the entranceway, waited until the man came out, another picture, the man not even looking at him, in dark sunglasses and into a car, he felt regret, disgust, shame deepening by the moment until there was his father, his brother, his mother, he turned the camera around to face him, shut his eyes tight, opened his mouth wide, and pressed the button,

IV

resettlement

the sun on the clean snow set the valley aglow, assaulted his eyes as blackstrap hawco ran toward the white pasture at the side of his house, climbing the fence, one leg, then the other, tumbling over into the stretch of snow separating their yard from the butlers', he raced clumsily through the sticky snow, then fell face first, hands bracing himself, he remained still and breathed into the warmness between his skin and the cold ground, he thought of junior, deep in the ground, deep, deep in the frozen earth, the way he had been beneath the ocean, but now beneath the earth, not moving, he thought the hot tears he was holding back might pour at any moment and melt the field of snow, junior a hero, it made him stronger and sadder, that junior was a hero, his big brother, a hero, he focused only on that, bravery, but it was bad, too, wrong, he lifted his head and stared back toward the house, his father shovelling the snow away, scraping every speck of white from the front walk and then trudging around the house to the back door, shovelling there,

blackstrap noticed his father's slight limp, on cold days like these, the limp became pronounced and he thought of the story of how his father broke his leg on the trapline and set it himself, waited for it to heal, then walked out on his own, walked out in a blinding storm and appeared in their house the very night that blackstrap was born, the story reassured him, gave a special magic to his birth, stories towered above his father, not like others who spoke words, but did nothing, like in school, all the words from other places that had nothing to do with him, he leapt up from the snow and raced back toward the house, over their fence, one leg, the other, falling, up on his feet again, he stopped, thought he should stay clear of his father, watched him, shovelling steadily, he went a little nearer, testing, his father not even seeing him, until blackstrap said: 'i'll do it,' woollen mitten held out, 'is done,' jacob replied sharply, without looking up,

blackstrap moved his foot back from where his father was vigorously shovelling, sweat on his father's forehead, angry, he wanted to help, but his father would not allow him, he watched his father's face fighting against something, jacob's lips turning tight and bloodless,

'jacob,' a voice behind him, jacob straightened at once and glared toward the voice, saw that it was their neighbour, lloyd butler, a portly man in cap and suspenders, stood on the path with a beagle not far behind him, the mutt sniffing at the ground in quick sloppy circles,

'i jus 'erd,' said lloyd,

jacob nodded in acceptance and continued shovelling,

'we all be move'n in da spring,' lloyd went on,

'move'n?' blackstrap said,

jacob would not look at his son, resettlement, no control over it, no say about being hauled off his land, his roots, this terrible wonderful place so close to the ocean, he had heard through rumours where they were going, a place called cutland junction, closer to a hospital and bigger schools and with better roads, he had been there three or four times before and knew one man from up that way; the man who used to deliver the coal, isaac tuttle,

'move'n where?' blackstrap asked his father,

'g'wan inside,' jacob barked, without looking at the boy, blackstrap glanced at lloyd butler who was showing his sad face as the boy moved near the back door, but did not enter, instead, he raced down the hill, toward the water, then up the rocky headland with rugged stunted spruce he sometimes grabbed hold of for support, along the snow-covered goat's path with patches of brown grass bent above the surface, striding up, securing his footing, then having to bend forward, to grab, steeper and steeper, and slower, but never slipping once, toward the top, up over the lip, where, in the summer, he found the bones of small dead animals brought up there by the gulls or crows, it was a pure white headland now, blazing like the uncovering of one enormous bone bleached by the sun,

blackstrap stared back at his house, far below, the fenced yard, the wholeness of his house set beside their small barn, and the shed where the nets were hung to dry, the other houses, spaced apart and rising up from the valley, he counted them, ten, more houses up over the hill, toward the school and church, but he could not see them, he pulled off his green and white woollen mittens and watched the steam rise from his hands, wafting about like vapour in the windless air,

a stare out over the water, the deep blue horizon to his left that settled along the paler blue line of sky, and in the centre of his vision the back of bell isle, the ragged straight-down cut of long narrow land, an island off the coast of an island, with its iron ore riches, set offshore only for the purpose of tempting his brother away from them, junior had been dead for five months, and his mother with a baby soon on the way, and now they were moving, he would have to leave his friends: paddy murphy, tommy bishop, harold butler, benjamin taylor, he would not even be able to race up the headland again to look out over the place that had caused his family such hardship and grief,

a change in his heart, like the way the wind turned, no longer toward but away,

good riddance,

entirely not, junior hawco, unaware enough to ask: what order to events, when he steps from the room it scrambles, before and after one and the same, never again permitted to touch the certainty of this:

the priest's words: 'the earth moved and a line was divided and one of our native sons was swallowed up,'

silence, a sob, a cough, a rustle of clothing, tears, as the community sat still in pews,

'jacob hawco junior was a fine young man, a sensitive and an intelligent young man who cherished life, a brother, a son, a friend who was appreciated by all, a young man who cared for those of us fortunate enough to know him, always willing to lend a hand, who went out of his way to help the elderly and spend time with them, to listen to their stories, an altar boy who, for years, served up here with me in this very church, and then, as he grew in years, a man who set out to seek his fortune, finding work to do his part for his loving family, a man who knew his obligations, and now . . . a man who valued life to such a degree that he could not see it destroyed, who gave his own life to save another, in death, junior hawco remains the man who adored life, junior hawco, a man of faith and action, now becomes one more commendable thing to us: a hero for all eternity,'

emily hawco heard the priest's speech repeated in her dreams, her son in the wreckage of confusion that blocked his progression back to her, it was all a mistake, junior smiled at her, it was someone else who had been killed, mom, i was only gone away for a while, mistaken identity, junior smiled boyishly, his eyes gleaming with such clarity, always the perfect child, he sat at their kitchen table, patiently explained the misunderstanding while eating a slice of homemade bread and molasses, hungry, devouring the bread, it was all so easy, so foolish, how can i be dead, mom, he said in that voice she craved to hear again, i wasn't even there, i was away, just to look at him, to marvel at his face,

i miss junior,

waking to the darkness, emily listened while the voice from her dream faded, a presence beside her, junior, older than ever, her fingers reaching out, no, jacob's face, breath from his lips, she stared at his shut eyes, hoping that it might still be junior, finding his way home, but it was not, and she rose to her feet, as though to move away from the bed would be to leave behind the muted panic and calamity that was fixed there for her to rest with,

'oh, god,' she whispered, choking on a sob, seeing, by the faint moonlight swelling through the window, her breath lingering in the air, her eyes on jacob's sleeping form, his body beneath the blankets, his thick fingers on the pillow, the desperation of winter, the chill, why her son, why such coldness, such darkness and deadening of spirit, why not him, jacob, the one who would not die,

she had been told that junior saved a man, a man named shab reardon, and had lost his own life in the doing, her thoughts were inflicted with images of the deed, the accident, the underground quake along the faultline that ran directly toward bareneed, this man, shab reardon, one of the miners had told jacob that shab hadn't even taken the time to pay his respects at junior's funeral, jacob had cursed the man, raging around the back yard, kicking things over in the small barn, cursing at the injustice,

"'e's a mean, 'orrible man,' maude butler had told emily, and junior had saved him, 'a drunk 'n da worst sort 'o bully,' it was so much like junior to do such a thing, emily thought, why so much like him, tears flooding her eyes, if shab reardon had been a judge or a senator junior would probably have thought twice about being so brave, no, it wouldn't have mattered to him,

'junior,' she whispered, the word cut to silence, she wiped at her eyes and sniffed, then quietly trod toward her stool positioned before her mother's three-mirror vanity, sitting, she watched her ghostly reflection sink into view, wondering about her ugly life, the pain in her heart and stomach that compounded to gather torment in her entire body, raising a hand to her forehead, she weakened further,

a deep breath, junior's final letter to her rested beside her bottle of white shoulders that he had brought on his last visit, her mother's comb and brush set on the doily, the photograph of her mother and father in england, their old house, a stately manor, she raised junior's letter in both of her hands and read about the people of bell isle, the sad people that junior was taken with, drew into his heart and loved as kin,

a tear dropped and landed with a gentle flicking sound, puckering the paper in a starburst shape, she glanced at the dark mirror, the vague shadow of jacob in bed, the sound of his breathing, he rolled over, settled, not sensing her absence, she knew that junior must have loved this man, in death, she found the need for honesty, not truth – truth always belonged to someone else – but honesty was needed now, with junior's death, she found no need to lie to herself any longer,

but why such a horrible man, why would her kind, gentle-minded son do such a thing, why love such a horrible man,

her fingers holding the letter, junior's long delicate fingers in the casket, all that they could find of him, all that remained after the cave-in, and then the explosion, dynamite set off by an overturned lantern, his four fingers arranged on the lacy pillow, loose, but in the shape of a hand, she had spaced them herself, set them apart by exact distances, as calculated from memory,

V

not what is wanted to be known of shab

shab reardon called to one of the workhorses, making a noise with his lips and whistling at once, stepping nearer the wooden stables built into a recess off the main corridor of iron ore rock, a cavern of black tinged purple and red with the ragged walls chipped away as though under the tools of a sculptor, he moved along the horse's length, nudged its head with his shoulder, then grabbed the long nose and steadied it between his elbow and side, holding on as the horse tried to jerk its head upwards, shab bore down against the rising force, his face smiling into the animal's eyes, as though in friendly yet challenging recognition, one front tooth missing and the muscles in his arms as thick as fence posts,

in the wrong body, junior thought,

shab cradled the horse's head in place while its hooves shuffled back and forward,

junior felt this a sight inextricably linked to love, an image to put into slow words in the dark, telling his lovers in later years, this kindness toward his other, watching junior while shab released his hold on the horse and laughed, 'atta b'y,' rubbing the horse and reaching into his pocket for a fresh carrot plucked from the earth on the way to work,

'best 'a kind, right,' he said to the horse, feeding it the carrot from the open palm of his hand, then smoothly rubbing its throat, 'some 'orses, buddy,' he winked at junior, 'down 'ere dey never see da light o' day, blind when dey go up, born in 'ere, dead in 'ere,' shab seeming proud of that, 'nut'n more ta it den dat,'

'yes,' was all junior could manage, tired and burnt around the edges, his ability to summon the usual choice string of words eluded him, shab watched junior, smiling in friendship, chuckling, waiting for such a comment,

'you aw'right, or wha', buddy,'

'yeah,'

shab came away from the horse and slapped his arm around junior's shoulders, squeezing with his big hand and leading him from the stable and into the rushing scraping sounds of ore being shovelled into the cars, of men spitting and blowing snot from their nostrils in the hollow, tunnelled resonant echo of sound,

'let's 'av a mug up,' shab insisted, pulling junior along,

'i forgot my lunch,'

'da's awright, b'y, you can 'av me own, christ, ya worries too much,'

junior glanced at shab's grinning face, an utterly different man when sober, harmless, almost boyish, lost, an orphan, junior had heard, growing up without father or mother, knowing nothing of how to get along, responsibility, only drinking to make his way clear of himself, to prove himself other than himself, drinking until every last cent of his wages was spent, pissed away and proud of it, nothing but a poisoned mind,

lucky man, junior thought,

'i got a drop 'a tea in me t'ermos,' shab nodded down at his lunch box, 'gertie's young one gets it fer me, finest kind, right, being tended to like a king,' he winked at junior, 'lard over everyt'ing,'

junior watched the gouged contours of the black and red rock, perceiving the sloppy geometrical texture of the clawed edges with a startling vividness, he breathed breath that knew of seclusion, limited oxygen, he was far underground, far beneath the ocean itself, sixteen hundred feet of earth above him, plus the weight of the sea, its true depth unknown, bearing down, tension in the centre of him, the land knowing, keeping count,

new management, despised by the workers, had been brought in to squeeze a profit from what was left of it, management thinking only of dollars as market forces bore down on them, while the lowest of the low, the muckers, the slaggers, the face cleaners, all worked like devils, management soon gone, packed up, shipped out, money in the bank on the mainland,

junior stared down the shaft, if they kept going the way they were digging they would hit the underwater mass of the headland in bareneed, start a vertical shaft and come up at the pinnacle of the headland, with a view of his parents' front yard and the other houses, where gardens grew, livestock roamed and clothes flapped on the lines, the thought of digging toward them urged unease,

junior found it hard to breathe, in such depths, he sometimes lost his breath, not hearing what shab was saying as he was pulled along, the jagged shadowed surface of the rock as they moved forward, a blur of seemingly impenetrable grey and red they were violating, turning redder and redder, rock to the sides, above them and at their feet, a sudden sprinkling of dust as shab jogged ahead, turning to face junior and slamming his fist into his palm, joking, playing with him, the men tiny and far off behind the bulk of shab's big body, goodbye,

'come on, i'll take ya, ya fuh'k'r,' shab shouted at junior, grinning widely, that missing tooth, that face, it reminded him of blackstrap, *naive and powerless, no sense of direction, possibility, just a hole he crawls through, one way and back, a mine, a cave, above or below ground, straight ahead, what bliss to be so finite, so adequate,*

sprinklings of dust, the air stopping dead in junior's lungs, stilled, every sound in the mine shutting down, the rumble, tiny and far off, miles above or below, to all sides, from where, then the whinnying of horses, as though galloping through the earth, the rumble heavier, vibrating into the soles of work boots, the clatter of steel falling, picks and rods, the shadowed edges releasing, the crack wanting to close over, the weight of the broken earth, the noise of shifting, eyes toward the low ceiling, toward rock, toward the sea, toward the sky,

junior hurled himself forward, the new-found easiness of his drifting body, already half dead, as he knocked shab backwards, the collapsing of the black-red rock, the undoing weight of earth rushing loose to pound junior's spine, walloping him, snapping him down, a calamity of boulders, dust and noise releasing steadily, not moving again, and then smaller rock, harmless and vagrant, dirt, big and little sounds, a river of a landslide of a clay spill, the air popping from lungs, once, like a paper bag blown up and slammed against the knee, echoing off, one sound only for him, the surface of the penetrated earth re-forming, and he in it now, a widening of the faultline,

shab blinked away the dirt, swiping grains from his face, blinking, he spat, the noise of no harm to him, noise only, how could it, hands already braced to stand from the ground, ahead the dust sprayed out in both directions, thick, lingering dust he could not see through, coughs from other men stood in wait, for the clearing, for the affirmation, rocks shifting as on a beach, a wave, clicking, he covered his eyes and opened them again, spat to clear the grit from his teeth and tongue, against the haze he moved through, the whinnying of the horses, plucking the blue and white handkerchief from the back pocket of his overalls and holding it against his mouth, the rubble that he tripped into, blindly tossing rocks away with one hand, three feet of refuse before him, workers tilting and ducking out of shab's way, he clawed, slicing fingers, snapping and tearing fingernails off, to find a six-inch clearing, the hair on the back of junior's head, the dirt in his fair hair, dead hair, junior's fingers uncovered, trying to move, shab placed his hand there and the other men were upon them, worried, wondering, talking in tones rarely heard, seeing shab's face covered with dark red dust and the clean wet trails running from his eyes straight down the length of his huge face, as if someone had taken a brush and painted him into disguise, into tears, into sorrow, never before, never again, he would see to that, junior's fingers stopped beneath his, he swiped the tears away, the love away, the roar,

springing to his feet, he glared at the three men, breathing through their handkerchiefs, stifling their muddled coughs, one of them glancing overhead, men who should be dead, stricken from the record, his roar at them through the grey haze, never to see him, not like this, he shoved two away, bellowing louder, bodies tripping backward to bash against the rock face, soundlessly in his ears, worthless, life, one big palm slapped against each chest, he then turned, staring down, deeper, junior's hair in the rubble, not wanting men too close, to see what had happened to junior, his single friend, clawing rocks away, breaking more fingernails, breaking fingers, breaking hands and arms and shoulders, there he was, uncovered, junior, dead, his face untouched, beautiful, dear christ, dear mary, mother of god, sweet virgin in the heavens, a rumble as great in him as that in the earth, shab spun around to shout and lurch forward to shove the men further away, 'fuuuhhhkkkkkkerssss,' who cared about the falling rocks, shab stopped them, pinned them overhead with a roar that would not stop throbbing from his mouth, the spill of a lamp, and the boom of nearby dynamite, they said, set off by flame and the quaking repercussions of shab reardon's rage,

'end of story,'
   'it's all there ever was,'
   'goodbye then, say goodbye,'
   'to who,'
   'all the friends you never had,'
   'like us,'
   'yes, only so long, these thoughts we're having, caught or gone,'
   'the voice as two, always talking,'
   'say goodbye now, lover, say the end,'
   'why me,'
   'i'll say it then,'
   'what,'
   'the end,'
   'thirty letters and a period to go,'
   'you're gonna cream your jeans'
   'i can't—'
    '   ,'

In order to learn the details of all that happened between Isaac Tuttle and Blackstrap Hawco, I read the unpublished book, Always the Infant/Toujours l'Enfant en Basâge, written by Constable Pope/Pierre LaCrosse when he was incarcerated in Cutland Junction Maximum Security Penitentiary in Newfoundland. In the manuscript, Pope explained the events of the day when Isaac Tuttle was taken into custody. The sections where Isaac Tuttle travels through the woods are copied, in part, from his journal entries written during his two months hospitalization at the Waterford Hospital in St. John's. Sections of the now-famous videotape of Karen Hawco were found on the Internet, her identity validated by her brother Glenn, who helped with the reconstruction of that scene.

1992

Cutland Junction

I

The trees smell of God

5.42 p.m. Constable Pope parks the cruiser along Cabin Road. Adjacent to a narrow tree-shadowed path that leads down into the woods. According to the given description, this was where the break-in took place. He waits and watches the cabin. Then hears the giddy scream of a child through his opened window. He leans out and pushes the vehicle door shut. Carefully with both hands, to listen. Through the autumn sunlight, in the narrow gaps between dark spruce, fir and speckled birch. He witnesses the flashing movements. A blue sweater. He steps away from the car and takes the path. Catching a scent of sweet wood smoke or trash burning. The freshness of the air giving the smoky odour fullness and reach.

A blonde-haired girl of seven or eight in a blue sweater plays by the side of the cabin. She sings and scrapes the dirt at the end of the driveway with a rock gripped in her hand. She outlines a small circle and jumps into the centre of it. Then she notices the policeman, immediately rushes ahead to greet him, as if he is an old friend who was expected. But then halts.

Constable Pope smiles at the girl's pretty face. Her big blue eyes and cherub lips. A picture-perfect child.

'*Bonjour*,' she says, holding a shredded slice of white bread in one hand, a stone in the other. 'You're a policeman.'

'*Bonjour*, yes, to you.'

'I'm in French Immersion. I can speak French. My mom says I can get a job better if I speak French.'

Delightfully caught off guard, Pope slowly asks her a question in his native tongue.

'*Oui*.' The girl points toward the cabin.

'Very good.' Pope looks ahead. 'Your mom and dad are at home then?' He regrets having said 'home.' The instant the words leave his mouth. He knows – by the fierce clarity in the child's eyes – that each of his words will be challenged. And corrected.

'This isn't our home, *monsieur*,' says the girl chidingly. She points back at the cabin and laughs, *like the tinkling of a wind carillon*, Pope tells himself, *a jingling of broken Noël bulb glass*.

'They're in the woods,' the girl says. '*Forêt*.' Her expression more reasonable now as she comes nearer to stare up at him. One eye squinting. 'You're here about the bad men, right?'

'What bad men?'

'The *bandits*, robbers.'

'Ah, yes, of course.' The thought of robbers. A smile to Pope's lips. He reflects on the image the child must be thinking. A man dressed in black. Black eye-mask and black cap. Black pants and black turtleneck. One leg raised. Sneaking through the window. A flashlight in one hand. A sack in the other.

'How long ago for your mother and father to leave?' The thought of them leaving the child alone troubles him.

'I don't know. Leave where?'

'Into the trees. *La forêt*.'

The girl shrugs. She drops the stone and lifts one empty palm, shrugs, holds the pose for a moment. She looks at the piece of bread in her other hand. 'They're just down in the woods. They go there a lot, leave me here to play.'

'You don't care that I wait?'

'I don't care. As long as you don't touch me,' the girl insists. She hears the quick trill of a bird and jerks her head in the direction, her big clear eyes searching into the woods. Pope notices her lips parted slightly in amazed concentration. '*Oiseau.*'

'I won't harm you.' Constable Pope offers a kind expression. Honesty. Although it is difficult to hold. He is nervous, considering the possibilities. How this child could claim he has done something. The precocious sort. It would be wiser to wait in the car. To avoid the mess that might be made of this.

The child shifts her attention back at him. 'You're really handsome, *beau*,' she says, seizing hold of his hand – her small fingers so cold – and dragging him toward the trees. 'The squirrels are over here. I've got stuff for them.' She raises the flap of bread and waves it in the air, beaming up at him. '*Pain*. That's what bread is called in French. Like pain. Maybe we can catch the squirrel and keep it for a pet. You have some kind of cage, right?'

He looks back toward the police cruiser. A cage, yes. *Un camp pour la fille.*

'Say something in French.'

'I don't know. What?'

'Tell me a story, that's what, like when you were a little *garçon*.'

Constable Pope recalls a story, one that was told him by his grandfather. He begins. It is not so long. It is like a parable. While telling it, he is reminded of Karen Hawco. It is a story about death in the woods. Peril fashioned in a benign way for a child. *Un conte de fées.*

The little girl watches Constable Pope's mouth move, catching the familiarity of a word here and there. 'I know that one,' she interrupts, smiling more and more at what she can pick from it. The name Karen is spoken. The name sticks out because it is in English and a girl in her class is named Karen back in St. John's. *Je violerai Karen. Dans son cul.*

The little girl tries to understand, but cannot. It is all going by too quickly.

Blackstrap Hawco hears the noise ahead. Through the trees, he cannot see. But a thrashing like a wounded animal. Its final moments caught in wilderness hold. Only to tread closer to find it on its side, struggling with terror eyes or stopped. Another blast ending it.

Last night, Blackstrap had gone to Tuttle's house. Shotgun in hands. The door kicked open. No one. Nothing in darkness. Tuttle's bed empty. Blackstrap had wrecked the room. Money under the mattress. Newfoundland dollars. Canadian dollars. All stuffed away in a hole in the boxspring.

He sat in the living room chair beside the shrine. Not even noticing it was there until later. He waited. Lights clicked off until morning made its own. And then outside where he found fresh bootprints. Down the lane and into the woods. It was there Blackstrap took up the trail. Suspecting that Tuttle was hiding. Knowing that Blackstrap would be tracking him.

It is not so difficult to follow a trail. An escape route that leaves its mark. Tuttle's path frantic. A man scrambling off without purpose. A wide trail of destruction through the trees. Branches snapped as though a moose had passed through.

Blackstrap pauses to listen.

The whimperings of a man toward the east. A sob.

And the grey clouds close over. What sun there was in the distance. It hides behind.

It begins to rain.

The trees smell of God.

Pain the Purifier stitches complexity to the name of Thing. More than crawling up off his knees. All dead once alive centuries of it making birth sucking him to stumble and dribble he scrambles to stand. Out of cave, burrow, nest, the step and the snap of What. Here in the absolute. His own Book built from the snap of the other shut. Sky. Tree. River. Colour. Animals never marvel at. Alive only to sniff and search. Intuition no invention. These whorebastardtwatfriggers. Head bowed. Plumb inside to nose loose the dirtiest of words: Soul. No slang explicit enough to twin. No higher animal higher than itself.

Isaac gawks up. Hands and face scratched filthy. Bits of brittle leaves stuck in hair and clothes. From moving all night in near darkness. Only moonlight. One cockthrobbingburstforward. Always forward for what might be made to happen. Never a plan hinged to action. Who he has wounded. Made no one. Who will come for him? He stills himself. Heart to hold his burning breath. The voice. Birds. Tittering. With pinprick dicks. Why so hard to say? Insects with 10 x tinier dicks. And microscopic cunts. Impossible to imagine. Who fucking invented fucked? Each Thing asking from trees, earth, water. All as one misunderstood echo. Drilling the tight-lipped confessional holes into a viscous smudge. Fish in the swim. Eggless dead to bacteria its own living Thing. What we invented. I am not blessed. Every creature. I am not blessed, yes. Every hole punctured. All sounds of bloodbeat. Connection dotted to rapture. No clamorous decree to Saviour. NotStarve salvation when finally decoded. Reamed into decodation. Heartbeat. Buggered into assembly and disassembly. A string of throbbing pearls strung toward the blazing sun. Grey and raining now in its grim Christness. Consuming yet and yet blessedly giving. Hovering this maze of a court so warm in the autumn chill. They are sleeping. These litters born. They are sleeping as YesFuck watches over YesFuck. Always, YesFuck to continue. Adolescent urges forging the industrial ingenuity of abortion. This patch of land trapped in where he fucks the slit in the earth that is his burial.

Isaac says, 'Yays.' Bloody clump of tongue come unglued alive with the rend of pain.

How else to know? If not spoken if not done.

Blackstrap pushes down an evergreen bough. Leaning to step, he sights a small clearing ahead. Where a tree was blown over by wind so strong it splintered. Blood on the jagged stump.

Tuttle has fallen there and been pierced by the grey branches pointing up. Not stopped though. The trees could not stop him. Not an animal that big.

The rain barely makes it through the mesh of overhead limbs. Rain gives everything a smell. There is light up ahead where the clouds have parted. A warmth. A sharpness where Blackstrap might see more clearly than before to better take aim. The fur. The mud. The filth. Whatever that must stop breathing.

Isaac Tuttle crosses himself, a flurry of arms. Whose arms, not his. Left and right crossing the tripping rush of wilderness. He plummets a blur. What will happen next? Cursing the message. Meaningless. Only to know, to hear and mis-exact the segregation of sacred utterance. Slap the calamity of sound no measurement. Broken gestures. Something to look forward to to quit toward. Isaac whimpers. Exile burning in his cheeks.

Pray to that his tongue a sticky gob of paste his mouth a jar in which to store his eyeballs. He tries to stir the tip. Stiff it hurts thick spilled along his chin. Blood and black afterbirth the effects. We come together to join hands and commiserate. How miserable were our lives yet so astonishingly beautiful if only our eyes punched out. Not by what seen but haven't.

How deep da cut? he himself aware of walking into through it to its source. These fuck-ugly pray-ers exorcize the dead from nearliving. Half awake in obliteration and counting down from 1,000,000 in slow motion to . . . If a Thing can count that far and then you are due. Unwashed all men born smooth-foreheaded in the arms of ignorant mothers learn their duty. Plugged thoughtless by sleepless disease and time the simple time the period the era. Excuses for plunder or sentimentality he remembers of course he would perish a wasted shell. But he would remember scrambled in disarray his brain faltered one memory with the face of another. A man in a room with nothing less and less of nothing. Set in order only his death finally there is order. Zero blank X. Scarlet-black gash in his mouth that he treads toward to enter Zero blank X. Nothing beyond morphine administered. His dying moments life's lie. Painless nothing in white and the soft-shoed step of 'nurrrrssseeee!' God created the end so it might end he says over and again. He has cried to believe but the end never ends. Only Zero blank X. Blank meaning multiply.

Constable Pope notices movement in the woods. The vague sound of a man in distress.

'What's that?' asks the girl worriedly. 'It's the *bandit*!'

'Stay in your place.' Pope treads alongside the cabin. In the back, there is a propane barbecue and wooden lawn chairs. A circle of planted flowers. A small white plastic chair.

The girl has followed after him. 'It's a black man.'

'*Qui?*' Pope asks, distracted, noticing the girl. 'Sit over there.' He points to the chairs.

'A bad man.'

Confused, Pope nears the edge of the woods. He hears another sound, one not so much in pain. He checks the girl. She has moved toward the chairs. But she is not sitting. She is standing.

Ahead is a small bank. Pope digs the edges of his boots in and descends, faster toward the bottom. Now lower than the child, he checks her again. She has come closer. He raises his palm to her and she trembles.

'I'm afraid of the black man,' she cries.

'*Qui?*' Constable asks, irritated.

'*L'homme noir*. I saw him on television. Stealing.'

How to answer that? There are no black men here. Not his place to instruct the child.

The girl hurries to the edge of the bank. Her hands joined in front of her, her feet moving up and down, wanting to run.

'Stay,' he says. 'Please.' He ducks under a branch.

'Are you there?' the girl calls.

And Constable Pope sees the bulk ahead. Through the trees, a head turns toward him. A man's head where he is hunched over a woman. Not so frightening. Not so terrible. A robber of not so dangerous a sort.

Ah, oui, thinks Constable Pope. *Famille.*

Stumbling through woods for innumerable hours. Tired now in body. Impelled toward an opening. The other side. It is here. There. You drown. You burn. You suffocate. Bitch says. Bitch says. Bitch says. YesFuck. I am here. For only you. Voices discerned. Playful laughter far up ahead, the delicate sound sifting through blazing leaves and evergreen boughs. The sunlight itself, splashing him in the face. Awakening pain and fingers curled. Sweet innocence of voice. When he was young. He is moving. That much is known. Toward a single sound capable of scouring him clean. If only a child. If only a son. If only a daughter. Not such a pillar-crash of inner ruin. He blinks his huge eyes, glasses lost miles ago. That time with Emily. Out of pity. In silence. In a way never understood. Neither of them admitted to. An act never spoken of. But nine months later. His? He will not say the name. Lipchewer. Fleshrotter. Arselicker. A blur of colour and sound that he grunts toward the back of his head.

A young girl.

Pose. Frozen in that.

Red red red lips caked with make-up, groves numbered in close up.

Up.

She bounces.

Light as the breeze.

Things he could tell her. If his tongue did not sting. So fiercely. The. The Lord. Lord. Incites the purified, the driven. YesFuck. Wake up. 6.00 a.m. Each day until the day. The. An infinitely small speck of recognition. Unearths itself, dirt blown up ahead. Lord. They advance through the forest with a cup and a pill.

And remain steady, patient, for growth will come.

Ahhh, it surges out of him, focusing, listen. He has stopped. It is still. It is exact. A forest, wilderness, city, cabin, apartment, house that he is stopped in. He sees. In these man-made or natural-ceilinged and open-skied compartments. It is him alone framed outside of this.

Blackstrap stares down the length of shotgun. Notices the trees have begun to thin. A view of objects beyond the woods. Outside the life of the forest. A different world. Unreal how it is found. The side of a cabin. Like it does not belong. Other people. A police car. The shapes of objects that do not fit in. The back of Isaac Tuttle's head. Lower. Through his shoulder blades. The space to the left. Where the spray of pellets would pop through. To make mush of the heart.

$1.50 for the shotgun shells. This is what Blackstrap thinks. Write it up in the book. As a debt. If he pulls the trigger. The entire world will hear.

*

Cabin up ahead. Just there. How many feet? Twenty. His cheek takes the lash. A branch with a stinger. For YesFuck. Half-eaten bodies. Nailed to walls. Built around JuicyPlum. JewySlum. Jerusalem. A count of lashes to open him. How many? Twenty feet. Her. How many? To her. Her is always him. Her to suffer. For him – a gutless wonder. Crows ripping at flesh. He has stopped counting. Wishing for another. Life. What is seen and wanted. The land. Always occupied wrongly. Thoughts – whip-snapping here to there. Unbounded by continents, divided by theology.

And thank you.

The child's laughter closer. City child in the lie of the land. That flourishes. Through the bounty of YesFuck. FuckYes. The child-drawn scribble. Portrait of the fisherman. Behind him, an ocean. The cunt suck pull of sea. And thank you. Thank you. The fishing grounds. No longer now. Empty. Cunt suck pull of the sea gone slack. Beyond shore.

Haggard whore. Biblical exactitude and majesty. For the seas shall empty. How not to believe? A walk across an ocean. Once. With feet floated by fish.

Crown-sanctioned
scroungers.
Out of foreign ports.
Overseas.
To vanquish.
God's country.
New Found Land.
Beneath a crow-wing flap
of a flag.
Of unholy bone-gnawers:
Piecemeal progress.
Who from where?

YesFuck in the tower. Says nothing. Smells the spillage. Dreams of killing. His skull a glistening fist.

Isaac lifts his head, unsticks his eyes to the opening through trees. Flicker. Unreal. He stands and trips again. Hands bracing ahead for the fall. One hand onto a hard thick root. The other penetrating softer space. A woman's mossy hair, through her giving flesh, like warm dough, implying his hand deeper.

     Life to life stiff nipple
     Entanglement
     His prick one thick pulse
     Bobs when fingered, willing
     to burst and blossom
     a bouquet of bleeding hearts

Falling too deeply, he must tell. The child everything before he is too old. Too much of a shrunken apple before she takes the bite.

     Any second now.

'Dad?' The girl calls into the trees. Her high-pitched voice tingling with fright. 'Police man?' Panting sounds. Pawing noises through the branches. And she trembles on her feet. The face rises toward the bank. The bulk of something. And the girl screams. An animal. No. A monster coming toward her. Slasher Eddy. Slasher Eddy. With a blood-black face.

     Constable Pope is now near. The girl lurches for his legs. Hugs them and screams without letting up. Slasher Eddy. Pointing. Slasher Eddy.

     'It's okay?' Pope says tentatively. More troubled by the girl's electrified overreaction than by the hideous sight of the man. He touches the top of the child's warm head. Squints into the slanting light that mingles with dust through the limbs and trunks. Revealing the dark flashings of a human form. Gurgling or growling. Until it makes it up over the bank at the edge of the clearing. The staggering body. Large white eyes against the stained and bleeding face. The squinting exaggeration of expression that could only belong to Isaac Tuttle.

     The young girl lifts her face. Away from where it was pressed into the fabric of Pope's pant leg. Mouth shut and silent. She peeks toward the woods. Screams again. A shrill sound that carries far across the land.

A great wounded bird. Behold, he cometh with clouds, is Isaac Tuttle, his eyes shifting within a clotted face of bright-red and brownish-black streaks and scratches, to stare woundedly at the sky. *And every eye shall see Him, and they also which pierced Him. And all the kindreds of the earth shall wail for him.* He nods okay.

'Ashley?' a man's voice from the woods at the back of the cabin. Hurrying out of the trees, 'Ashley?'

A woman calling unsteadily, 'Ashley,' forceful and yet troubled.

The man and woman step quickly from the woods. Scrambling up over the bank alongside the cabin. The woman rushes to the girl and scoops her up. The woman's blouse unbuttoned beneath her rumpled jacket. Revealing her pale blue brassiere and rounded cleavage. Her breath racing and erratic. The man is startled. Stops in his tracks. Flushed as he buckles his belt and scans the scene. Not expecting a policeman. Not knowing. Coming close to inspect his daughter. Touching her arm. Caringly tilting his head to stare into the child's fear-struck face.

'What is it?' he asks, out of breath. His throat dry. Almost choking on the words. He notices the man near the bank. Jerks back. Then to the RCMP officer, 'What the hell's happening?' he demands. Outrage overcoming embarrassment.

'It's okay,' says Constable Pope. 'She had just a small fright.'

'A fright!' says the man.

'Isaac Tuttle,' Pope calls out.

Isaac tilts his head, freezes, hears the calling. Caught, his jaw churning from side to side as he speaks out from the disoriented swirl, the sound a mash of thick liquid rasping. A blurry outline. One thought for these unfocused people, through the punching bloodbeat along the veins in his temples, *Christ 'av mercy on yer souls, ye frightened sinners.*

'You go to the hospital,' says Pope. Eyeing the half-dried blood beneath Tuttle's chin. 'We'll find out who did this?'

Isaac Tuttle bends his head sideways and watches Pope, sniffing the air. He shrieks, throwing his arms up into the air.

The girl's scream recedes. Followed by the sound of a door slamming. The mother has taken the daughter inside. Footsteps in the grass. Pope turns to the man in his beige down-filled jacket.

'Where'd he come from?' the man asks. Searching into the trees. The mesh-work of naked branches. Speckled orange leaves and green boughs extended from brown-splotched tree trunks.

Isaac Tuttle shifts his tongue, the pain provoking anger. He steps for the girl's father, but Pope grabs his arm.

'Mr. Tuttle,' says Constable Pope. 'I think we move on.'

The man snickers. Straightens his wire-rimmed glasses.

Pope turns with the wounded man in his grip. Leading him. Patiently up the leaf-strewn path into the blaze of colours.

'I knaw sssy worh, 'n ssy layor . . . ssou hanst not 'are ssem whiss are ehil . . . ye fuh'r.'

'You know that I was robbed,' the man says accusingly. Voice raised to be heard above Isaac. His tone insinuating a connection between past and present.

'I'll come back later,' Pope announces. Recalling the man's name from the radio dispatcher, 'Mr. White.'

Blanc.

'Okay,' Mr. White allows. His breathing steadier now. Reasonable, 'I'll be here waiting.'

Isaac Tuttle shifts his jaw, one side to the other as they step up the path, alongside the dense cluster of trees and onto the open dirt road. No longer blocked from the wind, their clothes are cooled, their faces freshened.

Startled, Tuttle turns to squint into the gust. Emily Hawco stood by the police car, her grey hair, once a beautiful black lustre, swirling around her head, her white arms twisting listlessly like flimsy tentacles moving to a song sung by her perished children, her body still young beneath her gauzy gown, her expression one of compassion, of pity. She beckons to him with a vile grin.

Isaac strains back from Pope's grip, stops himself from moving closer to the car. *T'was a wind like dis dat took her*, he chews out from his tongue, *da screech of her dead infant*. But only he makes sense of it. A gurgle of mush and blood, his mouth sticky.

'This way, please.' Pope pulls him along. Opening the rear door. He settles Tuttle in the seat.

Turning to gape at the window across the seat. Emily Hawco bent close to the glass, her grey face dusty and greyer in patches, her parched lips opening and closing, opening then closing, rotted, splitting pink, like a blossom, a bloom, she feeds like a fish effortlessly swallowing minute specks until – revitalized by the sight of him – she is made girlish again.

'Isaac,' she whispers, 'what have you done to me? Not as I was. What you have done to me, to Karen?'

Isaac Tuttle bursts out sobbing. Hears the driver's door open, a uniformed man shifting in, then the door shutting. Captured, he warns himself, *detained fer me beliefs*. He will be executed. A child's voice calls, wild, escaping, fleeing toward the cruiser, 'I want to take a picture,' one hand slapping the glass, her small face pressed into the window.

'Hey,' says the child, banging the glass with her hand. The city child. Her mother lifting her off, further ascension that rises with Isaac's heart, now stolen away. A camera to the child's face.

The engine is engaged. The cruiser pulls out. A blur of shifting landscape speeding up. Only Emily Hawco in focus beyond the glass drifting along with them. Her palms filled with heartbeats that echo into the cool glass.

II

Out of the woods and out of place in a locked,
antiseptic room

The hospital door is shut. Karen has been admitted.

Her brother, Glenn, at the door now. The private room he had taken care of. Turning the metal lock to hear it softly click.

'One last look,' he says. A heavy bag on a strap over his shoulder. He lays it on the chair. Fresh air coming off of him from outdoors. He pulls the long zipper. Takes out the video camera, balances its weight on his shoulder, and aims at Karen. Lying back on the bed in her blue hospital gown.

'What're you doing?' She gently shakes her head. Not believing.

'Smile.'

'No, Glenn.' She holds up a hand.

The video lens draws nearer.

'Glenn!' She nearly laughs. Wanting not to be seen this way. By the camera. No make-up. No jewellery. 'No, okay?'

'Tell us what you're here for,' Glenn says, eye to the eyepiece. Interviewing the stranger.

'Nothing.'

'An operation. Isn't that correct?'

Karen's face reddens. 'Turn it off, Glenn.'

'You're not afraid of seeing yourself?'

'No.'

'What are you afraid of then?'

'Nothing.' Her image shaky in the viewfinder. 'Just stop.'

'What are you here for?'

'Breast reduction, okay? Now, turn it off. That's it.'

Glenn stepping nearer the bed, aiming the camera lower. A view of rumpled fabric with hidden weight behind it.

Karen turns her face away so she will not be captured.

'You don't want to interfere with art, do you?'

'Glenn, that's enough now.'

'Come on, smile.'

She snorts. Turns her face halfway back. Shows her teeth. 'Okay, I smiled. Turn it off.'

Glenn clicks the video camera off. He sits on the edge of the bed. His eyes on the camera casing in his lap, wondering.

'What's the matter?' he asks, raising his eyes. 'Don't you want this documented?'

'Why would I want that?'

'So you can see the difference,' his voice quiet, reasonable, convincing. 'Come on, Karen.' His eyes steadily on her eyes. 'It's important to me.'

'I don't want to be in one of your documentaries.'

'Why not?'

'I just don't.'

'Just a few more shots, okay?' He makes to rise, but holds himself. Her permission required. 'Please?'

Karen watches the little boy she grew up with. His face. Please.

'I need your help with this.' Standing. Smiling. Everything okay.

'Alright?' Tentatively, he raises the camera. 'Ready.'

'Just a second, that's it.' She looks toward the door. Reaches down and lifts the blanket up to her throat.

The camera to Glenn's eye. The flush in his cheeks. 'What are you having done?'

'Breast reduction,' said matter-of-factly. A patient in a hospital bed.

'Why is that?'

'Why do you think?'

'I'm not certain. Tell me in your own words, please.'

'They're too big.' Her cheeks a deep pink. Light red toward the centre like Glenn's.

Glenn tightens on that. The hum of the zoom. Holds on the colour. The complexion changing. Deepening.

'It's hard to tell.' His hand comes forward into the picture. The shot widening. His hand exposed, out from behind the lens. Pulling the sheet down. The blue hospital gown, the neck hole loose. He grips the fabric edge, carefully pulls, coaxing. 'Stand up. Come on.'

Karen sighs, 'Glenn, I don't want to do any more.' A deep breath. Frustrated, her eyes glazing over. 'I just don't want to, okay?'

'Come on, Karen. Now.' His voice changing, telling her. Do what you are told. Another voice, a hurried whisper, 'Come on. There's not much time.'

She watches the lens.

Glenn's face hidden. His hair. His chin. The other features unknown. Unimaginable.

Sighing again, she slips her legs over the edge of the mattress. Stands in her bare feet. The hospital gown plain and hanging.

Glenn backs up.

Karen standing there. Uncertain. She brushes back her black bangs with her chubby fingers. Her toes on the cool tile. Nothing underneath the gown. Her nipples stiffening to be seen like this. The camera lens for so many.

'Turn sideways.'

Karen shifts, her eyes fixed on the window. A view of hills and small houses. This far away, there is no movement. She thinks they all might be empty.

'We need to see why,' he says.

She checks the lens. Resigned now. Eyes saddened without challenge. 'Why what?' But she knows.

He zooms in on her face. On her lips. Parting. Unsteadily. The tremble. A breath.

She says: 'Why what?' Her teeth. Her tongue. The pink inside of her mouth.

He says: 'Why you're getting it done.'

'I told you why.' Words without a face.

'Show us.'

The camera pulls back. The hum of the zoom.

Karen fully there again.

She does not know what to do with her hands. She raises them. Shapes them over her breasts. To show or protect.

'We can't see.'

'What then? What should I do?'

'You know.' His voice in the dark. Remembered. A smaller voice.

'Take it off?' Her voice in the dark. Remembered. A smaller voice with questions.

'Yes.'

'Is that what you want?'

'Yes.'

A pause.

The lens aimed down, then slowly up.

'Will you leave me alone then?'

'Yes.'

Snorting, she gives a shake of her head. Her lower jaw pushed slightly forward. She watches toward the window. Those little houses. Forgotten people in them. She will not look at him. Will not see. The blue sky above the hills. The roofs of those houses all black.

'Just for a second,' he says. 'That's all.'

She reaches back and waits, then pulls the string. Moves the gown from her freckled shoulders. Holds the material tight.

'Let it drop.'

Still holding the material. 'I don't want this on TV.' Her serious face toward the lens. 'I mean it, Glenn.'

'Okay, no TV.'

She lets go of the gown. Her body naked. Remaining perfectly still. Gooseflesh prickling.

'Okay,' he says again. Breathing. Focusing. Zooming.

'Are you done?'

'Turn around.' A quick breath out that sounds like a word. 'Now.'

The hum of the zoom.

She turns. Body swaying to each slight movement.

'Stay like that. Stay.'

She stays.

'Sideways now.'

She turns.

'Stay.'

She stays.

'Lean on the bed. On your hands.'

She does as told, right away to get it done. Her face toward the white metal headboard. Her breasts hanging. Her bum stuck out.

The camera shifts in behind.

The hum of the zoom.

'Okay?' her voice shaky. Not looking back. Not knowing. Not allowed.

'Not yet.'

'What're you going to do now?'

A hand entering the picture. Touching there. The curl of a finger stroking the divide. A man's low, appreciative moan.

She stands and faces him. 'Alright?' Her uncertain reflection in the lens.

'No.'

'Yes. You've seen enough.'

His breathing.

Her reflection. Liking her reflection. Far enough away. Using it for now. The reflection's hands over her breasts to hide them. Raising them higher. The way they should be. Smaller. She sees them that way.

'Take your hands away.'

She sees herself doing it. *Your* hands, he said. Not *her* hands. Breasts

thickly sagging. The unevenness of wide nipples shrinking. The plump-
ness of belly. The wideness of hips. The tangle of pubis. Thinking of it.
The feel of air on skin. Every inch of it. Wet in an instant.

'That's enough now.' But her voice meaning not to. She slips one bare
sole a little over. The air touching her better.

'No, more, like before.'

She backs away from her reflection. From before and now. Sits on the
edge of the bed. Waits. Hands tucked between her knees. An
examination is what it's like. Documentation. Like when the doctor
took pictures after drawing on her breasts. Her shoulders slouched.
'Shoulders back,' the doctor had said. Other photos of breasts on his
wall. Big ones made smaller. Before and after. Her head swimming. She
lies down on the bed. Flat. Rigid. But more comfortable. Wants to be
told. Wants to be confined. Choiceless. She covers herself with the
white hospital sheet. Get it over with. She checks toward the door. It is
locked. A strong hospital lock. That feels better than just a knob to turn.
They will not be watched.

A whisper: 'Someone might come.'

'No,' he says, right away. 'They're all sleeping.' He pulls the drapes.
Shuts off the light.

'Are you sure?' Her dim, faraway eyes in the lens. Her whole body
fitting in that compact space. Barely seen. The light strained through the
curtain.

'Yes.'

'I don't want to get caught.'

'You won't. You know what you like to do. Remember? Show
everyone.'

She bends her legs. Her knees rising. Her soles flat on the bed. The
hospital sheet slides away. Her knees pressed tight together.

'Show me, Karen.'

Edgily, bit by bit, she opens her legs. 'Like this?'

The hum of the zoom through near darkness.

'Yes.'

'This is bad. What you're making me do.' Her fingers sliding down.
On her thighs. Touching. Holding her glistening self open. 'See? This is
what it looks like.' Then rubbing. Working in. The wet click of two

fingers. A deeper voice in her head. No longer a whisper. She stops. 'You know I'm fucking knocked up, Glenn.'

The close-up.

'Do it.'

Fingers stuck in there. Numb. Sheening at the knuckles.

'Remember?'

'Yes.'

A moan with her fingers stroking in and out. 'Yeah . . . you remember, don't you? When I was knocked up before.' An intake of breath. A shudder. 'Knocked up, like a dirty mommy whore. Remember, Glenny? Look. Look at it. You wanna feel how wet it is?' Her legs wider apart. 'See?' Another gasp. Fingers stabbing. 'Come here.' Her body jerking once in response. 'You wanna put it in me, Glenny. Huh?' Muscles holding taut. 'Awww, you wanna suck sissy's big titties?' In darkness, as though fitfully in sleep. 'Ohhhhhhh, fuuuuuck, yeahhhh, seeee, meeee.' Adrift. Afloat. Higher and deeper. Brighter and darker. Blacker and blacker.

'What you were, are.'

What she is, was.

What is she ever, but that?

Body easing back. Legs closing. Her face relaxing, turning away. Having learned never allowed. A look of not knowing where she might be. Awoken from unconsciousness. Staring at what is not now.

Who he is.

Glenn clicks off the camera. Lowers it. His face out in the open. Nervous now. 'After,' he says, turning. Needing to be rid of it. Stashing it back in the bag. Zipping it up fast. 'You can watch how you were before.'

Blackstrap Hawco stands at the foot of his father's bed. The old man's jaw white with stubble. His eyes on the ceiling as if aware that Blackstrap has been up on the roof. Patching the shingles. A leak that had been dripping on Jacob's forehead. Not knowing what it might be. His eyes fixed on the sounds of hammering. Still echoing in his head. A gust of wind rattles a loose pane in the window. Blackstrap turns that way. Unknowingly places his tar-stained hands on the cream-coloured wooden footboard. He stares through the window. Clouds sweeping along up high. Travelling that way since this morning. The wind only now easing down to settle closer to land.

The old man makes a brutally distraught sound. But there is no fitting expression on his face. Only his jaw nudging upward, sucking without lip movement.

The wind rattles the pane again. A moment later, the old man blinks. Makes the tormented noise a second time. Half growl, half hiss. His face the same as ever.

Blackstrap Hawco moves to the side of the bed. Stares down at his father's dull grey eyes. No longer pale and cool blue like his own. Blackstrap waits, then says:

'Wha's the matter, Fadder?'

Nothing.

He wonders where Isaac Tuttle was taken by the mountie. What was done to Isaac. Constable Pope had already been by. Asking him to repair Tuttle's house for the damage done with the backhoe. He'd have no part of that. Isaac Tuttle in the Waterford from what Blackstrap has heard. He'll find him there. Enough of Isaac Tuttle. Hearing for years how Isaac Tuttle owned the Hawcos' land. How Isaac Tuttle lusted after Blackstrap's mother. How Isaac Tuttle was a saintly man. Handing over a parcel of land. And the only reason they took it was because it was larger than the piece they were intended to live on. The one offered by the government. Joining Canada on the eve of April Fool's Day. If that wasn't joke enough. Smallwood having a grand laugh in Hell. And then a decade and a half later – relocation. They had been their own country once. Their own people. And now, according to his father, the country overrun by towelheads and chinks.

His father's favourite rant: 'Not like now, a province full 'a Newfoundlanders made to be lazy children by da fed'rul gover'ment. Da U.I. cheques 'n da Moratorium money for keeping away frum da fishing. Bunch 'a fuh'k'n cowards vote'n "Yes" in da referendum. Da on'y province besides dat Charlottetown one it were named affer, 'cause dey're scared shitless 'a losing gover'ment money. Bawl'n about how we're robbed blind by da fed'r'l gover'ment, den get'n nice 'n comfy suck'n on Canada's tit. Canada ripped da spines right outta us. All words now, all mout', not the ghost of a backbone left in most men. 1949. God-forsaken year.'

Now, the vacant expression on his father's face. Another relocation of sorts.

A rock in Blackstrap's gut that turns heavier when he remembers. The way his father changed from the time they left Bareneed. Not so much to glimpse as a boy. But now, older, looking back, he can see.

Blackstrap notices the locket on a silver chain around his father's neck. The catch down around front. Reaching, he undoes the clasp. Sliding a hand behind the old man's neck, he carefully lifts his head. So as not to make his father realize. He pulls the chain free. Opens the locket to see the photograph of the girl and boy. They had died. In mute wonder, he stares. Lips pressed tightly together. Then he snaps it shut. Fastens it around his own neck.

'Lo?' a voice from down the hallway. A woman's voice. Blackstrap tucks the locket away inside his shirt. Shifts only an inch or two to acknowledge Mrs. Shears. The old woman coming since Karen disappeared. No doubt having run off to St. John's. To stay with her brother. Like she did when things got too much for her. Too much what? he wondered.

He regards his father. Thinking this the wrong thing to do in the presence of a woman. To stare at his father only highlights the man's weakness. He turns toward the window and steps there. The cool of the locket felt against his chest. Fingertips on the low cream-coloured dresser beneath the glass. Blackstrap scans the crocheted doilies and the old bottles and cases of powder. His mother's. The smell still with them. Nothing moved from its place. Jacob Hawco railing so fiercely against change that change overtook him.

The familial throb of defeat. Who's responsible for this? Blackstrap wants to know. Only the anger that needs directing toward some other thing or body.

'I'll look after 'im now, me love,' says Mrs. Shears. A voice behind him. A slight struggle in the way she says it. Pulling her arms from the sleeves of her coat.

Blackstrap leaves without word or gesture. His scuffed and nicked steel-toed boots sounding against the runner in the hallway. Over the bare hollow-sounding floorboards where the carpet ends. Out onto the unevenness of the path. Made from rocks hauled from the beach in Bareneed.

III

There is no understanding

Being wheeled to the operating room. She remembers lying face-down. On the carpet. In the spare room. A place far away now. Feeling far away. Back in Cutland Junction. Feeling numb. The sedative. If only she could be this way. A staring blank. Her cheek against the soft blue pile. The shameful aching between her legs. The afterthrob. Eats up her entire body. No period. No blood. A baby. The desperate, enfeebling plunge. Toward disgust. And anaesthesia. A video. A baby. Gone.

The door to the spare room had opened. Blackstrap stood in the light that spilled across his wife. Her orange T-shirt and naked lower body. The heaviness of her white skin. The thickness of her legs. He had listened to her sobs. Stood silent. Not knowing which way to move to give comfort. Not understanding what had changed her. Only discouraged by his lack of control. Over things. He had lifted the cigarette from his lips and held it pinched between the tips of his thumb and index finger. Wondering what to say to her.

'I hurt,' she had cried into the carpet. After the fact. After crawling from the kitchen. To this room and collapsing. Knowing that Blackstrap was standing there. Knowing and hating that his eyes saw. But could not see. The battered baldness of her thoughts. 'I hurt . . . so much . . .'

Blackstrap had stared down at his wife's naked backside. The dark pubic hair showing through. Her pale flesh shivering.

What's the matter, woman? he had said to himself. Never facing anything like this before in all of his memories of his mother and his

288

grandmother, Catherine. Nor his first wife, Patsy. Wondering what it was that made his wife so sad. Something she had seen on the television. Things she saw there often made her cry. She looked like a woman he had seen in one of those movies that she rented at the video store. A desperate woman never happy. More nervous by the day. This person sobbing on the floor.

Blackstrap took a draw on his cigarette and thought of bending down to her. Trying to say a few words that might make her feel better. But she would probably slap him away. Explode in a rage. Not wanting him close at all. Not wanting him saying anything because he never did understand.

The thought making him angry. Karen thinking herself the centre of everything. Thinking herself more complex than anyone could ever possibly be. All the attention she tried to get. Concerned about no one except herself. And proving just that the next day by being so selfish as to disappear. Without so much as one word to Blackstrap. Not so much as a scribbled note. Nothing.

They had already sucked the baby out of her. Yesterday. At the clinic downtown. A taxi there. A taxi back to the hospital. Who would ever know? It took only a few minutes. She had been awake. She had watched the doctor. He had not said a word to her. He had done what he was trained to do. She thought of having a car fixed. Up on a ramp.

She is not scared. Moving through the hospital corridor. The nurse who wheels her along might be her friend. The nurses seem like friends here. Nice people trying to be always kind. Taught to be kind. They will put her to sleep. They will watch her eyes shut. Like a child. Like a baby. A hum like a sing-song. The gurney hits the operating room doors. A number of people in masks. Stood there preparing. They look at her. Like she is something to be welcomed, something to be done.

'How are you feeling?' one of them asks. The mask fabric moving over the hole.

'Okay,' she says.

'Good.' The mouth hole hidden.

All of the mouth hole hidden. Except hers open.

A needle slipped through the skin on the back of her hand.

'I want you to count backwards from ten.'

'Okay . . . Ten . . .'

IV

Missing persons

Karen Hawco, age 32, 5 feet 5 inches, heavyset, black hair, blue eyes, has been reported missing. Constable Pope thinks over the reported details. Then holds the soft features of her face in his mind. An attractive woman. Quiet. Not what he would call 'heavyset,' but mildly plump. He is surprised to learn he has genuine feelings of concern when he hears she has gone missing. He had been thinking of her when he entered the detachment. The news is an affront, as though he has been caught in the act.

Karen Hawco's husband once missing, now the woman herself. They must be fighting, he suspects. They always run off and turn up later. Absence and the heart growing stronger. Back for more.

Pope is sent to talk with Blackstrap because of the officer's prior contact with the Hawcos. Blackstrap is under suspicion. His history of violence. A confrontation at sea with foreign boats recently. People in the community, even some of the officers at his station, look on him as a hero. A lunatic would be a more fitting word. *Fou.* The damage done to Isaac Tuttle's house with the backhoe. Rumour has brought him here. The boys at Wilf's New Place passing stories around. Karen unseen for some time. No one dare ask Blackstrap. They know he will not talk about family. Personal talk is no one's business. His wife could be missing for ten years. No one would hear a word of it from Blackstrap.

The boys pass around possibilities: Maybe she went off to her mother's in St. John's or maybe to her brother's. But, no, Aggie Coombs saw her being taken away by a man in a car. A strange man. Maybe her brother, someone suggests. Naw, he never looked like her brudder, says Aggie. The way he was getting on. That was the last anyone saw of her. This from Constable Pope's notes. Not like Blackstrap to harm anyone though, Aggie had insisted. He never raised a hand to no one. And he wouldn't pay anyone to make away with her. Not like him to do that sort of thing. Maybe that woman of his, that townie, just packed up and left the way Patsy, Blackstrap's wife, had, although some claimed that Blackstrap had kicked her out. The true story. No one knows for certain. 'No,' said Aggie, with a sorry intake of breath. 'No one ever knows da trute of udder people's misery.'

Blackstrap's eyes are trained on Constable Pope's cruiser. Where it pulls up along Cabin Road. Stops no more than ten feet away from the idling backhoe.

Blackstrap sits atop a large grey boulder. Jutting out from a barren hill adjacent to the site. He follows the officer's step from the car. Observes the officer moving around the cabin site, unaware of Blackstrap's position. Blackstrap smiles from his vantage point.

Closer to the machine, Pope glances around, hands on his hips. Blackstrap sits still. His expression levelling out again. Until the policeman scales the landscape. Sees Blackstrap sitting up there, using one heel to kick mud from the other boot.

'Hello,' Pope calls up.

Blackstrap nods without offering Pope any particular attention. Finished with the dried mud. He glances up at the light grey sky. Trying to find the sun. But sensing the clouds are too thick. He raises a hand to shade his eyes against the muted brightness.

'I think you say your wife is missing,' Pope calls outright, having no patience for Blackstrap. For this sort of Newfoundland man, how Blackstrap believes that RCMP officers are nothing but a nuisance. No right telling him what to do.

'I don't think so,' Blackstrap says plainly. 'I never said such a thing.'

'I think people say she is not home. They say that.'

'You think?' With this, Blackstrap glares at Pope. Stares through a moment of harsh silence.

'You file a missing person report?'

'No.'

'Maybe someone want to.'

'Who?' Blackstrap wipes at his nose with the back of his hand.

'To find her.'

'Not why, who.'

Constable Pope shrugs. 'Is she gone or no?'

'If she's gone, she'll find her way home.'

'Maybe she needs help, is lost somewhere.' Pope glances across the land.

Blackstrap frowns at this. Stares off at the breadth of the barrens and evergreens. Rising toward low hills and grey skies. The tower of the penitentiary. A stray glimpse of walls through the thinner patches of trees. He turns his head back. Straining to see the view behind him. Holding the rock with his hands and searching the distant deep-blue water beyond the wilderness. Miles off. Thinking of his father, once a fisherman. Not a fisherman anymore. Not anything.

'I would like some information.' Pope's voice impatient. 'Could you give that for me?'

'Go get some,' says Blackstrap.

'From you, I mean.'

Blackstrap shakes his head and spits off toward the grassy bank studded with large and small boulders. 'Lost,' he says with disgust. 'She's no more lost than that Christly rock.'

'She not a missing person for you?' Pope shifts on his feet.

'No,' says Blackstrap. Almost growling out the word.

'People say she is missing.'

'No, you're the missing person, buddy.'

Pope laughs dismissively. 'Very good.' Straightening, he glances at his car. 'You think I don't know what that mean?'

'You speak English?'

'I am speaking English. You see. Speaking it. Now.'

'What you're speaking is something I wouldn't have da gall ta serve up as English. It's da dog's breakfast.'

Constable Pope does not understand this remark. But he assumes, by Blackstrap's tone, that it is not complimentary.

'Maybe you would come to the office with me.'

'Office? It's called a detachment.'

'You can come then.'

'You got no reason for that. Don't gimme yer bullshit, Frenchie.'

'What about Isaac Tuttle? The hole you put there.' Pope points toward the distance, in the direction of Tuttle's house.

Blackstrap checks the road. A pickup truck passing by. He doesn't recognize who it is. He pulls on one of his doe-skin gloves, the worn fingers sealed with silver duct tape. 'Fucking mainlander.'

'What?' Constable Pope takes a step forward. 'What you just say to me?'

'Where you from anyway?' Blackstrap asks, fitting his other hand into his second glove.

'Quebec.'

'Kaybec, eh? You got the pissy face of someone from Toronto.'

'No, Quebec.'

'Kaybec.' Blackstrap chuckles. 'You must be French then. I could hardly tell.'

'All RCMP officers speak—'

'I wasn't asking about *all* of nothing. You speak French, or what?'

'Yes, I do,' Pope admits.

'Kaybec. Bunch of frogs always get'n their way, ruling the fuh'k'n country. Separatists.' He stabs a gloved finger at his own chest. Above his heart.

Pope shakes his head. 'That's none of my business.'

'What?'

'I need to ask questions about your wife. That's everything today.'

Blackstrap Hawco turns his attention to his machine. He knows by the lagging sound that it will soon stall. The idling pin in need of adjusting. He watches it. Like his stare alone might set it right. But it dies. Cursing, he climbs down the rock. Jumping with one gloved hand against the boulder. Landing perfectly upright on his boots. He strides toward the backhoe.

'*My* woman,' says Blackstrap, brushing close to Constable Pope. 'Just in case ya got no idea where ya are, yer in Newfoundland, Frog, so don't fuh'k widt me.'

*

293

Karen's chest exposed. Breasts the only thing of her body seen and drawn upon. Lopsided Xs and uneven lines toward the shoulders. The scalpel slices a round incision. Mimics the shape of the left nipple and areola. The flesh is lifted away. Still connected to its underlying blood vessels and nerves. All intact. It sits by itself to the side. Another slit. From the bottom edge of the areola. Skin splitting apart. The gash running vertically to the crease underneath the breast. Yellow red purple innards. A curved slice across the breast's bottom round. An incision in a gentle arc. Mirrors the shape of your breasts. The fat, glandular matter and skin cut out. Removed. The nipple stretched by gravity is reduced. Your nipple and areola are relocated to their new spot. Skin from above and below the original incisions is now pulled together. Sutures installed. Your recovery will be brisk.

Blackstrap opens the bottle of beer while he stands at the kitchen window. He watches a shaggy orange, black and white cat stroll along the edge of the treeline. A stray. Its head big. Its fur thick. A tom. He can hear the low hum of an engine nearing. An all-terrain vehicle. No doubt Paddy Murphy on his way. Paddy could smell a bottle of beer before the cap was even popped.

The stray veers off the path and returns to the woods. Blackstrap leans nearer to see to the right. Where the railroad track has been taken up. A red ATV comes into view. Lurching ahead and navigating a sharp turn off the gravel bed. Going over on one back wheel and then tipping all the way. Paddy leaping sideways and landing in the lower boughs of a spruce tree. Paddy gets up right away. Like nothing has ever happened. Goes to the ATV, rights it and climbs on. His helmet seeming bigger than his skinny body.

Blackstrap had bought him the ATV. It was a mess when he got it from Ira Coombs. Blackstrap had worked on it. Finding new tires and putting a new engine in it. He had also bought Paddy a helmet and made him wear it. After Paddy's first accident that got him twelve stitches across his forehead.

The movement of black high in a tree. Blackstrap's attention caught by it. He thinks a crow might be settling there. Or lifting off. A lone crow. One for sorrow, he remembers. Looks to see a black garbage bag tattered and snagged in the higher branches. Stirred only by a bit of breeze.

The ATV bucks to a stop in front of the shed and Paddy gets off. He tugs at the helmet strap but can't get it loose. He pulls up on the helmet but it won't come off. Blackstrap takes a sip of beer. Snorts in amusement. Almost spits the beer out in the sink.

Paddy finally manages to get the strap loose. Hauls off the helmet and carefully lays it on the seat of the ATV. But he misses and the helmet hits the ground. Wobbles a few feet before settling. Paddy heads toward the back door. Bangs on it. Comes in. All the same action. His body making noise. In the porch, he bends and unlaces his boots. Out of breath and exasperated by the time he's done.

Blackstrap pulls another beer from the fridge. Pops it open. He hands it to Paddy who takes it and gives a small shy grin. Showing off his missing front tooth. Before sucking back the bottle.

'Thirsty,' says Blackstrap.

'Cripes, it's some hot out,' says Paddy. His thin bangs plastered to his forehead.

Blackstrap looks at the window. It's almost winter. The air cold. Crisp. He sits at the kitchen table. 'What's all the news?'

Paddy stays standing. Not the sort to ever sit. He folds his arms and leans against the counter. Crosses his thin legs. Unfolds his thin arms.

'Billy Fowler's on a job in Mackinsons and needs a door.'

'How much you tell him?'

'Ten bucks.'

'Good.'

Paddy winks. Drinks back the beer. Knows he's done good. Proud to be of assistance. The bottle emptied now. A satisfied sound through an opened mouth.

'He needs a staircase, too. You got one, right?'

'I got that staircase from a hundred-year-old house on Shearstown Line. Byron Pelley's.'

'Behind the shed.' Paddy nods. Tosses his thumb toward the kitchen window. Just to show that he knows. Folds his arms again.

'Let's load it up. Take a few for the road.'

Paddy goes to the fridge. Squeezes two beer bottles into his front jeans pockets. Takes two more in his hands.

Outside, Blackstrap opens the shed. He flicks on the light switch. Moves in alongside the stacked junks of wood and salvaged windows. Toward the doors in the back.

'He want steel or panelled?'

'Steel,' says Paddy. Stood in the open doorway. He lays down the bottles on the concrete floor. Bends to tie up his laces.

Blackstrap checks one of the old window casings. Thought he saw a crack. But it was only the reflection of a web overhead. 'Billy need any windows?'

'Never said.'

Blackstrap lifts the door and carries it out.

'Dat a new welder?' Paddy moves out of his way. Eyes on the welding machine just inside the door.

'Got it from Kelly's Shop closed down in Carbonear.' Blackstrap walks to the pickup and puts the door aboard. 'Kelly's gone off ta Alberta. Gimme a hand with that staircase.'

Paddy loads the beer bottles onto the passenger seat. Then trails unsteadily after Blackstrap. 'Moose,' he says. Stopping dead. Pointing at the ground.

Blackstrap comes back. Watches where Paddy is pointing. 'A calf by the looks of it.' His eyes trace over the hoof prints. Track them off toward the woods.

Paddy checks that way, too. Then looks at Blackstrap's face. Wondering what might be done about it.

'No time for that now,' he says. Thinking of the moose steaks in the deep freeze. In the basement. Enough for a while yet. Nothing to do with all that extra meat.

Paddy nods. Follows after Blackstrap to the back of the shed.

The staircase there on the ground. Grass growing up over it. 'You tell him how much?'

Paddy shakes his head. Frowns.

'Hundred-year-old stairs.'

'Twenty bucks,' says Paddy. Shrugging. Hands in his jeans pockets.

'Sounds 'bout right. Let's load 'er up.'

They bend and lift the staircase. It's damp underneath. Where it was set against the grass for a year or more. Not so heavy for two men to handle.

In the pickup, Blackstrap watches the road ahead.

'They locked Isaac Tuttle in the mental,' says Paddy. Pops open one of the beer bottles. On the seat between them. Drinks from it right away.

Blackstrap says nothing. Waiting.

Paddy sniffs. Swallows another drink. The bottle half empty. He looks at the level through the brown glass. Then he pops open another. Hands it to Blackstrap who pries it down between his legs.

'The Waterford. Went fuh'k'n nuts.'

Blackstrap lifts the bottle. Takes a drink. His mind on the highway leading into St. John's. Planning the fastest route. Once done with the door and staircase.

The call comes in and is forwarded to Constable Pope's desk. Brenda Sparkes from community relations at the Health Science Complex in St. John's.

'We have a Karen Hawco here,' she says. 'Not in emergency, but admitted for surgery. Residence listed as St. John's though.'

'Why is she there?'

'Elective surgery. Can't say much more.'

'Thank you.' He hangs up. In the hospital for surgery. The case should be closed, but he thinks of Blackstrap Hawco. The lack of care he showed for his wife. He considers putting a call into the St. John's Constabulary. To have the woman's identity checked. How would he justify it? There is not enough evidence to proceed any further with the investigation.

He looks at his watch. St. John's is less than an hour away. His shift over in fifty minutes. He considers requesting authorization to travel to St. John's. He might suggest that the woman is in a state of disorientation. He knows her. He might help ease the conflict. Instead, he tells the commanding officer that they have found Karen Hawco. She is having routine surgery.

The file is considered closed.

When his shift ends, he changes in the detachment locker room and exits by the back door. Climbs into his car. One hundred and twenty kilometers all the way in. He barely notices the landscape. A flash of mossy barrens and boulders and density of evergreens. Karen Hawco's face forefront in his thoughts.

He is on Kenmount Road in St. John's before he realizes. He takes an exit onto the Parkway and heads for the Health Sciences Complex. He pulls into a visitor space and feeds the meter. Enters the building. Asks at the booth for Karen Hawco's room number. He is given the number without question: 314 west block, fifth floor. He takes the elevator up with another civilian visitor and follows the big blue signs.

Finding the desired corridor and approaching the doorway, he sees a man leaving 314. The man is of medium height and carries a large shoulder bag. Brown hair. He resembles Karen Hawco around the eyes and lips. He does not watch the man as he passes. The doorway is left open a crack. Pope pauses, struck by a sense of dislocation. One place to another in a flash. A wave of unreality that recedes at his will.

He gently knocks on the door. No answer comes. He leans in.

The woman is in the bed. Her eyes shut. Her face a sickly pallor. The colour of post-op. Greenish-yellow.

He steps in further.

The woman makes a muffled noise. Then another. She is just coming to. Waking up. She opens her eyes and stares flatly at the man. A man she does not know. Then a look of slow wonder on her pale face.

'Karen Hawco?'

Her soft voice barely heard. Maybe a 'yes.'

'You remember me?'

Cash in his pocket. The staircase and door dropped off. Blackstrap fills the tank of the pickup. Paddy back there with Billy to lend a hand. Working for smokes and beer. And maybe, if lucky, a bit of whiskey later in the day. A kitchen table with a bottle between them. Smokes and conversation until the wee hours.

The nozzle clicks off. Blackstrap goes inside to settle up. Rayna, the girl behind the counter, pays him no extra attention. She's grown up over all those years. He knew her when she was a baby. What she didn't know. She might be his. He never asked for sure. Her mother, Pamela Goobie.

He pockets his change. Takes a look at Rayna. Memorizes her face. Not a hint of him in her. Then gives her a nod.

A man just like any other man paying for his gas.

Outside, going down the step. He notices that it's uneven. He backs away from it. A shoddy job, that stair and railings. A bit of rot down along the trim board. The clapboard not overlapping. The water trapping there. Being drawn in to rot the sill. He tries to think of who built the structure. Someone working for Isaac Tuttle. He remembers that it was Fred Peddle. A man who'd slap anything together just to get the job done. Money-grubber. Not a stain of pride in him.

Blackstrap gives up on the idea and climbs into his pickup. Starts it. Shifts to drive. Heads out for the highway. St. John's. The Waterford. Isaac Tuttle. The fucker.

With a current population of approximately 150,000, St. John's, the capital city of the province of Newfoundland, was only a small but thriving port town when it burnt to the ground twice in the 1800s. Shortly after Patrick's arrival, he became one of the many hundreds of Irish workers employed to rebuild the town. While Patrick was busy with his often highly introspective exploits, Rose Cavanagh's pregnancy took on a magical quality, as documented in the infamously outlandish journal entries of Bishop Flax.

1886

Where Patrick Lambly arrives in a charred St. John's and witnesses a drop from the gallows

The sky in the distance, toward where Patrick suspected the harbour might be, was polluted with a lingering mass of greys and blacks. The clouded disturbance plumed from land and hung in a broad area, surrounded by an expanse of otherwise blue sky. *For it was newly daylight and pristine*, thought Patrick, *unfortunate and unbecoming with smudge*, understanding – despite his vaguely inebriated state – that only one thing might be capable of causing such a pestilent expulsion. *Smear, not smudge*, his mind corrected, bargaining with himself for a more fitting word.

Perhaps the exact word might be: Fire. Yet who really cared for these exact measures of things? Far better for a poet to be ambiguous and at war with common intention.

Since first sighting land, a curious crowd had gathered on the deck of the four-master. From miles off, traces of smoke could be detected on the breeze. As pessimistic, foreboding comments were passed from one passenger to the other, the mood that overcame the gathering was pervasively grim, for what else could be felt when faced with the sight of their supposed place of landing burnt to the ground?

Lament and woe and the thrilling flutter of tragedy in the breast,
for – at last – life had delivered what had been secretly expected.

Ask Mary Snow, thought Patrick, who stood off by herself. Ask her of her feelings about arriving at this unspoiled place of promise. With her eyes downcast since her abusive ordeal with two British soldiers, her mind appeared ruthlessly torn to expose the gape she stared into. She lingered near enough to no one. No matter how much kind attention was extended by the ladies on board, Mary Snow shirked away.

There she stood now, off toward the foremast, the silent one among the drone of gossip and speculation, a shawl wrapped tightly around her head and shoulders. Rarely did she make such a showing of herself. With the craft nearing land now, she fidgeted, seeming greatly agitated, and cast her eyes round, no doubt searching for Ferrol, who was otherwise occupied.

As the four-master neared the narrows, a giant chain – comprised of links as broad as a man's chest – became evident. The vessel, swinging its sails around, barely slowed to a pace sufficient to endure the chain pressing against its bow and not having it rip entirely through the wood. The chain was strung across the air and at a height to wreak enough havoc upon a ship's hull as to send it to the bottom of the sea.

Casting a look in one direction, and coughing at the wafting stench of smoke, Patrick saw, through the hazy grey that soon thickened and drifted to clear like fog, the chain running off to the north where it was attached to an alcove in the cliff that rose, in an etched, jagged incline, five hundred feet above them. The opposite end of the chain ran to the south and was fastened to the south-side craggy cliff that rose to less of a height. Beyond the chain, and the narrow, protective opening allowed by the gap in these cliffs, the masts of wooden ships and steamers could be seen cloaked in smoke where they were anchored to the docks in the calm belly of the harbour. Sighting those boats, Patrick was brought to mind of the *Venus*, the vessel they had originally departed Ireland on, further north on an uncharted point, where it was set afloat by Ferrol, with dead Americans on the deck and blood spilled aplenty. It was only Ferrol, having risen from his incidental state of unconsciousness to obliterate the American lot, who was permitted to enfold Mary Snow in his arms and comfort her.

Beside Patrick, Mary Snow, having drifted nearer, coughed and wept silently at the sight of the plain of sooty black. It would all be amusing if it were not so blatantly pathetic. Patrick thought to touch Mary Snow in reassurance, yet feared an outburst and an attack upon his being. Where buildings and houses once stood, there were now charred sticks poking up like huge decimated tombstones, chewed into pitch by some monstrous gargoyle, the ground saturated in smutty, black spew.

The giant chain remained fastened before them. Gradually, as the vessel, unable to be reversed promptly, pressed against the chain, the links drew groans from the wood and snapped a board or two above the waterline, thus provoking a round of yells and gasps from the on-deck passengers, before the vessel eased away in a lagging liquid bob and reverse lure.

As far as Patrick was concerned, the chain could remain in place. There were other, more lively places where they might land. No doubt there were villages, as in Ireland, up and down the coast. Why not try another port with a bit of unburnt colour? No doubt there might be other masters just as willing to enslave in those districts. Yet Ferrol, miraculously recovered from the gunshot wounds that barely penetrated his flesh and were picked out of his thick hide by the fingernails of two spinsters, and no less the worse for the devastation he had enacted upon the American sailors from the *American Pride*, pushed up from the rear to investigate. First, he studied Mary Snow's face and offered a few grumbles of consolation, then checked the sea to offer a 'fack this' and 'fack that' before climbing onto the rope banister and making a leap for the barrier chain which he snatched hold of in both his hands. Wildly swaying back and forth from the momentum of his propelled advance, he hung with one hand, as though in playful jest with himself, and waited a few moments until he was adequately stabilized and well-humoured. There was little movement or talk on board as all watched Ferrol progress, hand over hand, toward the cliff. The passengers appeared to be struck with awe, yet were also filled with fear of the place to which they might soon be entering. Ferrol, growing smaller and smaller, followed the chain to the flat of land where the final link was secured and fell onto the rocks.

In time, the chain dropped with a snaky splash,

a fuse lit by water
trailing along the width of the sea.

The passengers and crew stood in wait, wondering what unexpected feat might occur next. Absurdly, as the circumstance seemed quite dire, jokes were passed back and forth and backs were slapped by the ignoramuses of the lot. Dim-witted men still drooling in admiration of Ferrol made calls into the space that separated the heroic from the lot. After Ferrol's bare-fisted slaughter of the Americans as they boarded the *Venus*, a scene that would be spoken of daily and for decades on various continents, the specifics altered and made into greater impossibility, with Ferrol alternately named as a god or a demon, the passengers and crew had invested their complete faith in him and allowed him to undertake the captaining of the four-master, *American Pride*, despite his minimal knowledge related to such affairs. The crew had given him the required information and he had caught on at once, nodding in a clipped fashion and chortling at the easiness of the understanding, anxious to get on with the duties associated with his new station. A mere two days later he would take not another word of advice, adamant about tackling any imminent challenge under his own steam.

Occasionally, a drift of smoke filled the air, harshly invading the lungs. Coughs sprang from the passengers who were forced to cover their mouths and shield their burning eyes, while others, including Mary Snow, retired to the lavish berths that had been afforded the Americans on that beautifully stolen ship, now ransacked, with any removable item or object of value that might be unscrewed or pried from its foundation shoved away into the ship trunks or bags of the Irish passengers to be used in barter upon shore.

Patrick watched ahead at the smouldering remains, cursing himself for leaving Limerick while filling his mind with punishing images of his wife and children clutching hold of each other in the sourly oppressive stillness of their dark hovel. The thought of them increased his thirst, as did the invasive smoke, and he removed the flask from his hip pocket, a silver vessel carved with an unrecognizable insignia lifted from one of the bodies of the bastard American sailors, and drank until it was half drained. There was a vast store of rum barrels still on board, despite the continuous merriment they had drained from them, night after night at sea, out on that gorgeously drunken night water and under those gorgeously drunken stars that mesmerized the mind with heavenly clarity. Over the past week, there had been endless celebrations and toasts to their good fortune, while the stories of Ferrol's courageous rage were retold from every angle as seen through every set of eyes, and luck was not only expected but said to be predestined to visit each passenger upon reaching their new home port.

With the rum fresh in Patrick's throat and belly, cleansing away trepidation, he assured himself that, yes, this city would be fine. What more harm could possibly come of it? And, yes, he would send money back to his family in due time, once he sold the items he had salvaged from their lovely American ship. And once the money was depleted from the selling, he would send money from his employment, if, in fact, the master to whom he had been indentured was still drawing breath in the charred city. If not that master, then another one who might be more than a negligible pile of ash.

More rum, he thought, draining the remainder in his silver flask, becoming even more of a free spirit.

As the speculative mutterings of misunderstood direction became more prevalent, there came sight of a dull splashing that progressed toward the vessel and there was Ferrol swimming with great strokes back to the boat, where he soon climbed up over the side, and with a grunt of consternation and without a nod to anyone, trod – in his sopping clothes and with glistening head – up to the captain's bridge where he ordered the sails swung around.

In time, they edged through the narrows, between the towers of ancient wind-and-sea-chiselled rock and into the thickening grey hollow that was the mouth of the harbour.

All was in ruin, save for two stone towers up on the rise of what might have been a basilica, the single building seemingly unharmed by the devastating blaze that had blackened everything to ash.

The noise of coughing rose as the tears streamed down the faces of all on board, stung by the soot, as they docked at the foot of the charred city of St. John's,

a hideously sullen mystery,
looming larger and blacker,
and as far removed from the immaculate,
wrapped in its enchanting affliction as it were.

Rose Cavanagh began to show in October and planned ahead. The baby taken by the fairies, an infant of fair skin and fair hair, had been replaced by a black-haired girl with brown eyes and teeth that grew in black and rotted before the growth was due. Three months later, when Rose's pregnancy began to make itself evident, the changeling screeched for three days, shredding the air with its noise in a more vigorous fashion when in Rose's arms, as though wanting less and less to do with its counterfeit mother. At night, the screeching could be heard throughout Bareneed, rising and ebbing up and down the coastline as though carried on the back of a great desecrating bird. It robbed the residents of their sleep and clutched the village in the grips of ill ease. It frightened birds from their nests, where eggs were left abandoned, and spurred animals to flee the nearby woods, where traps and snares were discovered bare each day.

It was rumoured that the wail of the baby had set a curse over the settlement, the older and more grizzled of the men and women, professing in their ancient language, no longer understood by the youth who had been born on the rock of Newfoundland, that the baby must be tended to with the appropriate remedies. She was to be wrapped in cloth, the entirety of its body, from head to toe, and dipped in vinegar, sprinkled in sugar and baked in the oven for not long enough to scorch it too fiercely. No, they laughed among themselves, it were but a joke, that remedy. A good fit of laughter was had with faces etched in lines and chins curved by time and eyes made sappy by death and love and injury and acceptance and the waning of all of this lost again and again, settling on what other but acceptance. Only to laugh. Yet in austere reality, as the younger people were worried for their survival, it was decided that – for the sake of self-preservation – the infant must be smothered in its sleep, catch the dying screech in a pillowcase, tie it at one end and let it float to the moon where the face might swallow it, for not only was the screech driving life away from the area, its harrowing, dispiriting call was certain to infest the baby that Rose was presently carrying and any other baby that was living in the womb of any woman who heard or felt the infant's piercing lament. As luck would have it, while the residents were secretly speculating on the best means of putting the infant to death, by fire, water or stone, the baby perished on the eve of the third day of its outburst, with Rose feeling nothing for the loss, other than confusion and, as was steadily becoming one of her fundamental attributes, guilt.

Yet this was not enough. Dementedly suspecting that the fairy infant had been the offspring of the daughter, Elizabeth, as opposed to the mother, Rose, the villagers lured Elizabeth away and dealt with her in the woods where she was roped to a tree and left to the hands of her kin, the fairies. In time, as suspected, the girl screeched in the same manner as the perished infant, the voice of them one and the same, sprung from their misbegotten bloodline. On returning to release the girl from her bindings and offer burial, it was discovered that she had vanished, transported off by the fairies. Sighting her removal, the hearts of the villagers were lightened as they were now secure in their belief that all would return to normal.

Despite the suspicions of evil infestation, the infant was permitted burial, without the rite of holy sacrament, behind the cemetery beside the damned remains of Tommy Cavanagh. For a full day, the muddled screeching could be heard by wanderers strolling near the cemetery, the sense of suppressed and suffocated rage shivering the ground beneath their feet, and, again, the villagers were troubled by a predicament that cried out, yet again, for more pervasive action. On the second day, however, following Rose's dream of the baby clawing through the ground to gnaw at her husband, Tommy's rotting body, the baby was silenced. It was this flesh that made the screeching stop, this eating, it was said.

Rose was shunned by the other women and children. Even the naked children, who she had blindly and despondently taken for her own, avoided her, and ran off to occupy another room in one of the tilts where a place was made for them, as was the welcoming tradition. It was only the twisted boy, a body which remained nameless in its deformity, who kept pressed against the wall, watching what might happen with the changing form of the woman who was growing to the point of bursting.

With Rose's husband and daughter gone and with the village unwilling to provide nourishment for her, her body wasted away, her belly alone continuing to grow. Her pregnancy, while anticipated with both dread and starving, hysterical curiosity, arrived at the end of its nine-month expectancy, yet there was no birth. Rose had taken to her bough bed and was tended to by the twisted boy who lingered near, watching Rose's face and fiercely chattering in an unintelligible language about some personal menace that existed in a land private to him. On some nights, the twisted boy slept by Rose's side, thickly curled up on the floor with limbs cast off at all angles. Other nights, he went no one knew where, hobbling about across the fields and into the wilderness, returning with murdered things, snuffed out of existence by his carnivorous leer alone, to feed the woman with the bauble belly.

In the middle of the tenth month, the sense of fullness turned excruciating. Rose's back ached so terribly that the roots of her teeth felt as though they were scratching, prying, gouging deeper into her unhinging jawbone. She sweated continuously and was fed food collected by the twisted boy whom Rose could not bear to look upon. Any face was painful to watch. The mere movements of her eyes were enough to make her plea with the Creator for mercy. She ate only what was required, for the food made her feel ill, poisoned, its taste akin to nothing she had ever encountered.

The twisted boy came and went, chattering and groaning, and nodding while he rubbed herbs and spices on Rose's forehead in the sign of a broken, one-winged cross.

On her eleventh month of pregnancy, Rose's skin turned green, and her fingernails fell off. The roots of her hair grew out grey and she urinated continuously without moving, her back punishing her with gruelling pain. Her face had shrunken to such a degree that she was unrecognizable as herself or any other form, and her arms wasted away to the thinness of twigs. In time, her hair collapsed from her skull as she seemed to age a decade a month.

The twisted boy continued with his vigil, polishing the pink glowing belly with a lotion made from spit and all manners of human and wilderness excretion. It was said to be fit to drive the baby out. Hands lifted beneath flesh and knees and elbows stirred. There was constant movement, as though there was not a baby inside Rose, but an entirety of civilization, churning and moving and evolving from the state of her woe into a less worrisome state of something else entirely.

The twisted boy touched the hard, shifting limbs, fastened under skin, trying to clutch hold of them, and laughed in a guttural frenzy of excitement that made him straighten, loom larger and more erect, and then shrink back to his previous position of contortion when the final horsy hiccups of laughter were swallowed down his throat.

When the four-master docked at the Job Brothers wharf in St. John's, a crowd was gathered to greet the vessel. There seemed to be much fuss brewing, for a murmur rose up at the confounding sight of the unanticipated four-master. Store owners and fishmongers stood in wait, speculating and pointing.

From the deck, Patrick watched the crowd

> with the great black skeletal backdrop
> of the charred city
> still warmly radiating behind those onlookers,
> who stared seaward,
> as though we might be a sight stranger
> than the gloomy bluster they near perished in.

Most were overcome with the occasional fit of wheezing or coughing, while others shifted on their feet, for the ground still breathed heat beneath their leather soles. Up and down the line of carriages, horses sneezed, and shook their heads, jangling their fittings. Regardless of the manner of the merchants' attire or the height or weight of their physique, there was one thing they all had in common: eyes trained on the line of men and women that moved down the gangplank, wondering which would be their labourers and hoping for the most strapping or becoming of the lot.

Other men were present, in their soiled Sunday best with hats in hand, to meet their wives and children whose new-found presence before them would make their days a percentage more bearable. There was much celebration, despite the harsh linger of smoke that collected soot in their nostrils and lungs.

Patrick stood on the dock in uncertainty, wishing he might have a draught from his flask, but a show of that sort might prejudice him in the eyes of his employer who, no doubt, lingered near. Bodies brushed by him, taking up with their escorts. He noticed Mary Snow being met by a tall broad man who roughly took her arm and led her away. Patrick checked around for Ferrol, but could catch no sight of him.

While the labourers continued to disembark, Ferrol made his way down the plank, treading with his meaty arms wrapped around a barrel where he plunked it beside Patrick to the chuckles, outright cheers and eventual applause of the passengers and crew.

'Rum fer all,' he shouted, the merchants understanding the word rum, for it was the exact equivalent in English. The men turned back for the boat, as though having forgotten their bounty, and rolled or shimmied barrels down the plank, one for each labourer, although some went back for a second, as there was a fortune of them, no doubt recently looted from a trading ship by the American pirates.

A man toward the front of the crowd began shouting for a spell of quiet, and then the names of the men were loudly and clearly spoken, one by one, putting an end to their merriment and congratulatory remarks. Each singled-out man stepped forward, on legs unaccustomed to the steadiness of land, and was met by a merchant's servant on foot or a merchant himself, who, after casting his eyes over the shape and size of the body before him, merely turned, expecting the Irishman to follow on his heels. The rum barrels were left where they sat, the merchants unwilling to accept what they suspected to be ill-gotten cargo taken on as baggage.

When Patrick's name was shouted, he reluctantly stepped forward. For the fortification of bravery, he had gone a touch overboard in his consumption of rum as they neared shore. A tall, slim man dressed in a long coat and a bowler hat, and with a once-white handkerchief to his mouth, glanced him up and down.

'Patrick Lambly,' said the merchant, lowering the handkerchief only briefly to confirm the allocation.

It were me name 'fore da voyage,
spoke he in broken Irish,
yet I've adopted anudder now.
Call me Prince Patrick if ye wish
son o' da great king Ferrol.

He pointed a wavering arm back to where Ferrol was unloading the barrels and stacking them on the wharf beside the others. Wiping his hands together, Ferrol took a suspicious glance over the Irishmen being committed to their masters. With a condemning scoff, he then turned and stomped back up the plank.

The merchant shook his head. 'Speak English. And plainly, not in song.'

Patrick nodded, understanding the word English. He winked at the merchant and gestured to the barrels by his side. 'These'll need escorting. The liddle ones.'

The merchant, done with paying the ship's master, shook his head. 'I won't have any of that. Come.' In haste, he turned toward the carriages and strode off, only glancing back when he reached his vehicle to see Patrick still stood there, watching down at the barrel with a look of dour and calamitous uncertainty

for the ruination o'
me bounteous expectations
for the kindest of loves cradled
within those curved staves

and waving his arm at the barrels, he bade them farewell, going so far as to devoutly blow them a kiss and pledge his eternal commitment and adoration.

Soon, the screeching from Rose matched that of her perished infant and sacrificed daughter, Elizabeth. Yet rather than drive the birds and animals from the wood, Rose's cry appeared to beckon to them, for their numbers increased as they arrived in abundance. The traps and snares were filled each day, not one life-taking hole left unstuffed, and the goat and cow and chickens in the yards produced offspring in startlingly unnatural numbers, the screech seemingly inciting them toward rampant copulation.

The villagers, rather than suspect Rose's cry to be the foreshadowing or laying down of a curse, and riding on the changing tide, as the hordes were eventually wont to do, took the screech for a sign of prosperity and celebrated their new-found gift. 'T'anks be ta da Lard. T'anks be ta Awmighty God,' could be heard muttered extensively through the village when thoughts of the fresh extravagance disburdened a resident.

Animals were brought on ropes to the doorway of Rose's shack to hear the screech and then were led away, back to their yards or stalls where cow and goat might give birth to offspring numbered as high as four or five at once. The additional two pregnant women in Bareneed were coaxed near to the withered and screeching form with the shining distended belly, to touch the glistening orb that had a stench of mucous and seed filth.

The twisted boy officiated over the proceedings, speaking in his unintelligible language and grunting this way and that while the villagers commiserated with him about his day and night duty, or praised him to the high heavens for being party to the miracle of the screech.

The crows that had once alighted on the roof of the shack in staggering numbers, their claws scraping for a grip on the crowded surface that was a moving, living feathered cloak of black, were driven off by robins and finches and other birds of previously unseen shapes and colours that were diverted from their migratory paths by the gorgeous resound of the life-giving screech.

At night, fires were built outside the shack and instruments were tuned to the pitch of the screech. The music derived from the noise was chaotic and barbarous and tipped the singing and drinking beyond the celebration of life toward its murderous undercurrent that knew of the truthful need of its own perishing. Men and women were murdered at the edge of the woods to make room for new life. A war had come about, whereby animals multiplied fiercely in the ravage of attack while the people became removed from one another.

Jealousy of wealth, previously unknown to the residents of Bareneed, sprang up as ships arrived to load the copious numbers of livestock and pelts. From the credits written down by the merchant, lumber and windows were purchased from the merchant's mill, and each tilt was built onto, receiving a second storey, which gave the tilts the look of proper houses, although they remained less than that.

Above all, the merchants prospered, buying the goods for the cheapest price and reselling at a commendable profit to other merchants along the coast. It was a marvel for all to see, and ships arrived so that those on board might watch up at the sky at the miracle of birds and the meadows and valleys that were overrun by rabbits, partridge, moose and fox. They watched in marvellous disbelief yet would not set foot on shore for fear of having the screech enter them too deeply.

While the people of Bareneed towered among the animals, they were little different in their intentions. When not hidden away in bush, house or barn, clutched together in the breakneck throes of coupling, they stood in the fields with their hands jammed down their trousers or up their skirts, then over their ears, waving at the ships for moments at a time and grinning at the money-giving visitors who had come to witness the lusty bounty bestowed upon them by the screech.

The wood was milled to the north of St. John's and carried to the merchant centre by horse and carriage. Other materials were offloaded from ships docked from Boston and Halifax. The majority of the reconstruction was financed by funds received from Governor Harvey's appeal for relief abroad. The call of distress was briskly answered by Great Britain, the United States and the British North American colonies. The Peel Government, although in the throes of dissolution, committed £5,000, with an additional £25,000 pledged by the incoming government. At once, the Nova Scotian government delivered £1,000, while the citizens of Halifax collected £1,500 to be set toward the purchase of provisions. The total amount of donations reached approximately £41,000.

With these large amounts of capital arriving daily, Patrick was often in the company of labourers who speculated on the most proficient means of making off with portions of those funds. *Naw all of it*, the workers would jest, *I'd be satisfied wid jus' a wee bit*, while rubbing their thumbs and forefingers together. Conversations were laughed over in the public houses, with nothing coming of it, other than a sorry head in the morning and the grumbling or blearily silent return to raising walls.

Although this was not the work expected by Patrick – he had assumed it would be in the netting or curing of cod – he fancied the act of building. From it, something substantial, something created, might be walked away from at the end of the day. In the outdoors, working among men, while the *Sassenach* supervisor wandered about inspecting the progress, the occasional rum nip was passed secretly between the men as a remedy to the back-breaking boredom of hammering. With the alcohol alighting their senses, the men spoke openly of their elaborate adventures at sea and at home in their villages, yet confessed there were meagre stories to be had in a town of this size, only ceaseless work and the foolish yarns of urban exploits or the grand tales of currency passed back and forth between the merchants who visited to watch the erection of their new premises. The men laboured for weeks on end, sleeping only four or five hours each night.

During these months of reconstruction, Patrick learned the farcical story of the great fire from the workers who had been present at the disaster. It was said that the fire was started by an overturned glue pot in the shop of a cabinet maker on George Street. The wooden frame of the shop went ablaze and the adjoining tenements were quickly engulfed. At once, the fire alarm was sounded, yet it took near half an hour for the fire engines to arrive at the scene. By this time, an entire block was spouting flames while the firemen moved about in fits of inaction for they were prevented from proceeding with their duties for want of water.

The story was told in varying tones of drama and comedy, for the event was rife with ineptitude.

Governor Harvey, in an attempt to create a gap that might dam the further spread of the fire, had ordered a derelict house on the south side of Water Street to be blown up with gunpowder. The resulting explosion, rather than exercising any sort of relief, only further exacerbated the situation by sending chunks of glowing, fiery timber of varying sizes for blocks in all directions, which rained down, most notably, on several churches and the Roman Catholic school.

'Dis be da sort o' moronic leadership we be afforded,' one fellow labourer griped. 'Dis miserable colony be run by da usual lot of *Sassenach* crooks 'n 'alfwits.'

It was said that over half of the total population of 30,000 had been left homeless and this was evidenced by the roaming men, women and children who stood in the streets staring at the construction with tormented eyes, or wandered in a ravaged state of sleeplessness and ceaseless annoyance and disquiet.

It was months before the scent of greasy soot would dissipate. And each time that Patrick Lambly thought of St. John's, after he had fled the place, he would recall the town as a grim, smouldering smear of black that would not leave the skin, no matter how often the hands were washed. The faces always with a smudge or the blackness passed from hand to hand during the clasp of hands in friendly meeting. There was no way to be ever clean of it.

He had been under his master's servitude for near six months, rebuilding the stone walls of the Anglican church on Church Hill, when word reached him that Mary Snow, the woman who had travelled with them aboard the *Venus* and then the *American Pride*, had been convicted of murdering her husband, James Snow, of Port de Grave. According to rumour, she was to be hanged from the drop erected at the west end of the courthouse. At once, Patrick thought to tell Ferrol of the occasion. What might Ferrol think of such a thing, and what might the man do in reaction to this, obviously, unjust deed? Yet Ferrol had been a mystery to Patrick for months, disappearing for long stretches without explanation or penalty, it seemed, only to arrive back at work when it suited him.

The nip of winter was in the air and the stone walls they had been labouring over were now erected, leaving Patrick and the crew to nail up the inner wooden walls. In the cold, it became difficult to swing a hammer steadily for extended periods without having the tool catapult from the half-numb hand to deliver an unsuspected blow to some nearby innocent. Labourers steadily bore the marks of such injuries on their faces and bodies. The cold was beginning to grow unbearable and men soon lost fingers and toes to frostbite, despite the fire barrels that were kept lit within the structures.

So it was with relief that the men were given leisure time to witness the hanging of Mary Snow, a rarity in the colony. Women were infrequently hanged, and this one, who was with child, had come near to being pardoned due to her delicate condition. However, in the end, it was only the scheduled whipping which was stayed. A tactic that seemed overly harsh, as the lash might have been seen to injure the unborn child should the lash inadvertently strike the belly.

A huge crowd had congregated around the grounds of the stone courthouse, the sight of the erected gallows causing a stare of famished speculation among those gathered in wait. The mass of people was so extensive that Patrick suspected that every resident of the town was present to witness the event. There were men of high office in tailored suits and coats and ruddy-faced labourers in patched cast-offs. Women in flowery hats and furs were flanked by servants and nannies who tended to the children who reached with their arms and demanded to be lifted for a more panoramic view. The homeless were everywhere, like grey blots amid blots of glorious colour. Three boys in floppy hats and shabby clothes, worn threadbare at the knees and elbows, clung to the iron fence that marked the property of the church Patrick had been labouring over. They clutched stones in their fists and whistled, trying to scale the bars to hang from the top vertical rail. The volume of conversation rose steadily, the ruckus charged with the taint of grim conjecture. Gradually, the buzz fell to silence as though a wave of deadness had wormed its way through the crowd.

Mary Snow, a small figure in the distance, appeared on the bare stage of the gallows. She was dressed in a black crêpe gown with jet beads fastened up the front. The gown, which neatly obscured the bulge of her belly, had been donated by one of the noted ladies of position in the city. There had been many offers of such gowns and yet Lady Bowering had been chosen as the lucky donator, having been more soundly connected with officials in the government.

Mary Snow stood upon the stage and allowed her hands to be bound behind her back by the executioner. The sound of her remote weeping carried out over the crowd, with Patrick, at such a distance, catching only the occasional high disquieting pitch of it. She was weeping weakly, the roll and ebb of the sound evident in the crisp air. Puffs of breath issued from her mouth, for her breath was warmer than most, although as the entertainment carried on, Patrick noticed the thickening of the puffs of breath escaping each and every mouth.

Patrick expected a hood to be placed over the woman's face, as was the procedure for men who were hanged, yet this courtesy was not afforded the woman. She was Irish, after all, thought Patrick, and he felt his chest tighten with emotion at the thought of her words spoken to him after one of his poetic rants along the journey before she was savaged by the American soldiers: 'Ye 'av a fine tongue fer verse.' Hearing those words in his mind, he felt impelled to press through the crowd to free the woman. Yet she had murdered her husband, hadn't she? Wasn't she due severe treatment? Or had her husband brought it on himself? He recalled how Mary Snow had been taken away by a large man on the dock. Had that man been her husband? Either way, it was some sort of puzzling, convoluted lover's tale. Another man had been involved, who had been hung in secrecy a month or more ago. A bald-headed man, according to description, who laughed outright as the noose was opened around his neck. Patrick took a swig from his flask and cast a glance to the side, seeing Ferrol there, having appeared out of nowhere. Patrick offered the flask to Ferrol, who, without removing his eyes from the gallows ahead, gave a slight shake of his head and raised a stern hand. So unlike him to deny himself a bit of morning libation.

Overhead, a stone arced through the air and clattered and rolled against the wood while one of the boys laughed in mockery. Ferrol searched toward the source. A few others in the crowd, men and women, chuckled at the exactness of the aim. Another boy hurled a stone and a dull crack was heard, as it had struck Mary Snow on the skull, her head tilting slightly, her face marked by a look of dumb bewilderment. This sound brought forth greater laughter,

> of the sort lurking to rupture and burst forth
> when the brutal ugliness of the world
> was cast in humour, as was not often enough the case.

'Dis be da worse sort o' offence,' Patrick quietly whispered, yet was shushed by a woman behind him who poked him in the back with the tip of her widow's parasol.

316

'Faaaack,' said Ferrol in agreement.

Patrick drank more as the noose was opened and loosely placed over Mary Snow's head. With a tug, it was fitted snugly to her pale throat. Now, as realization hugged her neck, her weeping turned to open tears and cries for mercy, begging for the sparing of her unborn child. The child, thought Patrick, the prodigy of one of those dead Americans. At the sound of this plea, Ferrol made a step forward yet was held back by the tightly packed crowd, his eyes trained on the woman, as though his stare alone might forestall the tragedy.

Another stone clattered on the wooden staging. This time, there was a greater ripple of amusement, while Ferrol thrust deeper into the seemingly impenetrable mass, not caring who he might jostle aside.

Ears ringing in expectation, Patrick took another drink and turned away. He heard a prayer being recited by a derelict old man with shut eyes, who Patrick noticed in passing, and then the trap door opened and the hush of the crowd became its own dead-still, living entity swarming to hide in the heart and mind of each living person.

An instant of regrettable exclamation that held him from within and without. The pull of the crowd's breaths united as one as though sucked into a furnace of hell where their thoughts now delivered them. And yet, in a single moment, they were relieved, for they had committed not one wrong deed. It was the woman, after all, who had taken the life of a man, the woman who they would fear no more, the woman who, it was said, held a bastard child in her belly.

A lone voice then sounded, issuing from above his head, so that he looked to see a man standing on a box and calling out into the crowd: 'In the presence of a multitude its comparative loneliness chills the heart. Hear this. The value accompaniments are forgotten in the ideal grandeur which gathers round the scaffold on which the last penalty of the offended justice is endured. We are alone here this day. Alone in multitude.'

The voice continued as Patrick, in a state of blur and distraction, paused at a shop up the road and knew not at what he was staring, until his eyes focused and he saw a china doll displayed in the window, its head on an inquisitive angle, its skin white, its eyes watching him. *What are ye saying ta me?* Patrick asked. He drank from the flask and felt dire woe punish him with a force akin to the assemblance of his own cursed

317

birth and cursed death, an obliteration, a mastication, an erasure. A poem made of this as witnessed in his father's and mother's tormented eyes.

He finished the flask and, with hands shoved deep into his pockets and head hunched as though repelled by the clarity of the vivid air, he trod off under the persistently blackening gloom of self-recrimination.

A crust of speckled white, a cackling hag and a three-handed infant

The animals that flocked to Bareneed wreaked havoc upon the lands, chewing and trampling the yards to muck. The birds that filled the sky, as their own winged, ever-present colony, drifted inches apart, wingtip to wingtip, without collision, and shat upon everything and anyone who ventured out of doors. It amounted to an infestation of life. The plague of defecation carried illness throughout much of the settlement and, by causing upset to the bowel, drained the life from the weak. In the years to come, the episode was spoken of, not without a generous heaping of humour, as the Reign of Shit, a play on words that referred to the reigning merchant, Master Lawton, who had had the unfortunate luck of being born with a number of textured moles on his face.

As the sky was blackened by the ever-present squall of winged creatures from all corners of all continents, the sun was blocked and the stars masked. To the great fortune of the farmers, what remained of the harvest, that which was not eaten by the marauding gangs of wildlife, was soon due and so the requirement of sunlight mattered less and less. However, the fertilizer, while suspected of aiding the crops, soon wilted them, burning the stalks from any vegetable in root. There were burials each and every week until only a handful of residents remained, many having fled to safer locales, while others stood steadfast, professing in their mother tongue that they would not be driven from their patch of land. It would not be Ireland all over again. Not here in this new-found land that had become the perishing hope of many.

The coming cold was longed for, as the remaining residents prayed that the chill might drive the animals off to burrows and birds to warmer climes. Yet the creatures, rather than bounding off to the forests, dug their ways into abandoned and occupied houses where they sat, alert and watching, as though not only kept from sleep by the screech but appointed its sentinel.

While some accepted the animals into their homes, particularly the fox and rabbits, as it was believed that the murder of such creatures under a person's roof would bring woeful luck upon the household, others smashed the creatures to pulp wherever they sat.

In time, the remaining residents no longer heard the screech as it became part of the natural world, a pitch that all other sounds were judged against, its own uniform silence of sorts.

However, on the thirteenth month of Rose's pregnancy, the residents of Bareneed, growing weary of the animal overpopulation and the continuous need for slaughter, professed that it was the life-giving shrieking itself that had dammed forever Rose's ability to give birth. If the screech itself could not be stopped, then the creations that came from it should be struck down by whatever means possible.

Birds were shot from the air until all munitions were expended. Boys built slingshots from the limbs of trees and, with heads turned blindly away, fired rocks, then checked to see what they had felled. There was grease and fat glistening on every set of lips, meat stuck between every set of teeth, and feathers stuffed in every homemade mattress and pillow.

Yet the sound, no longer its tame, natural self as dead creatures filled the fields, rang to shrillness, varying in tone and oscillating higher, toward insufferable pitch, then lower to a bone-rattling hum. The locals, at the end of their tethers, now turned to Bishop Flax, who, upon returning from his reverential voyage up the coast, was baffled by the turn of events, and proclaimed that the screech, rather than being the product of agony, was, in fact, sprouted from a font of womanly bliss procured from the increased duration of this miraculous pregnancy. He sent a letter by boat to St. John's, summoning the finest doctor to Bareneed to officiate over the imminent sacred event.

Each day, while awaiting the arrival of the doctor, the bishop stood in the foot of the valley, below Rose Cavanagh's shack, and near the edge of earth where the sea rolled onto shore, in a reverie of holy exclamation, his arms thrown out to his sides, while the remaining residents, observing this behaviour and taking it for instruction, did likewise, tilting back their heads, in mirror of the bishop, and accepting the shit as that which they now took for a wash of resplendent light.

It was only the twisted boy whose demeanour remained unchanged in the face of the invasion of wing, paw and hoof. He stood in the outside, laughing and hiccuping at the screech of the birds that was in harmony with Rose's screech. The birds covered him in excretion until he was caked in a crust of speckled white with only his yellowed teeth and eyes hauntingly showing through. The twisted boy knew of the prodigious marks and signs. He knew of the riotous sounds of hoof and wing, for these were ever present in his eyes and mind, only now making themselves evident to the misguided flock that clucked and squawked in accord with the once lower creatures.

What he suspected to be the morning after the hanging, Patrick woke without knowledge of his whereabouts. The nip of cold had awoken him. He was in a room with half-burnt walls bashed open higher up and a ceiling patched with grimy rags that leaked dim light from beyond. His view of the ceiling was soon blocked by the buckled, rumbled, lumpy face of a hag that was smeared with soot and grinned openly with a mouth full of mismatched teeth, as though in putrid mockery of the gaping ache in Patrick's head.

'Yays,' the hag was saying, dipping her chin, 'yays, lad, ye were da fittest o' da lot.' A cackle as her shadowed face leaned back, and Patrick became aware of her nakedness, the wrinkled sag of her bosom and the lined slackness around her belly, and he sat up to face the stench of her that wafted to him as she shifted her legs. She nodded and nodded, as though her head were bobbing on water, and another female with long, straight black hair, one not so old, of what age Patrick could not exactly determine, perhaps thirteen or fourteen, although her countenance implied one more aged, rose from beside him and stared with large eyes that soon shied back down away from him, until her head was at rest again. With her steady gaze fixed on the length of his arm, she whimpered and purred and slid her thumb into her mouth.

'She were trapped in da fire,' said the hag, hawking spittle into her hands and swiping them together for warmth. She then sniffed there. 'T'were no 'ope 'a rescue 'til now. Ye 'av come, avn't ye, ta tak' us?'

Patrick shut his eyes to pull together memories from the blackness yet there was not a familiar image that might bridge the gap of travelling to this place. What hell? spoke a voice barely heard in his head. What fresh hell is this? It was only the roaring cough through the charred walls that brought an inkling of memory's relief. Ferrol. These were Ferrol's people. Women he had spoken of to the men at work. Survivors gone mad from the fiery vision, their brains scalded with torment. They had taken possession of the shells of the houses left standing, just as other homeless wanderers had, until ordered out by a constable or the demolition man.

There was a mix of low coloured light in the room, the shades strained through fabric. The window, covered with a torn rag, blew in and flecks of white invaded the room, settling on the blackened floor. With that gust, the hag and the girl huddled nearer and savagely pressed into him, their fingers clawing into his flesh for blood warmth, so that he grimaced and flinched away.

The hawking and spitting and muttering of 'fack' became more pronounced and Ferrol stood in the doorway that had been chopped through with an axe. The younger woman of the two crawled from the bed. By her step, Patrick saw the smutty markings along her back and the blackness of her soles, lifting one by one. She crouched over a bucket in the corner, all the while with her haunted eyes trained on Patrick with a look of longing that guarded against his escape.

What muddied hell? he thought.

> It were I strung from the gallows
> that snapped me kicking and broken kickless
> through the drop, this wrecked place of intercourse
> where I awoke with slatternly mind.

'Pádraig,' called Ferrol. 'Are ye more den a wee tad widt da living?'
Patrick remained still, his head thick and sogged. 'No,' he said. It was all he could do to simply breathe without the back of his skull dissolving. With three quick strides, Ferrol was upon Patrick, yanking him to his

feet. 'Ha. We'll make our way off den 'n pretend we're still o' dis world. Dey'll never know out dere. Buckled up as dey are by da snares o' commerce.'

Tormented by the sudden movement and wavering grounded in nausea alone, Patrick watched, with paining eyes, Ferrol's indefeatable smile. 'Off?' he asked, his mouth a wet ash bin.

'Nuff 'a dis blood slavery. We'll run like fack'n rabbits ta da shore.' He reached into his pocket and pulled out a worn and stained note. On it was written one word: Bareneed. 'T'was where me *dlúthchara*, Cian Shea, settled. *Nocht Riachtanas*.' And he laughed at the joke.

The girl was back from the bucket and curled and huddled into the hag. Patrick watched them shivering together until they were calm, the hag's face beside the young one's whose eyes were now closed. 'Ye were nearer ta dead in da days past dese, *a chailín mo chroí*,' said the hag, stroking hair from the girl's cheek. 'No more now dat yer 'ere in ruination's place.'

Ferrol watched the two naked women with a quiet sadness that bordered on the sacred, then snatched hold of Patrick's arm and dragged him around the corner to the outside.

Beyond the walls, snow fell white, the flakes large and only occasionally disturbed by a gust of wind. The snow must have been falling for some time, for it had masked a good portion of the expanse of black and fresh lumber walls of the newly erected with a welcome purity.

'Bury da facking town in da white o' angels. Dat be me plea dis morn,' said Ferrol, slapping Patrick on the back with a vigour that rattled every thought in Patrick's head into broken bits of chaos. He found that he was staring at a lamplight pole as there was something his mind appeared to recognize. He focused and held himself still to realize the letters of his own name, spelled out in Irish with its duplicate in English beneath it. Carefully, he leaned nearer to examine what it might say, with Ferrol only now taking notice, pulling his eyes away from a passing carriage that he had been straining to see the occupants of. He muttered a few words under his breath, 'Dat's what we be need'n,' and made nearer Patrick who was reading the poster.

Patrick struggled with the words. The notice appeared to be a warning. A time was given: *Nóin*. And a date: *Samhain 15ú*. Noon on

November 15th, 1886. The word 'house' and 'wife and children.' He recognized the name Limerick.

'Wha stink o' *cac* be dis now, Pádraig?'

The name of his employer, Master Job, was stated. He had heard of such notices from the other men when he questioned why they did not run free of servitude. If a man took it into his head to disappear and did not reappear on the date specified, the courts would seize the home of his wife or relatives back in Ireland to pay off the remainder of the debt of his transport. Papers had been signed stating such, although the men knew little of what it was they had applied their name to before embarking on the voyage.

How long had he been away from work? If this notice had already been posted, then he must have been gone missing for at least a week.

Ferrol tore the notice from the pole and gave it some consideration, then he regarded Patrick's blank face. 'Wha' be it?'

'Nothing,' he said in a voice barely heard.

'*Faic*.' Ferrol crumpled the paper in both fists and pitched it up into the snowfall, where it rose into the sky yet made no sound on its descent or landing. 'We'll be needing a carriage,' he said, turning to glance at the charred house where the youngest of the two had her ruined face showing behind the jagged bits of heat-blurred glass. 'A nice one widt red velvet tassels in da windows 'cause you an' I 'r da facking royalty 'a dis sorry paradise.'

When the visiting physician, Doctor Morgan, arrived at Bareneed, not only at the summoning of the bishop but also in accord with his custom of embarking on frequent humanitarian missions, he was faced with a vision that he believed to have been the exaggerated product of rumour. The sky above the village was alive with winged creatures and the land was smothered with animals. In the air, there was the faint pitch of a scream that made him poke at his ears as though to pacify an itch.

The doctor's open boat was made to wait a full hour to secure a place at the dock, as there were five ships anchored in the bay awaiting loading or offloading.

The man who had run the doctor up the coast from St. John's, a thin big-eyed fellow named Eamon Oliver, passed no comment on the sight.

With stubbly jaw opened a crack in tremor, he merely shook his head every now and again as though perplexed by the debacle.

The ships moved to a slower pace, as the crews, fascinated by the activities in Bareneed, lingered longer than anticipated, capturing live rabbits and larger creatures to take away as souvenirs, meat for slaughter, or as magical gifts for their children.

When the doctor's open boat finally managed to dock, the sun was waning in the sky, striking the blue water in a vivid fashion. To the doctor's great surprise, Bishop Flax himself was on hand to greet him. This was rarely the case, as the bishop generally sent a messenger to escort the doctor to where the bishop sat in wait.

The bishop made no reference to the astonishing sights that had overtaken Bareneed, instead plunging ahead to the matter at hand while the doctor climbed from the boat.

'There is a pregnant woman,' stated the bishop.

'Yes,' said the doctor, reaching back for his bag which was handed up to him by Eamon Oliver, his eyes then distracted by a moose that was ambling down toward the water. It made it nearer the shore and, with an awkward splash, dropped in and, with great head and rack raised, swam up the coast.

'Her name is Rose Cavanagh and she is in her thirteenth month of pregnancy.'

Because the words had been spoken by the bishop, the doctor expected them to be of a serious nature, as the bishop was not one to dabble in the comedic. With eyes now fixed on the bishop's unchanged expression and, perhaps, overcome by the bizarre sights he was facing, he could not help but explode with hilarity.

No doubt, what the bishop was repeating were the words of the ignorant Irish locals, only a tad more civilized than the Beothuk savages who lived nearby, and so backward as to be unfamiliar with the correct method of something as elemental as counting. However, after collecting himself and begging to be forgiven of his ignorance, the doctor was perplexed to see that the bishop's face was now struck with a look of even harsher sternness. Was the bishop out of his wits? This was quite disconcerting, for not only had he now vexed the bishop, but a fox had nosed its way near his foot and was sniffing at it, then nibbling

at it, so that the doctor cautiously pushed it away with the toe of his
other boot.

The bishop, seemingly done with conversation, turned on his heels
and gave the directive: 'This way,' to a space directly in front of
himself. He led the doctor off of the wharf, where the sun glistened on
the chilly blue water beyond, and up over the valley that a fitter man
might have had no struggle climbing. In fact, the doctor made it
without strain, weaving through the mass of life, but the bishop was
breathing deeply through his nostrils when they arrived at the door to
Rose's shack.

Not once, on the climb, did the bishop take notice of the silent birds
overhead or the creatures that he was forced to step around, as though
unwilling to give notice to this unadulterated grade of creation, while the
doctor's eyes went here and there, not able to linger for too long, despite
his astonishment, as another pair of creatures soon caught his attention.
They were mating everywhere, as the pitch of the screech grew louder,
making the doctor cringe, shut his eyes and cover his ears.

The twisted boy met the bishop in the doorway. Of all the visitors
who had entered the tilt over the duration of Rose's screech, it was only
the bishop who caused the twisted boy any consternation. A flailing of
limbs and garbled hoots and hisses that resembled a cross between a
reptile and a parrot were guaranteed.

As though in challenge, the twisted boy stood in the doorway,
blocking the bishop's way.

'He must be Church of England,' muttered the doctor, not checking
the bishop for reaction, but pressing in by his side to see if the twisted
boy might allow him entry. 'I'm a doctor,' he said, holding up his bag.

The twisted boy laughed, as though it were an asinine joke, then
shuffled aside, allowing the doctor entry, yet slipping back into place to
secure the doorway. The twisted boy laughed again, exposing overly
pink and bulbous gums that were stuck here and there with a few
crooked teeth, and pointed at the bishop's face,

'Damnú air!' slurred the twisted boy, sucking in air. 'Damnú air!'

Knowing the meaning of what was spoken, the bishop turned away,
his face burning red with rage.

Inside the tilt, the doctor, taking one look at the girth and blackened state of Rose Cavanagh's being and grimacing from the shrillness of the screech that rang in his ears, sought then to believe the gossip, although refused to accept the pronouncement of thirteen months. Impossible, for there had never been anything of the sort. The patient might have been weeks over, even, at the absolute most, a month beyond her due date, but she could not be thirteen months into her pregnancy. A woman could not endure a thirteen-month trial.

Examining the fragile, screeching form of Rose, whose voice suddenly popped hoarse, her throat so raw that it appeared to glow from within, shining a scarlet pink through her neck, as though a lantern were lit in there, the doctor thought to cut the infant out of Rose at once, wondering if the mother might survive the ordeal, for there was not much left of her, other than her belly and the hole of her gaping mouth. The rest of her body, having shrunk and withered, seemed lost in the rumpled mash of rags, grass and boughs that had been delivered as gifts by the people of Bareneed.

The doctor turned to the sound of blabbering and saw the twisted boy, with head thrown back to stare up at the sky, spring from the doorway. The doctor, relieved now at the lessening pitch of the screech, as though the mere presence of the man of science had muted its intensity, was compelled to follow after the twisted boy.

As he came to a clear view through the doorway, the doctor witnessed the twisted boy pointing upward with two fingers held so close to his face that they appeared fastened to his cheek. The doctor and the bishop, their breaths suddenly frosting in the air, for the temperature had dropped to a skin-burning low, watched to see what might have been causing such excitement in the twisted boy. There was nothing noticeable, for the sky was masked by the wavering drift of birds.

Disregarding the boy's attention as the ravings of a lunatic, the bishop turned away. The doctor was about to do likewise when his eyes caught sight of a fleck of fluff that might have been a piece of feather floating downward. The fleck descended directly above the twisted boy, who now opened his mouth and shut his eyes and hummed unevenly, in rising harmony with the screech, all the while waiting for the fleck to land. And land it did, directly in his opened mouth. With the flake swallowed and melted, the ground around the twisted boy began to sparkle white, its range of snowy brilliance expanding until the entire valley was covered in frost.

'Snow,' spoke the doctor, his already harrowed mind vanquished of the possibility of further expression.

Ears pricking up and with an inward gasp, the twisted boy turned and was, at once, saddened, for the blanket of snow that had been cast from the labyrinth of his veinwork had caused the screech to lower its pitch even more.

Soon, it would be gone completely, as the time of passing had arrived and was set to decline in the exact manner that the twisted boy had foreseen, thirteen years ago at the time of his birth.

It was the wrong season to attempt such a foolhardy run in an open boat. And the night only made it more of a daredevil's feat. The cold was pure misery to the flesh. Ice froze in Patrick's nostrils then melted with his breath, only to freeze again. Previously, while climbing in the boat, he had made the mistake of laying his hand upon one of the oar cradles and his skin had frozen fast to it. It was only when Ferrol splashed salt water on the bond that his hand would slowly pull free, but not before, in a fit of panic, he had torn part of the skin from his palm. His ears and fingers were burnt and throbbing from the cold. The snow that was now blowing was wet yet spiked with tiny pellets at the centre of each fat flake. If they did not find seclusion soon, he knew that his hands and ears would be tender for days to come, and the skin on those appendages would come loose. He checked his hands to make certain they were not yet tallowy white. They remained a raw pink.

Patrick blinked the melted snow from his eyes and regarded Ferrol, who seemed none the worse for the biting chill of the night. He rowed and watched ahead, then checked the shoreline, which was vaguely evident through the grey.

Patrick thought of turning back, yet that would mean the end of him. He would not let another day pass where he would be slave to a *Sassenach*. If he need perish, so be it. If his family's home need be taken, so be it. They would be settled somewhere, eventually, by family within the village. Not another day would he remain in the keep of the bastard

Englishmen. Better a lifeless chunk of ice adrift on a sea of dire adversity than a dead-eyed living cow.

Shifting on his slat, he became more aware of the panging in his ankle and shoulder, which he had suffered earlier that eve from being slammed about in an overturned carriage. Ferrol had stolen the carriage from a newly built carriage house near the basilica, and driven it with wild abandon out of the city until the snow on the road became a hindrance. Unsatisfied with his impeded progression, he had whipped the horses until they whinnied and laboured ahead over uneven ground, prancing and jumping until the carriage was tossed over. They had then trod off on foot to a nearby cove where Ferrol made off with a boat from a cluster anchored and afloat.

Why Patrick had come along with Ferrol, of all people, was an inexplicable mystery to him. If he chose to flee, why allow himself to be accompanied by the biggest, baldest man known to him? Wouldn't they be looking for Ferrol, as well? Although, did anyone actually know Ferrol's surname? In fact, was Ferrol his name at all? Once, in a public house, talking over a pint, Patrick had asked Ferrol about his family back in Ireland.

'Naw,' Ferrol had said with a big-lipped frown and a silent stare straight into the limited distance of the wall behind the bar. 'Naw family.'

'No wife, no children?'

No reply. A drink from his pint.

'Who is your family?' Patrick asked. 'Mudder. Fadder.'

'I cum from no one.'

Patrick laughed. 'Every man has a mudder.'

'No family. I have no family. No *teaghlach*.' And that had been the end of it, for a fiddler had struck up in the corner and they had both turned to watch the old man, seated at a table, whisk his bow across the strings to enliven the place with smiles of kindred recollection and foot-stomping merriment.

The shriek of a fiddle string echoed in Patrick's head, as though it had come to him from out over the grey water.

'How far?' Patrick called, his face stinging and numb in one cheek, his eyes practically shut against the gnaw of the surging wind, his fingers aching. He bunched them dully into fists and brought them to his mouth to exhale on them.

Ferrol pulled the woollen cap from his head and handed it to Patrick. 'Put yer hands in dat.'

'Yer head'll freeze.'

'Got nar blood in me head ta freeze. Facking lack o' brain.'

Patrick watched the faint image of the snow gathering to melt on Ferrol's head. The muted glisten of it while the bald man continued broadly rowing, staring across the water. Further out to sea, there was movement of light, and Ferrol stopped rowing and sat utterly still.

They watched as the vessel, veiled behind the downpour of grey snow, drifted by, ignorant to their unlit presence.

In time, the snow abated and the sky cleared. The temperature dropped excessively for Patrick was now trembling uncontrollably to the point of spasm. The cracks he heard resounding in his ears might have been his bones snapping from the insufferable cold. Yet it seemed as if Ferrol heard the sounds as well, as he was searching toward land in the direction from where the snappings shot out toward the water.

'Just dere,' said Ferrol, nodding toward a patch of land that unlike the land surrounding it, which glowed with snow beneath a moon that permitted sight for miles, was cloaked in shadow.

Checking the sky, Patrick saw what appeared to be a shifting flutter of strangely formed cloud.

As they neared the village, cracks and snappings turned to booms like the report of gunfire. Patrick suspected the quiet town might be at war. Yet there was not a flash of gunpowder nor any sign of smoke other than that which streamed from the occasional chimney.

'It's da timbers in da houses,' Ferrol said, passing by a lone schooner anchored in the bay, 'shrinking in da brutal cold. Dere's a'ways moisture in everyt'in, ye know dat?'

Patrick tried shaking his head yet the action was more an erratic jerk that carried on as trembling. He heard the lap of the water against the wharf posts and was brought relief. Soon there would be warmth, if mercy was to be expected of a single person in Bareneed.

When Ferrol climbed the makeshift ladder up onto the wharf, he heard the feathery sweep of a multitude of wings and gazed overhead to see darkness aswell like a black sea. He then turned to a view of Patrick still huddled in the boat as though his arse were frozen to the slat.

'Me feet're gone lame,' he barely spoke.

'Yer look'n a pretty shade o' blue.' A boom behind him. Ferrol spun around, only to laugh at the foolishness of his body's over-zealous reaction. He climbed back down into the boat and hoisted Patrick over his shoulder, took him up the ladder. On land, with an arm over Ferrol's shoulders, Patrick was then led up the valley that was crowded with sleeping or frozen carcasses of varied shapes and sizes. Sighting the peculiar landscape, Patrick assumed he had abided an insufferable extreme and slipped into delirium.

They made their way briskly, with Patrick's feet barely touching the snow-covered ground and Ferrol kicking the occasional frozen rabbit or weasel out of the way as though the practice was familiar to him. Others were snapped underfoot, the sound of little bones cracking making a path of noise toward the clutch of houses. Of the ten houses, only one was recognized by Ferrol as a duplicate of his friend, Cian Shea's, house back in Kilkenny. Instead of clapboard along the front there were shingles and the chimney was to the left of the front door, unlike the others which were to the right.

It was in this house that Rose Cavanagh was laid out on a table that had been scrubbed clean for the surgery.

Doctor Morgan had just set the tip of the scalpel to her belly and was drawing it in a horizontal line when Rose came out of her inhuman reverie, her eyes twisting in different directions and her sucked-thin teeth snapping off while she chewed down on a strip of leather.

Morgan had performed few caesareans before yet was familiar with the procedure from observation at the Poole Institute of Medicine, where he had trained before venturing overseas. He continued with the horizontal incision, and was startled to see – before the line had reached its terminating point – a fist rise out, two sizes larger than that belonging to the average newborn. Another hand reached out, desperately grasping at the air, and then what he thought must have been a foot, but was, in fact, yet another hand. The third.

Astonished, his fingers let drop the scalpel. It clattered on the kitchen floor, for he could expect nothing less than abnormality and deviation from the circumstance. He checked Mrs. Kearney, the midwife in wait, who blessed herself and ran fretfully from the room.

The physician, recovering himself, reached in and lifted out the baby. It was near twice the size of the average infant, sixteen pounds if it were an ounce, and was jerked back as its hand became stuck on something. The physician searched into the slit to find that the infant's hand was fastened to the hand of another baby. Relieved by the obvious explanation, Morgan gently pried the fingers from where they were entwined around the second infant's hand. 'Twins,' said the physician with relief, calling out, 'Twins, Mrs. Kearney.' He smiled at the mother, yet received no reply, for the murmuring screech, which had calmed to a sound resembling a boiling bubble in a pot, had waned from Rose's throat, and she appeared to be dead.

All was silent, save for a riotous pounding on the front door.

Emily Hawco is killed by a memory and Jacob Hawco does not know who is born. It is sad how everyone cannot remember and cannot forget.

1981-1986

(March, 1981)

Jacob answered the phone. It was a new beige-coloured one from the telephone company. It was heavy and dinged when the receiver was laid down. A man had come and run wires from the kitchen, up along the ceiling trim and then down along the baseboards. The phone had been hooked up for Jacob so it would reach the table beside his chair, just within reach.

The phone rang all day and Jacob picked it up. 'Blackstrap? Naw, b'y,' he remorsefully told whoever might be on the other end. 'He's not 'ere.' A pause as the image from the TV screen blurred over. ''E passed on.'

The voice at the other end: 'Are you saying he died?'

Occasionally, Emily was present in the living room and patiently waited on Jacob's answers, so that she might clarify the misunderstanding, insist that Blackstrap was alive.

'Yays, were in a mining accident,' Jacob confessed.

'No,' said Emily, hand out for the phone, to assure whoever might be calling that Blackstrap had survived. The only survivor. The single and sole survivor of the tragic ordeal. He had been rescued. She was certain of it, despite what was being said and reported. A misunderstanding.

'Who am I speaking with?' the voice would demand of Jacob.

'Who're ye ta ask?'

'This is . . .' And the reporter's name was given along with the name of the radio station, newspaper, magazine or TV station. The names spoken in a way that meant they mattered enough to be given nothing short of the truth.

'Yays,' Jacob confirmed. 'It be da sad trute.'

Emily watched as the receiver was hung up. She watched the receiver until it rang again and Jacob picked it up, his eyes on Emily for a second, then on the TV screen.

The television reported the news as fact.

Emily with her hand out for the receiver, but Jacob never giving it over.

'Blackstrap Hawco, the sole survivor of the *Ocean Ranger* tragedy, has died in a mining accident. At this time, further details are not available. As we receive information, we will pass it on to you. Stay tuned for updates.'

Jacob checked the television screen then turned to see Blackstrap stood in the doorway. Jacob nodded and winked in camaraderie. Then shifted his eyes to see Junior stood by the window looking out like he used to when he was expecting snow. The boy always knew when there would be a storm. He would stand there and wait. 'It's coming,' he would say, face tilted toward the sky. An image on the TV screen. A boy with his tongue out, catching snowflakes. The arc of falling snow beneath a streetlight, each flake separate and forming a pattern. A memory close enough to feel.

'It's okay,' said Ruth. 'It's okay, Daddy.' She sat on Santa's lap and rubbed the stubble on his chin with her little hand, her voice smooth, not the unending screech it had been. And Santa smiled.

The wind howled outside the window, and all at once the sea began tossing the boat around on Channel 3, and sleet pattered in a sheet against the windowpanes. Thrashed about in the sky, ice struck and clung to electric and telephone wires. It struck and clung to the limbs of trees. It covered the snow and everything in a thick coating of ice that snapped branches and wires, and plummeted the world into darkness, then shone metallically the next morning when the sun rose to display nature in its calm brilliance.

'It's okay, Daddy,' Ruth whispered into Jacob's ear when he woke in his chair, fresh from the darkness with the sunlight on his face. She reached out to a dog on the screen. And the telephone rang. And the pounding on the door. And Jacob never anywhere but in there.

(January, 1984)

'Da subway fare in New York jus' went up ta ninety cents,' Jacob said in a bewildered tone. He was answered by a voice he could not recognize, but knew. He sat up straighter in his chair to rifle through his pocket, to confirm his suspicions. Taking out a handful of change, he stared at it in his palm, poked the coins around with his finger. Always an American

333

nickel or a penny finding its way to mingle with the Canadian coins. 'Did ye hear 'bout dat?'

'No,' said a woman somewhere. He looked at her, confused by the way she had grown so old or not old enough. She was dusting photograph frames with faces in them. She picked them up and dusted them with a feather duster, then set them down again. They each had a place on the sideboard.

'It were seventy-five cents 'fore,' Jacob said, with a plea in his voice.

'Yes,' said the woman.

'We won't stand fer it, will we?'

The woman dusted another frame and held it longer than the others. 'Dat bastard Smallwood's rob'n us blind.'

'Not blind enough,' said the woman, her voice a crackle from the speaker beside the screen.

Another woman coming by to turn down the volume.

(May, 1984)

The warm rains had melted the snow and thawed the frost. The ground was soft beneath foot. The wind pounded the house. The structure shuddering, but remaining solid, having been constructed by a skilled boat-builder from Port de Grave. The house's slate foundation and wide thick boat-planking made it a structure of endurance, even more stable now that the top storey had been removed.

Emily looked up from the book she was reading. It did not hold her attention. She felt the need to skip ahead, to reach the end, to have it done with. It went on too long, was poorly written, and full of factual and typographical errors. She was seated in the grey chair in the small living room. She cast her glance toward the kitchen and listened to Jacob puttering around out there. On windy nights such as these, Jacob became restless. Emily imagined that he was thinking of the time he was tossed into the brewing black Atlantic many years ago. That had been when they still lived in Bareneed.

It was on a night like this when they carried him into the house. They had come up the grassy pasture that rose from the ragged brown rocks that were more a part of the Atlantic than land. The wind had been raging outside and the men, in their glistening oil slickers, called out against the elements. They hurried to lift him up the stairs and into bed. Emily had watched the deathly colour of his skin. She had felt the spirit-shiver that whispered it was over. She had imagined Jacob's body laid out in the parlour. The wake she would have to endure. She could not bear the thought of him dead. It shook her terribly, making her cold with fear, as though the mere thought edged her nearer to death itself. Her lips had chilled blue. She had trembled when she bent to him to find that his trembling was much worse than hers.

'More blankets,' one of the men had called back. All of them stood with the water dripping off their slickers and boots. A puddle fully surrounding them.

Jacob had watched her with scared eyes. That look. It could not be Jacob. Another man unseen.

That had been in 1964. Two years before, Junior, away working in the mines, had been killed. So, it must have been Blackstrap that Abe Stuckless had been shouting at for more blankets. Blackstrap had to be ten or eleven years old then.

Emily heard Jacob moving a cup and saucer from the cupboard, and wondered if he knew what he was doing.

'Drop 'a tea?' he called.

'Yes, love one,' Emily replied, thinking, *He shouldn't be at the stove.*

Two days after the madness of the capsized boat, Jacob, pulling through as the warmth gradually re-entered him, had carefully swung his legs over the side of the bed and slowly sat up. It was a painful chore, but Jacob would have no further part in weakness. Not in front of his son. He would show the boy that he was unharmed, that there was nothing for the boy to worry about. His father could not be taken as easily as that.

Emily had watched from the doorway, the father and son unaware of her presence. She had heard Jacob's voice lingering on words as he explained the drama of what had happened and then explained, in a lower tone, the merciful bravery shown by the man who had saved him. His voice was controlled and sorrowful, not fast and bold as was his nature.

Emily had watched her husband carefully studying Blackstrap's face. There was a quietness between them, before Jacob smiled toward a low, thoughtful laugh and kissed Blackstrap on the cheek. The single time she had ever seen Jacob kiss his son. Blackstrap's eyes had remained fixed on the wooden dory in his hands, the dory that his father had long ago carved for him. A toy cherished by the boy. And Jacob had hugged his son fiercely, as if holding on through the terrifying calamity, holding on as the waves crashed and smothered his ears and the wind thrust to snatch away his breath with thousand-pound bursts of water.

Emily had to stop herself from moving into the room to embrace them. She had remained still, with the warm trails creeping down her cheeks and, in the way that Jacob would have wished for her to do, thanked the Lord for His mercy.

The kettle began to whistle and Emily rose to help Jacob with the tea. She didn't want him to burn himself, as he had done on previous occasions. With tea cup in hand and a biscuit on a plate, he would then return to his shows.

June 1, 1984 Weightlifting record of 1,211 kg set by Alexander Gunyashev of the USSR

June 2, 1984 Actress Jill Ireland marries 'Death Wish', undergoes radical mastectomy

June 3, 1984 *Swamp Thing* and *The Cage of Queens* win at 38th Tony Awards

June 4, 1984 'Born in the NRA' released by Bruce Springsteen

June 4, 1984 Extinct animal successfully cloned from own DNA

June 5, 1984 Cellular radios introduced commercially in 20 major cities

June 5, 1984 Sikhs' holiest site (Golden Temple) attacked by order of Indira Gandhi

June 8, 1984 Dead at 88, composer Gordon Jacob regrets nothing

June 9, 1984 Disneyland celebrates Donald Duck's 50th birthday

June 9, 1984 Homosexuality decriminalised in the state of New South Wales, Australia

June 10, 1984 Incoming missile shot down in space by US missile for 1st time

June 11, 1984 Illegally obtained evidence may be admitted at trial if proved it would have been discovered legally by more honest means, Supreme Court rules

June 14, 1984 No women allowed to bake decides Southern Baptist convention

June 15, 1984 Roberto Duràn knocked up by Thomas Hearns

June 16, 1984 100th consecutive 400-meter hurdles race won by Edwin Moses in under 24 hours

June 17, 1984 Pierre Trudeau succeeded by John Turner as chancellor of Canada

June 18, 1984 Skokomish Indian Tribe of the Skokomish Indian Reservation in State of Washington files to incorporate

June 19, 1984 US painter, Lee Krasner Pollock, blotted out at 75

June 20, 1984 Actress Estelle Winwood (*Miracle on 34th Street*) lives miraculously, until 99

June 22, 1984 Secretary-General of NATO, Joseph Luns resigns from Mensa

June 24, 1984 Homerun mark of 265 set by Joe Morgan in basement

June 25, 1984 17th Miss Black America, Lydia Garrett, 24, is crowned without incident

June 25, 1984 Philosopher Michel Foucault (*History of Sexuality*) dies of AIDs at Plato's Retreat

June 26, 1984 Shuttle *Discovery*'s first amusement park ride aborted at T-4

June 26, 1984 World astonished at marriage of Tiny Tim

June 27, 1984 Set of Bond movie *A View to a Kill* destroyed by villains

June 29, 1984 *Conan the Destroyer* reviewed in *New York Times*: '. . . special effects aren't bad . . .'

June 30, 1984 Cocaine growers in Bolivia fail at recouping coup

June 30, 1984 Great Britain mints last sixpence (circulated since 1551)

July 2, 1984 Composer, Ramiro Cortes, hits career low note at 50

July 3, 1984 Launch of Dolphin rocket off San Clemente Island hits whale

July 3, 1984 Against their will, women forced by Jaycees to be members, Supreme Court insists

July 5, 1984 Supreme Court hints that evidence obtained with defective court warrants can now be used in criminal trials

July 7, 1984 Marriage of Frankie Valli to woman in bikini sparks vivid memories

July 11, 1984 Air bags or seat belts to be used in cars by 1989

July 11, 1984 Bophuthatswana re-elects Lucas Mangope as Four Seasons' top valet

July 12, 1984 Geraldine Ferraro becomes 1st woman VP candidate

July 13, 1984 After 7 shows, Walter Mondale quits Rod Stewart's tour

July 14, 1984 USSR scores 41% in Nuclear Test at Eastern Kazakh/ Semipalitinsk

July 16, 1984 Phil Hickerson & The Spoiler beat Dutch Mantel & Porkchop Cash at Mid-South Coliseum

July 17, 1984 Pierre Mauroy calls it quits as grand pastry chef of France

July 18, 1984 21 McDonald's patrons killed by James Huberty in San Ysidro, CA

July 19, 1984 Lynn Rippelmeyer becomes first female captain to move 747 across Atlantic via telekinesis

July 19, 1984 Youngest heart transplant recipient, Holly Roffey, discovered living in England

July 20, 1984 Javelin record broken by Uwe Hohn of East Germany

July 21, 1984 Robot kills human in US

July 22, 1984 Tour de France won by Victor Hugo

July 23, 1984 First black Miss America, Vanessa Williams, no longer Miss America when nude

July 24, 1984 Denny A. takes Mary B. to first AA meeting

July 25, 1984 Svetlana Savitskaya becomes first woman cosmonaut to waltz in space

July 26, 1984 *Psycho* inspiration, mass murderer, Ed 'Psycho' Gein, dies of mass injuries at 78

July 26, 1984 Pioneer of public opinion polls, George Gallup, considered dead by 74% of Americans

July 27, 1984 British actor, James Mason (*Lolita*) dies of insatiable lust at 75

July 28, 1984 Los Angeles pretends to host 23rd modern Olympic games

July 29, 1984 No events on this date

July 30, 1984 2.8 million gallons of blood spilled by Alvenus tanker at Cameron, LA

July 30, 1984 *Santa Barbara* cannot believe its own premiere on NBC TV

July 31, 1984 One-armed actor Bill Raisch (*Fugitive*) loses other arm and entire body at 79

July 31, 1984 *Entertainment Tonight* is so wonderfully, absolutely thrilled with Leeza Gibbons' first appearance

August 2, 1984 Nuclear test tutorial scheduled at Nevada Test Site by US Secretary of Education

August 3, 1984 New York Stock Exchange trades four million baseball cards

August 3, 1984 A new look at death suggested by AMA

August 4, 1984 *Purple Rain* by singer formerly and latterly known as Prince, hits #1

August 4, 1984 Republic of Upper Volta legally changes name to Bourkina Fasso

August 5, 1984 Actor Richard Burton bows to thunderous applause of bloody grand cerebral hemorrhage at 58

August 7, 1984 US singer, Esther Phillips' ('What a Difference a Day Makes') lonely nights are through at 48

August 7, 1984 Yellow Peril takes Olympic gold medal in baseball over Arrogant Yanks

August 8, 1984 Actor Richard Deacon (*Dick Van Dyke Show*) dies stuttering at 62

August 9, 1984 Decathalon record set by Batman in California

August 9, 1984 Bogus Doctor Sexual Assault story aired on BBC

August 10, 1984 Zola Budd's heel becomes obstacle for Mary Decker during 3,000 m Olympic run

August 11, 1984 US publisher, Alfred A. Knopf, dies regretting TV at 91

August 11, 1984 President Reagan jokes he 'signed legislation that would outlaw Russia forever. We begin bombing in 5 minutes'

August 13, 1984 'Arabic-African Disunion' treaty signed by Morocco, Libya & Israel

August 14, 1984 PC DOS version 3.0 released by IBM

August 16, 1984 Auto maker John Z. DeLorean acquitted on cocaine by federal jury

August 17, 1984 Youngest heart transplant, Holly Roffey, dies at 4 weeks

August 18, 1984 *Veterinary Times* publishes breakthrough article on persistent orf in rams

August 19, 1984 Ronald Reagan nominated for best supporting actor at Republican convention in Houston

August 22, 1984 Volkswagen makes last Rabbit Pie

August 24, 1984 LPGA record for 9 holes set by Pat Bradley with a score of 8

August 25, 1984 Truman Capote, liar, (*In Cold Blood*) dies at 59

August 25, 1984 Soviet gymnast great, Viktor Ivanovich Chukarin, dies at 62

August 27, 1984 *Coronation Street* actor, Bernard Youens, dies king of non-working classes at 69

August 28, 1984 Professors W. Michael Reisman and Oscar Schachter tangle

August 30, 1984 Transient Management Workshop sponsored by Pentagon

August 30, 1984 2-day Sotheby's auction of rock memorabilia begins in London

August 31, 1984 Pinklon Thomas beats crap out of Tim Witherspoon for heavyweight boxing title

(September, 1984)

Emily woke in the darkness to the sound of a small cry. Bolting up, she listened, thinking it might have been a dream, but then heard the sound again. The faraway cry of a baby. Immediately, in a fit of action, Emily rose from the bed. What was she to do? Was she fully awake yet? She paused, listening, while she carefully pulled on her housecoat. The sound was Ruth's. Any baby's cry, in a store, on television, in church, in another house, it was Ruth. Sixteen years ago. Any baby's cry, always Ruth's.

The sound again. And the entirety of Ruth's life and death. How Ruth had cried as a baby, how she had come so near dying in infancy. The warnings from the doctors. The specialists who came to examine her. That cry. It was not like the other baby's. She thought Ruth would die from screeching. But, no, Ruth had lived so that Emily might have those five years of memories: her little girl's life.

The cry again, muddled beyond the walls. Not Ruth. How could it be? Emily shut her eyes, listened, felt incredibly sleepy.

Ruth. Her twisted face.

Emily stepped toward the bedroom door, tying her housecoat belt at her waist.

It was not until Ruth was two years old that Emily heard the news on the radio, the truth about the drug. It was the drug Emily had been taking after Junior's death. A drug that the doctor had prescribed for Emily, so that she might forget Junior's death. 'This will help you cope,' the doctor had said, handing her the sheet of paper. And she had done exactly as told. She had had the prescription filled in the pharmacy next door to the doctor's office. The pills did help. They tucked her neatly away from herself. And left her removed. She had been able to function, but she was sealed within herself. She had been taking the pills when she was made pregnant with Ruth. And she had kept taking the drugs because they judged the world harmless. The drug that had reduced the pain to less than the wholeness of herself had made Ruth what she was.

The sound. It was no longer there.

Emily had awoken from a dark dream she could not remember. Her bones ached for the disturbance that had blinded her to the dream's significance. She stared back at her bed, at Jacob. Not a movement from him. With lips parted, and quietly drawing breath, she listened. There was no sound. There never had been a sound. Had there?

No. Nothing.

Slowly, she removed her housecoat, and settled back on her pillow. Sighing, she pulled the blankets over her. It took a moment to find warmth again. Eyes shut, she felt fully awake now, and opened her eyes to watch the ceiling. She waited for another sign, her memory filled with the sweetness of Ruth's face. In time, her eyes grew sleepy, her breath deepening. Her arms clutched hold of Ruth. She sank like a perfect stone, weighty and with barely any resistance, down through the buoyant water.

In the morning, Jacob discovered that a grey and white cat, a stray, had made a home of their shed. It came out to meet him, giving him a fright that forced the cat to flinch back, hunker down and hiss. At once, Jacob searched around the slate foundation for a possible point of entry. But he could find no hole where the cat might have squeezed through. No broken windows either.

The cat would go near no one, only meowed halfway between a hiss and a cry when anyone stepped into the shed. Its teeth were longer than those of a domestic cat and so Jacob knew that it was from wild stock. Thoughts of shooting the creature crossed his mind, ridding the grounds of that savage thing that he took as a bad omen, particularly because he saw its sagging belly and knew it was filled with kittens. Just what he needed, a litter of kittens to shove into a bag and fling into the sea.

'I'll shoot dat bloody vermin,' he warned Emily. 'If it not be gone by da perishing o' da day.'

Emily's fondness for animals, particularly strays, compelled her to plead with Jacob. She managed to get an extension on the terms. Three days. After three days, Jacob vowed that he would do away with it. Kittens and all, if need be.

'Dun't let it near yerself,' Jacob told her. 'It's rife wid disease.'

'Okay,' Emily agreed, not telling him how the cat had already rubbed up against her when she delivered table scraps of fried egg and bacon from breakfast to the shed. The cat's thick, grey and white fur was stuck up in many places, its vicious-looking eyes slanted up at the ends. Pink discharge hung from the fur on its rear legs, and Emily wondered if that was normal.

'G'way, ugly beast,' Jacob said threateningly when he went out later in the morning to carry junks of spruce from the shed. The cat came near, circling around his feet so that he had to kick it away. It had lifted off its feet and into the air. Regardless, the cat kept winding among his legs, as if attempting to weave an invisible knot.

'Wind warn'n on fer t'night,' Jacob said, his tone making the warning seem even more severe. It was the way he spoke lately. Always wanting things to sound worse than they might be. He said this while coming in from the shed to noisily drop an armload of wood into the bin beside the stove. He wiped at his forehead and sat at his chair. His elbows set against the tabletop. He scratched at his grey stumble with his thumb, and watched Emily preparing lunch. Homemade bread with butter and blueberry jam, a piece of dark blackberry cake with the ginger he liked, and a pot of black tea.

Emily shook her head a bit. 'I don't much like the wind.' She moved to the fridge to take out the milk and saw the postcard from Toronto that Blackstrap had sent. Only their address on there, written in someone else's hand, and their son's name signed in the sloppy way that made Emily smile. He was never one for school, she thought. Just couldn't sit still. And he would not let me teach him. He rejected it at all turns, creating a tension between them that was always present. Her disappointment with that side of him made her sigh in an offhand way. If he had stayed in school, and went to university, he might have been a doctor or a lawyer. He might have had a better life.

'Blackstrap should be calling again soon,' she said.

Jacob frowned and ran one hand over the white oilcloth with pale red flowers printed there. He brushed at them as if they were crumbs and thought on his sixty-fifth birthday. He would be getting his Canada pension cheque in a couple of months.

'Bloody government,' Jacob griped. 'Useless buggers. Dun't have a clue 'ow ta keep hold of its people. Every'n off on da mainland.'

Emily laid the milk on the table and glanced at her husband before stepping to the stove. 'Don't start now,' she said. 'You'll have a stroke one day the way you go on.'

'All this talk of Hibernia. Oil. Where's da jobs? I'd like to say a thing or two to that Smallwood fella.'

'It's Peckford, Jacob.'

'Wha'?'

'The premier's Peckford now.'

He looked at her, baffled, then dismissed it. 'Government's one big crew 'a liars that're all stuck on themselves. Half-ass beauty queens 'n actors. I'm poisoned with it. The likes 'a dem. Yes, Pickford. Yer right. Em'ly. Him widt dat big cigar in his puss all da time. Da sight of 'im turns me guts.'

A plate of thickly sliced white bread was laid on the table. Jacob grabbed up a slice. He buttered it in the palm of one big hand, then briskly bit off the corner.

Emily laid out the cups, then the teapot, before sitting across from him.

'We been screwed by da bloody government since Smallwood's time. He were da biggest crook dat ever lived.'

Emily watched Jacob, exhaustion coming over her. She was living in the years of Ruth again. The cry she had heard in the night had transported her back to that place. 'He did some good things, too,' she quietly offered, the voice of reason. 'Established the university.'

Jacob grumbled and tore off another bite of bread.

'He was an extremely intelligent man.'

'Aack. Intelligence is fer dose with no mind fer real work.' He stared at the oilcloth, wiped at his mouth with his hand and took another bite of bread.

343

'You can call him what you want, but I believe he helped Newfoundland. He was considered a great man by many.' Emily poured his tea then filled her own cup.

'Wha' da hell's got inta ye, womb'n? He were da greatest con man dat ever set foot on dis sacred soil. A bloody Nazi down in da States first widt dat feller frum Cuba, if ye knows anyt'in 'bout history. Joining Canada, destroying Newfoundland, and then moving everyone away from where dere families were raised up fer generations. Resettlement! Just making sure that there were less money going out ta da communities 'n more going into his own pocket.'

'I think you're wrong there, Jacob.'

'Naw way.'

'Smallwood wasn't a Nazi.'

'He were a Nazi.' Jacob Hawco chewed fiercely, thinking in silence, watching her. 'Cripes, b'y, he were.' He finished his bread and made a lot of noise slurping his cup of tea. When he was done, he stood and sulked out of the room without saying another word.

In the back yard, Jacob picked up a few scraps of damp papers that had blown onto his cut grass. He moved to the front of the house to make certain that no litter had spotted the lawn there. The paint on the house was holding up. He studied the barn-red colour and the white trim. Everything immaculate.

Returning to the back of the house, he loaded more wood into the shed. The cat appeared out of nowhere and he kicked it, harder than intended, hurling it across the shed so that it hit the far wall where the birch junks were stacked. He paused with the armload of spruce to make certain the stray was not seriously injured. The cat stayed where it was for a moment, then rushed from the shed, its legs a blur. Jacob was sorry for what he had done, cursing under his breath, 'Christly no good son of a bitch Smallwood. T'ank God fer Mr. Crosbie. T'ank Jesus he put him outta dere. Ye can say all da bad t'ings ye want 'bout Crosbie, he's still a saint in me own eyes. A bloody saint.'

September 1, 1984 *Force of Evil* actor, Howland Chamberlain, dies as himself at 73

September 2, 1984 Wang Chung plays Coliseum at Phoenix, AZ

September 3, 1984 28-year-old Chicagoan wins $1.99 in Illinois state lottery

September 4, 1984 $32,074,566 raised by Jerry Lewis in 19th Muscular Dystrophy telethon

September 5, 1984 *Discovery* 1 lands on Edwards AFB, 21 die

September 6, 1984 Grand Ole Opry singer, Ernest Tubb, drowns in Dolly Parton's cleavage at 70

September 6, 1984 Live remote telecasts from Moscow undertaken by *Today* show

September 7, 1984 Cricketer Don Tallon, (great Queensland & Australian keeper) loses final game

September 8, 1984 Composer René Bernier plays without accompaniment at 79

September 9, 1984 John McEnroe defeats Ivan Lendl

September 10, 1984 Kennedy Space Center begins sale of *Discovery* meal deal

September 12, 1984 Badly injured in a car crash, singer Barbara Mandrell appears speechless

September 13, 1984 Shimon Peres and Likud co-form Israeli government

September 14, 1984 Bette Midler and Dan Aykroyd lip synch as hosts at first MTV awards

September 15, 1984 Henry Charles Albert David Thomas Edward Peter Frederick Jake, son of Princess Diana, becomes third in British succession

September 16, 1984 *Miami Vice* accused of high ratings, white suit sales persist

September 17, 1984 Brian Mulroney sworn in as Canada's 18th Matriarch, accepts bonnet from John Turner

September 18, 1984 1st solo balloon crossing of Atlantic completed by Joe 'Madman' Kittinger

September 19, 1984 Agreement to transfer Hong Kong to China by 1997 signed by law firm Britain & Britain

September 20, 1984 NBC TV premieres Jell-o commercial *The Cosby Show*

September 20, 1984 23 killed in suicide car bomb attack on US Embassy in Beirut

September 21, 1984 Pope John Paul II visits Canada

September 22, 1984 Marriage of Brussels Princess Astrid to Arch Duke Franz Ferdinand of Austria

September 23, 1984 *Hill St. Blues*, *Cheers* and John Ritter refuse Emmy Awards

September 24, 1984 'No More Lonely Nights' released by Paul McCartney

September 25, 1984 Competition between Xenopus satellite I sequences and Pol III genes for stable transcription complex formation spirals out of control

September 25, 1984 Diplomatic relations resumed between Egypt & Jordan

September 26, 1984 Sanctions against South Africa vetoed by President 'Home Boy' Reagan

September 28, 1984 Sally Shaffer files an application with the Board of Review to institute further appeal

September 29, 1984 Cars park 'Drive' at #3 on Billboard charts

September 29, 1984 Betty Ford Clinic welcomes Elizabeth Taylor's addiction without shame

October 1, 1984 After two-year break, Gary Trudeau's *Doonesbury* comic strip resumes high-brow exclusivity

October 2, 1984 First FBI agent, Richard Miller, dejectedly charged with espionage

October 4, 1984 US government shut down by budget problems

October 6, 1984 LPGA Hitachi Ladies British Golf Open won by Yoko Ono

October 6, 1984 US palaeontologist George S. Simpson fully sinks himself into job at 82

October 7, 1984 Striking umps return from God knows where

October 8, 1984 Iron Maiden plays the first of four sold out shows at Hammersmith Odeon

October 11, 1984 Dr. Kathryn D. Sullivan first US woman to walk across space

October 11, 1984 Geraldine Ferraro (D) & George Bush (R) debate affordable health and organic products

October 12, 1984 Hotel where Margaret Thatcher stays bombed by INLA

October 13, 1984 $6 million won by thoroughbred John Henry in lottery

October 14, 1984 LPGA Smirnoff Ladies' Irish Golf Open won by Superstar Billy Graham

October 15, 1984 Central Intelligence Agency's Information Act tested on animals

October 16, 1984 Black Tibetan Buddhist Desmond Tutu wins Nobel Peace Prize

October 18, 1984 *Discovery* moves to bad neighbourhood in Vandenberg

October 18, 1984 October declared National Head Injury Awareness Month by Press Secretary of the United States

October 19, 1984 Jerzy Popiełuszko, Polish priest, kidnapped and murdered

October 19, 1984 Accidental self-shooting of Jon-Erik Hexum on set of *Cover Up* deemed anti-Hollywood

October 20, 1984 Valley Parkway All Purpose Trails completed in Cleveland Metroparks All Purpose Dump

October 21, 1984 François Truffaut, director, dies of mind-boggling brilliance

October 23, 1984 Ethiopian famine caught live on NBC

October 23, 1984 Lunch vehicle moves to launch pad

October 24, 1984 Colombo crime family sees 11 members arrested, coiffed and released

October 25, 1984 Discovery of Hepatitis virus signals end of liver

October 25, 1984 Chancellor Rainer Barzel resigns due to flagrant dishonesty in West Germany

October 26, 1984 Baboon heart transplanted into 'Baby Fae'

October 26, 1984 *Leave it to Beaver* actress, Sue Randall, dies at 49

October 29, 1984 New York Marathon won by Orlando Pizzolato (2:14:53) and Greta Weitz (2:29:30)

October 30, 1984 *Tiger Fangs* actress, June Duprez, dies at 66

October 31, 1984 Prime Minister of India, Indira Gandhi, assassinated by 2 of her own deeply confused bodyguards

(November, 1984)

The wind pounded the house so violently that no one could sleep. Emily tried to read in bed, but the book shook in her hands each time the wind gathered itself and struck the house. Winds were gusting up to 120 kilometers an hour. She had heard it on the CBC news. Finally, she laid the book down on the side table and stared at the moulding high on the wall across from her. Jacob was out in the kitchen, mad with her because of an argument they had had about Blackstrap being the way he was, having to go away. Jacob said it was her fault that Blackstrap left. 'Why?' she had asked, but Jacob could not explain. His eyes had searched around the floor, seeking an answer. 'So high 'n mighty,' he had finally said. 'Merchant's daughter 'n a bloody Protestant ta boot.' He had then blamed her for all of their children being gone. Why did he think this? It was cruel. It made no sense. Regardless, she feared that it all *was* her fault and felt herself wilting with guilt and mortification. When Junior was small and she was pregnant with Blackstrap, she had imagined all of her children living in Bareneed, each with their own house. She had imagined a large family with daughters and sons gathered at Christmas and at birthdays. And twenty or thirty grandchildren, so that if one was lost there would be plenty of others to fill the space. Her family in one place. Not in the earth or on the mainland. She was deeply sorry for her part in it, but she also felt her blood rising at the thought of Jacob's accusations and stubbornness – which had grown worse over the years. He would argue about anything and, most times, his argument would be based on twisted half-truths.

To calm herself, she shut her eyes and let her thoughts drift north, to the Arctic. Her decade-old plan of engaging her own dog team and going off alone into the white wilderness, where she would live in a canvas tent with only the barest of necessities, had been scaled back as she aged. Not far from her sixty-eighth birthday, she had decided to make the journey with a travel group. The bulk of the money she had saved was still hidden away under her mattress. She had seen an advertisement in *Reader's Digest* for an Arctic excursion. She had written away to the address and booked her passage. She would have to travel without Jacob. He would be dead set against it, and she could not bear the burden of him on such a voyage.

Thinking of leaving on her own hurried her heartbeat. She opened her eyes and saw the shut bedroom door. The window above the bed cast shadows of tree limbs there. Always movement, however faint, even in darkness. A trail against an expanse. The trip was scheduled to take place in two months, in the new year. In the Arctic, she would fit with the place of white removal that she had read so much about. The clarity of wide-open coldness, the purity of that. She imagined herself moving off from the others until absolutely alone, lying down in the snow and staying put, not to die but to somehow live. It had been sixty years since she'd travelled, when she sailed across the Atlantic from Liverpool with her parents. All of the time since then, kept busy with her family and sorrow, then kept to herself.

She reached to shut off her lamp. The click to utter darkness and the living shadows more pronounced on the bedroom door. Settling on her side, her mind was helplessly alert. The secretive thought of leaving filled her with both fear and anticipation, her heartbeat increasing even more, until the beat was intruded upon by a tiny sound, a faint, high-pitched calling. That baby sound again, she thought. She sat up, switching on the light and listening. She recalled the cries that Ruth made at night, how birds would often crash into the window of her room, seemingly drawn by the sound. The tiny bodies on the dark night ground outside the house. There would be crackling in the bushes as animals too appeared more frequently. Mice, shrews and rats were a source of grief then. She had forgotten about that. It had been peculiar at first, but then had been explained away, simply become part of their life.

Hearing the cry repeated, Emily convinced herself that it was only the cat, out in the rain and wind. She recalled Resurrection, the cat that Ruth had always played with, that had always been in the house. The cat that Ruth would let in, despite the protests from Jacob. And where Jacob had found it after Ruth's death. Frozen by the back door, snow and ice stuck to it. It had been hanging where it had got caught up in an old fishing net laid out over the back railing. A hideous signal.

Rising from the bed, Emily slipped her feet into her pink slippers and quickly fitted her arms into the sleeves of her white housecoat.

Jacob watched her as she came into the kitchen, his gaze then fixed unforgivingly on the tea cup he held in his hands.

Emily wondered if he was mad at her or whether his anger had shifted to another recollection, another target, as it frequently did. The immigrants who were flooding into Canada, the people in Quebec who wanted to separate, the . . . Anger so easy for him now. Anger and spite fit to occupy the space left by his own receding existence.

'The cat,' she said.

'Don't worry 'bout it,' he scolded, giving her a hard, injurious look. 'Is dead. I dealt widt it.'

'Why don't you go out and let her in the shed? She must be locked out.'

Jacob laughed. 'I wouldn't put a dog out in dis, let alone gw'out in it meself. She's snarl'd up in dat net. 'N I'm not one ta do da untangl'n. 'N I'm not putting a dead cat in da shed ta rot in da spring. Dat wicked smell come'n out ta meet ye. Da ground's too hard fer bury'n.'

With futility, Emily watched him, talking into his tea cup, and was reminded of Uncle Ace. The man who had disappeared. The body never found, and here he was now, sitting there, that man no different from the other. Only the gift of speech.

'I'll go then,' Emily said, stood closer to the table, unmoving, seeing if her declaration might spur him to action.

Jacob gave no word. He watched through the corner of his eyes as Emily moved toward the back porch door, out into the porch, and began opening the outer door.

'Jaysus Christ, I took care of it, I said. Dere's no point ta worrying 'bout a dead cat. Even if she were full o' kittens. Dey died wid 'er. Hung dere like dat.' He rose with a furious curse and moved for Emily, seeing her reaching for the storm door, her body jerking forward as the wind snatched hold of the barrier and slapped it open. Emily flying from the house, out, hurled into the air by the thrust of the wind, her steady grip fixed on the handle, then letting go.

Jacob raced ahead as the door slammed back on him, striking the side of his head. It hurt not a bit. He slapped the door back open, stepped down the three concrete steps and was inclined back by the wind, held still, held up in a slow lean forward, suspended away from the woman on the ground. She was something to him. A body. He strained a look around for the police. Not there. No one with cameras to take a picture of the victim. He struggled with his footing, leaning more and pushing forward as if bending the force with his entire body.

Released, he knelt close to where the woman had landed on her side against a slate flagstone, her eyes open, staring along the grassy line of the earth as the cat sprang up behind Jacob, meowing and rubbing against his hip, circling and arcing its body, rubbing forcefully for such a little thing, purring and sounding its hellish infant cry. He shoved it aside and watched the woman's face. The woman who stayed in bed all the time. The woman who read books. He knew her. Emily Hawco. He would like to get to know her, if he could.

The cat came nearer and he took it by the throat. Strangled its cry in the howl of the wind as it savagely bit and clawed at his hand. Allowing the injury for a pointless count of moments, he then smashed its skull against a rock.

And the babies came out of her and the babies came out of her and the babies came out of her, each one from a different father.

November 2, 1984 Margie V. Barfield, US murderer, first woman electrocuted in 22 years

November 3, 1984 Anti-Sikh riot in India eradicates 3,000 in just three short days

November 4, 1984 *Waltons* actress, Merie Earle, dies of lethal wisdom at 95

November 6, 1984 Mondale (D) humiliated by President Reagan (R) re-election

November 8, 1984 Special Meeting of Mankato City Council, 4:00 pm, quorum present

November 9, 1984 88 shots in Islander game regarded as outlandish, Isles 45, Rangers 43

November 11, 1984 Father of Martin Luther King and US vicar, MLK Sr, dies at 84

November 13, 1984 Little David Levy finds his 1st comet

November 14, 1984 H. Bruce Stewart's Applied Math lecture: *The Geometry of Chaos* spell-binds globe

November 15, 1984 Baboon's heart gives out, 'Baby Fae' dies at 3 weeks

November 16, 1984 The dead John Lennon releases 'Every Man Has a Woman Who Loves Him'

November 19, 1984 334 die when liquid gas tank explodes in Mexico City

November 20, 1984 50 billionth hamburger flipped by McDonald's

November 22, 1984 Smithsonian Institute receives sweater from *Mr Rogers' Neighborhood*

November 25, 1984 Uruguay presidential election won by Julio Iglesias

November 26, 1984 Guy LaFleur retires after 518 goals & 14 years with Montreaux Canadians

The wake was held in the parlour. The room that no one ever entered. Kept clean and perfectly in order only for death.

Every adult from the community attended. People from areas around Cutland Junction. They arrived from Brigus. Bareneed. Port de Grave. Mourners travelled over from Cupids. From as far away as St. John's and Carbonear. Others flew in. Relatives who people barely knew. Who believed they should be there out of obligation or necessity.

The Hawco house was packed with visitors. Women fussing at a table where all sorts of food was laid out. There in glass and plastic bowls. Turkeys and hams and slabs of roast beef. Dainty sandwiches with the crusts trimmed. Desserts of every sort. The cellophane peeled off the tops.

The old people were escorted on the arms of their sons and daughters. They stood there to look at the body. Expecting what they saw. Yes, that's her, they said. Others silent or tutting to themselves. Visitors telling some stranger who they were. Explaining where they came from. Related to this one or that one. The son of so and so. And then a string of other names from other lands. One attached to another. Leading to Emily Hawco in a coffin.

Everyone needing one final look. Out of respect. Or to tell others they were there. What she looked like. What Emily Hawco was done up like. Who did her face? A lovely job. Right like herself. You wouldn't even know she was dead. The way her fingernails were painted so perfectly. Not a chip out of them. The rosary beads wrapped around her fingers just so. The coffin was second-rate though. And there was a sparseness of flowers. A pity when someone like that's dead and there aren't enough flowers.

Jacob was seated by the coffin. He looked up and took the hands offered him. Watched the faces with fragile hope. Tried to remember what each person meant to him. He saw the face back in Bareneed. Emily there. Hanging clothes from the line. Pregnant. Her hair in the breeze. Turning to look out over the water toward Bell Isle. He explained to everyone how Emily would still be living if they had not moved. The pastureland of Bareneed. Old houses boarded up. His eyes reflecting that. Other houses moved. The collapsed rock foundations remaining as a sign of what once was. Emily buried in the frame of one foundation. That's where she should be buried, he said. This place killed her.

'It's all over now,' he told them. His hand with a bit of a tremble. Older than his years. 'T'were a good life, dough.'

'She died in her health,' one woman sighed.

Jacob Hawco had bought the most inexpensive casket. Claiming that she was being buried in it. Not displayed for the rest of all eternity. Not in a showroom. And that there'd be nothing left of it soon enough. Once it was in the ground. And the bugs had a go at it. Some thought his comments crude. And he questioned himself on them after they were spoken. Wondering why he had gone so far as to say such things. He said this aloud. To others later. To Blackstrap. Not knowing if he was speaking or thinking.

Blackstrap had offered to pay for a better casket. One that cost more. Bigger handles. Shinier fixtures. His money from working on the mainland. Up along in Toronto.

'No need o' dat,' Jacob had said.

'He ain't dealing well widt it,' one elderly woman whispered to another. 'And where's Blackstrap?' said another. 'Where's dat only son of deirs? Junior and Ruth both gone, bless their souls, only Blackstrap. Dey drove 'er to 'er grave. Dose dead children of 'ers. A mortal shame.'

'Out getting drunk probably,' said another. 'Dat Blackstrap Hawco, if I knows him.' Making sounds of shame. 'Naw,' said another. 'He's at da cemetery in Bareneed. Russell saw 'im on da way up frum da wharf.' 'Doing what?' asked one. 'You wouldn't believe it if I told ya.' 'Wha'?' 'I'll tell ya dis much, he's dig'n.'

December 3, 1984 Union Carbide poison gas emission in Bhopal, India kills 2,000

December 3, 1984 Wisconsin sees oldest groom, Harry Stevens, 103, wed Thelma Lucas, 83

December 5, 1984 10 Kanaken killed by French machete-wielding colonies in New Caledonia

December 6, 1984 2nd hostage killed by hijackers aboard Kuwaiti jetliner

December 8, 1984 *Saturday Night Live* tolerates Ringo Starr

December 9, 1984 Mariel Hemingway marries Stephen Crisman in fit of inner serenity

December 10, 1984 Superman discovers first planet outside our solar system

December 11, 1984 *Doug Henning and His World* opens with *Revenge of the Nerds*

December 11, 1984 Colonel Maawiya Ould Sid'ahmed Taya dazzles relatives with Mauritania military coup

December 13, 1984 1st stroke suffered by artificial-heart recipient William Schroeder

December 14, 1984 *Monday Night Football* punts Howard Cosell

December 15, 1984 *Vega 1* launched by USSR for covert summit with Halley's Comet

December 18, 1984 Sweden beats USA at 73rd Davis Cup in Gothenburg

December 19, 1984 Release of *Pumping Iron, II*, film on female bodybuilders

December 19, 1984 Wayne Gretzky, 23, youngest pinball champion to score 1,000,000,000 points

December 20, 1984 33 unheard-of Bach keyboard compositions excavated in Yale library

December 22, 1984 4 black muggers shot on New York City subway by Bernhard 'Don't Bug Me' Goetz

December 22, 1984 'Like a Virgin' by Madonna hits #1 for 6 minutes, then feels 'used'

December 28, 1984 11,700-year-old creosote bush auctioned at Sotheby's

December 28, 1984 Sam Peckinpah, director, dies of one hell of a fucking adrenalin rush at 59

December 28, 1984 28-year-run of TV soap *Edge of Night* finally bridges daylight

December 29, 1984 3 escaped convicts take Carole and Syd hostage

December 31, 1984 Car crash claims arm of Def Leppard drummer Rick Allen

December 31, 1984 Quitting UNESCO, US cites winding down of education, science and culture at home

(*January, 1985*)

Emily's death breathed wasted life into Jacob. He thought of her at all times: the simple passing moments they had spent together, the ease of their lives in the presence of the other. Each recollection more vivid than the reality of the moment. He dreamt of her and woke smiling with forgetfulness, the sheets beside him unoccupied, the weak frustration congealing in his bones. Dead and no longer with him, she grew exact and full-blooded. He often feared sleep. Other times, he longed for it to never end. He wondered how long he had been sleeping and rose from bed suspecting it might have been weeks, months or years.

Blackstrap, back in Cutland Junction for the funeral, had told Jacob that he planned to stay home, to not return to Toronto, saying he had enough weeks for his stamps. He would collect U.I. if it came to that.

Where Jacob once thought, *No bloody U.I. cum'n inta dis house*, he would say nothing to discourage his son. Blackstrap near now at whatever cost.

With Blackstrap to drive him around, Jacob began collecting items from other communities. Old furniture tossed out to accommodate newer pieces. Washstands, bureaus and sideboards that needed fixing up. He cluttered up his living room with them, wanting to fill up the house, to squat himself in tight, or force himself out.

It was while carrying a green sideboard in the front door that the phone rang. He left it alone but it kept ringing. The sideboard had been salvaged from Shearstown Line. It belonged to a Church of England minister back in the 1800s. Most of the old houses were being torn down on the Line. New bungalows going up everywhere.

The telephone kept ringing, drilling into his nerves. Finally, he stomped toward it and grabbed it up.

''Ello?'

'Hello, may I speak with Emily Hawco, please?' A man with a British accent that brought Emily's father to mind. But it couldn't be him. He was dead.

'No.'

'Is she not home?'

'No.'

'When would be a good time to call?'

'Never.'

There was a silence, and Jacob thought to hang up.

'Could you pass along a message?'

'No.'

'It's just that she's due on the Arctic Excursion '85 and we haven't yet received the final instalment. We can only hold her place for a few more days. The tour commences in two weeks.'

'Tour?'

'The Arctic Tour. I'm sorry, would you mind having her call Mr. Norman? She has my number on the literature she's received.'

Jacob hung up. The Arctic. Who was trying to sell them the Arctic? Some shyster. If the fellow called back again, he'd give him an earful.

In the days that followed, Jacob painted every room, but left his bedroom the shade of pink Emily had chosen. The books on the shelves remained untouched. He cleaned the room daily, the dresser top uncluttered with only a few of Emily's bottles and jars and the crocheted doilies and the grey rosary beads with swirls of white, like glassy marble that belonged to his mother. The room held her smell. It was a medium-sized room with much clear space. He sat on the edge of the bed with his palms placed flat above his knees and looked around, thinking of her body in that space, moving through it as she dressed.

Then he stood and went out into the hallway, immediately having to turn sideways to fit past the old armoire pushed up against the wall, and next to that a pine washstand just like the one they had used down in Bareneed. In fact, it might even have been from his house, left behind for newer furniture. He moved out into the kitchen with its groupings of long, thick-glassed cola bottles and blue bottles on the counter, and the two tables, one on either side of the room. Jacob opened the cupboard door for a tea bag and the bag of flour fell out with a thump and spilled everywhere across the counter. A vast plain of white without a mark in it.

Tiny footprints soon seen there. Whose? A tread toward what?

His knees jittered at the smell of fresh-baked bread. It fed his nostrils from nowhere and his knees went weaker. His hand against the flour-covered counter. His head bowed. Eyes open, he stared at the field of white that went on for eternity. Then up at the bread box on the counter. The silver box that showed a warped reflection of his knuckles. The image of Emily stood behind him.

His footprints in that field of frozen white with what trailing after him?

Emily?

'I have to bake,' she said.

'Why? . . . Why, Em'ly?'

'We have to eat.'

(*Summer, 1986*)

Jacob remembered the time he was stuck on the trapline with a broken leg. He had been removing the snare wire from around the neck of a woman from Nicaragua. And his foot had slipped through the snow. He had fallen. On his back, he had seen the white falling from the boughs of an evergreen. The white plume thickening in the sky. A trail following the *Challenger*'s explosion. Thirty seconds following lift-off. He had dragged himself along the trapline, back to the lean-to where he would set his leg to mend. In the lean-to, made from evergreen boughs, toward the back, he had stored the $30 million worth of weapons that had been secretly sold to Iran. The money from the sale had been given to the Contras. Lucky for him, he had managed to pull through. If it weren't for the cases of Coca-Cola and Frito Lay potato chips he would have been a goner.

(*Winter, 1986*)

Jacob looked at the baby. He was unshaven. There were stains on his shirt. His fingers were yellowed with nicotine. The glint of humour had faded from his eyes. They were sad and wrinkled downward at the corners. He had been beset upon.

The sight of the baby made his head tremble. He watched its face. Then he looked at Patsy who was holding the baby. Ruth. All grown up.

Jacob stared at the baby. Shook his head.

'Wha'?' he said, not seeming to get the meaning. He checked Blackstrap as if for explanation.

Blackstrap said nothing.

The baby's name: Junior. He died.

Jacob turned away and set his hand on an old washstand. Pushed up against a wooden headboard in the corner by the window. 'I got dis from an ol' barn down 'n Bareneed,' he said. His eyes went to the baby.

Not mine.

Patsy stood there. Blackstrap stood there. He's not mine. I know he's not mine. I knew it all along. The baby in Patsy's arms. That baby, again.

The baby began to fuss and Patsy left the room. Wandered into the kitchen.

'Is dat Junior?' Jacob asked in a whisper when Patsy was gone.

'Jacob,' said Blackstrap. 'That's what we named 'im.'

'Junior,' Jacob said, turning to look out the window. 'Junior ta some'un.'

The smell of fresh-baked bread.

Emily in the window. Turned to smile at him.

God help me.

(?)

Dere were a man name 'a Brent Linegar. He worked for the merchant. He were a drinker, like a fish. Dirty collar done up and dirty tie straight and knotted proper. He wore white gloves. Shined his shoes even dough da sides were practically out of 'em.

He would finish up widt his work. I'd see 'im keeping books, widt his pencil, every number perfect. He'd be done 'n 'e'd go off ta 'av a drink. All days all night, he'd wander off 'ome, hardly a stagger to 'im, but 'e never knew where he were, 'e'd wake up in someone else's bed widt his shoes laid neatly to one corner, side by side 'n his white gloves off 'n laid one atop da udder on the bedside table, wrong house dough, well one night 'e wandered 'ome 'n no one saw 'im again, we searched everywhere fer 'im, but dere were no report of 'im. 'e were never outside, 'e weren't da sort ta fall down,

da merchant, yer mudder's father, alan, were on vacation, 'e went somewhere sunny on a ship, ta boston or furder sowth, when he came home 'n opened da 'ouse 'n brought his suitcase to 'is room he heard yer mother screaming, when he went to yer mudder's bedroom, dere was brent linegar, frozen solid, 'e were, looking well preserved and neat as anything,

dat's a good story, ain't it,

Jacob Hawco was part of several uprisings against the merchants in Bareneed. He was named as a chief instigator in one document, although, as far as I could determine, he evaded arrest and trial. Despite being separated by unfortunate circumstances, Emily and Jacob would be reunited in the years to come.

1937

Where Blackstrap's father, Jacob, turns twenty and Emily's father is taken away

Zack Coffin, president of the Bareneed branch of the Fishermen's Protective Union, stood at the counter of the Bowering Brothers store. He had come to demand a look at the books that Alan Duncan kept with their expenses written out. William Coaker himself, who had visited Bareneed the previous night, had taught Zack about the crooked ways of digits as figured by the merchants.

Jacob Hawco was on hand to give Zack support, despite the fact that Jacob's mother, Catherine, had discouraged him from being seen with Zack, warning about the FPU and how it was organized at the Protestant Orange Lodge, claiming the union was anti-Catholic. The newly arrived parish priest, Father Burke, too, had made a point of discouraging Catholics from joining the union, claiming that Coaker was a 'threat to society' and condemning the 'materialism' of the union's demands. Jacob went along however, knowing that a change was due in how things were handled. At the FPU meetings, it was detailed how the merchants had taken advantage of the fishermen for decades, rigging the prices so that people came away with nothing more than the clearance of their debts for the most basic provisions (mostly clothing and food) conveniently purchased at the merchant store.

It was the weekend, so Emily Duncan was behind the counter. Weekdays saw her practicing piano, baking in aid of the Protestant church ladies, and knitting mittens and hats for the poor children down in the most impoverished section of Bareneed, the cove nearer to the shore that her father referred to as 'the gut.' She had been arranging tins of Gillett's Lye in the wooden cubby holes that comprised the back wall, having replaced the steel funnel with another, the previous having been purchased earlier that morning. A tricky bit of business, for she had to stand on a stool to reach where it was, and avoid the other articles that hung around it: the lanterns, kettles and rugs. When the bell rang over the door, signalling Jacob and Zack's arrival, she had spun around to see who it might be.

'We're 'ere ta see yer fadder,' said Zack, in his lackadaisical manner of speech, while Jacob stood back, checking over a pair of overalls that were neatly folded among others on one of the divided wooden shelves.

'I'm sorry, he's not here,' Emily replied, but her eyes took a peek toward the open doorway at the rear of the shop, for from there came a rummaging sound.

'I t'inks 'e is,' said Zack.

Emily noticed Jacob stealing a quick look at her. He had always been the one to stand up for her at school when the Catholic boys hurled stones at Emily and sang out: 'Dirty Protestant.' He had been the quiet and darkly handsome older one who had chased off the taunting boys, allowing Emily a clear run home up the hill toward her big house with its view of the bay. Friendless, she had grown up with her books, the British classics: *Wuthering Heights*, *Jane Eyre*, *Pride and Prejudice*, which were ordered by her mother from St. John's, and which she read again and again, the prevalence of doomed romantic isolation striking such a deep chord in her heart, the stark British landscapes so much similar, in brooding sentiment, to those in Newfoundland. She had spent most of her time in her room, warned by her father to keep clear of all those beneath her social standing (which seemed to be everyone), while watching out the window at the valley of shacks, with the fishermen dressed in greys and blacks, and striding about with their arms hung at their sides. She dreamed constantly of returning to England to live in that soulful place of her books, for despite the grimness of the tales, there was also a sense of monumental stature and importance that seemed lacking in this outpost.

Lately, she had taken to going for walks into the hills and making notes and sketches of the flowers and trees in her journal. Occasionally, she would come across a rabbit, fox or moose and would stand in wonder at the suddenness of life in all its vivid clarity. The fox, no different in size than a small dog, would sometimes remain still, studying her, and, once or twice, had even made movements toward Emily, which had both startled and thrilled her.

Presently, her father made more noise from the back room. She heard him muttering, as though he were searching for an item beyond memory's grasp. She looked at Zack, who stood, snorting breath through his nostrils, his cheeks turned a lovely shade of dusty pink, like the hue of a flower petal. She then checked for Jacob, who was now deeper toward the back, pretending interest in a few bolts of material and rolls of wallpaper that were laid up against a baby's high chair. Although Jacob had hung around with the other boys, he had rarely attended school in those early years when Emily first came to Bareneed. He was too busy salting fish or off in the woods cutting wood with his uncle Ace, the madman who never spoke a word to anyone.

'Emily,' called her father, coming out of the back, his eyes briefly on the two men before realizing they were of no importance and so he went up to his daughter, his attention cast toward the ground, as though he could not meet her eye.

'These two gentlemen are here to see you.'

'What?' Alan glanced them over. 'These two.'

'We're here 'bout da books.'

'Books? What books?'

'Da ledgers.'

'The ledgers are there.' He pointed to the two ledger books that were for sale in a cubby hole behind the brass cash register.

'No, yer books. According ta Mr. Coaker we 'av a right ta look 'em over.'

'Coaker!'

Emily backed away, her hand sliding along the lip of the long counter. She thought it might be a good time to leave, as her father's voice had adopted an edge of hostility.

'I'm Coaker's man 'ere.'

'Is that so? Well, I'm aware of the procedure.' At once, Alan turned and trod off toward the back room. The door was heard opening. A few moments passed and then the door was slammed. Alan Duncan reappeared with a weighty black ledger. He set it down on the counter. 'Zachery Coffin. Correct?'

'Yays.'

'Good. I'll be pleased to show you your accounts, but those of the others are of no consequence to you. In fact, they're confidential and without the authorization of—'

'I'll see mine, too,' said Jacob.

Alan Duncan squinted toward where Jacob Hawco lingered at the back of the store. 'Aw, Mr. Hawco. Yes, of course, I'll dig out the records of your uncle, Ace Hawco, as well. I believe he still hasn't settled. There was the question of his debt a few years ago, yet my efforts to collect on behalf of the establishment proved futile. It seems he had no house to call his own, according to the deeds. The house that was once his was demolished and rebuilt as yours. Correct? Or so the deed states.'

Jacob stared. He tilted his head slightly one way, aware of Emily's eyes on him, yet unwilling to meet hers.

'How clever,' added Alan Duncan.

'I'm twenty year old.'

'What?' Irked, Alan furrowed his brow.

'I'm twenty year old.'

'And? So?'

'I believe your daughter's of 'bout da same age.' He did not so much as look at Emily.

'What?' Alan said with a huff, his eyes flashing toward Emily, locking and then dipping to the ground. 'I . . . what?' In confused confrontation, Alan then glared at Jacob, but could no longer meet his eyes either. It was known that any talk of his daughter turned him into a stuttering idiot.

Alan Duncan left the room and returned with two additional ledgers. The three books were opened in a row on the clear counter and the three men went over them, with Zack figuring additions and subtractions on pen and paper.

The entire inspection took over three hours, and when Jacob and Zack departed, Bowering Brothers store owed Zack's and Jacob's families over one hundred dollars a piece.

*

362

Amanda Duncan thought through the details that she would include in her letter to Annie Gull. She was seated at her writing desk with a view out the window toward sea, her pen poised in hand. Her eyes were trained on the horizon as though this searching look might arouse an image of Annie and what might be best written to her. Dusk was settling over the sea while her mind illuminated their excursion by train from St. John's to Brigus.

Dear Annie:

I hope this letter finds you well. It has been almost ten years since my last missive to you. I had been warned by Alan that any word of our new location might be of dire consequence. However, all seems well now and I cannot put off writing to you any longer. Enclosed with this note is the letter I wrote to you all those years ago (but never posted for fear of repercussions) on our arrival in Bareneed from St. John's.

I will write more about Emily's growth and education in the time to come. Please forgive my silence, although as a mother I fear such behaviour might be entirely unforgivable!

Faithfully yours,
Amanda Duncan

Dear Annie:

We have moved to Bareneed, an outport in Newfoundland, where we have set up shop in hopes of helping the poor fishermen. We ventured to Brigus by a special train and were most comfortable; Alan & I had cabins with beds next door to each other & a washstand – just like a tiny ship's cabin. Emily bunked down with me and took great delight in watching out the window at the landscape flashing by. We had an observation car and a dining saloon and our own kitchen. Our train ran up & down inlets of the sea, & along lakes & in & out of coves. The land itself is $1/4$ water. I must send you a map that will show you how wild it is. 6,000 miles of coast with most of the outports accessible only by water.

From Brigus, we transferred to a boat to Bareneed, where we were met by a crowd and a doctor working away with a little girl who had just been drowned. As you might imagine, such a meeting immediately put a damper on any good feelings of arrival. The sight of the little girl greatly upset Emily, for she stated that, in time, the girl might have been her dear friend. I later discovered that the girl was one of 11 children & there was nothing in the house – not even a shift in which to clothe the poor little body for the coffin. The poverty of the people and the size of their families are both appalling problems. When hearing me complain to Alan about the grievous state of things, Emily was quick to offer one of her better dresses for the little girl's burial.

In Bareneed, the fishermen are unorganized and are in fact serfs. For 300 years, they have been existing, and the major part of their earnings have gone to create about 300 wealthy families, one for every year of occupation. And that system of sweating still exists. It is a dreadful problem. The people are so apathetic – they have suffered so long there seems to be no energy in them.

Since arriving, I have been trying to help with the local schoolhouse and have made some inroads. The children are taught everything. At my suggestion, school now begins with the children washing their hands, faces, ears & necks and brushing their hair. Then they all clean their teeth. All of this is an entirely new experience for them.

This is a cruel county in many ways. Life is maintained by killing something – fish or seal or deer or beaver – or birds – and from their babyhood the children learn to kill. The result is indiscriminate killing. The caribou is supposed to be protected. The poacher goes out & kills, not one, but as many as he can, and then leaves the corpses rotting on the ground, just taking titbits for his consumption. The same with birds. They shoot for the sake of killing. The same with salmon in the rivers. They poach the salmon – 'jigging' they call it – and often leave them lying on the bank – just kill for the sake of killing. And yet they are highly religious people.

In St. John's, I learned that the numbers of baby seals destroyed in the annual hunt are enormous. They say it is a dreadful scene. The seals cry pitifully just like babies, & tears come from their eyes. The big seals are shot; the babies are killed with one blow of a club. It must be ghastly. This year the fleet has taken 190,000 – and 20,000 large seals. One ship came in with over 50,000 white-coats, i.e. baby seals, on board. They only bring the skin for the fur. The carcass is left on the ice. A man comes home from sealing with £20 in his pocket and goes straight on the dole. And this though we have got 100,000 people on the dole of the island's 280,000 occupants. There is a general demoralization among a people who, a generation ago, were self-respecting, self-helpful people like the Scotch.

What is needed here is education, and we are arranging for that.
Faithfully yours,
Amanda Duncan

There was a celebration in the Coffin house that night. Jacob was present, but his mother refused to attend, claiming that Zack had made an error, how could a mere fisherman know more than a merchant. There had been some mistake, she warned. 'Mark me words,' she had said spitefully. 'No good'll come frum it. Yer fadder tried ta take on da merchant back in '23 'n dey left 'im on da ice ta perish. Speak'n up on'y gets ye an eternity o' silence.'

The party lasted long into the night.

From her window, Emily witnessed the lanterns burning in the Coffin house, the only throb of light illuminating that small spot in the valley. And further up from the valley, in her father's store, which was nearer their own house, the light burning there, as well, her father not having come home for supper.

Occasionally, throughout the night, Emily could hear the music rising to her, lifted toward her mansion on the slightest breeze. She sat by her window in her wingback chair and read her book, her concentration impinged upon by a hoot or holler or a sharp stroke of fiddle note that escaped when the back door to the Coffin house was opened and shut. So much merriment issuing from that isolated dot of light and the blackness surrounding it. The headland at the edge of the valley and at the cusp of the sea, looming toward the sky, blacker than the sky, as though it were a piece of black felt sheared out and set there. And beyond the headland, the vastness of water, which shimmered a fainter black, a streak of moonlight trailed across its surface, running from the horizon toward land and connected in a straight line with Zack Coffin's house. Lantern light in the windows. Shadows moving about, and shadows stood steadily or stumbling around in the Coffin yard. Emily smiled at this touch of serendipity. It made her sleepy and, for reasons unknown to her, filled her thoughts with images of Jacob Hawco. The look he had given her earlier that day. The dark foreboding thrill of it. Bad girl, she told herself, smiling with secret feeling, naughty girl. And her eyes dipped back to those neat rows of words.

That night, she dreamt that she was dressed in a colourful gown, and at her feet were shades of black and grey. The shades moved and she thought she might be on the sea, stood atop the flutter of water, being stirred by fish, yet as the disturbances increased and began to rise, she saw that the shades of grey and black were men, ascending from the water, carrying nets and knives, yet utterly harmless as they trod past her, as though they were spirits or she were a ghost, either of them meaningless to the other. When she woke in the early morning, still in her chair, and gazed out her window, she saw a ruckus at her father's store. A group of men were gathered outside. She heard the smashing of glass as a rusty barrel was lifted and tossed through one of the front windows. The noise appeared to provoke the men, for their actions became more demanding, leaning toward ferocity.

Emily's mother, Amanda, burst into the room. 'Have you seen your father?'

Emily shook her head, watching her mother turn at once. She followed after her, down the hallway and descending the staircase.

'He never came home last night. Stay here,' said Amanda, as she opened the door and left, heading along the path toward the front gate. She unhinged the latch and briskly advanced down the lane.

Molly Gilbert, the servant girl, was standing behind Emily as she turned from shutting the door. There was a look of fret on her face. 'Wha's da matter?' asked Molly.

'Something at the shop.'

Molly cast her eyes in that direction, as though she were able to peer through walls.

'Dey figured it out,' said the servant girl with a worried expression.

'Figured what out?'

'Da light in yer fadder's store.'

'What?'

Molly paused, her mouth held slightly agape. Then she said, 'It weren't burning all night fer nut'n.'

'What? Tell me what you know, Molly. Please.'

The servant girl fitted her hands into the pockets of her apron and watched her shoes.

'Molly?'

'Dey says 'e were at da books, miss.'

Jacob Hawco, Zack Coffin and the five others – all awake since the previous morning and fortified by an extended evening's consumption of spirits – loudly fled the scene and headed for the wharf. They stopped inside the flake house to partake in the morning ritual of a ladle full of festering cod liver oil from the wooden barrel where the livers were tossed upon gutting. Once each man had had his share and wiped the smear of oil from their chins and whiskers, they leapt aboard their dories and headed out into the bay. There was much merriment and knee-slapping and vile cajoling aimed toward the shoreline.

They steered in the direction of Boghopper Bight, passing the flakes where the salted cod was split and laid out to dry. A few boys were there turning the cod over; a dog was kicked away from chewing on a flattened cod tail.

The men, while out on the water in a fit of rowdy foolery, soon went to work without thinking, setting their lines and jigging cod a safe distance from shore. Throughout the day, they passed several bottles of rum back and forth. When the rum had been depleted, one of four jugs of moonshine – previously hidden in one of the craft for just such an occasion – was revealed to a boisterous round of cheers. The cluster of boats sat prettily in the bay while the late summer sun deepened, toughening the fishermen's skins and casting the flesh in a tinge of mortal majesty.

The men remained on the water until dusk, filling their boats with such an abundance of cod fish that they were buried deep to all sides.

And the cod, not nearly dead, but slowly dying in the unbreathable air, flicked in slippery spasm around them. The laughter derived from being waist-deep in the silvery flopping was life-giving.

While the men tried not to think of it or have its mention spoil their spell of liberation, each one knew in his mind that the ranger would be called in. But if they stayed away long enough, all would most certainly be well. Without doubt, in time, all would be forgotten and forgiven. Deciding to make their whereabouts unknown for a stretch, they headed for a camp on Long Squat Island. Tilts were built there for a stopover journey along the way from Bareneed to Dog Island, where the salmon ran in the spring.

During the night, the men emptied the remaining jugs of wickedly potent moonshine and swapped stories, cursing the merchants and the authorities who would soon show themselves in Bareneed. A few men, drunkenly mistaking talk for a call to action, stood at once and made threatening, staggering gestures toward the others, who were inadvertently taken for enemies. Fights seemed destined to break out, as families pledged to destroy other families in the name of some ancient misdeed that was loosened from their murky bloodlines and now, in the thin of things, flowed more swiftly to the bubbling surface.

Jacob Hawco watched it all in silence, thinking of Emily Duncan and what she might feel about the renegade attack upon her father's store. Did she care for her father or what happened to the business? The Duncans never seemed to be a close-knit family, not like the others in Bareneed. There was a chance that Emily might even admire him for doing what he did. Was she thinking of him in her comfortable house, worried for how he had gone missing?

There was shouting down toward the water, as shadows fell against one another. Someone tumbled sideways and another tipped away and fell to the rocks. Those still capable of laughter found it lowly jiggling in their chests, prompting another sloppy pull at the jug and unintelligible shouts toward the water.

'E's right lovesick,' said a voice. It was Zack Coffin, stood above Jacob, his face half shadowed by the glow of the fire, his body swayed by the flicker.

Looking up, Jacob drew on a bottle of moonshine. He even found himself chuckling, which was entirely out of accord with his usual disposition.

Zack spoke toward the gathered shadows crouched before the fire. 'Dat Duncan young'n give'n 'im da eye when we were in da store.'

There came head-nodding laughter from the shadows beyond the rich orange shades of firelight. Glimmers of faces, wide-eyed and open-mouthed, practically unrecognizable, wavered in the night. A mouth hawked a gob of sputum onto the fire and the sizzle came louder than expected.

In denial, Jacob shook his head. He pulled a knife from his boot and showed it to Zack.

'No injuns here, brudder,' said Zack, staggering back into the greater wash of light and then into the concealing dimness. Gone.

The shimmer of the blade created wonder. Jacob put it away, slowly gathering through the numbing dawdle of alcohol that he had once had a knife in his hand.

Soon, in what might have been minutes or hours, there came further sounds of commotion and cursing, and the smacking of flesh against flesh. Then a splash in the black water. Comments were passed back and forth in a mishmash of inebriated accents. A body rose from its place near the fire. An arm braced against the beach rocks that rolled and clicked, shifting to dump the body on its side.

Jacob took another pull from the jug and watched toward the distance, thinking that the far-off speck of light he saw might be from the bedroom of Emily Hawco. But, no, he soon felt that he was on his back, and what he mistook for Emily's vigil light was nothing more than a star as viewed between the edges of clouds.

In the morning, when Jacob awoke, he found that he was covered in stench. Rising from the boughs where he had been sleeping, having no idea how he had managed to move himself to that spot of rest, he felt weights, one by one, drop off of him, as though chunks of flesh were giving way. Highly unsettled by the sensation, he searched the ground to see cod fish dead along the mossy growth at the edge of the beach. Along the rocks and dirt and grass there were fish in various forms of mutilation. Some were headless and gutted, others skinned with the patterns of their bones along their exteriors as though turned inside out.

The beach was slathered with fish innards. The buzz and swirling lift of flies added disquiet to the spectacle. Along the treeline, there came a few dull thumps as fish fell from the higher boughs, stirred by a rising breeze that felt as fresh as mint on Jacob's face.

A few of the men were already awake and stood perplexed among this baffling slaughter. Bereft of language, they watched Jacob step into their midst, then stared toward open water, only now noticing a large bulk on the shoreline near their boats.

A body level with the waterline, its clothes and hair sapping wet.

Jacob trod nearer and crouched, knowing by the soggy stillness that things were not right. He turned the body over. Zack Coffin, dead drunk, his face white.

No, Jacob said in his mind, rattled by an inner shiver. Not dead drunk, but dead. He looked to the other men who stared breathlessly, eyes on the body then shifting to other disbelieving eyes.

Seagulls cried above the beach and the men stared up to see a flock wishing to settle on the scene and feed off the carnage.

Zack Coffin. Murdered or drowned, no one could rightly decide.

In time, as all were roused, the men turned from disbelief to argument over the doing, accusing one another of what might have been rightly withheld in their minds.

All of it useless, this talk, Jacob had pointed out and, with the help of another, loaded the body aboard Jacob's boat.

In a procession of wretched-souled silence, the men steered their dories back toward Bareneed where the headland loomed above the settled living, evident even from the distance of ocean miles.

'There's a'ways tragedy sprung frum such t'ings.' Catherine Hawco was working in the garden, bent over in the midday sun, weeding the beets. She divined movement overhead and peered toward the sky, squinting to see a pattern of birds plummeted from the pale blue, down toward the shore, seemingly disappearing in the ocean. 'Da ranger were by 'bout dat foolishness up on da hill. Ye'll be paying fer dat window. Mark me words.'

Jacob watched his mother, his head filled up with the death of Zack Coffin. A death no one on shore yet knew of. They had buried him at sea and sunk his boat, bashing a hole through the bottom with the rock anchor. That body, with stones in its pockets and its boots filling up with the weight of the sea, disappeared under the surface. Forever watching that sinking sight, Jacob could not speak of it. And never would. The tragedy brought to mind his Uncle Ace, what Uncle Ace had faced to silence him those ten years ago, for Jacob felt that he, too, might refuse to utter another word. In that deadened state, he sensed himself at communion with his uncle. Where was he now? Jacob wondered. Always off somewhere. Wandering the land, he would be gone for days. He might be on the trapline. He might simply be huddled in a spruce lean-to somewhere. He might be dead like Zack Coffin.

'Yer fadder were a twin 'n I were warned, when I were but a liddle girl, 'bout da misfortune dat would come from union widt 'im. I t'ought nut'n of it. A young maid like I were. Dere's nut'n wort' believing in den. Only headfirst inta all da mistakes ye'll ever make. It were only misery dat were heaped upon us. First it were yer fadder, Francis, 'n now Uncle Ace gone off widout a word as he be wont ta do.'

It was the first Jacob had heard of Uncle Ace being his father's twin.

'I shuddn't even be tellin' ye such t'ings. No good ta jinx us, but widt dem both gone da harm be taken away. Men're a bloody nuisance, is what.'

'A twin,' said Jacob, staring up the valley toward the Duncan house, his eyes first catching on Zack Coffin's house. Had word reached that household yet? There was not a sign of life in the garden or in either of the windows.

Catherine paused and stood with a groan, pushing her hand against her back. She picked a piece of grass from the front of her bleached-white apron and stared at it, her eyes brightening. 'Well, Blessed Virgin, a four-leaf clover.' She winked and grinned at Jacob. 'I'll press dat in da bible fer safe keep'n.'

Jacob said nothing, his gaze on his mother's fingers twirling the clover.

Girlishly, Catherine looked at her son, her eyes gradually darkening while she dropped the clover into her apron's front pocket. She raised her hand threateningly, and Jacob leaned away. 'Dun't 'av me ta smack da face right off ye. Involved in dat foolishness up at da store. 'N udder t'ings, too, I can see da lie in ye a'ready. Wha' else?'

Jacob shook his head.

Catherine stared for a while, until Jacob could stand the investigation no longer and gazed away.

'Git,' said his mother. 'Git in da 'ouse, g'wan.' She shooed him off, made a boot stomp toward him and flicked an arm in his direction. 'G'wan.'

Backing away, and with his mother's fierce gaze still set on him, he turned and trod toward the back porch. He went through to the kitchen where he saw his mother out the window, stood in the same spot. She watched up the hill at the store, and dragged her sleeve across her brow. Then, straightening, as though newly aware of a presence, she spun and glared right at him with burning eyes, then raised her hand again as though to deliver upon him a sound clobbering.

Isaac Tuttle had come by the store with a box of holy cards, rosary beads and medals of saints to sell to Alan Duncan, and had been alarmed by the boarded-over window and the presence of the ranger. Any sort of altercation turned him into a fit of nerves, for he suspected that the trouble from it might be said to be the product of his indirect doing. And he could not be put in trouble's way. If the ranger ever darkened their doorway on his account, his mother and father would take turns thrashing him until there was not a trace of life left in him.

It was only to obtain an order from Mr. Duncan and then he would be off. Years before, when he was a boy, he had sold the holy items door to door in the area: Bareneed, Port de Grace, Cutland Junction, Shearstown Line. He travelled by horse and buggy, doing so since the age of ten when he had finished his schooling. But, now, with the convenience of the shops, he went about his sales in that fashion.

Even the voice of the ranger was a menace to Isaac. He would have fled the shop and endured none of it had it not been for Emily Duncan stood behind the counter, her face somewhat white from the shock of the violent action brought upon the store by the vandals. The names of those involved had been called out by her father, for he had seen every one of them from where he was secretly stood in the corridor leading to the back offices.

On the mention of Jacob Hawco's name, which was called out in the

372

gravest, most severe tone by her father, Emily appeared to wince and shift uneasily on her feet. Isaac took notice of this because he was aware of Emily's fondness for Jacob Hawco, having heard stories of how Jacob had protected Emily through the years.

The ranger took down the names and assured Alan Duncan that the perpetrators would be brought to justice and no further happenings of the sort would be expected or tolerated, by God, as he was now taking up residence in the community for the safety's sake of the Duncans' persons and property.

The ranger then left, tipping his hat to Alan Duncan, smiling assuredly at Emily Hawco, and casting a suspicious look toward Isaac Tuttle on his way out.

'Tut, tut, tut,' said Isaac Tuttle, in an uncharacteristically bold manner. 'Mischief makers.' He gave Emily a clumsy smile, hoping it might offer a bit of reassurance. Lifting his brown case onto the counter, the one he had been given as a gift for his twentieth birthday last month, he unfastened the catch and went about laying out his goods. Alan stared at the lot, his mind so occupied that he saw not a single object. Emily stared there too, her thoughts elsewhere.

'Which would ye like?' Isaac enquired. 'Dere's a fine market fer such icons in da holy persons of Bareneed. Ye knows me mudder were frum 'ere before we moved ta da Junction. We got relatives still 'ere. Ye c'n be sure 'a dat.'

'Leave a bit of each,' Alan said shortly, and, distracted, turned for the back room. 'Emily will look after you.'

With that, Isaac turned his sheepish eyes to Emily. He went over the words in his head: *I brung ye a present. I knows ye likes ta settle down widt a good read in da even'n.* Yet the more he shuffled through the words, the more convoluted they became until he blurted out: 'Brung sumt'n good, ye likes reading, yes.' From his box, he daintily lifted out a paperback. It had a lurid cover that, now revealed in Emily's presence, took on a more vivid, explicit connotation and made him blush. When the book first arrived by mail, he had hidden it away, not wanting his mother to see it. He had ordered it expressly for Emily, for the woman on the cover resembled her to a certain degree. If his mother knew of the existence of the book or of his fondness for Emily, she would whip him fiercely for

373

his sinful thoughts and deprive him of meals for a week. His sinful thoughts were, she would scold, no different from intention and deed itself. One and the same. 'Ye 'av sinned,' she would gravely state, watching his face as he passed into a room or sat at the dinner table. 'I c'n see dat in ye. Dere's no hid'n injurous t'ought frum a wicked son's mudder.' And she would name the quote's exact place in the Good Book.

While studying the book cover all those days prior to his journey to Bareneed from Cutland Junction, he had looked upon the woman on the cover as Emily. The slip that the woman wore was cut low in the front and the hefty curves of her bosoms were pinkly apparent.

'Oh,' said Emily, her tone implying that she was distressed by the cover.

Isaac gave a hard swallow. 'Is a romance,' he mumbled.

'Yes, I can see.' She raised her eyes from the cover to Isaac's grimacing face, and she smiled if only for the sake of soothing his obvious unease. 'Thank you.'

'I'm . . .' he stammered. 'I got 'er . . . ordered in . . . I . . .' And he saw in her eyes something distant and plainly apparent, a question that tore at his very existence and made him flee the store, his body thrusting through the screen door, his boots jangling bits of broken glass on the ground. Away he went to the lane behind the store where his horse and carriage waited. He climbed aboard in sobbing hatred of his being, leaving all his holy icons in the cherished hands of his beloved, while he muttered a string of ugly sentiments against himself for all of that day and night, and into his sleep and the heartlessness of the waking morning.

That night, Jacob lay in bed watching the ceiling. From beneath him, through the vent in the floor, there rose the sound of his mother's low rhythmic muttering in the kitchen. Quietly, he tossed back the covers and knelt beside the vent, leaning for a view through the iron slats. There was his mother, knelt at the kitchen table, her hands joined in prayer and resting against the table edge. A length of rosary beads hung from her hands. The lantern was turned so low that the scene was golden.

At first, Jacob felt fear rise in him, fear of what God might think of

374

him, fear of the outcome of Zack Coffin's loss. But as he listened and let himself be guided by the undulations of his mother's prayers, he pleaded for forgiveness and experienced a calm. He remained on his knees with his head bent toward the grate and, with eyes shut, joined in with the pattern of his mother's recitation, for he knew it by heart, having heard it from the time of his infancy.

This way he remained, until the sound of his mother's voice shouted out to him: 'Get da Christ back in bed.' And he leapt away from the grate and buried himself in the covers.

Emily Duncan continued to work at the store, for her father spent more time away, his nerves, no doubt, having been badly accosted by the attack. She had heard by letter that the window was soon to be replaced by an order from Mr. Bowering.

On the morning of the scheduled replacement, Emily stood on the step, having witnessed the ship's arrival through the unsmashed plate-glass window to the other side of the door. The large window was carried up over the valley by two men who had attentively taken it down the plank of the ship. Much to her surprise, she noticed Jacob Hawco, with cap on head and one hand in his pocket, the other holding the handle of a wooden toolkit, trailing up behind the two men.

Arriving in the store's yard, the men set down the glass, leaning it up against the side of the store, then tipped their hats to Emily. They surveyed the sign hung above the front door, one of the men checking the name against what was written on a piece of paper pulled from his back pocket. Satisfied, they went back to the boat, without further word to Emily.

Jacob, barely greeting the two men on their way down, continued on until he reached the store. He glumly tipped his cap to Emily and set down his heavy toolkit near the steps before studying the boarded-up window.

Emily was struck speechless by his presence. At first, she had been happy to see him and had even flushed with excitement, but now, for reasons unknown to her, her flush was tainted with animosity. She felt herself growing vexed with him. Folding her arms, she watched while he used a bar from his kit to tear the lengths of wood from where they were nailed over the window frame.

Shifting her eyes toward the distant wharf, searching for the other men to see if they might be returning, she noticed Jacob's mother stood out in her yard. She was faced toward the store and stared without movement, her body posed plainly yet with the tension of intent.

The noise of splintering wood drew Emily's attention back to Jacob's work. Questions stirred in her mind, and she desired clarification. Why had he come? Why was he doing this work? Was it an act of penance or an act from the heart? Were his acts genuine or spurred from the cold mechanics of obligation?

By the time the two other men returned with their toolkit, Jacob had removed all of the wood. The gape of the window hole intrigued Emily. It was a sight rarely seen, that remarkably clear view of the items in her father's store.

Jacob stood off to the side, while the two men gave him some consideration, but seemed inclined not to question him. They worked in silence, removing the bits of glass that remained jaggedly obtruding along the frame. They then went about retrieving the new, cumbersome piece of glass from the side of the store.

Emily had gone back into the shop to tend to a customer. Done with wrapping the purchase, she offered the change with her thanks and followed the customer out to the top step. A few men and a woman, along with several children, had gathered to watch the installation. Emily tried not to let her eyes drift toward Jacob, who stood off to himself, yet she could not prevent it. There he remained, watching the window be hoisted into place as though he were lord over it all, as though what the men were doing required his all-knowing approval. Perhaps he had come to smash this window. What was to prevent him? Emily checked toward her house up on a higher rise and thought of striding off to get her father, but that would only muddy things up. Her heart, betraying its basic physiological function, became nothing more than a torment to her.

Again, Emily peeked toward Jacob's yard to see Jacob's mother still positioned in her garden. A flock of birds flew overhead, drifting in varying formations of unison toward the north. A cat ran up the beaten path and then disappeared into the taller grass, lifting its paws higher. Nearer to her, a boy passed comment about the cost of candy. Emily responded to him and he poked in his pocket, extracting a few coins and worrying over them.

Sensing Jacob's eyes on her, she flittered her gaze that way to catch him in study of her. He continued staring, boldly refusing to let up. Unable to hold Jacob's gaze any longer, Emily hurried back into the store.

When the men had finished sealing the window, they came to face where she lingered behind the counter and announced the completion of the task.

'Thank you,' she told them, hoping they would go off and allow things to return to normal.

'Come 'av a look,' said one of the workers, a thin man who was livelier and more forthright than the other. With a lopsided smile, he tilted his head toward the doorway and stepped off, checking back to assure that Emily was following after them.

Outside, Emily went down the step, noticing that Jacob was missing from his post. She faltered back, needing to shade her eyes from the blinding reflection of the sun in the glass.

'Very nice,' she said.

'A'right?' said the thin worker.

'Yes, thank you.' She took a look at him.

He grinned and nodded, highly content to have her approval.

The other man had already wandered off down the trail and the thin man bowed his head, spoke his goodbye, and joined his partner. With the two men gone and the glare of the reflected sun still in her eyes, she was uncertain of the figure that emerged from the side of the store. She assumed it to be Jacob and stepped so that the glare might slide out of place.

Jacob Hawco trod close to the glass and seemed to be staring through it or at his own reflection. Emily could not be certain.

'What are you watching there?' she said, hotly, finding her voice.

Jacob turned as though expecting the question. 'I saw sum'n in reflection.'

'Um-hmm.' She found herself tapping a foot. Again, she folded her arms across her chest.

'Fleeting, it were. Dat's da word, I suspect. Fleeting.'

'What was it?'

Jacob trod a few steps closer to her.

'Some sort o' t'ing. A feeling it were.'

With the mesmerizing blueness of Jacob's eyes on her and with the lushness of his voice in her head, she thought she might be overcome. Her breath sank and sank as though dropped into the sea where she finally pulled it back with a deep sigh. In the position where she remained, the sun's reflection again brightly slipped in to startle the eyes, as the sun was travelling, or she had shifted in uncertainty, without knowing.

'What sort of feeling was this?' Emily managed, dumbly shocking herself at having spoken the words, the flush high in her cheek feeling more and more like fever.

Jacob came nearer, his hand extended with something balanced in his palm.

Emily thought it might be a stone, and she suspected more openly that he had come to smash the new window. Glancing toward Jacob's yard, Emily saw that his mother was gone. She checked Jacob's palm, wondering if he meant her family harm. What lay in his palm was, in fact, a stone. A white stone, slightly bigger than an egg and rounder.

'Dat white stone,' he said, holding his palm out to her. 'It were me mudder's frum down da line. She said ta pass it ta ye.'

'Why?' Emily let her arms fall and even considered outstretching her open palm to him. Before she thought she might, she had done it. 'Am I supposed to toss it through the window?' She said this saucily, which made her head jerk in a gesture of challenge.

Jacob set the stone in her hand. It was at once cold from the earth and warm from him. And it was lighter than expected, as though hollow in the centre. She shivered, as gooseflesh rose to provocative life on all surfaces of her body.

'It c'n't do much damage,' Jacob professed. 'Ye pass dis frum one ta anudder.'

'What feeling?' she quickly asked in a quieter, confused voice, remembering his earlier remark.

'Dey say it brings on fergiveness.'

Emily lifted her eyes from the stone to him.

'Forgiveness for what?' she asked, beguiled to the point of weakness, her gaze centred on his eyes and face.

'Ah,' he said with a smile that was more of an injury to himself than a signal of joy. 'Neidder of us 'av a clue, eh? Wha' cud ye 'av done? Nar one wrong t'ing. 'N me, I'm as innocent as da lamb.'

The following week, there was more commotion. The day after the trouble at Bowering's store, Alan Duncan had locked himself in the den of his house and refused to show his face, not even to open the store nor to meet with the ranger who required Alan's signature to bring charges against the vandals.

Emily was the one enlisted to carry on business as usual.

A week later, Mr. Bowering himself arrived, followed by two men in long coats and gloves who made their way directly to the store, for a long-scheduled visit. Dissatisfied with the state of the shop, which had suffered a few more assaults, despite the presence of the ranger who, at various turns, had found himself bound and gagged and dumped in the woods, Mr. Bowering and his cohorts made their way to the Duncan home.

Emily's mother later told her that Mr. Bowering and his men had demanded that Alan join them for discussion, but Alan had refused, claiming that they were not about to capture him so easily. If they were here for the girl, she was at the usual place of business.

Mr. Bowering and his men had then returned to the store and removed the cash from the safe in the back room.

'Someone will be here,' he told Emily. 'To deal with your father. He's clearly out of his wits.'

Since the passing of the stone to Emily, Jacob had not come near her. She thought that he might have been embarrassed or was waiting for her to visit him, which would be highly unorthodox. Her mind played with the possibilities to the point of utter distraction and torment. It were as though a spell had been cast over her, and Emily suspected that it might have something to do with the white stone, which she carried in the front pocket of her apron and often fondled, and Jacob's mother, Catherine, who was regarded as a healer by many in the community. Emily had heard stories about Jacob's mother from the servant girl.

Catherine Hawco's past was rife with peculiar happenings, and the Hawcos in general were said to be the product of some mythological bloodline.

Regardless, Emily waited in hope and anger. When not serving customers or restocking provisions, she stood at the shop window, pretending to watch the water, yet glancing toward Jacob's yard where she sometimes saw him at work in the garden or coming in or out of the small barn. Whenever Jacob looked toward the store, Emily would turn away to pretend straightening items in one of the bins until a time when she thought it safe enough to courageously peek a look.

Three days following Mr. Bowering's visit, a boat arrived at the dock with two tall and broad men, who, after joining ranks with the ranger, burst down the door of the Duncan study and took Alan Duncan by force, strong-arming him away to the boat. He raved and roared while the dour or grinning faces in the Bareneed windows and yards watched him go.

'Dere he be,' they muttered. ''Taken from whence he n'er belong'd.'

Emily continued running the shop, expecting that it might all come to an end. Her mother assumed as much, as well, although they would not speak of it. They kept up appearances and went about their routines, until, ten days later, when the mail arrived, a letter was received addressed to Mrs. Amanda Duncan. The letter was from a solicitor representing Mr. Bowering. The contents advised them, in so many words, to vacate the premises by the stated date.

The shop was to be taken from the Duncans and run by a new family by the name of Harmen.

They were given a week to clear out their belongings, and, so, one week later, the furniture from the Duncan house was moved by cart down to the wharf where it was loaded aboard a steamer. Emily and her mother were scheduled to travel on that boat, as well, leaving Bareneed for St. John's where prospects appeared brighter.

Jacob Hawco, observing the progression of events from his place on the wharf, fixed his eyes on Emily Hawco as she stepped aboard the steamer. He was ribbed by a few of the younger men while others kept silent, understanding the loss.

Emily Duncan, while aware of Jacob's presence, would give him no attention. Her embarrassment and acrimony prevented her from meeting anyone's eyes in farewell, for many of the residents of Bareneed took profound pleasure in the leave of the two high-and-mighty ladies, and went so far as to make derogatory noises: cackling and hissing and booing.

Emily Duncan and Jacob Hawco would see nothing more of each other for three entire years.

The year of 1962 saw the death of Junior Hawco, the birth of Ruth Hawco and the Hawcos' relocation from Bareneed to Cutland Junction. Jacob chose not to join the others from Bareneed who were meant to move to Burnt Head, instead settling on the nearer Cutland Junction. 1962 was also the year that many believed was the first of many times that Blackstrap Hawco died.

1962

despising the living

summer air mild and warm, the sun pristinely shimmered on gradients of blue, clarity in jacob's boat, stood against the bottom slats, he stared the furthest possible, palest blue sky a line atop dark blue, water's steady depth and volume, sloppy density bobbing the boat gently beneath his feet, ceaseless swelling and ebbing that with the wind's roar might blacken and arch eighty feet skyward to swallow any ship,

but not now with such a sky,

junior killed in the mines of bell isle,

scanning water, he sighted bright orange buoys, stepped nearer the wheelhouse to engage the engine, guide the wheel, circle close to one buoy, but not reach over to retrieve it, instead lingering in silence, calling on merciful recollections, emily and blackstrap, bargaining against despair, junior, his namesake, he stared down the water, dazzled by its implied texture, drawn by waver, wanting blackstrap out here now, to squeeze his shoulder and make it real, but he would not ask the boy to come, walking away, hating them for junior's death, despising everything, most of all the living, and worst of all among the living – himself for existing, adrift on a sunny day,

the ocean's terribly beautiful danger generations sailed over, patrick hawco taken, uncles or cousins lured deep too, water granting sustenance while depriving them of one another, clashing wind with water, neither force claiming victory, in the stead of elemental triumph claiming men as their minuscule prize, what not taken in and consumed by the sop,

lost in thought, a low purring soon in consciousness, a screech from above, looking up for wings, troubled by a flash of light beaming in his eyes, so bright he squinted, not where the sun should be, this radiance, the glare of reflected sunlight, blinding him to the presence of a drifting mass, lines of orange clapboard vivid in noonday brilliance, two storeys high, square house, soul-startled, believing he had drifted so close to land, rocked by wayward yet false sensation, movement not his, he darted a glance toward shore, still miles off, fifteen feet from his craft, a floating house towed by one small boat, quiet engine barely buzzing, the man waving as he neared, his silent family crowded on board, grim outlines stone-still and resistant, a second house, its colour white, trailing behind the first orange one, and another, barn red, ocean littered in line toward the disappearing distance, houses coasting for points further down shore, the first house edging boldly close, the man in the boat uttering no word, the women and children huddled together on the slatted seat at the rear, woman watching jacob with trapped eyes, forced transport, three children finally waving, jacob waved back, his arm languidly through the air, no land beneath them, the house in passing, jacob watched up, the second-storey windows, again sunlight glinting there, reflection of the blue sky, mirror-image of a gull, clear and perfect, as though sky extended itself within the confines of that house, he followed its effortless progression, then another house, faces in boats exactly as the others,

if dere were but a wind, jacob told himself,

isaac tuttle with cap in hand would not sit at the table, the seat emily blankly offered, out of obligation, that was all, he watched emily busy herself washing dishes in the plastic pan, then the flowers he had brought for her, lying flat on the table, stuttered an apology for junior's death, having found the job for junior in the first place, put in a good word with reg prescott, the mine manager on bell isle, not heard, the apology, not a word clear enough to know, isaac filled with troubled sincerity, he grimaced every so often, his eyebrows knitting together in confusion, his eyes squinting to stare at the floor, he moved his cap around in his hands, then peeked at emily, the baby due any day now, she set dishes in her glass-doored cupboard beside the daybed, wiping the plates in smooth, circular motions, she was thinking of junior, a baby, how she washed him in the tub, held his head up, gently wiping the cloth along his chubby pink skin, that smile of his, that pure look so different from blackstrap's,

the back door opened and isaac flinched a look, expecting jacob, but there was blackstrap, stepping in, making great noises in the back porch, rifling through tins of screws and nails resting on a window shelf, finding what he was after, he rushed out, the boy so violently focused he did not even notice the visitor, *at least it were not him*, thought isaac,

out in the yard, blackstrap spat off into the grass, stomped toward the small barn, entering its dimness and heading toward the side wall where a red bicycle rested against the wide planking, bending there, he fitted the tiny screw into the hole in the chain guard, the first screw too loose, sloppy in the hole, the second one with the wrong thread, he stood in a huff, and stepped back from the bicycle, hands in his pockets, turning, he kicked at an empty paint can, it clanged around before wobbling still, a tentative position on its side, wishing to knock down anything near him, the entire barn if need be, to bring back the dead,

he glared at the bicycle, it had to be fixed, and he needed a battery to put inside the silver light casing, too, he could not read the worn sticker on the back of the seat but suspected junior's name spelled there, if it said 'jacob' or 'junior' he had no idea, but understood well enough who it belonged to, and it needed fixing, he grabbed the bike by the handlebars and wheeled it out into the yard beside the long patch of vegetable garden, stared at the seat, the worn red and white covering, a hint of grey stuffing along the left edge, the bicycle just about his size, he checked the dirt road slanting up toward the far-off church and schoolyard, tommy taylor and harold butler rolling screaming down on their bikes, both of them with brush cuts to keep the lice away, seeing blackstrap in the yard, they skidded to a stop beyond the limb fence at the edge of his yard, dust rising, they watched it fill the air and settle,

'you gotta new bike,' tommy taylor called out, but when they kept watching they knew it was junior's old bike,

blackstrap faced the bike the other way, toward the water, let go the handles and it rolled a few feet, moving on its own wobbly balance down the grade before, falling on its side in a twist, he gave it a kick with the heel of his sneaker, 'you com'n,' harold butler tilted his head toward the direction they had just ridden from, 'we're go'n up bald rock,'

blackstrap studied the two boys, then jerked a look at the fallen bike before turning away and heading back into the barn to slam the door and glower in silence,

the headland crack along the faultline had widened since the rumble in the earth, junior's life taken by it, for years the boys of bareneed, on dares, had tried entering the hole, only the smallest of them capable of going so far, before bawling out and getting yanked back by others, but now with the crack widened, boys of fourteen or fifteen could aptly fit,

blackstrap, scaling down the cliff's ocean-side, was first to discover the wider split, he thought it might be some sort of trick, by how the sun was hung in the sky, but as he reached his arms in, he found that if he leaned a little nearer, his shoulders would fit through, he stared ahead into the limited light, airless black as it stretched off, he squatted on his belly and crawled forward, shifting knees as best he could and squirming to inch ahead, arms out in front of him, no way of turning to see the light behind, only blackness and sprinkling dirt he pressed deeper into, fearing he might suffocate, but liking the feeling of that fear, the snug enclosure with the fright, two of them suiting each other,

blindly edging forward, wondering if the hole might end or shrink to a trapping space, a slower creep ahead, until reaching where his shoulders became tightly fitted to the rock, he could not budge another inch, how far ahead, to the hole on the headland's south side, the hole they often attempted to enter as well, but never could, not a sign of light from it, his eyes felt strange, staring into blackness to see absolutely nothing,

he kicked with his boots and jerked to shove ahead, the rocks close around his face, the crumbling dirt, the struggle jamming him more soundly in the hole, he wondered how far he had come, no way of looking back, the air not much of anything, impossible to take a deep breath, his squat ribs, his hips lifted to back out his upper body, but nothing worked, he was stuck, the hard-edged rough rock to all sides of him, yes, he thought, settling at last, his mind growing sleepy, this is where i belong, the service was held at bareneed catholic church, up over the hill from the hawco house, father connolly spoke in a calm voice, recalling the young man's intelligence and unique gift for observation, the learned gentleman described how junior hawco grew up just down in the valley from this church, how junior was top of his class and a caring young man, the priest cited examples of junior's kindness, his willingness to always lend a hand, his intense curiosity and years of volunteer work at the retirement home in bay roberts, his goodness toward others, highlighted there now by the giving of his life for another,

'a hero,' father connolly announced, in a stately manner, 'a good son, a treasure to be loved, to be cherished, and remembered in our hearts forever,'

the canadian, norman park, had flown back from the mainland to pay his respects, other miners travelled from bell isle, forming a delegation in the back, sad worn faces with bowed heads, a fallen comrade, a young one, the worst kind to go,

norman sobbed into a handkerchief, then coughed and straightened his neck, the men not watching him, leaving him be, norman gazing toward the altar, the casket, its crafted bulk, its new weight, its permanence, he thought back to junior hawco's face, recalling shab reardon's drunken violent sprees at dick's club on the ferry wharf on belle isle, he wiped at his eyes, it was more than he could endure, never such tears before, not even at his own father's funeral years ago,

'nineteen years old,' the priest said, sustaining that reflective note, pausing, he stared toward the heavens,

a few sobs broke out from the front of the church, making the space sound hollow, empty, but filled to the rafters, men and women stood at the back, spilling out through the entranceway, not a sound, what to say, when to cry,

'and now a change, always the certainty of change, the community itself soon to shift, one place to another, a new beginning, junior's death, he's found his place, with God, you see it does not matter where we are, as long as we have faith and know in our hearts of our final resting place, where we will be together again when the Lord calls us home, our true home, our only true home,' in the front row, jacob hawco gritted his teeth, he could not take much more of that babbling ramble, he shut his eyes and squeezed emily's hand tighter, squeezed the tears from her eyes,

'junior has left us, but he has not really left us . . .'

norman turned to his side and, with handkerchief covering his mouth, excused himself through the line of standing men, such heart-wrenching morbidity that sucked the breath inward,

the air was cool outside, the sky clear, bright along the tips of spruce that ran off to either side of the road, leading down, beyond bareneed, the road running for miles before connecting with the conception bay highway, moving further east, norman could be in st. john's in an hour,

he stepped away from the church, away from the hearse parked by the door, not far to go to the graveyard and the old tombstones, many from the 1800s, some of them no more than pieces of jagged slate stuck vertically into the ground, something once scraped into their surfaces, he turned away, walked toward his car, over a hundred parked cars and pickups, the community in mourning, all of the vehicles empty, he scanned the makes and models, then saw a black ford galaxie 500, its sides coated with red dust, a man in the driver's seat, the inner compart-ment hazy with smoke, a big man, hunched over the wheel, shab reardon rolled down his window and tossed out the scorched yellow filter of a cigarette, norman noticed that the car was idling, a beer bottle tipped back, then flung into the trees, making a faint whistling sound as it whirled and scraped among the branches before tinkling into the lower brush,

he can't be waiting for me, norman thought, nearing his own car, he caught sight of shab's eyes following after him, *he must be here for junior*,

he flinched and sobbed aloud as shab barked, 'what're ya do'n here, fack'n fruitcake,'

norman climbed into his pontiac and engaged the engine, pulling away, he checked his rearview once, then twice, nothing coming, shab staying where he was, norman thinking, *junior protecting me, even in death*, the radio was playing a love song that did its best to make his heart ache, wiping at his face while cruising slowly past the trees, then into the connecting community of cupids, the scattered houses, the inlet and the wharf with the small boats tied up there, the rugged hills and bluffs spotted with rocks, surrounding him, the rising clumpy barrens, a postcard picture that junior had no place in, norman kept driving until it was gone, and he was on the highway, heading west for the mainland ferry, an eight-hour drive away, leaving the island behind,

voices through the hollowed earth, the muddled sound at night, dead miners dreamt, faces red with dust, solemn tearless eyes aglow, in darkness, the harmony boomed beneath the atlantic, through the ragged shafts of shut mines, number 4, number 3, and soon number 2, the iron ore tankers sunk, resting in sediment, hulls torpedoed by nazi submarines, rusted like iron ore dust that the ghosts toiled among,

   miners sang steadily for junior hawco, an echo through the underground chambers, the resonant, iron-tainted harmony, a dull nocturnal heartbeat, slow as cold molasses,

> *we'll rant and we'll roar,*
> *like true newfoundlanders*
> *we'll rant and we'll roar*
> *on deck and below*
> *until we hear rumbles*
> *inside the mine tunnels*
> *when straight through the rock wall*
> *to water we'll go*

shab reardon's drunk doe-eyed gaze searched the face of the girl-child sat upon his lap in tousled embrace,

   'be t'ankful,' said he, giving nil a big hug and bouncing her on his knee, 'roof o'er yer head, food on da table, a family ta look after ya,' he checked off toward the open door of the bedroom, gertie seated on the bed with the smiling baby boy, while shab took a draw from the cigarette held between his fingers, he mussed up the girl-child's hair and pecked her on the cheek,

   'give's a smile,' he said, searching nil's face for expressions of love, the girl-child smiled for him,

   he tickled and then hugged her again until she giggled and hugged in return, 'ye be t'ankful,' said he, ''member dat, always be t'ankful fer what ya got in dis sorry existence,' and in the centre of his mind, the thought of another man's death relieving him,

My grandfather, Blackstrap Hawco, failed in his first stab at murdering Isaac Tuttle. His unsuccessful attempt to enter the Waterford Hospital in St. John's occurred three days before visiting his ex-wife and son and daughter in Heart's Content. Although Blackstrap's initial murderous exploit did not come to fruition, he tried again three weeks later, his frustration mounting by incidents described below.

1989-1994

(*September, 1989*)

There are boats on the screen. They sail out into the night toward some impending danger. Jacob can tell by the music that something is going to happen. He can tell by the strings of the violins. The low rumble of the bass drum. Tension and fear. The boats continue to sail out. They disappear until there is nothing but blackness.

Jacob waits.

'Why are you crying?' Emily asks.

Jacob opens his eyes. 'It's Blackstrap,' he says. 'It's on da TV. What he done. A miracle.'

'Shhh,' says Emily, cradling Jacob's head. 'Shush-shush, my darling, you know that's not real.'

And his sorry eyes staring up at the memorable blank of her.

(*July, 1992*)

Jacob is on the Bareneed wharf. He knows where Blackstrap will tie up. The place for Blackstrap's boat. There is such a large crowd on the wharf. He can barely find a place. But then the crowd recognizes him. They make a path to allow him a view. Right up front. Blackstrap Hawco's father. The crowd mutters. Hands are on his shoulders. Squeezing his arm. A few applaud him. Your son, the hero, they say. It doesn't take long for the people with cameras to catch on. They ask him questions about Blackstrap. Questions that he cannot answer.

The boats are larger dots now. Sailing from the horizon. Recognizable. Seven minutes away. The crowd begins to applaud and cheer. A roar goes up. A roar to the heavens.

'Did he mention anything to you?' asks one reporter.

'Mr. Hawco, what do you think of your son?' another wants to know. 'How does a father feel when something like . . .'

He sees his son in the lead of the boats. Only a few minutes up the bay. He swipes the tears away. The backs of his hairy hands doing the job. He keeps swiping them clear of his eyes. He hasn't cried like this since he was a teenager.

'Why do you think no one has undertaken this sort of action until now?'

'Do you think this will affect government policy on . . .'

'The cops are here,' says someone.

Jacob looks over his shoulder. Four RCMP officers at the back of the crowd. And more coming in cars. He faces the water. The scent of the ocean being pushed forward. *Bareneed's Pride II* glides alongside the wharf. Wood skimming against wood. A perfect docking. And the other boats soon find their places. When Blackstrap comes out of the wheelhouse. The cheering and whistling hurts Jacob's ears. Blackstrap tosses the rope to his father. Jacob catches it. Ties it around the gump.

'Get dem inta da fish plant,' Jacob shouts above the racket on the wharf. Pointing and nodding at the Portuguese stood on deck. 'Just the right size fer splitting 'n salting. Da smaller ones we'll feed ta da dogs o'er da winter.'

Jacob offers his hand and Blackstrap takes it. Up he rises. Looking the same as ever. His feet on the wharf. Everyone leaning near. Wanting to shake his hand. Pat him. Touch him. He doesn't like much of it. Uncomfortable in the centre of everything.

Then there are cameras and tape recorders in his face. Blackstrap watches his father's eyes. And his own eyes glaze over. Not having any of that.

'Christ,' says Jacob, pawing away his tears. 'Ye've turned me inta da worst sort o' crybaby.'

(December, 1992)

A quick journey at Blackstrap's speed. The drive from Cutland Junction across the slushy Trans Canada Highway. Down through the rolling pastures and shacks of Shearstown Line. And into Heart's Content. In less than an hour he is there. But first he must pass through Sculpin Cove that has no cove. Nor ever did. Then Broke-up Beach. Jagged as a mess of exploded rocks. The road running close to the Atlantic. The loose greyish-green ice at his right. Glowing blueness beyond. A blinding winter sun in a cloudless sky. The water soon lost behind a hill. The snow-laden trees as he rises further inland. And higher up. The curving hill with Dead Soldier River below him on his left. Over the crest of the hill and down into Bay Roberts. A larger town with two strip malls. Two supermarkets. Two hardware stores. Two gas stations. Four fast food shops. One RCMP detachment. One arena. Where he used to watch hockey games as a boy. The boys from the Bell Isle team always the ones to beat. Beyond the traffic lights. And up another hill. Levelling off. Past Ascension, the high school. Then steeply down. He cruises across the flat land of Spaniard's Bay. Again, the ocean at his right. The hills of snow-covered spruce. To his left ridges of rock stuck out here and there. The church high on a steep cliff. Towering right above the road. Through the barrens of Tilton. And the long stretch. Before the rusty hull of the shipwreck. The *Kyle*. The boat that used to bring people up and down the Labrador. Left there now in the shallows as a sight for tourists that signals the beginning of Harbour Grace. The older houses well kept. One old house. Something called a bed and breakfast. The country-living spirit catching on. From the covers of magazines Blackstrap has seen in drugstores. Then inland. Again a curving rise. The lifting and falling of the land that Blackstrap pays no mind to. Yet takes as a presence to be dealt with.

More snow on the road now. Whiter. Thicker. The sky grey. It snows for a few minutes then stops. He rolls on. Listening to Kris Kristofferson on the radio. The sky blue again. Coming upon the grey smoke of the incinerator drifting across the road. Then up a steeper hill. The sign for a radio station. Another RCMP detachment. Then racing down around the sloping valley that cups the town of Carbonear. The ocean a huge U nestled into the land. Up the wide gradual hill that winds for minutes to his right. With its expansive view of land and water. A peninsula that must be Bay Roberts in the distance. Back toward the east. Across the flat desolate barrens that run on forever. Beyond Victoria. And into Heart's Content. Again, water. This time, on the other side of the road, on his left. A long narrow harbour. A proper bay with a wharf and fishing boats. No confusion. This is where he is.

Blackstrap Hawco knows the house. He has been inside many times. Years ago. And is certain that Patsy is in there now. He can sense her behind the walls. Knows that she moves within the comfort of her parents' home. Memories of when they were first dating. Her parents then alive. Welcoming him into their home with open arms. They had heard of his Uncle Ace. The remarkable stories of his triumph against Mr. Bowering, the despised merchant. They were aware of his father, Jacob, and the tales of him on the traplines and on the ocean. And his part in the attack on the Bareneed merchant shop. Patsy's father had told the stories to Blackstrap. Details that Blackstrap was not even aware of. The addition of a spirit who spoke to Jacob when his leg was broken on the trapline. A woman who some thought might have been Jacob's mother, Catherine, warning him of the cold that ate at the dead. Making the stories sound thrilling, monumental and unforgettable. Patsy's father adding his own bright points here and there. Raising his eyebrows. The white hairs long and swirling away. Narrowing his eyes, suspicious of whether the listener understood. Jabbing a finger to poke the scene alive.

Pausing with a frown, and a nod of agreement, 'Yays,' while drinking his rum without ice or water. And then the yarns of his own ancestors' triumphs, their reckless and unbelievable tales of survival in the face of the most wicked bile that nature could heave at them, their blasting and carving up of large animals that threatened one life with their own, and the netting of limitless fish in savage seas that could never muster the might to swallow them, merely spit them back onto land to endure more torment.

Done with his long and extravagant tale, Patsy's father would sip his rum while his wife, a large, solid woman who moved with a dark silence about her, tended to her chores. Not tending to Patsy's father the way he would have liked but out in the back yard after supper splitting wood for the fire, replacing a foot valve down in the well, milking the goat or weeding the garden. Blackstrap would see her through the kitchen window while Patsy's father tipped the bottle to their glasses, and Patsy waited, coming into the kitchen again and again to gripe about their lateness getting to the dance they were meant to attend. While the two men immersed themselves deeper in rum and the intoxication of memories that shrouded them in self-settling hues. The wife would be bent there for hours, flinging stones behind her to crack against the side of the small barn, tearing out weeds and checking them with her earth-stained fingers, devoting careful attention to the garden that was no longer there.

Nothing growing. Now. From the patch of earth that had once been. Made fertile by Patsy's mother. Snow-covered, but that patch always greener than the rest of the grass. In the summer. The soil remembering.

Driving by the house. Blackstrap sees a young boy playing in the snow. And thinks of his brother. Jacob Junior. And the years long ago in Bareneed. He will not remember. Stuck in the crack and his last breath. But here now. Here always.

It is Sunday. Quiet and still. And he feels a longing for his dead brother. The recollection of times spent together. At play. He knows that the boy in the yard is his son. Without needing to see his face. Hidden in the hood of his blue snowsuit and wrapped with a scarf. Tied around his mouth and nose. He knows by the way the boy moves. The way he pounds something against the ground. And the shape of his body.

Blackstrap drives by slowly. The boy does not look up. From the mound of snow he now pats together.

Tires on wet pavement.

Driving on. Blackstrap leaves Heart's Content. And thinks of continuing. Moving through the barrens. Until his sense of solitude couples with the feel of the land. To disappear in sudden desolation. To drive forever and reach nothing. But he finds his foot pressing into the brake. He pulls over onto a wide shoulder. A straight deserted piece of highway. With snow-covered barrens on either side of him. Only the burgundy hip-high bushes poking out from the ditches. He begins to turn the big Tornado around. Having to curve the wheels and reverse. Move forward. Reverse. Curve the wheels. Tightly one way and forward. Finally free. Facing the direction from where he has just come. The gear shift clicks down to drive. Telling himself it will do no harm to visit. His daughter must be walking by now. A pang that he has kept in check by distance. Showing Patsy how he could survive. Without her. And he has. No more of her lip. Her nastiness. The boldness of Patsy's mother's silence. Finding voice in her. But not crossing over to action. Laziness. All her energy in talk.

The driveway just ahead. Not ploughed. Not shovelled. The snow with tracks in it. An old car up to its undercarriage in snow. He pulls over and ahead so not to block the vehicle. Who owns that? he wonders. Not Patsy's. Maybe a man's. Hearing the sound of the stopping car. The hum of the idling engine. The boy jerks his head up and watches toward the road. There is a familiarity to the large green two-door. Recognizing it. The boy lifts himself from his knees. His hands hanging by his sides. His fingers covered by the rounded edges of blue waterproofed mittens. He steps toward the car. The material of his snowsuit making a wispy sound. And stands a few yards away. His head tilted back slightly. To see beyond the edge of the hood that hangs down.

Blackstrap opens the door. Steps out. He is not wearing gloves. And he feels the cold on his fingers. He thinks of putting them in his jean jacket pockets. But wants to keep them out. In case the boy might welcome him.

The boy watches. He does not move.

'How ya doing, Junior?'

Jacob Junior steps forward. For a better look. He stares. Three years ago. Patsy pregnant. And gone. Junior almost seven years old now. Junior. Looking confused. Not surprised when he says, 'Dad?'

Blackstrap does not nod. Why should he? And the boy runs off. Races toward the back door of the house where he crashes in. Blackstrap catches sight of the kitchen window no more than six feet to his right. He sees Patsy stood there with Ruth. His daughter. In her arms. The name she had chosen. His dead little sister's. Out of respect. Patsy still had that. But now she seems angry. The way her mouth moves. Her head turned to see him. The way she flicks back her thin head. He is not certain if the motion was meant as an invitation to enter. Or done out of habit. Left over from the time when she had long hair. Her face seems harder now. Stricken. Sharper cheekbones. She stares at him. And he cannot determine what it is that moves in her eyes. Before she shifts away to watch Junior in profile. She nods down at Junior. Her face aware of Blackstrap. Of Blackstrap stood there. Watching into her life. Suddenly.

Blackstrap hears the muddled dullness of her raised voice. Behind the glass, 'Yes, yes, Junior, I sees 'im.'

It is an awkward visit. The policeman at the foot of her bed. Karen feels caught doing something she should not. The policeman says she has been reported missing. She wonders who reported her. Blackstrap? She doubts it. She cannot imagine him. Behaving with hysteria. She wonders why the policeman is in the room. He does not seem to know.

What happens next.

'I'm not missing,' she says. Her throat sore. Dry. A croak.

'Yes.' The policeman nods. He stares toward the window.

'Where's your uniform?' Her voice barely heard.

The policeman looks at her. It takes a minute. His eyes shifting to think. 'I change to come here.'

Karen raises her hand from the bedsheet. Touches her hair. There is more to this. A policeman in a hospital room. He has found her. Now, he should go away. Because everything is fine.

'I'm fine.'

'Yes,' the policeman agrees. 'Well . . .' He nods and backs away. He points toward the door. 'Good that you are fine.'

She moves her head to watch him. On his way out.

'Goodbye.'

'Bye.'

He leaves and turns to walk up the corridor. Brightness out there. A nurse passes.

Karen raises her hands. Places them on her breasts. The flatness. Bound within gauze wrapping. Beneath her hospital gown. The policeman still there. In her mind. Tall. Standing in her room moments ago. Something else he wanted. She wishes she had told him to stay. A quiver in her.

The nurse enters to check on Karen.

'How you feeling?'

'Okay.'

The nurse smiles. Almost meaning it. A nice woman. She takes Karen's temperature. Does her blood pressure.

'When can I go?'

'Tomorrow. We just need to check the bandage for a while. Can I have a look?' The nurse nods at her chest. 'Just undo the back.'

Karen undoes the string. Behind her neck.

'Can you sit up a bit?'

Karen tries. Rises a little. The nurse takes down the front of her gown. The nurse lifts back the edge of the bandage. Peeks in. 'Okay.'

Karen's eyes on the open door. A man passing. Watching in. Flowers in his hand. A child behind him. Skipping. She glances at her chest. Flat. The doctor had told her to expect it. Gravity will have its way, he had said. I don't go smaller than a C cup.

'Okay,' says the nurse. 'You can lie back.'

She turns her face away. Then looks at the nurse. Still there. Karen tries a smile.

'You'll be fine,' says the nurse. She shifts to see a man in the doorway.

It is Glenn. With his shoulder bag. He raises a plastic shopping bag. 'I ran out of tape.'

Karen says nothing.

The nurse leaves.

Glenn steps in. Shuts the door. Lays the bag on the chair.

'What did the nurse want?' he asks. Checking the door. A tapping there.

'Come in,' Karen calls out.

The door opens a crack. The policeman, again, sticks his head in. He is looking right at her. Something behind his back. Then he notices Glenn. 'Oh, sorry.'

'It's okay,' she says.

'I was thinking to ask if you need a ride. But you have . . . I see.'

'This is my brother, Glenn.'

The policeman nods.

Glenn nods. Not happy about the intrusion.

'They thought I was missing,' Karen says to Glenn. Laughing a little. Hooking greasy hair behind her ear.

'They?' asks Glenn.

'The police.'

'Oh.'

'I don't know if I need a ride.'

'I can drive you back,' says Glenn. 'Not a problem.'

Karen sees the hint of something pink. Behind the policeman's back. In his hand. A stuffed animal.

The policeman notices her eyes. At first he doesn't want to show her. That's how it seems. Then he does anyway. 'I found this. Lost by someone. Up on the floor there.'

Karen smiles. It is a puppy. A pink puppy with floppy ears. 'I leave it here in case, you know.' He carefully steps into the room. Lays the puppy on the bottom of the bed. He nods. Backs away.

'When are you going back?' Karen asks.

'Tomorrow. I see some friend tonight.'

She looks at Glenn. 'Save you the trip.'

'I don't mind.'

She is beginning to feel better. Although groggy. All this competition.

'Tomorrow,' says the policeman. 'I ask again.' He backs into the doorway. Nods politely. 'Okay?'

'Okay.' Karen smiles. Numbness in her breasts. She is aware of.

The policeman takes a look at Glenn. Looks at the bag on the chair. The zipper open. The edge of the video camera visible. His eyes change. He checks Karen. Nods and leaves.

'You,' Karen says to Glenn.

'What?'

She waits until she is certain. The policeman is gone. 'Out,' she says. Pointing to the door.

Glenn laughs. 'What?'

'I'm going to scream.'

'What?'

'I'm going to scream now, if you don't leave.'

Glenn chuckles.

And she screams. That sound and footsteps. Running.

'Tell us wha' ya wants first,' Patsy says. "fore I let ya in.' Her hand holding the latch of the screen door. The toddler, Ruth, braced in the crook of her left arm. Inside the house. There is the sound of a television program. It's all plain to him. Too plain for him to want.

Blackstrap studies the girl. His children taken away from him. No real reason given. Patsy just wanting to move. To get away. Blackstrap didn't want to move. Cutland Junction was his home. Patsy made all the noise. He said very little. Then Patsy moved. Maybe he should have said more.

Gone one day.

The girl much prettier than her mother. With curly brown hair. And big brown eyes that stare right at him while she sucks on two fingers. He wasn't there when she was born. Never saw her as a baby. Blackstrap glances down at Junior. The boy has pulled back his hood. His hair damp. His cheeks burning red in two uneven circles.

'Just a visit,' he says. Not looking at Patsy. He smiles at Junior. And is pleased to see the boy smiling back. Shyly. But meaning it.

'So say hello 'n leave. No one bees interested in seeing you.'

Blackstrap turns his eyes on her. Patsy's expression steady. She sniffs and leans slightly to one side. Supporting the weight of the child. Patsy scrawny in her jeans and white V-neck pullover. Dark rings under her eyes. Sick rings. Not the woman he knew.

'Can I come in?' He has tried his best to ask forcefully. But it does not come off that way.

Patsy checks his eyes. She licks her lips. Thinking.

'I got company,' she blankly tells him. But there is more to it than that. Something else in her voice.

Blackstrap nods without really meaning to.

'Just Rayna.' Patsy sees the shift in Blackstrap's eyes. She watches them change again. Smiling and crinkling in the corners. Just like his father's. So that she smiles too with memories of better times. She tosses the screen door open on its spring. And turns. 'Come in den.'

Blackstrap takes hold of the door. Steps up. Into the tiny square porch that leads directly into the kitchen. The house smells the way he remembers. Despite the absence of her parents. A bag of sliced white bread on the kitchen counter. And a few thick round slices of bologna. Junior making a sandwich. The knife rattling in a jar of mustard.

Blackstrap glances at the porch wall. A big wooden outline of Newfoundland with a row of pegs pointing out from it. A few jackets hung there. Patsy's father made it years ago in his shed out back. Blackstrap leaves his coat on. Steps into the kitchen. A plump woman in a grey tracksuit at the table. Pulling on her coat while she stands. Blackstrap nods at her. And she gives a sour smile. Obviously having heard things about him. Knowing who he is. Where he has come from. He doesn't know her. Someone new to him. Someone he does not want to know. Poison by the looks of her.

'I'll call ya later,' she says to Patsy. Then glances at the TV on the counter. The one Junior watches while biting into his sandwich. An argument going on there. A big black woman pointing at a skinny little white man. Words bleeped out. 'Don't forget ta tape da soap fer me.'

'Spot on,' says Patsy. And the woman laughs at this. Moves toward the back door. Where her eyes check Blackstrap over. Again, she smiles. This time in a secret way. Playing with him. Hinting at other things out of Patsy's view.

'See ya,' Rayna says to Blackstrap. And is gone.

Moving to the corner of the kitchen. Patsy groans as she sets Ruth down on the floor. Junior stands next to a chair. Chewing bites from the sandwich. Eyes on the screen. Then steps out of the way. When Blackstrap stomps the snow from his boots. Junior's eyes on the TV again.

Sitting, Blackstrap takes hold of the boy's arm. And carefully pulls him back to the place where he was. 'No need ta move, Junior. It's just me.'

The boy looks from TV to his father's face. He smiles and inches closer. Until he is almost leaning against the man. Blackstrap lifts his arm and sets it along the boy's shoulders. Junior smiles. Warms to this. His smooth-skinned face aglow. Not a word out of him. His eyes then back on the TV.

'How's things?' Blackstrap asks. Gaining confidence. Finding acceptance where he feared. What would most certainly be denied him.

'Ya wants a cup of tea?' Patsy asks. Stepping away from Ruth. Across the linoleum. And reaching for the cupboard.

'That'd be fine,' Blackstrap says. His eyes skimming the new flooring toward the edges. Where the mouldings were nailed in place. 'When'd this get done?'

Taking down a mug. Patsy glances over her shoulder. 'Few months ago.'

He thinks he should have done it. If he knew. He could have done it for her. Saved the cost of labour. Or maybe there was no cost of labour. If she was hooked up with someone new.

'It was filthy,' she says. 'Rayna's brudder done it.' She offers a bit of a smile when he looks at her. And so her words do not scald too badly.

Rayna's brother.

He watches Patsy slide the kettle onto the burner of the electric stove. And he thinks of the old pot-belly stove. Once there. Patsy's mother always at it. Not a word in her mouth. The heat unbearable in the kitchen. The way Patsy's mother liked it. You'd have to haul your sweater off. Or faint from the heat.

'Don't ask about the stove now,' Patsy says. 'Yer jus like yer father always wanting to hang on to everything. Every bloody broken-down bit of nuisance.'

'Was a great stove,' he says. Encouraged by how she knew what he was thinking.

'That old thing!' She shakes her head. And turns for the counter. Stares at the mugs.

The audience makes a ruckus from the screen. A lot of them boo. Some of them cheer.

Blackstrap thinks of his mother's stove. And he thinks of Karen. So that he must shift his eyes to the floor again. To hide what he knows is showing. He hears Ruth babbling. Knocking toys together. Looking there, he finds that she is not watching him. She is watching the TV. The flicker of light. Just another man to her. Sitting at a table in a room. He squeezes his arm tighter around Junior's shoulders.

'You know my brother was called Junior,' Blackstrap tells his son. 'You were named after him.'

Patsy lays a plate on the table. He sees that it is stacked with fresh buns. The scent nearer to him now. He has missed this. His mother never knew how to cook. When she came from St. John's. From

England. This he knew. Because his father often said it. The daughter of a British merchant. His father said that, too. But she had learned to cook. And bake. And was made to be just like any other bay woman. Taught by his father's mother. But smart too. Sharp as a tack. Karen had not turned out that way. She had the brains. And was different. Better. But without knowing how to abide. How to be thankful. How to count her blessings. How to . . .

'You wan' mashberry jam, or blueberry?'

'Mashberry,' he says. Not looking at her. Not wanting to give her too much. Now that he has gained a bit of ground. Still pissed off. Still bracing control. Even though he understands that it is he who has come back. The thought making him uneasy.

'Did I ever meet him?' Junior asks. Drawing his eyes from the TV.

'Yer father's brother's dead, Junior,' Patsy says. With her back to them. Reaching into the cupboard for the plastic tub of margarine. As simple as that.

'Oh,' Junior says. Quietly.

Blackstrap takes offence to Patsy's bluntness. The tone of her comment bringing up memories. Harder times between them. He checks the boy who is watching him. Curiously. Chewing his sandwich. Only the crust left now. And he sees his brother there. The spitting image. The genuine want to know. And outright friendliness that always won out over his brother's sadness.

'Yer just like him,' Blackstrap says. ''N he was one hell of a great man, tough as nails and sharp as a tack. Like yer grandmother. And a hero. The best kind of Newfoundlander.'

Patsy comes up beside the table. Looking at Blackstrap's arm around her son's shoulders. Her face does not change. Shows no reaction.

'I could've sworn that was yer old man talk'n,' she says.

Blackstrap thinks of Jacob. He glances at his boots until he hears the whistle on the kettle. Feels the boy shifting beneath the weight of his arm. His small shoulder must be uncomfortable. Blackstrap lifts his arm away. Straightens his legs beneath the table. Looks toward the window. And stares at the snow. He does not know what to say about the man. About his father who has been struck down. By something no one recognizes.

'I was just saying to Rayna about when all da oldtimers is gone, then that's it fer Newfoundland.' The whistle of the kettle. And the sound of Patsy. Dragging it off the burner.

Blackstrap mumbles, 'Utter bullshit.' Not wanting to hear such nonsense. He looks to see Patsy turn with the kettle in her hand. He slathers margarine on a bun. Puts it back together. Chews into it. The smell and taste of it. Doughy. Warm.

'Don't be talking with the language around the boy.'

Blackstrap casts a stray wink at Junior. The curse has captured the boy's attention. And Junior smiles. Proudly nodding his head. Winking back. As if they now have a secret between them.

Patsy lines up two mugs on the counter. And pours in water. 'Yer father's one of the few true Newfoundlanders that're left, Blackie. The oldtimers. How's he doing?'

Coughing. Blackstrap straightens in his chair. And leans an arm on the table. Carefully. He studies the boy. Ignoring Patsy's question.

'You're a true Newfoundlander, Junior.' Blackstrap nods once. Seriously. 'Right?'

The boy nods in agreement. 'Yes, sir, I am.'

The mugs are laid on the table. And Blackstrap glances up to see that Patsy is shaking her head. Frowning as if out of pity for him, while she takes a seat.

Blackstrap lifts his cup to his lips. Glances out the window he had been on the other side of minutes ago. Lowering his mug, he looks at the boy. The boy's eyes glued on the TV. The boy's head leaned toward his father.

'Don't listen to yer mother, Junior.'

'Blacky!' Patsy slaps his hand. Lightly.

'Listen to her 'bout other things, but not 'bout this one.'

Patsy watching him. A question in her eyes. 'Wha's widt you?' she says. 'Da way yer talk'n.'

He reaches for another bun. Tears it apart with his fingers. Butters it generously. And chews. Looking at the bun while he eats. A good thing. Or a bad thing. Her words. He wonders.

'That missus frum St. John's teaching ya how ta talk right. Or'd she kick ya out?'

He stops chewing. His eyes sting her. His mouth even. His expression hard.

'Don't be talking about true Newfoundlanders,' she says. In defence of herself. 'Yer mudder was frum England sure. That's probably wha's da matter widt ya. Where ya got yer uppity nature frum.'

Blackstrap eats the other half of the bun. His jaw working quickly. He sips his tea. Clicks his tongue against his teeth. Cleaning them. Thinking of having a cigarette. Working against the unrest he feels toward Patsy. He thinks of leaving. Of storming out. Of bolting to his feet. And smashing his chair against the table. But that would not be him. He was trying to be new.

'Quiet now,' is all he says. And Patsy stands from the table. Knowing what it means. When these words come from him. Knowing what might happen. She moves to the counter and straightens things away.

Blackstrap looks at his son. Then at the small screen. Another woman shouting at a man. Charging from her seat. Pointing at the man. Going for the man. A big woman being held back.

Blackstrap watches Junior's eyes seeing.

'Junior? What's so interest'n in those strangers' lives?'

'Huh?'

Patsy slaps off the TV button.

Junior stares at his father. 'What?'

Blackstrap says nothing. Listens to the quiet in the kitchen. A crackle of static, from the black screen. He sips his tea.

Junior newly interested in Blackstrap's presence. The heat of his movements. The vigorousness of his chewing. He glances at his mother. Sees that she is watching Blackstrap too. Watching the back of his head with a look in her eyes. Junior cannot place.

With the drugs there is clarity. Isaac Tuttle sees a table for a table. His hand for a hand. He wonders about faith. The bible they have given him. A book. The bible he had pleaded for when he was brought in. Held by two big orderlies. A book. Delivered to him. To hold on to. To hug. Not ever a book. But God. The Bible.

Now, only a book. Words on thin sheets of paper. Something to read. Stories.

A doctor had visited with him. Stood next to the bed. Then sat on the chair. A man whom Isaac did not know. Asking questions. This stranger. Wanting to know. What was the matter? He had answered with memorized words. The doctor trying to look into Isaac's eyes. To see what was in there. Beyond those words.

'Do you hear voices?'

'Do you see visions?'

'Do you smell smells?'

Yes.

Yes.

Yes.

He was alive, after all. Wasn't he?

He lies on the bed and watches the ceiling. The big tiles can be counted with simple numbers. There are thirty. Six rows of five. He is frightened by the easiness. By the simple truth. By the thought of losing what he believed in his chest. Deep in there. What had driven him forward. Has stopped.

'You will have moments of clarity now,' the doctor had said. 'The medication should do that. And what you have believed in might vary. Be prepared for a different view of things. Simpler, maybe.'

When he first took the pills. He had felt God leaving him. Moment by moment. Pulling away. Dying. God dying horrifically. With rage and accusation and heart-breaking sorrow. And he had felt the tears warmly dribbling down the sides of his head. The tears in his temples wetting the hair. Freshly washed and combed by a nurse. Lying there. Face washed. A mass of gashes. Scabs. His stitched tongue a constant aching throb. Being cleansed. Being cleaned. Your face will heal in time.

With God unthreading from his bones. An image he stopped before it fully came to him. Lying flat in bed. His eyes shut. He could still imagine. What he saw was the church in Bareneed. Where he had stood out front. His arms raised and receiving. The morning before Emily Hawco on the floor in the kitchen. No, Blackstrap's wife. He knew now. The difference. And he was deeply pained to see what he could not believe. Ever possible. The new sign out front. A bed and breakfast. Four stars. It was the saddest sight. The saddest thought he had ever had. His arms raised to a bed and breakfast.

He was no longer a church.

'If everything works out,' the doctor says one day, 'you might be able to go home in the new year.'

Isaac presses his palms flat together. Pushes harder in hope.

'Would you like to go home?'

Home, thinks Isaac. No longer is there that place. A house, but not a home. If it is only Me.

It is dark when Blackstrap returns from Heart's Content. The visit has worked out well. And he knows that there is hope for the return of his family. He will block Karen from his mind. She has been gone for months. Living with a mountie in Bay Roberts. He's seen her once or twice. In the drive-through line at the coffee shop. Nothing to do about it. Taken up with another man. Living that way. Move on.

When he pulls into his father's driveway, he sees old Mrs. Shears waiting in the window in her coat. And then out in the doorway in an instant.

Far off, there is the sound of a siren. Blackstrap steps from the car. Feeling the cold night air. The too-still night air. Too crisp. Sharpened for clarity. For tragedy.

'I called the ambulance,' Mrs. Shears shouts.

Blackstrap knows that his father is dead. Before Mrs. Shears has a chance to tell him. And instantly he believes his visit to see Patsy has caused it. He should never have gone. Never given in. Lowered himself.

Shutting the heavy door of the Tornado. He hurries toward his father's house. Already questioning everything in his head. Mrs. Shears fretfully follows after him. Whose fault is this? The telling of this heart-stopping truth?

'What happened?' he asks. Moving away from Mrs. Shears. Fast down the hallway.

Only now the old woman begins crying. He hears her sobbing somewhere behind him. 'Merciful Lord.' While he steps into his father's bedroom. The smell of his mother hits him. Fiercely. Stops him like running into a wall. His mother. She has been there. Lingering now at his father's side.

Mrs. Shears has lit candles in the room.

Blackstrap leans over his father's bed. Takes his father's hand. Cold. Feels for a pulse. Like he was taught to do in the safety course for the oil rigs. Nothing. He dips his head near his father's mouth. No breath. He joins his fists and strikes his father's chest. His father's face has changed. Again, he strikes the chest. What once was him. Has left. Again. Now. What lies. On the bed beneath Blackstrap is not his father. And again.

The siren nearer. Mrs. Shears gone out to meet it. Men soon in the room. They get by him. They push him back without looking, saying, 'Please.' They go to work.

'What happened?' Blackstrap says. This time a whisper.

'It was his time,' says his mother. Not Mrs. Shears.

Mrs. Shears tries to speak, 'He said somet'ing. Numbers. Da temperature, time or something. Then 'e shut his eyes.'

Blackstrap turns to look at her. The men at work around him. They have him on a gurney. Strapping him in. Lying there with his father. He gets up.

Mrs. Shears is a small woman. Who now holds her hands over her heart. As if a pain is there.

'I writ 'em down,' she says, tears glistening on her face. 'Poor, poor soul.'

'What?' Hurry. If the gurney is to go. He should be on it too.

Calming herself. Closing her eyes. And taking a few quick breaths. 'I writ 'em down.'

Blackstrap can only manage a quick look at his father. The candle-light across the features of a dead man. The way he moves only when the gurney moves. A rustle of paper from the pocket of Mrs. Shears' smock. The gurney being wheeled out. He follows after it.

'47 degrees, 33 minutes,' she says. '53 degrees, 14 minutes.' She pushes the note at Blackstrap. Paper in front of him. He is at the front door. But he will not take the note. Will not touch it. He checks Mrs. Shears' eyes instead. She watching a ghost.

'He just kept on repeatin' dat,' she says, fretfully. 'Da temperature. Da time. Were it? Like a countdown.'

Blackstrap glances at the numbers and words. He heads for his car. Climbs in. Follows after the ambulance. The lights flashing in his face. 47 degrees, 33 minutes. The siren. 53 degrees, 14 minutes. From his father's stories of Uncle Ace. Latitude and longitude. A ship's bearings. Co-ordinates to chart its return. When out on the uncertain ocean. Back to the safe enclosure of Bareneed bay.

(*July, 1993*)

Junior watches his father chopping wood. He thinks of the axe and he thinks of blood. *Camp Kill.* The teenagers who were chopped up and stored in the wood shed. Their heads hung on steel hooks. A dog licking up what was dripping on the floor. He stands on the top of the wood pile. Eight-foot lengths of spruce and fir. Stands there still and watching. Hearing the splitting sound as the heavy axe cracks through a wide junk. Picking up one half, Blackstrap sets the open half to face him. Up on the block. Splits it again. The quarters neatly flying away to either side. He glances back at his son. Checking for a second. His son seven years old. Blackstrap thinks on the years and numbers, counting.

'Neat chainsaw,' Junior says. Watching off toward the wood horse and the pile of cut junks in the sawdust. He thinks of wrestling. One man in a mask. Another in a cape. Holding a chainsaw. Revving it outside the ring. He looks toward the shed where a hole was dug with a shovel. Yesterday searching for worms. Trouting with his father up at Middle Gull Pond. The hole. The open earth. He thinks of his grandfather buried in the ground before Christmas. A crowd gathered around all the old tombstones. Expecting the worst to come out from behind one.

Blackstrap picks up the other half of the junk. Splits that one. The quarters flying away. Landing on the ground with a dry, hollow sound.

'Can I go in and watch some TV?' Junior climbs down from the pile. He has heard the sound of buzzing. Maybe a wasp. He steps closer to his father. 'Can I?' He checks back to see if something with wings is following. He listens. No buzzing. 'Cartoon Saturday,' he says to his father.

Blackstrap nods without looking. He stares off at an angle. Toward the back of the house he built for Karen. The house ruined by what he had heard of her. Isaac out now. Back in Cutland Junction since last Monday. Let out of the Waterford. Released. Something he has been thinking on for days. That house vacant now, having moved Patsy,

Junior and Ruth into his father's house. All of them together since December. It had been a good Christmas for the children. Good for everyone except him and his father. The need for family at a time of death. No greater bond.

'No one ever home over there,' says Junior. Pointing toward the beige bungalow.

Blackstrap lifts the axe and swings into another junk. He hears the wooden screen door open. Thinks of his father. That sound. That creaking opening a memory of him stood there.

Bending, he gathers the splits into his bent left arm. Walks into the back door. Into the kitchen. Sets the wood down in the steel tray beside the old woodstove. His mother used to bake bread there. The stove where his father stood. Cooking once his mother was gone. Patsy likes a fire at night. Even in summer. To sit and drink tea. And talk about her parents. His mother liked a fire in the evening. His father, too.

Blackstrap hears the volume from the television. Patsy's distracted voice, 'Jus' wait a second.' He hears her coughing. Walking into the living room. He sees Patsy sat on the old highback couch. A blue cloud of cigarette smoke hanging in the air. Junior standing there. Watching the TV screen, dimly interested, waiting.

'Where's Ruth?' he asks.

'Down fer a nap.' Patsy turns her head. Offers brief attention before tapping ash from her cigarette. Shifting her eyes back to the screen. A young man pointing at a television up on stage. On the TV, there is the screen image of a woman. In a prison jumpsuit. People sit in chairs to either side of the television. A grey-haired man with glasses holding a microphone in front of the young man's face. The grey-haired man pushes his glasses up on his nose. Smiles evenly. Trying to be reasonable.

'That woman killed all her children, ate one of 'em.'

Junior looks at his father. Looking for what? Reaction. Permission. Then the boy slowly sits on the couch. Next to his mother. Eyes trained on the screen.

'What happened to cartoons?' he asks.

No one answers.

A commercial for laxatives comes on. Smiling gentle people. Not a care in the world. Now that they've got themselves unstogged.

'Did you see *Terminator 2*?' Junior asks his father.

Blackstrap shakes his head. Surprised by the television's picture. Sharp and bright. All the time his father watched it. Still like new. It was the same set his father bought for Patsy. Back in 1984. When Blackstrap and Patsy first moved in to stay with Blackstrap's father. To watch after him. Then, after Patsy, there was Karen. The one his father never liked. Still married to Patsy, his father had grumbled. He had liked Patsy. Her sauciness. Her spirit, he called it. Spirit reminds him of wind. He thinks of his mother and the back door he has just come in through. The wind that snatched the door she was holding. Threw her from the doorway. The earth that killed her when she struck it.

His mother on the ground. His father in the doorway.

'Get me a pipsi, Junior,' Patsy says, eyes on the program. The intro music for a second. Then a question being asked by a man about love.

Patsy coughs and coughs. Stabs out the cigarette.

Junior passes close to his father. On his way to the kitchen, 'I saw *Terminator 2* eight times.'

Blackstrap shifts his eyes back to the television. The human horror. No TV if he had his way. But what would Patsy do then? He moves for the kitchen. Follows after Junior.

'Give that to yer mother,' he says, gesturing toward the can in Junior's hand. 'And come on out back.'

Junior frowns.

Blackstrap watches his son go out into the living room.

'Mom, Dad says I have to go out with him.'

'Junior,' Blackstrap barks. Heading toward the back door. Not wanting to hear any more protests. Shoving it open and out. Striding across the yard. Past the pile of spruce rails and the sawhorse. Alongside the shed. Toward the treeline where he pauses. With hands in his back pockets to look for Junior.

The boy runs toward his father. The tall grass beyond the sawhorse slowing his stride. 'Where we going?'

'Into the woods.'

Junior stares to the right of Blackstrap. 'Is there a path?'

'There's no need. Come on.' He ducks beneath a low limb. Treads into the brush. He breathes in the sweet smell of the trees. Eyeing the fallen grey trunks with brittle grey branches. The ones he collects for kindling. The branches easily snapped off in his hands. Thirty feet in, he bends. Grabs hold of the long trunk of a fallen evergreen. Grey-dry and without needles.

'You look fer others. Haul 'em out.' Blackstrap drags the tree. Tangling a bit in grass. Its limbs catching in the ground. Against the rough bark of other trees. He pulls until the branches free themselves. Catch again. Another tug. Continuing with the effort until he is in the clearing. At the back of his father's house.

'Junior,' he calls. He listens. Lifting the dead tree, he tosses it toward the sawhorse. Where it bounces softly. Bobs.

'Yes,' a small voice. Muddled and round-sounding through the woods.

'You com'n?'

'Yes.' The sound of struggling and then silence. A few moments later. The sound of quiet crying that startles Blackstrap.

He hurries into the woods to find the boy bent there. His small back jerking with sobs.

'What's the matter?' Blackstrap asks.

'Look,' Junior says. Lifting his hand. Showing the scratch.

Blackstrap grabs hold of the hand. Stares at it. Then squints meanly at his son. 'That's nothing.' He watches the boy. Huge wet tears rolling from his eyelashes. 'Give that foolishness up. That's nothin' ta cry over.'

The boy wipes at his eyes. Tries his best to blink them clear.

'There's no need.'

The boy nods. Then flinches at the sound of snapping behind him. Scared of the woods. Scared of what might get him. Someone always running away. He twists around. Searches through the screen of trees. A killer. A madman with a torn-up face. Born crazy and deformed. Making noises not words. But only a moose lumbering along. The languid snap-cracking of limbs and brush.

'Shhh,' says Blackstrap. Hand on the boy's shoulder.

The bull pauses to look at them. Turns its steady head. Balanced with the elaborate weight of antlers. And watches with utter disinterest.

Junior moves to stand. But Blackstrap holds him down. Presses firmly into the boy's shoulder.

The brown bulk of the moose shifts. Its back as high as Blackstrap's head. It steps speculatively. Lifting its nose with a slow swaying motion. Its antlers rustling the branches above.

Junior's breath makes noise in the air. It wetly shivers with fright.

The moose stares intently at Blackstrap. Then dips its head from side to side. As though understanding what is there. The wish for a shotgun. It backs off. Turning its heavy head. Angling its long legs forward. Lumbering deeper into the wilderness that breaks apart. For its entry.

Junior looks up at his father. Smiling with relief. And wiping at his eyes. 'That was something, huh?'

'A lot of meat on 'im,' Blackstrap says in a way that makes Junior laugh. The boy feels happy to have survived. Happy to see his father smiling at him. Not disappointed after all. He looks to where the brown bulk of the moose has gone. Barely visible now through the tangle of branches.

'He's getting away,' Junior says. 'Get your gun.' Speaking the words he believes his father wants to hear. But they ring false. And Blackstrap looks down at him. Hurriedly, he takes hold of the boy's tree. 'Stay here. I'll get da shotgun.' Dragging the tree out himself to prove the point. The ease with which it can be done. Then into the house and back out again. The screen door slapping shut. His shotgun in hand. Cartridges slid into the chambers. Snapped shut. After the moose. Back into the trees. Where he finds Junior. 'Come on.'

But Junior not following. Junior staying put. Junior terrified.

While Patsy sleeps, she dreams of her son. Junior sits at their kitchen table. Back in Heart's Content. He is armless. Ruth, rolling on the floor, is armless, too. Patsy's breath is harder to catch than expected. Not knowing where. A pain she cannot find. Blackstrap has taken the arms away. Afraid that she will eat them. She is laughing and crying at once. Wakes with a noise in her throat. In tears, turning in bed. In darkness, she strikes out at Blackstrap. Hits only the empty pillow. Mutters his name in accusation. Blackstrap not there. Where are her children's limbs? She knows she will not eat them now. It will be okay. The weight in her chest a dream.

A deep breath. She coughs and rises from bed. To make certain she might not be dreaming. Blackstrap is not carting off the limbs. Is he? Woozy and unstable on her feet. She steps into the children's bedroom. Tries to stifle her cough. Sees from the light through the window. Junior and Ruth are sleeping. Soundly beneath their blankets. Their bodies exact. She kisses each of them on their cheeks. On their foreheads. Then steps down the short hallway to the kitchen. Blackstrap not there. Sound coming in from the outside. She notices the front door open. The outer screen door shut.

Out in the dim front yard. Littered with hubcaps, sections of fallen fence, debris from cars . . . She calls quietly. Still tingling from coming awake. From that place. The stars above her. 'Blackie?' A cough. That one deeper. It hurts her chest. The chill of the night more noticeable. She steps out further. Sees a light from the bungalow next door. Light cast on its manicured front lawn. The big bay window is lit. The white sheers parted in the centre. She sees the dark outline of a man stood there. It could be anyone. He does not move. A black shadow that begins to scare her. Something in his hands. Something like a shotgun. She calls, 'Blackie,' into the night. And the man in the window. The black shadow. Turns its head toward the sound. Almost in recognition.

(November, 1993)

They are watching the news when Alphonsus Hawco appears. In handcuffs. A stranger's view of him. Not like himself. It takes a second to know it's him being led out of a police car. A policeman on either side. One holding Alphonsus' elbow. Guiding him along. Alphonsus watching straight ahead. How can it be him? There. Like that. Taken from their home two days ago. Now, on TV.

The announcer says: 'Once heralded as a Newfoundland hero, Alphonsus Hawco, also known as "Blackstrap Hawco," a vigilante who fought for the fishing rights of fisher people in this province, and a survivor of the worst nautical disaster in Newfoundland history, now a player in yet another tragedy, a tragedy that appears to be of his own making, the hero now with blood on his hands . . . Murder in Cutland Junction.'

Patsy glances at her son's face. She lights a cigarette off the butt of another. Wonders if she should turn off the channel. But decides that he should know. What people are saying. What his father is being charged with. So he won't be ignorant. She takes a swig from the cough syrup bottle. Sweet and bitter at once.

'Hey,' Junior gasps. Pointing at the screen. Flickering with colours and movement. Darting his shocked eyes toward his mother. In his head, those images. 'That's Dad.' He stands from where he has been sitting on the carpet. And slowly steps backward. Away from the screen. Toward the couch. Toward his mother. One hand coming to rest on the cushion near his mother's leg.

Patsy watches too. Sighing deeply. Knowing that something like this would happen. Sooner or later. Blackstrap always heading that way. A wheeze wanting to be a cough. She clamps it in. Takes another drink from the cough syrup bottle. Life going bad. When it had seemed to be going good. Everything snaking out of control. The police. A dead man. Because she had expected good things. Good things were not possible.

Not now. Anymore.

When the news story ends, Patsy says, 'Was an accident, Junior.'

'What happened?' Junior's face ticking with emotion. He tries to hold his anger. 'What . . .' But soon falls against his mother. Crying outright. Arms tight around her waist.

Patsy holding him. Wheezing in his ear. Not wanting to cough. Thinking, *And you just got him back. Poor little soul.*

'They're gonna put him in jail,' Junior sobs.

'I don't know.' She kisses the top of his head. A terrible ache in her stomach. A watery burning feeling that turns to nausea. Shakes her head to deny it. Make it go away. Please. Rising from somewhere deeper. Moving Junior away from her. She stands from the couch. Has to hurry to the bathroom.

She will not look in the toilet. When she stands from her knees. She knows the scarlet colour would frighten her.

'Mom?' Junior's voice. From behind the door. 'You okay, Mom?'

'Yuh, fine, just something I ate, sweet'eart.' She retches again. Nothing coming up. But acid. Revulsion. A low desperate moan in her throat.

Tiny drops of pink on the toilet seat. Wiping her mouth. Wiping the seat. She tosses the tissue into the water. Flushes it. The water swirling down. The sound making her feel weaker. Insignificant. Frightened. To expect so much. Even inside her. Admitting now with this news of Blackstrap. News she already knew before. Once in her mind, every-where now. Broadcast. Him taken away. Ruth watching him go. Her tiny arm held out. Fingers opening and closing. 'Bye, bye, Daddy.'

With Blackstrap gone, Patsy feels horribly ill. Who will care for her children? She will not cry. *Fuh'k.* Weakness. Then greater anger. *Fuh'k, no.* She stomps her foot as a threat. Clamps her teeth together. Turns to see her thin, yellowish-green face in the mirror. And curses God.

(April, 1994)

Karen knew she would eventually find herself. In this place. Only a matter of time. To muster the courage to face him. Perfectly honest about where she was going. Telling Kevin of her plans. And he was reasonable about it. Kissing her. And wishing her well. Supportive. A quick visit before they left Newfoundland.

'I just want to clear some things up.'

'Yes, I understan',' he had said. Smiling at her. And touching her arms. Holding them gently. Always gently. How lucky was she to have found him?

An understanding husband-to-be. What every woman dreams of. A man in a uniform. Tall and handsome.

An old guard in a grey uniform unlocks the main steel door. It is painted green. Freshly painted, perhaps by one of the prisoners, she imagines. *Their chores, when not hammering big rocks into smaller rocks.* The guard not looking directly at her. Out of respect. A friendly man. Holding his arm out every so often. To signal the way across the inner courtyard. Surrounded by the walls. Leading her toward a room. Along a compound with wire-mesh windows.

'Careful,' says the guard as Karen steps up three wooden stairs. Enters a door into a small room. Two long wooden tables and wooden chairs. *Old heavy chairs*, she thinks, finding it strange. With the newness of the structure. *Maybe they took them from some older place,* she tells herself. *A place where they used to hang people.* She has to press her lips together. To stop from giggling. She must be nervous. She wonders if she can get through this meeting. Without laughing in Blackstrap's face. So happy with her life. Even this place cannot smother it. She coughs lightly. Sits where the old guard gestures with his arm straight out. His head slightly bowed. Backing away. Apologetic for having to be in her presence. In this place.

Karen joins her hands on the tabletop. Moves her thumbs around. She is wearing a pretty spring dress. Bright and flowery. Cut low in the front. A push-up bra. Her skin tanned from the Hawaiian Sun solarium. Her hair dyed Natural, Ultra-light, Summer Blonde. Her contact lenses tinted True Hazel. Twenty-five pounds slimmer. Blackstrap might not even recognize her. Then she hears the door open. Is startled by the sound of boots stepping. The freshness of outer air breezing into the room. She looks up. *Sweet Jesus!* She had forgotten his solidness. Not his bigness. But his impenetrable sense of being. The power of his eyes. The piercing quality of his stare. The roguishness of his face. *All of us,* Karen thinks. *Here, in this room, for him.*

A younger guard follows behind him. Moves over to the corner. Stands there.

Blackstrap waits near the table. His hands are not cuffed. Karen thought they might be. Should be. There is only a table. No glass between them. Not what she expected. What she imagined from movies. Talking through a telephone. Not enough distance. Separation. He sits directly across from her. Open air between them.

Right away. He knows who she is. Smiles at her. A corner of his lips rising. In a way that tells everything about her. What has she done now? What to herself? His eyes, bright and cool blue like his father's. *He is a man,* she thinks. *Stuck somewhere. A dependable specimen. Locked away for killing a man . . . who raped me.* This is real. The thought exhausts her. A shiver troubles the back of her neck. Her shoulders twitch in reflex. She shifts in her chair. With him right across from her. That close. Watching her. Not a word out of him. He could reach out and touch her. She puts her hands off the table. Down in her lap. She has lost her voice. She tries to say: how are you? But the words lodge in her throat.

She blushes now. Is humiliated by him. Feels ashamed. For the way her body is. A body he always liked. Never complained about. And the baby. Kevin's baby. Due in six months. *It should be his baby*, she tells herself. *Even this, all wrong. Why isn't it his baby? What went wrong?*

Her life perfect. Perfectly changed.

'You lost a pound er two,' Blackstrap says. The look in his eyes. Wondering what is up. 'Hair's longer.' He nods slightly as if in agreement. 'Different colour.' Avoids glancing at her chest. But he knows.

'Yes,' she manages.

'What da fuh'k did you do with yer eyes?' He lifts two fingers. Scratches at the stubble on his right cheek. Laughs a bit. Leans his head to the side. Glancing over his shoulder, he eyes the guard. Stood against the wall with his hands behind his back. The man stares toward the other wall. Trying to be invisible.

'Jimmy,' he says to Karen. Tilting his head toward the guard.

'Oh.' She looks at him. 'Hi.'

'Hello, missus,' Jimmy says, smiling nicely.

'Jim used to be a fisherman,' Blackstrap says. 'Down in Bareneed.'

Karen picks up the line. 'Wasn't everyone, once?'

Blackstrap nods. Stares for a stretch of time. 'I helped build dese walls, 'member?'

'Yes.' And Karen finds herself aroused. By the mere set of his shoulders. His position in the chair. The way he straightens himself now. Holding his shoulders back a touch. Like he will tap a tune out on the table with his fingers. The way he says very little. Only watches her. Knowing her better than any man ever has. Knowing her the moment he first laid eyes on her. For the way she was, not is. Not now. Was. *On this table*, she thinks, blushing. *Right now.* She would let him. Wasn't he allowed such a visit? Wasn't there a place in the prison for one last time?

'You okay?' he asks.

She could break down. By the way he has spoken those words.

'Yes.' She smiles for him. Capped, whitened teeth. Paid for by Kevin with not a mention of cost.

Blackstrap's eyes turn sad. They seem worried for her. Concerned. A sigh through his nostrils. He bows his head. Stares at his fingers flat on the edge of the tabletop.

'Thank you,' Karen says. For the death. For the murder. No, for him caring. For him doing.

Blackstrap presses his lips together. Keeps his head bowed. When he looks up. He turns his face away. Eyes glassy.

Karen shakes her head solemnly. What sort of creature are you?

And Blackstrap looks right at her. Searches her eyes, harshly, lovingly. Searches her eyes to see what she has done to herself. Not what she thinks of him. But if she is okay.

'I'm . . .' Karen cannot say the words. She notices his fingers. His gold wedding band back on. Married to Patsy instead of her. Still married. All of this she had wished to forget. She had come here to make a clean break. Now, she is filled with hope. By the thought of them behind these walls. Locked away. Together. Goodbye. With the baby in her. Goodbye. How does she ask? She will not. She did not come here for that. She knows that she came for something else. His forgiveness. Why? For what? Not the tugging away to be released. But the tugging away that tightens the hold.

'Where you been?' he asks. And she has no idea what he is talking about.

'What d' you mean?'

'Where'd you disappear to?'

Her breasts ache. Throb. As if someone has punched her. As if her entire body has shrunk protectively. Around the baby. It was a dream, or is this a dream? Her features collapse beneath the make-up. No matter what she does to herself. There is no protection against him.

Blackstrap knows about the other man. The policeman. RCMP. The Frog from Montreal. Constable Kevin Pope. What sort of name is that? For a Frenchman. For a separatist. He has heard these things. He looks away, toward the window. He can read everything in her face. Sense the slightest shifts in expression. Mine the deeper truth. As he might sniff the changing air. Hours before rain. And bluntly comment that a downpour was coming.

There is nothing she can do to change that.

'What'd you come ta tell me?' he asks, still staring out the window. Snow along the grass in patches. The coolness lingering into April. No early spring in Newfoundland. Not ever.

'I'm sorry,' she says. Her voice cracking. Strength draining. What left to do, but leave. She braces her hands to stand. Looking toward the guard. In a small voice: 'Can I go now, please?'

'I just have to call someone.' The guard named Jimmy picks up the phone on the wall. Presses buttons. Then speaks lowly. She will not look at Blackstrap again. In the corners of her eyes. She sees that he is staring at her belly. The slight rise. The new life. But she does not want him to see now. The mistake. He will not meet her eyes. The baby a shame so near him. Her breasts. How will she feed the baby? Who will feed the baby? Not her. The doctor had told her.

The door behind her opens. There are two doors to the room. One for visitors. One for prisoners. Karen turns. To see the apologetic older man with his sloppy moustache. He nods once and gestures with his arm. His jacket seeming a touch too big. The sleeves extending down over his wrists.

Karen walks toward the old guard. No last look at Blackstrap.

'Don't come around no more,' he says, speaking plainly. 'There's nothing holding you to me.'

Struck in her heart. An exhale close to a sob. She follows the old guard down the stairs. Across the yard. Heading for the steel door. The guard smiles and nods sadly. When he finally looks at her. After the door has been opened. And she has stepped through. He wants to say something. What? Some final word. Something about why she is here. Finally, the old guard says: 'He's not a bad man.' And the steel door closes with a loud sound. Final. A noise that makes her feel as if *she* is the one barred in. Stepping back to capture a better view. Of where she has come from. The high concrete walls she now fears. The barbed wire coiled along the top. The parking lot behind her. And further on, the woods. In every direction. The paved road that leads only to here and stops. This place built for him.

Cars parked in a flat parking lot. She gets in hers. Starts the engine. The new car. Kevin's. Drives off. Her eyes in the rearview. The towering walls in the middle of forest. A make-work project. Built by the locals. Men Blackstrap knew and told her about. Fallen on hard times. After the collapse of the fishery. A rise in crime. In desperate acts. The government knew. They would need a prison to keep the men.

She watches the road. But sees Blackstrap being led back to his cell. Not a word from him. Not a gesture to anyone near him. Stepping across the threshold. His door shut. His face behind bars. Watching out. Just like that. Never moving again. Not even needing a breath. His misery so complete.

Goodbye, Karen Hawco. With the baby in her.

'We were talking about criminals in school today,' Junior tells Patsy. 'A policeman came in and I was asking him about prison. He had the same name as the Pope.'

'Mmm.' Patsy watches her son. From the pillow where her head rests. She carefully licks her pale dry lips. Searching her son's face. Then shuts her eyes against the drought.

Junior looks down at Ruth. Stood there. Staring back up at him. Rubber boots on her feet. The ones she will never take off. No other clothes on. Except the baseball cap on her head. His father's.

'Hi,' he says. Smiling at her. Playing up to his mother. A trick he learned from the time Ruth was born. Brought home from the hospital. Junior trying for that extra bit of attention. Because of the baby. 'You need your diaper changed, Boo-baby?'

'Dewnrr,' Ruth says. Smiling wildly and smacking her hands together. Then reaching both hands up for him. Opening and closing her fists. 'Dewnrr. Dewnrr. Da-da.'

He lays her on her back against the floor. The toddler moves her legs to kick and wriggle. Then grabs a nearby slipper. Holds it in both her hands. Studying it closely for a while. Then pushing the edge into her mouth.

'Don't move,' he tells Ruth. Then looks at his mother. 'When can we go see Dad?'

Patsy shifts her head to one side. Attempting to shake it. But the action is cut short. Too tired, medicated. Heavy thoughts, *He only cares 'bout his father. Junior.* Images of Blackstrap. Meanness like the cancer. Because he has drawn the shadow over himself too. Put himself away. Not there for her or the children. She has not called social services yet. She cannot bring herself close to the thought. Turning her children over to strangers. What will happen to her children? She has seen all sorts of horror stories on *Oprah* and *Geraldo*. She wishes her parents were still alive. Had not had her so late in life. So they died when she was in her late twenties. Her mother, then her father. Finding no point in surviving his wife. There was her mother's sister, Aunt Frances. But she was too old now. Kind and wonderful. But too old now to care for children. Who could she ask? Her friends back in Heart's Content? Her mind swims over their faces. Female friends. Unmarried or with their own children. She would ask. She would beg.

The pain Patsy feels welcomes death. The unbearable discomfort and nausea. But not the thought of leaving her children. In the hands of others. That makes her illness consumptive. Well past this earth she will leave. Well past her body. Her sickness ruining the lives of her children. Eating up their lives, too. She moans. Perhaps there is a special hell for parents. Who leave their children unattended on earth. She moans again, her mouth open. Shifting, she shuts her eyes.

'You okay?' Junior asks. Looking up from wiping Ruth's behind and legs. With the scented baby wipes. Patsy can smell the scent. Sweet. It turns her stomach. Her festering head.

Fear in his voice? Patsy asks herself.

'No, I'm 'kay.' She manages a smile. Looks at him. Amazed by how beautiful he is. How beautiful her daughter is. They are perfect angels.

'Should I call the doctor?' Junior slides the new diaper under Ruth's bottom. Fastens the sticky flaps. The old diaper looks heavy when he lifts it. Closes it over.

'Stinky,' he says, as Ruth rolls over onto her belly. Pushes herself up to her feet. Comes close to the couch. Where Patsy is lying and reaches up. Grasping and grasping. 'Mam, mam, mam . . .'

'There,' he says. Taking hold of Ruth's hands. Ruth lifts her shoulders in a shy gesture.

'You wanna watch some TV?' he asks.

'TB,' Ruth squeals. Crouching and springing up. Bouncing from one foot to the other. 'TB.'

Junior checks his mother. Hurt by how she is quietly crying. He presses close to the edge of the couch. His arms dangling uselessly by his sides. Ruth grasps the blanket Junior has put over his mother. Pulls on it as she tries climbing up. The movement pains Patsy. She makes a noise. Ruth stops. Rests her head on her mother's thin, seemingly hollow, chest. Junior nibbles at the side of his thumb. Smiles at his sister. While her head stays there. Her thumb in her mouth. Big eyes watching him. His mother's bone-thin hand coming out. From under the blanket. To settle on Ruth's head. To stroke her soft hair.

(June, 1994)

The airplane taxis down the runway. Karen watches the St. John's airport. A small, brick building. The gas trucks. The distant tower. Forest along the perimeter. She stares toward her carry-on at her feet. Beneath the chair in front of her. Then feels a hand settling on top of hers.

'Nervous?' asks Constable Pope, caringly. Watching her eyes.

'Yeah.' She smiles. Happy to show her white teeth. Taking her hand away from him. Still with thoughts of Blackstrap. Not leaving Newfoundland. But leaving him. Her belly making her uncomfortable. Five months pregnant. She sets both hands on the rise. Very noticeable now. The maternity clothes she needs to wear. Pants with stretchy waists. She watches her fingernails. Glued on. Red. Polished. That stroke each other. Shiny. But hard to feel. Amazed that she has agreed to go away. To Montreal. She's never travelled before. Never out of the province.

'Montreal is nice place,' says Pope. Eyes on the oval window. The plane moving. 'A good vacation to go.'

The airplane roars along. Pressing her into the seat. Roaring faster. Then tilts her back. And up. The feeling Karen gets when she lifts away. The weightlessness in her legs. Her body light. A natural flush rises in her plump cheeks. She hates the colour. What it does to her skin. She looks out the window. Her eyes trouble her. As the island drops further beneath. Ugly land. Tangles of trees. So deep green they are black. Ponds. Lonely roads. Houses clumped together around water. In the middle of nowhere.

Her stomach shrinks. Rising. The coast evident from this high up. The broken shoreline. The steep cliffs.

Leaving Blackstrap. The island behind.

Karen understands. That this was always meant to be. Far. Far away.

Far. Far away. Where there are real people. And real things to do. Bright lights and tall buildings.

Constable Pope will show her new places. Has already mentioned. Place des Arts. Musée d'art contemporain de Montréal, Place Jacques-Cartier. Old Montreal. With its cafés. Cobblestones. Horse-drawn carriage. A romantic. European sort of place. Like the sort she read about. When she was a teenager.

A row of limousines waiting outside. *Sorte.* Dorval airport. Limousine. *Limousine.* The same in French. Karen recognizes it.

Constable Pope steps toward the limo. As if it is something done every day. And the man. *Bonjour.* In the uniform smiles. Touches the shiny beak of his black cap. Opens the trunk to load their luggage. The limousine smells nice. Newly rich. And luxurious. The radio low. Karen picks out a few words: *Crise. Pistolet. Sang.* Karen holds Constable Pope's hand. Tightly. Love wells up in her chest. This life she has been given. For him and the baby. Three together. And she leans toward him. Kisses his cheek. *Officier. Tueur. Femmes. Évasion.*

'Happy?' Constable Pope asks. Reacting with pleasure.

'Yes.' She kisses him again. Perfume in her nostrils. 'This is perfect.'

The limousine dips through a tunnel. Resurfaces along the divided highway. Lanes on each side. Factories with logos Karen recognizes. Glowing high. The place where they manufacture things.

Eyes fixed on the foreign sights moving by. Beyond the window. So refreshing to see something. She does not recognize.

At the desk of the Queen Elizabeth Hotel. Karen is flabbergasted by the opulence of the open lobby.

The hotel clerk signals. Says something toward another desk. Where men in uniform wait.

Constable Pope nods, '*Oui, merci,*' then smiles back at Karen.

Away from the front desk. The elevator arrives. A man on there. *Bonjour.* And Constable Pope steps inside. Allowing Karen to enter first. *Bonjour.* The look of her. She says, *Bonjour.* Not exactly right. The bulge of her belly. The man glancing there before stepping on. He is with a woman. With an ugly face. Who whispers in his ear. The man is attractive. Karen wonders what he sees in her. A white mink coat. A face impossible to make over.

When they arrive at their room. Karen is surprised by the plainness of it. Not impressive at all. Not as nice as expected. Having heard from her father. Years ago. That this was *the* place to stay. She recalls some of the French phrases. That he always repeated. Taking pride in his bilingualism. He worked for a security firm. Their head office in Montreal. And so visited the city regularly. Bringing back stories of gangsters. Bank robberies. Smoked meat. Delis. Fashions. Women. His hands at night. Stories in her ear. And his hands at night. In the dark. And more stories made up or not.

'You want look around,' Constable Pope suggests. Standing by one of the beds. 'See sights?' He turns on the television: *Couteau. Marteau. Scie.*

'Sure. Just . . . I have to use the bathroom.' In the bathroom with the door shut. She pees. Then stands. Looks at herself in the mirror. Beyond the door. The television: *Fou. Coup. Corde. Prenez garde.*

A hotel room, she tells herself. A shudder going through her. For some other reason. She turns sideways, And smoothes her smock over her belly. Her dyed-blonde hair. Her plucked brows. Her fixed nose. Her teeth. Her contact lenses. She loves herself. Now. For once. She loves herself. Almost exactly enough.

Never. More natural. Never. More at ease.

Out in the room again. She finds Constable Pope stood by the window. Flipping through a magazine about Montreal. The television on. She moves in beside him. Closer to a bird's-eye view of the city. A wide street with solid grey buildings. To either side. People moving everywhere. She had noticed in the airport. And out on the street. The way people dressed. The men in sharp suits. Women in expensive fashions.

In the limousine. Constable Pope had asked the driver to cruise up St. Catherine Street. Wanting Karen to catch a view of the action. She had watched out the window. Seeing the clothing stores. The mannequins lifelike. Standing on their hard feet. Or hung. The deli windows. With meats. And cakes. And pickled peppers. Hanging. Businessmen coming out of doors. Tugging on raglans. Or holding umbrellas. Chatting in a language foreign to her. They had passed a large building at their right. With a great expanse of grass in front. Constable Pope had pointed it out. Place des Arts. And had listed jazz musicians. He had seen there.

'St. Laurent just up not far,' Constable Pope had indicated. Nodding his head toward the windshield. *'Prenez une droite,'* Constable Pope had called to the driver. The limo had turned right.

They had passed a fast food restaurant. A cinema with XXX. And then in the doorways of a variety of shops. She had seen women in tight skirts. With frizzy blonde hair. Done up with make-up. Too much. She had seen a black woman. With a red tube top. And black skirt and nylons. She had stared at the black woman. Stared. The black. Woman had watched. Her pass. Waving to the limousine. And laughing.

Karen had tried not to stare. But could not help herself.

'Not very nice,' Constable Pope had said. *Putains.* Peeking a glance at her. Watching the whores. Smiling. She had felt a twinge of hatred. For him. Why had he come this way? On purpose. It had been on purpose.

Then further ahead. Flashing lights. Police cars. A covered stretcher being wheeled from a doorway. The limousine around a corner. Gone.

Standing in the hotel room. She turns away from the window. Constable Pope watching her.

'You are doing fine?' he asks. Nodding to answer for her.

'Yes,' she says anyway. Glancing around the hotel room. Feeling like she should not be here. Why? She deserves it, she tells herself. It is like fear. *But I am good enough to be here.* And thinking of what Blackstrap might say about this place. Why Blackstrap? Why him always in her head now? From the television a covered stretcher being wheeled from a doorway. What they had seen. Out the window of the limousine. Police speaking in French. The falseness. The lack of character. The province Blackstrap hates. The French. Canadians.

'We go.' Constable Pope. He holds up a finger. One minute, he means. Steps into the bathroom. His wallet on the dresser. Money stuffed in there. Next to change. Keys. The bathroom door locks. Karen stares at the money. Moves closer to count. The wallet in her hands. Opening it. The bills. Twenties and hundreds. So much money. It

425

makes her feel better. Puts her at ease. A credit card. Gold. She lifts it out to see. The numbers. The name: Pierre LaCrosse. Not Kevin. Not what she calls him. Not Kevin. It must be his name in French. The other credit card. The same name. His photo ID. The same name. Never has she looked inside before. His wallet.

The bathroom door unlocking. The wallet back where it was.

'We go now,' Constable Pope says. '*Explorez.*' Coming out. Seeing her by the bed. He takes hold of her hand. His fingers joined with hers. Something Blackstrap would never do. Never. Hold her hand. Never touch her in public. No shows of affection. She hates him desperately. With a longing that makes her shake. Her head in a way barely seen. Why him?

'What?' Constable Pope asks.

'Nothing.' She fakes a little smile. Aware of her teeth. The cost of them. Kevin had paid for the contact lenses too.

'We eat Greek tonight. Okay?'

'Sure.'

Constable Pope takes his wallet. Does not think twice. Puts it in his pocket. Tilts his chin at her. Smiles charmingly.

Karen follows him to the door. The television left on. A woman's face from a picture. Another woman's face. From when she was living. Then another. And another. One photo. The face the same. *Disparu.*

Reaching to open the door. But the door is locked. The chain put across. She watches Constable Pope check the knob. To see that it is unlocked.

No, locked.

Together she sees them. Hand in hand. Walking down the carpeted corridor. Toward the elevators. Arriving there. Constable Pope pushing the button. And staring at her face. Another woman's picture. And another . . .

'You like it here?'

'Yes,' Karen says. 'Yes.' The elevator. But not the elevator.

The locked door. The hotel room. The hotel. The city. The province. The country.

Not who he said he was. His name in French. She tells herself.

'*Putain,*' says the man.

426

Blindfolded on the bed. She is naked. Mouth crammed with cotton. Taped over. Arms tied above her head. Legs roped to footboard posts. Her body. An X. With a hump.

The scars around her breasts. The bruising. Constable Pope watches there. The scars. Around the rise of her belly. Not fully healed yet. The fat sucked out.

Constable Pope thinks: *Transformé en l'animal pour tuer.*

She shakes her head. She.

He says. In English. For her. 'Made into the animal to kill.'

She cannot see. Nothing of her. Of him.

'*Boucherie.*'

He reaches into her. He reaches deep into her. He reaches himself deep into her. He reaches himself deeper and deeper into her. Until his hand has hold. He takes the heartbeat.

Screaming. But not heard. Whose voice?

She read this in a book once. She saw it on television. A picture in a magazine. She read it in a headline.

A holiday.

She was beautiful. Done over. Dead.

She was made up nicely.

Screaming without sound.

Wasn't she? Dead. Or death pulled out of her.

My baby.

Mon bébé.

Moi.

In her adult years, Emily Hawco feared that something had not been right with her childhood. Her father had made veiled references to discrepancies throughout her lifetime. It was not until Alan Duncan was on his deathbed that Emily learned the truth, as it related to her, of why they had fled Liverpool.

1953

St. John's

The lunatic asylum and a father's death

The train ride from Cutland Junction to St. John's was an agitated blur. Emily tried watching out the window, her eyes registering the impression of ponds and forests, sights that would normally reassure her, yet her slack concentration disallowed appreciation. The news of her father's critical sickness had delivered Emily to the brink of new and sudden realization. Over the years, where her father had existed in a realm of madness, he had remained essentially unreal to her. However, the thought of his impending death, of his total abstraction, brought him to a fullness that was lacking for decades. What was there to erase if not a man?

Emily had tried reading the paperback novel that Isaac Tuttle had given her to take along for the journey, a book written by John O'Hara which described an alcoholic's pitiful decline from society's favour. Isaac always with a lesson to pass on. This one, no doubt, aimed at Jacob's fondness for drink. Isaac never touched a drop. She shifted her eyes from the words to the window. Isaac like a child, really, the thought of him prickling a sensation of fear and excitement through her. How could he seem to have existed from the time of her first memories in England? Those shadows of thoughts that were her constant dreams.

Travelling away from her home, on the miles of track through the wilderness toward uncertainty, she moved her eyes to the book to forget.

Although she was seeing the words, the corridors behind her eyes, through which the words usually made smooth passage to her mind, were broken in places so that the words often slipped through. The lulling tremor of the train made her sleepy despite her anxiety at what might meet her at the termination of her journey. She dozed into the vast openness that transported her off, yet would be jostled back to the closeness of the compartment and the stare of a young man in a shabby coat watching her chest from across the way.

Aware of the young man's stare, she felt her breasts ache with fullness. The thought of Blackstrap made her nipples leak and, so, she vied to keep her mind from him and the guilt she felt for leaving him in the care of Elizabeth Coffey, a young woman from Bareneed who had a new baby of her own. A wet nurse, she would be called, by Emily's mother. With a faint shake of her head, she studied her lap. The book open there. Where she was going was no place for a baby.

Since learning of her father's forthcoming and most certain demise from Dr. Frazier Murphy, the psychiatrist at the lunatic asylum who had sent the telegram, the world had come alive in a most painful manner.

At the station in St. John's, she disembarked the train and waited for the porter to retrieve her single case from the baggage car.

When the porter handed the case to her, she enquired: 'Is there a streetcar running to . . .' She caught herself before stating the lunatic asylum, or the Hospital for Mental and Nervous Diseases, as it was properly named, adding, instead, while she pulled on her gloves, 'Running west, along Water Street.'

'Streetcars stopped running in '48, missus. There's a bus.' The porter pointed toward the front of the station where a number of travellers were already gathering across the street. Riding on the streetcars with her father and mother as a child in St. John's was one of her earliest memories, clear and complete unlike the muddle of what was left behind in England. Following their move to Bareneed, her mother would take a trip twice a year to St. John's to shop. During those excursions, they rode from one end of Water Street to the other to visit the select shops where her mother bought her a new dress or shoes, her outfits always distinguishing her from the other schoolchildren in Bareneed whose clothes were worn and tattered, handed down from brother to brother or sister to sister in the long line of siblings that comprised the majority of outport families. Because the clothes distinguished her, they also made her an easy target when she left the one-room chilly schoolhouse each day for the boys' rock-throwing. Done with her downtown shopping, her mother would then hire a cab to visit with Mrs. Hickman, a friend of her mother's who had established a charity foundation in aid of the new St. Claire's hospital. Her mother would help out with plans in any way she was able, donating money as well.

Emily carried her bag and joined the others at the bus station across the road, avoiding the interest of a woman wearing a green bandanna and a shabby long black coat who stood near her and boldly eyed her up and down.

'Wha's in da case?' asked the woman, her mouth filled with spaces where teeth were once lodged.

After a shunning moment of thought, Emily said, 'Personal items.'

'Aw,' the woman scoffed, staring directly into Emily's face, squinting and making up her mind. 'Visit'n den, ye must be. Is dat it?'

'Yes.'

'Where ye from?'

Emily was about to say England, something in her, perhaps an urge to dominate this woman and thus briskly silence her, reared up, but she restrained herself and politely said, 'Bareneed.'

The woman gave a swift sharp shake of her head. 'Nev'r 'erd of it,' she griped, as though her pronouncement did nothing short of obliterating Bareneed from the map. The woman then leaned back, studying Emily's hair and coat. 'Lovely coat ya got dere, missus,' she said, no doubt, meaning for it to be taken as a compliment, but making it sound as though it were a criminal sentence.

'Thank you.' Emily held her case in front of her waist, both hands gripping the wooden handle, and stared off into space.

The bus arrived fifteen minutes later.

As Emily boarded the bus, the woman followed in close pursuit. It would be a chore to avoid the woman now. She searched for a seat in which someone was already positioned by the window, so as to prevent the woman from sitting beside her. There was an old man with a pointy chin and salt and pepper cap, his thin hands placed meekly on his lap, seated about halfway down the bus. She chose the space next to him and sat.

The old woman took position in the seat directly across the aisle and leaned across, patting Emily's shoulder to get her attention, and grinning as though their talk at the bus stop had set them up as fast friends.

'Where ye off ta, me duckie?'

'Just up the road.' Emily tilted her head in a forward direction.

The old woman gazed ahead. Done with her fruitless search, she faced Emily again and said, 'Dat's anywhere sure.'

'Bowering Park,' Emily admitted, which was directly across the street from the lunatic asylum.

'Aw,' said the old woman, her eyes cast toward the case that sat on Emily's lap. 'Ye 'av'n a picnic?'

'Yes . . . I mean, no.'

'Now, make up yer mind, maid. Which it be?'

'No.'

The old woman leaned to gawk up into Emily's face. After much consideration and as the bus passed alongside the tan buildings which comprised Littledale Convent, the woman commented, 'Yer not frum dat place ye said.'

Losing patience with the woman's enquiries, Emily looked at her.

'Where ye say?'

'Bareneed,' Emily said sternly.

'Naw,' said the old woman, straightening in her seat with a huff and folding her arms. 'Dat's nut'n but a wick'd crock o' lies.'

Emily regarded the woman who would no longer meet her eyes, which was fine with her. She sat in stillness, facing forward and considering the velvety texture of a woman's black hat in the seat ahead of her. A moment later, she felt the old man's thin hand slide over to rest on her knee while he watched through the window and commenced humming merrily, inclining his head one way as though to signify interest in a sight beyond the pane. The hand patted her knee as though in friendship. Not wanting to cause a scene, Emily gently shifted away as much as possible, toward the very edge of the seat, yet the old man's hand remained where it was. It did not budge another inch. It simply rested there, the warmth of it seeping into her flesh. She checked around for a place to move, but the woman, seated half on and half off her seat with her boots in the aisle, was blocking the way.

Searching the windows on the other side of the bus, she found that the perimeter of Bowering Park was now visible. The rolling field and then the edge of the pond where a swan house had been erected.

'I got a daughter,' the old woman professed, "bout yer age. She were snooty like ye too. T'inks she's a princess. Royalty. Butter wouldn't melt in 'er mout'.'

Emily kept her eyes on the windows across the aisle as they passed the first set of gates for the park, then peeked at the old man's hand on her knee. The touch of that hand seemed to shrink every muscle in her body and set every nerve on edge. Yet she could not bring herself to look at the old man's face nor issue any sort of curt warning.

The bus would soon stop at the lunatic asylum.

'She's in dere,' said the old woman.

Distracted, Emily looked at the old woman to see where she had indicated.

The old woman was peering at the red-brick building. 'She's in dere, in da Mental. Widt all da udders of her royalness.' Reaching up, the old woman's fingers curved over the rope and pulled down. A bell dinged. And the bus pulled over. The old woman was already on her feet and Emily, despite her reluctance, would need to exit at that stop as well and follow after her.

In haste, Emily stood, watching the old man's hand fall away and return to meekly rest atop his other. Flushed and addled, she turned and waited impatiently for the back doors to hiss and fold open. From her position behind the old woman, she could smell a scent of stale perfume off her. She thought she sensed something astir in the greasy strands of the old woman's long hair.

Out on the sidewalk, the old woman turned to face Emily who avoided her, instead gazing across the street. There was Bowering Park, with its expansive landscape featuring deep-green metal statues of moose, Peter Pan and a soldier from the First World War with his arm stretched back to pitch a grenade, rivers with waters cascading over rocks, a multitude of flower beds and shaded paths beneath imported trees. Emily continued watching that way, as though admiring the prettiness of the park, until the eyes scrutinizing her through the bus windows were swept along by the vehicle's progression.

When the bus had taken a corner further along, Emily turned, hoping the old woman had stepped off. However, just like Emily, the old woman was facing the red-brick building, its construction angular and intimidating. The same daunting vision as when Emily had last seen it. Six years ago, she had left in tears, vowing never to return. Her father had said hurtful things to her, malicious and obscene. In his delusional state, he recognized her only as a little girl. The conditions in which he was living were unnatural. His wild, unkempt behaviour terrified her. She could not bring herself to see him again, the memory of his furious face, with its spittle-encrusted mouth, still haunted her.

'Who ye got in dere?' asked the old voice.

Emily regarded the woman who was now tilting her head toward the building.

'Pardon?'

'No need ta pardon me. I ain't done nut'n.'

'Oh.'

The old woman grinned. 'T'were a joke, me duckie. I said, who ye got in dere? I knows ye got someone in dere. No need ta pretend udderwise. Yer fool'n no one, 'cept yerself with dat sort o' snotty foolishness.'

Emily would not say it. Could not say it. She could not manage the word.

'Ye can tell me. Dere's no shame in dat. Dey're all no crazier den us.' With that, the old woman gave a peculiar giggle. 'Tell us, g'wan. I wun't tell no liv'n' soul.'

'My father,' Emily quietly admitted, tears of confession warming her eyes.

'T'ought so,' said the old woman. 'Ye got dat look about ye o' a fadderless child. Come on,' the old woman encouraged, taking hold of Emily's arm and pulling her along, only to stop dead in her tracks almost at once. With mouth agape, as though a realization had reared up to challenge her, she spun to contemplate Emily's face. 'Ye sure ye've not got a room booked in dere fer yerself?' she asked with an overly concerned face that soon rounded out with impish laughter. Practically toothless was her grin, widely uncovering bald, gleaming gums.

Watching the old woman's expression, Emily found herself perplexed and then disburdened by a quick smile. However, any relief that she felt was short-lived, for treading toward the steps of the asylum, her knees began to tremble. She shifted her case from one hand to the other, yet this did nothing to vary her body's state of anxiety.

One of the women in uniform announced to Alan Duncan that a visitor was waiting outside the door. In a reasonable tone, indicative of her calling, the nurse assured him that the visitor was a woman, his daughter. Emily was her name, and she would cause him no harm.

'Yes,' he muttered. 'I know.' Although he did not know. Not exactly.

The visitor, the woman, entered the room with a case in her hand.

Alan Duncan had been expecting a child. Hopefully, he had been expecting. His cheerless eyes searched the woman's face until he found the inklings of a more youthful being. Younger than him, that was all. There was little left of her, but he was able to reconcile himself with the few collected traces.

'Emily,' he said, desiring to know her more than his dwindled sense of recognition allowed. That name on his tongue. It came of its own volition. It was an intrigue. He was about to ask: *Did they take you?* but could not bring himself to do so.

'Yes.'

Alan watched the woman, his mind feeling uncharacteristically clear and lucid. A clarity had come over him, all at once, upon word of the woman's arrival. At first, the sensation alarmed him, as though he had been far off in another world, and been yanked back into this one to face the brash accumulation of a painstakingly incomparable reality.

'How are you?' he asked to centre himself around his own voice. That was the right thing to say. If he had possessed the strength to do so, he would have smiled in compliance with the ritual.

'Fine.' The woman laid her case on a chair toward the door and stood there in her coat and hat.

What was there to do now? Why had she arrived in the room?

How peculiar it must be to her, Alan thought. Leather straps holding his thin wrists to the bed frame. His old head, with only a few grey wisps of hair across the yellow scalp, tilted on the pillow, chin dipped down, trying to fully see her. The smell of him, the length of him beneath the sheets, the thought of him. A white room, in a bed forever.

Alan continued studying her. A woman like any other, one that he was meant to claim as his own, and, perhaps, felt a yearning to do so. Concentrating, he made an effort to welcome the attachment. Yet the child was missing. 'How are you?' He might have already said that. A woman, not a child.

'Fine.'

'I see.' He tried to guess at her age. When had he seen her last? Yesterday? No, longer. A week. A year. Before he was born. Misery, he thought. Medication and misery. And never a child in here. Never one. Not ever. The squeal of laughter skipping in the corridor. Little hands grasping his.

The woman had been thirteen at the time, when they wanted her back. Was thirteen a child? No, not in those years. Thirteen was a woman.

'How are you?' she asked. Or was it him? Or was she merely aping him, mocking him? Her face gave no sign of it.

He offered no reply to the question, instead saying, 'They've taken something away, you know.' The words presented themselves, without gathered thought, to both him and her. 'If not you, then me.'

The woman gazed over her shoulder, then around the room.

She must have been in her thirties. No longer thirteen. The gap in between, a life of insidious complications that required management and endurance.

'What?' asked the woman, almost with reluctance.

'This dying.'

'Pardon?'

'Dying. I'm not afraid to say it.' He waited, his eyes fixed on her, unfamiliar with the meaning of what he might be wishing to express, as though his mind, the reason for his being and being here specifically, continued to be kept at a distance from himself, for his own good. 'That word in the mouth. It won't jinx anyone, anymore than it already has.' Yet a frayed sense of intuition was guiding him. The woman was magnetic. He could not draw his eyes from how her figure stood out against the white wall. 'This sickness that's killing me . . .' His voice trailed off, as he realized he was not talking to a nurse or doctor. This woman was something unlike that.

The woman nodded, seeming to understand but, perhaps, doing so in the interest of self-preservation, so as to not complicate matters. Was that how it worked? He remembered these subtleties. These translations. Not so base and vulgar now. He chuckled at what he saw. The chuckle pained him. 'Oh!' He shut his eyes, smiling. A man lodged in the throb of one silent laugh. How old am I? he wondered. His eyes closed. It went on for years, this wondering.

'Whatever it might be,' his dry lips said while his eyes opened. 'Eating me up. It's taken away the mess.'

Emily stood speechless before the foot of her father's bed, her hands joined before her, the large wooden buttons of her coat still fastened. It was stifling in the room. She glanced toward the radiator and thought of placing her hand on the iron. She suspected it might burn. Noticing the bars on the window, she regarded her father again. His eyes were beseeching her, yet she would step no nearer. She watched him, expecting his face to darken toward that bestial expression she recalled with such despair, yet he did not spring from the bed, he did not pace the room, tossing his arms here and there and muttering accusations that she was not who she said she was: another child. He was taken away, so she, too, must have been taken away. How could she not have been if he was not there to watch over her, to protect her from harm? He did not bellow filth at her now. There seemed to be not an ounce of strength left in him. This was the end. She sensed the quietude that she knew was her father's knowledge of his own impending demise. Finally, he was broken, benevolent, cowed by the certainty. Whole human beings away from himself.

'I could care less.' He smiled and his teeth were a deeper yellow than his skin and two were missing, one front tooth and another off-centre on the bottom. 'It's killing the torment. Not me. That's worth the effort, isn't it? Death in the mouth.'

It was not the mouth Emily remembered, neither as a child nor from her last visit six years ago. Where had her father's teeth gone? she wondered. Had he lost them, bashed them from his mouth off some hard object in a fit of rage or had they been extracted? She searched around inside herself to discover what she might feel for him. A dying man who resembled no one she knew. Yet she loved him. Love of the sort that was sutured layers deep, the layers of love for her husband and children growing over that love. Yet she did. Yes, love him.

Watching this woman, Alan Duncan was surprised, for he recalled this woman as a baby and as a child. Her birth. The complications involved because her mother, not his wife, was of a tender year. Her first day at school. Her tenth birthday party. The stopwatch start of when she was expected back. They said tenth or – at the latest – thirteenth. Between one date and the other, any moment in between she would be lost to them. Hadn't they moved when she was young? Fled because of this. England. Newfoundland. The city of St. John's and deeper into the backwoods that people mistook for a picturesque seaside. Bareneed. That word. Was it a place? Or an expression? So many years scratched away like an eraser over pencil markings. A breath, the remnants blown from the page. It was as simple and as forgotten as that. The shadings of an imprint remaining. Debris on the floor that others trod around. How the years went away. Every day died silently, without ceremony. No funeral for the passing minute, no liturgy conducted over the gaping grave of the perished hour. The imbalance balancing itself now. There it was, his life. There it was, always in the distance, nearer now, his death. And the secret that stood there, perfectly defined against the white wall.

Emily watched her father sleeping. She hoped that he was only sleeping. His chest rose beneath the white sheet. She gazed toward the shut door and thought of leaving. It would be much easier to return on the train. Follow the route back to where she had come from. But wasn't she doing that now? She watched her father's form beneath the sheet and thought of Jacob, how her husband had forbidden this visit. Forbidden if not in harsh commands but in silences. Thinking of home, of Jacob, Junior and the baby, her breasts began to leak again. She sensed them let go and glanced at her chest, hoping that the tissue paper she had stuffed inside the front of her brassiere would absorb the embarrassment.

Alan Duncan, thinking of the woman, the woman who was named a name he and his wife had smiled into being, was dead with sadness. Breathing and dead with sadness. Tears pouring behind every inch of his skin, collecting at his fingertips, if only to touch and burst. His daughter, Emily. The secret. Forgiveness was meant to be exacted here. He would restore nothing, yet there was the need for it. He opened his eyes. Dead with sadness. If I am to die, he thought, I am to die. I will be as gone as nothing. Look at the life of her. What does that mean to me? This woman I had named and saved. She knows nothing of it.

He would tell her this: 'Do you remember the dock in Liverpool?'

'Yes,' she said at once, as though expecting those exact words.

Emily watched her father's eyes. He was seeing into her and she into him. Neither knew the true meaning of what they remembered together, for what they remembered together was not the same.

'We left.'

The door to the room opened and a nurse leaned her head in. She checked over the situation, smiled at Emily and leaned back out, quietly pulling the door to.

'They don't want the truth,' he said, his voice quavering, faltering. Not a stain of interest in the departed nurse, while he continued with his probing search of Emily's eyes. 'Merely whatever is convenient. Whatever they say it does. It is a pronouncement.' His eyes went to the window. His life was a story he told himself to believe. He would not share the story because he was of his own invention and not meant for others. But the secret that was his life was not for the grave, for he could not keep it there with him. The worms and maggots would eat his secret, piece by rotting piece, strip by tattered strip. It would come away from his bones. The secret would be dissolved and that would be the end of him. For there were secrets in the flesh, secrets that pumped the blood, secrets that shaped thought, secrets that drew each breath into the lungs. The doctors wanting the secrets so that they might make life plain. Here was his secret. He shifted his eyes from the window to the woman. There stood the beginning of the disclosure of his secret.

Her.

The one they said was his daughter.

'I have told this to no one before.'

The woman took one step nearer the bed. That was all it would take, an admission, to draw people nearer. Another secret closer to another secret. The secret wanting to be known by the secret in another.

'On the dock in Liverpool, there were two men. Do you remember, Secret?'

'Yes.'

'Their names were George Chapman and William Gull. Georgie and Willy. They were brothers, even though they never shared the same surnames. These two men knew you. They kept separate names because they were hiding from each other.'

The woman, the secret, straightened on her feet.

'Do you know how they knew you?'

'No.'

'They were your uncles, yet not related to me or your mother.'

The woman, the secret, appeared confused. That was customary in the beginning of the progression of the revelation of the secret.

'Do you remember those two men?'

Emily tried to imagine their faces. She had little trouble doing so, for they were always as vivid to her as if she had witnessed them in the hours past. She wondered why and felt icicles beneath her skin, for now she knew that they were linked to something other than her father. They were linked to her. One of her earliest memories had been of that dock, but only because those men had been involved in even earlier memories.

'Your secret will take the place of my secret here.' Again, he moved his eyes toward the barred window. 'The two men had a sister. Her name was Annie. There was a circle of men in Liverpool who I had fallen in with. They were business associates. They knew Annie from an early age. She was kept by them, they told me. At the age of thirteen, Annie conceived you. She was secreted away to an elderly woman in a parsonage in Lancashire. You were born when Annie was fourteen. This history I was told. As Annie was under the financial and social protection of this group of . . . gentlemen, you, too, became their protégé. Georgie and Willy were the collective threat. They did the bidding of the circle of gentlemen. I have no recollection of why I told them I would harbour you, perhaps it was for reasons of protection, or perhaps perversity, perhaps a bit of both, a man's heart is not that easily divided . . . For whatever reason, I told them that I would take you in and keep you for them. An import, they called you, a conversion. This would be our secret. Your mother could not conceive. She was incapable. I took you home and assured her that you were ours. A child in her arms. An infant whose parents had met with unfortunate circumstances. Your mother asked no questions. The questions were blanched from her mind, at the sight of you.' His eyes, slowed by age, illness and trepidation, scoped across the room to settle on the secret's image. 'Her face. You should have seen it. Your mother's face watching you. And you watching her.'

Emily felt as though she were being driven back from the bed, back toward the wall and floor at once, although she was not moving. Bits and pieces of this information she had heard before, all of it taken as the ravings of a madman.

'On your tenth or thirteenth birthday you were meant to be returned to Annie and the circle of gentlemen. If you recall, as I do, you celebrated your tenth birthday here, in St. John's. Your thirteenth in Bareneed. The year I was removed to set up lodgings here. If we had remained overseas, you might have found yourself in a place much like this. One of the minds of others in here might have been yours. A circumstantial substitution.'

Emily had often argued with herself over memories. She had heard people claim that their first memories were from an age of five years or so. Yet Emily believed she had recollections of being in a crib, as an infant, despite others' insistence that such memories were an impossibility. Now, as she had in the past, she recalled the face of a young girl, a friend of the family in England. Never had she once suspected the face to be that of her true mother. She thought, of course, that the girl looking in at her, standing above her, was a girl who had visited, a girl who had nothing more to do with her, a girl with a face that betrayed existence, for she was timeless. A girl who remained a girl in Emily's mind. Her mother. A girl.

Emily found herself repeating the word 'Mummy' in her head. How was any of this to be verified if her mother, Amanda, the only mother she truly knew, had passed on? It was out of the question, and this sense of drastic uncertainty and – somehow – failure sank through her entire body, threatening to suck the breath from her lungs.

'Shortly after leaving Liverpool, I heard that Georgie and Willy were murdered. An anonymous letter arrived in which it was stated that my name was on a list, that my address was known. Of course they knew my address. What more proof did I require than the letter in hand? At once, I sought out an address far removed. Bareneed. The letter stated that my food or water would be poisoned. That my family would be hunted. I had to escape, and it worked. You were not harmed. Were you?' Alan Duncan turned his eyes to the secret.

The secret, wiping at her eyes, slowly shook her head.

'Your mother, she grew to despise me. But you were never harmed. I see that now. Thank God. My food and water. It seemed they were safe, despite what I suspected. Under the protection of this institution . . . Regardless, I have been poisoned.'

Emily watched her father until she could no longer bear it.

'It has been an exceedingly slow poisoning.'

Emily turned away and went to her case. Opening it, she sniffed away the tears and searched around for the black and white photograph taken by Brent Linegar with his new camera. She found the envelope containing the photograph and slid it out into her palm. Captured there was Junior, holding a baby in his arms and smiling. The sun was in his eyes and one eye was completely shut, his head tilted on an angle as though to shun the brilliance, the tall grass behind him, the slatted corner edge of their house. Blackstrap in Junior's arms. Emily had meant to show it to her father, so that he might know the two boys, at least in image. But now she was made nauseous by the prospect of his eyes roaming over the appearance of her sons. They were children, just as she had been. She glanced back at what she'd thought was her father.

'What have you there?' he asked, with a lightness to his voice, as though the story was now told and done with, and they might be not only fair-sailing blood relatives, but friends.

Emily considered turning the photograph around and bringing it near to her father's face. His eyes fixed on the black and white surface. How far into it might he fall?

Who is this? Alan Duncan would think. Who are these boys? Nothing of what he would see of them he would know.

Emily slid the photograph back into the envelope and put it in her case. Her knees were wobbling. She shut the case and moved it from the chair. Then she dropped down onto it. Seated there, in her hat and coat, she put her hands to her face as though to hide.

A room, thought Alan Duncan. A weeping woman. A dying man.

The secret changing hands.

Bareneed

Uncle Ace kills the creature in the box

The flicker from the sway of a single candle flame gave illumination to the kitchen table. Vaguer light lent dim visibility to the far reaches of the room. Uncle Ace was seated in his motionless rocking chair toward one corner, his grim face unchangeable in the subtle shift of shadows cast by the creeping and ebbing light. Steadily, he watched toward where the creature was set down in its box beside the stove. The creature made not a sound even though it stirred awake. It searched with its eyes. It seemed to know and not know at once. It sniffed to recognize the space it shifted in. The creature would soon chew. It was good at chewing.

One creature eating another. A full stop. He was a man. He knew that much. His hands were a dead giveaway. The grasping fingers of a man. Hands that could hold artefacts. Tools. Food. Weapons. As was the case throughout his long-standing years, he suspected something skulking in the corners of his eyes. He took it for a trick, yet it was not. What moved always in the outermost line of his peripheral vision was often a bug. In this case, a carpenter, its grey back sectioned like armour, searching out a hiding place for the fall. The carpenter bug found its way inside with the cold, like mice, like rats, like hornets and blue-arsed flies. There were creatures hidden everywhere in the house. Behind ceiling mouldings, beneath wallpaper, tucked away in attics where they chewed themselves a nest. Hiding away from the killing weather. Their home. A man had to permit them. Why should they cause him unrest? Who was he to say

442

otherwise? A mouse snapped in a trap. A bug underfoot. The crushing smear. He took it all to heart, yet – in doing so – experienced an even greater urgency to destroy. Love and kill. Keep the heart removed from it. Flesh was meat, no matter what god was said to govern it. When face to face with a murderous animal. Try to reason it was worth more than yourself. Worth sparing with its teeth and claws in you, like hunger, like desolation, slaughter to put food on the table. A moderate heart was a luxury, not for the caring, but for the eating.

Uncle Ace pressed his thick, blue-veined hands into the armrests of the rocking chair and stood. It was enough to be on his feet. He often suffered from dizziness and a throbbing at the base of his skull. Whiteness sheeted across his vision with any sudden movement and he would forget everything. He stood still, waiting for his brain to allow sight, his eyes clearing to a view of this room.

The creature in the box by the stove shifted its eyes to give him attention. It was a round, soft creature from which no challenge would' be expected. He had taken this creature from the house of a woman. The creature was being fed there. He had taken it from where it was sleeping, and brought it here. The creature had not seemed to mind. It made no noise.

There came the sound of a larger creature from overhead. Footsteps and shifting. A sound or two from a mouth or nostrils. Whatever it was might be sleeping. Tossing itself from one side to the other. The house tipped by wind. Not a threat in its present form.

The scurrying and clawing of life in a wall.

The progression of the carpenter bug, thriving on the rot, with its grey armoured back that would not prevent its own crushing, inching toward the table leg.

Seven blue-arsed flies nestled beneath a sheet of wallpaper with its edge slightly unglued toward the ceiling moulding. They would sit in your hand and not fly, made sluggish by the accumulating chill.

A hornet hibernating in the sleeve of an old coat in the back porch.

A man inside, kept safe from the biting wind that hammered the walls. It was preferable to be in here than out there, although something told him he would fare better being blown about. Facing every punch of the wind.

Uncle Ace stepped nearer the box by the stove. The creature's mother was nowhere to be seen. Usually the creature's mother was near, but the creature's mother seemed to have been gone for a time unknown. There had been a number of them in a nest. His memory of such things. There were bottles that the creature sucked from. What was it? This thing. He trod nearer. The creature watched him. There was no threat, but once it grew larger, there might be a challenge. One day the time would come. Larger and larger until its needs surpassed a meagre amount and the power that was held over it would dissipate. It would encroach upon the requirements of others. It would make demands and strike out at those nearest to it. Proximity of the heart, he thought, his eyes fixed on the creature's chest. Proximity of one heart to another. Never to forget the others' passing.

Now was the time to make away with it, before it gained the upper hand for all of its life, hiding inside one, hiding inside another. It was the stink of men that he sensed from the creature. How the creature might live off the stores of others. Not so young then. Not so cuddly. The creature would occupy space in its mother and father. Take up more and more space.

Uncle Ace trod nearer. The creature's eyes were upon him. He stared and stared, growing agitated, breathing harsher. Beast upon beast. Club it to death. Deliver blows until nothing remained, save the act of forgetting.

The creature's eyes shifted from him toward the doorway. Uncle Ace turned to see yet another creature, larger but still not full grown. Two to kill. No. Two to kill him. The larger but not full grown one with its eyes on his hand. He was holding the weapon. The one he needed before, in the first place. The one that would have saved him. He laid it down on the counter where it made a clatter and caught the soft glimmer of the lone candle flame. Little creatures surrounding him. They would not take him down. He was the bigger of the three. The larger now.

The one in the doorway stalked in and took the smaller one from the box, eyes warily fixed on him. 'I thought he was at Coffey's,' said the small creature.

Uncle Ace watched them go out together, through the door. He looked back to the box. The creature still in its place. The one he had been after. Grey and long with a bald tail. He raised the weapon from where he had laid it down. Both hands held the handle high. Then he squatted and thrust at once. Nothing felt as the tip went through. The creature pinned there, to the bottom of the box. Done. He checked over his shoulder. Footsteps slowly treading upstairs.

Rising from his crouch, Uncle Ace watched the creature jerk in spasm. It was a dance, a jig, a trick that everyone might, one day, learn the steps to. Funny, it was. He had seen it before. Men engaged in that painful flailing of limbs. How many living things in the room now with him not counted?

When the jig had stopped, he yanked the weapon loose and picked up the still-warm creature in his hands. He went out the back door and through the front yard, past a sleeping mongrel and down the slope of Bareneed toward the headland. Under the blue spill of moonlight, he climbed up the headland, clinging to rocks and small trees until he reached the top. He watched out over the night ocean, the moonlight on the black water, a glistening streak that absolved his heart of every troubling crime.

The creature was not so heavy in his hands. He clutched it in his right hand and pressed it to his heart. Its pain would equal nothing short of his own. He moved toward the edge of the headland and stared down. He might fall forward, tumble and plummet for a count of final seconds before smacking the rocks, smacking other surfaces, harder and softer, in a blind thudding, until the water stopped him.

But he did not fall. Not this time, like all the others. He crawled down the far side of the headland to where the hole ran from one end to the other, the hole he crawled into as a child, barely capable of fitting through. A faultline that was said to be the place where Newfoundland, the island, would break in half one day if struck by the foretold tremor. He found it, big enough to barely fit into. Head first, he leaned into the narrow cavern, shoving the dead creature ahead of him as he progressed. Knees and elbows working to take him deeper into the rock, inching into the squat, dank confines until he could shift no further, nor could he move backwards. It was a place to rest, to hibernate. Warm as it was. Safe from the wind and the snow that was sure to gust in the coming months. Where he would spend the winter, safe from others, others safe from him.

With the dead creature, he shut his mind off to the other live ones that journeyed down the hole ahead of him, to worry over his face and scurry on legs that tracked upon him in time.

There he slept, waiting for division to open up the rock and expose him.

Junior sat on the edge of his father's bed with Blackstrap in his arms. His father's snoring pitched and rolled and thundered toward choking.

'Hey, Blacky,' Junior whispered, watching the baby's face. 'Where'd Uncle Ace go? Did you see Uncle Ace too?' The baby's eyes searched around the dark room. Junior mentioned his uncle only out of fear, as though to talk about the man might lessen that worry. Blackstrap's eyes kept wandering, then fixed on Junior's face.

Junior checked his sleeping father, but would not wake him. Would his father believe him about Uncle Ace? He absent-mindedly rocked the baby in his arms and sang the song he remembered hearing from his mother:

> *Silent Night, Holy Night*
> *All is calm, all is bright . . .*

'You like that, Blacky?'

> *. . . Round yon virgin*
> *Mother and child*
> *Holy infant so tender and mild*
> *Sleeep in Heeeavenly peeeeeace*
> *Sleeee-eep in Heavenly peace*

Junior's eyes shifted to the doorway. There they remained, while he plainly uttered: 'I don't think Uncle Ace is really dead, Blacky. How can I see him if he's just a ghost like Mom says?'

St. John's

Any number of names

In the morning, Emily rose startled from bed in her room at the Welcome Arms. Confused as to where she might be, she threw back the covers and stood, her breasts paining her, the front of her nightdress wet with milk. A sour odour rose to her. She stepped before the mirror above the basin and saw the stains. Loosening the straps of her nightdress she let it drop and felt the fullness of her breasts. She leaned nearer the basin and prodded her nipples, rolling them and then squeezing them, until dots of milk appeared. She took hold of her breast with both hands and pressed her fingers into the flesh. Jets of milk shot into the sink. Doing so, she could not help but think of Blackstrap, but also of Jacob who had tasted the milk and commented on its flavour, taking a liking to it thereafter.

Having relieved herself sufficiently, she then dressed and ventured immediately by bus to the lunatic asylum. A deep-seated sensation of breathlessness and ill ease kept her fretting on the entire forty-five-minute ride.

The psychiatrist on duty, Dr. Frazier Walsh, was summoned by the nurse at the station when Emily requested a visit with her father. Stood in wait, Emily began to tremble, her head swimming with weakness. She remembered that she had not eaten breakfast, as her thoughts were with Blackstrap and whether he was being properly cared for. A baby. She tried to remember his face. She should never have left him, even though he was in capable hands with Mrs. Coffey. A woman not Blackstrap's mother. Emily began to perspire, droplets rising along her brow and hairline. If only she could be home now. Home with Blackstrap and Junior and Jacob. A house with them in it. This imagining connected her to a dream she had experienced last night. A dream of her house and family. Junior and Blackstrap had looked nothing like themselves. In fact, they were the exact same age. Twins, eight years old. And when she entered the room, they merely regarded her with indifference and asked her where their mother was. How to remember now? Her mind jarred at the thought of their true faces. She could not recall them and the vacancy frightened her.

'Hello.' Dr. Walsh, the lilt of an Irish accent evident in that one word. He placed a hand on her shoulder as though he had known her for years.

Emily shifted her eyes to that hand. The long fingers and trimmed nails.

'I'm sorry to tell you, but your father passed during the night.'

Emily made an involuntary sound, while Dr. Walsh went on to explain that every effort had been directed toward notifying her during her father's final hours the previous evening. However, she had not left an address where she might have been contacted.

Dr. Walsh then gestured her to his office. 'Come and have a sit.'

Seated behind his desk, the doctor watched Emily as though he might know the truth of her existence. Her head swam while she wondered whether her father had told him about her, and she flushed with embarrassment, fearing that she might faint away. What if he asks about my children?

'Are you going to be alright?'

'Yes,' she heard herself say. The sound of her own voice in her ears only heightened her weakness.

'I'm very sorry about your father, Emily.'

She could barely manage a nod. 'Thank you.' She bowed her head, her hands there in her lap.

'I have to say I'll miss him.'

Emily focused on the doctor, drawing out from within herself.

'He was an interesting man, and I know he cared for you deeply. He always had a way of showing that.'

For whatever reason, perhaps because she had been removed from him and thus suspected that he was removed from her, in thought as well as location, she was caught off guard by the doctor's admission. Her head gave a slight shake.

'It was always another name, but I knew it was you he was talking of. Any number of names. Victoria. Betty. Elizabeth. Emily. He had delusions of harm coming to any number of young girls. He used different names, but I suspect he was referring to you in these cases.'

Again, Emily lowered her eyes, for she had begun to cry.

'I'm sorry for your troubles. Here.' He handed her a handkerchief.

Emily took it and dabbed at her eyes.

'I often wondered what kept you away. There was a record of your visits from several years ago. I had been meaning to contact you about it shortly. I only took over here five months ago.' The doctor paused. 'What I suspected was that he might have harmed you at some point?'

Emily sobbed, 'No,' and shook her head.

'I needed to ask. He seemed to fear that his association with you might harm you in some way. Any idea why?'

Again, Emily replied in the negative, and pressed the handkerchief tight to her mouth to smother her sobs.

The doctor leaned back in his chair. 'Your father was a brilliant man, Emily. He had a highly complicated story for me every day. It was always a chore to sort it out, always entertaining though.' He gave a caring, boyish smile. 'I'll miss him.'

'Yes,' she said, not knowing why she agreed. Who knew more of him? This doctor or the dead man's supposed daughter.

'Alan spoke freely of everything under the sun, yet he had a great secrecy about him.'

'Yes.' More tears, and an open sobbing she could no longer restrain.

And so it remained, the matter of her father without clarification, her mother passed on, as well, the history of her existence left to her own mind to formulate.

Bareneed

What is buried with Emily's father

The funeral was intended to be a quiet affair. After her father's death, Emily had worried over where to bury him. Into what plot of land should he be interred to embrace eternal peace? Finally, she decided that Bareneed, where her father had been removed from all those years ago, a secluded cove that he claimed as a hideaway for safety's sake, would be fitting as his final resting place.

During the days leading up to the funeral, as more and more people visited to offer condolences and to share stories of her father, she felt badly distressed. She could not sit still, her thoughts scattered and undecided. These stories. These memories of her father from the mouths of others. She did not want their words bringing him back to life, enlivening him in ways she had never known. The people spoke of kindnesses expressed by him, credits given at the store to the highly impoverished. Children presented with clothes and boots. Emily would notice herself watching Junior with a puzzled expression. And the baby was an entity that she could not fathom.

''E never show'd no one da books back den 'cause so many were owing,' explained one old man, while stuffing half a cookie into his mouth in the parlour. Crumbs falling. The cookie half chewed and pushed to one side, rounding out his cheek. 'Dat's why dey hauled 'im off, dat bloody rotten bastard, Bowering.'

Emily dreaded the thought of enduring the burial, and wished she could do it alone. She wanted no further thoughts of her father. She did not want Jacob there. She did not want her son and the baby present. She did not want to be seen.

As she arrived at the church, she was astonished to find every pew filled. Despite her father's position in the merchant store, Emily suspected that respect was due him, and that respect would not be cast aside by a single living soul in the community. This is what she thought. But what she found out was that they were there for her. They told her as much. They touched her arm and they hugged her. They gently took her by the shoulders and watched her face with sad understanding. They warmly held her hands for moments on end. They were in tears for her. They wept for her. 'So sorry about yer loss, me love.'

Watching her father's casket be lowered into the earth, Emily wondered on the mystery of him being buried. A madman. A man who told stories to suit himself. A man who invented the truth. Where was she in all of this?

The young woman, Annie, who was said to be her mother. She remembered that childlike face as her father went into the ground.

How to find Annie? Emily had not even thought to ask her father for the young woman's last name. How ever to know her? The possibility now lowered into the hallowed earth of Bareneed.

The poems in these sections, while not entirely the creations of Patrick Lambly/ Hawco, were found with his belongings. Because the scraps of paper were hand- written with lines crossed out and additional words added, I can only assume that they were partially his doing. The renowned scholar of Irish immigration to Newfoundland, Jon Bannion, has confirmed that portions of the poems were taken from lines penned by various great Irish poets.

1896

Bareneed

How the Hawco name fell from the sky

For Patrick, the drink was no dire problem, as decreed by most, but rather an elixir that untangled the snarly words that poorly mistreated his thoughts when sober. In a decent state of inebriation, the once rough-edged, tormenting bits of words became an elegant gush that poured out of Patrick with as much sublime spirit as the rum he effortlessly poured into himself.

Since the loss of both feet to frostbite ten years ago, he had been inwardly off balance, the derelict portion of his soul ballooning larger to make waste of his life, with time spent outside the public house committed exclusively to the scribbling of verse.

Patrick Hawco were the first words he had written on a piece of wood, after recovery from the surgery to his feet. As luck would have it, behind the Sheas' front door where Ferrol had knocked that first night in Bareneed, there was a physician of high caliber attending to a woman in extended labour. Once done with delivering the twins, the physician had taken a look at Patrick's bloodless feet and pronounced that it was they that should be removed or, in time, the entirety of Patrick's being.

The name Hawco had been chosen by Ferrol, for as they were entering the doorway to the Shea household that full decade ago, a thud had sounded behind Patrick which had been a hawk dropping from the sky. Its wings frozen stiff. Ferrol had kept the hawk and had it stuffed as a token of their good fortune.

The boys that Rose had given birth to on that night when the birds fled from the sky, in a mad torrent of escape, as though snipped free from their tethers, and the creatures dead and living vanished without movement from the loving cup of the valley, were given the names Francis and Ace.

Rose, while assumed to be not strong enough to survive the ordeal, where she muttered on her deathbed, balancing on the precipice between life and the hereafter, eventually recovered from her agony and, while lacking memory of any of her ordeal, spoke in hushed tones of mysterious events that no one managed to comprehend. Where was the twisted boy? she kept asking, yet no one knew of whom she was speaking.

As Rose's condition remained precariously frail, her twin infant boys were watched over by Margaret Shea in her childless home, where she treated the infants as her own and heaped motherly love upon them. However, a few days following their birth, and much to the terror of Mrs. Shea, the twins went missing in the night, supposedly abducted by the fairies, as appeared to be the fate laid out for all of Rose's offspring, yet they were missing for only a single night and were brought back the following morning by Ferrol, who refused to share the story of their recovery. In reply, he recited some verse, no doubt the invention of Patrick Lambly, relating to the eternal damnation of his soul through acts of abominable offence to the heavens.

News of the return of the mirror-image infants, while a jubilant affair that brought consolation to the community at large, was quickly overshadowed by the discovery of Bishop Flax's disappearance by one of his ship's servants. To the great consternation of the faithful of Bareneed, Flax did not return to his ship nor was he found, by the search party that departed that day, in any near proximity along the coast. It were as though he had disappeared off the face of the earth. It was not until two springs later that two boys, engaged in dangerous play, as boys were wont to do, came upon human bones and tatters of his regal clothing stuffed into the crack that ran through the headland in Bareneed.

Both Rose and Patrick were nursed back to health by Ferrol who made a point of sitting in the tilt between the two invalids, feeding them water and food as best could be managed, and tending to the fire in the stone hearth.

It was in his delirium, following the amputation of his feet, that Patrick discovered his true voice and, according to Ferrol, spoke in verse throughout most nights with the intonations of a master poet. Such was the greatness of his fever-sprung poems that Ferrol summoned Michael Ryan, the literate cooper from down in the valley, to transcribe Patrick's words for safe keeping. These Ferrol kept in a wooden box that he gifted to Patrick upon his recovery along with a knife so that Patrick might leave his mark on the trees. 'Carve up da forest,' Ferrol commanded. 'Fill 'er widt dose ravish'n words 'o yers.' It was a world of true wonder to Patrick. Often, while reading the poems, tears would brim in his eyes, for the sentiments were so beautiful, filled as they were with the florid passions of the dead and dying. Not by my hand, he would tell himself. They could not be. Yet they were. *Is liom an leabhar seo.*

In his fever-damaged mind, Patrick valued the box of poems as his severed feet and carried them with him, wherever he went about on crutches fashioned from twisted tree limbs, reciting them in public houses while being held above the gathered men on Ferrol's shoulder:

> *Beauing, belleing, dancing, drinking,*
> *Breaking windows, cursing, sinking*
> *Ever fighting, never thinking,*
> *Live the life of Ferrol.*
>
> *Knowing short but merry lives,*
> *Going where the devil drives,*
> *Having sweethearts, but no wives,*
> *Live the life of Ferrol.*
>
> *Spending faster than it comes,*
> *Beating waiters, bailiffs, duns,*
> *No one's true begotten son,*
> *Live the life of Ferrol.*

There was no more glorious moment in Patrick's life than when his head was awash with rum and his mouth full of words from the scraps of paper on which his poems had been written by another's hand, the words sometimes changed and rearranged and made more precise by the accommodating currents of intoxication that swept him off while still conscious, barely there,

> *yet speaking from that realm*
> *where the aesthetically noxious*
> *had not entirely exacted its killing force*
> *upon that one good man.*

Often, while carving his verse into the benches or tables of the public house, he would be paused by a word linked to home, and the thought of his family back in Limerick would visit him, yet he would strip the thought bare with the word: safety. He was safe here. Master Job would never find him in this place. Not with his name changed by his great friend, Ferrol, who looked after all requirements. And, yes, one day he would make his way back to Limerick to set things right. There was always another day. Tomorrow or in the years to come. In fact, although there might very well be a shortage of bread or coins or love, there was – without argument – no shortage of days to look toward where matters might be put in order.

'Who 'a ye could argue widt dat?' he called out from his place high on Ferrol's shoulders. 'One day perishes 'n anudder steps right up widt a big fat beaming look o' conceit sladdered all over its puss like a gob of . . .' His voice trailed off, for the lads to all sides of him were already laughing and calling out in agreement.

Noticing this, he gave a generous smile and laughed himself, swaying while he raised his mug, toasting not only the lads but the brotherly sense of inner wealth, accumulated only through the intake of ale. In his head, he heard a voice that must have been his own, and there came with it another sound, the settling of waves upon a shoreline, the great suck of the sea mesmerizing him, so that his spirits were made morbid and he spoke quietly in Irish and with heartfelt intonation:

You wave down there
lifting your loudest roar
the wits in my head are worsted
by your wails.

In time, the twins were returned to Rose Cavanagh, and Patrick Hawco remained settled in the home and took the boys as his own. Having abandoned his own family, and knowing nothing of their current fate, sentiments of this betrayal found throughout his verse, he felt that if he were ever to be made father again it would be to children that were not rightfully his. A fitting cross to bear.

Rose was seduced by Patrick's poems. In them, she recognized a way of life that was known to her, for now, in these days that seemed too mundane for words, the lines formed a bridge to places of pure feeling where she believed she might unearth a dwelling akin to that magical realm of painful invention where she had resided before the birth of the twins. In belief, she worshipped Patrick and fell hopelessly, devoutly in love with him.

The twin boys, at an age of sensitivity that fostered concern for the infirm, would help Patrick around. They would follow after him, even from an early age, as though they expected something of him, for he appeared to be held in high esteem by many in Bareneed. In his black cast-off suit and faded collarless shirt, he would kneel with a gnarled stick for support near the water and face northeast. He would ask the boys to do the same, one to each side of him as identicals.

With the breeze from the sea on his face, he would tell stories of Ireland, of the reprehensible voyage across the water, of the heinous American sailors who attempted to sabotage their journey, of their uncle Ferrol's dramatic escapades, of the great fire in St. John's that left the world black to the touch (of the hanging, he would not speak a word), of his brave voyage of escape from enslavement during which he had suffered nature's injury that necessitated the lopping off of his feet. With the mention of this last point, he would cast a glance back up the valley, toward the houses clustered there, and his eyes would betray the sadness he felt for those who still slaved for the benefit of the master in that house at the highest rise of the valley.

It was through these acts and the thoughts passed on that Patrick became the boys' true father, for they recognized no other man as that, and found resonant reflection in his memory for the entirety of their lives.

The curse of the girl's vanishing

It was in their tenth year that Francis and Ace, having just departed the edge of the cliff where Patrick was engaged in his daily kneeling and what had become regarded as a rite of recollection for the other villagers knelt gathered with him, went into the woods and came upon a clearing where the sunlight was sifting down upon the ferns and bright green grass. At once, with a double intake of breath, they were stilled by the sensation of a presence.

Through the criss-cross shadows of limbs, a small figure could be made out. It was not until the boys stepped nearer, trying to keep their step silent against the living earth, that they discovered the figure to be a blonde-haired girl with her back to the boys. Taking her for one of the girls from Bareneed, they called out. Yet the girl would not turn to face them.

Treading nearer, they were startled by the screech of what they took to be an overhead bird. Staring skyward in unison, their vision strained by that upward elongated lurch, they determined that it was not a single bird at all, but two crows perched on the upper boughs of a spruce tree and cawing in duplicate. Two for mirth, each boy thought, having heard the pronouncement on numerous occasions from their mother. Yet reflected in their eyes as two and watched by two, the crows should have been taken as one.

When they drew their eyes back to the earth and searched for the girl again, she was nowhere to be found.

'Hello,' they called out, an echo resounding back to them that might have been one of their voices chasing the exact other to match it. The echo came back to them and entered their ears in perpetual vibration until they were forced to flee the forest to rid themselves of the irksome inner shiver.

That night, while eating stew, Rose watched the boys with extra interest, her eyes travelling from one face to the other.

'Wha' 'av ye seen?' she asked, for their eyes still held the faint impression of the blonde-haired girl clouded by present intention and action.

They both shook their heads.

Patrick's gentle snore, from his bough bed in the corner, grew louder.

'Wha'?'

'A girl,' Francis admitted, the first to speak of their sighting, and so the one destined to have a greater dealing in it.

'Where?'

'In da woods,' Ace piped up, pointing in the direction. 'She 'ad blonde 'air,' he added, trying to make up for the error of speaking second.

Rose sipped from her spoon.

Patrick snored louder until the sound became caught up in the table and the bowls of stew required holding to be anchored against the shimmy.

Rose, casting a look toward Patrick, reached for one of his stick canes and whacked him soundly across the back, where he whimpered and was silenced.

'Tell me of it,' she said to the boys, pointing a finger to one face then the other. 'Every scrap o' wha' ye 'old in yer liddle 'eads.'

That night, the curse of the girl's vanishing was lifted by Rose's deeds.

In keeping with the directions discerned from one of Patrick's poems, a medley of tradition and invention that was taken as spiritual fact by Rose, she wrapped the black glass rosary beads, gifted to her by Bishop Flax, around the skinned carcass of a rabbit, and ventured to the graveyard where the fairy changeling had been buried.

The twin boys followed after her, although uninvited. Their presence was noted by Rose yet she made no mention of it. At the grave site, she laid the offering at the back of the slate tombstone, on the front of which was etched with a sharp stone the specifics of the infant's death. Following a moment of reflection, and with a boy stood at either side of her, she searched for a thin stone around her feet and found the exact one required to fit neatly into her hand. Pressing its edge to the back of the tombstone, she scraped a horizontal line, then two longer vertical lines straight down, one from each end of the top line. At the bottom she drew another horizontal line, parallel to the top one and connecting the ends of the two verticals. Toward the centre of the door and off to the left, she drew a circle, a doorknob. Done with her doodle, she let the thin stone fall from her grip and watched the door, then cast her eyes toward the starless sky, her head cocked on an angle to best invite listening.

The two boys, curious of her actions, stared toward the night sky yet saw no obvious attraction. Turning her head, Rose then knelt and, pressing her palms to the stone, set her ear flush to the door. She shut her eyes and listened intently for near to an hour. The boys, growing weary, thought to sit, yet remained on their feet, not wanting to slacken the grip of the proceedings. Just when they were growing sleepy, they heard their mother whisper, answering in words previously unknown, words that were tested on the tongues of the boys as they recited what had been heard. Rose nodded once. Then opened her eyes, leaned back and raised her fist to the door to knock soundly, three times.

The dull clatter of knuckle bones against stone.

Done with her undertaking, she gathered the skinned rabbit and broke the rosary beads, sprinkling some from the twine onto the earth surrounding the grave. She then took the remaining beads and, on her way back down the valley, with the boys trailing after her toward the darkness of her tilt, placed each bead in her mouth, one by one, and swallowed. Three beads were left to cook with the rabbit, which Rose ate late that night with the twin boys.

The next day, after a sound sleep, where not one person stirred in the tilt, making not one movement nor one sound, Rose gave the boys instruction: 'Go ta da woods.'

Doing as they were told, they found the spot where they had first sighted the girl. There, they waited in hope. The scene was not so thrilling as the first sighting, for the sun's rays were not illuminating the space and so there was no such heavenly aura about the forest nor in their hearts. Regardless, in time, in the dimness of a clouded afternoon, a girl appeared. Although the figure seemed of the same size and shape, its hair was black rather than blonde.

The figure was in the exact position as before and turned without a word of beckoning from the twins. As she made her way to face them, there came a caw from overhead and the twins looked up to see four crows perched in the upper branches of a spruce tree.

The girl came toward them.

'Tháinig beaguchtach,' she said, in a tongue the boys barely recognized. They knew only that she was speaking in Irish, a language that the children thought hopeless, for it was an old and difficult language, and that she had said something having to do with loss.

The girl walked up to Francis and stood by his side. 'You have spoken of me,' she said in English.

'No,' said Francis, denying involvement from the very start.

The black-haired girl followed them home, where Rose stood in the doorway to the tilt, and studied the child as she neared. She then took her by the shoulders and investigated the features of her face.

'Were da sun shinin'?'

'No,' said Ace, hoping that something might have gone wrong, for, again, he felt only second-best in this venture.

'Wha's yer name chil'?' asked Rose.

'Caitriona.'

'Ah, 'n who tol' ye so?'

'Na daoine maithe.'

Rose put a palm to the girl's cheek where it remained for a count of minutes. She then turned to step back into the tilt where she set her hand over the flame of the open fire and turned her palm to see the outline left in smoke. As expected, it was of a different face from the one stood in the doorway, yet of not so great a difference as to banish the child from their midst.

The mutely glistening void of ebony

On the night of what many assumed to be Catherine's return, a gale blew, battering the walls of the Cavanagh tilt and rousing Patrick from his blank sleep.

The pounding of the wind shook the walls and the rain slathered the windowpane, blurring everything beyond when Patrick sat up and blankly stared toward the glass. The hammering on the walls became more distinct and rhythmic until he assumed it might be a person rather than the wind knocking on wood. The voice he heard was indistinct yet sounded as though it might be calling his name. He shifted off his bunk and grabbed his sticks, leaning and leveraging himself up and toward the door, not wanting the noise to disrupt the sleep of Rose and the children.

Patrick set one hand to the wall for support and, with great care, pushed opened the door, clutching the edge just as the wind thrust hold of it, yanking him out. In a brisk moment, both the door and his body were caught by Ferrol who quickly reinstated Patrick to his previous position. Uprighted, Patrick squinted at the two faces drenched with rain. One smaller, the other bigger. Cian Shea and Ferrol in borrowed oil slickers. The world behind them petulant and storm black.

'There were a wreck,' said Cian, his head tilted in a manner of shielding, and his voice struggling to outdo the wind. 'Down off da cove.' He pointed toward the void that pressed behind him and stretched for an eternity to the point of relentless indistinction.

'T'were a Portugee vessel,' said Ferrol, raising his eyebrows in glee. 'Get on yer slicker, Paddy. Facking ha.' He clapped his wet hands together and squeezed until his muscles bulged through the slicker sleeves. 'Dere's port aboard.'

> The sea was a blackened throb
> made dark and malevolent
> by nature's ire.
> If not for the whitecaps,
> those sizzling crests of black
> beaten white by the punishing wind,
> that signalled division between sky and water,
> the entire scene would have amounted to
> nothing more than a swelling,
> mutely glistening void of ebony
> in which all was held
> with lamentable indifference.

Within that black gale, three men managed their descent over the cliff by holding a thick length of rope and giving careful attention to their footing on the sheening lips and crevices of each craggy rock. It was not a night for missteps as everything was sopping and slippery as though sealed in a viscous coating of primordial slime.

Patrick was first down on the shore, his hollow boots crunching into the beach rocks as his sticks dug in for steadiness, his socks wetly thick against the nubs of his legs, the phantom itch worsening by the moment. He glanced up at the two others, Cian and Ferrol, the former gradually descending the incline like a nanny goat, Cian's boots slipping and scrambling, certain to fall on Ferrol at any moment, who trod down the cliff facing as though across a field. It was a precarious situation unto itself.

Patrick turned to face the far-off thunder of waves striking cliffs. In the cup of the cove, there was greater protection from the wind, the waves not so treacherous where Patrick approached the punts, overturned on the beach, not caring which he might take a lend of for the excursion. Beyond the punts, the sea was a-swell, rising and tossing as though in fitful battle with itself.

> Battered by all forms of nature's distress,
> lashed by sheets of rain
> and muscle-shoved by the wind

Patrick flung down one stick and went about uprighting a punt. Crouched as he was, he was quickly blown over.

'Nar lazing about,' said Ferrol, yanking Patrick to his stubs. 'Dere's port ta be salvaged.' He stared out as the sea rose before them, seemingly higher than the earth itself yet remaining strangely in place.

'Fack,' said Ferrol, laughing in fellowship with the storm.

Patrick, squinting water from his brow and dragging the boat toward the water's edge, was soon aided by Cian and Ferrol. In the gale, she was barely launchable, for the swell of the sea hurled the punt back at every attempt, and near smothered the three men with five-foot-high surge.

In ignorance of the sea's true power, and the tumultuous bashing of the boat against all parts of their bodies, chests, legs, arms, groins, the three men battled on, finally managing to get the craft fully afloat, the punt smoothly, unevenly rising high above them while they hung on with their bent fingers, until, again, the punt was flung back onto shore, the wooden weight of her nearly snapping Patrick's right leg at the knee, as he had been sucked beneath her in his efforts. The panging was nothing new to him yet was none the more agreeable due to its familiarity.

'Get aboard 'er,' Ferrol shouted above the fizzling noise. 'Up. Jaysus, yer as lazy as a cut mongrel.' Again, Ferrol pulled Patrick to his feet and left him supported by Cian while Ferrol turned and made a roar at the punt, leaning into her with both arms and shoving her – against the thrust of the sea – back into the rising waves.

'Now,' shouted Ferrol, waving his arm to the others. Patrick hobbled ahead with an arm over Cian's shoulder, and Ferrol, seemingly having had enough of Patrick's lameness, snatched up his friend and tossed him into the rocking punt.

With the strict attention of the two lads now at work, they fully relaunched her, Ferrol and Cian wrestling with her, holding at either side while Patrick took up the oars and moved them around to no avail. One oar came up out of the water as she took a swell port side, Ferrol going fully underwater, laughing and shaking his bald head when the water dropped. Young Cian shouted something, but no words worked in the ramming crossfire of such weather's ferocity. He pointed back toward the cliff they had descended, perhaps wanting to return or warning them of the approach of others who might have in their minds a similar adventure, for there were glistening shadows spilling over the cliff and creeping toward them.

Patrick searched that way, collecting images out of the blackness, yet everything was vague and shadowed and smeared, only the solidness of earth offering any hint of reassurance, all matter around it agleam with inky turbulence. There might have been movement, yet whatever it was could likely be creature or human, deformed shapes shifting in the wicked dimness to rob them of their very souls, or nothing at all, a mere trick of the eye-warping landscape. Patrick blinked the sting of the salt water away and rubbed at his eyes.

He then yelled, yet the words were even unknown to him and barely discernible in his own ears. His cry might have been a demand aimed toward the other two, to get aboard the craft which was pulling loose from their grips, rising higher on one side and then on the other, Ferrol's greater weight about to capsize the craft which, again, was surging toward shore. The men floated and clung to the edge, at once in shallower water and then in deeper, their boots over underwater rock while their bodies strained to keep her from being heaved ashore.

Cian and Ferrol leaned ahead to gain control, stopping the punt's advance toward land, shoving her out until they were waist-high in water, then almost chest-high, waist-high, head-high, and spitting and wiping and blinking the sting of salt away. They clung until the sea came fully alive beneath her, then, in unison, the two pulled themselves free from the suck of the sea, up over the edge of the punt, the weight of each man distributed to either side, perhaps preventing the capsizing of the craft, yet allowing sloshes of water to pool in the hull.

Patrick rowed with vigour, pointlessly thrusting against the tide that demanded his return to land. His face strained with the effort while he was pelted with rain which he tucked his head against. Despite his constant labouring, the craft was heading nowhere except where the sea inclined.

He slaved to row in the direction Ferrol pointed. The scratchy waver of Ferrol's rough voice calling out, until he took hold of the oars and relieved Patrick of his station. At that point, with oars in hand and hunched in effort, a change came over Ferrol. Propelling the oars into the black water, his face strained to the point of wicked trans-formation, the tendons in his neck becoming pronounced, his teeth bared in fits of exertion, his eyes settling deeper into his skull, his muscles expanding beneath his open slicker and soaken shirt so that they tested the fabric. Rowing and growling, Ferrol laughed with the resonance of the deepening wind itself.

Cian – clamped about the bowels by a generous degree of fright – was seated beside Ferrol, wondering of his place in the venture. With his bare hands clasped tightly to the board beneath him, riding the vessel, he watched in one direction or the other as the sea swelled around the dory, the massiveness of it rising in disconnected peaked and rounded divisions, blackly bent and throbbing as though to its own intention, each patch churning out of rhythm with the other so that the sea would both rise and sink on all sides at once.

Words were called out to one another yet no one could make clarity of the utterances. There was only the flat pitch of a voice and Ferrol's rumbling laughter that broke like a nature sound in the sky.

Ferrol laboured harder, rowing, grinning enthusiastically, as though he were born for that likely sort of voyage, while Cian wore a worried expression and continued clutching the board, swiping the stinging spray of salt from his face, and checking back toward what might have once been land yet was now nothing actual. Blue lipped, he tucked his hands under his arms for warmth, but quickly put them back to the boards as he was violently tilted portside.

Patrick Hawco had learned from Ferrol that the Portugee ship had struck rock in the shallow of Critch Gut, yet when the punt was out so far, bobbing and thrusting from one end to the other, land became governed by illusion and direction was entirely vanquished.

Insofar as there was only one fitting action in the craft, Patrick and Cian keenly, hopefully watched Ferrol rowing, heaving his need into the effort while his swamped face grinned in the light of the whitecaps. Ferrol turned his head toward what might have been east and shouted in that direction. Nothing heard, as though the power of Patrick's ears had been stolen away. When Patrick searched that way, he saw the glisten in the air. No doubt wood of a ship's hull. The dark lines of slats that appeared vertical yet might have been at various horizontal angles depending upon their own position.

A roar in the sky that must have been Ferrol's cheer.

As they neared, the swell of the waves rose to the rim of the punt and a body thudded the side, an arm reaching into the punt and then swallowed back by the plummet of the swell.

It seemed that Ferrol might not have seen the body for he was laughing with greater wildness and bending forward, reaching with his arm as though to clasp hands with something living. Patrick was made to lurch forward to grab for the oar that Ferrol had released, to prevent it from being forever lost in the water. Holding fast to the oar, his eyes were trained toward Ferrol's reach, seeing the curve of wood strapped together by rings of iron. A barrel rammed the side of the boat with astonishing force, then drifted back, plucking away any merciful thoughts of its contents, forcing Ferrol to lurch for it in a peculiar flailing of limbs that resembled a jig. Leaning, his grip missed its target and his body straightened in agitation. At once, he stood, his feet set as anchors against the punt while the others cast wary looks up at him, fearing that his movements in the jerky craft would lead to their peril.

Ferrol stared toward a target, the grin widening on his face while he raised his arms straight above his head and dove in.

Cian, shouting a noise that was nothing, made a spasmodic grab for Ferrol, almost losing himself, as well, to the sea.

At once, Patrick snatched hold of the other oar, drew both into the punt and laid them to rest. It was now necessary to extend his arms to each side of the boat and hold tightly to ensure not being flung from her.

On the open sea, the lash of the rain was incredible and the salt water spray near blinded his eyes so that he could barely perceive anything through the blur. He leaned toward the side and scanned the water to discern that Ferrol was nowhere in sight. The watery swell strained his eyes with the hypnotic illusion that such motion was impossible, his brain confounding him with the sight of the liquid disorderliness rising and setting at once to various heights and depths. Frantically, he glanced around as a barrel – hurled out of the nearby blackness – struck the side of the punt, crushing his fingers where they were securely gripped to the edge. Cringing with misery, he withdrew his hand and was tossed to the other side, banging his legs against the hull. In that position, blinking away the rain, he searched over the starboard side. No sign of Ferrol as another barrel smacked against the lip of the punt with such force that there was a shuddering and splintering of wood.

At once, Patrick caught the whiff of port. The barrel had sprouted a leak and was gushing into the boat, faster than the rain. Behind him, another barrel pounded the bow. On his back and twisting around, he caught the desperate look on Cian's face. In the company of this younger man's fear, any remnants of Patrick's bravado were cauterized to expose rawer sentiment. With Ferrol gone, this was not so much an adventure now as what appeared to be a jaunt into intended jeopardy.

Another barrel rose alongside them, hoisted by a swell that shrank and dropped the vat into the boat where it shattered the bones in Patrick's legs. The pitch of his scream was deadened by all manner of nature as he desperately shoved to remove the barrel that, perhaps for his own good, kept him pinned within the punt. He saw the rain-drenched Cian stand to help or search around for a means of escape, and shouted out a protest, his hands going up, all to no avail, for in that single ill-chosen moment Cian, with limbs fluttering like the wings of a tormented bird, was dumped overboard.

Frantically searching over one side then the other, for the craft was now being tilted in every direction, Patrick learned that he was surrounded by barrels, their slick wooden staves rising above him and falling and swirling in the discord of the sea.

Another barrel struck the bow, its end flipping over, knocking him from his slat, before it was carried away, back out into the sea. His legs pinned, he fell sideways into the punt. Salt water sloshed into his mouth. It stung twice as badly, as now it was cut with port. He thought that his lips might be split. As much as he desired to, he tried not to swallow. The barrel that had trapped his legs was spilling from its side. He reached ahead with one hand and felt the flow of port, somehow cooler than the rain. He cried out for help, whimpering the names of his loved ones. Then he merely cried.

Trapped sobbing, his head tilted back to stare at the black sky which was wet and malignant, he heard an answer to his cry; a seagull or some creature in flight screeched from the blackness, the sound rising, swooping, nearing, until Patrick decided that it was not a gull at all but the rhythmic recurrence of a triumphant laugh, as though Ferrol had boarded the shipwrecked vessel and stood upon its deck in glorious claim. His calls of 'Faaaack, faaack, faaack' soon ran together and became sharper, cut with the screech of a gull and a crow, and faded, faded, faded . . . until the sea brought forth a wave that slammed into the punt and flipped her upside-down.

After unknown moments of deafness and unaccountable deadness, and with a gasp frozen by the sea, Patrick discovered himself once again in possession of his senses. He had resurfaced to find that his hands were holding on to a barrel, that bodies, dead and slumped, were clung to similar barrels, that the barrel continued leaking and was pouring onto his numb face. Shivering with fear and in the watery grips of frigidity, he was pained by the suspicion that the sweet and sticky fragrance of port might be blood. He opened his mouth as he was floated above other barrels and lifeless bodies, then dropped into a hollow, as though in a complex pattern of living maze, winding his way through a labyrinth that drew him here and there and rose and fell beneath his torso and smacked him with the disunity of hundreds of barrels set loose and afloat around him, being hurled and tossed like balls, above him and then below him, the world of water unformable, undefinable, unliveable.

Laughing and crying, he drank as best he could from the gushing port before a bone-smashing blow was delivered to the back of his skull. A barrel punched his neck and then another hammered his face, crushing his cheekbone. He was slugged in the chest. He was battered in the shoulderblade. Bashed once again along the hairline split in his skull.

On his back, floating in silence's embrace, his opened head and mouth filling with salt water and port, Patrick Lambly's eyes were ignorant to the unfathomable count of barrels drawn toward the violent eddy that sucked him under and buried him in the tumbling and rolling swirl of precious cargo.

> The drenching night drags on, Siobin,
> harrowing my head.
> No stock, no wealth
> This storm on waves nearby
> Where towering crests collide
> in recollection.
>
> A daughter, Claire, a son, Angus,
> Cold and dead to me these years
> Though burn they do as embers now
> upon my sea drunk lips that will not
> die in this drenching night.
>
> Three faces in my shattered mind
> My love, my life, my penitence.
> How fitting that the mongrel,
> baying in the swim for distant shores,
> succumbs to the echo of its own pursuit.

Book Two

1971–2007

Chapter I – 1971

Helter Skelter

(April, 1971, 17 years old)

Charles Manson is being led from the courtroom. His eyes look like they could scare the fur off a cat. He has just been sentenced to death. Charles Manson and his family. The family lived together in a hippie commune, away from the rest of the world. The family came into the city to slaughter a pregnant woman, a movie star with long blonde hair and a pretty, movie-star face. The family used the woman's blood to write 'PIGGIE' on the bedroom wall in a home in the United States. The movie star's husband is a movie director. The way the reporter is talking makes it sound like the movie director is strange. It was no surprise the movie director's wife was killed and butchered. Only a matter of time. Part of a weird movie that the director might, one day, direct himself. His own doing. It was bound to happen, even though it was – without doubt – a terrible, terrible, *terrible* tragedy. A shock to the community at large. What the family has done is the fault of a song by the Beatles called 'Helter Skelter.'

On the television, a woman with a shaved head shouts into the camera: 'It's gonna come down hard. Lock your doors. Protect your kids.'

Blackstrap Hawco is seated on the living room couch. His father, Jacob, watches the news. He looks over at Blackstrap. 'You got any of dem Beatles 8-tracks in yer car?'

Blackstrap merely shakes his head, then wonders if music can do that to people, make them kill each other, make them cut off all their hair, make them look like they could eat you if the moon hung just right in the sky.

Blackstrap's mother, Emily, stands at the entrance to the living room with a dish in one hand. She has been drying it with a towel, drying it over and over with a swirling movement. But now she stops. She watches the TV screen.

No one says another word.

The television is a new 25-inch Electrohome console with mahogany wood. The four legs that press into the carpet look almost pointed. Jacob has bought the television with money earned from the seal hunt.

Three faces continue watching the screen in shocked disbelief. Then Blackstrap looks away, toward the window for a view of the outdoors, his eyes wanting to shift back to the flickering images. He stands and goes to the window.

Outside, there is not a hint of a breeze. It is snowing ever so lightly, big flakes covering the roofs of the old and new houses. Big snow, no snow, as the saying goes. A rare spring snowfall. Smoke thickly rises from the chimneys. The snow settles in the boughs of the evergreens stretching for miles to the east, west, north and south of Cutland Junction.

(December)

The seven people beyond the window are wearing cloth masks and several layers of clothes, one piece over another, to disguise themselves. They hoot and holler and make screeching noises as they approach the house. Blackstrap has not been expecting them, but they often arrive without warning.

The crowd makes greater noise as they near the back door and hurl it open, the cold winter air briskly following them into the porch.

A knock sounds on the inner kitchen door. One of them calls out: 'Any mummers 'llowed in?'

Blackstrap, who is stood in the kitchen doorway, smiles to himself.

With a wink to Emily, Jacob rises from his chair and opens the door. The mummers are pulling off their boots and leaving them in a pile. With exaggerated gestures, they hurry in, fiddles and accordions in hand, and begin dancing around, playing a brisk rendition of 'Mussels in the Corner.' De-de-de-de-de-de-de . . . de-de-de-de-de-de-de . . . de-de-de-de-de-de . . . 'Mussels in the corner.' They disguise their voices, talking in deep or high pitches as the music reels out and the mummers perform foolish steps of dance around the kitchen, clapping their hands, bending their knees and scuffing their heels. Dancing in circles, arm in arm, the mummers appear puffed up because of all the clothing. Two of them pull Emily from her chair at the table, where she has been sitting quietly in thought, and hurl her around in dance.

Emily tries her best to smile, but her heart seems not to be in it. The disguised person doing the jig has a pillowcase over its face with eyeholes roughly snipped out. A green woollen hat is pulled over the top of the pillowcase. The person is wearing three layers of clothing. A sweater over a woman's dress. And mittens on its feet that make stepping without slipping a tricky chore. This becomes part of the dance, another slapstick addition to the merriment.

The final notes of 'Mussels in the Corner' drop away and another tune starts up, one Blackstrap can't pin a name on, although he's heard it a hundred times if he's heard it once. Back when his father used to play the fiddle. He wonders who the people might be, going through a few names from the community. If he saw the car they came in, he'd know right away.

Out in the living room, the hi-fi radio continues playing. Blackstrap leans back a little to catch scraps of lyrics and bits of the tune from 'Brown Sugar' by the Rolling Stones. Before the mummers' arrival, Blackstrap had been in the living room – the room that has recently been built onto the side of the one-storey square house to make room for the television – listening to 'Stay Awhile' by the Bells, the sweet whispering voice of the female singer always does fine things to his head. If he can only find a woman who sounds like that. The voice makes him feel sleepy. Makes him want to touch a woman in a dark room.

His mind on Agnes Bishop. Her gentle voice. The long smoothness of her dark blonde hair. No one but her for as long as he's known. Since the time they moved to Cutland Junction and he went to school for those first few days, before he dropped out to stay at home and look after little Ruth, who had been born all twisted up and blind. His mother still sick from Junior's death. Never the same, and needing help with Ruth. His mother with no energy then. Eight years ago. And little difference now. The way Ruth was born having to do with the new place, Jacob and Blackstrap suspected. Cutland Junction. Being forced to move from their home. And then little Ruth's death. That had made his mother even sicker. Cutland Junction had.

One day, Blackstrap plans to move back to Bareneed, onto land they still own down there by the ocean. He's already checked at the records of the town hall. It's only to save for the building materials. He had planned to move there with Agnes. That was the way it was meant to go, an unspoken understanding between them, or so Blackstrap had thought. But Agnes has other ideas now.

He remembers kissing her out in the coldness on his eighteenth birthday last week, after she'd given him the new trouting pole and reel, all wrapped up in birthday paper and her joking about him never figuring out what it was. Not in a million years. That's all he's ever had of her, that kiss. It was a kiss with all of her body and heart in it. A kiss that was slow at first, then faster, in need of something more, some sort of telling, then slower, creating a feeling that made plain the fact that he never wanted to look at any other face except hers. Her hands on his cheeks. Her eyes on him.

It was after that kiss that she told him – in a voice that could've cut him in half with its sad sweetness – that she was going away to university.

The sight of the telephone hung on the kitchen wall reminds him that he is supposed to call her. He has a Christmas gift for her, a ring that was meant for baby Ruth, that had been sent by one of his mother's relatives, an aunt named Annie in England, when Ruth was born. To be saved. Blackstrap had wanted Agnes to have it. Now that she is going away he can't bear to see her. Her family moving to the mainland at the end of January. Her father already working up in Fort McMurray, Alberta, wanting the whole family to join him. Mr. Bishop had enough of being away without them, only coming back for special occasions, like he was back now for Christmas. That was what Agnes had said. Her last Christmas in Cutland Junction. Their house up for sale. A sign with a 'Sold' sticker on it, the house already bought by Isaac Tuttle.

Blackstrap watches the mummers dance. His thoughts on Agnes, what she might be doing. Plenty of relatives at her house exchanging presents. No presents exchanged here. His mother's relatives all in England. She doesn't have much to do with them, only the occasional letter arrives from that aunt. Emily's mother and father both dead. On his father's side, Uncle Ace has been missing for seventeen years, dead,

474

everyone assumed, since Blackstrap was a baby. And Jacob's mother, Catherine, had passed away before Blackstrap was born. He'd never known either of them. No presents from them. No big family around like most of the other people had in Cutland Junction.

Agnes in her house. The house soon to be empty. Blackstrap turns his thoughts away from her and thinks of people barging into his house. The way it has been for years. Mummers. Friends and neighbours walking in the back door for a bit of entertainment. He thinks of the Manson family in the news all the time. Everyone wants to know all about those crazy murderers. The woman who has been killed. A baby. Words written on the walls with blood. The noise before his eyes. The shaved heads. He stares at the movement. How far off are people from killing? How dangerous are they? The thought fascinates him. It is almost exciting, the absolute wildness of it, but he doesn't let it dig in any deeper than that. He concentrates on what's right before him, right before his eyes. Not a bit of harm possible here. Not with these good people.

Jacob is clapping his hands, winking and smiling at the crew of seven that spin around the kitchen and try to make light of everything. When one of the mummers – a man by the size of him wearing a woman's brassiere out over his green zip-up coveralls – approaches Blackstrap and takes him by the arm, Blackstrap follows along and gives a few steps before inclining away and drifting back to where he was leaning in the doorway. A new smile on his lips. A good one. The mummer keeps dancing a jig, bouncing his elbows and clapping his hands, kicking up his feet, while the others call out encouragement.

Rum or cherry syrup are poured for everyone, and plates of dark and light Christmas fruit cake are laid out by Emily. Despite the fact that she mourns what is missing from Christmas, she always takes the time to prepare the cakes, to do her baking, what is expected of her, as she was taught to do by Jacob's mother, Catherine, all those years ago, to do what is expected of her, before she returns to her bedroom and the darkness.

Jacob goes about trying to identify the mummers, calling out names that are denied right away with quick shakes of the head. He laughs and points. Glass in hand, he drinks back more rum. His cheeks and ears glowing pink. Three days' growth of beard on his face and his eyebrows all over the place.

There is not a worry in the kitchen. Not a speck of it, despite the fact that the fishery has failed that summer and the anti-seal-hunt movement has got its way, the know-nothing mainlanders managing to turn the seal hunt into the slaughter of big-eyed babies. They are a smart crew, though, for playing on people's emotions and hauling in the dollars. As good a job as any, Blackstrap supposes. They're on the television and radio all the time looking saintly, trying to sound like if only the baby seals could be saved from the 'barbarian Newfoundlanders' then the world would be a more decent place. At first, it was just a bunch of snotty mainlanders making all the ruckus, but now scientists are on the television and radio too, saying that the seal population has dropped by almost half over the last twenty years, and the only way to save the herd from extinction is to stop now.

Stop the slaughter, they say. Stop the slaughter now.

Quotas have been set for the coming sealing season.

By the looks of it, Blackstrap might be making his last trip to the ice this spring. He's gone for the past two years, since he was sixteen, working right beside his father. The red fanning out on white. It will only be one of them going this year. Probably Blackstrap, leaving his father behind, back on land to putter around.

Blackstrap can't help but think: That's only the tip of the iceberg in the bad news department. It's hard times right across the island. Paper mills shut down on the west coast. All of it being reported on the St. John's TV news. The American army base in Argentia laying off seven hundred employees. And, worst of all, Newfoundland's on the brink of bankruptcy, close to one billion dollars in debt.

It said on the TV news that just last year some newspaper in Toronto wrote that Newfoundland should be put under Federal Trusteeship because Premier Joey Smallwood, the last living Father of Confederation, the man who hauled Newfoundland – bawling and kicking – into Canada in 1949, is making a shambles of the economy.

He wonders why this is all happening, who is at fault. He feels like Newfoundland is doomed. He feels like someone is trying to kill the whole island, strangle it to death. Why is it in such hard shape? With all the fish and all the forests and all the mines.

Jacob doesn't seem to have a worry in the world. Everything runs off

476

him like water off a duck's back, since Smallwood was defeated in the recent election. It was only by a narrow margin and Smallwood has since refused to step down, but Jacob still takes comfort in the fact that Smallwood lost, even if the premier won't hand over power. Arrogant bastard, Jacob calls him. Nazi.

Dance, thinks Blackstrap. Kick up your heels. He takes a swig of his beer, then tips it all the way back, draining the bottle. Discouraged by the easy laughter, he scoffs quietly and lays the bottle on the sideboard, leaves the room.

Outside, Blackstrap's 1970 Ford Galaxie 500 is parked alongside his father's pickup truck. He can hear the muffled sounds of the fiddle, shouts and clapping, from behind the walls, as he makes his way down the driveway. The night air still and sharp. Another vehicle is parked on the side of the dirt road. The big white Chrysler – Andrew Fowler's by the looks of it – that all of the mummers came in. Parked halfway across the road. No doubt the lot of them are three sheets to the wind.

Blackstrap climbs aboard his Galaxie 500 and pulls shut the heavy door. The new car smell still lingering. He looks across the seat to where Agnes usually sits before sliding over to lean close to him, to kiss him on the cheek. He bought the car last year, before all the bad news found its way to them, out of money earned from crab fishing with Roger Barnes.

He had liked the Galaxie's black colour and the sleek look of it under the lights in the showroom. But most of all, he admired the way the salesman had described the car, running through its features like the car would be a friend to Blackstrap: 'A V8 engine with three-speed column shifted automatic transmission. Power steering. Three-hundred-and-ninety-cubic-inch big block.' All of that was impressive, but what had set Blackstrap's mind on buying the car was the crowning touch that the salesman had used by describing the car as having 'an aggressive stance.' The salesman had said: 'You won't be let down by this baby's aggressive stance.'

Blackstrap sits in the seat, his mind in the brightly lit showroom in St. John's. Soon, he wonders where he might go. Not far. It's Christmas Eve. If it were any other night, he'd take a run into St. John's, go downtown, just to get lost for a while. But not tonight. Christmas Eve, a bunch of bullshit. Any day now, this place gone for him. He'll be forced to head to the mainland because of the sorry state of things. People from around Cutland Junction, Port de Grave and Shearstown Line already up in Ontario and Alberta. Rumour has it that several more young men will be heading off soon, nothing to keep them at home. Ted Bartlett and Ray Foley are already gone, just before Christmas. Jobs waiting for them up along. Jobs in Ontario factories or in the oil business in Fort McMurray. Pockets of Newfoundlanders everywhere in Canada: Galt, Toronto, Calgary . . . And there's no sense sticking around Cutland Junction for Christmas when there's no money for presents.

Blackstrap reaches for the half case on the floor in front of the passenger case. He tears open the flap and pulls out a bottle, the neck between his fingers. He uses the opener on the chain hanging from the radio dial and pops the cap. Taking a drink, he switches on the radio. Christmas songs on most of the AM channels. Then a station playing the Bee Gees' 'How can you Mend a Broken Heart.' He tries the FM rock station. Gordon Lightfoot's voice, pure and smooth and full of hard luck all at once:

> If you could read my mind love,
> what a tale my thoughts could tell.
> Just like an old time movie
> 'bout a ghost from a wishin' well.

The sound of Lightfoot's voice snags on something in Blackstrap and he turns up the volume dial, making full use of the new speakers.

> In a castle dark or a fortress strong
> with chains upon my feet
> you know that ghost is me.
> And I will never be set free
> as long as I'm a ghost that you can't see.

Blackstrap starts the engine. Revs it. There are shadows cast on the snow from the kitchen window at the side of the house. Dancing shadows. He revs the engine some more, feels the power lift in front of him. The solid roar of it beneath his feet. Then he backs out of the driveway, takes the dirt road up, and around the grove of evergreens toward the centre of Cutland Junction. Down into the valley then uphill, waiting to catch sight of the bungalow. At the top of the rise, the new Bishop house, built out of money made from work on the mainland. Built to be sold and move on. He watches Agnes' house while he passes. The Christmas tree in the big window. The cars parked in the paved driveway. He could pull in. Park his car and go in for a visit. Agnes' mother. A nice-looking woman always kind enough when he visits. Like she's happy to see him. He slows down. Thinking that Agnes might look out the window, see him as he passes by, as he rolls by for a final look. He presses his foot into the accelerator.

Beyond Cutland Junction, he follows the highway. Black-green spruce running as shadows on both sides of him. And takes the turnoff for Bareneed. Follows the pock-marked road that leads down from the highway. And ends at the ocean. Glad to have left Cutland Junction behind. The Christmas lights that make him feel lonely. Christmas always makes him feel left out. Isolated. Thoughts of Junior and Ruth. Gone off. Leaving him with just bits and pieces of them.

Most of the old houses down around Bareneed harbour, the ones abandoned after relocation, are black and desolate, unoccupied for almost twenty years. But he notices there are a few with lights on. Some people having moved back to their homes and living on welfare. The houses circle the arc of the harbour. Dark shells staring toward the ocean with blinded eyes.

Bareneed cove is a bay of black water beneath a massive headland ten times blacker than the sky. A few boats are tied up around the community wharf that has fallen into a state of disrepair. Blackstrap shuts off the car's engine and climbs out. Only the sounds of his breath and bootsteps over the hard ground. Then a few sounds coming from across the bay, skimming the water. The toot of a car horn. A loud bang that might be anything. He heads for the wharf, minds his step, and casts off the lines before stepping down aboard his father's boat, *Bareneed's Pride*. The sense of the movable sea beneath his boots puts him at ease. He steps into the small wheelhouse and starts the engine, sails around the headland towering above him at his right, then out to sea.

It is not until he feels the boat moving faster than he intended that he realizes how angry he has become. At first, it was a pleasure to be free of land, but then came memories of how Agnes used to ask to go for a ride in the boat. Just two of them out on the water at night. Her behind him while he was at the wheel. Her hugging him. Nothing behind him now. No one holding on. His mind filled up with the idea of Agnes leaving. Making him and the boat heavier.

Having cleared the headland, Blackstrap sees the widening of the bigger inlet to his left, and, far across it, tiny lights shine from the houses of Port de Grave. To his right and back a bit, the dilapidated houses remain perched along the Bareneed cliff. He can barely make them out, only a few lights burning. His family's house moved from there just after his tenth birthday. The top storey torn off. His bedroom – that used to belong to Junior – and his parents' bedroom, all rebuilt on the lower floor. Torn off because the house was too big and would be easier to move. Uncle Ace's house still there somewhere though. It's hard to locate in the dark, but he has an idea, catching sight of what he believes to be the roof edge. Blackstrap's been inside that house. Years ago, he thought of saving it, rebuilding it, back to the way it was, but the rot has made that impossible now. The sills gone, the structure leaning on one side. He'd be better off tearing it down and building a new house on the land. A one-storey bungalow with a concrete basement.

The vague shadows of the abandoned houses deepen Blackstrap's rage. Out at sea, with the houses fading into utter blackness, he feels himself drawn into that shadow as it seeps through him. He is on the water, in a boat, and he is stogged full of fury. He steers away from Bareneed, keeping the land over his shoulder, not looking back, while he aims toward Port de Grave where he might tie up and have a listen to the men and oldtimers gathered on the wharf.

Port de Grave.

Bareneed.

It is Bareneed he has come for.

Not Port de Grave. No more news of closures passed around. No more words from mouths that won't do a thing about it. Men with no guts or balls to go out there and do something. Fight someone. Fight who? he wonders. Someone. Anyone. His anger gets the best of him, and what he has been ignoring over his shoulder, the dark remains, draws him back. He swings the boat around, turning the craft in a wide arc toward Bareneed's ragged cliffs that rise up eighty feet. White foam from the surge of the ocean in the distance despite the absence of the moon.

What comes into Blackstrap's head is an image of his brother, Junior, under the water to the east, bits of him still buried in the caved-in iron-ore mine, then an image of his little sister, Ruth, dead from a disease that came from his mother's pills. Not from Cutland Junction like they suspected. Pills. Ruth's misshapen face, her laugh, her crooked, blackened teeth. Too soft. Her teeth too soft, the doctor said. Her bones too soft. He remembers. Her blind eyes that knew him when he was near. Both his brother and his sister dead. And his mother living like a ghost, stuck in this life without the faintest hint of joy or pleasure.

And his father laughing it all off.

When his father dies, Blackstrap will be the last one of them. The last Hawco. The last one. He increases the throttle, feeling the engine thrusting beneath his boots, and aims straight for Bareneed, for the rocks and the cliffs and the white foam that grows whiter.

Agnes.

The last one.

He flashes on a memory of the crack in the headland that they used to crawl into as boys, just big enough for him to fit through. No turning back. And slightly to the east of the crack, the cave that you could run a small boat through. And above it all, the pasture where the goats, cow, horse and sheep grazed, all of it under darkness now, beneath a black sky capable of suffocating any man's spirit.

Speed increasing. The black wall of cliff no more than a hundred meters ahead. Jagged rock coming to him.

The rock.

Fantasizing about a shipwreck, like he used to as a boy, the splinters of boat wood, the thick mast and the sail cloth in the water. Fantasizing about surviving. So he can save the other people who are near death. Like his great-grandfather, Patrick Hawco, after coming all the way from Ireland, perishing in the sea on a stormy night in an attempt to rescue crew members from a wrecked Portuguese vessel. Where were those men now? The ones he had saved? Who would rescue him from this?

Who?

Where are the men who have been saved? And what are they thinking?

Sixty meters from blackness. The bow of the boat cutting the water. Blackstrap broods on his mother. His mother and her sadness. Always in her room, in the darkness. She might as well be in one of those black houses in Bareneed. He will die with what has been taken from her. He will go down with it. Without hope. But he cannot make her worse. He will not allow it. The pain he would cause her. He glances down and sees a small hand on the throttle, a girl's twisted hand. His skin prickles as the hand slides the throttle back a touch. He turns to look. No one.

The engine slows. Fifty-five meters away, but still steady toward collision. Uncertain of the force of the impact. Never having felt such a thing. Even just to know this destruction. The girl's hand no longer there. Rock reaches out to both sides of him, carved by the persistent sea. No way of turning with rock to either side of him.

His hand, frozen, greenish-white, snow-covered.

Fifty meters. Forty-five. What will become of the tale without him to do the telling? It will be told by others. And they will change it as they see fit. He considers leaping overboard. Forty meters. His body rigid with indecision. If he jumps, he will last only a few minutes before hypothermia sets in and the ocean kills him.

More and more of the sky now blocked out by the pure blackness of the cliff rock. Deadening sound. A shadow solidifying.

Thirty-five meters.

Near total blackness. White foam darkening.

Agnes.

Thirty meters.

Rock.

Twenty-five.

The last one.

He glances at his hand. The veins in it rising, the sheen of sweat on his skin. His fingers. He lifts his hand and turns over the palm. Then he looks in front of him.

His legs frozen stiff. A whiteness and a roar.

End of story.

Beginning of story.

'You're not very smart,' says the little girl, looking up at him. She has an accent. Not like a Newfoundlander. She sounds British. Proper enough to confuse him.

'Why's that?' he barely asks, hanging there, uncertain, but brightly awake in the night air. The tiny lights from miniature houses glisten far across the water.

'You think you're a Christmas bulb. But you're not, *are* you?'

Blackstrap laughs the freest laughter ever known to him. Easiness that evacuates his head, and puts nothing in there but clarity and fresh air. But, soon, the coldness makes itself known. In his hands, then on his face, and his body begins to tremble while he watches his little sister. Ruth with her eyes that stare at him. Seeing. Eyes so blue watching his face. And he is ashamed.

She looks nothing like his little sister, but he knows it is her. She holds a candy cane with one of her woolly mittens. The candy cane stuck to the fuzz of the wool. It is white with red stripes that smear when she licks or sucks. She's wearing winter clothing. Ear muffs. Boots with white fur around the tops. The rubber soles on a rock, and she's trying to not fall over. Her left foot, the most unsteady. She wobbles a bit. The rock sloppy beneath her. It clicks against another, and her arms shoot out to catch her balance. She checks down at her feet, like nothing is the matter. Just to look. To see. Then bites off a bit of candy cane, crunches it with her dark teeth, looks up at Blackstrap.

'You don't even shine,' she says. And she is going to smile, and he will see her teeth. The black rotted teeth. They will be uncovered once her lips part. But there is white. A hint of white. A glisten . . .

As his trembling increases, Blackstrap feels that his arms are uselessly heavy at his sides. His eyes come back to him. He falls together with the weight of his own body and sees the tiny lights far across the black water in a new way. They are real houses. Not miniatures after all.

Across the inlet. Port de Grave. There as it was meant to be. A fishing community.

It is a mess. That's what he is in. His feet hanging beneath him. His boots not touching ground. He moves his legs around in air. His arms reach back to find the needles of a spruce tree, then reach up to check the branch that the back of his woollen sweater is snagged on. The sweater that Agnes knitted for him last Christmas. The first one she ever made, helped by her mother. A bit too big for him, but he always wore it with pride.

There is something else holding him up. Something in his chest that is keeping him suspended. He slides his fingers over the front of his sweater and feels the sharp edge sticking out. Near where his heart should be. A tree limb like the sharp end of a broken bone. He wonders if it is a stick or a rib.

Either one means fear. Without feeling.

It is then that he knows he is dead. Slow, careful fingers on his eyelids, shutting them.

And wakes on the shore, his hands in the freezing-cold water and his numb cheek on a rock. He tries to sniff but it is only a mess of flesh that makes a sticky clotted noise. He struggles to take a deep breath but something is blocking it. A wall that surges up until he coughs out water. He is sinking, has been sinking, twenty or thirty feet down, and is now rising, being pulled toward the surface, pulled and sucked upward by a pressure to all sides of him, pressing in on him, holding him and expelling him at once, wanting and not wanting him.

He breaks the surface and his face is freezing, frozen. Sealed within a chunk of ice.

He is dead.

Up in the tree, stuck.

Christ.

Christ.

Christ.

How seriously is he injured? He bucks ahead and waves his arms, kicks his legs, pulls himself clear of the branches and falls. Landing on his boots, he crouches at once to gain balance while he slides toward the steep incline of cliff, almost tips over. Forty feet beneath where he has been thrown, the wreckage of his father's boat, his eyes hurting to watch the drop. The white fizzle. He grabs on to a rock, tears two fingernails away from their skin. Clinging on, his other hand goes to his chest, touches there. The sides of his boots dug in. He checks his fingers for blood. No sign of anything in the darkness. He sniffs his fingers. Tries to see what might be on his dark hands. Only darkness. But is there wetness?

Far down below, no one to pull gasping from the frigid sea.

And above, the little girl climbing the bank. Her back to him. One elbow bent. A hand raised to her mouth. Chewing. Crunching. Up and over. Gone away from what she thought, but has failed to happen.

Walking up the side of the house, he glances in the kitchen window, straight through the hallway, past the doors to the two bedrooms and the bathroom, to the living room. He sees his father asleep in a chair, facing toward the TV screen.

At the rear of the house, Blackstrap grabs for the back doorknob and twists it to find it dead stiff. Stuck. Jammed. The knob must be broken. He tries harder and feels that it must have been locked, by accident. His eyes on his hand just to be certain.

He waits, wondering what to do. There is no way of getting the icy tremble out of his bones. The knees of his jeans are stained with dirt from his climb up the hill. His hands and fingernails ache with cold. His mind unsteady from the shock of collision and the sight of his dead sister. Have his parents locked him out, already knowing about the smashed boat? He hears a lamb sounding in the distance, from Bishop's barn to the north. The sound travelling in the crisp air. Then the moo of a cow. A small dog barking, wanting to be let in. A car door shutting. An engine starting.

He pulls on the knob, rattles it. Maybe he should knock. Knock on his own door. He's never done that before. A first for him. He raises his fist and knocks. His body trembles and he thinks his lips might be blue, his eyes no longer his.

A few moments later, he hears someone on the other side of the door. The click of the lock coming undone. The door opens and Jacob stands there with a confused look on his face.

'Yer mudder must've locked it,' Jacob says, turning away with a disappointed shake of his head.

Blackstrap makes no comment. The less he says about his mother, the less he admits to. He enters the kitchen while his father quietly returns to the living room. Blackstrap stands in the kitchen, alone, walls surrounding him. It feels wrong. His life. The emptiness in his body. He moves nearer the stove to be warm. The deadness in him settles down. And suddenly, he is hungry, starving. He makes himself a sandwich of homemade bread, dropping the mustard bottle on the floor and cleaning up the spill.

'What was dat?' His father from the living room.

'Nuth'n.' His own voice, the sound of it foreign in his ears.

He uses paper towels and the floor still stinks of mustard. He takes the key off the can of corned beef and fits the metal tab into the key slot, turns the key, peeling back the tin.

He eats his sandwich and pours a tall glass of cold milk, chugs it back while looking at the cluttered table. The smell of beer and cigarettes crowding the air. Every now and then, his bones give off a shiver. He gets a whiff of mustard. His back to the heat of the stove.

When he walks past his parents' door in the hallway, he hears his mother shifting in her bed. Up ahead, in the corner of the living room, the coloured tree lights are on, the presents arranged beneath it. His eyes go to the TV screen.

A man is talking about how the United States has invaded a place called Laos. Something about the Ho Chi Minh Trail. There are people being interviewed who are in tears. American soldiers are dying. Coffins. Bombs dropping. Protesters. Hatred shouting for Peace.

Jacob looks up from the television. 'Where ya been keep'n yerself?'

'Jus' around.'

'See anyone?'

Blackstrap shakes his head.

Jacob looks back at the television. 'Yer honey called.'

Blackstrap feels as though his knees might buckle. Agnes. The smashed boat. How to tell his father. He keeps it all at bay. Won't let it get to him. Agnes in his head and then his mother and how she always tries her best to like Christmas. But he knows she doesn't. He knows this in his heart. Admit to nothing. His father watching television, trying to keep his eyes open. He looks at the Christmas tree.

'Who were da mummers after?' Blackstrap asks, licking his lips, his hands still half frozen.

Jacob chuckles, wakens, eyes on the television. 'N'ver figured it out. Crafty buggers.'

Images flickering in the dark room. A ship has been lost in the Bermuda Triangle. A picture of the ship appears on the TV screen. Right away, Jacob stands and turns up the volume, goes back to his chair. The story has a mysterious sound to it. Other strange things have happened down there. The reporter mentions something about UFOs. When the story is over, Jacob says: 'Turn dat down, will ya?'

Blackstrap steps in and turns it down.

'Naw, right down.'

Blackstrap turns the grooved button until the volume is gone, only pulsing light in coloured shades, like the bulbs on the tree.

'Dat put me ta mind o' yer grandfadder Francis.' Jacob faces his son, smiling in the half-proud way he does before telling a tale. 'Speaking o' strange t'ings. I got a call frum some feller at da university in Sin John's. Dis feller claims dat a man by da name o' Francis Hawco, same name as yer grandfadder, lived on da sout' coast of da island fer years, livin' off shipwrecks.'

'Shipwrecks.'

'Yays. Dis university feller come across dis diary whilst he were diggin up dirt somewhere fer da university.'

'When'd you hear dat?' Blackstrap is not certain whether he should believe his father. It might just be a story. Something made up. Something invented. Or having to do with the ship he has just wrecked.

'Christ hallmighty!' Jacob sits up straighter in his seat, presses one hand into the armrest. He shifts his eyes toward the ceiling, trying to think. 'It went right outta me mind, dat call. Ye were out shrimpin' widt Aubrey Boyd, so it were . . . when?'

'That was six months ago.'

'Wha'? Jaysus Cripes! I fergot da gist of it. Wha' was it?'

'Francis Hawco.'

'Yays. Da t'ing is dat dis feller mentioned somet'n queer 'bout dat diary.'

'What?'

'In 't dis Francis Hawco says he got a brudder name 'a Ace. So chances are it's da very same Francis as were me fadder.'

'Did you tell Mudder?' The tremble practically gone out of him now, only in small fits and spurts. His hands almost entirely warm. He tries to hold himself still, hoping his father will not notice.

Jacob squints toward the wall across from him. He frowns and shakes his head. 'Dun't t'ink so. Anyhoot, dis feller got a ship's diary he said I could 'av a peek at. I wrote 'is number down somewhers.' Jacob looks around the room as though he might be able to cast his eyes upon it. 'I dun't believe a speck o' it. Dem university fellers're a'ways mak'n t'ings up. Couldn't be me fadder's diary, 'cause he n'ver learned how ta write 'n 'e perished when he were out on da ice.'

'You should call 'im.'

'Wha' fer?'

'Don't ya want ta know about yer father?'

'Me fadder? 'E froze ta det, perished while swilin'. Dat's wha' Uncle Ace tol' me, 'n dat's da God blessed trute or else Uncle Ace wouldn't breed a word of it. Mus' be anudder Francis Hawco dat university feller is on 'bout. 'N anudder Ace. Dey're a stunned bunch, dem fellers. Dere brains're all muddled up frum being stuffed full 'a too much heducation.'

On his way to bed, passing by his parents' room, Blackstrap hears his mother whispering behind her door. The sound of her voice draws to mind the tone of his sister, as she spoke to him on the cliffs of Bareneed. He slows his step, trying to listen. Suddenly, his mother calls out a name that sounds like 'Alan.' She calls it again, louder. Blackstrap checks back toward the living room. His father sitting there, nodding off, snoring, the silent television flickering across his face.

'Alan,' his mother calls, her voice a panicky whisper. 'Junior.'

The bedroom door is open a crack. Blackstrap pushes it clear a bit further, looks in. His mother is sitting upright in bed. Light from the hallway has swiped across part of her white face and over her long, wavy hair that hangs down around her shoulders. In the corner of Blackstrap's eyes, the uneven throb from the TV screen.

'Alan,' she says. 'Get it.' She raises her hand and points to the corner of the room. Her wrist seems limp and her hand droops there.

'What?' Blackstrap quietly asks, coming fully into the room.

'Get it,' says his mother, pointing to the corner where there is nothing.

'What?'

'Get it, get it. In the freezer.' Her voice seems different, clipped short, like she's half drunk, or half asleep, but alert at the same time. Anxious. Her voice sounds like it knows what it wants. It's sure of everything, even if it makes no sense.

Blackstrap's mind scrambled by what he should do. He slowly goes nearer the corner, stands there.

'In the freezer, put it in the freezer. Get it.'

'Get what?' He reaches back, into thin air, to let her know there is nothing there.

'The numbers.'

'The numbers?'

'Get the numbers,' she says, louder now, growing angry. 'Get them in the freezer.' She lowers her arm, sits there with both arms on the bed covers. She is breathing through her nose. She is watching him, her eyes staring straight at him like she's disappointed.

'I dun know . . .' he says.

She shakes her head a bit, like shaking it all the way would be too much.

'Mom?' he says, trying to wake her. She must be dreaming. Sleep-walking sitting still.

'Awww,' she says, fed up, and lies back down on her side.

Blackstrap waits, but there are no other words.

Soon, his mother is sleeping.

He backs out of the room, trying to be as quiet as possible. Not wanting to wake his mother back to the scene he does not understand. The chill has re-entered his bones. His mind inflicted with new fright.

In the bright bathroom, he spits in the toilet, then pisses and brushes his teeth. The toothbrush snaps in two in his hand, the broken end almost cutting his face as it shoots away, hits the wall then drops to the floor. He picks it up and throws it into the wastebasket. He notices the empty boxes for the bottles of pills his mother buys: 222s with codeine. Three empty boxes. His mother has been taking them for as long as he can recall. She buys them from the new drugstore in Port de Grave. The one with the doctor's office in it. The pills, his mother says, are for her headaches.

Blackstrap lies in the dark. When he thinks of Christmas, he sees Junior and Ruth together, even though it never happened. Junior dead before Ruth's birth. Why all of them around the tree? He tried to look after Ruth the way he knew Junior would. Christmas always brings this back to him. His father done up like Santa Claus. Blackstrap knew the difference, but there was no way of Ruth knowing. Every year for seven years. Done up like Santa Claus. Even on that last year, that seventh one. In the hospital. Jacob in the Santa suit. Ruth's slow blind eyes, barely able to move, but the smile came anyway, slow and full of love when she heard the 'ho-ho-ho.' No Santa suit after Ruth's death. Years later, he found it in a box out in the shed. A nest for a family of mice. Why a Santa suit for a blind girl anyway?

The boat is gone. He should run away tonight before his father finds out. He wonders at the time. It must be close to midnight. Midnight mass last Christmas. They did not attend service this year. And Blackstrap did not mention it. It was always his mother who made certain she got them to church when it was necessary. The weekly Sunday service that he used to attend as a boy was no more. Blackstrap's father had hauled him off to church a few times, despite his mother's unwillingness to go. He did it almost angrily, as if to spite his mother. 'We're home frum mass,' he'd call when he came in the door, pulling off his Sunday suit jacket. Blackstrap avoided church if he could. Ever since Junior's funeral he could not stand the place. Too close to God. Too near Him for anybody's good. Too close to hating God.

Last Christmas, they had sat in the pew and Father Connolly had announced that they had a special treat for that night. A youth choir was visiting from St. John's. It had been arranged by Mary Wells who also arranged the annual turkey teas. Candles had been lit in all the stained-glass windows and up on the altar. As was always the case on Christmas Eve, there was standing room only. Men leaning against the wall behind the last row of pews, done up in their suits and coats, chatting quietly, a few low laughs, a whiff of booze here and there as you passed close by.

At first, Blackstrap hadn't noticed what was up front, in the corner. A group of young girls in white blouses and black skirts with red bows in their hair. Just as his eyes caught sight of them, the lights had shut off in the church and candles gave off the only light in the high-ceilinged building.

The voices of the young girls rose at once. It was like a humming at first and then the words: 'Siiiilent night, hooooly night, allllll is calm, alllll is bright . . .' drifted high out over the crowd. The sound was something to hear. It brought a contented, heart-warming smile to Blackstrap's lips. He glanced at his father's face and saw the same sort of look, like he was witnessing one of the sweetest and most sacred things imaginable. But when he checked his mother's face, he saw in the candlelight that her eyes were glistening. She stared toward the group of singing little girls and the tears spilled, sheening on her face, running free, until she wiped them away with her palm.

That was the last time Blackstrap's mother attended church. And it was only a few months later that Blackstrap and Jacob stopped going to Sunday mass.

Blackstrap clears his mind of the memory and thinks of Agnes. He turns on his side and stares at the wall. His guitar leaned there. He feels like sitting up and playing a quiet tune. But the image of his wrecked boat pins him down and the tremble stirs in him again. He wonders what he will tell his father. What people will think of the accident. Will they know it was him? Who in the houses down in Bareneed might have seen him?

Agnes. The centre of everything that gives him pleasure and displeasure. He draws his straying thoughts back to her. And reaches down inside his underwear to steady himself with her in mind.

In the morning, Blackstrap wakes to hear his father putting wood in the kitchen stove. The solid clang of metal against metal as the round damper is slid back over the hole. The noise of Jacob's bootsteps against the wooden plank flooring.

Blackstrap stays where he is, staring at the ceiling. Christmas morning. The wrecked boat troubling his spirit. If he had a dream while he slept, he cannot recall it. There is no Santa Claus. There hasn't been since his tenth birthday. Their first year in Cutland Junction when he told his mother and father there was no need to keep up with the foolishness. He knew the truth of it. The presents were hidden in the cupboard under the stairs that went nowhere now. The North Pole was nothing but snow. He'd been told that by one of the boys in the new school he was soon to give up on. Going off into the woods instead when he left with his bookbag in the morning.

His mother will not be up yet. She always sleeps late, even on Christmas morning, or maybe even longer on Christmas morning.

Blackstrap throws back the covers and climbs out of bed, his socks still on, his jeans and salt-and-pepper sweater, his thick short hair sticking up in different directions. The dampness at his knees has dried. Deeper regret takes hold of him as he recalls last night in more detail. His mind bringing him back there against his will. Even worse now on an empty stomach. Terrible regret and fear.

Out in the hallway, he passes in front of his mother's room. Not a sound inside. He goes into the bathroom and relieves himself. And the smell of bacon reaches him, his father cooking Christmas breakfast. Eggs. Bacon. Pancakes. Toast. Cinnamon rolls. They'll eat a big load and then sit in chairs or lie down on the sofa lamenting the intake of every morsel.

When Blackstrap enters the kitchen, Jacob is quick with 'Merry Christmas.' He reaches out and musses up Blackstrap's hair.

'Merry Christmas,' Blackstrap quietly responds, straightening his hair.

The boat. He cannot check his father's face. Meet his father's eyes. Look to see what might be there.

'Let's get at dem presents.' Jacob rubs his palms together.

Blackstrap heads for the back door and goes outside to smell the air. It is fresh. A clear morning. Every morning, he steps outside to get a sense of things. In the distance, there are church bells. Snow in the trees, the limbs full and heavy. It must have snowed while he was sleeping. Quiet snow. Heavy, gentle snow. Tracks in the snow toward the barn. A cat's paws.

'Give yer mudder a call,' says Jacob when Blackstrap returns to the kitchen.

'Sure.'

'Dose presents need da wrap ripped right off 'em, 'n fast.'

Blackstrap knocks on his parents' door. 'Mom?'

No reply.

He knocks again, listens. Nothing. He goes back to the kitchen. 'She's not getting up,' he says.

Jacob doesn't respond. He sniffs and clears his throat. Turns strips of bacon around in the black skillet. The fat sizzles and pops. Jacob swipes at his arm. 'Christly fat, *fuh'k* dat burns.'

Blackstrap knows that his father is angry because his mother cannot get up, cannot get over Junior or Ruth. His mother has been crippled by their deaths. He's heard his father's voice behind the bedroom door, rising in argument. 'Nut'n left o' ye but get'n up 'n going back ta bed. Yer lost in da past. Lost yer joy. Get yer head outta da past, womb'n.'

Blackstrap sits at the table and pours himself a mug of tea. His father goes through the motions, his actions louder than usual. Finally, done with getting things together, he turns and heads for the hallway.

The telephone rings. Blackstrap looks at it, thinking on whether or not he will answer it. Someone about the smashed-up boat.

'Get da Christly phone,' Jacob calls back.

Blackstrap bolts to his feet and lifts the receiver from the arc of its steel cradle. ''Lo?'

'Hi,' says the lovely voice on the other end. 'Merry Christmas.'

Agnes.

'Fer Christ's sake, Em'ly,' Jacob gripes from the bedroom. 'Christmas morn'll be gone da once.'

There is silence. Strained.

Blackstrap listens, aware that something is the matter. He holds the receiver away from his ear.

'Blacky?' says Agnes' far-off voice.

'Em'ly?' says his father, worried.

Blackstrap stands perfectly still, listening.

'Em'ly! Lard Jaysus Christ! Blacky!'

Chapter II – 1972-1973

The Munich Olympics

(March, 1972, 18 years old)

They leave under the cover of night. Blackstrap drives the pickup while Jacob sits in the passenger seat with a stack of Tory leaflets on his lap and a staple gun in one hand. He clicks the handle of the gun in beat to his thoughts. He watches ahead through the windshield, his eyes intent on coming deeds, while the car rolls down the valley into Cutland Junction.

"Ere,' barks Jacob in a whisper, hurriedly tilting his head toward the slushy side of the road.

Blackstrap stops the pickup and Jacob scrambles from the passenger seat, leaving the door open while he slaps a leaflet on a power pole and fires a staple into each of its four corners. In four seconds, he's back in the pickup, the cold air trailing him in.

'Go,' he says, 'drive,' watching the pole, his head turning as the pickup rolls ahead. Done admiring his handiwork, he searches the side of the road beside him.

"Ere,' Jacob says, the passenger door already open before the pickup is fully stopped, the asphalt moving beneath him. He leaps down. And Blackstrap hears the snap of bone. Jacob tilts with a groan and goes over as Tory leaflets wildly flutter into the air.

'If dat bastard Smallwood weren't driving da province inta bankruptcy and using da money ta repair roads instead, I wouldn't 'a snapped me leg in half in a Christly pot'ole.' Jacob pauses a moment, while the doctor wraps the wet rolls of plaster cast around his leg. He stares ahead and searches around inside his head, then he chuckles. 'Reminds me of a story yer brudder Junior, God rest 'is soul, tol' me years ago. 'E always loved ta tell a story.'

494

The emergency room in Carbonear is practically deserted, the curtains drawn around the narrow stalls and empty beds. At first, Jacob had refused to visit the hospital, opting to continue putting up flyers. But while the cutting pain continued and Jacob sweated buckets, Blackstrap told him that if he didn't get it checked, gangrene might set in and he'd lose the leg.

'Dun't be so goddamn foolish,' Jacob had gritted through the pain that was making his eyes go wild. 'Dey'd never get dis leg off me. Like ta see 'em try. Christ! I been t'rew worse, in a woods widt creatures try'n ta chow down on me.' But, after a while, Jacob just sat there in the pickup seat, his face covered in sweat, his fingers gripping the Tory flyers as spasms swept through him. Blackstrap had just driven to the hospital, despite his father's half-hearted protests.

In the emergency room, Blackstrap searches his father's face. It's the first time he's heard his father mention Junior's name in the ten years since his death.

Jacob quiets down, looking around, like he's only now realizing where he might be. He chuckles again. The pain not so bad, it seems. The medication kicking in. A shot of something as soon as he got in there.

Blackstrap waits. The doctor rinses his hands in the sink. He's dark-skinned, from somewhere in Pakistan by the looks of him. 'Keep a good eye on those potholes when you're walking next time,' says the doctor, smiling.

'Tell dat bastard Smallwood. Son of a whore.'

The doctor laughs. 'Let it dry a while before you go. Twenty minutes ought to do it.'

'Let me tell ya dis story, doc. Got a second?'

'Yes, one second.'

'Junior knew a feller name 'a Hedley Basha who worked in da mine office over on Bell Isle. Junior were in da office one day on an errand 'n Hedley Basha were in dere bawling like a baby on da telephone ta 'is wife. "Marjorie," he were bawling. "Marjorie, Marjorie, I broke me leg." Junior couldn't believe dat da man were sitting dere on a chair lookin' perfectly fit. "'E weren't in any sort o' pain—"'

A nurse enters the close quarters of the cubicle. 'They need you. Bed four.'

'Excuse me.' The doctor looks at Jacob's leg, then leaves.

Jacob frowns, checks down at the plaster cast, seemingly vexed with it. 'Dis is gonna be itchy, mark me words.'

Blackstrap waits for the rest of the story. He hasn't heard it before, strangely enough. But Jacob will not continue. Blackstrap knows his father won't utter another word until the doctor returns to the stall. They wait in silence. Blackstrap checks over the walls. Picks up some of the instruments. Looks them over. He studies a chart. Inside things with words printed next to them.

The doctor does not return. Finally, a nurse appears in the curtained section and tells them they can leave. 'Come back and see us in a week.'

On the half-hour ride back to Cutland Junction, Jacob keeps his mouth shut. He rubs the cast every now and then, lifts his hand near his face, looks at his palm, at his fingers.

When they arrive home, Emily is at the kitchen table, staring at the floor. She watches Blackstrap come in and lean on the counter. He folds his arms, his eyes on the back doorway. The sounds of Jacob lumbering up the driveway, not wanting any sort of assistance. Even refusing the crutches that were offered. Emily stands when she sees Jacob appear, struggling to move the way he is. 'What happened?'

'Wolf chewed me leg half off, 'fore I blinded 'im widt me own piss.' His hand on the kitchen door frame. He turns away to face the hallway, seeming to wonder where he'll go now.

'What?'

'He broke it in a pothole,' says Blackstrap.

'A pothole?'

'Jumping from the pickup.'

'Everything okay?' She frets after Jacob, touching his arm.

'Nut'n to it,' says Jacob, pulling away, and limping off to make it seem worse than it might actually be.

He stops to take a few breaths, stays there like he's confused. He turns back for the kitchen. Blackstrap tries helping his father, but Jacob swats at him, 'Paws off. I can manage.' One hand going for the table edge while he shuts his eyes to let Emily catch a full whiff of his torment. 'I could do widt a bit of a lie down,' he says, turning and heading for the bedroom, with Blackstrap near his side. It takes a while to get into the bedroom. Jacob drops down on the edge of the bed, lying back. 'Christly cast. Leg made of frigg'n stone.' Exhausted, Jacob watches the wall. Then, remembering, shifts his eyes to Blackstrap. 'I were tell'n you 'bout Junior.'

Emily stands in the bedroom doorway. A shadow masking the hallway light behind her.

'Dun't get yer knickers crooked, womb'n. Ever'tin's right rosy.'

'Can I get you something?'

'A beer.'

'Did the doctor give you painkillers?'

'Shot me widt sum'tn dat a beer'd go right lovely widt.'

'You shouldn't drink with that then?'

'Whatever ye say, b'y.'

Emily backs away and is gone.

'Shut da door,' Jacob tells Blackstrap. 'G'wan.'

Blackstrap does as instructed.

'So, dere were dis feller dat Junior tol' me 'bout, a feller widt da snapped leg. Jus' like wha' befell me. He were on da phone 'n—'

Bright light spills over Jacob's face, and Blackstrap turns to look toward the bedroom doorway. Emily comes into the room with a bowl of soup.

'You should eat this now,' she says. 'I've had it on the stove all day.'

'Naw, I'm fine.'

Emily stands there with the bowl in her hands. 'You both look guilty of something.'

'Guilty?' asks Jacob. 'Dun't be so foolish.'

Emily watches Jacob's face until he can't take it any longer. 'Awright,' he says, 'I'll have a drop. Lay'er dere.' He points to the bedside table.

Emily sets the bowl down.

'T'anks, me love,' he says.

Emily gives him a tiny smile and glances at Blackstrap. 'Hungry? It's late.' Her hands joined in front of her.

Blackstrap shakes his head.

'You're never hungry. I know, you just eat to eat.' She waits, taking quiet pleasure in watching Jacob and Blackstrap. 'The stove needs some splits when you're ready.'

497

'Okay,' says Blackstrap.

Emily turns and leaves.

'Shut da door,' says Jacob.

The door clicks shut.

Jacob looks at the bowl, turns up his nose. 'Fine soup, but I ain' got no stomach fer it. Da pain robs a man of his will ta slip a morsel o' food inta 'is trap.' Jacob shifts his gaze toward Blackstrap who's now leaned against the wall. He then eyes the rocking chair beside the bed. 'Have a seat why dun't ya. Yer making me nervous stood up dere.'

Blackstrap does as his father says.

'So.' Jacob glances toward the door, waits, listens. 'Hedley Basha were bawling and bawling. Everyone in da office were lookin' at 'im. 'N Junior couldn't believe 'is ears. "Me leg is broke," says 'Edley. "Me good leg. I broke me good leg." Good leg? Junior were wondering. What's he on about? But it were jus' den dat Junior noticed what were resting on da top of da office desk beside da phone.'

'What?'

'It were his wooden leg, snapped in two.'

Blackstrap chuckles.

'Ooooow, Marjorie,' says Jacob. 'Ooow, I broke me leg. Ooooow. Me good leg.'

'So what happened?'

''Is wife bought 'im a new leg from 'ome. But it weren't as nice as da one dat broke off, as da first one were belonged ta 'is dead fadder who 'ad it 'anded down ta 'im from 'is fadder before 'im. All miners dey were. Tough as nails, but not too handy widt dere legs by da sound o' t'ings.'

(May, 1972)

When Blackstrap pulls his father's pickup into the lane, he sees a yellow VW Bug parked up further in the driveway. He thinks of backing out and parking on the road, not wanting to bar the vehicle in, but decides against it. Whoever owns the car should've known better. He looks in his rearview, the load of spruce and fir he's just cut from the west side of Coombs Hill blocking his view. A few clumps of snow stuck to the bark. Snow still in the woods, not melted yet like it has from the wet fields and roads.

His own car, the Galaxie 500, is on the other side of the house, up on a ramp. The front axle snapped. He leaves it there, not wanting to fix it. It reminds him of Agnes. He had bought it with her in mind. Only three months since she's left for the mainland with her family. And the pain still there in his gut whenever he thinks of her face. She used to call and tell him about everything that was going on where she was, the other Newfoundlanders she'd come across, the difference in the stores and land, but he didn't have much to say now that she was gone across all that distance. And all the things she told him only made him feel more and more like she had deserted him, that she was having a good time, a good life without him, while he was miserable. The more he heard, the more he was silenced. Every word drained out of him by her descriptions. He couldn't get over being angry with her. Agnes must have known it because she stopped calling. She'd sent him letters, too, but he'd stuffed them away in the secret box he kept on the top shelf of his closet. No time for trying to figure out what they meant.

His stomach grumbles and he plans on something to eat before delivering the load of firewood to Isaac Tuttle. Tuttle wasn't home when he tried him earlier and Blackstrap wasn't going to leave the load there and then chase after Tuttle for the money. It's peculiar that he's delivering wood to Tuttle, when Tuttle used to deliver coal to them down in Bareneed. The need for fire never gave up on anyone. Blackstrap recalls Isaac's truck that used to pull up in his family's yard. He used to watch Isaac shovelling coal into the chute that went down into the crawl space under the house. The fine black dust hanging in the air like a big smudge of something waiting to settle. He'd always be the one to go down through the hatch in the kitchen floor, and come up with a pail of coal.

Blackstrap scratches his sideburn with the back of his thumb. Climbs out of the pickup. When he passes by the VW Bug, he sees a small plastic girl with a grass skirt on the dashboard. He's seen one before. The girl wobbles when you drive. On the passenger seat there's a book, a blue cover with a white seagull on it.

In the kitchen, a fellow in a pair of jeans and a brown velour shirt. He's at the kitchen table with Jacob. The fellow's hair is down to his shoulders and parted in the middle. He has on round wire glasses. Like the type the Beatle, John Lennon, wears. There's some sort of old book on the table. The young fellow looks at Blackstrap and gives a big smile. He stands from his seat and – with an eager jerk of his shoulder – offers his hand to Blackstrap.

Jacob is already smiling. He's been in particularly good spirits since Smallwood finally resigned as Liberal Party leader back in January. That means a new leader and another election. No doubt, Smallwood will be given the boot this time. That victory has practically obliterated any mention of the wrecked boat. His father had ranted and raved when he heard the news from Jimmy Shears. The boat gone from the wharf and the scrap of it found near shore. Wrecked. The police had been by to investigate. Blackstrap had assumed that his father would know it was him. But it could have been anyone because a set of keys was always left on board. No insurance. No boat. But Blackstrap was saving to buy another. Jacob was saving. There was talk of Ted Hutchings, a distant cousin, selling his boat for so much down, so much every month to help them out. But Jacob didn't like owing anyone money for anything he had. Credit was a curse, he said.

'Bill Riche,' the young fellow announces.

Blackstrap looks at the hand. Shakes it without giving over his name.

'Dis be da feller I tol' ye 'bout.'

'Who's that?' says Blackstrap. Moving to the kitchen sink to wash his hands. He thinks of his mother while he runs the water. He wonders if his father has checked on her. The pump cuts in from the back room. He doesn't hear what's said in return. He soaps up his hands but the blackened sap doesn't come off his palms and fingers. He watches out the window, then shuts off the tap. What he needs is gasoline. Gasoline'll wash anything from his hands.

'. . . mentions da whole tale 'ere,' Jacob is saying.

'What's that?' asks Blackstrap. Drying his hands in the dish towel.

''Bout yer gran'fadder, Francis. It be 'im affer all. Me name's in 'ere. I dun't get da gist of it dough.' The lines deepen in Jacob's forehead and around his eyes. Although he smiles again quickly. 'Dis feller's been read'n me bits o' it. Francis lived off dem shipwrecks on dat perilous stretch o' water 'long da southern shore, got all 'is needs from wreckage.' Jacob laughs. Slaps at his knee. 'Christ. Ain't dat 'larious?'

Blackstrap stands by his father's chair. His eyes on the old book. The cover is made of leather, faded black. The edges are worn, black to dark brown, and look soft.

Bill Riche opens the cover. Shows Blackstrap the inside. Riche watches Blackstrap's face with pleasure. While he goes about turning the yellowed pages with handwriting on them.

'It's something, isn't it?' says Riche.

Blackstrap grunts. Turns away to check the breadbox.

'We found it in the wall of an old house on the Southern Shore. Wrapped in linen. A woman's dress with lace embroidery. We were able to make it out. Maybe a wedding dress.'

'Yer granfadder were slaughtered by Beawtuks.'

'Well.' Riche faces Jacob. Then glances back at Blackstrap who is smearing butter on a piece of plain bread. Then pouring molasses on top from a cardboard box. 'I don't think he was slaughtered by the Beothuks, really. There's no mention of any sort of—'

"'E were in da cumpany o' dem. Says so.' Jacob thumps the book with his fingertips.

Blackstrap holds the slice of bread in the flat of his palm. He bites off an edge. Chews up the salty fat taste of butter. The iron sweetness of molasses.

'But there was—'

'No doubt dey murdered 'im in 'is sleep. Bunch o' savages.'

'He mentions in his journal that he traded with the Beothuks. What is fascinating, however, is that we believed Shanaditti was the last of the Beothuks. Well, not "we" particularly because we've heard reports of Beothuks surviving Shanaditti, but this is documented proof. Extremely valuable.' He raises his eyebrows. 'From an historical standpoint.'

'Slaughtered 'e were.' Jacob drags a finger across his own throat. Then winks at Blackstrap when Riche isn't looking. Torment the poor townie. Good for a lark.

Blackstrap chuckles while he eats.

'There was no mention of animosity,' Riche quickly points out. Getting worried now. Needing to convince everyone in the room that the Beothuk wouldn't do such a thing. Indians not savages anymore. Not in these savageless days.

Tricky word, Blackstrap thinks. Animosity. He knows what it means, still chewing.

'He died, didn't 'e?'

'Yes.'

'Christly Christ!' Jacob slaps the table, making Riche flinch. ''N dere were Beawtuks 'round dere. Pro'bly scalped da 'air right off 'is 'ed. Made a purse outta it or a toy fer one of dere liddle baby savages.'

'Yes. Well—'

Jacob doesn't say another word. He leans back in his chair. Folds his arms and tilts back his head. Point made. No argument.

Bill Riche says, 'But there's also mention of a woman in the diary. A ghost at that. Can you then speculate that the ghost killed Francis Hawco?' Riche checks Blackstrap. Like Blackstrap might understand, might go along with him, being the younger of the two Hawco men.

Blackstrap stares. Then shoves the rest of the bread into his mouth. Sweeps his palms together. He picks up the diary. Turns the pages. Butter stains here and there.

Riche's hands jerk in the air. Shoot toward the diary to hover near. His head bent on a pleading, suffering angle.

Blackstrap swallows. 'This ours now?' he asks. Looking directly at Riche for a second.

'Well, you have some rights, of course, but we were hoping you might consider donating the piece to the Newfoundland Museum in St. John's. It's an important artefact in that it relates certain stories about the Beothuks. Any sort of literature on the Beothuks is quite rare. They're all gone, you know. The Beothuks. Slaughtered. We killed them all.'

'Wh-wee?' sputters Jacob. 'Wha' sort of bullcrap are ye on about? I never laid no finger on any Beawtuk in me life. Frum what I 'erd dey were sweet liddle fellers though, if da trute be known. Right cute.'

Blackstrap watches the young man from the university, detecting a trace of an accent. Proper like, almost British. Blackstrap licks a finger. Flicks over a page.

The noise of the page turning sounding like a rip. It almost makes Riche come out of his skin. His hands flinch up from the table.

'Where you from?' asks Blackstrap.

'St. John's.'

Blackstrap studies Riche's face. Unconvinced. He flicks another page. This time with even more crumpling force than the first.

'My parents are from England,' he admits. Like he's almost proud of it. His eyes trained on the journal.

'Teachers, the lot of 'em.'

'Yes.' Riche smiles. 'Professors. How'd you guess?' The young fellow straightens his glasses. They look too small for him. The stems pressing into the sides of his head, maybe leaving dents all the way through to his skull.

'Me wife's lot were frum across da big drink too,' says Jacob, but not like it's meant to make them closer.

Blackstrap snaps shut the diary. He keeps it in his hand. Wanders down the hall to check on his mother. His mother likes books. She used to read all the time. He remembers from when he was younger. She read books and letters. Wrote letters in return. He brought them to the post office for her. Stood in line in the morning. But there isn't much of that now. Her door is open a bit and she is sleeping. He hears her breathing. During the run of any day, he often stops there. Just to listen for her breathing. To make certain the air's going in and out. Ever since they had to take her to the hospital in an ambulance. It was close that time. She might have died, if the ambulance hadn't arrived when it had. That room in the hospital. Visiting her with nothing to say. But loving her. Loving her and frightened by the possible loss of that love. Frightened like he was mad at her for what she did.

Everyone knows now. An ambulance racing with its sirens blaring and red lights flashing. Past every house in Cutland Junction on Christmas morning. His father told his friends and the women gossip mongers, anyone who called trying to find out the news, that it was heart problems that had caused her spell of affliction. But they all knew better. It was heart problems, alright. The torment of a broken heart from burying two of her blessed children. The women in the community all knew about that. The men could say whatever they wanted. The men could go on with their lives. But the women knew what it really meant to stare dead-struck into that hollowing loss. It was a wonder any woman ever outlived it.

Blackstrap edges open the door to his mother's room. With book in hand, he steps in.

Out in the driveway, the truck is down more on the driver's side than the passenger's side. Blackstrap must have busted a spring with the load of wood on. Always something to bother a man. Climbing aboard, he sits behind the wheel and revs the engine. He thinks of his mother and the way she reached for that book. The look in her eyes when she heard what it was about. Waking up. Waking from a dream to something like an emergency. Alert. The secrets written in its pages. He wouldn't mind knowing what's in there himself, but would never ask her to read it to him. Not like he's a child or anything. She might offer sometime, if he hints around a bit. He watches through the windshield while Bill Riche talks on and on to Jacob, both of them in the driveway. Jacob backs Riche away from the house, toward the yellow VW. Riche hoists the strap of his woollen purse up on his shoulder while Jacob nods reassuringly. Agreeing with everything Riche says, Jacob pats him on the shoulder and keeps nodding and agreeing.

Jacob even opens the car door for Riche who keeps talking.

A slow smile grows on Blackstrap's lips. His father always with a bit of the devil in him.

(March, 1973)
The envelope is addressed to Jacob Hawco. Blackstrap can tell that much. He knows his father's name from seeing it on bills over the years. Hawco and the letter 'J.'

'You gonna sign fer it?' Fred asks from behind the post office counter.

No good can come from signing for a letter at the post office. Everyone knows that. His father warned him years ago about such things. 'Avoid it like da plague,' he'd said. Blackstrap glances at the envelope. A logo up in the corner with words printed under it.

'Who's it frum?' asks Blackstrap.

Fred glances down at the envelope. 'Memorial University,' he says, tapping the envelope with his fingertip. 'Sin John's.'

Blackstrap checks over his shoulder, toward the big window and beyond. Jacob sitting in the passenger seat of the idling pickup. His window rolled down while he talks with Larry Peters.

'Hang on,' he says without looking at Fred. He goes out through the glass door into the frosty air. When he opens the driver's side, his father looks at him, a smile on Jacob's face from his conversation with Larry Peters. Larry Peters keeps talking, breath misting while watching toward the sky, then pointing over his shoulder. Something about a bunch of seals that've come ashore on the slob ice down in Bareneed. A bunch of locals down there feeding them with table scraps.

Jacob checks Blackstrap's face. He straightens his baseball cap and waits.

'Letter ta sign fer,' says Blackstrap. 'Frum da university.'

Jacob shakes his head once, then goes back to talking to Larry Peters, telling his own story about seals and the sorry state of the seal fishery now. The bastard mainlanders with their half-assed celebrities trying to make away with the seal hunt.

Blackstrap shuts the driver's door and goes back in.

'He want it?' Fred asks.

Blackstrap shakes his head.

'Sure?'

Blackstrap says nothing more.

Fred pokes through his drawer of rubber stamps and lifts one out. He turns it over to read the letters, then raises it and smacks the envelope. The letters in ink on the front spell a word.

'Refused,' Fred says, laughing.

Blackstrap takes the rest of the mail, and leaves, irked by the memory of that young fellow who came with the diary. That letter was about the diary. It had to be. There's no way that Blackstrap will be giving the book back, not after finding out how his mother cares for it. How the diary has got her out of bed and seeming to be more alive than he can remember for years. She talks about it with him. The things that have happened to Francis Hawco, things no one knew before, like it makes her excited. She's even asked him to drive her to St. John's so she can go to the bookstore. He'll take her there after getting the mail. All he has to do is drop Jacob back home. Jacob avoids St. John's at all costs. 'Da cars 'n signs 'n ever'tin confuses me eyes,' he often says of the city.

Jacob says 'take 'er easy' to Larry Peters and leaves his window open, the air breezing in, sweet and crisp in the nostrils. They drive in silence, down into the valley and up again, tires thumping over the railway tracks and then curving east toward their road. Blackstrap glances at the dashboard clock. The train on the Carbonear line not due for another two hours.

'Letter frum da university—' says Blackstrap.

'Where?' Jacob eyes the mail on the seat between them.

'Refused it.'

Jacob stares through the windshield, the land moving to both sides of them. His eyes shift back and forth, while he thinks hurriedly. 'I'll burn da frig'n t'ing,' Jacob finally says, "fore I let dose scoundrels 'av it ta sniff at 'n paw over. It's about me fadder, written in 'is 'and. Wha' good is it ta da likes of dem grave robbers? Want'n ta own pieces of every'ns life like dey ain't even got one ta call dere own.'

Chapter III – 1974

Patty Hearst

(March, 1974, 20 years old)

The far-off sound comes from several directions at once, bouncing off the icefields. A sputtering like something mechanical repeatedly chopping into the sky. As the sound grows louder, Blackstrap looks up from the fat and blood. Stares south to see the dot of the helicopter. Slowly lowering toward the ice where the men from the *Newfoundland Breaker* are at work skinning seals. He tightens up his thoughts and curses under his breath. They have been warned that the protesters were on their way.

Twelve days in a boat trapped in three-foot-thick ice. Not making a cent and fearing for the worst. The ice scraping and crunching at the sides of the longliner. Spooking the hell out of everyone in their sleep, waking them to listen. Because two vessels had already gone down. Their hulls crushed by the pressure. Six men lost on one boat. The others rescued by chopper.

And now to face this.

The sky is a brilliant blue. Cloudless. The exact same throb of blue everywhere. The sun, burning overhead, causes the red to blaze against the snow. A perfect day for a visit from outsiders.

'Just ignore 'em,' Captain Hynes calls out. 'The whole spoon-fed lot of 'em.'

As the helicopter nears, all sound is smothered by the punching sweep of the rotor blades.

A television crew from the Canadian Broadcasting Corporation is on hand to document the arrival. Their helicopter had already touched down over an hour ago. With a reporter and film crew, wandering around the ice, trying to get important pictures. The worse the better. Stick their camera right up the seal's arse if they could. The reporter, a man Blackstrap has seen on television, asks questions. Some of the men answer shortly, grunting from their labour. Just to be polite. Others treat him like he doesn't even exist. No time for explaining what's important about making a living. What the seal hunt means to them. Why, sir, I just luvs da seal hunt. I truly does. How much, you ask? Well, b'y, I'd marry 'er if she'd 'av me, in me fil'ty blood-'n-fat-soaked rags. Yes, b'y, I would.

The noise from the approaching helicopter increases, making the seals yelp louder. When Blackstrap peeks up from the dead seal clamped between his boots, he sees the camera aimed at the helicopter that has just landed. No more than seventy feet up the ice. Blackstrap goes back to sculping the pelt away. A clean whispering slit, from throat to tail. When he looks up again, he catches sight of a silver-haired man. The leader by the looks of him. The way he stares out over the ice. Like he's stepping into a kingdom that once belonged to him, that had been magnificent. Occupied now by bloodthirsty barbarians. A true monarch, if there ever was one. Another man climbs out behind the first. Followed by a younger man and a woman. They look like they don't belong anywhere. Except in places of their own clean making. Spectators. Zipped up in brand-new winter gear. Spotless. Hair combed just right for the cameras. Nice sunglasses. Expensive ones made by companies owned by poofters. So they don't go snow blind.

Blackstrap's sunglasses he bought at the corner gas station. From a counter rack for $3.99. He doesn't like the sight of the woman most. By the looks of her, she's never been to a place like this. And she will make a mess of herself. Because there is nothing to do here but slaughter things. Work. Why would anyone want to come and watch, if not because they've got time on their hands? Time to burn. Money to burn. Other people's money to burn. Other people's charity. Luxury time.

That place just not bred into the woman's head. Not a place for women or soft men wrongly dressed in clothes they think proper for the climate. Too warm for a day like this. Too warm if you plan on working. Getting your hands dirty. Nice clothes to be wearing if you want to stroll around, looking concerned and God-awfully wounded.

The cameraman hurries toward the helicopter. Another man with a microphone on a stick follows along. And the reporter comes up the rear. The reporter is shaking hands with the silver-haired man. The Lord over all cute creatures.

Blackstrap snorts. Looks down at the seal. Sculps away the hide. Rolls the seal over. A slosh of blood on his boots.

The helicopter engine is shut off. The rotor blades slow with a whine. Then comes the sound in his ears. He notices now because he is listening with the ears of the new arrivals. The shrieking of baby seals. A sound that will bring tears to the woman's eyes. Their bawling makes it sound like they're in pain. Even when they're not. It's just a sound they make. Doesn't matter if they're being killed or not.

The RCMP officer moves toward the new arrivals. The silver-haired man hands the officer a piece of paper. The officer looks it over while the reporter waits. The reporter checks the cameraman and the man with the microphone. Making sure everything is set up the way it's supposed to be. He points to a cord. One of the other men straightens it out.

The officer gives back the paper. Moves away. The four people from the helicopter roam toward the patch of men around Blackstrap. Off on an excursion, out for a jaunt in the fresh air. He feels his shoulders go tight. He becomes aware of his hand holding his sculping knife. The screeching as plain as anything. Points of sound on a deaf white field.

One of the men brings down a club on the head of a young seal. And Blackstrap feels disgust. Sounds of disbelief from the new arrivals. Cringes and Gasps Incorporated.

The way these people react makes him feel lousy.

The silver-haired man leads the group. He's talking like he's humble. But he's got something important to say. Like he's a sweet guy that everyone should listen to because he's put it all together nicely. He's thought it all out. The clear voice of informed reason. Every word said just so, written down somewhere for him. Maybe written out by his own hand before he says the words standing in front of a mirror. Watching himself to see how others will feel. He's an important guy. Knows he's good-looking. A charmer. Silver-tongued. He's from a group called Keep It Green. The green must stand for money. Because they make a good living. Trying to shut down other people's lives. A respectable racket to be in. If you're a know-it-all snotty mainlander. A colonialist. A bigot.

The taller man, behind the silver-haired man, comes up to one of the sealers. Introduces himself. His voice can be heard everywhere. It's a voice born for making speeches. The man's a senator from the United States. Here as an observer, he says. He talks like he's the most level-headed man alive. Like he wants to hear all sides of it, for the sake of the people he represents. His American countrymen. But he already has his mind made up. He's been brought aboard. He's just looking for ammunition to make his argument stronger, to get a ban on seal pelts in the US. The Newfoundlanders ignore the senator. Continue with their work. A senator is nothing to them.

But it is none of this that bothers Blackstrap. Not as much as the sight of the woman. Looking around at all the spilling red. Like she's stepped into some wide-open, cunt-ugly nightmare. Born to be slaughtered. Every living thing. The sound of the crying seal pups. She's horrified. Not a child ever pushed out of her. That's how she seems. A life too important for children.

The blood on the snow.

The red on the white.

The honest spillage.

The need to eat.

What he thinks

is he'd like to fuck her.

Right there in the mess of it.

Then she catches his eye.

'Christ!' Blackstrap mutters. How to hold the knife now. How to make it look not so bad for her. He feels like dropping it, kicking it away from anywhere near him. Not mine, missus. Instead, he stabs harder. Stabs when he doesn't need to. Stabs at the carcass until blood is flicking everywhere. Spraying because the heart is still pumping. He will not silence it.

And his face is made blessedly warm.

A radio in one of the helicopters must have been switched on. Because Blackstrap suddenly hears music. Words plainly carrying across the still expanse of ice. Something about everybody kung-fu fighting.

The woman steps up alongside plump Billy Taylor. He's already huffing just to have her so near him. Like she's contagious. Billy tries leaning away a bit.

'How does that make you *feel?*' the woman asks, her voice unsteady. Not her place to ask such a question. Why didn't she know that? Live the sheltered life, stay in the shelter.

Or bent over in the doorway of the chopper. Taking it from behind.

'Move outta me way, missus,' says Billy with a voice that sounds half choked. 'I'm tryin' ta work here.'

The woman waits, watches Billy labouring to keep up with the others. Tears already on her face. She slowly raises her fingertips and carefully dabs the tears away. Then, with head tilted despondently, she turns and steps away, up beside Blackstrap. He sees her leather boots. New as they can be. Expensive brand. They must've cost hundreds of dollars. Her feet must be really warm. Too warm. Her feet are probably sweating now. Stinking. Her toenails clipped nicely though. Painted pretty. Someone probably does it for her. She has on a pink snow suit. Expensive too. The brand name on the pocket. On her head, she's wearing a hat that looks like it's made out of beaver. Or maybe that's just her hair. The style of it.

'How do you feel about what you're doing?' asks the woman. Her sad voice with an accent he cannot place. An accent clear as water. Pure and unmuddied.

Blackstrap does not answer. There is another seal near him. A fat harp seal baring its teeth. Hissing. Jerking ahead to bite at him. He steps in front of the woman. Catches a sniff of her perfume. Pretty is what it does to his insides for a second or two. Then he raises his club and smacks it in the head. Crushing its skull. He rolls it over. Slices its belly while it flinches around. Not the cleanest view now. But worst for her. Show her the worst. He growls a little for good measure because it feels right. That sound in his throat. He even thinks of licking his fingers. Her question making him into a savage. And while he stabs at the seal, he hopes the blood will shoot out at her. It doesn't. So he rolls the carcass over onto her boots. And lets the insides spill and slosh. The steam rising for a good whiff.

He looks up at her. His red face. His grin. His evil laugh while he drags an arm across his lips, smearing a clear patch for a kiss.

The woman stumbles back. Her stunned expression. Frightened. Aghast, might be the right word. Those toenails inside those boots. Those perfect toes treated to everything. This little piggy went to market, this little piggy stayed home . . .

What do you eat? Blackstrap wants to ask her. 'There's blood in everything,' he says. More to himself. What the fuck do you eat, you teary-eyed, manicured, made-up whore? Bend over.

But the woman hasn't heard. She stares hard at his eyes. At the way he's watching her. How is he watching her? With a threat. How he is holding the sculping blade. Without looking behind herself, the woman backs away more, her boots leaving red prints. There is a shout from the senator. Because the woman is about to trip over a four-hundred-pound harp seal. The silver-haired man doesn't notice. He's being interviewed, his mouth not knowing how to stop. Because he's so good-looking. Because he's practiced at his trade.

And the woman trips. The woman falls. Good solid ice packed hard. So the woman doesn't have to worry about going through.

The senator can't get to her in time. The four-hundred-pound harp has already made a snap at her face. Tore a chunk clean from her cheek. The woman doesn't scream. Like she's never learned how. She is horrified though. Her gloved hand to her cheek. The blood brilliant on her white mitt, dripping away onto white. Her big eyes looking there. Her own blood. Then to the men who have turned to watch.

The silver-haired man keeps talking. The reporter holds the microphone and nods. The silver-haired man makes a circle in the air with his hand. Gesturing out over the icefields.

The harp jerks ahead and bites the woman's fingers, clear through her mitts.

Billy Taylor starts toward the scene, his short legs struggling.

The senator tries getting close. But the harp won't let him. Whipping around, its jaw snaps and snaps. A whitecoat bellies near. Nips at the woman's hair. Messes up her hairdo. Pulling it loose from how it's pinned in place.

Now, the woman's screaming.

Blackstrap steps nearer. The other men have gathered round. And the reporter has finally shifted his eyes from the silver-haired man's face to notice the commotion.

The scream.

Not the baby seals.

The woman.

Everyone's moving now, as fast as they're able. Because something is screaming. Maybe they can make a good stash of money from it. It does sound desperate enough. The screaming. Effective.

The men do nothing. Blackstrap Hawco. Billy Taylor. Andrew Coombs. Peter Galway. They watch the woman surrounded by seals. Feeding time at the zoo.

The senator snatches a club. Starts beating at the seal. But he doesn't know what he's doing. It only pisses off the harp seal who growls and gets angrier. Snaps at the senator's shin. Chews on the woman's boot. She's huddled up in a ball.

Her blood.

Or the blood of a seal.

Who knows.

Other seals gather around and screech at the woman. They probably think she's one of their own. Screaming like she is.

'Do something,' wails the senator, poking at the seals. But frightened too. Needing the men, the murderers, to do their job.

The reporter is turned with the camera aimed at what's going on. The world that will see how the woman was treated. The famous footage that will travel the globe in no time, to be spoken of as an indignity.

Blackstrap steps forward. Raises his club. Crashes it down on the head of the harp. The skull giving way. On the heads of the whitecoats. On the heads of the greycoats. Everything soon dead around the woman. Limp. Everything stopped. Only the woman moving. Whimpering. Crawling through the stillness. Only the woman saved. The sobbing woman spared.

She is helped up by the senator. By the silver-haired man from Keep It Green who looks overly worried. Maybe a lawsuit on the way. No speech prepared for this. He says something like: what else could be expected?

The woman is led away. Crying. Her tears not for the baby seals now. But for her fucked-up face. 'My finger,' she's blubbering. 'Get my finger.' The senator comes back to search for the finger. But it's been eaten. Inside the belly of the harp. Blackstrap cuts open the huge seal. Fishes around in its stomach. Nothing. Slits it across its throat. Finds the finger and hands it back to the senator.

Full of the seal's insides.

'Thank you,' says the senator. Like Blackstrap has done a great service for his country. For the US of A. He might even get a medal for it. Holding the finger in his palm. Eyes on it. Precious and revolting. He hurries over to his wife.

Blackstrap nods. *Not your world*, he thinks. Junior's voice filling his head.

Tiny dots
On a field of frozen slaughter
Witnessed from what once was
Thought of as the Heavens
The lesser come for it
For gulls when gone
Beak tip to the stilled
One inside another
With beating hearts

What you eat
When at your table
With a family kept alive
By (your) lies

(September)

Blackstrap stands on the rooftop of Andy Coffin's house. Andy's pole and brush lodged in the chimney. Too much creosote caked inside the stainless steel pipe. The woodstove not drawing like it should. Blackstrap had been driving by in the pickup, saw Andy up there. He had pulled over, rolled down his window to watch Andy struggling. Hearing him cursing on the pole. Andy's mom and dad too old to be up on the roof, so Andy's father, Billy, stands on the road. Hollering out instructions and comments, and enlisting the advice of anyone passing by.

'I believe Santy Claus never made it up outta dere las' Chris'mas,' calls Andy's father. A terribly thin and slightly stooped man with a few days growth of grey on his sunken cheeks. 'Ain't dat da trute, wha'?' He laughs. Looks at the other two people gathered by his side. Their heads staring up at the rooftop. 'I dun't believe Santy managed a swift escape, wha'?' Billy laughs again, toothless and trouble-free. 'Wha', eh?' He laughs and shuffles nearer to Mrs. Wells who's stood there in her plastic rain bonnet. Despite the absence of clouds in the September sky. Andy's father wheezes. Stares at Mrs. Wells' face. Puffs on his cigarette while shifting his attention down at her mauve slacks. 'Lovely pants ye got dere, Missus Wells.'

Blackstrap grips the chimney pole above Andy's hands.

'Okay,' he says. 'Go.'

They yank at once, and the pole edges loose. Then slides free. Blackstrap notices the pole is made of copper pipe soldered together with joiners.

Andy lifts a thin ten-foot length of limbed spruce tree. Shoves it down the chimney. Battering at the creosote blockage.

'Fuh'k,' says Andy, ramming the spruce rod against the dead-end blockage. 'Christ!' He pulls the rod out. Shines a flashlight down there. Blackstrap supposes it's hard to see too far down. Because it's daylight out.

Billy stares up at the roof with his jaw hanging open. 'Shock'n stuff,' he says to the two others. 'Wonder Santy didn't go right crispy widt da fierce heat.'

Andy grabs up the mason jar of gasoline. What he's poured from the canister in his shed. He unscrews the lid and dumps the contents down the chimney pipe. He tilts his chin up at Blackstrap. 'This'll do 'er.'

Blackstrap looks toward the east. He can see the roof of his house. Barely there in the trees. And a length of the train tracks beyond. The sound of the train in the far off. On its way from Holyrood then on to the Badger line. Not yet visible. He wants to be down for when it comes through. So he can feel the rumble in the earth.

Andy lights a match. Lights an old rag.

'Spark 'er,' Billy calls out. 'Watch out down dere, Santy.'

Andy drops the lit rag into the chimney hole. Nothing happens. He puts his face over the opening, waits, staring.

The lick and the roar at once. A pop and a whoosh. Practically invisible. Except for the scorch.

Chapter IV – 1976

Viking 1

(May, 1976, 22 years old)

The Caribou Lounge is hazy with cigarette smoke. The muddled ruckus of conversations and bursts of laughter. The brief applause has just died down. Blackstrap stands on the raised stage, looking out over the crowd with his guitar in hand. His fingertips warm on the neck of the guitar bridge. He slides them back and forth. Once. Picks at a few strings without meaning anything by it. While he watches the different bodies and faces. Most of them familiar to him in various ways. The song has just ended. And people are moving back to their seats at the long tables in the hall. The scraping of chairs against tile.

Andy Coffin is behind him on drums. His face not quite healed.

Never will be. Burned smooth that way. And Pete Gilbert is on Blackstrap's right with his bass. As usual, the Saturday-night dance is packed to capacity. Drawing people from Cutland Junction, Shearstown Line, Port de Grave. And beyond.

No one ever thought that Blackstrap had such a voice in him. For someone who never said two words to most. That's what people were saying during the breaks for the first and second sets. They slapped him on the back. Told him what a fine job he'd done. It being his first time up on stage. Right on, b'y. Finest kind. People buying him beers or glasses of rum. Winking when the drinks were handed over. Months ago, Blackstrap had given serious thought to joining the band. Deciding against it at first. But then Andy Coffin had kept coming around. Asking him to play. And Blackstrap found it hard to say no to Andy. Especially with his new face. Blackstrap had thought that Andy might go into hiding after the burn. But it was the complete opposite. Like Andy wanted to be seen even more. Like he made a point of getting around. And getting right up in your face, too. He even took up smoking.

Andy had heard Blackstrap play guitar in midnight mass last Christmas. The first time in years Blackstrap's mother had led them back to church. Emily getting involved. Wanting Blackstrap to play guitar because the priest had mentioned the idea of a folk mass. Like the ones they had in St. John's. Young people enjoyed them. It opened the church to young people, the new priest explained. Made them feel more involved in the ceremony. Music has always been an integral part of the church. No harm in modernizing. Blackstrap's mother in church more often now. Telling Blackstrap she finds it peaceful to sit there in the quiet, sacred feel of the place. The wonder, she has said. The glorious, solemn wonder of those statues and crosses. All of it so ancient and ceremonial.

What Blackstrap likes most about being up on stage is the way the women's eyes keep steady on him. He likes the feeling of that. But he has to look down after a while. Watch the pick in his fingers hovering over the strings. It's too much to handle. Too many eyes on what he's doing. He looks at his boots. Smiles a little. Trying to remember the next song. Until he hears Andy Coffin's loud voice, calling out 'Black Velvet Band,' behind him.

Blackstrap leads them off with the opening chords. Slower than the traditional version. He peeks up. Sees a few smiling women in their seats. The ones not dancing with their heads swaying a little to the music. And some of the others grabbing a glance at him over the shoulders of the ones they're dancing with. Even turning their heads to keep eye contact.

Blackstrap shuts his eyes. Sings with velvet intention: 'Her eyes they shone like the diamond . . . you'd think she was queen of the land . . .' thinking of Agnes Bishop. Wishing she were there to see him. To hear this. He sees her eyes in all the eyes of those watching him. Maybe word will get back to her. Last he heard she had moved from Alberta to Nova Scotia. Where she was studying to be a doctor. Dr. Bishop. He opens his eyes to witness a sea of couples waltzing. Young and old alike. Couples close together. Waltzing in slow circles in the dim light. The sense of it settles his heart. The way they move together to the music at his hands. If they could stay that way. Always close and dancing. If life were only like that. Down in the back, a few others laughing and being rowdy. That sours him. Because it looks like the beginning of a fight. Most times there's one. Has to be one with the usual lot. He suspects Andy Coffin is paying particular attention to the scuffle. Watching with his eyes that look lidless now, wanting to join in if something breaks out.

Blackstrap keeps singing. Trying to keep those thoughts from hardening the lyrics. Only the words and the meaning, and the feeling from the meaning. When the door opens toward the corner at his left. His eyes rove that way. A woman coming in. And he knows her right away. The sadness and the sinking and the joy. And he misses the lyrics. The words escape him because they mean nothing to him now.

Jeans and a loose pink top. Boots. Leather purse over her shoulder. She watches ahead toward the tables. A few women wave excitedly to her. And she calmly waves back. Not so wound up. Gentler. She smiles. The women who were waving all point toward the stage. And the woman turns to look. At him. In wonder. Not singing anymore because she is there. She stares with those eyes that know him from childhood. Not the eyes of other women. The eyes that have been watching him all evening. But with the eyes of Agnes Bishop. She smiles in the way he remembers best. And he tries, but cannot sing. His voice lost while the

517

band plays on. So the people can keep dancing. So the song doesn't end so badly.

'Where's *Bareneed's Pride*?' Agnes asks. Glancing around the community wharf.

'Smashed up years ago,' Blackstrap says, like she should know. In fact, he's certain that she knows because she was in Newfoundland when it happened, even though he never spoke to her before she went away. She never heard of it from his lips, but she's heard of it. He's sure of that, and her asking now is only to make it seem like she has forgotten. It has slipped her mind. Being away, in her new life, has made her pretend to forget, because all the things from here, from Bareneed and Cutland Junction, cannot amount to anything compared to the really important things in her new life.

The idea of it irks him as he digs his boots into the side of the bank. The bank that used to be much steeper. A dead drop down to Bareneed beach. Until the grade was angled off. A make-work project years ago. A new wharf. Building a wharf on top of a wharf. The way it used to be. Money for doing nothing really. Only because people were out of jobs and needed to do something. He fast-steps down toward the shore. Keeping his balance. Trying not to tip his beer bottle.

'Aunt Myrtle told me, but I wasn't sure.' Agnes carefully stepping from the top of the incline. 'You know what she's like.'

'Yeah.' An intake of breath. Like the way things are is the way they were meant to be and there's nothing to be done about them. Steady with the beach rocks underfoot. He watches up at Agnes. Her figure stood there against the dark sky. He can't see her face, only her profile when she turns a little and watches the ground. Blackstrap making certain she doesn't slip. Her sneakers down over the bank. The momentum rushing her toward Blackstrap who catches her. Just to be safe. Her in his arms. He lets go right away. Because of the way she watches him. Too good. Too bad. He tips back a drink from his bottle. Then hands it to Agnes. Old friends despite everything. She takes hold of it, but doesn't drink. Her eyes filled with interest and worry. Not what he wants.

'How?' she asks.

'How what?'

'How was it smashed?'

'Don't remember.'

'Yes, you do.' The tease of a smile. Genuine or not.

'Storm.'

'Was it stolen?'

That had been the story that came out of it. That's what people were saying. Stolen and smashed up by young delinquents.

He shakes his head.

'Who was in it?'

'Me.' He admits this for her. Not for anyone else ever.

'Were you alone?' Interested now in the truth of what happened. She has a careful sip from the bottle. Slowly hands it back to him. The way she is looking at his face. Different. He knows that she is thinking of him in the water.

He nods, recalling the feeling of heading for those rocks. His eyes on her now, knowing it was about her. Him almost dead. But feeling good now to have Agnes back. Worried a bit for him. How much? Not enough. Back in the place where they used to come. Feeling sad. And a little angry. His thoughts going to years ago. Their plans for a house. An old house in Bareneed all done up. He wonders if she is home for good now, but he won't ask. His eyes go to her hand. He wants to hold it.

But, instead, he turns away a little to get the pain out of his back. When he walks, his back and right leg still hurt. From the fall off the ladder. On the drive from the Caribou Lounge. On Shearstown Line down to Bareneed beach, Agnes had asked about Andy Coffin's face. Blackstrap had explained about hauling Andy down the wooden ladder. Blackstrap pulling Andy close to the edge of the roof where the ladder was set. The cursing and sounds of misery. And the smell of burned flesh had scared the hell out of Blackstrap. Regardless, he had managed to position Andy on his back. With his head close to the eave. Then Blackstrap had stepped onto the ladder. Taken a few rungs down. His upper body still above the roof. The only way to get Andy down would be to grab him under the arms. And slide him down the rungs. People had gathered at the base of the ladder. The ambulance was on its way. Coming from Brigus or Bay Roberts. That's all that mattered. He wouldn't listen to anything else. The calls to be careful. The voices telling him. Andy's father trying to climb the ladder. All of that just made him nervous. He kept blocking it out. Something had to be done right away. He couldn't stand the sight of pain. He couldn't stand looking at Andy lying on the roof. Gritting his teeth and beginning to sob. Trying to touch and not touch his face. The roof not a place to be. He had pulled Andy's arms until Andy's face was beneath his. Then he hooked his arm under Andy's left arm. Wrapped it around Andy's chest. Then backed down the ladder. Taking the weight of the body. The smell of charred flesh nearly a retch in his throat. Like a God-awful barbecue. As he slid Andy down. Easy at first. Until Andy's legs and then his boots made it from the roof and all of Andy's weight was on the ladder. And instead of keeping straight up, Andy's legs swung toward the ground. The back of Andy's head in Blackstrap's face. The smell of scorched hair. Andy made a sound. And the weight yanked at the muscles in Blackstrap's back. Blackstrap held on. Holding the body weight in against him. A mistake. Trying to move. So that Andy could get his scrambling feet on a rung. Blackstrap with one hand on the rail. Squinting with the pressure. One hand around Andy's chest. Muscles tearing up in his neck and back. The weight too much. He tried squatting Andy against the ladder. And clutching on to the ladder with his left hand too. But he missed his grip. Drifted away in a motion that could almost have been stopped. But not quite. Gravity pulling. Weightless and weightless and weightlessly heavy to the ground. Holding on to Andy. Hugging him from behind. So that he would land on Blackstrap. Then came the slamming. Rattling. Rock-hard ground smack. The crack to the back of his head. Skull harder than earth. How that was made. Andy on top of him. The crowd of people around him. Looking down. He was fine. He could not yet move. But not dead. The crowd picked Andy up and helped Blackstrap to his feet. He could hear the ambulance in the distance. His back hurting. His head a mess. A rumbling in the earth. The train passing through. Before he realized the ambulance was in the driveway. And the paramedics took Andy away. Asked if Blackstrap was okay. Checked him over. Sat him down to be sure. Because people said what happened. Blackstrap not saying a word.

Nodding. Fine. Yes. Then the ambulance gone. All of it in what seemed like seconds.

Andy's sister had driven her mother and father to the hospital. Following after the ambulance. And after a session of spinning in his head that gradually focused, Blackstrap got back in his pickup. Took a good look up at the roof while people on the street still watched him. The height making him feel sick in his stomach. Noticed that there was smoke streaming from the front eaves. He drove home. Called the volunteer fire department.

Eight months ago. Andy's hands not too badly burned where they had gripped the inner brick edge of the chimney. Still able to hold drumsticks. His face a different story. His face able to hold the attention of anyone in a room.

Agnes watching Blackstrap finishing the story. 'You've got a great voice,' she says. Because she had finally heard it. It had come back to him after her smile at seeing him. 'It's beautiful. When'd you start that? You never sang before.' She nudges him with her hip. 'Not to me.' A sweet smile that makes him want to sing. That reconnects the two of them just like that. But he won't sing. Not like this. In the dark. In the quiet. He stares out over the calm water. Shrugs. He feels the heat in his cheeks. He looks up. Over his shoulder at the headland. A hole in the deep-blue sky. He's heard something about an excavation company wanting to dig into the headland and truck off loads of fill. Turn it into a pit. But the government has said no. Despite the fact that most workers in the area wanted the project to go ahead. For the sake of the jobs. But an environmental group led by Mrs. Foote kicked up a stink, and the project was cancelled. For once, Blackstrap sided with the protesters. Without telling anyone what he thought.

'Why didn't you ever sing for me?'

'I never sang.'

'Until when?'

'While ago.'

They both look out over the water. A sound of small waves brushing up against the shore. A thousand trickles in the night. Beach rocks quietly shifting. No wind to speak of. Plenty of stars. No moon and no clouds.

Blackstrap turns to look for the moon. *I never sang until you left.*

'What?' Agnes asks. 'What're you looking for?'

'The moon.'

'It's over there.' She points, remembering where it should be. Knowing even after having been away. Fitting back with the place she knows. 'I used to come here and watch it. Remember?'

He should have known too. Maybe he did. Maybe he wanted her to find it for him. His head not right after that fall. Certain memories weaker or gone. Direction sometimes changing without him knowing. He nods. 'How long you home for?' He finishes off his beer. Reaching back, he flings the bottle toward the ocean where it plunks into the water.

'Five days.'

Five days.

Then gone again.

That's not enough. Not enough time. It makes him feel even worse. Like he might say something bad to her. Five days. Leaving him. He takes the other beer from the pocket of his jean jacket. Pops the cap off with the rim of his belt buckle.

'I'm starting my internship.'

'Dr. Bishop.' It comes out wrong. He takes a mouthful of beer. Looks at her. Swallows. Proud of her despite everything. Watching her like a challenge. Another mouthful. You're something else. You'll always be.

Agnes smiles in a way that says she's had a few drinks. Her heart coming out more. Her goodness better than ever. 'How're your mom and dad doing?'

'Fine.'

She knows it's not true.

He knows she's really asking about his mother. But it's his father she should be asking after now. He seems the sick one. His mother getting better. Stronger. Planning on something. She's told him about the Arctic. How she wants to go with dogs and a sled. How she wants to see all the white stretching off for all eternity. A secret between them. Promise not to tell your father. His father faltering. Forgetting.

'Who're you staying with?'

'Aunt Myrtle. Mom and Dad are back too.'

Blackstrap wishes that he had a boat. He wants to take her on the water. And feel the calm sea beneath them. In a boat. Out with the water and the sky and just him and her. Anchored over in Deep Gulch beyond the cliffs. Sitting on the deck and watching her face in this blue light. With the water beneath them, life would be fit to stand.

If he'd known, he would have gotten the key to Andy's boat. If he'd known they were going to end up here. But there was nothing in his head about plans when he saw her. When he talked to her. No plans when he was next to her.

He turns to look at her face. The headland behind her. And his breath drops out of him. Her face. He can't stop looking. The sight of her face softens every spot in him. Her eyes watching his eyes. Wanting to say something. Hiding something and going softer. Prettier. Still. Sorry. She looks away. So sorry. Raises her left hand to put her hair behind her ear. The glint of a ring in that blue light. On her ring finger. A diamond.

Blackstrap's nose grows warm. He takes a step away. Further down the beach. Watching the rocks. The beer bottle cold in his hand. He chugs back the rest of it. Holds the empty. Stares at the empty he can almost see through. The brown glass. He had been thinking about gathering driftwood for a fire. But that's no good now. He wipes at his nose with his shirt sleeve. And grips the bottle by its stubby neck. Hurls it up into the air where it rises then drops, popping to pieces on the beach rocks.

Then he looks back.

To see that she is still stood there.

Not calling out his name.

Not stepping after him.

He can barely make her out.

Mostly in shadow.

Then black.

Never there at all.

Nothing but an outline.

Like the headland behind her.

As he keeps moving and angles away toward the bank. Her shadow slips aside. Slips across the water with moonlight on it.

For all of his years.

That is how he remembers her most.

(July, 1976)

Blackstrap sits in his Galaxie 500 with his eyes on Agnes' old house. He is parked across the road. The tires resting on bulldozed land. An old fisherman's house once there, in place of the car. The slate foundation, bits of wood and brick now buried beneath the earth. A house that had been moved up from Bareneed back in the 60s. Moved in sections on a flatbed and reassembled. Torn down now. He was one of the two men hired to pull it down. Hammer and drawbar. Three days' work. First day, up on the roof, watching out for rotted boards while the other fellow tore out the inside walls. Almost went through the roof twice. Caught himself. The roof gone with only the dark rafters left. Then the west side wall of the top floor. Beating out lengths of board. Full one inch thick and a foot or more wide. Old boat board. That's how they used to build the houses. Most of it pine, darkened by age on the outside but still good board, light and dry and blonde with an orange tint inside. Smashing it loose in sections with the clapboard attached to the other side. The walls falling in chunks. The flies were the worst of it. On the second day, the front wall of the top storey. Gone. Stood there with the land spread out in front of him. Agnes' old house always there across the road. He wishes it was her house he was tearing down. The sky going on forever, the trees too. The other fellow at the chimney, knocking it with a sledgehammer. The whole works tipping a bit. The mortar loose. A few starlings swooping up out of the top. The other fellow not able to get the chimney down. Too careful, too watchful of his feet. Blackstrap went over and stood up on a chair with pieces of the floor gone beneath him. And smashed the brick until the whole length of it went over. Tipping out and falling to the tall grass with not much sound at all. The bottom storey taken down on the third day. Only thing left were the old milled studs, rough and rounded on their edges, two storeys in length. So dark brown they were almost black. They took them down and saved them for the guy who was tearing the house down. He wanted them for something. Paid in cash. Plus Blackstrap's share of the scrap wood. For burning. And old furniture he brought home to his mother. Because she likes old furniture. He didn't know at first. The first few pieces he brought home. Cut up for burning. Good and dry and made to rage the fire. But when his mother saw the pieces stacked near the stove, she bent toward them. Ran her hand over the old varnished surfaces. Even picked up a few pieces, trying to figure out how to put them back together. Looking up at him with an expression. Like he had done her harm.

'Alphonsus,' she had said. That name she never called him. 'Did you do this?'

After that, he brought back the pieces of furniture in one piece. To see what she might want to keep. His mother found a place for each one. In the living room.

A new bungalow soon to be built in place of the old fisherman's house. The lumber stacked there for cribbing in the concrete foundation. Trees chainsawed down in a wide area. So the roots won't bother the house. So the bugs don't get too thick. So the crows don't nest and bark in the early mornings. Plenty of construction. With everyone leaving. Not many left to do the job for those staying anyway, wanting to remain despite everything.

The bonnet of Blackstrap's car glimmers under the moonlight. Blackstrap washed and waxed the car that morning. He hears the whistle of the last train leaving for the night. Just as a car goes by in front of him. Dodge Dart. Clunker of a car. Heavy like a tank. Like a locomotive. Mildred Piercy at the driver's wheel. On her way to the Thursday-night card game at the fire hall. Blackstrap glances at the clock on his dashboard. The second hand revolving smoothly. Like it's in water. Mildred's late for cards. Maybe she's not going there at all. Maybe she's going to Walt Coombs' place instead.

Watching the big window, he expects to see Agnes step up to the glass. Alone in that house. Some true part of her living on in those rooms. A ghost that knows no better, only where it should or must be. The thought brings to mind Ruth. That night he smashed up his boat. Her hand on the throttle. He would swear that it was all real. Not just his head haunting him, but her. He thinks about Agnes up in Halifax. Considers flying there to find her.

Why did Agnes go to the beach with him? When she was home. Why did she want to be with him? To torment him? What was in her mind then? Her stood on the beach. Nothing to her when he left and waited for her in the car. Not a word between them when he drove her home.

Earlier that night, Andy Coffin had called. To tell Blackstrap that he'd got Brent Parsons to agree to play fiddle in their band. Andy's half-plugged voice through the telephone. Blackstrap was almost used to it now. The fiddle always interested him. It had been his idea to add one to the group. A couple of years ago, he'd dug out the fiddle that used to belong to his father. Started practicing. But he never stuck with it. Too much practice involved. Not as easy as the guitar. Although he told himself that he'd go back at it one day.

There was something else too that Andy Coffin told him. About Agnes being engaged. An announcement printed in the *Evening Telegram*. Even though Blackstrap had already known. Had heard it from the boys at Wilf's Place. He had gone out and bought the paper. Found the photograph. The picture of Agnes. So close beside another man. Her hands on his shoulders. Someone telling her to pose that way. It made his eyes burn. And both of them smiling. Like Blackstrap had nothing to do with them at all. The man's name was Peter MacLeod, Andy told him. His hair was combed just so. He had on a suit. And a tie. He had a likeable face. Not a face that was easy to hate.

Halifax. It isn't that far away, he thinks, taking up the newspaper. From that place right next to him where Agnes used to sit. Tears out the photo and lays it on the seat. He can drive it in two days. Ten hours to the ferry in Port aux Basque on the west coast of the island. Across the strait. And then how far from North Sydney to Halifax? He isn't exactly sure. No more than half a day. If he remembers his maps.

He takes another look at the empty house. Then at the photo on the seat. Another car goes by. A Ford pickup with Johnny Gosse at the wheel. Going where? Who knows. He picks up the bit of newspaper. Folds it and stuffs it away in his wallet.

Chapter V – 1977

Gary Gilmore

(January, 1977, 23 years old)

Blackstrap hears this on the radio: 'EMI Records fails to renew the contract of punk rock group the Sex Pistols.' Driving in his car. Seeing nothing but the snowstorm to all sides of him. The way the headlights stretch into the blizzard. Show him nothing but white. He wonders who the Sex Pistols are. If Sex Pistols is another name for cock. If an animal stepped into the blinding white, its eyes would be electric green or orange. Then it would be struck down. Erased. Out in a blizzard that made the land. One huge terrain. Where cars and machines were invisible.

Halifax was nothing like he'd expected. He hadn't realized there were bay communities around Nova Scotia. Places like in Newfoundland. On his first few days in Nova Scotia, he had driven around to some of them. They had old houses and fishing boats tied up. Were called villages. But it wasn't like Newfoundland. The people were different. In another place, Annapolis Valley, there were apples being picked from trees. Apples everywhere. They grew red apples there. Not that far from Newfoundland. A nine-hour sail across the Atlantic. Where it was only possible to grow crab apples. That much of a difference in the weather. The snow had been the same. The winter blizzards. But people told him that spring came earlier there. He thought he might see it for himself. But he ended up not staying that long. If he had stayed, he might have been arrested.

His first night in Halifax, he had been in a bar. Met a man with a neighbour from Newfoundland. The man said that he liked Newfoundlanders. They were hard workers. Good people. Trustworthy. Reliable. Interesting things to hear from a man. A few beers later, the man offered Blackstrap a job on the Halifax docks.

'Doing what?' Blackstrap had asked.

'Lifting,' said the man. 'Nothing to it.'

He had slept in his car that night. Stretched out on the back seat nearly long enough to get comfortable. But colder and colder as the hours went on. And the beer waking him up to go outside and piss in an alleyway.

The next morning, he showed up with only a few hours' sleep and wandered around, looking for the man. He was about to give up when he found him. Worked eight hours loading boxes into a truck. The foreman found him a room in an old house down past the train station.

He drank more than usual when he wasn't working, and couldn't bring himself to look for Agnes. It was the loneliness that led him to the bars and kept him half-snapped most times.

There was a naval base near where he worked. Sometimes he saw the navy men going around in their uniforms. He gave some thought to enlisting. Getting the hell out of Halifax. Off of land altogether. One way to get back to the sea.

In the blizzard. In the quiet car. On his way home to Cutland Junction. He shakes his head at the thought of chasing after Agnes. What was he expecting? To take her back to Newfoundland with him? A foolish idea now.

He imagined going out to sea. On one of the big grey frigates where he used to see them tied up behind the wire fence. Two weeks after landing in Halifax, he went into the recruitment office. Talked to the recruitment officer who turned out to be a nice fellow. Bright and friendly. Mannerly. Not nasty and shouting. Like expected from movies.

'Where you from?' the officer had asked Blackstrap.

'Newfoundland.'

'A Newfie? Good for you. My wife's from there. From Glovertown. Pam Greening.'

Blackstrap shook his head. He didn't know Pam Greening. Only Pam Kearney from Shearstown Line.

'Here's an application, if you're interested.' The officer slid the paper across his desk. 'And some information here. More pamphlets over there.' In a room with posters on the walls showing men in uniform doing different things. 'Spend any time on the water?'

'Yes, sir. Plenty.'

'Perfect.'

Blackstrap had taken the application and glanced at one of the posters. Big grey ships at sea. He knew some of the words on the application. But knew it would be impossible to fill out the entire form. He imagined the look of it with his scribbles in only some of the spaces. Also, they would know he couldn't read or write when they interviewed him. Or maybe they wouldn't ask. Wouldn't need to know. He wondered if you had to read and write. It was a question that was hard to ask. Did it matter?

Five months ago. When Agnes was back in Newfoundland. On their pickup ride from the Caribou Lounge to Bareneed beach. She had mentioned the name of the university where she was studying.

On his day off, three weeks after landing in Halifax, he finally found himself in the right frame of mind. Something that just needed to be done. He went to the university campus and walked around. Feeling like he wasn't allowed there. But no one bothered him. No one asked him a question. They thought he might belong. Not so different from the others. Or that he worked there. Maybe he worked in maintenance. Or fixed furnaces in the buildings. Maybe they thought that. But he was the same age as a lot of them. Why would they think he wasn't just like them?

When he first visited campus, he thought he would come across Agnes. Right away. As easy as pie. He feared it in a way. Feared seeing her walking right in front of him. In this new world of hers. But there were thousands of people coming and going. Watching their faces, it hurt his eyes. All that steady movement. It made him think of time passing, and he wanted to leave.

But he had forced himself to find the medical building. Gone in there. What to do next? He had found the classrooms. Looked in the small windows. They were like movie theatres. Hundreds of people in there watching one person talking. That had been enough. He went to a bar and drank to steady himself.

He visited campus again. Six times over six weeks. Finally feeling comfortable there. Thinking he might be able to do it himself, become a doctor. It didn't look so hard. These people with books. He found the bookstore and went inside. The stacks of thick hardcover books in the aisles. Cardboard tags hanging off the front of the shelves, in front of each stack. People picking up the books and opening them. Their eyes skimming the pages. Others were just walking around and talking. Normal people dressed different ways. But then he'd see them reading.

He never came across Agnes. He thought that he might run into her in the bars down around Barrington Street. In the Seahorse Tavern where he liked watching the oldtimers drinking and talking. A few of them had been in WWII, and he overheard stories. Old men still rattled by the memories. One of them in tears whenever he spoke of it. Every day no matter what. The story of how his friend went out for him on a mission. A fighter pilot who never came back. In his place.

But he never did see Agnes. There were several times when he thought he saw her alone at a bar. Drinking beer after beer, he might look around and see a woman who had long, sandy-blonde hair. Was the same size as Agnes. But the face. The face never the same. Impossible. The eyes different. The chin too wide or narrow. The lips smaller. The cheekbones not so high. There were plenty of opportunities when a woman squeezed in next to him at the bar. Plenty of young people around. The bars crowded. A woman would look up at him. Smile. Her money in her hands to buy her drink. And he would nod to be polite. But that was it. The way a woman watched him. One who wasn't Agnes. He'd feel poisoned by the attention. Then he'd sip his glass of draft. Something new to him. Cheap, pale, watery beer that they never had back in Newfoundland. Beer that they poured from a tap. And people bought by the glass or jug. It was a party beer. A beer that was swallowed fast. Because there was nothing to it. He kept drinking.

Then he would walk down Barrington Street. A mile east. Toward the railway station. The trains he sometimes looked at in the yard. Remembering the earth-heavy rumble from home. From in his yard when the train went by. Always hookers down that way across from the station. He liked the attention they gave him. The way they joked with him. He liked the honesty of their words. The easy movements of their bodies. But he never went home with them. He lived nearby and they knew it. Sometimes, he would stand against one of the old stone buildings. The corner of South Street or Tobin. Light a cigarette. Just to watch what was going on. Cars coming and going. Headlights slowing. Some of the hookers were in hard shape. Every now and then a woman would disappear. Another woman or two would take her place. They would be the same. But they would be different. Taught to behave like they were made for one thing. Walking around in clothes like that. Where did they come from? Who let them do this to themselves? Where were their mothers? Their fathers? These women were alive. They were blessed. They were beautiful in a way he never thought possible.

One or two would be beaten up. Not in front of him, but off in one of the cars. He couldn't understand that. What sort of man would do that? From under what dark rock of shame?

He wanted to go up to some of the cars. Stick his head in the window. Right there beside the hooker and look at the guy. Check the guy over to see that he was a nice fellow. Maybe just a bit lonely and pathetic. To look into his eyes. To make sure the guy, sitting there in the shadows at the steering wheel, wanting to drive away with a woman, was harmless. Either way, it was sad. One long silent curse at someone. And it was mean.

He would stand there. Smoke his cigarette. The sole of one boot up against the stone building he was leaning on. Sometimes, he would take a few steps ahead. And he would see the eyes in the car, shifting from the hooker to him. And the car would move ahead a little. And the hooker would look back at him. Like he was a problem. A nuisance.

One time, he moved ahead when one of the girls was shouting. A new girl named Bonnie. Only a child by the looks of her. Younger than Blackstrap with that make-up making her like something from a nightmare circus. A man with her by the hair. Trying to pull her into the car. Blackstrap had run toward the man. And the man had raised his arm and an explosion let go. Blackstrap had stopped. Struck by something. The man gone with a screech of tires. The girl on the sidewalk. The other women tending to her now. Taking her off to make sure she was okay. Not a tear out of her. Just quiet. The world quiet around him. The other cars gone after that sound. And he had remained. Thinking he was hit. But there was no wound. He looked over his shoulder at the building. A gunshot that had missed him. Then he was on the ground.

The women looking down at the scene. Like someone might have been killed. Another beer was what he needed. He was fine. They stood over him and watched his eyes slowly shut.

The bars in Nova Scotia had different names on them. The beverage houses would close early. Sell only beer. The cabarets would stay open much later. Served beer and liquor. It was a place where he could get a shot of rum. After the beer had given him all that beer could give. There was a cabaret up across from the artillery. A few streets up over the hill from Barrington on Brunswick where he went late at night. They had a dance floor there. He liked to watch women dance and think of Agnes. The women didn't remind him of Agnes because they were nothing like her. They were only female. None of them could be anything like her. Agnes wouldn't dance the way they did. Dancing because people were watching. She would dance because the music was making her. Doing it to her body. Into it. Like she used to dance with him. Listening to the music. Watching his face. His face and the music making her dance. A bit of a smile on her lips when she looked at the ground. None of them talked the way she did. They seemed fake. Giddy and foolish. They were in it for something. It wasn't natural. But sometimes he'd feel okay about it. He'd have a few more beers. Then start drinking rum. And he wouldn't like to watch the women dance. He'd shoot back the rum because they were interested in him. And that was the thing to do. There was no stopping him. That was the message. He'd keep drinking. To kill something off. To make the way they were watching him go away. The women serving bar were impressed. They had secret conversations about him. There he was, shooting back rum after rum. In a small plain glass. No ice. No cola.

After so much rum, he'd leave the bar. Find a pay phone outside. He'd call the operator and ask for a number for Agnes Bishop. He'd say, 'from Newfoundland.' There was never a listing. He wondered if she had a phone. He'd ask for numbers for the places where they stayed on campus. The residence? the operator would ask. Yes, he'd say. That's it. The residence. Then he'd call the different places. Ask for her. A young woman answering a phone. Who he thought might be Agnes. No one named Agnes Bishop lived there. Were they lying? Because she didn't want to talk to him? He began to suspect that she didn't live in the residence. That she lived in an apartment somewhere. Maybe with the guy. That rotten fucker, MacLeod. Or she wasn't even in Halifax. He began to suspect that *she* had lied to him. That she wasn't studying medicine. That she was doing something else. Just to confuse him. Studying to be a she-wolf, or a taxidermist. What he'd like to do to her if he saw her now. Those hookers in his mind. It was ugly, getting uglier.

He started buying flasks of Newfoundland Screech. Carrying them around in his pocket. He couldn't find her. He hated where he was. He loved where he was. If he had enough drinks in him, he loved where he was. Nothing to do with him, nothing to do with his father and mother. Nothing to do with Newfoundland. Nothing.

He'd rest his back against the stone building and drink from his flask. The women leaned in the car windows. Talking like they already knew the man. Friendly as anything. Their new best friends. Money. Money was the real whore. He gave them money when some of them asked and he had a little extra. But it was never enough to change anything.

When his flask was empty, he'd wander over to the station yard. Walk around the big engines and cars. Run his hand over the steel wheels. Want them to roll out of here. He'd touch the train body. Talk to the train. 'Go,' he'd quietly say. Like it was an animal that recognized him. Just him and the train under moonlight.

Then he'd go back to his room. The hookers would say goodnight to him on the way. Like they were normal. Nice young women. Like they might be his sister in a room. In a house at bedtime. And it was time to say goodnight. Simple and sweet as that. It would bring tears to his eyes. Something like love in him. The sounds of them saying goodnight. One after the other. Goodnight, Blackstrap. They knew his name because he wanted them to know it. Goodnight, Blacky. Sleep tight, honey.

Going into the rooming house, he'd always be quiet. He wouldn't trip up over the stairs. Taking them one at a time. Quiet as a mouse. He'd get in his room. Shut the door. He'd sit on his bed and watch the wall. A small room. In a city that seemed stuck between old and new. He'd fall back on his bed. Look at the stupid ceiling. He shouldn't be there. He didn't want any of it. He'd put his arm up on his forehead and talk to himself. He'd turn on the bed. See himself in the full-length mirror on the closet door. His dim reflection. His mom alone in her room. Back home. His father in the house. The house surrounded by trees. His brother and sister dead and buried. The points on a map. The distance traced from his house in Cutland Junction to those two plots in Bareneed graveyard. His head a mess. The hookers. Agnes. His work on the docks. He'd go to sleep, but never sleep all the way. Agnes. Just don't be a whore. Like those women. Agnes. Sleep. And the steady thump of a bed against the wall next to him.

On his eighth visit to campus, nursing a hangover on his day off, he went into the medical building. Knowing the doors to enter by. They were made of steel and glass. The layout of the building familiar to him. He knew where everything was. He went to the cafeteria in the basement. Bought an egg sandwich. A milkshake in a box. He shook it and sat at a table in the corner. So he could see everyone. He noticed that his hands were dirty. Grime beneath his fingernails from the grease on the forklift. He'd taken to fixing it on the dock. There were black lines of dirt in the lines on his hands. He couldn't scrub it off. The people who came and went were all clean. Dressed respectable. Even the ones who seemed dirty were just trying to look that way. They didn't get dirty doing anything. Long hair or long beards. Old clothes. Others looking perfect. That's why they were there, wasn't it? Or maybe for all sorts of different reasons.

He was chewing his egg sandwich. Checking the way a young guy was dressed. When he saw someone in the corners of his eyes. Agnes coming into the big room. Not a different set of eyes. Not smaller lips or thinner chin. Agnes. The rush of her right there sped his heart. She was with another girl and a guy. MacLeod, the guy from the photograph. All of it real to him now with their bodies close together like that. He looked down at the table. Not wanting to be seen. His heart thudding in his chest. His palms turning sweaty. Why here? What was he here for? Feeling like a jerk caught at something. The noise in the cafeteria went up a notch. The egg sandwich lost its taste as his mouth went dry. He raised his eyes to find Agnes. She seemed to have more energy. Talked more than she used to. Like she needed to keep talking. To pretend it was alright. She talked in a way he never knew. Not like that with him. She never talked so much. Acting like any other person in the room.

Blackstrap watched her going down the line. Picking out what she was going to eat. She had a tray that she carried. Her eyes searching for a table. Ahead of the other two, she led the way. Her eyes scanned near his table. Then ran right over him where he was sitting. She didn't recognize him. Why would she in this place? How would she ever know him? In his baseball cap and unshaven face.

He watched her sit and talk and eat. The conversation was full of laughs. He had no idea what it was about. One of the saddest things he ever saw.

When she was done, Agnes left with the guy from the newspaper photo. Blackstrap followed after them. There were others around. No one seemed to notice anyone. He stayed far back and watched them talking. He couldn't hear what they were saying. Which was fine with him. They were close. He could see that much. They reached the end of the hallway. Went up a wide flight of stairs. He kept after them. Up the stairs and down another hallway. Two of them stopped outside a doorway where other people were waiting. And they kissed goodbye. Their lips like that. Meant to be. For how long? Blackstrap's body wanting desperately to stop them. Agnes went into the room. And the guy walked on. Blackstrap's eyes burning. He looked at the number over the door: 214. And then he followed after the guy.

At the end of the corridor, the guy went down a flight of stairs. Blackstrap followed to the bottom floor. The guy was walking along with doors to all sides of him. Near the end of the corridor, he turned and pushed open a door. When Blackstrap got there, he saw it was a bathroom. He waited. Watching the symbol of a man printed on wood. He wondered if it was done with a stencil. It looked that way. He pushed the door open and went in.

The guy had just finished at the urinal and was looking at his book bag on the floor. Then he went over to the mirrors and sinks. Washed his hands. He spent a good minute washing his hands. Rinsing them off. Practicing to be a doctor. He was watching his face in the mirror while he kept soaping his hands. He frowned. Seemed disappointed with something.

When Blackstrap came up to the next sink, the guy looked over and nodded. Gave a little smile that was friendly enough. Blackstrap nodded back. He ran water over his hands. Dried them with the paper towel. He was done before the guy was finished. Then he stood close. Watching while the guy turned off the tap with a paper towel. Before folding it over and drying his hands with it. So that when the guy turned, he stood facing Blackstrap.

Blackstrap reached back for his wallet. He opened it. Flipped through the plastic sleeves with the pictures inside. There was a school photo of Agnes in one of the sleeves. The one she had given him when she graduated from high school. He held it up. He pointed at it, his breath getting troubled. And the guy's eyes went there. He shook his head when his eyes moved back to Blackstrap.

'Is that . . . ?' asked the guy. But he didn't finish. He shifted a little. The thoughts in his head doing that. But it looked like he was trying to get away. 'Where'd you—' To get out of whatever this was he was in.

Blackstrap shifted too. To keep facing the guy. He looked at the picture. Agnes. And his breathing turned hotter in his nostrils. And the heat came to his face. Agnes. The way the guy had spoken. The sound of his voice. She's not yours, Blackstrap said to himself. She can't be yours. Not by the looks of you.

The guy's face was confused. 'How . . . ?' His eyes went to the waste-basket. Like he wanted, more than anything, to get rid of the paper towel in his hand.

Blackstrap thought to say something. To explain. His throat contracted. He swallowed. Go home, he warned himself. Back to Newfoundland. Just go home and leave what is changed alone. But his hand shot out. And he shoved the guy. A quick slap with his flat palm. Like a punch in the chest. The guy stumbled back. Hit the paper towel machine with his shoulder. He winced and shook his head. His eyes going angry. His lips tightening up. The guy not so innocent now. Not so easy-going. Not so gentle. He looked mean. Ready to fight. That was all Blackstrap needed. He grabbed the guy with both hands. Pulled at the front of his shirt. Flung him sideways toward the open cubicle. The guy ended up right in there. Banging around with his arms out. And as Blackstrap turned, he saw another fellow stood by the doorway. Having just come in.

'Hey?' said the fellow by the door.

Blackstrap ignored him. Went after the guy in the cubicle. Had his arm across the guy's throat. His knee against one leg. His teeth clamped shut. Agnes' name. That's all there was in his head. Her face. Shoving his arm in tighter. When he saw the face turning purple, he flung the guy against the other wall. The steel making a racket. Echoing in the hollow bathroom. Someone was pulling at his arm. The fellow who had come in. Blackstrap swung around and smacked him. Drove him back toward the sink. He heard glass shatter. Maybe it was one of the mirrors. Pieces fell to the floor. He raised his fist and hit the guy. Spring-loaded muscle. Pounded him in the face. In the stomach. In the nose. In the cheek. Like a ricochet that wouldn't ever stop.

Blood was running from the guy's nose. From his lips that split open. On his teeth. He could see the blood coming with every punch. With every time he pulled back his fist. Smearing across his knuckles. There was more blood. Red as anything. It kept him going. Spreading. Flickering on the wall. On the white toilet. Seeping into clothes. Not a breath out of him. He saw the toilet. The water. Shoved the guy's head in there. The water going red. Cloudy trails. He felt hands on him again. The fellow he had thrown against the mirror. And another guy. He spun around. Hit two of them. One fell down sideways and never got up. The other just slid back a bit. He was bigger. Then Blackstrap saw the guy from the photo. His head out of the toilet on the floor. Bleeding. He turned away. Saw the guy's book bag over by the hand dryer. He went to it, reached down, grabbed it and ran. Through the door. Out in the corridor. People looking at him. At his aching hand he was flicking a bit. He checked back over his shoulder. No one coming after him. The other two helping the guy on the floor. In blood. Maybe. Reminding him of that woman. On the ice floes. The seal hunt. That woman. Who had been torn by seals. Her face on television. In the newspapers. The stitches. Claiming it was the sealers. Claiming it was him who had done it. Barbarians. Him with the club rising up. The men gathered round. The club coming down. The reporter only seeing so much on film. It looked like him. Clubbing the woman. The famous footage that ran on TVs around the world. The police paying him a visit. The other sealers telling the police it was Blackstrap who saved the woman. Finally, no charges were laid. But the nuisance of it all the same. And no one knowing the truth of the reported lie.

He kept running. Then slowed down. Went back up over the flight of stairs. Found the classroom Agnes had gone in: 214. He remembered. He sat on the bench outside. Breathing hard as his heartbeat. Watched the door. Hoping that no one would come along. Not Agnes. Not yet. He needed to get his heartbeat settled. There were a few students waiting outside. To go in or to meet someone coming out. They looked at him every now and then. He got up and set the book bag in the corner. Far enough away, so that it seemed left behind. He should wash his fist. The left one that he had used. It was throbbing. Maybe something broken. Blood on it. If he did, it would be too late to see her. He would miss her. On his feet, he watched toward the doorway. Then up at the clock. The second hand smoothly revolving. How long before she would come out? He tried wiping the blood in the back of his jeans. Dissatisfied, he put his hands in his jean jacket pockets. A sharp aching pain in his bones. With a steady pulse in his skin. The skin scraped open by bone or tooth. His breathing not so bad now. He checked down the corridor.

No one coming.

No one seeing him.

No one pointing.

He sat on the bench again.

After a while, he heard an ambulance siren. From out around the building somewhere. It brought him to his feet. It might not be an ambulance. He checked for the doors that would take him out. A wall of them down over four wide stairs. He went outside for a while, walked away and found a bench. Watched the building from a distance for signs of trouble. All those windows. He shouldn't stick around. But he thought he might never see Agnes again. Not ever another chance.

When enough time passed to be safe, he went back inside. The classroom doors had just opened. A rush of chatter and movement. It was difficult to see Agnes. But she stopped. A book bag over her shoulder. Talking with another girl who left after a few seconds. He sat back on the bench. Nonchalant. Agnes looking around for someone. She seemed a bit confused as she came toward the bench. Her eyes right on him but not seeing him. Then she slowed down as she realized. As she came to believe that he could be there. Was there. Across all that water and all that land.

He was there.

She started to smile.

And it was gorgeous.

'What're you doing here?' The smile bigger now. She sat right next to him.

He shook his head.

Then she saw something in him. He had no idea what. What his face was telling her.

'How'd you find me?'

'I just came.'

'Easy as that.' She laughed a little.

He watched the floor, the tile. 'You told me where you were.'

She wasn't saying anything. So he looked at her. Her eyes were on his hands. He was fingering his hurt hand without knowing it. Knew better than to look at her then.

'What happened to your hand?' She reached out. Touched him. Like she was going to take his hand in hers. Like it was the thing to do. Natural. The way it used to be. Her looking after him. Always concerned about the slightest thing. But she stopped. Just when her fingers touched.

Because the wound was fresh.

Because the blood was new.

'Work.'

'You're working?' But something about her didn't believe him.

When he glanced up, he saw her scanning the ten or fifteen people still hanging around outside the classroom.

'I'm gonna join the navy,' he said.

Agnes said: 'Oh,' in a quiet, surprised way. She seemed disappointed, which made him feel better. Gave him a little hope. But when she checked his hand again, it made her stand up. Pull away from him.

'Did you see Peter?'

'Who?'

She looked down at his face. She touched her lips. And he saw the diamond ring. 'He's supposed to meet me here,' she said quietly, her voice going even lower toward the end.

It was enough. It was all. It was Peter over him.

He stood from the bench. 'Nice to see you,' he said. In a voice not nearly his own. 'I've got to get to work.'

'I've got another class.' She peeked at the round-faced clock on the wall. 'You're living here,' she said.

'Just a while.' He stared at the tile. 'Until the navy.' Couldn't keep his eyes on hers. Revealed like that. Too much to take. Too much there for the both of them to see.

'You're joining the navy.' She looked confused now. Really confused. No idea what was going on. 'I have a class.' She checked her watch and started walking off. 'Where are you?'

He supposed she meant: where are you living?

'In a room.'

'A room? I have to go. Where?'

'Where you living?' he asked.

She looked at his hands. 'With a friend,' was all she gave over. And the way she said it. Protecting herself from him.

He should have washed his hands. Like the guy did in the bathroom. Taken time to wash them, to be prepared.

Agnes raised her hand to wave. But not all the way. Her eyes worried while she turned. He watched her go off into the crowd of students. He just stood there as she went around the corner. Her head not turning for a view of him.

He went back and collected the book bag. Took it to his room and dumped it out on the bed. Books. A calculator. Pens and pencils. A chocolate bar. Scribblers full of notes that meant nothing to him. Worse than nothing. Saw himself in the mirror by the bed. He tore the scribblers to shreds. The guy's handwriting. It turned his stomach. He'd never thought of asking the operator for a phone listing for Peter MacLeod. But that was enough. He'd done all he could do.

Blackstrap burned the university books. In the fire in the barrel they had going outside on the docks. Some of the other men wondering what he was doing. 'Why you burning books?' Flip had asked. 'You taking courses or something? I guess, not anymore.' He hadn't answered. And

Flip had just watched. Eating a bag of ketchup potato chips. Checking down toward the bottom for chip crumbs. Tipping the bag back to finish whatever was left. It was break time. 'You could probably get money for them.'

Now. Back in Newfoundland. In the white blizzard. With nothing to hold his attention. He cannot help but remember.

In Halifax. A month after the fight in the university washroom. Blackstrap had seen a poster for a Christmas comedy show. With a man in a yellow rain hat and yellow sou'wester. The man had a goofy expression on his cross-eyed face. And his bottom lip was pulled up over his top lip. The man's name was Dicky Spurrel. They called him the Pride of Newfieland. The poster said: 'If you're a Newfie, show your pride and come along to hoot and holler. For the best Newfie time with all things Newfie.' There had been the first winter snowfall the previous night. Watching the snow made Blackstrap lonely for the island. He didn't have enough money to go home for Christmas. So, he bought a ticket to the concert. Went along to see if it felt right.

He drove across the bridge from Halifax to Dartmouth. Found the place where the concert was set to happen. He arrived a little late because he wanted enough beer in him to make it through. When he stepped in the big club, a fat woman with a change box on a table tore his ticket in half. He was surprised to see it was a country and western bar. The tables and chairs were almost filled. He stood at the back. Where a bar ran along the full length of the wall. And ordered a beer.

The guy in the yellow rain hat and slicker was on a small stage. Up toward the front. He was strumming a guitar. Singing a song called 'Goofy Newfie.' Blackstrap looked around to see the people. He recognized the features. The craggy faces smoking cigarettes. The easy laughter. The shared hilarity. One to the other. A lot of them from Newfoundland by the looks of them. He was surprised to see the people laughing. The bartender was chuckling when he handed Blackstrap a beer.

'Funny stuff,' said the bartender. Tipping his head in the direction of the stage.

Blackstrap paid for his beer. Took back all his change. His hand still hurting when he closed it. To put the change in his pocket. He should have had it X-rayed, but he never did. Maybe there were bones broken. He tried to put it out of his mind. Picked up the beer in his right hand and swigged it. Watched the guy on stage. At the end of the song, the guy's pants fell down. To show off his underwear with baby seals on them. The Pride of Newfieland bent down to pull up his pants. And flicked something from the stage at the same time. A rubber fish. It flew into the audience. A woman caught it and laughed. Raised it high. And wagged it around. Threw it back on stage. The Pride of Newfieland grabbed the rubber fish. Started kissing it. He pretended that he was toothless. Smacked his lips together. 'Some good,' he said. He winked and tilted his head. Laughed like an inbred idiot.

Blackstrap looked at the bar. There was a display of the guy's albums with a sign that had a price on it.

There was a bit of a ruckus. Blackstrap turned to see the guy pulling a woman from the audience. She had short curly hair and was plump. Maybe in her fifties. Her cheeks flushed pink. She was a good sport by how she was accepting it. Nodding her head and straightening the bottom edge of her top. The Pride of Newfieland made her kiss the rubber fish. 'Shut yer eyes, now, missus,' said the guy in a screechy sort of voice. 'Ya gotta kiss da cod. 'N den a shot of Newfie Screech ta keep up yer strength. Den you'll be all Screeched in. An honorary Newf.'

When the woman shut her eyes, the guy winked at the audience. Winked with both eyes. Like he didn't even know how to do it properly. With his tongue sticking out his mouth. And his mouth going from side to side. The audience laughed and the woman peeked.

'Now, dere's no peeking, missus. Jees, b'y, yer right saucy, ain't ya?'

She shut her eyes again. And from the pocket of his slicker, he took out a rubber dildo. 'Now, missus, ya gotta give dat cod fish one more smooch 'fore ya can be a real Newf.' He nodded at the audience as he brought the dildo to her lips. She kissed it and opened her eyes. Then pulled her face back. The Pride of Newfieland let his mouth hang open with laughter. And buckled forward a bit. Slapped his knees. Stomped his boots. Did a little jig around in a circle. He gave the woman the rubber dildo. 'Da way yer holding dat, looks like ya had a bit of practice, missus.' Then he sent her on her way. The woman went off trying not to hold the dildo. Like it was contaminated. 'Ye'll be t'anking me later,' he said, and the audience applauded and laughed. Laughed so hard they had to swipe tears from their eyes.

'What da fuck're you doing?' Blackstrap muttered. Then took a drink. He began walking toward the tables. Stood at the rear of them. Then he drifted left. Made his way toward the wall that would take him closer to the stage. He stopped halfway and leaned on the wall. He wanted a closer look at the guy's face. The guy had a beard and moustache. The guy put the guitar strap back over his neck. Said: 'How ya doing now, b'ys?' He raised a beer bottle from the table his props were on. Chugged down the beer. Hands slapped the tables to encourage him. People hooted. Called out. The place went wild with uproar. When he was done, he flicked his head. Like he'd just come up from underwater. From going down. And being rescued. 'Some good, b'y. Dat's da finest Newfie juice I ever tasted.'

The audience shouted in agreement. Lifted their beer bottles. In tribute. Everyone with more than one bottle in front of them. The tables littered.

Blackstrap moved closer to the stage. No more than fifteen feet away in the shadows. So no one really saw him. Only a few people at the tables nearest, giving him a nod. In it together. He drank his beer. As he got closer to the guy on stage, the guy became clearer. Blackstrap could see his face. See that he was just a man pretending to be something else. His face showed its true self. Every now and then for a second. A guy making a buck. A guy doing an act. He was probably not even from Newfoundland.

'Where you from?' Blackstrap called out.

'Wha'?' The guy squinted, looking around the audience. 'I t'ink I heard a cat meowing.'

'Where you from?' Blackstrap shouted. Like a roar. So everyone could hear. And the place went a little still.

'Where'm I from?' The guy made another stunned expression. Held it for a few seconds. Looked around everywhere to make it last. To get the laughs. He crossed his eyes. Then said: 'Where ya t'ink I'm from?' The audience clapped and laughed. A man in the back called out: 'That's right.' Then Dicky Spurrel looked toward Blackstrap, waiting to see what might be said next. A comedy sketch in the making.

'You're not from Newfoundland.'

'I were born in Newfieland, honest ta God. Cross me 'art 'n 'ope ta die of whiskey t'irst.'

'You're not from Newfoundland.' Blackstrap's hand was aching. Of no use to him the way it was. He tightened up his fist. But it wouldn't close all the way. He noticed a shadow by his side. One of the bouncers.

'Honest ta be jessus, I is.'

'You're a fucking joke.'

'I truly hopes so.' The guy winked at the audience. Then broke into a tune. About a woman who loses her drawers from the clothes line out around the bay.

Blackstrap moved a little closer to the stage. The shadow followed him. Then a face leaned near.

'That's enough of that,' said the shadow.

Blackstrap looked at the face. Because it was a true Newfoundland voice he heard. He did not know the face. But he knew the voice. Not like the one up on stage. The retarded monkey.

'You're from Newfoundland,' he said to the big fellow.

The big fellow nodded. 'Any more outta you and you'll have ta leave, buddy.'

Blackstrap finished off his beer and studied the empty.

'Don't try it.'

Blackstrap shifted his attention to the bouncer's face. 'What part of da island are you from?'

'St. John's.'

'Figures.' Blackstrap laid the empty bottle on the table nearest him. The guy sitting there looked at the bottle. Then up at him. The guy with his sleeves rolled up. Beer belly. Tattoos. Hair greased back. Smoking a cigarette. That look in his eyes: Who're you to tell me anything? A solid sort of Newfoundlander.

Blackstrap walked away. Back toward the bar at the rear of the hall. Toward the exit. Leaving, he heard the lyrics: 'So kiss me arse, so kiss me arse, 'n we'll be wed in da marnin'.'

The blizzard before his eyes. From everywhere at once. There is no telling whether the car is on the highway or not. Just a field of white. He has to slow to a crawl. Or risk having his front wheels go over a bank. A tense, uncertain journey. And still three hundred miles to go. He is heading east, having just passed Gander when the blizzard thickened. He wouldn't stop in Gander though. He wanted to keep going. He wanted to get home.

Chapter VI – 1979

Three Mile Island

(July, 1979, 25 years old)

Blackstrap has already cut two loads of wood since he walked into the trees. The sun just up when he got there. The heat fierce in the woods. Not a breath of air. Not a hint of breeze. Black flies in clouds. Spitting them from his mouth and lips. His body feels as though it's made of nothing but hot flesh and sweat. Only the strong smell of snotty var, white spruce, black spruce and the rare blonde birch cut down. And the stillness when his chainsaw quiets. The sound of birds up high. Past the peak of mosquito breeding. And the black flies are the menace now. Smaller, no sound. Blackstrap's hands are covered in sap and bites, tiny blots of squashed flies smeared black and red. Flies squashed in the sweat on his cheeks and neck. Sweat stings his eyes. He swipes at his forehead with the sleeve of his flannel shirt. While holding the revving chainsaw with one hand.

He is cutting a spruce. Thirty feet high at least. The spring on his safety broke earlier that morning, so he has to be careful of kickback. The teeth seem duller than usual. He thinks he might've hit a rock. Covered in bog. When he was limbing out the last tree.

While he's cutting, the chain snaps, winds like a snake lashing out. Then coils back tightly into itself. As luck would have it, the chain stays clear of his leg.

'Jesus, Jesus, Jesus.' He shuts off the saw. He turns away, already walking because he remembers there's a spare chain in the pickup.

He treads down the trail, littered with cut boughs, and sees his truck through the trees. A glint of sun he thinks might have come from his vehicle, but is reflected from another pickup, pulling alongside his. A government logo on the door. His jaw stiffens while he mutters another string of curses.

The forestry officer is out of his pickup and next to Blackstrap's. The forestry officer is wearing short sleeves. A luxury to be in the woods with short sleeves. What sort of forestry work is that man doing? Working on a nice tan. Not being eaten alive by flies.

'How ya doing?' the forestry officer asks.

'Great.' Blackstrap opens the passenger door of his pickup, lays the saw on the seat. He paws around in the glove compartment until he finds the white box with the new chain in it.

'Popped your chain,' says the forestry officer.

Blackstrap makes a sound that means the same as disinterest and no kidding.

'It's a hot day.'

Blackstrap finds the ratchet set down on the floor. Popping it open, he takes out the fitting for the chainsaw bolts and spins them off, then removes the plate. The broken chain has jammed in the already broken spring of the safety, has done more damage. He is going to have to snip the spring to get the saw to work again.

'Trouble, hey?'

'Yup.' He goes to the back of his pickup. Reaches over the edge to lift out the tool kit. He opens it. Fishes out the pliers. Shuts the box. Then tries snipping the wide steel spring.

'You're going to have to cut that right back.'

'Right.' He lifts the chain bar to get it out of his way.

'Nasty.'

Blackstrap is about to turn on the forestry officer. He doesn't mind too much that the man is there. Doing nothing and stinking of fly dope. He just wishes the man would shut his mouth. He takes a moment to calm himself. Says quietly. 'Out fer a run?' He stops what he's doing. This is all slowing him down. He needs to take three loads out by sunset. Then he's got two cars to fix. A starting motor in one. A dent to tap out and polyfill in the other. And a split boat trailer to weld for Jimmy Parsons. Blackstrap checks the man's face. 'Out fer the good of yer health?'

The forestry officer smiles. Mirror sunglasses reflecting a warped view. 'I doubt that.'

'No?'

'Well . . .' The officer looks toward the trail where Blackstrap has come from. Blackstrap looks there too, to see what the officer might be seeing. Nothing. No sight of cut trees. But what else would Blackstrap be doing in the woods with a chainsaw?

'I was wondering if you have a permit.'

'Fer what?'

'Cutting wood.'

'I never cut any wood.'

'Really?'

'That's right.'

The officer takes off his sunglasses. His eyes going to the chainsaw. 'What were you using that for?'

'I was carving.'

'Carving?'

'Statues.'

'Really?'

'Yays, really. Totem poles. I'm three-sixteenths Beothuk.'

The forestry officer smiles widely. He's not a prick, by the looks of him. Seems easy going. He hooks the earpiece of his sunglasses in the open front of his shirt. 'You know there's a fine for cutting wood without a permit.'

'Never heard of it.'

'Unfortunately that doesn't mean it doesn't exist.'

Blackstrap nods. Smiles a little. A real smart aleck. But he's not snarky about it. Trying to be friendly. That doesn't make it so bad. It's like he recognizes something in the way the man talks. His face. Now that he's getting to know him. Maybe not a townie after all.

'Where you from?' Blackstrap asks.

'You know Bareneed?'

Blackstrap's eyes steady on the officer's face. 'Heard of it.'

'That's where my family's from.'

'What name?'

'Taylor.'

'Taylor . . . Tommy Taylor's little brother, Mikey.'

'That's right.'

Blackstrap grins. Slaps the man's arm. 'You know the Hawcos from Bareneed?'

'Sure do.'

'Well, you don't recognize this one.'

'You'd be Blackstrap.'

'That's right. What's Tommy up to?'

The smiling light leaves Mikey's face. He checks toward the treeline. After a moment, 'He passed away.'

'Sorry to hear.'

'Car crash.'

'Really sorry 'bout that.'

'I heard about Junior.' Quiet, squinting eyes back on Blackstrap. 'That's a shame.'

'Yeah.' Blackstrap shifts his eyes toward the horizon. The tips of spruce trees against blue. All the way to the unseen edge of the island. 'Where'd you move to?'

'Resettled to?'

'Yeah.' He looks at Mikey again.

'Up to the Labrador. I'm living in St. John's now. Drive out every morning. It's a nice run. But I'm thinking of getting a place down in Bareneed. Old houses cost practically nothing.'

'Little Mikey Taylor.'

'I think we might even be related. Cousins or something.'

Blackstrap laughs loudly. A bark that goes out over the clearing. 'I've heard as much. Somewhere down the line.'

'Well, it's good to see you.'

Blackstrap stares. Remembering water at the end of land. 'You got a boat down there?'

'No.'

'There's space to tie up.'

'Maybe one day. When I can afford one.'

'Tell me about it.'

Mikey Taylor with his eyes on Blackstrap's chainsaw now. 'Well . . .'

Mikey Taylor wondering what to say. '. . . that course came in this year. You should take it.'

'What for?'

'Safety precautions. Forest management information. That sort of thing.'

'Forest management.'

'Save the trees.'

Blackstrap searches back at the woods. One tree and then another, going on in all directions. 'There's nothing but trees fer hundreds of miles.'

'You cut them all down, they won't be there anymore.'

'It'd take 'til the end of creation to cut down the trees on this island. 'N by that time they'd be grown up again.'

'A lot of trees alright. A hundred and twenty-two thousand square kilometers of 'em. One-third of the island. I learned that years ago. But each tree is special.' The forestry officer grins.

Under different circumstances, he might enjoy a beer with Mikey Taylor. In fact, he's feeling thirsty now.

'How long's that course?'

'Three weeks, I believe.'

'Haven't the leisure time.'

Mikey Taylor chuckles. 'Yeah, it's a nuisance.'

Blackstrap likes the sound of that. 'How're yer mudder 'n fadder?'

'They're still fit.'

'They must be in their nineties.'

'That's right. Mom still tends the garden. Bakes bread every week. And Dad's out in the boat. Can't keep him off the water.'

'Good to hear.' Blackstrap goes back to his saw. Snips the safety spring back closer. The chain should work now. He puts on the bar. Fits on the new chain. Aligning the teeth with the running groove. Sets the cover back on. Pulls snug the bar while ratcheting the two bolts tight. 'Well, you have yerself a nice day, Mikey Taylor,' he says, then turns with the chainsaw in both hands.

'I will. Now don't you go back in there.'

'Wouldn't think of it.' A few steps toward the path.

'I mean it. I'll have to fine you. I'll look the other way for now. But you can't go back at it. Sorry.'

'How much is the fine, Mikey?' He turns to see Mikey with his sunglasses back on.

The forestry officer tells him the amount. It's too much to handle. More than what he'll get for a couple of loads of spruce. And the second fine is even higher.

Blackstrap stares at the forestry officer. He yanks the cord on his chainsaw. It starts. The teeth are long. Sharp as razors. They will cut through any tree in jig time. A pleasure to have a new chain. Chunks of wood coming loose on the cut. It makes life easier. Like going through butter. No need to sharpen for a while.

The officer looks at the saw.

Blackstrap revs it, studying how the chain spins around. Listening to make certain it's moving freely. The spinning of the spokes. Chain oil lightly spitting toward the grass. Everything fine. He shuts it off.

'There's a load of wood in there I came across. When I was on a walk. Birdwatching was what I was up to.'

'I thought you were carving.'

'Yeah, while I was birdwatching 'n carving. Multi-talented, I am.'

'It'd be a good idea just to leave it there.'

Blackstrap nods. 'Sure.' He returns to his pickup and lays the chainsaw in the back. Packs away his tool kit. Slides it in on the floor of the cab. 'See ya, Mikey,' he says, shutting the passenger door.

'See ya. It was good talking.'

'Maybe I'll see ya in Bareneed sometime.'

'Yeah, that'd be more like it.'

Blackstrap goes around to the driver's side. He gets in and starts the engine, backs up, swerves around, straightens on the rough grassy road, and heads out. The pickup bounces over the ruts in the grass. He glances in the vibrating rearview, the forestry officer's blurry truck following after him. When he makes it to Fox Marsh Road, he turns right and heads for the highway. A steadier view of the forestry officer in the rearview, the government truck pulling out and going the other way. A few toots of his horn. Blackstrap drives for a few miles then turns around, circles back.

He passes the forestry truck coming towards him, about a mile from the turnoff into the woods road where his cut trees are waiting. Mikey with his shades on. But Mikey doesn't do anything. He doesn't wave or make any sort of notice. Blackstrap watches in the mirror, but the forestry truck just shrinks away. And a bigger truck looms in the distance, thundering toward him. A big truck loaded to the top rails with wood for the lumber mill in Tilton.

Blackstrap works in the same patch for four days. Until a different forestry officer shows his face. Tells Blackstrap all the same things. Confiscates his wood and fines him.

Chapter VII – 1981

Charles and Diana

(January, 1981, 27 years old)

They fly out in a big orange helicopter from St. John's airport. Twenty men on board in survival suits and ear protectors. Their boots set down beside them. Blackstrap is hoping for a good view. An occasional ship. A sailboat. A tanker. A trawler. But there is only grey. Fog or clouds for two hours. There had been a stir of excitement about flying out. But the edge is gone off his hangover, so he sleeps most of the way. Just like the other men. No chance of talking with the noise: nin-nin-nin-nin-nin. The constant high-pitch whining of the turbo blades. His head muffled from the ear protectors. Noise kept at a distance. But hearing himself too clearly when he breathes through his nostrils or clears his throat.

Somewhere between sleep and waking, he feels the chopper begin its descent. Out of the fog with the water in sight. A vast field of greyish-blue with a tiny speck in the far distance. The men in the other seats begin to move around. Sit up straight. Coughing and stretching their neck muscles. Watch through the side windows. With the rig that far away, it seems the chopper would be too big. A dangerous trick to put something so huge down on that speck. But as the chopper nears, the rig looms larger and becomes a possibility.

The mass of steel with its derrick poked up. Looking like no ship at all. More like something ancient and new, a man-made monster. The offshore drilling platform, the *Ocean Ranger*.

The sea is fairly calm today. Only whitecaps and grey skies. But he has heard stories of the weather. And has been there himself. Not on that rig. But on the water in January. Out for a lark just to see what the water was like. A foolish boy lost in an open boat. A memory best kept behind a screen of white. What the water can do to anything afloat. The worst sort of vicious winter storms gather in January and February. The months of shipwrecks. The *Carlysle*. The *Yarmouth Town*. The *Parry Sound*. All gone. Never the months to travel on water if avoidable. Time to be at home, in the warmth, with the angry sea out there on its own.

Take it or leave it. A job on the rigs or another trip to the mainland. And there was no going away if he could avoid it. He had signed up at the hiring office out on Bowering Road in St. John's. One hundred dollars a day. A Texan in a cowboy hat who must have been six foot five. Pacing the office and talking. Asking about experience on the sea with his big Texan drawl. Checking a paper to let you know if he made you a roustabout or a roughneck. Better to be a roughneck, said a young fellow next to him. The young fellow had introduced himself as Billy Cullen. There was a form to fill out. One that Billy filled out for Blackstrap. Lending a hand when he saw Blackstrap not doing it. 'You remind me of me brudder,' Billy said. 'He won't fill nut'n out either. You never saw someone so stunned.'

The chopper approaches the landing pad. Centres itself in the white circle. Tilts and drifts from a push of wind. Holds there, straining, before it levels off again. Sinks down steadily until touching.

A ship like any other ship.

The chopper door opens and the men climb out. Blackstrap's feet on the steel. He wants to get his boots back on. Pull the survival suit off. A nuisance the way it fits.

Off in the corner, he notices a man in a silver space suit. Holding what looks like a thick hose or a cannon aimed at the chopper. There's a window in the front of his silver hood.

Blackstrap waits while the rotor blades wind down.

Another man is there in a hard hat. Shouting above the helicopter. A voice with a drawl: 'So, you're the new crew. Git on down and git your overalls and git on up to the drill floor. No time for pause with money burning away. Oh, yeah, I forgot to say "welcome."' A smile meant to be something other than a smile.

They head toward a set of stairs and go down. The blun-blun-blun of engines in the steel walls and floor. To Blackstrap's right, an office with a guy sitting in a chair. A big bubble centred inside a glass on the wall. To the left, another room with a wall of radios. A guy with a telephone receiver in his hand. Another door with a red cross on it. Then into a room where other men are waiting. The off-duty crew ready to fly back home. Blackstrap wonders why they're there. What they're waiting for with the chopper up on the pad ready to lift off.

'Git them suits off,' says the man with the drawl. He's come up behind them. The new arrivals remove the survival suits and the other men put them on. A few exchange stories while they do it. Two suits left over because there are only eighteen men going back. The steward shows up and takes them out into the corridor. Blackstrap glancing back over his shoulder to see the old crew climbing the stairs up to deck. Then the new crew clangs down another set of metal stairs. Crew quarters. A notice posted behind plexiglas. Four brass screws holding it to the bulkhead outside his door. He sees it in passing. Doesn't check it out, thinks maybe he should, but doesn't want to look like a know-nothing.

Right away they change into their overalls. Put on their hard hats. They introduce themselves. Billy Cullen, Fred Rumsey, Johnny Cole and him. All in one room. A bunk each. One stacked on another and a small table between.

'Let's go,' says the drawl out in the corridor. 'Almost noon. Let's go now, ladies. Come on down.'

'Who's that?' Blackstrap asks Fred Rumsey. Because Fred has been on the rig before.

'Senior tool pusher, Willy Cuntz. Last name's sumt'n like dat. From Mississippi.' Fred frowns. 'Worst sort 'a prick.' The others follow after him. 'T'ree t'ings,' says Fred, holding up three fingers. But there are only two because one of them is gone. Nothing but a stub. Billy Cullen is close by, trying to get closer, listen carefully. Wanting to hear anything that might be important. Curious eyes and always licking his lips. 'Number one . . . Now, lis'en. Number one, never get between anyt'ing that can or will move. Number two, never turn yer back on a piece of drill pipe. And number t'ree, always watch out fer the person yer working widt. Got it?'

Billy Cullen nods while walking.

Johnny Cole doesn't pay attention. Not a care in the world. Only interested in the rig. The walls. The rooms. Grinning like it's the finest thing he's ever seen. A fancy hotel in a big city.

Blackstrap keeps looking straight ahead. Up the stairs.

The men join the others on the drill floor. Right away they get to work putting drill pipe together. Thirty-foot lengths screwed into each other. Three of them making one long length that's stored vertically off to the side in the derrick. Blackstrap watches Fred fit them down into the hole. Machine clamps grabbing hold of each length and screwing it together tight. Just to be certain. The solid mechanics of it impressive.

'Ten t'ousand feet down,' shouts Fred. 'Two miles.' A good-humoured tilt of his head. He looks toward the driller in the drill shack. The driller's hands on levers. Calling out: 'Watch yourself, boys.' All the while, the foghorn is going. Hnwwww-hnwwww-hnwwwwwwwwwwww. Dot-dot-dash. The letter 'U' for danger, Blackstrap knows. Why a warning signal? Maybe just to alert other vessels that they're sitting where they are.

Putting lengths of pipe together for twelve hours. Near the end of the shift, with the fluorescent lights on above them, giving the space a fake daylight glow, a piece of chain lets go. It whips toward bushy-haired Billy Cullen. Blackstrap yanks the young fellow down just in time. The chain rattling and snaking off before losing its energy and settling against steel. The wildness gone from it. Someone put a sloppy knot in the chain. One of the new guys. Fred Rumsey shakes his head at what might have been. A constant string of things that might've happened. And then things that do.

Starving at midnight. Steak and fries from the cafeteria hot line and some apple pie from the dessert table. Blackstrap sits on one of the benches. A photograph of the *Ocean Ranger* hung at the end of each long table. The one he's watching shows the drill rig in a calm cove somewhere. He stands and tries reading the words beneath it. Until Billy Cullen comes up and reads them aloud, 'Ocean Ranger in Port Alberni, British Columbia.' Blackstrap sits back down. Checks over his shoulder. Billy Cullen looking at another photograph. The Ocean Ranger under tow. Being pulled by a ship on the smooth, blue water.

'I heard why dere were only eighteen men in the crew goin' out,' says Fred.

Billy Cullen, not wanting to miss anything, returns to the table.

Blackstrap chews some steak and bread with butter. Watches Fred.

Johnny Cole watches, smiling while he eats.

'Duanne Foley and his brudder got put off on a supply boat.'

'Why's dat?' asks Johnny Cole with a laugh. A guy who laughs at most things. Skinny and tall. Wavy, coal-black hair and a long face. A mouthful of big twisted-up teeth.

'Dis new senior tool pusher. Cuntz. Fired 'em. He were brought in ta get t'ings going. You and you, Pat Hopkins told me, dat's what Cuntz said, You and you, yer not working hard 'nough. I'm running you off this rig.' Fred does a good impersonation of Cuntz. Good enough to get a few chuckles.

Blackstrap cuts another piece of steak. It's pink in the centre, the way he likes.

'What'd Duanne do?' asks Johnny, drinking milk. The question like he wants the punchline to a joke.

'Nut'n right away. Dis new pusher figures he'll play tough guy 'n show us. So, Duanne were sittin on his bunk when Pat Hopkins came in and Duanne were just out of prison. Duanne's from Torbay. Got a job to please his parole officer. So, he's shaking his head saying "It's ain't right. Not fair, buddy." Den he gets up and leaves the cabin. Just like dat. Had enough of it. Pat follows after him to Cuntz's cabin. Duanne gets in there, hauls Cuntz outta bed 'n beats da shit out of 'im.'

Blackstrap swallows the lump of bread in his mouth. Puts a piece of steak in there. The rig is swaying slightly. Just barely enough to feel.

Fred goes quiet and Blackstrap looks over his shoulder. To where

Fred's eyes are looking. Cuntz there, walking through the cafeteria, checking the men.

'Tell ya da rest later, b'ys,' says Fred.

A shower and bed. Dreams of nothing except a blackness with forms that almost take shape. When Blackstrap wakes, there's a storm blowing. Strange energy in the air. Electric. The hum of the locomotive engines vibrating through everything. Fluorescent lights burning his eyes with brightness. When he passes the radio room, he sees a few men in there, waiting to use the phone.

He eats breakfast then watches Billy Cullen and Johnny Cole playing ping-pong. Johnny whacks the ball and Billy ducks and covers his head. Johnny laughs. Blackstrap catches the ball where he's sitting. Tosses it back. There's a video on the television about a flying machine. The *Gossamer Albatross*. A strange-looking contraption with big wings. And a guy inside a glass box pedalling. It manages to cross the English Channel and win a prize. Powered by pedals that drive a two-bladed propeller. It takes 2 hours and 49 minutes. The voice on the screen says. 'Achieving a top speed of 18 mph and an average altitude of 1.5 meters.'

Madman, thinks Blackstrap. Fucking madman. But wonders about the mechanics of how it might be done.

The screen is suddenly switched off. Cuntz up there for the safety meeting. The men gather, sitting around while Cuntz talks on and on. A routine he's gone through a hundred times before. Nothing but words for the sake of saying them.

At the end, the men ask questions that Cuntz has no time for. Fred Rumsey has a few concerns. Broken locks. Breakdown of equipment. They've been calling the rig the Ocean Danger for months. Soon after it arrived from drilling off Ireland a year or so ago. 'Eight fingers gone in two weeks, b'y,' says Fred.

Cuntz seems outraged. Furious by the steaming redness in his face. 'Don't you call me "boy" or I'll run you off this rig.' His voice getting louder, shriller toward the end. His finger pointing. Jabbing at the air. 'You just do your job. Do your job. Everyone. And keep your fingers on your own hands.'

Blackstrap wonders: Whose hands could they be on except our own?

The men are concerned about the storm and high winds. The rig shifting more than usual. Never felt so unstable before, one man comments, barely loud enough for Cuntz to hear.

'This rig cannot sink,' shouts Cuntz. 'It was built by the Japanese.'

Twenty-one days on. Twenty-one days off. He is surprised that he has survived and made it back to land. The unsteady helicopter ride to shore. Watching the rig turn into a fleck in the mist and fog. Battered by high seas. Solid as a rock out there in the middle of the Atlantic. Then the chopper up into grey turbulence. The gut and nerves not wanting any part of it. Out that far on the sea with the fear of death so near. Fishermen do not sail to sea in winter for a reason. Those words in his head, again and again. Fishermen do not . . .

But the money. Pockets stuffed with two thousand dollars in danger pay, he rents an apartment in St. John's. An old house on Military Road, divided up into units. Across the street, there's a church where he sometimes goes to pray. The Newfoundland Hotel is only fifty feet away. Signal Hill behind the hotel, up high on a steep incline that forms one of the cliffs framing the harbour narrows. An intersection divides the church from the hotel. Around the corner is Gower Street with row houses painted all different colours. The streets parallel to Gower run gradually lower toward the harbour. Duckworth Street. Then Water Street. Then Harbour Drive skirting where the big boats are tied up. It takes him little time to familiarize himself with the geography that is considered downtown. He walks wherever he goes, investigating the bars and clubs, and favours a bar down on Water Street called Martha's where all sorts of people drink: businessmen, workers and young people. He likes the mix of it, how they all get along.

Blackstrap buys furniture from a shop on Water Street. A mattress that he puts on the floor, a couch and a coffee table in the living room. A truck delivers his order right to his door. The men won't let him help bring the stuff in. Something about insurance. They do it themselves and Blackstrap watches, trying to stay out of their way, feeling embarrassed.

Living in that house, he soon discovers that the place is not properly insulated. The ceilings are too high, the space impossible to make warm

557

with electric heat. Sometimes when he wakes in the early morning, there is a thin layer of ice on the toilet water. The windows are tall and expertly made with intricate mouldings, one window in the centre and one on each side, a box that protrudes out. The living room window gives him a view of mature trees in the back yard. The bedroom window faces the street. People walk by on the sidewalk near his window. He watches them go by without them knowing he's seeing them. A fancy place, once lived in by people with money. There is a mantelpiece where a fireplace must have once been, but the hole is boarded over.

What to do with his spare time? He buys an LTD Crown Victoria at the Ford dealership on Elizabeth Avenue. The man in the brown suit wants to give it to him on credit when Blackstrap says he works on the rigs.

'Credit?' Blackstrap asks.

'Yes, nothing down and 2.5 per cent. You can't beat that.'

The way it's explained, Blackstrap thinks he might be making money on the deal. He signs his name and drives away, exploring the outports fifteen minutes outside St. John's: Torbay, Outer Cove, Middle Cove, Flatrock, Portugal Cove . . . The places are much like home. Same square houses circled around bays. Same narrow, winding roads and paths. Same decent people with no thoughts in their heads of being anything other than what they are. Men and women comfortably settled into the land. Not ever wanting to go anywhere else.

One Saturday, he parks on the ferry wharf in Portugal Cove and watches across the water. The sheer cut of land that is Bell Isle. He gets out of his car and climbs up on the finger of rocks that makes the breakwater. The winter air harsh on his face. Ice rimming the shore. There are houses perched on the cliffs behind him. Built there years ago by fishermen. The nearer the water, the better. They bring the openings of caves to mind.

The ferry is on its way from the island, seeming far away but not that much of a distance. He scans the land around him, the cars in the line-up, the workers in overalls near the dock. Each time he checks the water, the boat is bigger.

When the ferry pulls in, Blackstrap decides to take it to Bell Isle and have a look around. He's never been there before. He drives up the hill, parks at the back of the line-up and waits for the horn to sound. What to do in a line-up? Sit still. A car pulls in behind him. He notices it in the rearview. A teenager at the wheel fixing his hair. Blackstrap switches on the radio and rolls down the window for some fresh air. There's a baby bundled up in a stroller, out for a walk with its mother. A few baby sounds reach him above the music. Down near the shore, two boys are throwing stones high into the air. Out past the ice. Blackstrap watches where he thinks the stones might fall. Then they plunk into the water.

Soon, the cars start moving ahead. He rolls down until levelling off at the ticket booth. He hands the man his money through the window. A ticket for the vehicle covers the driver too. The man nods and silently checks out Blackstrap's car. A schedule is pinned to the glass in the booth. Times for leaving and times for returning.

'How often the ferry run?' Blackstrap asks.

'Every twenty minutes.'

'Sounds good.'

Pulling into the belly of the ferry is an interesting experience. He likes the sound of the ship when he gets out and shuts his car door, takes the metal stairs to the observation deck. The hum of steel underfoot brings the Ranger to mind. Back out there soon in the void of ocean. Gulls circle near the railing. Blackstrap looks back at the land. The two boys are still there, trying to skim rocks across the ice now. They laugh and shoulder each other for a better position.

The ferry nudges ahead and begins to drift. The engine suddenly vibrating louder. Blackstrap watches the boat's reflection wavering in the water. He stares until he thinks he can see forms down there. When he finally looks up, he notices the red in the distant cliffs. Iron ore. The mineral that once made the place so valuable, that drew people to it from all over the world. He keeps his eyes fixed on the approaching land. An interesting preoccupation to try and tell how many more minutes until they dock. The land slowly gaining depth and height. Soon, he senses it growing over him. The towering cut of the cliffs changing the sound of the boat's engines. He goes back into the belly of the ferry and climbs into his car. Other people are returning too, starting their engines.

The ferry coasts in, strikes the tires attached to the dock, gently rocking everything aboard for a second. In time, the big door is lowered. Cars move ahead of him until he is waved an okay by one of the workers.

Rolling off the ferry, he feels his wheels touch earth. Movement solid and steady again. He follows the cars up the steep hill, passing the slope of the graveyard on his left with tombstones facing toward sea. No problem for the Crown Vic to make the incline. The car seems to lean into it, gradually reaching the flat of the land. A scattered store and house here and there. Small barns with horses and cows or an occasional goat out in a yard, seeming to not belong. Clothes on a line even in winter. Children play in the yards. The clothes they wear remind him of the 1950s. Pants not jeans. Pullover sweaters. The girls in old, worn dresses and coats. He senses himself adrift in time. Locked in a forgotten era.

At a convenience store with a cola and beer sign, he buys a half case. Then drives on into a town square where most of the shops are boarded up. There are only so many roads. Red gravel on the shoulders. Not much snow down to cover it up. Not knowing what he came for, he cruises around, taking it all in. A beer bottle stuck between his legs, the other bottles jingling in the case on the passenger seat. He takes a swig while watching the large yards with grey wooden fences. The tall grass. The old houses built away from each other. Many of them abandoned. Two huge dilapidated barns with concrete foundations set side by side.

Eventually, a road leads him to an open area where a large hole in a cliff is boarded over. He parks, watching it, knowing what it is. No one going in or out of there now. Whatever was left down there is down there for good. This was probably where Junior had worked and died. The mine closed decades ago, but there are still stacks of iron ore rock. Piles of them covered with patches of snow. What are they worth? Not enough to even bother taking away.

He finishes his beer and slides the empty into the slot. Then he stares at the barred entrance, not knowing what to think. He wonders if there's a way inside. No doubt there must be. Children would have found a space big enough to fit through by now. His fingers reach for the handle to get out. But he waits, wondering what he might do. Then he thinks of his fireplace back in St. John's. Boarded over too. He uncaps another beer with his belt buckle and drinks it. With the car idling, he shuts off the radio and rolls down the window to listen. Nothing outside. Nothing on the cold wind. He keeps his eyes on the barred entrance, drinking and imagining. What's there to see down there in the darkness? Hollow shafts cut deep. Then he backs away and drives off, shaking his head.

By the side of the road, he spots a pile of cut brush. Evergreen boughs stacked above the snow, the needles off, the branches gone grey. He pulls over and loads his trunk with them. Then he shuts the lid and looks at the trees running along the side of the road. A long string of evergreens, the leaves gone from the other trees. 'Wilderness tapestry' his mother used to call it. The trees and the moss and bushes in the woods. He takes a breath of the air, the freshness of it on his skin. He lumbers back to where the boughs were stacked and heads into the woods. Pushing branches back, he checks over his shoulder until a view of the road disappears. He unbuckles his belt and unzips, slides his jeans down and pisses. Watching the moss and fern and bush, untouched by the snow, he shakes himself off but keeps his fingers there. The woods never failing to arouse him, the chilly air on his exposed skin. In his mind, he undresses Agnes. He has her do whatever he tells her, until he is finished and somehow sadder than before. His sperm left on the forest floor. Something he has thought to do since he was a boy.

Back in the car, he heads for the steep hill down to the wharf. There's a short line-up for the next ferry. He parks and leaves the car there. Walks over to Dick's, the bar and take-out, where he orders fish and chips at the counter. His hand slowly spins one of the stools while he waits. A few sounds coming from behind him. He checks over his shoulder. A little passageway connecting the take-out to the bar.

'Seven minutes,' says the large, pink-cheeked woman. 'You want gravy?'

'No,' he says. 'Seven?'

'Dat's right. Seven minutes. I gots it down ta a science.'

He smiles a little and turns, treading through the passageway.

The barman gives him a nod. The room is wide open. Tables and chairs, and a pool table off to one side.

'India,' he says.

The barman watches his face for a second, then uncaps the bottle of India Beer.

Blackstrap studies the label. A big, black Newfoundland dog on it, just like the one on the plastic clock behind the bar. He looks at the bartender, not knowing what to say. It makes him finish off his beer more quickly. Then he goes back to the take-out. By this time, his order is bagged and on the counter next to a few others.

'Yer late by a minute.' The woman lifts the order in the palm of her hand. Blackstrap chuckles and takes it from her. The bottom of it promisingly warm. He pays and carries it to his car where he rips open the brown paper bag and lifts off the wax paper covering. The smell hits him. Malt vinegar. He eats the thick French fries and puts on more salt. He does the same with the crispy fish. Thirsty, he uncaps a bottle of beer from his case and drinks it down. Then he goes back into the bar, leaving the car where it is.

'India.'

The bartender nods, already reaching for the bottle.

Blackstrap drinks that one down and orders again, missing one boat after another.

With Dick's filling up, he watches the men and women talking and joking with one another. He looks around for Junior. He wants to ask the barman if he knew Junior, but how would he? The barman looks like he might want Blackstrap to ask him something. Taking another glance around, he sees the tables becoming occupied more and more, a waver in his head like the boat's passing reflection, and Junior finally there, smiling toward the back, near the jukebox, stood by himself, as usual, stood off alone.

Blackstrap hears himself laugh under his breath. He feels good for reasons unknown to him. He feels the best he has in years. Among these men and women he does not know. Their friendly and rowdy noise in his ears. Nearly satisfied, he orders a round for the bar from his Ranger money. The bartender uncapping beers or pouring glasses of rum and nodding toward him.

He counts out the bills and feels somehow worse. The sight of that money being handed over. For what? When it's all rung through, the barman tells him about the last boat, tipping his head toward the dock. Toward the windows that have darkened on the other side.

'Last one?'

The barman nods, hands on the bar, waiting for his decision.

'I'm gone then,' says Blackstrap, going out into the night toward the long string of cars. Some vehicles with their dome lights on. He passes faces in their windows, behind the driver's wheel, or in the back seat. People of all sorts. Interesting to look at with a few beers in him. An old man and woman, watching ahead. Silent with each other for how many years? A man by himself, turning something on the dashboard. A bunch of young fellows with a few girls. Laughter. Tons of easy laughter. He smiles and finds his car right up front and climbs aboard.

On the ferry deck, he watches Bell Isle fade off into a blackness not so pitch as the water, only the pinpoints of lights from the houses. He thinks that he has left his mark there. His sperm spilled in the woods, booze in everyone's bellies. He leans to look over the railing. The dark sea rushing by. A thought in his mind to jump, the magnetic urge drawing him into the sea. Not now, he thinks, and returns to his car, staying there behind the wheel, his head filled with memories of his brother, until the time to drive off.

The long road through Portugal Cove connects him to St. John's in darkness. He navigates his way and finds his street, pulling a U-turn to park outside his apartment. Inside, he stands in his living room. Alone is how he feels. Removed. Wherever he walks around, his boots make a hollow sound. He sits on the couch with one arm draped over the back. He stands up and looks out the window. The trees lit by a streetlamp off somewhere. He checks toward the boarded-up fireplace. Why would anyone want to do such a thing? He hears footsteps above him, walking across his ceiling toward his bedroom. He follows after them and drops down on his mattress. The cough of a woman reaching him. He falls asleep and dreams of exactly what he has done that night.

On Sunday, he goes to church service, listening to the young priest who has a nice way of talking. He stands in the line-up to shake the priest's hand on the way out.

'Peace be with you,' says the priest, both hands holding Blackstrap's.

'Thank you, Father,' he says, feeling comforted by the touch. His boots squeak the snow underfoot as he treads across the parking lot.

The hairs in his nose go brittle when he breathes in. He wanders around, his hands shoved into his coat pockets. Downtown is deserted. He stares in the windows, not wanting anything he sees. There is nothing to do, except watch the boats in the harbour. He brushes some light snow off a steel gump, sits on it and rolls a cigarette, smokes it. Foreign sailors pass him by. They are dressed in long coats or thick sweaters. They speak a language that sounds harsh.

Sunday night, he goes to night service and there is a different priest, one he does not like as much. The older priest seems strict and humourless. The story he tells has nothing of himself in it. There are fewer people in the pews than at the morning service. Blackstrap goes back to his apartment and kneels on the mattress, lies back, watching the ceiling and listening for the woman above him. In time, he hears her footsteps, not as hard as before. He thinks she must be barefoot. Then music begins playing that he can barely hear. He falls asleep trying to imagine what she looks like, and wakes in the middle of the night. Listening to the silence, he feels that the house is dead around him. He tosses and turns for an hour and a half before being able to get back to sleep.

When he arrives home from buying a stereo on Monday afternoon, there is a woman going in the main door ahead of him. She holds the door open for him. She's dressed in a long purple coat. Her hair is short and copper-coloured. She wears small glasses. There's a briefcase in her hand and a bag of groceries dangling from the other. She smiles at him in a friendly way.

'It's bitter out,' she says.

He nods and makes a sound of agreement, setting down his boxes to shut the outer door. A few dried boughs stacked on top of the boxes.

His apartment door is directly ahead on the main floor. Hers is on the second level. There is another apartment downstairs, entered by a back door in the yard. Sometimes, a man comes and pounds on the door, shouting to be let in, but is never admitted. The woman glances back as she steps up the shadowed stairs, giving him another smile. She is a professional, by the looks of her. She works in an office.

In his apartment, he unpacks the stereo and moves the coffee table against a wall. He hooks up the speakers and puts on a cassette. The speakers deliver the music with perfect clarity. The cymbals, the thump of the bass, the guitars and vocals. Everything crisp, even with the music down low. He bends near the mantelpiece and taps it with his knuckles. Hollow. A board, plywood by the looks of it, over the hole. There is a hammer under the sink, left by whoever was there before. He uses the claw to remove the half-inch round trim. It snaps in places as he pulls it off the top, bottom and sides. Then he tries using the claw to remove the board, but can't get it under an edge. The plywood is too tightly cut and snuggly fit. So, he stands and swings back his steel-toed boot. The impact crumples a hole in the centre. He kicks again and then bends, yanks the splintered, caved-in plywood away. The hole is clean. He leans to look up the chimney. Too dark to know anything for certain. But the bricks look in fine shape.

Bunching up some advertising flyers, he then breaks the boughs, laying them on top. He strikes a match and watches the fire grow. It crackles with the flames vaguely visible. Standing, he checks for smoke, but smoke doesn't seem to be flowing back into the room. Satisfied, he leaves the apartment and crosses the road. He watches the house, slowly backing up with his hands in his pockets, until he is deep in the church parking lot and can see the chimney. Thin smoke rushing out of it on the angle of the breeze.

Back in the apartment, he wishes he had a telephone. He would like a pizza. Something he has taken a liking to after drinking downtown. He thinks about eating while listening to music and tending to the fire. The boughs crackle nicely and he wonders about sparks on the carpet. He lets the fire go out and leaves for a pizza and a screen for the fireplace.

In the porch on his way out, he meets the woman coming in. They face each other for a few moments. The door shuts behind the woman, the wind doing that. She doesn't bother checking to see what might have happened. There seems to be no need to move. The woman watches Blackstrap's eyes. She's not wearing glasses this time. She has green eyes with flecks of brown that fill Blackstrap with astonishment.

'Well,' she says, with a happy sigh and moves aside. 'We live in the same house,' she says.

Blackstrap cannot get the meaning of this. All he can say in reply is: 'Yes.'

'I'm Susan.'

He shakes the hand she offers. 'Blackstrap.'

'Really.' She seems to approve. She nods a little. 'Blackstrap. How's your new stereo?'

'Good.'

'I like your music.'

'I'll turn it down.' He smiles because he's not certain what she really meant.

'No, that's okay. Tom Waits is great.'

'Louder then?'

'Sure.' She laughs and the sound opens Blackstrap's heart wide. Her laugh and her lips remind him of Agnes. His muscles relax because he finds simple peace in watching her face. She is older than him. How old, he cannot tell. Sometimes she looks younger, too, or prettier than the moment before. But she must be ten years older, at least.

'You've got a fire going?' She checks his blue and black flannel jacket. 'I can smell smoke.'

'The chimney works.'

'Mine is boarded over.'

'Mine too.' A moment later he laughs because of the way she's watching him. 'Not anymore.'

'I was going to ask how you managed that. It works?'

'Yup.'

'Maybe mine does, too.'

Blackstrap waits. The woman doesn't say anything and his mind finally puts it together. 'I can have a look.'

'Really? That'd be great.'

'I wasn't going anywhere.'

'You want to come up now?'

'Sure.'

She hoists the bag in her hand. 'I'm making supper. I'll pay you in food for your services.'

Blackstrap goes directly to Susan's mantelpiece. Hers is in a different location than the one in his apartment. He looks up at the encasement built around what must be a brick chimney. He assumes it's connected to one of the other chimneys he saw coming out the roof. There is a screen in front of the fire box, even though it's boarded up. Why is that? he wonders. For looks maybe. He glances around the apartment. It's done up nicely, like she's been living there for a while. He checks over the couch. Lots of pillows. There are plants hung from the ceiling in knitted holders. Posters framed on the walls. It feels like a one-room home.

'You have a hammer?'

'Sure,' she says from the kitchen.

Blackstrap can see her from where he's crouched. She shuts the refrigerator door and brings him the hammer. Watching her step toward him gives him a peculiar feeling. The two of them alone in a room. He becomes aware of the fact that he does not know this woman. Her slim hand coming toward him to pass him the hammer.

'Thanks.' He works slowly. He does not break any of the half-inch round. This takes a while. The longer the better, to try and impress her. He lays the strips aside after tapping their finishing nails out so the sharp ends won't cut her hands or fingers. He gets a screwdriver and carefully works the edge of the plywood loose until he can lift it away. The space in there is clean. He leaves her apartment and goes down to his, brings up some branches and newspaper. He builds a fire and places the screen in front of it.

'Well,' she says, coming up beside him. She hands him a beer, like she's known him all her life. 'Isn't that something.' She has another beer for herself. She taps hers against his and searches his eyes. 'Fire-maker. You should rent yourself out.'

They stand there drinking beer and watching the fire.

Susan turns to look at the room. 'Nice light. Orange shadows.' She makes a sound like she's considering something. 'Almost like sunset.'

Blackstrap notices movement through the window. Snow falling, big flakes drifting down lightly in the dusk.

'Major storm coming,' Susan says. 'Good thing we have a fire.'

He looks at her and she is watching him, the bottle rim to her mouth, her wet lips coming away from sipping.

'At least we'll be warm.'

In the days that follow, Susan continues to cook for Blackstrap. Dishes he never tasted before from other countries. Food from Morocco, India, Mexico . . . She uses fresh herbs and spices from a store named Mary Jane's. A health-food store, she calls it. 'Ever try a smoothie?' she asks.

'No,' he says.

She puts one together for him in a blender. The blender makes more noise than he wants to endure. 'It has yoghurt, bananas, ice cream, cinnamon . . .'

When he tastes it, it reminds him of eggnog. It's like liquid dessert.

'Good?' She wants to know.

'Um . . .' He tastes more, not knowing whether to swallow or chew it first.

'You like it?'

He doesn't say anything. He takes another drink, waiting to answer. His eyes go to the table. There are pictures of performers and other people there. She notices him looking at them.

'Do you like his music?' Susan asks.

'Who?'

She gives a name and nods at the photograph.

'I don't know.'

She goes to her stereo and puts on a cassette. It's like country and western music with a flavour of Irish in it. It makes him want a beer, not a smoothie. He lays the glass on the table. Too sweet for his stomach.

There are big envelopes on the table with Canadian government logos up in the corners. 'We're sending him to Europe.'

'Why?' He looks right at her face. 'What'd he do?'

She laughs lightly until her lips part. 'On tour. The Department of Heritage is footing the bill.'

'Oh, yeah.' He has no idea what she's talking about.

'Do you play guitar?'

'No,' he says, not understanding why he answered right away, or why he lied.

'I thought you might play guitar.'

He asks himself why she would think that and glances at his hands.

By the end of the week, they are sleeping together, but they do not have sex. Blackstrap sleeps soundly in Susan's bed. Her sheets are soft and she has heavy quilts that pin him to the bed. She touches him under the covers, puts her head on his chest. She kisses him on the cheek, then on the lips.

'Goodnight,' she says sweetly. 'Lover.'

Weeks later, Blackstrap wakes one night, incredibly aroused with all of his senses charged. He slides on top of Susan and rests his head on her shoulder. He raises her long lacy nightdress and gently parts her legs. What drives him to do this seems more natural than breathing, the sensation without complication, reminding him of safety and boyhood. Not a word is spoken, only their eyes set on each other. He thinks he might cry from the way he's feeling, from the way Susan is content to watch him so peacefully this close up.

When he is done, he kisses her on the neck and rolls away. She touches his arm. How he has found himself in this place with her is a mystery. They say very little to one another. Each day, Blackstrap comes upstairs and knocks on her door. Susan smiles and lets him in. They sit on the couch with the fire going. They watch the flames. They eat and go to bed. Although he knows little about relationships, he suspects he has come across something impossible to find.

'You're going back out there,' Susan says when he shows up at her door with his duffel bag. 'It must be freezing cold.'

'It is.'

'When are you going?'

'Now.'

'Why didn't you tell me before?'

He says nothing to this.

'It hasn't been twenty-one days?'

He nods, thinking that she looks like a little girl.

'Really? Let me drive you to the airport.'

'I got a cab downstairs.'

'You don't need a cab.' Just like that, there are tears in her eyes. She wipes at the tip of her nose. 'What do you need a cab for? When will you be back?'

'Twenty-one days.'

'Right.' Her eyes wetter. 'Twenty-one days . . . Be careful, will you.' She kisses him on the mouth. Her lips are hot and wet. She hugs him and kisses his face, his cheeks, his lips again. She runs her hands over his body and through his hair, her tears smearing on his skin, whispering, 'Please, please, be careful. Please.'

(February)

Up on the drill floor, the weather is a curse. Snow melting against machinery, then freezing in clumps. Snow banking up. The roustabouts de-ice the working area, and try shovelling the snow away. The steel floor is a slippery mess. The men continue to put together pipe. The wind catches the top end of a pipe length and tosses it toward the drill shack. The driller ducks inside. The pipe bounces off the roof. Billy Cullen slips and falls. Hits his head. The hard hat protecting him. Blackstrap helps him up. He looks at the driller, then up at the derrickman. But he can't see the derrickman through the snow.

Cuntz screaming: 'I got ninety thousand dollars invested in this rig. If we don't find oil soon, I am going to *lose . . . my . . . money*.' His voice rising to such a high pitch it's almost a squeal.

More pipe gets loose. Billy Cullen slips again. Snatches for his hard hat wobbling away. The pipe falls three feet from where he's trying to get up off the floor. It bounces and clangs around while Blackstrap makes a grab for it. Billy's gloved hands sliding on the deck.

Johnny Cole laughs it off, yanking Billy to his feet. 'New legs on ya?' shouts Johnny.

Fred Rumsey says nothing. Bent near the drill stem, he loosens the slips to draw up the pipe. Ten thousand feet down. Deep into water, then a shaft cut into the ocean floor. Gouging into rock and earth where the oil is buried. Working with the stinging lash of snow on his face.

Later that night they are playing cards. Earlier, when he had passed the radio room, Blackstrap remembered it was Valentine's Day. Men waiting in the room. He never put his name down to use the sea-to-shore telephone last night. A long list of men calling home to their sweethearts. Valentine's Day usually nothing he ever paid attention to.

Feeling regret now, Blackstrap cannot get Susan out of his thoughts. He should have bought something for her before he left. If he had known that day was coming. She is nearer to him the way she is off at a distance. He thinks of them in her upstairs apartment. The fire going. Both of them at the table, eating food off of dark blue plates. What he wouldn't give to be there now, because sadness is seeping into him. Sadder and sadder until he thinks of Agnes. Never can he seem to get clean of her. Snagged in his heart, the way her memory pulls.

Twenty-one days, twenty days, nineteen . . .

The storm has picked up and is turning ferocious. Blackstrap remembers when he fixed Susan's fireplace, her saying how they might be snowed in. It never happened but they pretended, not leaving the apartment until Susan had to go to work in the bright winter morning.

February on the Atlantic Ocean. These sorts of waves were not meant to be endured. Hurricane-force winds. The barometer steadily dropping.

Susan and the fireplace. The living room solid beneath their feet. A house built on earth.

There is a feeling of disquiet in Blackstrap's bones. In the water of his body. If these men, most from fishermen stock, were ever out in a boat when this gale started up, they would have headed for shore at the first whiff of it. They would have known better. Otherwise, they would have perished. But the Yanks know even better, their 'better' adding up to dollars. Sixty-, seventy-foot waves. Never in a boat. But this is a boat. A ship anchored at four corners. A ship designed to endure the extremes. The biggest and sturdiest oil rig in the world. So says the information behind the plexiglas screwed to the bulkhead outside Blackstrap's room. He took a few moments to finally check it over just after coming off shift. Billy Cullen there at his side like always. More noise than usual in the radio room when he passed. With the weather being what it is. Billy reading, 'The *Ocean Ranger* is designed to withstand simultaneously 115 mph winds, a 3-knot current, and 110-foot waves. The helicopter deck will be rated for a Sikorsky S-65 helicopter. The *Ocean Ranger* will accommodate 100 men in its living quarters and will drill at the 80-foot draft in water depths up to 3,000 feet when equipped with 3,000 feet of anchor chain.'

Blackstrap wonders who wrote those words. If the man had ever stepped on a boat.

The cards are dealt out.

'What happened widt that story?' asks Blackstrap.

'Wha' one?' asks Fred Rumsey.

'The guy who punched Cuntz.'

'Yeah,' says Johnny Cole. 'Wha's up widt dat? Widt Duanne?' He says the name Duanne with a toothy twang.

Billy Cullen looks at his cards. Frowns like there's nothing but bad at the end of the story. 'Duanne and his brudder. Dey were sent off on a supply boat.'

'Yeah,' says Blackstrap, tossing out two cards.

Fred Rumsey deals to Blackstrap. 'Cuntz put Duanne 'n 'is brudder in a net basket 'n had da crane operator hold dem out over da rig. Supply boat down below, bobbin' around. A blizzard blowing. Told da crane operator to hold 'em dere. An hour and a 'alf in da basket. Out over da sea in a blizzard.' Fred deals more cards to replace the ones thrown out by the others.

No one says another thing for a while.

'Dere were almost a riot over dat,' says Fred. 'Dem fuk'n Yanks. Da Newf'nlanders were gonna kill 'em all. Wipe 'em out.'

Blackstrap bids, tossing in a few chips.

Johnny Cole folds.

Billy Cullens bids. Then raises.

Fred says he's out.

Blackstrap sees Billy Cullen.

'Full house,' says Billy, laying down his cards. Proud as punch.

Blackstrap lays down his cards. Four aces. His face showing nothing. Never. And then the slow smile that can't be helped when winning comes like that.

The men look at him. The ace of spades edging away from the others. A vibration in the table.

'Jesus,' says Fred Rumsey. 'Lucky frigger. What're the fuk'n odds?'

Blackstrap looks at the wide splay of chips. A few of them in the pile begin to slide. A little to the left. The quiet threat of an avalanche. An illusion. The body tipping. A ship's movement. Not supposed to be that way. Not what he suspects. Not on this rig.

The men all look at each other. Their faces registering surprise. Instantly grim. What about the ballast system? Everything always upright. As steady as a hotel. Never anything like this. And the stomach-aching dread as the room begins tilting. Coming awake. Coming alert. Rising.

'Christ,' says Fred Rumsey.

All of them on their feet without knowing.

The cards and chips slide along the table. Hands go out to prevent the chips from spilling. But it's too late.

'Fuh'k,' says Johnny Cole. 'Who owns what now?'

The chips fall onto the floor. Clatter around and roll toward the bunks and lockers.

Johnny Cole watching them all roll.

A siren starts blaring.

Blackstrap's arm on the bunk edge. He checks the porthole. Black in landless darkness and fizzles of grey almost white. A wave hits the glass. Three feet away, he can feel the force of it.

The lights flicker.

Off for a while.

Then on.

At once, the men move for the corridor. To join the sounds of other men already hurrying up toward the office. The sounds of disunity and confusion. Where the bubble in the glass is no longer centred. Across the way, the radio room is full of men. Men already there to call their sweethearts. Others there now, too. Ones without sweethearts.

Why hadn't he thought of buying something for Susan? He had seen the hearts in the stores. The advertisements for the special event, but he couldn't have picked out a card. He didn't know what it might have said. How badly he was in love with her or not, printed there for her to read.

There is much fast conversation.

Jack, the radioman, saying: 'There is a serious problem. We need to get people off now.'

'Where're da lifeboats?' says Billy Cullen. Barely words through a dry throat. Knowing nothing now. Not having learned about this. His head a mass of fright. His young voice not hiding the scare. His worse nightmare never expected. Sounding even younger. A helpless boy.

Blackstrap looks at Billy. Sees Fred Rumsey's face. Snatches of other men's alert expressions.

Then the lights go out.

The rig tips more. Bodies fall against him. The radioman is calling into darkness: 'Mayday. Mayday . . .' But nothing at the other end. His words going nowhere.

A light sweeps through the room.

A light in a tunnel.

In a shaft.

In a mine.

All faces turned that way.

'Come on, boys.' It's Cuntz with a flashlight. 'Let's get to the lifeboats. Move.'

Blackstrap remembers the two survival suits. In the room across the way. He goes in there and catches a flicker of orange. From the flashlights sweeping around. Another light on now in someone else's hands. He grabs both suits and follows after the push of men. Up the stairs to the drill deck. One of the survival suits caught on something. Or someone trying to tug it away. He holds on. A blinding blizzard with savage wind. The howling blackness. The air wet and mercilessly stinging. A barrage of needles. The men press against the wind. Some of them in shirts and pants. Faces dipped to be shielded. Trying to look everywhere, even up. Eyes squinting. Others in green or blue overalls.

He sees Billy Cullen and grabs him.

'Here, get back under,' Blackstrap shouts, dragging Billy back toward the stairs. The noise of steel straining. Like wood that cannot snap. Only bend. Creaking. The sharp groan felt in the fillings of his teeth as the rig tilts more and a wave sweeps behind them. Up onto the deck. Eighty feet above the sea. Men washed away. Gone before anyone realizes a thing. The impossibility in an instant. Blackstrap sees as he turns, hurrying now. An arm in water. A leg. The back of a man. Gushing by. No way to try for them. He pulls Billy fully into the door. Down the stairs with water sloshing in after them. Along the corridor. Leaned against the bulkhead. He struggles to get his suit on. There are men in the darkness. Flashlights up the stairs. Inside the door. Flashes of Billy's face watching it all. Men not wanting to go out. That open door and the fierceness of the weather reaching him where he is. More water pouring down the stairs. The smell of it where it was not meant to be. In here. The stink of salt water and oil below deck.

'Get ta da boat,' says Blackstrap. But he cannot see Billy Cullen. Only a voice coming back to him. If there was one. Up the metal stairs. 'You dere? Billy?!'

'Yes.' A voice behind him. Following after him. Up the stairs. Up to the door. The flash of a lightbeam. He looks back. Billy's face. Terrified. No orange suit. 'Where's yer fuk'n suit?'

Billy doesn't answer.

'Billy!'

The temperature nips at the flesh. Waves pound the *Ocean Ranger*. The deck floor is awash. Blackstrap wonders what comes next. The ugly tilt of the rig. A place on a boat. The cold will kill him. He knows this. Without the suit. His mind on his chances. They are zero. If this rig goes over in the black rising swell of Atlantic. He stumbles sideways. His feet slipping. Ice washed over and over. Freezing thicker. Growing. Shoots out his arm to brace himself against a steel wall. Falls against it. His feet almost going out from under him. Eye strain in the darkness. Billy Cullen on top of him. Holding on. Fingers dug right into his flesh. The pound of a wave. Against a cliff that will go over. A group of men at the lifeboat. Fifteen feet away. Only one lifeboat on this side. The side leaning toward the water. The other two, on the other side, would be unlaunchable. Swung in against the rig, the davits wouldn't work.

Who designed this fucking thing?

The fucking Japanese.

Fred Rumsey in there. In his overalls. A plaid shirt. The sweep of flashlights. Illuminating flecks of snow. White and dead moving. Waving him over. Light full on Blackstrap's face. Shivering over him. Blinding him. A greater sense of unknowing now. When the beam moves away. Billy Cullen lit up too. While others try to board the boat. Fred pulls them in. Shouting. Enough room for almost everyone. Before two other men. Right in front of Blackstrap. Greg from Heart's Content and Peter from St. John's. Men trying to climb into the boat. Are hit by the thousand-pound wash of a wave. Their feet flipped out from under them. A bully trick. Bodies tipped and swirled. Ramming them forward. Toward the derrick. Spray in Blackstrap's face. Stinging. Blinding. A mouthful of it because he was shouting to them. Like the others. He wipes at his eyes. His mouth. Hawks and spits. Vomits without even bending down. A bone-rattling shiver close to a sob. He thinks of crouching to hang on better. Another wave pounding. His hands already half dead. Losing their grip. When the sizzling wave pulls back from the platform. Greg and Peter are gone. His boots soaking wet. Feet frozen stiff already. No feeling in his toes.

There is a noise.

More shouting and crashing. From another direction.

Blackstrap turns to see nothing. Black white sky. A shadow coming from the other way. A shimmer from the other side. Then a bulk of something. One of the lifeboats launched. It bounces by Blackstrap's head. Not a sound of it in the wind. Just the silent fullness of it, gaining. Until it smashes against the deck. Cracking and splintering as the men spill out. Five of them flat on the platform. Sliding in the wash of water. Fish in the bottom of a boat. But their faces. Others trying to rise to their feet. Washed away by smaller waves. Big enough to pull them to the edge. And over the railing. Arms and hands jerking for a grip. And calling mouths open. Gone in the black drop.

Hold . . . fucking . . . on.

The body picked up carried high in the water. Lost. Then a face. Surging around Blackstrap's boots. An arm, a hand, snatching, almost pulling him down. He backs away. He lets go his hold. The count of the next wave. 'Go,' he shouts to Billy Cullen. Rushes and grabs for the lifeboat. With the weight of Billy not knowing. Grabs hold to the handle. No idea how many men the boat holds. Sixty or seventy. The boat has been lowered to the deck by one of the men. But the waves bash the door. Fill the boat with water. Make it impossible to close the door. There are men in there. Soaking wet. Trying not to get sucked from their places. Then the two up front are swept out. A tumbling fall into the sea. Eighty feet down. Speckled-white blackness to blacker blackness. Bodies tinier. Blackstrap gets Billy Cullen in there. Billy Cullen there in his hand. Frozen to him. Shoves him in. Snapping the ice that bonds them. Then tries climbing up. His leg in someone's hands. Trying to climb up on him. Or hold on. He will fall back from the strain. Into the black sucking pull of gravity. Andy Coffin on that ladder. What will he hit if he drops now? Falling for all eternity. The arms let go and he is in. His stomach turned by the possibility of dangling. There is no more time. Pulled in by Fred Rumsey. Chances not so zero now. The rig listing more. A man puking next to him. All over his suit. The sound of retching as men slide away. In the waves. The howl beyond the opening. The big rig leaning toward the water. A monstrous jungle of steel about to go under. Like a ship after all. Just like a ship. A creaking, straining ship and the snapping of anchor chain. The snapping of steel no stronger than wood.

'Shut the door,' shouts Cuntz. He's in there. 'Now.' The boat is sealed. Like a capsule. How many men in the boat? Blackstrap does not know. Their feet in water. The stink of bodies. The sounds from mouths unheard before.

In the muffled lifeboat. The breathing of the men.

Heavy panicky breath in different beats.

Terrified. He hears his own most. Eyes searching around. Trapped but maybe safe.

Fred Rumsey. Billy Cullen. Johnny Cole. Sealed in. Other men too. The lifeboat rocks. Water in the bottom of it. The men trying to keep their feet up.

'Where?' says one of them. Johnny Cole. And starts trying to rock the boat.

'Ready?' says Cuntz. 'I'm launching.' Flashlight beam on a button. His finger pushing.

Why?

Suddenly, the lifeboat moves. At a speed unknown. Maybe swept away. It descends. Slowly? On ropes, he supposes. Two ropes. Then drops. Plummets. Sucking the breath out of Blackstrap. Not a sound from any of the men. Except for Billy Cullen. What sounds like a bit of quiet crying. Only enough whimpering to jut out. Under the pressure of the fall. Blackstrap holds to the sides of the boat. Presses his arms there. Waiting. Until they slam against something. The end of the davit ropes? What? It might be anything. The rig. Above them? About to come down. Another boat. The ocean. Have they landed? It's all the same. A hard wall. The damage. The blackness. The noise. The neck-aching jolt upon impact. Smashed. They hit so fast. He might have broken something. Parts of his body hurt by quickness and objects unknown. Men tossed against men. Hard. Like punches. He might have gone unconscious. He might have for a while. But now it appears they are afloat. They are turning over. Rising with the sea.

Grunts and gasps. Shivering in the throat not like anything from men.

Away from the rig. Blackstrap tells himself. Get the fuck away from the rig. Even upside-down. If that's how he is. He sees them being hurled against the tilting platform. Swept back onto its deck. Through the window. The water-blurred flashes of lights from the rig. Lit like a horrible Christmas tree. Lights back on. Why? Listing. The lights burning out. Beneath the water. The rig listing at a forty-five-degree angle. A snatch of it. On its way under. Or a dream. In the Atlantic Ocean. The boat surging away. Propelled. As though under engine. A swallowing wave from the sinking rig.

The freezing cold seeping through as they slow. So that it feels like water is entering. They all check for wetness. The walls. Their hands at their numb feet. Already wet. But it is not water coming in. It is only frost. Its intrusion. A tiny hint of itself. They will soon be frozen. They will soon be dead. Each and every one of them. Only a matter of minutes. How many minutes in the water before death? They had warned him. The only man in a survival suit. An extra minute or more. If he could think.

Through the window lights approaching. The bob of lights. They do not know how far they are away from the rig. If it is the rig they are returning to. Eyes frozen over. The smell of shit thicker in the air. Fred Rumsey is praying to the Virgin Mary. 'Pppray fuh-ffor us sss-sinners. Nnnow, nnn . . . at th-the hour . . .' His teeth chattering.

Blackstrap's mother and father. There in his mind.

'Sh-hut up,' shouts Cuntz. 'Shu-uh-ut up, or I am gggoing to lose muhy *mind*.'

Who will punch Cuntz first? Not an arm raised. Only because of the numbness. The God-awful discomfort of men close together freezing and shifting inches to keep warm. Groaning. Head hung down. Billy Cullen vomits again and cries for his mother. The pinch beneath the skin. Every inch at once. Pinching. The torment of warmth leaving him.

The lights bob. It might be a supply boat. Or it is only them bobbing. It might be a rescue boat. Billy Cullen tries wiping at the window. It is freezing. A view through ice. The only window. Too small. For the grim sprawl of the view.

'Ccc-uh-ccan't ssee,' he says, bawling, an opened mouth, a hollow held that way for a while. Then more weak pawing at the window. 'Ssss-uppuhpuhly bbboat,' his voice filled with trembling joy. 'I th-think.' The words barely made out from the chill. The joy. Face aglow on the edge of a flashlight arc. The other men in desperate pain. Some of them still. Dead from the drop. Leaned one way or another. Dead from the cold. Men rubbing men. Shaking them. Butting up against them. Leaving them. In horror, they realize. Fred Rumsey shaking his head. His eyes shut. Johnny Cole punching the inside wall.

'Stttay awwwake,' Cuntz threatens in a low voice. The flashlight falls from his fingers. The beam shining up. No one able to reach for it. To hold it. The shadowed light on Cuntz's face.

The rattling tremble in Blackstrap's bones. Cold and fear. He does not know. A volatile mix. There is little difference between the two. No feeling in his lips. Agnes. Her face in his head. Dear God, how did this happen? He asks her. At this point. Either might do him in. Cold or fear. Might kill Billy Cullen. Fred Rumsey. Johnny Cole.

'Ssuh buh-oat,' says Billy Cullen. Smiling numb lips. 'Is.'

The flashlight switched off and on. By Cuntz who has managed to lift it. Using his wrists. Stiff fingers bent at angles. Distress signal. Off and on. The switch raised against his face. Like a strobe. So Blackstrap's eyes hurt to move. The carnage inside this sealed shell.

It is upon them.

The boat.

They strike the side of it. And they are tossed into each other. An elbow in the face. Blackstrap's nose smarting. Blood pouring out. He sniffs it away. Warmth. Sniffs up. Wants more of his own blood. On him. Helping him. But his blood is not warm. Not that he can tell. Nothing left of his stomach. A pit sucked into itself. The dread of the final end.

Billy Cullen reaches for the release. Smiling. Poking at it. Lame. His fingers useless. Good.

'Nnn . . . Nnnn . . . No.'

It's okay. It's alright. Look. The supply boat.

No one can call no again, in time.

Too cold are they to say.

The latch.

A hand with fingers that feel now.

Feel one final time.

The door pops open.

Water gushes aboard. Weather cut from chaos takes the space. A snatch of a million fleeting razors. The freezing ocean as water and wind. The blast in the face. Skin and bones dead in seconds. The chewing howl. Eyes frozen fully shut. And the boat sinks. The men are in the water. Arms and legs useless to swim. They sink. Silently, they give in. Men gone from themselves.

The harrowing chill attacks. Every nerve. Blackstrap's brain unusable. Just like that. Two minutes. No more than two minutes in the water. In a survival suit. Before he is dead. That time. What was it? They were told. Already cold enough. They were warned. This is all he can almost think. Before his mind goes. Unconscious. He floats. Bobs and rises. His head in it. The shrieking rage in his deaf ears. Him or the weather. They are one in this. His body drops. Sucked low. By the vast slow pull of black water. The supply boat high above him. If he could look up, his eyelids almost stuck. The blur of boat descending through crystals. Lower and lower until level with him. Almost on its side. Moments uncountable. Then the boat beneath him. Down, down, in a deep watery hole. And him raised high on bobbing blackness.

Billy Cullen tossed toward the boat. Bashed into the side. His head cracked at the neck. Then open. Swallowed. Wet like that. His hair with blue ice in it. The other men swept off. Blackstrap has no sight of them. A blur. The salt water blinding. Burns and freezes his face to the point of snapping. A finger poked through him. A hole. By the wind with its tiny fierce icy pellets. Trying to shatter him. A patter on glass. And the fucking howl. His life and Agnes. Why, Agnes? The harrowing fucking howl of the wind. Making watery madness of the sea. He cannot keep it out of his mouth. He can barely see. Gone again. The supply boat. Rising and falling. Frozen dead. A hook in front of his blank face. Metallic. It sticks to his cheek. Freezes to him. Tears away. A hole poked in him. The wound sealed. Almost level with the ship. Then the hull high above him. A hill of black rolling water. Floating on his back. Suddenly awake to see the hook gone. If that's what it was. The salt in the cut. And he rises. I am dead. The hook comes again. Catches between his arm and side. Now lured toward the supply vessel that drops in a rolling hole. Down he goes. Dragged after it. Down and down. The ship rising again. He drifts away. He rolls over. He sleeps. He thinks there's something floating. Billy Cullen. If he could move his arm. Something like fur. Wet and lifeless. The back of a head. Hair. Or a drowned dog. Nearer to him. Being gathered to him. No body with it. No head. Hair or fur. Or something growing in the water. Blooming. Something alive. Or dead. Living in this mess. He sees two men on board. Drenched by the waves. Aglisten. Amelt. Being rocked forward. Then gone back. Tilting. There. In his face. The rusty bottom of the boat. The wind and noise. Roaring. The bottom of the boat to come down on him. He shuts his eyes. They already are. Burning. Something cold touches his face. Something metallic. He opens his mouth to say . . . The salt water gushes in. He swallows. He gags. He cannot turn his head to struggle to breathe. Chokes. Feels metal on his teeth. Frozen to his lips. He closes his mouth. Bites down. With whatever strength left in him. He goes under. His head lifts. His mouth, a plug of ice. A metal hook centred there and stuck. Frozen. The point pressing inside his mouth. A great weight in his neck. His head tilts. Pressure in his left cheek. Then a popping without feeling. The thick hook going through. Drawn above the water. He rises. His body spins backward. Is pulled toward the supply boat. His arms numb at his sides. He rises more. Whether on a wave or on a hook and rope. No idea of knowing. His neck about to snap. From the weight. Cheek tearing more. The hook frozen in his mouth. The tip broken through. In the corner of his eyes.

His body against the hull of the supply boat. Barely nothing to hear now. The weight of himself in his neck. Hanging. No feeling there. Against something though. A man's hand reaching down. Nothing to sense. Who are they lifting? Except in his teeth. His teeth still living. Still hard and alive. He bites down. Another hook finds his dead leg. He is tipped sideways. Goes underwater. A body appearing beside him. A man moving. A man who could be anyone. A man with a face he does not know. A man in a survival suit like him. It might be him. Is it?

Any man he does not recognize, but recognizes as every man. Grabbing him. A man from the supply boat who has fallen in. The man is lifting Blackstrap. A man on the boat reaches over. Takes him. Pulls him aboard. Lies on the metal. Slides quickly. Hits something near him. Stops. The man above him tries for the other man. But he is lost. Then there again. So that he is rescued. Hauled aboard. Shouting in his ears. Questions and curses. Erased in the wind. In black fizzle. He is lifted to his feet. They are both taken away by another man. They are led off at once. Hunched over. Squat down and hurrying at rocking angles. Weight shifting. The sea beneath the boat. Changing form. Behind the stormy thickening slant of grey flecks. Blackstrap barely sees. A black wave-wall to one side. Glistening and bleary. Stretching up in a towering rise. To come down on them. But it does not. It hesitates. It waits. Then gives up. Gone. Back from where it came. Lurching them. Toward the supply boat's cabin door. On the way. Hammered by another wave. And the three of them go over. Slide toward the edge of the vessel. Strike it. A shoulder busted. A leg snapped. He does not know because he cannot feel. Beyond the dead damage. The blunt popping inside. The man who had been in the water. His rescuer on his knees. Holding on to Blackstrap. The other man has hold of him. The sea water clears from the deck. As they tilt sideways to face the water. Looking directly down at it. Falling. Hitting metal. His body buckled. But not over the edge. And the man holding on. Above him. The man's legs dangling. Until the boat levels. And the man rests back against the deck. Then hurries to stand. Rushes across and grabs Blackstrap. Yanks him to his feet. Again. Three of them on their way to the cabin door. Pitching one way as gravity angles. He rises from his feet. What gravity? Nothing between him and the deck. He settles again. Afloat? Was he in the air? Adrift? They lean against the tilt. Lean to walk. Are held still. Are held frozen. Pressure. Then gravity shifts once more. And they swing forward. Barely able to maintain balance.

Inside. They put him on a bunk. Dead tired with this thought: He has been saved. Dead tired with the sickening rocking. They leave him to someone. A man. A woman. Back out into the storm to rescue others.

And there is Agnes Bishop. It is she who has found him. It is she who raises her fingers to his face and shuts his eyes.

Junior with his lips to one of Blackstrap's ears. Ruth with her lips to the other. A whispering harmony: 'Mommy appears in the hospital doorway. She cries as soon as she sees him. So unlike him to be in bed. Resting. He would be furious if he knew. How can he just lie there? She takes hold of his hands.

'Mommy sits by the side of his bed. She recites from memory the journals of Francis Hawco. The shipwrecked man they thought was dead. She leaves out the part about the woman. The ghost. That part belongs to her. She explains, word for word, about the abandoned ship. Floating in the distance. Not a soul on board. She wonders where Blackstrap might be now. Watching his face. On which shore is he lying. Along the perimeter of this island.

'Daddy sits in the corner. "Who is it?" he asks. Mad. His words hot with anger. Staring at Blackstrap's bed. Junior at the window with a camera to his eye. Raised to the outside. Ruth banging her arms together. Her hands dead at the ends. Flopping like flippers. And screeching in silence. Her mouth. A circle the machinery beeps from.

'My only son, thinks Mommy. You die with your children. That part of you that first went over to them. That was taken. That was freely given. It dies. Yet when a child is sick you come alive with caring. Nothing matters of yourself. Other than the child's return to health. That possibility. Praying they were well. Nothing in the world is of consequence. The newspaper dares to report on insignificant matters. The radio, the television. They are filled with the cares of the living. They torment you with their irrelevance. But if this one dies, this son, this boy, this child, everything will be lost. It will be reported in the newspaper, on the radio and television. I will have ceased to exist. I will cease. I will die for the hope of Heaven.

'"I will die for the hope of Heaven," Mommy whispers. Eyes shut in the dim hospital room. Her hands holding Blackstrap's hand. Careful of the IV. She prays: "I will die for the hope of Heaven." And she hears from her mouth the "I" and sees that it is her again. It is not about Blackstrap. But about Mommy. The loss she might experience. And with this realization, her heart eases. Her body, once rigid, turns supple. Her lips part while she watches her son's face.

'It is not about me.

'It is about him.

'In the morning. While Mommy sleeps in the chair by his bed. Blackstrap's eyes open. He has seen everything. Haven't you. Seen it all. He has heard everything. His mother. Mommy. His father. Daddy. His brother. Junior. His sister. Ruth. Hello, Blacky. The living and the dead. Which one is he now? Why do you survive us, always?'

Out of the coma, Blackstrap lies in bed. Wondering where he was. All that he recalls is water. The bed is afloat. He wants out of it. The hospital tilts. The window is masked at night with blue. Water thrusts there. Pellets. He shakes his head on the pillow. A dream of his mother and father. His brother and sister. Trapped in this room with him. And he tries to keep the tears from pouring. One or two come anyway. Before he can hold them back. He rubs his face in the pillow. His mouth open.

Billy Cullen. Johnny Cole. Fred Rumsey.

Susan.

He wants out of the hospital. Despite his weakness, he needs to walk. He needs to see Susan. He feels that she has been harmed by the storm. He feels seasick. His stomach unstable. He wants to be in Susan's apartment. The fireplace. The food. Everything rises and ebbs. He moves his hands to see they are bandaged. Wrapped in a clump of white. Two fists of blizzards.

He needs to get a message to Susan. But cannot speak. Again and again, he dreams that she is in danger. Because of him. He does not know her last name. Her telephone number.

His mother is there always. She smiles at him. She loves him. She is not like herself. Her face. He thinks that she is younger. That he is younger. Ageless. Only to be alive. That does it. Alive. Or is it the other?

There is a crowd outside the hospital. Mostly people with cameras and tape recorders. They want what he's holding too dearly. The flesh-erasing memories. He has nothing to say. He moves past on crutches. Knows of his fingers gone now. One thumb. Three fingers. A count of what remaining. He tries not to think. His feet. Toes sawed off. They told him which ones. Not the big ones to keep him upright. He half listened or pretended. He never looked when the bandages were changed. To see what monster.

He sees men. Their faces losing colour. Men and women in motion. One foot before the other, they drain. Energy back into the sea.

Frozen men being offloaded from a ship.

Twenty-two bodies recovered.

That's what he sees in the place of things. Not in front of him, but in him.

Dead men floating in water. Already covered in ice. Stuck together in chunks.

He had been saved but had saved no one.

The sea a savage to those families forever.

What beauty in the water on a calm day.

It is cold outside, the wind bitter. But it is May. Spring. The sun above him in the blue sky. It puts a rattle in him. Not winter. People in light jackets. Sneakers. Shoes. He cannot stop trembling. Clouds over the sun. The coldest breeze imaginable. He cannot hold himself steady. His knees are the worst. His left shoulder still aches fiercely. Cracked in so many places. He wonders if he might not be here. Not fully anywhere since coming back to himself. There is humour or kindness in nothing. The elements not felt as they are. He leans more on one crutch. Opens the passenger door for his mother. With the fingers that have been left for him. Remains. The remains of him. What remains? He has to look at his hand. The stubs partially bandaged. Waits until she gets in and shuts the door. The blunt stubs. How many fingers lost on that rig? How many fingers collected in a box? He keeps his back to the reporters.

The calls. Mister Hawco. Other people stood there too. Wondering about him. The sealer who clubbed that American woman. Yes, it is. Where to move now on his crutches. The shouts all garbled and meaning one thing. Waves of noise with voices almost there. He is guilty of something. Then he opens the back door. Leans in the back seat. Pulls his legs in. Shuts the door. Keeps looking ahead. His father at the steering wheel.

The pavement rolling in reverse.

Then straightening to drive. Down the black strip of asphalt. Steady and unmoving. That night in the flat-bottomed *Seaforth Highlander*. Rising and falling on impossible angles. Water gushing and frothing in from all sides. It would not go over. But the lights of the drill rig on that angle.

No one else rescued. The *Seaforth Highlander* forced to head for safety. Where would that be? Land. A chunk of something rooted. The land he rolls over now.

Safety here.

Tires gripping the pavement. Smooth and forward. Traction.

The water beneath the earth. Rising and falling in his heart. His head aswim. Something deep in the earth always moving. The way he thinks has changed. Has it? He is frightened of everything. A sound from a passing child. Rushing in through the window.

The door is knocked upon. The telephone rings. The silver stem on the ringer turned down. A dull clatter. Blackstrap cannot spend a single peaceful moment in his house. There is no end to people wanting the truth about what happened. The only two eyes that saw. He will not give it to them. Because they do not want the truth, they want the story. He will not give over the story of those men who died. They did not die, they perished. He will not explain how those men perished. He will not give it to men and women paid to know the pain of others. To open it raw to everyone else. The wounds. The tears. The disease. The death. The loved ones. They are filled with maggots. That's how he sees them. Rotten, cunt-ugly fuckers. He sees himself at a table, staring. And he is sitting there, watching only his hands. Uncle Ace. His fingers missing. People entering the room. Then leaving. Shadows speaking in a language once understood. The stories he heard of his great-uncle sitting in his chair at the kitchen table in Bareneed. Not a word from his mouth. All those years alive. Not one word from Blackstrap's mouth. Only his eyes that would watch. Like they were narrowing to see. Straining to make something out in the lamplight. His father told him the way it was. Then Ace's eyes catching sight of the small growing bigger. Seeing too much. Widening. Not a single word. But now. Now, Uncle Ace finally says: 'N'ver ag'in.' Eyes wider. Seeing through the boiling black water that pounds down over him and stretches infinitely in all directions.

'N'ver ag'in on da sea.' His words Blackstrap's. But only for now.

Dead right, for now.

Water beneath his boots in the earth.

The book publishers call. The movie people. Wanting to buy the rights to his story. Jacob tells them that Blackstrap is dead. Whether to protect him or believed as fact. Blackstrap has no true idea.

He should be happy to have lived, but he wishes that he were dead. All of those men, heroic in their demise. The trembling voices of the families. The mothers, fathers, sisters, brothers, calling to ask him. Tell me anything. Did you see him? Did you see my boy, my husband, my brother . . . ? What did he say? Was it peaceful? Do you know where we can find him?

The lawyers at his door. He will not take a penny. Millions, they tell him. Someone must pay you for your pain.

They leave notes.

They send letters.

Psychological damage.

Pain and suffering.

Loss of limbs.

Not limbs.

Fingers and toes.

Post-traumatic stress disorder.

Millions. Never the need to work again. To worry about money. Never a worry in the world.

Imagine someone playing your part.

A famous actor.

Who would you want to play you?

For the sake of the dead men,

tell us.

He is terrified every moment.

Waking or sleeping.

Dusk through the window.

On the verge of tears.

A puddle.

A brook.

A pond.

A glass of it in his hand.

'I'm go'n away,' Blackstrap says, his voice in the darkness of his mother's bedroom.

'Why?' his mother says. Her hand coming up to touch him at that distance. There is movement in the bed as she rises to sit. Coming awake or trying. Hands held against her face, she rubs at her eyes.

He does not know why he must leave. A step nearer. A limp getting better by the week. No nearer than that. His only thumb running over the smooth tender nubs of his fingers.

'Why?' her voice chokes. 'Don't you have any idea?'

He shrugs. A feeling only. The need to be gone from anything known.

'Is it because you survived?'

He does not understand and does. What she is getting at. There is no sorting it out exactly. It only hurts his head to think anywhere near it.

'When you survive . . . they come after you. They want to know how it's done. Because they can't . . . Because they're not . . .'

Blackstrap stands near the bed and watches his mother. 'Not what?'

'Not surviving.'

Edging a little nearer to her, now that he is going.

'Can you tell them why?' She smiles kindly, knowing the answer already.

He shakes his head. 'No, Mom.'

'How're your feet?'

'Fine.'

Her eyes half seen in the dimness, shifting to his hands. 'When are you going?'

'Now.'

'In the night?' Her eyes skimming higher, to his eyes. 'You're not running away, are you, Alphonsus?'

'No.'

'Under the cover of night.'

'Flight at midnight.'

'That's it, is it? Up into the dark sky? It's not wet up there.' Her gaze toward the windowpane.

'Yeah . . . Maybe I'll stay up there.'

His mother's smile stretching strangely, slowly. But her eyes still on the window. Like he's out there somewhere. 'That's my boy . . . Let's hope it doesn't rain.'

Three hours before his flight. He takes a taxi to his old apartment on Military Road. He remembers where his LTD was parked on the street. It's gone. Another car sits there in its place. He has been away for months. Maybe longer. It is difficult to remember how one thing came after the other, or before.

He takes out his key ring. The key for the outer door was silver. Square instead of tapered. He cannot find the shape of it. His hand tries the knob and discovers it unlocked. The key to his apartment was gold. He tries one of the gold keys. Then another, but none of them fit. The lock must have been changed. With his ear to the door, he hears the murmur of a television show. Then theme music leading to something. He creeps up the stairs and knocks lightly on Susan's door. There is no answer. It sounds hollow in there. The way his apartment used to when he walked across the floor. He knocks three more times. Then leans against the hallway wall, his back sliding down, until he is sitting. Carpet beneath him, worn from continuous tread. He looks at his hands. The new shape of them. The dumb pain still there. The corridor dark. He listens for a noise behind Susan's door. There is only silence.

Standing, he waits a moment and tries the knob. Locked. He rattles the knob. More and more strongly. He pounds on the door.

He pounds until he thinks he hears a small voice buried beneath the noise.

And stops.

Listens. Holds his breath. Stares.

'Hello,' a child's voice behind the door.

'Susan there?' he asks, his tone desperate. His eyes look down because the voice behind the door is low to the ground.

'No.'

'Where is she?'

'I don't know . . . You woke me up.' The words said through a yawn. 'You were banging so fiercely.'

'Does Susan live here?'

'Yes.'

'Where *is* she?'

'She's *here*.'

'Can you get her for me?'

'I . . . can't.'

'Why?'

'Because she's just not, Blacky.'

Gooseflesh prickles Blackstrap's skin. 'Get her for me.'

'She's just not.'

'Not what?' Blackstrap touches the door, his palm flat to it. The door is warm. There's a vibration in it that might be the sound of the television below. He chews on his bottom lip then backs away.

'Because . . . what you touch, Blacky.'

Blackstrap hears himself breathing. Then the toot of a car horn he checks toward. The taxi beyond the walls. But only darkness in the upstairs hallway.

The voice smaller, more distant, with each word: 'Because . . . what you touch.'

He steps away, toward the stairs, and unsteadily descends. He shoves through the door. Fleeing.

Outside, the air is warm. Is it spring? Is it summer?

He checks his keys for the big silver one to his car. Gone. He wonders if he took the right key ring from the house in Cutland Junction. He watches up at Susan's window. A light flashing there. Dot-dot-dash.

Dot-dot-dash. And the child, the woman, the girl, the lady standing there, holding the hand of a pale man staring east, toward water.

Junior sits beside him on the airplane, watching out the small window. Junior sits beside him through everything he has ever known or felt. Blackstrap cursed by the sight of bicycles. By the sight of books and cameras. By the sight of all things touched by Junior. Cursed by the sight of toys bashed together by Ruth. Plastic, solid colours. Red. Blue. Yellow. White. Bashed together. Toys. And that shriek with no sound from her buckled mouth. A child in the aisle across from him. Its big eyes staring. Knowing his thoughts by how its top lip pulls up.

'It's about time,' says the child.

What? Blackstrap wonders.

'One of us got away.'

From what?

He looks over his shoulder. Leans toward the aisle to stare down the rows of seats. A rowdy bunch of Newfoundlanders toward the back. Drunk already. Cracking jokes and singing. Lewd remarks made to the stewardess. Words with double meanings. A bunch of raw laughter.

A flash goes off.

Someone taking a picture.

Black beyond the oval window.

A face watching another face.

Yonge Street. Both sides with tall and low buildings. The longest street in the world, Blackstrap has heard. It runs off as far as the eye can see. A steady flow of cars rolling north and south. Expensive and new. And the occasional limousine, creeping by for the show of it.

It had been no problem finding a job. With his experience on the Halifax docks. A job handling the cutting machine at a toilet paper factory run by blind people. Even with his fingers. One thumb gone. Both hands still functional. Spreading wider to do the job. The missing fingers a bonus. When the woman who did the hiring saw them. He had started out driving forklift. Like his old job. Gloves with the empty fingers. An obstacle course if there ever was one. With those blind people edging around. Some tapping with their canes. Others secretly feeling with their hands. Then he had been offered the cutting job. When someone lost a hand. At least he still had most of his attached.

On his time off, Blackstrap wanders the sidewalks. Anyone who meets his eyes. He tilts his head and winks. Solidly. In acceptance and in defence of himself. A hardness willing to give way. Trying to make himself feel more substantial. They do not respond. Like they know nothing of the greeting. Like they do not see him at all or are afraid of him. He has started on Bloor and worked east. Past Bay Street. Toward Yonge. Then south. With the waterfront in mind. He does not like spending time with the other Newfoundlanders. The ones who have moved up to Toronto and hang around a bar called the Newfie Club. They often act foolish and drink too much. As though it's their birth right to drink themselves into bleary states. Or beyond. Into unconsciousness. A joke. Complaining about a hangover the next day. They like to do nothing more than start fights and chase easy women. The uglier the better. Big-titted and slack-arsed. None of it ever raunchy enough to suit them.

He avoids those sorts of Newfoundlanders. Prefers wandering around by himself. Seeing things that surprise him. He likes to stumble upon the red and yellow shop signs in Chinatown on Spadina. He grows fond of the little people speaking in a choppy language he can't understand. All those little Chinese. Japanese. Whatever they are. Absolute strangers to him.

He likes to stroll down Bay and watch the businessmen in their sharp suits. Neatly cut hair. They move in and out of glass doors. Talking to one another with that look. Like nothing else in the world matters. Even their words in a hurry. Not even watching where they are going. Crossing streets as if by instinct. They keep talking and talking. No one runs them over. Cars screech to a halt for them. They don't even bother to look at what might have happened. A driver slapping a dashboard inside.

Blackstrap has a bad feeling about Yonge Street. The steady movement of the cars unsettles his stomach. Some kind of fake western town he's seen in a cowboy movie. All the low store fronts. The street deserted on Sunday. Newspapers and litter swirling around in vacant doorways. Bars closing too early in the night. What to do when the bars close. Just a big feeling of loneliness. And the heat. Christ! It is like living inside an oven. The steel and concrete and the air so thick and hot.

He swipes a drop of sweat from his nose. The nub of his finger dangling. He licks the drop away. Continues walking. His feet sweating in his socks. In his boots. He should buy a pair of sneakers. But worries about his feet in something so flimsy.

There's a bar up in the Eaton Centre. Maybe open now, if not soon. A picture of a horse's head on its sign. He's been there before. Plans to stop there for a beer or two. Then come back out into the sun. A day that's a little more comfortable. Everything more acceptable then. Alive with a new splash of interest. He dreads returning to his room on Brock Street. There's a liquor store close by. Attracts all the crazies. No shortage of them. A dime a dozen. So many crazies in one place. One or two of them live in the same house with him. He can only sleep there. And most times he's forced to take a bottle home to get any rest at all.

He passes a big grey hotel across from a parking lot. And knows he is almost at the Eaton Centre. A group of black kids leaning against the parking lot railing. They watch him in silence as he approaches. One moves away from the others. Walks straight for him. The black kid flashes what looks like a black plastic gun. Held under his jacket.

'Money for the subway, man.'

Blackstrap ignores the teenager. Keeps walking. He hears a long curse behind him. Spoken in a violent way. Words he's never heard before strung together. Learning to ignore what's headed for him. Like all the others.

Up ahead, a pretty girl in a skirt and blouse. A purse in her hand. Even at a distance, Blackstrap can see through the blouse. See her bra and the curves of her breasts. Maybe a hooker. Maybe not. He can't tell for certain. Maybe just done up to be sexy. Not really selling herself for money. But conjuring up desire. His breath shrinking in his lungs. He watches her face. The even whiteness of her skin. Like Agnes. Her skin. But this woman done up too perfect. Her lips outlined by pale red lipstick. Her eyes covered by large sunglasses that give her face sleekness and mystery. With his hands tucked in his jeans pockets, he turns to watch her pass. The length of her glistening sun-warmed blonde hair down along her back. Her high heels twisting into the concrete. While she passes the group of teenagers. They make noises and call after her. Without a glance back, she raises her hand, gives them the finger.

Turning, he sees a man in a wheelchair gliding along the sidewalk. Blackstrap stops to watch the man. The wheelchair has reminded him of Ruth. Of a stroller. Of babies. He smiles and winks when the man catches his eye.

'How ya doing?' Blackstrap says in passing.

'Alright,' says the man. His arms working the wheels. Shoulders put into it. 'Thanks for asking, man.'

When the wheelchair passes, Blackstrap turns to look at the man. People clearing a path for him on the sidewalk. Human contact. He feels good about himself. The way things should be. Say hello and get a hello in return. That man not so special. His mind filling up with Ruth. He had tried to teach her how to count. One, two, three. Over and over. Until she banged her arm down. One, two three. And she had laughed with her head hanging back. And he had cried with laughter. Because she was so beautiful. There was nothing he liked better than hugging that thin body. Those big eyes watching him. Knowing everything there was to know about him.

Up ahead, the sign for a bar. A man in a white shirt and black pants outside. Setting up tables on the concrete fronting.

'Open yet?' Blackstrap asks. Stood by the man's side. A touch too anxious now from the long walk to this point.

'No,' says the man blankly. His voice soft. His movements careful. Like a cat's. 'Not till noon.'

Blackstrap watches the man move off. Going about his duties. The man is dainty. A word Blackstrap's mother might use. Like a small spoon and fork his mother owned. Dainty. The man brings something to mind.

'Where you from?' the man asks half-heartedly. But smiling. Briefly looking Blackstrap up and down. Knowing by the way Blackstrap has spoken that he's from away. 'Ireland?'

'Newfoundland,' Blackstrap says.

'Oh.' The man smiles more. Nods. A special secret. He lays an ashtray on one of the tables. 'Makes sense. A Newf.'

The man reminds him of Junior.

Blackstrap wonders whether he should be offended. The tone that implies all is explained by that word: Newf. He licks sweat from above his lips. While the man sets chairs upright.

'Another fifteen minutes or so,' the waiter says evenly. He gives Blackstrap another smile that thinks itself cute.

'Alright,' says Blackstrap, suspecting that the man is a quiff.

Then the waiter pauses to lean with one arm on the table. He takes a good look at Blackstrap. 'I guess the bars never close in Newfoundland. That's what I heard.'

Blackstrap shrugs. The way the man is standing there. He looks like a woman. His face. He is a pretty man. Definitely a quiff.

'I hear they're open until three or four in the morning in St. John's.' The man folds his arms and nods. Almost like an accusation. 'True?'

'I'm not from St. John's,' Blackstrap says, shyly now. He wants a beer or to leave.

'Oh, but you must have *been* to St. John's.'

'Yes.'

'Where are you from then?' The man sets one hand to his hip. Like he's challenging Blackstrap. 'Hm?'

Blackstrap thinks of his parents' home in Cutland Junction. Then travels back further, saying, 'Bareneed.'

'Bareneed!' The man's mouth drops open. He shakes his head in amazement. Touches his hair with one straight finger. 'What a great name.'

Blackstrap glances in through the glass. A television is on in there behind the bar. A news broadcast. There is a map of Canada behind the newsman. The east end of the map ending with Nova Scotia. Newfoundland nowhere to be seen.

'Newfs are really great people. My sister has a friend from there, from Stephenville or something like that. Everyone knows one, I guess. That's what I've found. Either they're related to one, know one, or have one for a pet.'

Blackstrap offers a careful nod. Still not knowing if the man is being genuine or not. If he is being friendly or disguising his meanness. So many lilts in the tones people use in Toronto. People always complaining about something or someone else. What they do and to who.

'Only a few more minutes now.' The man tilts his head up. Winks. 'I'll let you know right away. Bet you could use a beer. It's soooo hot out.' He blows breath up toward his forehead.

'Thanks.' Blackstrap watches the man move in through the glass door. He thinks of sitting at one of the silver tables. But wonders if it's allowed before opening time. He looks across the street. To another street running perpendicular with Yonge. Trees strangely separated from each other. Growing up from concrete. So many people in the streets. Believing only in themselves. To be so separate from everyone else. He watches them walk by. Not a word to him. They stare straight ahead. Or chat amongst themselves. Not one set of eyes meeting his.

Chapter VIII – 1983

The Hitler Diaries

(September, 1983, 29 years old)
Blackstrap lays the old woman's packages on the kitchen table. The apartment is not large. There are paintings on the walls of the ocean with cliffs. A large hooked mat on one wall. An Eskimo on a sled. Huskies pulling it across frozen water. The shoreline in the far distance. The curtain is drawn across the window. On the back of the couch there is a cat. Lying there without raising its head.

'What part of Newfoundland are you from?' the old woman asks.

'Bareneed,' he says.

'Bareneed,' she says. Thinking about something while she takes off her long coat. 'What happens there? Fishing?'

'Used to.'

'Used to.' The old woman fits her coat on a hanger and puts it in the small closet by the door. 'Yes, there's a lot of "used to" in Newfoundland.'

'Everyone moved.'

'You're not in Bareneed now?' She gives her head a little shake. 'Your people.'

'No, Cutland Junction.'

'I left in 1950.' She casts her eyes around the kitchen nook. Until they settle on a four-shelf unit built into the corner. 'I was forty-one. I never went back, but I have photographs.'

She goes over to the shelves. Takes out an old album and sits at the table. She lifts a pair of glasses from a case. Puts them low on her nose.

'These were taken when I was a girl.' She opens the brown cover of the album. 'Sit down, go ahead.' The sheets inside are made of black matte. Silver corners hold the black and white pictures in place. A few of the corners have come unglued.

Blackstrap stands there not expecting to stay. He thought he was just helping. An old woman carrying so many bags. Now, there are photographs involved. And an apartment he does not know. A space he feels he wants out of.

'Please, have a seat.' The old woman's eyes go to the other chair. She smiles and nods, watches him with soft, friendly eyes. 'I won't keep you too long. I promise.'

Blackstrap sits and listens while the old woman begins to tell a story. Who is in the first photograph. What that woman means to her. Where it was taken. What sort of special day it was. What happened to the woman and her people. The next photograph. Verna and Bill. Where they were from. What they did for a living. One was her uncle. He worked in a mine in Buchans. Died of lung cancer. A horrible death, that disease. His wife remarried. Back in a time when that was frowned upon. She went to Boston on a trip and stayed there. Running away. Never to return. 'I don't know what became of her.' Another is of the old woman's mother and father. Stood together in some grass. The photograph is tinted brown and looks ancient. The woman in an apron. Black hair coiled and pinned up on her head. A hard face. The man with a cap on. His eyes in the shadow of the brim. They are stood as if they don't know what to do. Captured this way. Perfectly still when so used to moving. Out of place. They look almost ashamed to be in the picture. To be thought of in that way. And another is of her brother and seven sisters. One sister went away. Most of them stayed. Her brother was a fisherman. John. A sister, Betty, worked on the American base in Argentia. Another sister, Alice, was a teacher. The nuns just told her to teach. That was it. No university required back then.

All dead now.

She was the youngest. Her fingers on the pictures. That look on her face with her mind lingering in a memory.

One of herself as a baby.

Done with the last page, she shuts the photo album and remains quiet. Her hands on the front cover. Her eyes watching there.

'It's enough to hold in the head,' she says, moving her eyes to look at him. Happy enough to share what she's just said. A smile from her to prove it. But a smile not all the way happy, part of it sad too.

He does not know what to say. 'Nice pictures.'

This woman with a desperately wrinkled face. 'Yes.' She smiles again. 'They are. It's all I have of them.'

'My brother took pictures.'

'Oh. Would I know his name?'

'Junior.'

'Junior?'

'Junior Hawco.'

'He was named after your father?'

Blackstrap nods. 'Jacob.'

'Does he still take pictures?'

'No.'

'Oh.'

'He died in a mine. Bell Isle. Iron ore.' It is the first time he has admitted it. Spoken those words aloud. Why to the old woman? The stranger. He notices the woman's eyes going softer. He moves his thoughts away. Shifts in his chair. Too much to think of now. He watches the table and considers leaving. That is the urge that strikes him. To be occupied with something. Work. He wonders what he might do with his upcoming days off. He would rather work than have free time. There is a woman named Heather at the factory. Blind. He has no way of knowing what to say to her. Where would he take her if he asked? To a movie. Dancing. But her gentle smile. It confuses him how much he cares for her, with no way for her to ever see him.

He raises his eyes. The old woman is still watching him.

He looks down at her hands on the photo album. 'You never went back?' he asks.

'I won't go back to face what's been done. All I hear about is when there's news of some sort of find. Churchill Falls. They took the hydro power and gave back nothing. Quebec gets all that money now, selling power to the States. I listened when they found the iron ore. Gone soon, I told myself. And it was so. Bell Isle flooded with Canadians and Americans. Then shut down back in the 60s. Pulp and paper. Cut down the trees and ship them out. Now, the offshore oil. Do you know anything about that?'

He shakes his head.

For some reason, she looks at his hands. 'Oil will kill everything in the water. That big disaster there. The *Ocean Ranger*. You must have heard of that.'

Blackstrap shrugs.

'Everything in the water. Dead soon enough.'

Blackstrap thinks of his father. How he would like this old woman. How she sounds just like him. They would have a noisy conversation. Over tea. Voices rising hotly and, eventually, laughter.

'I won't go back to see what's done. What it's like.'

'The same,' he says right away. Then he thinks about it. 'No difference.' It is a mystery why he tries to make it sound good for the old woman. Like he is meant to defend the place.

'Yes, you see a difference.' She reaches and presses her hand against his. 'You do. It might look the same, but you wait and see. I see Newfoundlanders here. Come across them every now and then. I have a small circle of friends from back home. The men leaving because there's nothing left. New found land. New taken land. That's what they should call the place. Newtakenland.'

The old woman stares off, watches toward the curtain. Then she stands and goes over to pull open the drapes. Light floods in, so that Blackstrap squints to see. Gradually, a view of the old woman watching out the window. Old houses across the street. Low brick shop fronts.

With old signs over their doors and in their windows. Places where you can eat all sorts of cheap food. He never heard of any of it before. Can't pronounce the names he hears. Smells coming out to meet him. Dark-skinned people. He wonders how anyone fits in here all bunched together. The buildings and houses stuck right next to each other. No space between them. No land to own. No place to set a stretch of garden.

'Have you ever heard the story of the black sea?' The old woman turns and steps toward the kitchen nook. The cat raises its head where it's lying on the back of the couch. It looks like a stray he used to see hanging around his house back in the Junction. The cat stares right at him. Same colour. Same orange, black and white markings. Stares and then lowers its head. The old woman fills the kettle from the tap in the sink and carries it to the stove. She switches on the burner and sets the kettle down. Then she returns to the table to sit. One hand on the photo album. 'Have you?'

Blackstrap shakes his head.

'It's an old Newfoundland story.' She smiles in a surprised way. Straightens a little in her chair. 'You've never heard of it? I don't believe you.'

'No.' He hadn't. Heather in the eyes of this old woman. That's what he had been thinking about. Why with this woman so old? Those eyes not blind. But the same somehow. Too pale. Seeing too much, the same as nothing.

The old woman waits with her eyes on Blackstrap. Then down on the photo album.

Soon, the kettle boils and she rises to prepare tea. She carries the pot to the table. Then two cups and saucers. She pours him a cup of tea. 'One day the sea turned black and stayed that way.' Blackstrap's cup filled near the rim. She levels the teapot, moves it toward her cup and pours. 'On the sea, there was no longer movement, but stillness. Blackness. No longer liquid but a void that somehow kept a boat afloat.' Done pouring, she sets the teapot down. Spoons a cube of sugar into her cup. Pours in a little tinned milk. Her spoon makes a tinkling sound while she stirs. 'Help yourself . . .' Her hands tremble when she raises the cup to her lips. 'So . . .' Her eyes fixed on him in a way that makes him feel strange. Makes him aware of the fact that he's in an apartment with this woman he does not even know. A woman who had been struggling with her packages. He had offered to help. And here he is. A woman from Newfoundland. He does not even know her name. And she has not asked his.

'The men would go out onto the black sea and cast their nets to fish. They'd do this every morning, as they had done before for centuries. The nets wouldn't make a sound when they hit the black water. There was only dead silence.'

Blackstrap sips his tea. He realizes he has slurped it. The next sip he keeps quiet. The tea going down, warming him. He feels his stomach grumble. It is near suppertime. He carefully belches behind his shut lips. His mind emptied now. Only the story from the old woman.

'When the men pulled their nets in, it were as though they were dragging them through nothing. And when the nets came up on the boats, there it was: nothing. Just the holes. They'd return to shore and question each other about their catches, but every boat was empty. Not even a bit of seaweed. Eventually, they decided that someone had to go into the black sea. Someone had to see what was down there that was causing all the fish to stay away from their nets.'

Blackstrap watches the woman's wrinkled face. Her pale blue eyes bright and alive. Almost scary. Like they don't belong in the face at all. With each word of the story, Blackstrap grows more comfortable with her, the familiarity of her voice.

'So, the next day, one of the younger men, a man who was known for his strength and his industrious ingenuity, went out in his boat with his two brothers and father. They sailed out early in the morning, as they always did, to reach the fishing grounds before daybreak.' She pauses to look at Blackstrap's hands. 'Do you want a tea biscuit?'

'That's okay.'

'With raisins. You like raisins, I can tell.' She stands and goes over to the kitchen nook. Takes some tea biscuits from the counter. Lays them on a plate. She brings the plate and the butter dish over. Sets it in front of Blackstrap. 'I can't stand tea biscuits without enough raisins. Raisin bread either. The bread has to be heavy. Dense. And the raisins have to be measured exactly.'

Blackstrap takes a tea biscuit.

'Have some butter. Go on. I'd like to see you eat it. That's the boy.'

Blackstrap cuts the tea biscuit in two. Plenty of raisins. He uses the knife to blob on the butter. Then he takes a bite.

'Good?'

'Mm, yes, missus.'

'Not too much baking soda. Some people put too much in it and it burns the mouth. You know what I mean? I can't stand that.'

He nods. He knows exactly. But he did not know it was baking soda that did it.

'So . . . the men travelled under a black sky and on the black sea. Soon, it was only their boat and them that could be seen floating in blackness. The strong son said he would swim down and see what was the matter. They waited in the boat for daybreak, but the sky remained black. Everything remained black. Finally, the strong son said he would wait no more and stood and dove over the side of the boat. There was not a sound on his disappearance. He just vanished. And, of course, he never returned.'

'What happened?' A piece of tea biscuit falls from his mouth. He brushes it under the edge of his plate.

The old woman sips from her tea. Watches him with those young eyes in an old face. 'More men went out to try the same thing. By now, the women knew that the men would not be coming back when they went out on the black sea. There were tears when the men left. Women hugged their sons and husbands to their breasts for they knew that they were gone, lost to them, that the men would be taken.'

Blackstrap sits patiently and waits. He takes a bite. Chews. Swallows. Then he says: 'What happened?'

'That's all for now. If you come and see me again, I'll tell you the rest.'

'What?'

'I've got you now, haven't I?' the old woman says. A bit of the devil in her voice. She slowly stands and carries away her empty tea cup. Rinses it in the sink and gently lays it to rest in the rack. 'Thank you for your help. I'll need a little rest now. Storytelling always takes the good right out of me.'

Blackstrap stands and checks the old woman. He does not know what to say.

'I'll see you tomorrow then?' she says, still at the sink. Her back to him. She turns her head to give him a wink. 'There's another story I'll tell you, too. It's about a shrieking woman who gave birth after thirteen months. You ever hear that one? An Irishwoman.'

Blackstrap shakes his head.

'Ohh, it's a good one.'

The next day during work, Blackstrap is distracted. Lost in recollection. He almost misses the clearance call twice. Blind people wander near him. He doesn't see them. But they curve out of his way. Like they can sense his heat. He snaps out of it in time to keep them from the railing. Thirty feet from where he works, Heather at the control panel for the packager. All of the buttons in Braille. She must have them memorized by now. Everything in her fingertips. How sensitive they must be.

The thought of her fingertips scares him. How she sees with her fingertips. He imagines them removed. What then? It reminds him of disaster. But she is there. Working through it all. All of these blind people moving around him. Getting on with what must be done.

When he finishes work, on his way out, he passes near Heather. Her face more and more familiar as he nears. Close enough to smell her perfume. Her head turns a little while he goes by. Like she's listening and knows his step. Her lips are pink and full. But they don't smile. They're serious. Almost frowning. The colour of her eyelids like powder. Her eyes staring. Fixed like an animal on display. She listens after him. Her face turning more. He looks back to see her watching. He tries holding his eyes on hers. But can't bring himself to keep it up. Even though there's no way she can see him. Her arms by her sides. Her face made even more stunning by the blindness. Always as though she's waiting for only one thing that's needed.

Out in the fresh air, he heads for the old woman's apartment. It's not that far away. About halfway between the factory and his rooming house. He has a bad feeling about not doing anything with Heather. Every time he moves close to her, he tries to say something. But the words won't come out, and he can't stand himself for not knowing what he wants from her.

Before he knows it, he is on the old woman's street. He has already passed her apartment and has to turn back. He has been wondering why the old woman left Newfoundland. If she came to Toronto with her husband, she never mentioned. Why stay away like that? If she loves the place so much? He wonders about his mother and father. What they are doing now. He can get no sense of it from where he is living. No sense of what they might be doing in their house in Cutland Junction.

He is at the apartment door. He goes inside and looks at the buzzers for the five apartments. He remembers her number: 1A. The letters M-R-S. L-A-M-B-L-Y next to the button. He presses it with his ring finger. He has been thinking about the story all day. While standing at the control panel in the toilet paper factory. He has been trying to make sense of it. The image of the black sea. The blackness of it has sunk deep inside. To connect with a darkness already present.

The old woman's voice comes through the intercom: 'Hello?'

'It's me . . . From yesterday.'

The door buzzes and he goes in. Up over the one flight of stairs. He knocks on her door. The door opens a crack. And there is the old woman's face. 'Yes?' she says.

'Hi.'

'What is it?'

'I'm back from yesterday.'

'Yesterday?' She squints a little.

'I was here yesterday with your bags. Groceries.'

'Who're you?' The old woman stares. Her lips wrinkling around the edges while she studies him. Then her eyes brighten and she begins to smile. 'Ha. Just joking.' She opens the door wide. 'You've come to hear the rest of it then.'

Blackstrap smiles and blushes a little at the old woman's playfulness. 'Thanks.'

'Come in.' She steps back for him to enter. Anxious. Her hands joined together. 'It's good of you to come back. I thought I might have frightened you off.'

He wipes his boots in the mat, and they sit at the table. Again, the curtain has been drawn. The old woman does not open it. A small lamp is on in the living room. It gives off a cozy glow. 'Oh,' she says, raising a hand slightly. 'I forgot.' She pushes herself up with a low groan and makes a pot of tea.

Blackstrap takes a moment to look for the cat. But there is no sign of it. He notices a few books stacked beside the table lamp.

A tray of raisin buns is on the counter. The old woman puts them on a plate and brings them over to set on the table. 'I made raisin bread too. A loaf for you to take away.'

'Thanks, missus.'

'I'm cooking salt fish and potatoes later. Maybe some scrunchins, too. You'll have to stay.'

Blackstrap says nothing to this. Then nods. 'Okay.'

'Good . . . So, where were we?'

'The men went out in boats and didn't come back,' Blackstrap says.

The old woman chuckles while she sits, her eyes on Blackstrap's face. 'Right . . . The women would hug their sons and husbands goodbye . . . Was that where we were?'

'Yes.'

'Okay.' She straightens in her chair. Dabs at her lips with a fancy handkerchief. Looks at the lipstick stain. Then folds the handkerchief and tucks it away. Up the sleeve of her housedress. 'So . . . Each day, another man would go out, then another . . . But nothing given in return.' She shrugs. 'Except . . .'

'What?' Blackstrap clears his throat, and eyes the raisin buns.

'A few coppers. For every man lost, a few coppers would arrive at the household of the man lost. An envelope found on the doorstep with a strange stamp up in the corner.'

'From who?'

Again, the old woman shrugs. 'Soon, all the youngest men were gone, were lost. So, the middle-aged men were sent to see if they might find something in the black sea.'

Blackstrap shifts his eyes to the woman. His stomach grumbles and so he moves his attention back at the buns.

'Have one?' says the old woman. Nudging the plate toward him with her bony fingers. 'Don't be shy. Not around me. Take whatever you like. I don't mind.'

Blackstrap lifts a bun and bites into it.

'You want some table butter?'

He shakes his head. 'Why do the men keep going out, if the other ones don't come back?'

'They cling to hope, of course. Hope is what keeps them going. Up in the morning, out the door, into the black sea. Hope . . . One day, they say, one of the men will finally return with news of why the sea has turned black. And let's not forget the envelope of money that finds its way to the family of the man who vanishes. The coins keep the poor children from starving to death. The men know this, so, in resignation, they come to make the sacrifice.'

Blackstrap takes another bite. Hungry for more words. He sips carefully from his cup of tea.

'Eventually, the town has lost all its young men and its middle-aged men. There are only old men left and they can't go into the sea. The women give birth and when the boys grow into young men they go to the black sea. The mothers and sisters stand on the shore, staring out into the black void that the boats silently float through. The women won't even raise their hands to wave because waving had come to mean goodbye forever. Women lining the shoreline for miles and miles, stood there as still as anything with no expressions on their faces. It keeps happening like that, and there is never any news and there is no change. It becomes the way. The men are born to disappear in the black sea.'

'There's never any change?'

'No.'

'Do the men die?'

'Not really. They don't die completely.'

'What's in the black sea?'

'Nothing.'

'So where are the men then? Where do they go?'

The old woman stares at Blackstrap, her eyes losing their youthful gleam. 'They're right here.' She turns her head to gaze out the window. The curtains pulled. Not a stain of light entering from outside. Then the old woman looks back at Blackstrap. 'You're one of them, aren't you?'

Chapter IX – 1984

Ghostbusters

(March, 1984, 30 years old)
One thing about the mainland, Blackstrap can go almost anywhere by bus. This is an idea he appreciates. Because there is no need to travel over water. No longer on an island. He buys a ticket from Toronto to Boston during his time off. One week. A belated present to himself for his thirtieth birthday. While on the bus, he thinks of Heather. Then he thinks of Agnes and Susan. But the way he feels for Heather is different. Protective. Agnes does not need protecting. She is off with another man. Maybe that was what happened to Susan, too. Maybe she met another man and went off with him. Although a part of Blackstrap believes that Susan was just something he imagined when recuperating in the hospital. Someone his mind invented as a distraction from the pain. But her memory as real as anything. Forever in his mind, a stretch of grace between two shifts on the Ranger. Or had there been two shifts at all? He thinks there might have only been one. The memory of Susan like a warning though. Why? He cannot keep his thoughts there too long because he fears the island entirely now. Not just the water but Newfoundland. When he thinks of his life there it dissolves into a series of broken actions. Meaningless and scary. He should have asked Heather to come along, if only for the company. To keep his mind occupied and the creeping fear at bay. He wonders if there is any point to blind people travelling. He could describe things for her. Would one place be any different from another? Sounds, he guesses. Smells. The air. How would he describe what he sees? He begins doing just that in his head. The stone front of a building. The grooves where the stones are joined. An old man's long face. The way his hat sits on his head. The balloon in a child's hand. A red balloon shaped not exactly round. Red. Round. What does that mean? Just a shape. A colour like a scream. Or

a fast car. A siren. Is that what it means? When he turns from the bus window, he still sees these things in his head.

The opposite of blind.

An image there without seeing.

Heather, his twin.

After checking into the hotel, he finds the phone book in a drawer. Opens it and looks through the lists of tiny names. He goes over the pages. Searching for an 'H.' He knows the 'H' and how to spell 'Hawco.' The name torn from an envelope he keeps in his wallet. 'H.' Two straight lines down and a line across the middle. It takes ten minutes and then fifteen. Comparing the shapes of letters. One after another. He is about to give up. Slam shut the book, when he finds the pattern. He counts the letters that form the name. Five. The sequence the same. That's right. Then he counts the names with his finger. There are seven Hawcos before the letters change. And he wonders if he might be related. But he does not call a single one. It is enough to know that they are there.

He goes down to the fish market. The one the guy at the hotel told him about. Haymarket on Blackstone Street and Quincy market nearby. He wanders around. Aware of the crowds. The colours and faces. The smell of fish and sea. The sight of the ocean. The pull of the sea under a blue sky. Blue water not black now. Not towering high. His body wants him in it. That water wants it. What it did not already claim from him. At the edge of land. The toes of his boots over the lip.

Out of place for months.

His dazed eyes drawn away from the mesmerizing water. He scans the faces behind the stalls. They are friendly, as far as he can tell. Going about their duties. Their jobs. But they talk with an accent bigger than the words they're saying. They are not Newfoundlanders. Newfoundlanders talk quickly, wanting to get it done with. Why did he choose Boston? Was it because of the old woman in the apartment? What she said about her sister moving to Boston. Many Newfound-landers there. Why would anyone come here? To find a place where they could settle. Or settle for.

The different types of fish he does not recognize. Then he sees the codfish, and accepts the people in the stalls who want to sell it to him. The smile on his face that the merchants see. It is taken as a sign to do business. He does not want fish. What would he do with it? A full codfish. But he wants to let them know that he recognizes it. Codfish a part of his life from the time he was a boy. The sea in the background. Making him sweat more than the heat of the sun. He wipes at his nose. The noise of the people increasing as the day moves along. The chatter. His eyes wanting him out of there. Not knowing why he came now. His head begins spinning at the idea of where he is. How far away. A dot on a map. He should be back in Toronto. A place he knows. He should have asked Heather to come with him. She would have made him stronger. He could have whispered in her ear. Explaining the action. A darkness seeps through him. A feeling removing him from any known place. If harm came to him here there would be no one to save him. No one he knows. No one for miles and miles. A hospital? How near is a hospital? And will he end up in one again? Tomorrow he will leave. The sooner, the better. He is hungry. He needs a beer. That might be part of the problem.

His hotel is across the street from an Irish pub. A sign on the sidewalk outside. Inside, there are different types of beer from Ireland on tap. All in a row. Names he has never heard of. The people around him ordering: A pint of Guinness. Kilkenny. Caffrey's. Murphy's. A pint in a big glass.

He stands at the bar. Watches the barmaid pouring a glass of beer from one of the spouts. She looks up from what she's doing. Smiles to show him she knows he's there and not to worry. 'What's your pleasure, hon?'

Blackstrap thinks what to ask for. A stranger from away. He does not want to be seen as one. The barmaid with long black hair in a ponytail. The blackest hair he has ever seen. Skin as white as paper. He wonders about her accent while pointing at the tap she was using.

'Guinness?'

Blackstrap nods. The barmaid's accent is a pleasure to listen to. Fresh and fun-loving. Nothing like the bent and broken version of it back home.

'There's a fiddler playing later,' she says, checking down the bar toward a small stage in the corner. Other men at the bar waiting to be served. 'Kevin Roach, have ya heard of him?'

What lovely music to her voice. Dazzling to the ears. 'No.'

'No? There ya go,' says the barmaid, wiping her hands in the sides of her jeans and naming the price.

The black beer he drinks is bitter. It is filling, like a meal. A black smoothie. An invented memory? How is that possible? He does not want another. He watches what other people order. Points to a bottle of what looks like normal beer. His head swimming a little from the quick drink.

He pays the barmaid and raises the bottle. The new beer seems light. Nothing to it compared to the other. He has another swallow. Looks around. The place reminds him of leprechauns and foolish shenanigans. There are cardboard four-leaf clovers up on the walls. There is a pot with what looks like chocolate gold coins in it. The pot on a ledge over the bar. Is this what Ireland is meant to be like? There are big flags up on the walls. A golden harp on a green one. A bird with claws on a blue and white one. Wooden pillars in the place. Wooden tables and chairs with people drinking and talking. The faces almost like Newfoundlanders. It reminds him of Martha's down on Water Street. A real place? he wonders.

He checks toward the stage. A thin man stood there. Then bending down to lift a fiddle from its beat-up case. The fiddler is wearing a Montreal Expos baseball cap. A bushy beard and moustache, and big glasses. The fiddler leans into a microphone on a stand. He mumbles a few words that are flat and lost in the noise of conversation. This one looks like a Newfoundlander too. The fiddler taps his foot a few times, then jerks his arm into action. Heads turn at once. Faces smiling right away. Recognizing that sound, like it's theirs to claim.

The fiddler keeps up for five minutes steady. His arm a blur. Fingers shifting in a strobe of generations-old recollection. It's thrilling to watch. The smile growing on Blackstrap's lips. His boot toe tapping along without him even knowing. The genuine goodness of it. The people in the room clapping and cheering. Getting noisier. Hooting as the fiddler speeds up the tune. The bow tilting up and down in a dizzying see-saw. A few hairs broken and curled away. The smile growing bigger on

Blackstrap's face. Amazing to see a man play like that. His spirits lifting. He can't believe the quickness of that arm. The accuracy. The music jittering out of that wooden instrument.

When the fiddler's done, everyone applauds. Loud cheers and shrill whistles. People clapping with their hands held over their heads. The fiddler nods once. Pushes his glasses back up on his nose. The beak of his baseball cap down over his eyes. Then he starts in again. And the crowd gets even louder. More hands clap along. More feet stomp the floorboards. Orders for beer are shouted out. Blackstrap has another. The barmaid winks at him. All is going well with the beer and music in him. Everything in the entire world. Him and the fiddle music. And everyone else, too. All of them in it together forever.

In time, he feels the need for a bathroom, and finds the wooden arrow pointing downstairs. He takes the steps, his eyes on the walls going down. Black and white photographs hung there that stop him dead. They are of Irish girls in dirty old dresses. Children with smudged filthy faces. Boys with big freckles that look like they're saucy as dogs. But the one that shoots him through the heart, makes him put one hand against the wall, is a dark picture of a lone man kneeling on a grassy cliff. With the grey ocean behind him, the man is wind-blown, leaning on wooden sticks. There are children knelt around him. Listening. The man is wearing a black suit with an open-collared white shirt. It is not a new suit or shirt. The man has black hair and his features are severe. Carved by violent wind. Thrusting in from out at sea. The howling roar of it in everyone's ears. The push of it. He will not permit it to budge him. The children there for safety's sake. Rooted to the man's words.

The man looks the way Blackstrap feels at that exact moment. The man steady and enduring, despite the forces battering him. The similarity is so exact it nearly erases him.

Why is he in this bar? Why is he in Boston? Why in Toronto?

The land. The cliffs. The ocean, and that man knelt down. Twisted and shaped by it all. In worship and challenge.

Blackstrap wants to steal the photograph. Carry it away with him. He checks up the stairs and sees the fiddler coming down. The fiddler winks and tilts his head. Blackstrap does the same.

The fiddler moves by on his way to the washroom. Blackstrap studies the photograph a little more. Decides he might get it later. The stub of his finger touches the frame. It does not move. He sees why. Four bolts. One in each corner. Holding it to the wall. Then he goes to relieve himself.

The fiddler is pissing in the urinal.

Blackstrap steps into the cubicle. The door left open behind him. He pisses too, smiling at the noise in the water. Then he hears the bathroom door open and another man step in.

'That was some fine fiddling,' says the man in an Irish accent.

'Nut'n to it,' says the fiddler.

'How long you been playing?'

'Since I were t'ree.'

'Where you come from?'

The fiddler laughs. ''Av a guess?'

'Maritimes by the sounds of it.'

The fiddler laughs louder. 'Close enuff, b'y. Newf'nland. Not da Maritimes dough.'

'New-found-land. You're kidding. I've got an uncle from Chapel Arm. Bud Greene.'

'N'ver 'eard of 'im,' says the fiddler.

Blackstrap grins in the cubicle. Done pissing, he fixes himself up and waits until the Irishman is gone. Then he steps out. Made nicely alive by the beers he's drunk.

The fiddler is leaning with his back against the sink. Arms folded. 'Wha' part of da island you from?' asks the fiddler.

'Bareneed.'

The fiddler grins, his lower jaw coming forward a bit. 'I'm from Outer Cove, sure.'

They shake hands while Blackstrap gives the fiddler his name.

'Kevin Roach,' says the fiddler. He glances at a man entering the washroom. Then regards Blackstrap again. ''Awcos eh. A good strong Newfie name if dere ever were one.'

Blackstrap nods. 'Dat's right.'

They leave the washroom together.

'She's in a fine mess now,' says the fiddler, going up the wide stairs. A sad shake of his head. He glances back at Blackstrap. 'Da Rock.'

Blackstrap says nothing. Takes another look at the photograph he admires so much.

'Not fuh'kn much left of da island now.' Then the fiddler stops and adds with great seriousness: 'Still God's country, dough. Ya can't destroy dat place. Tough as fuh'k'n nails. God's country.'

'Finest kind,' Blackstrap agrees, following after the fiddler.

'Dat's right, 'xactly.' The fiddler climbs the rest of the stairs and steps up to the bar. 'Jeez, b'y, yer a sight fer sore eyes, wha'?' The fiddler slaps Blackstrap on the back. 'Wha're drinking?' he asks. 'Me old trout.'

Soon, Blackstrap and the fiddler are the only two people in the world. Talking at the bar like they were born in the same room. From the same womb. Separated at birth. One finishing the other's sentence. Talking about people they know or heard of. Cursing politicians and life-draining corporations.

'Da 'Awcos,' says Kevin, winking and tilting his head. 'A fine crew dey are.' A few moments of silence to watch Blackstrap's face. 'Dere's a ton of stories 'bout dem. Da 'Awcos of Bareneed. Christ, b'y.' He lifts his pint glass. 'To yer namesakes.' Tips it back. Swallows and swallows until the glass is empty.

They order plates of fish and chips. Eat them at the bar. Plenty of vinegar, salt and ketchup. The fries crispy and soft. Warm and golden. The batter too. And the fish flaky like it should be. More salt sprinkled on. Fries rubbed in ketchup and eaten with fingers. The grease licked off or wiped in scrunched-up paper napkins.

The fiddler talking while he eats. A name mentioned that they thought they might know. Frankie Power. The fiddler telling Blackstrap to remind him later. The story of Frankie Power in the snowbank off the bridge. Then everything washed down with beers. A few more pints ordered. And leaving the mess there. Off to another bar.

Walking the streets while a story's told. A gale that blew off Outer Cove the last time Kevin Roach was home. The night of the gale that washed a dog ashore. A big black dog that sat outside the door of a widowed woman. Waiting until that woman died. Then back into the sea. Swimming out to God knows where. Kevin himself had seen the mongrel. He tried feeding it, but it wouldn't eat a bite.

The wind begins to pick up, gaining enough force to jostle Blackstrap. So he has to shift on his feet.

'Cruel wind,' says Kevin. Hands stuffed in his pocket. Fiddle case under one arm. Kevin winks at Blackstrap. Then musses up his hair. 'What a fuh'kn time, wha'? Jaysus Christ, b'y. Wha' were da odds 'a run'n inta ya?'

'No odds.' Blackstrap grins.

'Anudder frigg'n Newf,' says Kevin, his eyes half shut. His stare unsteady. But his smile big and open. Wheezing a boozy laugh. What's stood before him in the streets of Boston. No greater gift in the world.

The rest of the night had been a blur. Women. Men. Beer. More music. A ruckus of conversation. The story of Frankie Power jumping off the bridge in winter. The fiddler with his hands straight up over his head to show how it was done.

'Frankie were stood up on da rail of da bridge,' Kevin Roach had said, chuckling to himself at the end of the story not yet told. He made a motion with his knees to jump. ''N down poor Frankie went. Straight as an arrow. Ahhhhhhhhhhhhhh.' The sound of Kevin's voice getting fainter with the fall. ''N den there were a poof. Right delicate it were. Den not anudder sound. Poof. In Frankie goes, inta da snowbank. Poof.'

'Buried?' asks Blackstrap.

'Da snow closed right over him. We stood dere waiting. 'N den we burst out, laughing our heads off. It were da funniest t'ing we ever saw. Until the fright set in. But even da fright couldn't bar da laughing.'

'Wha' happened?'

'We ran up da hill ta Tommy Gladney's 'n he came down 'n dug poor Frankie out.'

Then the only two men left in a smoky bar. Lights blasting on. Closing time before anyone knew it. That squinting brightness. No more beer served. The barmaid shaking her head. Scolding Kevin whose head wagged like a rag doll's. Watching the floor or drifting off. A cigarette burning between his fingers. 'Go on home, Kev,' the barmaid said, refusing to listen to any more of his stories. And a man there in the bar. One of the few left lingering. Talking and laughing. Someone who Blackstrap knew. That face. That glance out the corners of his eyes. It couldn't be. Billy Cullen. All cleaned up by the looks of him. A haircut. A confident smile. New clothes. Blackstrap staring like his eyes weren't working properly. Then needing to go over to him. Slowly because he was still unsure. Not wanting it to become an embarrassment. In profile it was Billy Cullen. Sure as shit. And as Blackstrap neared the face turned to show it was Billy Cullen. Not knowing Blackstrap. Not seeing him because one of them was good and dead.

Then out into the street. Another gust of wind shoving him. Almost blowing him off his feet. A taxi cab home. Where did the fiddler go? He had no idea.

Waking to morning. What part of it a dream?

A bus back to Toronto because he'd had enough.

On the bus ride to Toronto, he thinks of Kevin Roach. That fiddle going. That photograph on the stairs. The man on his knees. The music and the photograph in his head. His mouth tasting ugly. His head stogged with wet cardboard. His stomach damaged. His bag on the seat next to him to keep others away. Him at the telephone again. Lying on the bed with the receiver to his ear. Trying to call someone. Who? Heather. Heather back in Toronto. He knew her name from when she was called over the PA at work. Heather Cavanagh. He has no idea if it was her. But he talked to someone. The conversation broken up. The memory of it coming back to him in bits. Hurting him. Making him feel worse. But her voice low and understanding. Him saying God only knows what. A long-distance charge on his hotel bill. The cost unbelievable.

In Toronto, he catches the subway from the bus depot. Watching the faces. People on their seats trying not to notice him. All sorts of faces from all over the world. He can't stand the loneliness of it, and stares out the window. The solid blackness gushing by. His barely there face flashing in it.

Up from the subway into the bright heat. The two-block walk to his rooming house on Brock. There is a woman near the doorway. A strange look to her from a distance. Like she's lost. Homeless. But as he nears, he sees that it's Heather.

He wonders what to say. Is she waiting for him? Or is it a weird coincidence? She turns to face him when he is five feet away.

His footsteps slowing. Her head tilted back a fraction. Her eyes searching somewhere to the left of his face.

'Heather,' he says. A croak. His voice seeming unused for days. He coughs to break it up. Shifts the weight of his bag on his shoulder.

'Yes.'

'It's me. Blackstrap. From work.'

People pass around them. A steady flow of little Chinamen.

He will not ask how she got here. Because he suspects he might have asked her to come on the telephone. What had been said? His address given? He has no recollection. Only the beat of his words, the rhythm they sometimes took.

She says: 'Because there is death here.'

'What?' His eyes are hurting in the brightness. He wishes he had sunglasses. The movement around him makes it all worse.

'That's what you said.' The tremble of a smile. 'The poem. That line. Because there is death here. I know it.'

He watches her face. It is hopeful. Like the words she has just spoken matter a great deal to her. 'I can sense you in passing,' she says, her lips nervous. Only fractions of a smile at a time. Coming and going. 'Not just here. But always in passing.'

Blackstrap feels the gooseflesh creep. The same feeling as at Susan's apartment. That little girl's voice through the door. He checks over his shoulder. Across the street. A window with an old woman stood in it. Like the old woman with the story of the black sea. Mrs. Lambly. She had told him her name. Again and again, as though it might mean something to him.

Why are you watching me?

'I gotta go in,' he says, hoisting his bag for her to see. But she does not. So he says, 'Get rid of my bag.'

Heather nods.'

Blackstrap passes by and she follows on his heels. Feeling for the doorway frame with her hands. Nudging ahead with her foot for the threshold. The toe of her sneaker. The sole testing. He does not think he should help her. Touch her in any way that would confirm her condition.

He thinks she must not be entirely blind.

The door shuts.

'I can see dark shadows.' Her calm voice answering his thoughts in the dim, cool enclosure of the stairwell. 'That's all the light.'

Blackstrap climbs the stairs ahead of her. Taking his time. The smell of damp wood. The heat thickening with each step. He keeps checking back while Heather gradually follows. Careful with her hand on the rail. Not enough light for anyone. Creeping in from around the door frame behind her. Should he help her?

At the top of the stairs. One of the boarders, a man called Skinny Nix, opens his door to peek out. A look at Blackstrap coming up the final stair with his sports bag in hand. Desperately in need of sleep.

'Hey,' Skinny Nix says suspiciously. Watching through the door slit. Then smiling fast. The smile gone when he catches sight of Heather. His caved-in cheeks caving in more. His big eyes getting bigger. Sinking deeper. He nods at Heather.

Blackstrap takes his eyes off Nix. Too tired to waste attention on him. Turns to head along the uneven floor toward his room. But waits a moment for Heather.

'I got messages.' Skinny Nix slams his door. Opens it again right away. Slams it. Opens it. 'Liiiisten to me.'

Heather hurries her step at the sound of the outburst. Like a dog nipping at her heels. The floor tricking her. She stumbles, almost trips. Her hands out in front of her waist. Then gripping the wobbly rail.

Blackstrap reaches to help her. But she has already recovered. He shuts his eyes while searching for the key in his pocket. If only there was quiet and peace.

'Two days they've been calling. People from New-found-land. You want it, or not?'

Blackstrap checks toward the voice. A face he almost knows. Skinny Nix smiles nervously. Sharply. Then frowns. Staring at Blackstrap's fixed expression. Nix unmoving. Then he slams the door. Stays inside. Calls from behind the barrier, 'Your mother's dead, asshole. An emergency. Just face it. Asssshhhhhole.'

Blackstrap sighs in exhaustion and disgust. His teeth gritting at the thought of Nix. Talking about his mother. Clicks the key in his lock. He thinks: Out of his mind. Always saying these things. Out of his fucking mind . . . Opens the door and steps in. Not wanting a racket. Turning, he watches Heather hesitantly enter his room. Her lips parted as though listening for someone hidden. Blackstrap glances at her feet. Then studies the unmade single bed where Heather is staring. The sheets in disarray. The rumpled pillow. He lays the bag on the bed. Always best to ignore Skinny Nix. Everything he has ever claimed to be. Through his window, a view of chopped-up lettering on a storefront. Heather there. Hands at her sides. Not a toy in either one of them.

'This is your room.'

'Yeah.'

The stutter of a smile and her teeth revealed. Crooked. Jagged. Half rotten. She chuckles and changes.

Blackstrap hears the rattle of a knob down the hallway. The squeak of hinges. Footsteps toward his room.

Heather with one hand rising as if to trace the air. 'You said the poem and I knew who you were. I never knew before.'

The footsteps pause. An ear listening at Blackstrap's door. Fingernails tap. Fingertips rub against wood. A whisper, 'Hey, you okay?'

'Get lost,' Blackstrap barks right away. His voice scratchy and rumbling. His vision burned around the edges. He coughs. Pats his pocket for a smoke. His pack left on the bus.

'It was your father,' Heather whispers. Her eyes on the bible by the bed.

Something pounds the door, and Blackstrap cannot help flinching. Cursing under his breath. Skinny Nix punching. Kicking. Or hitting his head off of it.

Blackstrap strides toward the door. Throws it open. A smile twitching on Nix's thin lips. 'Oooooow, brought to a rise!'

'Get the fuck outta here, or I'll break yer fucking neck. G'wan. Off.' His arm shoots out. Pointing toward Skinny Nix's room. In his rage, he suddenly feels dizzy. The floorboards tilting, as though the house might be afloat.

Nix with his eyes on Heather who has not turned. In a long dress with faded flowers. Her back to them. 'He said you had to go home. I could barely make out what he was saying. He kept calling.' Nix talking to Heather, not Blackstrap. 'A long time since I heard his voice. You were gone somewhere, so I barely recognized it.' Skinny Nix drifts back, deeper into the empty shadowed hallway. His face frightened and frightening. 'Hawco. That's your name. I remember.'

Blackstrap slams the door. And the house steadies itself. The pay phone jingles on the wall down the hallway. The noise from the impact. Then it rings. Blackstrap hears Nix pick it up.

'Yeah,' he says, then calling, 'Blackstrap Hawco. Come get it.'

'Father,' whispers Heather. Drifting toward the corner chair where she cautiously sits. Like she has forgotten how. 'That poem was lovely, Blacky. Just like the ones you used to read.'

He remembers another line:

Meet me where I dwell.

And the one after that:

Because there is death here.

Blackstrap leaves the room. Skinny Nix stood with the receiver held out. He strides there and yanks it away. Nix flinching, but then giggling secretly. The fright a merry rush. His hand up near his face. Cupped over his mouth.

Whose face becomes the nightmare now?

Blackstrap says hello with eyes on the wooden floor. To listen to his father's voice.

'Is turrible,' says Jacob Hawco through the wire. 'Turrible . . . yer poor mudder . . .'

The floorboards tilting again. Holding the receiver tighter. Blackstrap feels a hand on his shoulder and spins to see Skinny Nix's face on an angle. The man's eyes dead. Licking his lips. Then chewing on a corner.

Blackstrap's stomach churns.

The cradle we grow toward.

'Cry,' says Skinny Nix. 'That's okay.' He nods intently. His hand slipping lower over Blackstrap's chest. Giggling. Then serious with a hand against the wall to steady himself. The slosh beyond the walls. 'Come on, cry. It's time. *All these years meant to happen.*'

Blackstrap lunges ahead. His grip on Nix's throat. Nix's back slammed against the wall. The house listing and slowly righting itself.

The sickening flow of gravity. Blackstrap raises the receiver. The cord too short. It drops. A fist now instead.

Nix shrieks and darts his face away. Eyes jammed shut. Lips pinched tight. Fingers shivering up near his lips.

Blackstrap snorts. His eyes searching for what? The fist held back. Held tighter to let go. His body slackens. Turning, he sees the telephone cord dangling. Picks it up and listens.

But his father has been disconnected.

'People dying,' Nix quietly says. Near Blackstrap again without a stain of fear. A smile of knowing and understanding. 'You have a family, they all die. Everyone except you. Isn't that right? Everyone except me or you.'

'Shut up.' Blackstrap bangs down the receiver. It misses and falls. His feet unable to walk a straight line. He sways off, into his room. Shuts the door. Twists the lock to be sure.

Heather seated silently in the chair.

A loved one charmed to always return.

He is thinning. That's how he feels.

'I used to love a boy from Newfoundland.' Nix already on the other side of the door. 'His name was Hawco, too. Did you know him?'

Blackstrap crouches and reaches under the bed. Shaking his head, he snorts and yanks out his suitcase. Tosses it onto the mattress. This close to tears. He shoots a look at the door. The chair without Heather. His lips tight with intention. Listening for one more word. One more fucking word. Nothing. Then he faces the window. The Chinese sign for a store. He does not know what sort of store it is. The old woman in the window. Heather's reflection. Never growing old. He turns for the chair. She is next to him. Her pale blue eyes. Her thin hair. She says:

'Who arrives in a flash of unknowing.

'The love only ever yours.'

He has a feeling that he does not know. That it can only get worse. That, in a few seconds, he will not have a clue who he is or ever was. Like his mind is filling with white. Soon to lean and spin him down. He is scared of his body. His heartbeat a gallop. He lowers his head. Shuts his eyes. A wave of white he will soon crash upon. He might pass out. Or has he? Arms around him. He will not look to see who holds him up.

'He was a sweet boy who died. A sweet, sweet boy. Before here.'

Blackstrap opens his eyes. Tingling white . . . clearing. A gradual view of his sports bag. His hand against the wall. His fingers weak. His arms powerless. The fright gone through him. He puts the bag in his suitcase. The sensation like an action almost done. He leaves his factory outfit. He takes the bible from the night table. The one his mother gave him. With her handwriting inside. He is frozen like that.

The bible in hand.

His father's voice in a storm of words. A story Blackstrap cannot remember. He tries, but cannot recall a single syllable.

The door thrown open from where he had locked it. Heather must have left. In anger. In terror. In tears.

'He died saving a stupid ignorant man like you. A stupid ignorant man.' Nix's voice breaks. 'He was a saint.'

Who? Blackstrap wants to ask. Who are you talking about? Who? Who? Who?

Heather asleep on the bed. Facing the wall. Her mouth open but not shrieking. Her back still.

Blackstrap turns from the suitcase. Treads across the room.

Straightening in expectation, Nix's expression goes hopeful.

'Who?' he asks. 'Tell me.'

'You know, don't you?'

'No, what're you saying? What?'

'Junior,' Nix glances away, forlorn. 'That sweet boy. I'm all that's left of him.'

The anger and confusion. 'What're you fuck'n saying?'

The bedsprings creak as Heather shifts. 'Junior,' she says. Rising from the bed on her elbows. Her head raised and turned. Eyes shut. 'Is that you?'

'What was he to you, dreary dearie?' Nix's eyes searching Blackstrap's. 'He was something to you. I can see that. Him there. Like me and her.'

Blackstrap's mind on the street. On a way out. On a way home.

'I know, it's *only in death you learn what should have always been intuited.* That's why this.' He raises his arm. To show Blackstrap the bruised pin-holes in his arm. 'You learn when you die. I found out that he loved me.'

621

His eyes shift toward the open door at the end of the hall. 'Because we're both dead, aren't we?'

Enough. Blackstrap slams the door.

At once, fingernails scrape the wood. 'You're just like him. You're afraid too, aren't you? What people will think?'

'*Every thing made for the living.*' Heather on her side. Blank eyes fully open and on him. '*Why is every thing made only for the living?*'

Blackstrap shuts his suitcase. Clicks the two catches. His breath hot in his nostrils. He turns away. Nix's face at the funeral, eyes that had been watching him. Twenty years ago.

But the door not shut.

'They said it was an explosion, but he just vanished. There was no explosion. Why only his fingers left?' Nix raises his own hand to stare. 'Why all of me now? Because of what you touch.' He checks Blackstrap's hands. The missing fingers.

Blackstrap grabs the handle of the suitcase. Storms from the room. Shoving past Nix who stares at the bed. He strides for the stairs, but Nix is after him. 'We look almost the same.' Nix laughs. Like an insane bird. A shriek that rings in Blackstrap's ears. Deafening. 'He's alive you know. In my bed. His hands all over me. That's how he left. That's how he got away. In that black pit he went down into. And you in the black sea. They thought he died, but he's here. Dead with me. Dead with you and her.' He pauses to catch his breath. Then shouts: 'You have to stay because we're family.'

Blackstrap stops halfway down. Looks back over his shoulder. Holds himself from racing back up the stairs and murdering the idiot.

Nix tiredly plunks down the stairs. Loosely holding the banister. One step at a time. Until gripping Blackstrap's arm. Bunching up the shirt material. Tears growing to spill over those caved-in cheeks. Sucked into the hollows. And gone.

Blackstrap jerks his arm.

'*He sleeps in my bed.* Go and see . . . What makes you so different? Why should you be able to go? Why you of any of us?'

Blackstrap gives up. Hurries down the stairs. Throws open the door. No ocean as he expected. Chinamen everywhere in the street. Crowding the cars. Chattering around him. Not an eye on him. Not a concern for what he might do. Millions of people in another country. The stink of that in the street. The food he has never tasted. And never will.

He searches for a cab. He waits. Hundreds of Chinamen blocking traffic. What to do? Run.

But need always the opposite. He finds himself dashing back in. Drawn up the uneven stairs. Two at a time. To hide in or destroy what might be familiar. Nix just returning to his room. He drops the suitcase. He spins him around and strikes him. Heather screams and falls. He kicks him. He punches her. They do not fight back. He kicks and he kicks. He looks at the bed. He sees him in the bed. She sits on the bed. He looks at them on the floor. She rises from the floor. He sits next to her. She is in the bed. He lays a hand on his knee. He leans near her. He knows him. So she does not move away. He falls back together.

Cutland Junction

Blackstrap had gone to Paul Harnett. Told him that his men weren't needed to dig the hole.

'It's done with a backhoe now,' he told Blackstrap. 'Men don't dig.'

'Okay,' Blackstrap had said. Stood in the undertaker's office. 'I'll take care of it.'

'Take care of the digging?'

'Right.'

'If that's what you want. Sure. You have a backhoe?'

Blackstrap gave no reply.

'And you'll need a permit.'

Three feet wide. Six and a half feet long. Seven feet into the earth. Working his way down with a shovel in the Bareneed cemetery. The space between where Junior and Ruth are buried. A shovelful of loose dirt tossed skyward. The ground made easier by the two holes to either side. Hoping not to strike any wood from the others. Hoping not to find them pressed in against him. But hoping and wishing he might. To make them deader or to love them dearer.

Down deeper.

Four feet into the earth. The full length. The cut of the shovel keeping everything even. He cannot stop until it is done. The sun warming the shirt on his back. The heat in his hair. His muscles aching. Going weak then stronger after a pause. The nubs of his fingers. How he must hold the shovel now. He doesn't even notice after a while.

By late morning, two children come to watch. A boy and a girl from the welfare houses down the road. Blackstrap can tell by the way they're dressed. A dirty look to them. A greyness to their clothes and skin. Not in school. Why not in school? He wants to ask. Deep enough to be in the shadows now. Able to bend out of the sunlight.

'Dig'n a grave,' says the boy. Like he knows exactly what it's all about. Just another day. Must be over five feet deep. Blackstrap can still see above the rim. Level with his neck. He pauses to glance up. The boy has a small bag in his hand. Brown paper with candy that he eats.

'Who's going in dat?' asks the girl. Wiping at her nose and snorting up. Then pointing at the hole.

Blackstrap looks at the girl. Her long hair greasy. Her face sweet as it is. He gives his head a little shake.

'Old person?' asks the boy. Eating a candy. Chewing it with big movements of his mouth.

'Yeah,' says Blackstrap. Going back to work. Digging in. The shovel blade making a steady sound that brings to mind a voice shushing someone. His mind fixed around a coffin shape. Only one size of a grave. No matter what's laid to rest.

'Mister or missus?' asks the girl.

'Missus.' His arms unsteady from tossing up the dirt.

The children say nothing. So he thinks they are gone. A dog barks somewhere off in the distance. A crow calls out. Won't stop for whatever reason. Then a blue jay squealing. Other birds too. Smaller by the sounds they're making. A crow overhead. The feathers whooshing in the stillness. He hears then sees when he looks up. The shadow passing.

'We never seen you b'fore.' It's the girl.

He tosses up another shovelful. The sweat dripping from his nose. His arms glossy with it. The lifeboat. Trapped in that. Digging deeper. Toward water. The clay tumbling onto his boots. Like handfuls of dirt tossed there. Sloshing around. What if there is water?

'Bill drives da machine,' says the boy. 'Dat digs dis stuff.'

His lungs burning, Blackstrap pauses to catch his breath. To swipe sweat from his eyes. To squint up at the boy and girl. High above him now. Stood there. Looking down at him. Not saying another word. Just staring. With the blue sky behind them. A few fluffy clouds. Not a word from them now. Not a breath of wind.

Two sets of eyes fixed on him.

Not really a question.

Not interested to know.

Just something being done.

Stood there for hours.

A photograph in a frame.

Until he feels the hairs prickle on his arms.

And the boy comes to life. Rifles around in the bag. Takes out a long jelly worm. Holds it out to the girl at arm's length. 'Last one,' he teases. Moving it around by her face. 'Suffer, maggot. Suffferrr.'

'Frig off.' The girl slaps at him. Misses because the boy leans away. 'I got a mind ta murder you.'

'Yeah, try it.' The boy pops the candy into his mouth. Chews. Crumples up the bag and tosses it over his shoulder.

'Someone's buy'n our house,' the girl says to Blackstrap. Arm out by her side. Pointing at the ocean. 'We're mov'n ta Sin Jahn's.'

'Ta da orphanage,' adds the boy. 'Cause our mudder says we're brats.' The boy spits off toward a place Blackstrap can't see.

'We come down?' The girl.

'Yeah.' The boy.

'What for?' Blackstrap leans against one of the rough clay walls. His shoulder pressing into it. The earth pressing into him. The shovel handle almost in front of his face. Both hands on top of it. Someone buried where he's standing soon.

'Have a look 'round,' says the boy.

Blackstrap checks the four sides. 'Not much to see.'

'Come on, buddy.'

'Come on, buddy,' says the girl. Just like the boy.

The boy squats and turns. His palms flat on the grass. Tries putting one foot into the hole. Dirt sprinkling down. His chest against the broken earth. He lets his other foot dangle. Then he drops. Falls without tipping over. Stands up straight. Dirt on his clothes. He dusts himself off. But there are smears of clay left. Looks around. Inspecting the job.

'Me,' says the girl.

The girl alone up there with her arms held out.

Blackstrap leans the shovel handle against the earth wall. Nowhere for it to fall. Except lengthways. He raises his arms to the girl.

'Jump,' says the boy. Laughing. 'Chicken.'

The girl squats. Still with her arms out. Uncertain. She leans forward. Just a bit. Leans back again. Not convinced. Still squat down. She shifts her sneaker toes closer to the edge. Leans forward. More and more. Her shoulders tipped ahead. Her face expecting something. Until gravity takes her and she drops. That fright on her face. Falling. Screaming.

Blackstrap catches her. The weight of her in his arms. Hardly anything at all.

The girl smiling now. Her face up close to him. Teeth rotted around the edges.

'Frig'n good catch,' says the boy. His voice louder and moist in the hole.

Blackstrap lays the girl down. She squats right away. Fingers the dirt. Uncovers something just there by her foot.

'Ugh,' she says. Already stood away and stepping further back.

The boy taking her place in a flash. Shoving the girl aside. She falls on her bum and stays there. Legs out in front of her. The cool earth. The boy digs. Small bones arranged in lines. All running parallel. Earth mixed in with them.

'Fish,' he says. Pulling it free and shaking the dirt off. The boy wags the skeleton in the girl's face. 'Dead fish. Ya wan' some? Dee'licious.'

'Stop.' She throws dirt at him. One handful, then another.

'Ha.' Then he throws the fish skeleton out of the hole. Wipes his hands together. Looks at the walls. Looks up. 'Ha,' he says again. 'Heyyyy,' he shouts at the sky. Listening to hear if it goes on.

Too much noise and movement. Too suddenly. Blackstrap's shoulders tensing.

'I'm tell'n Mudder,' says the girl.

'So. Screw dat. I'll punch yer lights out.' The boy takes hold of the shovel. Starts digging. Hits Blackstrap with the long handle. Trying to lift the shovel blade toward the opening. The dirt just falls back in. He tries some more. Keeps digging and lifting the shovel. The dirt sliding off the blade. Some of it into the boy's face. He spits and wipes at his eyes with his arm, but keeps at it.

'Hey,' says the girl. Still sat there. Her face staring up. 'How we get'n out?'

This is something that strikes Blackstrap. The girl looking at him. Her face gone white. Like that for what reason? Fear? The blood drained completely from her.

The fear in him.

To make or match it.

'Climb,' says the boy. 'Easy.' Digging at the walls with the shovel. Trying to dig a tunnel the other way. A hole about two feet in before Blackstrap notices.

'Hey.' Blackstrap snatches the shovel away.

'I was dig'n, buddy.' The boy pissed off.

'Up. G'wan,' says Blackstrap. 'You had yer fun.'

'Up,' says the boy. 'Right.' He tries climbing. Can't get a grip on anything. His hands pulling at dirt. Knocking small rocks loose. His feet climbing nothing. Loosening more dirt.

'Here,' says Blackstrap. Bending down. Meshing his fingers together. 'Put yer foot dere.'

The girl hurries ahead of the boy. Steps onto Blackstrap's hands. He lifts his arms. Tightens up his back. Straightening. Waiting for the pain. But there is none right away. 'Hold my shoulder.' The girl holds his shoulder. Stood there in his hands. Then he rocks her up and down. 'One . . . Two . . .' Blackstrap aiming away from the headstones. '. . . Threeee.' And up she goes. Screaming. Flying from the hole. Higher than the grass. Higher than the earth.

The girl drifts out of sight.

Followed by a different scream. Not the girl. 'Mother of mercy. Saints preserve us.' A visitor, no doubt. 'Sacred heart of Jesus!' An old woman from the nearby distance. By the sounds of it.

'Right fuh'k'n on,' says the boy. 'Put me higher.'

Patrick Hawco, Catherine Hawco, Ace Hawco. The names on tombstones scattered around the Catholic Cemetery. Markers white and weather-beaten. The facings worn thin. Unreadable. But people knowing who owns what. Someone always present to remember.

A quiet crowd gathered around the hole. Faces watching toward what will be put in the ground. Most of the faces familiar to Blackstrap. From seeing them around. But Agnes not there. The death of his mother. He always thought Agnes would be home for that. The death of his mother or father. Agnes leading to Heather. A paler presence. That rooming house on Brock. Not an idea of what happened. He keeps away from it. The three of them. And Susan. Susan in a room too. Which room? Where? The confusion chokes the breath in him. Blackstrap's eyes on the hole. The casket there. The words of the priest.

The graveyard is surrounded by dense spruce trees. Beyond the wire link fence. What used to be an old church. The steeple has been removed. Set down at the back of the graveyard. The cross at the top pointing north to south. When it should be pointing east to west. For all of Blackstrap's life. A wooden sign secured to the side of the building. Four brass bolts. One in each corner. Bareneed Bed and Breakfast. On consecrated ground. A four-star establishment with a patio built on the back. Big umbrellas with logos for alcohol makers. People drinking while the burial service goes on. That sort of loose laughter spilling out from there. Pure torment for those gathered around the body of Emily Hawco.

After the service, Jacob says he wants to walk down toward the old houses. The welfare houses and the ones redone. A number of them, the ones leaning toward ruin, have been bought by townies and Americans. There is talk of building a golf course. And developing some kind of adventure trail. A few of the houses have been restored. But there have been things added. Curly-swirls of trim up around the eves. Hanging planters. Big decks with barbecues and iron furniture. The houses look like the old square fishermen houses Blackstrap remembers. But they're done up. Like they've been made to look brand new in an old way. Clean, smooth clapboard. Double-hung vinyl windows. Painted colours never invented until now. A make-believe village.

It doesn't sit right with him.

Blackstrap silently follows along. Knowing no words for this. Only fuming pain that chars the rage. Deadens for now. Jacob moving slowly, although not old. Careful of his step. Blackstrap keeping his eyes off the balcony of drinkers when he passes. In the corners of his eyes. Men in baseball caps and white polo shirts. Women in summer shirts and slacks. Watching the world go by. Ice cubes jingling in a glass. Jacob looking there. Not saying anything in reply to greetings called out. Those people from somewhere else. Staying in a room in a church. Overlooking a graveyard. What they can tell their friends when they go home. Slept in a church. Ate breakfast where the altar used to be. What do they think they're saying by saying that?

Further ahead. Beyond the road that runs between tombstones and the old church. There is a perfect spot for picking blueberries. Cranberries and partridgeberries too. The blueberry bushes where they would pick buckets. Just by reaching down and grabbing up handfuls. Plump berries in the mouth. A different flavour from the different sizes and shades. Purple as light as pink and blue as deep as black. Every other tint in between. The autumn boil-ups they used to have in the clearing beyond the bushes. Making a picnic out of it. With Junior watching over Blackstrap. Eventually the two of them off playing together. Climbing the nearby dogberry trees. Up high in the branches. The sight of their old house from a distance. Down further in the valley. Beyond the dirt road and the bushes. Where the land slopes away toward what has become communal pastureland.

Halfway down, Jacob begins to tire. Forgetting the immensity of the land. Smaller in his mind because he knew every square inch. The rolling green pastures before him. The distant headland of black rock that towers from the earth. Spotted with twisted and squat-together trees. A piece of it gone toward the left. Dug away to be tested. The grey rock and shades of brown clay uncovered and showing. A trench shaped like a V. The earth fresher, brighter, the deeper the cut went. A quarry company given a permit to test the rock. Before it was all stopped by protesters. He'd heard all about it when he came home. And the ocean beyond. The thick flat slab of Bell Isle in the distance. The salt water in the air. Every morning, every day, every night. That salt water that used to fill his lungs. So sweet. Like honey in the blood.

'How long's it been?' says Jacob. 'Block'n it from life.'

Blackstrap doesn't get his father's meaning. He watches the headland. Remembering when he had climbed up there. After hearing of Junior's death. Then Ruth's death. The blind eyes open from not seeing to not seeing. Then shut. The desperate sinking shudder in his bones. The love still there. His little sister in a small box. But the hole the same size. What won't be filled up.

Now, his mother's death. In a bigger box. The hole cut the same by his hands. He wonders now if it was the thing to do. The right thing.

Everything taking its time.

They move further into the pastureland. The tall grass green and bent. The smell of someone barbecuing from one of those done-up houses. A herd of goats rushes to one side. Flowing like a startled flock of birds. Pounding the earth. Hooves instead of wings. The sound in the grassy earth. The feel of it travelling.

Jacob pauses by the foundation of their old house. Falters slightly as if losing his footing. The rumble of those goats in his black Sunday shoes. While he checks the blank space inside the square of stacked slate. And his hands come up to cover his face. His two huge hands covering his entire face. His face buried.

'Mudder,' he sobs.

Blackstrap watching his father. In his old suit slightly too small for him now.

And the herd of goats continues running. In a flowing pattern toward the edge of the cliff. But veering away together as one. Mere inches from the drop.

The next morning in his mother's bedroom. Facing those rows of books beside her bed. Staring at the titles. Whose lives in there? Blackstrap wonders. He takes down one book and flips through it to a bunch of glossy pages. Photographs of a four-master stuck in ice. Men in old clothes surrounding the ship. He suspects that they were explorers. Probably a hundred years ago. He suspects that they were trapped. He studies their faces. Men just like any others. He shuts the book and slides it back into its hole. If they did not die on that voyage then they are dead now. Who cares what they did?

He goes out to the kitchen. Jacob is sitting at the table. A small envelope in his hand with markings on it. Like a form to be filled in. He turns it over. Weight shifting as the jewellery slips out.

Emily's wedding ring.

A locket.

Two of these in his palm.

'Quincy MD gave me dis,' Jacob says, raising his hand a touch. 'Yer mudder said she never wanted it buried with her. It were fer yer wife, should ye ever find one. Dat's wha' Quincy said.' The look in Jacob's eyes. Like he can't believe anything. Eyes straining for a pluck at the truth.

Blackstrap lifts the locket from his father's palm. The thin chain dangling. Swaying. He opens the heart. Inside, there is a photograph of Ruth. An image of Junior in the other half. Blackstrap lays it on the table. The chain pooling. Jacob takes it up. Studies the small photographs. Then gazes up at Blackstrap. While he fits the chain around his own neck. Clips it at the back.

Blackstrap picks up the wedding ring. Holds it between two fingers. Some of his other fingers gone. Never a thought of rings. He sits in the chair across from Jacob. Thinks if he should try it at all. What it might mean to do that. He turns the ring over. Looks for an inscription inside. Not knowing why. He tries the ring on his pinkie.

It fits snugly past the knuckle.

Jacob feeling the locket at his neck. His palm cupped over it. Like a woman. That pose. He keeps his palm there and stares at Blackstrap.

Blackstrap watching his pinkie. The plain band of gold.

The smell of bread baking.

They both turn to watch the stove.

It is morning.

But then it is night.

Chapter X – 1985

Rambo

(June, 1985, 31 years old)

Patsy tells Blackstrap how she watched him come down the walkway. Between the desks in the unemployment office. Years later, when she is dying, she likes telling the story. It brings her comfort because it is about how they met. She tells the children, too, when Blackstrap is locked away. He was her third client that day. Ticket number 44. The number called out over the crowd of men and women sat waiting on chairs. She remembered because 4 was always her lucky number.

It was Patsy's first day. Her first summer job that her father got her. Being friends with Mr. Maher, the supervisor. She had a new car from the Ford dealership in Spaniard's Bay. A gift from her mother and father. She drove from Heart's Content every morning. The wide-open burgundy barrens tinged with blonde and green hilly grass. Wildly stretching in all directions. Then into Victoria with its old houses right near the road. Until barrens again. Up and gradually winding, down into the valley with the ocean and the sprawl of Carbonear to her left. Past Incinerator Road. The haze from burning garbage drifting into passing cars. Climbing another hill and down again, listening to the Bee Gees on her car stereo. Sometimes singing along. For the half-hour run to the unemployment office in Harbour Grace.

Both of the people she had interviewed before her third client were strangers. She was a little nervous, but trying to be in control. Knowing the questions she was meant to ask. Neither of the people too concerned about her. Friendly, in fact. Seeming to like her. Like she was special. Could do things for them. 'You'll be holding da purse strings,' her father had told her. Her confidence building. She was happy to have a job. The extra money in her pocket.

The man paused to search the five desks in the big room. Turning to look ahead at her nameplate on her desk. Then looking at her with serious eyes that somehow shocked her. The man was familiar. He was wearing faded blue jeans. A white T-shirt. The short sleeves tight around his thick biceps. A package of cigarettes rolled up one sleeve. He stepped over to the chair and stood there without sitting down. His form held in one hand by his side.

'S'posed to see you,' he said.

'Please have a seat.' Patsy motioned toward the chair with her hand. But the gesture seemed foolish in his presence. Having seemed natural with the others. Things turned awkward right away. A sense of threat. She was afraid of him and shy, too.

The man checked the chair. Then her. His thick hair was blonde. His face handsome in a rough way. She smiled, but the man glanced off across the office. Like it might be a trap. Like he was checking to see if anyone was watching. Then he placed his hand on the back of the chair. Pulled it out while he sat on the corner of it. Leaning forward. Still watching her face.

'Your form, please.' Patsy tried speaking clearly and properly. Knowing that she should cover over her accent. The way to get ahead, one of her teachers used to tell her. A woman from St. John's who taught at their high school, Holy Trinity. 'No excuse for ignorance,' the teacher had said. 'Just because you're from Newfoundland. There's no pride in dropping your "H"s.' She pronounced 'H' like aych, not haych. But Patsy's accent came through anyway. Here and there. She sometimes heard the sound of it after the fact.

The man didn't smile at her. He just handed over the form. And she saw that it wasn't filled in. She began to ask him why, but stopped herself. Remembering one of the points emphasized during her training course. A good number of the people coming into the office won't be able to read or write. Not wanting to embarrass anyone. She smiled again.

'Your name, please.'

'Blackstrap Hawco,' he said bluntly.

'Blackstrap,' she said, searching for a pen. Patsy found one under a form she had previously completed. 'That's interesting.' She wrote the man's name in the spaces provided. The name was known to her. From somewhere. TV. A newspaper. 'That's a nice name.' No, she thought, 'nice' wasn't the word. When she looked up, she saw that he was staring at her. Not pleased. And she felt the smile dissolve from her lips.

'Different,' she managed to say. Knowing now where she recognized him from. That oil rig that sunk. He was the only survivor. Famous for it.

Blackstrap had noticed Patsy Newell's long hair. He gave it but a glance. But admired it all the same. Like someone he had seen. A woman in the Sears catalogue. She was wearing a purple button-up blouse. And maybe a skirt. Blackstrap could not see. Her hair combed whip straight.

'Address?' she asked. With her pen hovering over the spaces on the form.

Blackstrap flipped the pack of cigarettes out from under his short sleeve. Tapped the box on the desk. He waited until Patsy thought he had not heard her. Until she began to ask again, 'Addr—'

'Cutland Junction,' he said gruffly. Sticking his thumb into the bottom slot of the cigarette box. Pushing up. Opening the fold. Crumpling off the foil covering. Tossing it for the basket. When he looked up, he saw Patsy studying his hair. The blonde already streaked with wide streams of silver-grey. He took out a cigarette. Tapped the end on his knee.

'Hav'n a good look?' He leaned slightly to the side. To pull out his Zippo lighter. Flipped it open with the butt of his palm. Flicked the flint wheel. One quick recoiling motion. Puffed the flame to life. Then snapped shut the casing. He slid the warm metal back into his pocket. His fingers almost making a jumble of it.

'No.' Patsy locked her eyes on his eyes. Her cheeks flushing red. She tried smiling, but it came out wrong. Saucy, maybe. The smell of the lighter and a newly lit cigarette.

Blackstrap noticed her two crooked teeth. One to either side of her front teeth. He noticed the brown freckles on her nose. Her fine plucked eyebrows. Lipstick, slightly purple to match her blouse. Eyeshadow too.

'Do you have your Record of Employment?'

Blackstrap looked away. He sat up in his chair. Put one leg over the other. He blew smoke at the floor. Left hand on top of his right one in his lap. Glanced up at her. 'No.'

'We're gonna need that.' She nodded, trying to be serious, but look pretty too. She thought the way he was sitting was almost like a girl. 'Where was it that you worked? Maybe we can request the record.'

Blackstrap stared down at his cigarette. Flicking the end with his thumb. Knocking the ash away. He sniffed and slowly rubbed at his nose. Twice with the side of his index finger. Thinking for a moment. Then he stood and put the cigarette between his lips. Closing one eye to protect it against the smoke as he gathered up his cigarettes. Folded the package back in his sleeve.

'Forget it,' he said. Glaring over at a chubby, middle-aged woman who had taken an interest in him. His eyes on her, unmoving, until she looked down at her desk.

Patsy watched his face. Then took notice of the woman. Her name was Viola. She was from Harbour Grace.

Stepping away without further comment, Blackstrap headed for the door.

Patsy wanted to stop him. To tell him to come back, but could not summon the courage to call out. To hear her voice shouting in the big office. She looked at the clock on the wall. Almost lunchtime. She stood from her desk to see six people waiting.

'G'wan,' Viola called to her. 'I'll look after dem.' She nodded toward the waiting people. ''Av yer lunch, girl.'

'Thanks.' Hurrying for the front door, Patsy hoped Blackstrap Hawco would be lingering on the steps. She was dying for a smoke too, after having Blackstrap smoking right there. But she wasn't allowed to smoke. Rules. There were tons of them in a government office. Closer to the door, she slowed her step, thinking he might still be there. Not wanting to seem like she was rushing after him. She opened the glass door and leaned out. Searched the unpaved parking strip in front of the building. Saw the back of him, the silver of his hair against the blonde, down by a big forest-green car at the far end. Luckily her car was parked right next to his. Her heart sped as she stepped out. Trying not to look at him where he was getting in his car. The sun bright and hot, and she felt it on her skin. Opening her purse, she slowed her step. Poked around for her keys. She heard the heavy door shutting. A muffler rumbling. A screeching of tires. Dirt and pebbles flicking back. Pinging off the other cars. Looking up, she saw that it was his car. Blue smoke hanging in the air. Drifting toward her until she was standing in it, coughing.

Him gone.

This is the story she tells. Years later. The God-honest truth, she swears to Junior. Little Ruth too young to know any different.

'And yer father so proud. Never a cent of unemployment coming inta dis house,' she says, mimicking Blackstrap. 'Well, dat's where we met. When he a'most gave in.'

And more of the story, most of it never told. Unfit for children's ears:

The big forest-green car is parked in the woods. Barely visible against the dark clot of trees, melding. Patsy is nervous to find herself here. Having just passed a vacant church at her right that looked haunted. A small graveyard surrounded by a chainlink fence to her left. All of this she has seen in the sliding arcs of Blackstrap's headlights. She looks at him. She is nervous and excited. The graveyard bothered her. She had held her breath while she passed. Like she used to do when she was a child. So the souls of the dead wouldn't enter her. She thought of blessing herself too, but didn't want to do it in front of Blackstrap.

She watches Blackstrap turn off the headlights that glare against the soft black-green tangle of evergreen boughs where the overgrown road keeps going on. Only a few houses with people in them, she's heard. Down in Bareneed. She wonders if they drive on that road. It must be rough to go over.

Blackstrap opens the car door and steps out.

'Where ya going?' she calls. But the door is shut quickly and with such force that she straightens in her seat. The darkness. She sees Blackstrap's shadowed body moving in front of the car. Hears him hawk and spit. Then his head tilted down while he lights a cigarette. The whoosh of flame gone. The orange dot bobbing. He had been talking about going back to Toronto while they drove down here. He worked up there in some kind of factory. The exact type of place he wouldn't say.

Glancing at the ignition, Patsy sees that the keys are gone. She rolls down her window and leans her head out. 'Hey?'

Blackstrap's voice dull, already far away, 'Don't be a scaredy-cat.' And he laughs. Not a good one. Almost like a bark into the night. 'Come on, womb'n. Udderwise da boogeyman'll get ya.'

Patsy pulls up on the steel handle and pushes open the heavy door. The sky is a moonless charcoal blue, but with stars. The rocky road leads downhill, in the direction where Blackstrap has gone. She follows it carefully, waiting for her eyes to adjust. Then seeing the darkness clearer. Walking slowly on her heels. Holding her arms out at her sides in case she loses her footing and falls. She has forgotten her sweater in the car. More and more scared stepping down the sloping land, she finally makes out the shape of a man. His back to her while he trudges blindly ahead. Not much to him but a shadow.

'Hey,' she calls. 'Where ya going?'

He stops to wait for her, half turned so that part of him is seen. He has reached the large, blasted-flat surface of stone where he used to play as a boy. Scraping designs on the stone with smaller rocks. Home base for tag and spotlight. Cowboys and Indians. Forts built nearby in tiny clearings hidden in the trees. Bareneed always down beyond. Never too far away.

He reaches out and takes hold of Patsy's hand. Meshing his fingers with hers. A few spaces where his fingers are missing. Smooth and strange. It almost makes Patsy pull away, but she catches herself.

Blackstrap leads her further into the grass. Curving away from the road that goes off to the right. Instead stepping toward a fence with grey wooden rails and large squares of wire. He finds the gate and opens it.

'Where are we?'

His voice beside her, strange out in the open darkness, 'Pastureland.'

'Any bulls?' She hesitates, feels her weight stopping.

His soft tug on her arm. 'Come on.' But he pauses to give her some time. 'What's da matter, ya don't like be'n out widt murderers in da dark?' He grins and widens his eyes.

She makes a noise. A yelp smothered in her throat. 'Stop it!'

And he laughs, heading on with her hand in his.

She goes ahead, to avoid being dragged, but leaning slightly back. She hears a sound, her eyes searching a nearby grove of trees. 'You hear dat?' she whispers tightly.

'Dat's da murderer I was tak'n about. I got a meet'n set up widt him.'

'Stop it!'

They rise up over a bank. And they are among the horses and cows. The solid shadows that do not stir as Blackstrap and Patsy pass. Moving down toward where the ocean is. The open gleam of it in the night. Lights from a few houses down deeper in the land.

Patsy can hear the dull surge of water, smell its nearness. The lights across the water on Bell Isle. And beyond, the more distant shore of Portugal Cove.

Blackstrap's voice, 'I'm go'n up dere.'

She sees his eyes.

He takes his hand from hers, draws it away.

'What about those horses?'

'Dey won't hurt ya, luv.'

He begins up the headland, his boots digging in at the edges. It takes a while and his body hardens on the climb. His fingers knowing how to work with the others gone. Up on the top, no longer the noise of him struggling. The sea and the land an eternity around him. The dark mass of Bell Isle against the blue-black water. Topped with lights. Like something afloat. The churn in his guts.

The lights of Port de Grave reflected in water to his left. All mirrored straight along the long strip of land. And the brighter lights of Bay Roberts on a slightly higher ridge behind that rising. Stillness that he breathes into. Not a sound outside his own body. Only the glassy black plain of water before him and the night land at his sides and back.

He hears Patsy's voice calling to him from below. But he hears it as his mother's.

Home. Their house in the valley.

He gazes up at the clarity of stars. Vivid points of light arranged against the deepest blue. The faint impression of clusters like dust. Far off. Like he can see millions of miles into space. The sight saddens him, troubles him. His feet on a rock. The truth of planets. He shies away from thinking that big. The swell of it roaring up in his head.

'Come up,' he calls to avoid himself. 'Fer a taste of the sky.'

He hears her laughing a little.

'Yer frig'n crazy,' she says.

Patsy Newell stood in the darkness far below.

If he doesn't look at the sky, he feels at peace up here. The water cannot reach him. Unless he plunges into it. A story he has heard about someone falling off the cliff. Hundreds of years ago. Someone from Ireland who drowned himself. The headland was named after him for a while. Tommy's Drop. Then it changed into some other name. For whatever reason. And another.

He feels how it might be possible. Nearer to the edge now. The toes of his boots a bit over. Made happy by the sight of that. The distance to the dark rocks and water. Nothing as powerful as what that drop might take from him.

With Patsy trailing after his bootprints to this place. Knowing now that she will follow him anywhere. Scare her and make her laugh at once. Hook, line and sinker.

Blackstrap has heard of a course he can take to drive a backhoe. There is plenty of work because men keep heading off to the mainland. Working for better wages. Why stay in Newfoundland when more money can be made elsewhere? The townies and mainlanders keep buying up land and old houses in Bareneed. They get everything for cheap because no one in Newfoundland knows what it's worth. He's heard a few mainlanders talking about how cheap the properties are. Them dressed in creased summer clothes meant to make them look casual. One of them wearing a strange hat. Like's he going hunting lions on a safari. They keep using the word 'cheap.' How cheap the old houses are. A steal. Right on the ocean. You'd pay millions of dollars anywhere else. For a view like this. Millions. They'd laugh and keep talking while Blackstrap did work on their places. Like he wasn't there. Tearing out old boards to put in new. Replacing split clapboard and nails with the heads rusted off. Jacking up a house on one end to dig out a rotted sill. Tearing tar paper off a roof and mending a soft patch of wood here and there. Nailing shingles on. Not black like the normal ones. The townies want them brick red or green. Something different to set them apart. As long as he's in Bareneed, he doesn't mind the people. He still feels at home there. Rebuilding the houses that might've fallen down otherwise.

He knows he doesn't need the backhoe course. He just wants to learn how to drive the machine. How long would it take? Half an hour. Just give him a backhoe and let him drive it. There are a few of them parked at night by one of the contractors doing work down in Bareneed. The townies not wanting to hire local guys. Bringing in workers from St. John's who charge twice as much for the same thing.

He thinks through all of this while he waits for another beer at the bar in Tommy's. Patsy wants Tia Maria and milk with a little straw. She has to have the straw or she can't drink it. He hands her the glass and she sips from it while watching him. Lighting a new cigarette off the butt of the old one. She likes her smokes.

The band strikes up. The boom of the bass drum in his chest. Patsy turns and watches. Blackstrap stares at the space behind the bar. Thinking about when he sang up on that stage. Playing when Agnes walked in. 'Black Velvet Band.' What he wouldn't give to see her now. Andy Coffin drunk most of the time. The bottle getting the better of him. Something the matter with his legs now. Rubber-legs, they've been calling him lately.

Someone taps him on the shoulder. He looks to see Patsy.

'Wanna dance?'

He shakes his head, drinks from his bottle. All the people in the hall from all around. Most of them know who he is. Especially after the *Ocean Ranger*. He wouldn't make a fool of himself by dancing. The band up there that he could be playing in. No time for music anymore. The guitar no good without all his fingers. And he won't be one of those freaks with a special talent. His picture in the paper because he can play the guitar.

Another beer and him staring at his hand holding the bottle.

Music sounds loudly in the large dance hall of the Caribou Lounge. The band on the stage in the corner is playing a Freddie Fender song, one that Patsy likes. They left Tommy's hours ago after Blackstrap started talking in a strange way. Going on and on with words that made no sense. Like song lyrics but too strange to make out. His voice almost singing, but not quite. Looking straight at her and speaking in that voice. Deep, complicated strings of words.

Patsy stands with her back against the lip of the bar. A short glass of rye and ginger in her hand. Her fingers on the two thin straws. She gave up on the Tia Maria. Only a few or they'd make her sick. She is half listening to the music. Half watching Blackstrap lean with one arm against the wall by her side. His head bowed down. Staring at the tile. He's stopped saying the strange words. They had been dancing to a slow song because those are the only ones Blackstrap will dance to, close and slow.

The boys had been buying him drinks of rum in sympathy for the death of his mother. And he had drunk them quickly. Pretending that he was alright, his expression unchanged. That was the first Patsy had heard of the death. Blackstrap hadn't mentioned it to her the first few times they went out together. Hearing that had been like a kick in the heart to her. Not knowing what to say to Blackstrap about it. He wouldn't look at her after she said, 'I'm sorry fer yer loss.' Wouldn't meet her eyes from that point on.

Blackstrap comes over to sit at the table. Two chairs away from Patsy. He stares at the crowd. Seeming unfocused. Lost with so many people all around him. Patsy watches his rough face with its grey and blonde stubble. Then his arms as he takes hold of the table edge with each hand and pushes himself up. Bracing a palm tighter against the beer-cluttered top for an instant before he turns. He carefully steps through the tables toward the back. Next to the bar where the crowd is thickest.

Right away, he returns to Patsy. 'Let's go,' he calls, stepping up alongside her. The band silent between songs, only the static of the crowd. He tilts his head toward the steel double doors at the front of the hall. The ones he helped install a few years ago. A new door box put in and a bit of rot needing to be cut out.

Patsy takes one last sip of her rye before slipping the thin straws from her lips. She lays the drink down because Blackstrap has already started off. His stride through the crowd surprisingly even.

Outside, he says, 'Gimme da keys.' Turning and leaning with his back against the building. His voice so clear in his ears out in the night. The muddled sound of the band starting up through the walls.

Patsy opens her small white purse. Digs around while glancing at him.

He looks at her, his face demanding, almost hostile. But he says,

'Don't worry.' Standing straighter. The air seeming to sober him. He makes a noise in his throat, the beginning of a cough. He hawks and spits, flinging his head in the direction of the saliva.

Patsy finds the keys. Holds them out to him in her closed hand. Searching his eyes. 'Ya alright? Blacky?'

Blackstrap stares intently. Something off kilter in his eyes. He takes hold of her arm and pulls her closer. Uses his other hand to bend open the fingers holding the keys.

'I'll drive ta Cutland,' he says, meaning she can drive herself home. If that's what she wants. Only so far.

Patsy follows after him. The soles of her white shoes skimming the gravel in the parking lot. She finds it difficult to walk in the tight white skirt. Attempting to hurry, she is forced to walk in a way that frustrates her.

Opening the driver's door and sliding in, Blackstrap feels cramped. Slides the seat back. Then the passenger door opens and Patsy climbs in. Her skirt hiking up, so that she flushes red and tugs it down as soon as she sits. The centre patch of her panties revealed for a second. Glancing at Blackstrap, she sees that he has been looking there. His face telling nothing. She buckles up, clicking the belt snugly into place.

'Ya sure?' she asks, touching his arm.

Blackstrap starts the engine. Staring through the windshield.

'Put on yer belt.' She reaches for it and pulls it across his chest. Clicks the buckle in place. Just as the car roars ahead. Out of the gravel parking lot. Blackstrap not checking either way.

Oh, God, Patsy says to herself. 'No,' she whispers. 'Blacky.'

Speed increasing, the car takes a curve in the road. The passenger tire sliding onto the soft dirt shoulder, then back onto the even asphalt. Nothing that cannot be easily controlled.

Patsy grimaces and worriedly peeks at Blackstrap. But his eyes are fixed straight ahead as if chasing after something he might recognize or pass through.

'What're ya trying ta prove?' she finds herself saying, her voice gone teary.

Blackstrap says nothing.

Patsy leans to check the speedometer. The needle between 100 and 110.

'Stop it,' she says, her fingers on his arm. Fingernails digging in. Shaking his arm. 'Stop it.'

Another glance at the speedometer: 120.

Blackstrap is thrilled by the speed. His legs turning lighter and lighter. The pleasurable movement in his crotch. He knows the road. Knows its length, but his timing might be off. Travelling at such speed. He spots the stop sign up ahead.

Coming crazily, unpredictably close.

Shearstown Line running perpendicular with the strip of asphalt they glide along. The yellow sign facing them with the black dots and black arrowheads pointing in either direction. Vivid in a flash. It is all upon them before his foot reaches the brake. He slams hard and fiercely cuts the wheels to the left. The car leans off, sideways, on two wheels, then none. Tilting silently up through the still air. Through the sign. A weightless drift that cannot last much longer . . . A wave descending. A shock of lost breath . . . Before impacting against the hard ground. Metal easily giving way. The shape of the earth indenting.

A crashing blur of chassis and bouncing crunching glass as Blackstrap and Patsy roll.

Black silence.

A plunge through ice.

Frozen, crystal mercurial and still.

The silence holds chaos back.

The dead men nudge him.

Blackstrap moves to free his breath. Eyes that see in unknown darkness. A moan beside him almost lovely. Instinct. A way out. He reaches for a handle, tries opening the door. Stuck, damaged, dented. Shoving it with his shoulder, it scrapes open mere inches. Something stopping it. Bodies. He pushes harder with his shoulder. More scraping. The green dashboard lights glow before his eyes. The headlights pan out in front of the car. No sea. No waves. The trees hold their branches like roots to the ground. But everything afloat. He looks at Patsy staring at him. Her dead eyes fixed on something beyond. But then she blinks.

Her lips blue beneath the pink lipstick. They open wordlessly. A quarter inch between top and bottom rows of teeth. They chatter in code.

Blackstrap tries the door again. Shoving at it. The grating into earth. The gouging. Only now noticing the ground at the top of the door. And his perception wobbles. Slides toward . . . what?

He looks at Patsy. His head heavier than it should be. Wanting to drop the wrong way.

'A'right?' he asks.

She turns her head and stares through the windshield. The ground as the sky beneath them. The earth dropped away and only space remaining. Patsy tingles everywhere. She thinks that she has had an orgasm. Her body alight. What that might mean frightens her.

Am I dead?

Blackstrap shoves harder at the door. Until it opens a foot more. Enough to squeeze through. He is suspended in place. Why? Searching his chest. The seat belt. He reaches for the buckle. Presses the button. And falls out onto the ground. Rolls onto his side. Bracing the clumpy grass and dirt with his hands. He lies there for a moment. The smell of the damp earth. Like in the grave he dug. Something wet on his hand. A slug. A worm. A maggot. His eyes watching the roof of the car. Level with his face. He stumbles to his feet to discover how damaged he might be. Stepping away from the car stuck there. Upside down. The metal crinkled and busted up. Not a new car anymore. He checks toward the road. Sees that they are eighty feet in from asphalt. Not a car in sight. He walks around to the other door. Opens it with a series of tugs.

'Careful,' he says to Patsy. Leaning in, he unbuckles her seat belt to help her out. His right hand behind her neck, his left behind her knees. He lifts her from the vehicle. Tipping her body until her head is higher. Her feet aimed at the ground. He sets her down. But holds her with one arm around her waist.

Patsy looks at the car, then at Blackstrap's face. A tingle of newer fright. A tremble everywhere in her face. Her knees give way. Blackstrap tightens his hold on her to keep her upright.

'Me car,' she whispers. 'Fadder's gonna fuh'k'n kill me.'

My car, thinks Blackstrap in his mother's voice.

Patsy has dirt in her hair. Where it had rushed in through the broken passenger window. Blackstrap gently flicks the sprinkles away. Then grips her shoulders and stands in front of her. Checking her clothes and body. His hands all over her. Touching places she barely feels.

Not a scratch on either one of them.

'I'm gonna . . .' Patsy's hand darts up. Turning, she chokes and vomits into the dark grass. Crying now. 'Me car.' Being sick has let loose the tears. Her head hanging forward. Holding her hair away from her mouth.

Blackstrap tries to touch her. But she leans away. Slaps blindly back at him. Sobs with her head bowed. Again, Blackstrap checks the street. No cars yet. He thinks of turning off the headlights. Goes to the driver's side and bends in there. Pushes the knob off. Night only. The moon soon giving its own scary light.

He steps up to Patsy in the quiet chill. Where she turns to face him. To see what he's going to do.

She wipes hair from her face and watches her smashed car. Backs away in fear.

Blackstrap steps in front of her. Following until she stops and looks at him.

'You okay?'

She shakes her head. More tears as she reaches for his chest to know if he's really there. A handful of trembling fingers. A wet sob caught in her throat. Blackstrap edging closer to give strength to weakness. Presses his cheek to her wet cool cheek. Patsy shivers her arms around his shoulders and hugs him. Crying louder. The rattle of nerves spreading. The nice smell of her hair. Her perfume and body heat rising to him. He leans back to sniff the clean air. Patsy's eyes on him, waiting. His eyes searching toward the treeline.

'Wha'?' Patsy looks over her shoulders.

The trees.

Blackstrap stares at one spot. Where something is moving.

I have slipped into the woods
And to find me will mean never
And then never, again

He shifts his eyes to her face. Determined. Set on forcing himself back to now. He lowers his lips to hers and they kiss. Their breath raging hotter in spurts and moans. Until Blackstrap feels Patsy's hand pressing over his crotch, into his jeans, rubbing the fabric. They kiss and touch with more urgency. Groping. They kneel on the ground then lie in the lumpy grass. Blackstrap on top. Sparkles of glass dust on Patsy's face. She simmers magically while she hikes up her white skirt. Presses Blackstrap's hand to her crotch. Rubs it back and forth. Her panties soaked. She unbuckles his jeans and he helps pull them down. A struggle until she rolls him over. Climbs on top and grinds against him. Feeling the hardness. Then draws aside her panties and takes hold of his cock, guides it in.

From where he is, Blackstrap can see on an angle. No cars on the road. But any moment now. There has to be. His hands on Patsy's breasts through the tight top. She rides up and down, pounding him, faster and faster as her mind glides away from here. Her wavy hair bobbing. Her face gone savage. She comes right away. Shudders until her body melts down and she holds him. Tightly. Not wanting to fall. Her lips on his ear. Her whispers unknown to him. Words as though talking in her sleep. Her ass slowly moving around. Straightening up, she begins grinding and goes at him again.

Blackstrap can't hold back any longer. He comes inside her because she will not get off him in time. Locked onto him. His eyes shut to see nothing. To only feel for once. He finds that he is holding his breath, and exhales.

They lie still until Blackstrap feels himself shrinking. He slips out of her. The need to protect, to cover up. He moves Patsy aside where she stays on the ground, half kneeling, staring up at him. Watching while he fixes his zipper and fastens the button.

The scene brightens while Patsy lies back, there in her hiked-up skirt. One breast exposed where her top is raised. A car coming up the road from the Caribou Lounge. The headlights stretching ahead, aimed right at them. Not too bright at this distance but enough to see the overturned car.

Patsy pulls down her top. She sits up and straightens her skirt.

The car hauls ahead onto the gravel. People get out right away. Their voices distant and quickly wondering.

Blackstrap helps Patsy to her feet. Then he just stands there, watching the people approach. Mumbling to each other as they check their footing over the dim ground. Shadows blocking and releasing light.

'What happened?' one man asks when he is near enough. 'What happened, Blackstrap?' and Blackstrap regards him. What is that man doing here? A neighbour from his community. One look is all he gives. Why does he want to know? He will not meet eyes with either of them. These shadows trying to pass over him.

The faces too sharp to watch. Words echoing in his head, with him just torn from a place where he was less than alive. His body ripped through a muddle to find his feet on stronger ground. Made new and wide awake. No way of looking at his own hands, his own legs, without thinking them possibly elsewhere.

A few minutes later, there comes the sound of an ambulance approaching from Brigus. A woman tends to Patsy who is crying a few feet away. Weeping into her hands. The sound of her tears makes him soft. Makes him feel responsible for everything that has ever happened.

Blackstrap's car is parked in the front lot of Ernie Green's Take-Out. Patsy eats her feed of wings and chips and keeps glancing at him, wanting to say something. Words there in her mouth, behind the mash of deep-fried food.

A car pulls up alongside Blackstrap's. He looks to see Donny Laracy, and gives a small tilt of the head. Donny nods. Ted Galway behind the wheel. Music blasts in the car, turning louder when Donny gets out. Shuts the door and goes up to the order window.

'I been in S'n John's,' Patsy says.

Blackstrap stops eating his fries, licks the grease from his fingers. His eyes on the dashboard clock, checking it against the time said on the radio. The announcer's voice talking about the weather for tomorrow, then 'Like a Virgin.' He changes the station to the middle of 'Born in the USA.'

'You remember dat night, da crash?'

Blackstrap watches her face, wondering what she might say next. It's something out of the ordinary. Something he's not expecting. The crash. How long ago was that? A week? A month?

"Member?' She turns down the radio.

647

He nods. He'd rather be hearing the music than her voice.

'On da ground.'

'Yeah.' But he doesn't remember. He takes one of the white napkins and wipes his fingers, but the napkin is soon soaked with grease. It tears in places so he has to use another one.

''N ya know.' She tries smiling, but it's nervous. It comes and then it goes. Her eyes go a little wider. She nods a secret. Then, without the slightest bit of warning, she bursts into tears.

Blackstrap looks at the car next to his. Donny getting in with the food covered in a brown bag, held upright to keep it from spilling.

'I'm pregnant,' she bawls.

His eyes on Patsy. The air sucked out of his lungs. His mind rushing back to that night. All he sees is the yellow sign with the black arrows. A blur and a tumble in the slowness of time.

'We did it dat night. 'N now I'm pregnant.'

'Jaysus.' He wipes at his mouth with the napkin. 'You sure?'

'Yes, da doctor told me, Blacky.' She goes from tears to anger. She slaps his leg hard. 'I'm knocked up, 'n it's yer fault.'

As if someone has stuck a plug in his throat, in his mind, too. Someone kicked him in the nuts. 'I—' He is going to tell her that he doesn't remember anything about that night. But he knows it might be the wrong thing to do. He checks the car with Donny and Ted, both with their fingers up to their mouths. Fries and chicken wings. Biting and chewing and washing it down with beer. He rolls down his window to toss out the brown paper bag. Gulls screech and head over from nearby where they're waiting. Walking or fluttering their wings between the cars. They screech and fight for the scraps.

Eyes on the rearview, Blackstrap starts the engine and backs up. Donny waves and grins. A mouthful of food behind his teeth. Blackstrap doesn't nod. He tries not to notice anything. Because nothing seems worth ever bothering with now.

'Wha're we gonna do?' Patsy says.

He straightens the car in the narrow lot. In front of him, a row of pickup trucks and cars waiting for their orders. A few gulls in the sky, circling the overflowing litter bins. He drives off.

After so much time, he sighs. He's thirty-one, and never planned on children. He watches the cars pass on the other side of the road. Maybe when he was younger, with Agnes. The thought might have crossed his mind back then. Patsy is making teary noises on the seat next to him. He just can't look her in the face, can't bear the sight of her now. A fucking curse.

'Wha's da matter?' she asks. 'Blacky?'

'Nothing.' Agnes is who he should be having children with. Not the way things have turned out though. A waste of a life now.

He feels Patsy's eyes on him.

Then she says, 'I'm not hav'n anudder abortion.'

Another?

The steering wheel in Blackstrap's hands. The car rolls on. The wheel turned a little this way, a little that way. Watching the road, but watching nothing. The word 'whore' in his mind, the word 'slut.' And Agnes there to taunt him. A pretty face in chaos.

Not a decision that he can make for himself.

Dug in so deep to both of them.

Chapter XI – 1986

Chernobyl

(*March, 1986, 32 years old*)

'Remember da time I broke me leg on da trapline?'

Blackstrap nods.

Patsy is at the stove. Her belly stuck out. Due any second. She comes over and takes up Blackstrap's pack of smokes. 'I'm some *fuck'n* hot.' She blows a breath up at her forehead and wipes hair away with the butt of her palm. Putting a cigarette in her mouth, she lights it with Blackstrap's Zippo. Then she clunks the lighter onto the table. Goes back to checking the big pot. Boil-up on the stove. Salt meat boiling since early in the morning. Every pane in the kitchen windows steamed up. Vegetables cut into pieces on the counter. Potatoes. Carrots. Turnip. Cabbage.

Blackstrap's father runs his fingertips along the tabletop. Looks out the window. He seems worried, concerned. A sky layered in shades of grey. It's been that way for days. A biting wind too, dampening the spirits. Pellets of grey snow begin hissing off the panes.

'I had it laid there up on da desk,' says Jacob, 'da wooden one. 'N I called yer mother on da telephone ta tell her I broke me good leg.' It is almost a joke, but not funny anymore, not after so many times.

Blackstrap drinks from the bottle of beer. He checks back to see Patsy. One hand on her back, the other on the counter. She waits and takes a breath. Then lifts a knife to start peeling potatoes, squinting to keep the smoke from her eyes.

Jacob nods, calls out: 'Em'ly?' No answer that he knows of. He shouts: 'EM'LY?'

Blackstrap endures the call.

'Em'ly. Jaysus Christ, womb'n?'

'She's not here,' Patsy says sharply.

Blackstrap looks at her, but she's still peeling potatoes like she hasn't said a word.

Jacob faces Blackstrap, a threat in his eyes. 'Yes, she is. Where's yer mudder? Out whoring 'round widt Tuttle? I knows more den anyone t'inks.'

'She's in da living room,' says Blackstrap.

Patsy checks over her shoulder, giving him a look. He shifts to watch out the window. Through the moisture trickling down, he can only see part of what's there. No amount of snow on the ground. The weather not what it used to be, not like when he was a boy. Snow drifts as high as telephone poles. The baby due soon. There's no point to driving backhoe in the winter without snow. Greg Wells with no work for him. He thinks about getting his own backhoe soon. Not buying, but leasing. He decides to get Patsy to check into it. Then he looks at his father.

Jacob nods, says quietly: 'She can hear me a'right.' He gets up and goes into the living room. The sound of the television being switched on.

'Em'ly,' says Jacob.

Music comes from the TV speaker. A woman singing in a commercial.

'Wha's fer supper?'

'... brand of canned ham you have ever tasted. Fry it, bake it, slice...'

'I'm half starved sure.'

And the voices cross over each other. The words all jumbled together eventually. Conversation hard to make sense of. His father talking to himself. The TV talking steadily. Never any rest. Never any silence.

Blackstrap looks to see Patsy, her eyes still on him. One hand on her belly, stubbing out the cigarette in the pile of peels. Her eyes accusing him for some reason. He can't figure out what. He looks at her belly, counting off the months, slowly trying to do the math, but no way of figuring it out so it makes any sense. Hotness in his eyes and mouth.

Blackstrap never was one for hospitals. The stink of them is always worse than any rotten smell. The clean stink. He hasn't been in one since the *Ocean Ranger*. The hospital in St. John's. Not this smaller one in Carbonear. He remembers his mother visiting, her face next to him when he woke up from wherever he was.

Shoot me, he says to himself as he steps up the corridor, before I go back in a place like this. Shoot me. His body cringing at the sights. His mind wanting out of the deathly feel of the corridors, aware of his hands and feet. The fingers and toes missing. He wonders where the fingers and toes went. Did they burn them up in a hospital fire with all the blood and shit and disease? He thought to ask at the time, but was afraid then. Afraid to ask anyone anything about himself.

He's heard the old men and women moaning and bawling from the beds upstairs. His mother took him there when he was a boy to visit Nan Duncan. He remembers her hair gone white, her soft eyes and face, then the pain stiffening her body. Trying to make it seem okay for him though. To ignore the pain and smile. Her voice with a proper accent. She would call him: 'young man' or 'Master Hawco.' The smell of spearmint off of her like the smell of chewing gum.

Shoot me.

He had been up the line repairing track. A part-time job that he got when Pete Galway left for Kitchener, Ontario. Pete's brother on the mainland with a job in construction that paid more money. Blackstrap had been replacing a section of rail when Charlie Coffin came down the line on the mini-car, anxious to tell him that Patsy had gone to the hospital in Carbonear. 'In labour,' he'd said, smiling like Blackstrap didn't know what he was in for.

That was a little over twenty minutes ago. Long enough for him to get back to his pickup and drive to the hospital at breakneck speed.

Maternity, he'd been told, second floor.

He takes the elevator up. Finds the nurses' station. His palms sweaty. He can't get the taste of death or disaster out of his mouth. Has the baby been born? He asks at the nurses' station. He gives over his wife's name. They give over the room number. Not born yet. The nurse smiles kindly. A nice-looking woman. Something special about her. He wipes his palms in his jeans when he makes it to the door. The right numbers next to it. He checks his hands. A mess of dark smudges and the stink of creosote from the railway ties. The baby. Born dead? This is what he fears most. Or what he expects, what he wants. No.

He goes in to hear Patsy cursing in the bed. 'Jeeesssus!' She notices him and her eyes burn with accusation. Your goddamn fault. He almost laughs. Then Patsy is overtaken by a wave of pain like his grandmother dying.

A nurse comes in and checks under the blanket. She says something to Patsy about dilating.

'Hold on,' the nurse says. 'You'll be fine.'

'I needs more drugs,' Patsy pleads. 'Fer Christ's sake! More dope.'

'I'll check with the doctor.'

Patsy glares at Blackstrap, her cheeks puffed out with rage. She growls in her throat, deep like an animal who needs shooting. It's nothing like what Blackstrap expected. From what he thought, it should be a quiet time. A joyful, loving one. The birth of a baby. That's how he's seen it on TV. A man and a woman holding a baby all wrapped up. Both of them smiling at each other. The woman a little sweaty.

Instead, Patsy there acting like a savage.

'We're going to take you now,' the nurse says, beginning to wheel the bed away. 'Are you coming?' she asks him.

The thought slams into Blackstrap's head. Coming? Where? To watch?

'You'll need a gown from there.' The nurse nods toward the shelf of folded green gowns. 'You have to put one on.'

Another nurse enters the room. And the bed is rolled by him. Patsy has just enough time to grab his hand while she passes, her fingernails digging in, tearing skin, stinging.

Smarting with pain, Blackstrap watches the bed go. Then he steps out into the corridor and half-heartedly follows after it. He suspects that's the thing expected of him, but he's not certain. The bed goes through a set of swinging doors by the nurses' station.

'You need a gown to go in there,' a nurse calls out. 'And a mask.'

Blackstrap looks toward the nurse who comes at him, a gown in her hands. It's the pretty nurse. 'Here.' She holds it open. 'Arms.' He fits his arms in. 'Coopy down.' He squats and she puts the mask on, hooks the loops over his ears. The heat of her near. The fabric of her uniform against her breasts. He looks at his filthy hands. Is that allowed?

'Okay,' the nurse says, smiling at him. 'Good luck.' She even pats him on the back. Half a pat and half a rub. He glances at the nurse's hands. Long, slim fingers with no rings. Her skin so fair it is almost white.

Blackstrap checks the nurses' station. Another nurse stood there watching him, smiling like she knows something he doesn't. She nods toward the swinging doors. But there is no anger in her, not like Patsy. These nurses are like different women. He remembers them from the other hospital when he was in. The same sorts of women. He almost fell in love with every one of them. The way they treated him with such care. Sweet and gentle. And the way they were with the drugs in him. The nurse keeps watching. He wonders what she's thinking. Then she shifts her eyes to the counter, reading some pages. The pretty nurse steps in behind the counter to join the other. And Blackstrap wishes he was damaged, wounded, half dead, if only to be in the hands of those women. To fall on the tile floor and be gripped by seizure. To have his heart explode.

'You're going to miss it,' says the pretty nurse.

Blackstrap goes through the doors and finds the activity by the noise. Another room he goes into. There's a doctor between his wife's legs. Two nurses there too. He stays close to the doorway, watching. At one point, when the head starts to show itself, he thinks he might be sick. His eyes flinch away. But then back again. Something he has to watch. The clump of bloody purple and colours unknown to him. A monster showing itself. His eyes strain and his stomach goes nauseous. He breathes through the mask. The stench. This birth. Birthing. He remembers kittens as a boy. The cat they always had. He must have been ten or eleven. Always the immature spring cat that had six kittens. The first litter usually seemed to die, except for one. Then the next litter in the fall. The ones that died on their own and the ones he tossed in the ocean in a brin bag. And the one that died and he put in the brin bag to throw away. Cold and stiff and small with the softest fur. His father and mother had touched that kitten to make certain. Hours later, when he picked up the bag to throw it out, the kitten made a shriek that scared the shit out of him. The sound had made his fingers loose their grip and drop the bag. There was movement behind the brin. When he looked inside, he saw the kitten blindly squirming around and mewing, its limbs almost useless. It had been dead; bone cold through the fur. And it had come back. A miracle cat, his father had said, naming it Resurrection. It became his father's favourite kitten then. A man who usually had no time for nuisances. His father said that Resurrection was magic, that it was good luck. But that screech it had made in the bag. The screech that let him know absolutely anything was possible.

More activity before his eyes.

A baby there, but not a sound from it. Where is the baby noise? It mustn't be alright.

Patsy with her head turned away like she's dead, the baby hovering over her. Held that way after Patsy had seen it. Hovering over her in the hands of the nurse. Then brought to the table by the wall and laid down. Blackstrap sees it, then sees its legs and hands, pink fingers and toes. The tiny movements of its messed-up face.

'He okay?' he calls out, not meaning for it to be so loud. All heads turn toward him. A shout from his mouth like he's found someone lost.

'Yes,' says the nurse, more to the baby than to him. 'He's just fine.'

It is something to see. A small one like that, coming out of a woman. A boy. The thought of it brings up a blur in his eyes, spilling down his face. No control over it at all. Not a speck of hope to pull himself together. Blubbering like a baby himself.

He sobs and swipes the tears away. They smear from his cheeks, leaving wide black trails along his face. The stink off his fingers. Creosote. Preservative.

(September)

It is one of the Newfoundland coins from his father's collection. A woman with her hair done prettily on the heads and a crown on the tails. The date 1865 under it. It is one cent. He knows because his father told him. The word Newfoundland is there too. Blackstrap holds it in his fist. He stands in the centre of the track between the two rails, each boot on the same oily railway tie. He has walked away from the crowd gathered on the platform in Cutland Junction. All of them there to see the last train pull in and then pull away, taking their jobs off down the line into the path cut through the wilderness. Cutland Junction's main source of employment on its final run. The CN train service losing money for years right across the island. All 548 miles of track being scrapped. But a promise from the provincial and federal government of new jobs for the area. A federal penitentiary. Maximum security. It was all on the radio this morning. A federal–provincial initiative jointly announced by Newfoundland premier Brian Dickford and Gaston Maudet, Federal Minister of Justice. The project to create 250 onsite jobs and a further 125 off-site jobs over a two-year construction period. Workers from the area will be given preference during the hiring process. And once the penitentiary is completed, the workers involved gain a special Unemployment Insurance package for an equal period of time. So they can be retrained. University or Trades College. A big chunk of land already being cleared for the site, off behind Isaac Tuttle's place on the back of Coombs Hill.

Stood on the track, Blackstrap remembers a painting he saw in a store window in Toronto a few years back. A street that had art galleries all in one rich area up near Bloor. People walking around dressed in fine clothes with their little, well-bred dogs on leashes. There was a painting of a black horse galloping head-on toward a train at night. A cloud of smoke from the train spread out across the night-grey sky. The train light on, brushing the rails with a faint bit of light, barely showing the horse. Blackstrap imagines the horse striking the train. Knocking it from the tracks or disappearing into the steel, going right through it.

He feels the faint vibration in his feet, the thrilling promise of an earth-heavy rumbling. 'Roads for Rails' is what they're calling it. Better highways for hauling up the tracks right across Newfoundland. The railway that joined Newfoundland to Canada. If not actually by land, then in a symbolic way, from coast to coast.

Newfoundland apart again. The thought of this should be inspiring, but Blackstrap can't stand it. It feels like a slap in the face. A personal affront. Newfoundlanders all being cheated in a clever way. If they are to be cut off from Canada, then let it be completely. The lyrics from a song fill his head. The voices of thousands of men blending in deep harmony: *Thank God we're surrounded by water.*

Ride the last train. It was made out to be an exciting trip. Something to enjoy. Something to celebrate. Get your tickets now for the last train ride. A thrill to be a part of it. As usual, everyone's way of thinking all arse-backwards.

The trembling leans toward a steady thunder and he catches sight of the train, far down the track. The black nose of the locomotive with its moose catcher grill toward the bottom. It would flick him aside like any animal if he never moved. A fitting way to end it, hit by the last train to roll across Newfoundland. The idea of it makes him burst out with a laugh. He looks at the Newfoundland coin in his palm. Then he squats and uses his two good fingers to set it on the gentle curve of shiny, silver rail. The coin stays there and he searches down the line. The locomotive thrusts ahead at a chugging speed. Why ever get out of its way? he wonders. He thinks of his son, his baby boy. The lack of sleep making him feel like he's always half in a dream. Patsy trying to leave the boy in his crib, so he'll get used to being there. The crying. The chug of the locomotive. There's nothing in him that makes him want to move. His boots flat on the ties. Squat down as he is, he feels deadened to the world.

The rumble of the locomotive fills his boots. He stares, mute and mesmerized. The string of passenger cars pulled behind it. He checks over his shoulder to see the slow bend through the trees that leads into the junction.

He turns to face the train. The coin staying steady on the rail, not even rattling. The locomotive there upon him like it never was.

A brilliant escape if there ever was one, but he's at odds to remember how.

Blackstrap won't work tearing up track. He was offered a job but turned it down.

On his day off from clearing ground for the prison, he sits in his pickup with his father. Both of them staring through the windshield. A case of India beer down by Jacob's feet. They watch the men pulling up the railway spikes, using tools imported especially for the job. Railway ties are up for grabs. Soaked in tar, they spring up everywhere in the junction, running up both sides of driveways or stacked to shape rock gardens. Other people saw the ties into chunks and burn them in their stoves. They burn nicely through the winter. Slow and lots of heat. The smoke blacker than usual. Black on the snow. And in his handkerchief when Blackstrap blows his nose.

In the spring, when the snow pulls back and the sun comes out a little hotter in the sky, Cutland Junction reeks of creosote. After a month of near steady rain, the water from the taps turns smelly and a little off-colour.

'The water's brown,' Patsy says, giving Blackstrap Junior a bath in the big plastic pan on the kitchen table. Blackstrap getting ready to go to work, taking his lunch tin and thermos, not checking inside to see what's in there. He prefers to eat onsite. Stay away from the house whenever possible.

Thermos in one hand, lunchpail under his arm, he sniffs the tinged water. 'Creosote.'

Patsy watches him. 'Well?' she says.

'Well what?'

'Where's it com'n from?'

Blackstrap takes notice of his wife. Most times, she's just there and he doesn't bother to see the details. But now her image comes at him. One hand on her hip. Saucy looking. Her head tilted one way and her eyes with brown bags under them. No sleep. He hears Patsy complaining about Junior on the telephone all the time. Her friends asking if the baby sleeps. If he naps a lot. If he's a good baby. A good baby if he sleeps all the time. None of it makes any sense to him. He hears the words in his head now. Her complaints. That's all.

He looks at Junior, splashing in the water, making baby noises. He kisses his son on the top of his head. Then he turns and leaves.

In the pickup, he looks at the house sat there with the trees behind it. His thoughts shifting to Toronto. The urge to take off, to drive to the ferry and escape the island. Leave it all behind like many men. Men pretending that the work was better on the mainland. But really running away, wanting nothing to do with the family they're stuck in. Heather in that room on Brock Street. Skinny Nix. The three of them on that bed. Heather with one, then the other. The grabbing and holding. The eyes staring up close. Creatures. That's what they were. Creatures slying at one another on a bed behind a shut door. His breath stuck in his chest. Find Agnes. Find Susan. These women removed from him. Which one does he want? He's not breathing, just staring at the house. No one in the window. No one in the doorway. The world sparkles white around him and his ears slowly go dead.

When he comes to, he's slumped across the seat. His head is heavy and his legs feel weak while he pushes himself up. The same place where he's always been. Parked outside his father's house. Since the Ranger, when he thinks of the past he sometimes passes out. He starts the engine and drives up the dirt road, trying to see what's right before him, while trying to forget.

The Department of Health is called in to figure things out. The water supply in Cutland Junction is sufficiently contaminated to be of concern. A study is undertaken to determine the source of contamination. Someone from the mainland is brought in. A company made up of environmental experts. Their fee close to half a million dollars. They hang around the community, going into people's houses, sniffing here and there, taking samples in jars and bottles. They even ask the residents for urine samples. Special gloves on their hands. White masks over their mouths. Poking around in gardens until the cause is determined. It takes three months for the study to be done.

The government issues a press release.

It's the railway ties.

'Bunch of geniuses,' Jacob tells Blackstrap. 'Ya can't pull the wool over dere eyes. Sharp as tacks, dem fellers. Prob'ly got three 'undred year 'a schooling betweenst 'em.'

The railway ties are all hauled away. Several options are introduced. The earth has to be moved, trucked off and treated. Then trucked back. Or new earth brought in. Or the people in Cutland Junction can relocate if they choose. The government will provide land in other communities. Their houses moved too, on flatbeds. All paid for by the government. Another proposal sees the entire community shifting one mile east, picked up and put down again.

Television cameras from the CBC show up to talk to people and capture the action. The reporter is the most interested person who has ever existed. Then another group of people with cameras arrive. A company making a movie about it. Not for theatres, but for TV. These people are young, with long hair and sloppy clothes. They keep asking about the children in the community. Are the children sick? Have the children exhibited any signs of abnormality?

The town council votes in favour of earth moving. Trucks come and go for months. Bulldozers and backhoes. Dump trucks. Eventually, every lawn looks brand new. Landscapers work alongside the construction workers, planning to make everything 'visually pleasing.' These are the words Blackstrap hears someone say. New sods are laid. Held in place with wooden pegs. Others in the junction opt for seed. Yellow sprinklers are bought for everyone as part of the settlement package. New wells are dug. 'Artesian or shallow?' asks the well-digger. 'The choice is yours.' Most opt for artesian because they're the most expensive.

The cameras for the movie figure this is the end of it. They pack up and take their time going around saying goodbye to everyone. Sadly, they have not found one sick child. Only false alarms of children with colds and the like. This makes them have to rethink their theme. But they're not worried. Being good sports, they even throw a little party in the town hall. Everyone goes for the free booze and food. The smell of dope outside, where some of the long-hairs are toking up. During the party, when people get enough booze in them, they keep asking when

659

they're going to be on TV. 'When will I see myself on TV?' The film people are a bunch of strangers, trying their best to fit in. They're friendly and seem well-intentioned, but they're in the junction to make a freak show out of it. They think the people are interesting. They think the people have character. But these stoned young townies actually think they're smarter than the people in the junction. Blackstrap knows that the film they're making will be about stupidity and ignorance.

By this time, construction has started on the prison. Blackstrap is hired to work the steel and cinder block. It's the second time he's been made to wear a hard hat on any job. He doesn't like it. It reminds him of the Ranger. He changes the white one for another colour. Lifting block and steel, he wishes he was welding. Better pay. Plus he likes melting things together, joining them to create something solid and unbendable.

When the prison walls are finished, the unit roofs are fitted in place. There's plenty of room to move around because of the open yard. The supplies are delivered to that central location where they are fanned out by the workers.

The pay is good. Because the union is involved. Everyone is made to join, and they all carry a union card. Some of the workers don't like the idea of it, but it's worth it for the money.

Business as usual, learning a few lessons here and there. But it's not until the bars arrive that things get really interesting. It's then that the workers start to catch the true shape of what's being done. They begin to realize. Up to that point construction was nothing more than cinder block cubbyholes. Small rooms with holes roughed in for plumbing. A building coming up from scratch.

The day the bars arrive, the men all stand around to watch them being unloaded by the crane. It takes eight men to lift one front unit. They carry them in through the wide open doors and up the stairs. It's a struggle that's barely possible with so many men trying to give directions. They face corners that the wall of bars must be moved around. No one planned on that. Someone says that the bars were meant to go in first, before the roof was set in place. The crane should have hoisted them in. A screw-up. But nothing slows them down. They just have to knock down walls to get the bars through and put them up again later.

The first set of bars, the facing of a cell on one of the units, goes into place nicely, fits like a glove in the space made. The bolt holes are drilled into the blocks. The anchors and bolts fixed and set. The door hole is open because the door is to be put on separately. They go out into the yard and carry in the door, four men holding one corner each, tilting it on its side to get in through tighter spaces. All of them sweating and grunting with their boots shifting over concrete. They fit the door on the pin hinges. It's hot in July and all the men working around make it hotter. The hard hat is a nuisance, nothing but insulation for the top of the head.

After they fit on the first door, they shut it. It closes and opens, its clanging sound distinct. No keys for the lock. Not yet. They're being shipped in by armoured courier that's driving from Ontario.

The second length of bars is lifted in the same way. While taking a corner, one of the men slips on a half-eaten bologna sandwich, and falls fast. When the load shifts, the other men scramble to shift with it. Calls of 'whoa' 'hey' 'hold on' 'Jesus' before someone else has to let go or be pulled down too. Then another man stepping back fast to get clear of the edge swinging up to almost smack his chin. The weight taking over. Blackstrap's boot twists in between the bars. He goes over to stop the ankle from snapping, and the bars come down on him. The hard hat protects his head from the fall, but a steel corner of a protruding plate gouges deep into his testicles when he hits the floor.

Whenever the medication begins to ease out of his system, he feels his stomach churn, and he dry heaves.

Patsy comes with Junior to visit, her eyes trying not to know.

'How ya doing?' she asks, like everything's the same.

The sight of her with the baby makes the pain between his legs throb. No one has told him anything yet, but he feels the news will not be good. They've told Patsy though. He can tell by looking at her. That's how it works in here. They tell everyone except the patient. That's how it was after the Ranger. Everyone knowing everything about his condition, or the possibilities of his condition, except him. The other men in the room probably know too. The way they watch him. They probably heard nurses or doctors talking while he was unconscious. After the surgery.

'Aaron called 'n said you'll get worker's comp. He's got it in da works.' She leans Junior near him. He kisses his son on the top of his head. His lips barely feeling. The nice baby smell. His testicles a dull ache. When he first woke, a thought hit him and he slowly reached for his penis, barely strong enough to work his hand down there. It took a while to find what he was after. Awake and then gone before awake again. The penis where it was supposed to be. Useless was how it felt. A tube in it, lower down a bandage. He wonders what happened. If his nuts are okay. But he won't ask anyone. He can't stand the sight of the nurses, sweet as they are. Trying to pretend they don't know why he's on the bed, his balls bandaged up, telling him that the doctor will be by to see him tomorrow, to have a chat. The beautiful, dark-haired nurse from when Junior was born in the same hospital. The one with the white skin. He's seen her in his room, or imagined it.

Patsy sits on the chair and bounces Junior a little. The baby has started to fuss. She puts the dumb tit in his mouth, and he sucks and watches Blackstrap, one arm reaching out to touch the rail. Grip it firmly and then Junior's small fingers just touching.

Patsy pulls him back. She doesn't say much more. She sniffs and looks at the wall. Then she looks out the window, more and more nervous to be anywhere near him.

He wonders how his father is, if Patsy is looking after him, cooking for him, making sure he changes his shirt every now and then. He waits for his father to come and visit, to show himself in the hospital doorway. He hopes the man does not. And he does not. He stays away. Even with his mind the way it is, his father knows better than to look his son in the face.

There is no way he can lift anything. The thought of picking up a half case is enough to crucify him. He can't even bend over without the pain shooting up the left side of his groin. The swelling makes his lower back ache mercilessly. His stomach feels pasty from the medication. His thoughts aswim in physical sickness. He stands in the shed and looks at his tool kit. He can't lift it. He stares with a haze in the corners of his eyes. He won't ask anyone to do it for him, so he squats and takes the tools out one at a time. He carries them to the front of the house where he fixes the cars. He drops the tools as soon as he gets there. His eyes shut at the embarrassment of the pace. His mind off somewhere.

A one-nut wonder.

His father up in the window, watching him, not a word about the accident.

Worker's compensation is not enough money. He wants a new boat. The one thing he wants for his father. The other boat given back because payments couldn't be made. There is talk of a settlement from the union because of his injury. The insurance company's working out how much a nut is worth. Soon to get back to him with the calculation.

Sometimes Patsy laughs about it. She can't help herself. No way of talking about it without smiling. After so much time has passed, it's not an injury anymore, but a funny story. She tells her friends.

A complete recovery, the doctor told him. Two or three weeks after the removal, you'll be perfectly normal again. The talk of a prosthesis. A fake nut. Most men have it done, the doctor explained, if they're active. Just for the look of it. But he decides against it.

Toward the completion of the penitentiary, a flyer is handed around informing workers that jobs are available as prison guards. Paddy brings a flyer to him. He gives it over and stands there with his hands on his skinny hips, licking his top lip. He nods once, patting the flyer in Blackstrap's hand, like he's asking what Blackstrap's going to do about it. A training program has been set in place. The completion of the ten-week course to coincide with the official opening of the penitentiary.

'Dat's a job fer you,' says Paddy, sniffing. 'Yer jus' da type.' He laughs, shifts from one leg to the other. 'Mr. Muscle.'

Blackstrap folds the flyer into four and lays it inside the open window of the car he's fixing.

'All yours,' says Blackstrap.

'Right,' says Paddy, making a small muscle and smacking it with his other fist.

Blackstrap goes back under the car.

'Wha' ya at under dere?'

'Dig'n fer gold.'

Paddy laughs outright. 'Muffler is it? Bunch 'a nuggets inside?'

663

Blackstrap makes a noise and puts out his hand.

Paddy hands him the tools without needing to be asked.

Rust sprinkles into his eyes. He blinks it away and blows the dust from his lips. One bit of rust stings and he blinks for a while before the blur goes. A set of clamp nuts are seized on. He'll need to torch them off. Pushing himself out from under, he gets a twinge running down his legs when he stands.

'You should give some t'ought to being a guard, dat's what I t'ink.'

A prison guard is not the job for him. Watching over men locked away, while the men hate his guts. He knows how it works. He's seen enough of it on TV to know.

He already has plans of his own. A new boat bought out of the insurance settlement. He'll have plenty of money from what he's heard. And all he needed to do was lose a testicle. If he'd only known that before. He'd have cut one out himself. Maybe he'll call the boat the *Floating Nut*. He's also working on getting his big rig licence. Patsy reads the books to him at night. The stuff he needs to know. She helps him study when Junior's napping. Blackstrap sits in class with others who don't say much, mostly younger men and a few in their thirties like him. He listens to the instructor and understands every word. The government pays him to attend the school. His father says nothing about it, not to his face anyway, but he says plenty to Patsy. He hears them at it in the kitchen. 'A licence fer wha'?' Jacob demands. Patsy slams a cupboard door, bangs down a pot. She leaves the kitchen with the baby and sees Blackstrap stood there, thinking about the book for his course where he hides it out in the shed. Looking in at his father at the kitchen table, he sees the man is vexed and muttering to himself.

Blackstrap drops out and drives a rig anyway. Whenever an offer comes his way, he lies about having a licence, grunts when asked if he finished the course. But everyone knows he didn't. They smile at the thought of it. That's Blackstrap, one says to the other. Just like himself. And he's hired anyway because people know he won't ever do a job unless it's done properly.

Chapter XII – 1987

Fred Astaire, Jackie Gleason, Liberace, Rita Hayworth Die

(?)

The pain pills and the rum and the world not there. When he thumbs a capsule into his palm. Washed down with a swig. Burning a trail for the capsule. Floating under, in him. Deeper in the dredge. What sealed in the capsule? How many men spill out when it dissolves? To feel so exactly. Awake and sitting grim-faced-staring for hours with a memory of laughing the night before. Bashing off walls and laughing. A cataclysm from calm room to room. A person flashing by. Speaking or moving or still. They don't know what it's like, those ones, the woman and the child. How would they know? But the father. An old man. Older than he should be. He does know. Because of his age. His time. His dissolution. Naked in front of the mirror. Artillery shot with the fingers gone. He holds them up. Running fingers over stubs. What war? A battle at sea. The toes not there either. The scar in his cheek that throbs when it rains. It rains and it rains and he stands in it. Drenched and breathing his head off. Only a hook to save him. Winched up. The legs dangling. Never drowning in earth. The hook to the story. An abomination. Soaken wet but not cold enough. To die. He screeches in laughter. A mouth open unstopping. A hollow. His mouth pooled with water. Wind. Ripples. A shiver unsteadying the surface. Who afloat in there if not him? Bobbing. The nut once in liquid smashed to smithereens. A sack less one tiny skull. What is this? Me? What? Look. Me? Look! Look at you! LOOK AT YOU! A bottle raised to his reflection. And a pill. Dropped on the carpet. Green. Like plastic on the outside. Bashed together. On his knees searching for green ones. Blue ones. Red. Bashed together. In his palm. Pills to play the room around. Words on the label he believes he can read. With eyes not often his. With him falling into walls at all hours. With one blank and artful expression chunked and crumpled up in his heart. He says what he feels. And his son not knowing him. Who is he? What is that crying man? What is this son? Shaking the baby and raging: 'Who is this son? Mine?' And Agnes or Patsy or Susan shouting for him to go. His grip no longer on the baby. Clutching after the woman. Who pulls away. Spinning him. A swirl a whirl a hiding in the room. The three of them there. One and the same. A heyt wuyver, he shouts. A heat waver. Tracking them at night. To aim. To leave. To go. Get out. Yer crazy. Get out or I'll call the cops. Her hands in his hair. Her nails. His hold on her. His hold on a bottle. Pulling and pushing. What muscles were made for. He falls to the floor. Slams to rattle everything. His face a clutch of chuckling. Words barely pressed through spastic lips, Y's, wha' muscles ma fr. The bottle scraped along the floor to his lips. He stares along that level line. A fit, they think, he is having. The cops called again and again and again. With him gone. And wrapped in bandages. His father unknowing itself. To watch that figure stooped, sitting, asleep in age caving in on itself. A man he knew as a boy. Which one is he now? The one who keeps changing because he cannot stop. Will himself to. Not what he ever knew. Why did time do that? The memories ribbed around what is changing. The heart. A mystery who once lived in the house. Now, out in the woods. Crackling and snapping like a fire of shadows. With him moving. He is the fire of shadows. Arms and legs shooting out to damage. Crackling his way through. Only in there. With the living things he cuts down. Tree or animal. Will he near the nature of the suffering he feels. Falling through wilderness growth and laughing and cursing. In perfect understanding so sharply attuned. Patterns in the bark in the leaves in the sky. He wakes in the woods. Cold. Damp. Staring up. Criss-cross of life blocking the sky. No forgiveness spoken in silence. Back in that house with the woods growing around it. The sun and snow and rain. The hovel. The hole. The hiding place. From the wilderness into it. Crawling or standing or falling. A fever. A chill. An ache. All at once for his hands searching like nothing for the bottle.

Which bottle? Where is it? Where? Where did you put them? No, you *do* know. You do. The pill cap trembled off. The rum unscrewed. Steadiness in what is put inside. To shut the inside off. Holding on to steadiness with eyes shut too. Silence is everything then. Better and better. Boot heels dug into certainty. Breathing easier. Not so bad toward muscle. Only time until up on his feet again. Yes, his house. His feet. His hands. In his house. The things he worked for all his life. Mine. For who? For what? And then loss. Because there are others. Regret for the less-than-that they give him back. Shouting at that woman. Why? Never enough are you. He does not know her. Who is she? What is she? What has she done to him? Into this. Me into this. Look at me. Roaring. Look at me. You fucking cunt. A king in no castle. A mite infesting what? Fucking hate you. Fucking hate you. And I hate you. You should be dead like the others. Oh, I hate you, too. Leave. Go. If that's it. If that's what you want. Exactly, yes. Exactly. Laughing and falling down over the stairs. But no stairs in sight. The police come. He comes back. He must to his house. Where else could he be kept? Barely lifting his head from where it is. And seeing. What is he seeing? He falls down again. The police put him away. He watches out through steel bars. Why have they trapped him with the door shut? Holding bars in his hands. Slit shadows in his eyes. Every object pressing in on him for space. Spitting on about the little that's left. No one understands a word. No one comes to his rescue. What is he saying? Spitting out words. He froths at the mouth. I am not. Not these words. Not mine. These words. Don't you say so. Head thrown back, he wails. He reads every-thing. On the walls in the room. These lists of conditions. These rules to live by. Reading but not understanding. That's the noise he makes. How to read without understanding. He shouts and points. A blurt. You should know. But not crazy. Me. I'm not. Take me home. Show me it. That's not it. I don't know that place. Not where I feel. Where are the ones where it's easy? Not to that place. Never to the place I can even begin to imagine. Not in the confines. I could never know. I could never say. People like me, help me, please. Who know what I am. In the back of the car. The policeman with his hat. Quiet now. Helping him into the house. Confinement. The wife. The son. The father. He the father and his father. The two of them. Him with what's left of him. In silence. In sorrow. In hating regret. Which prison to clang the door shut in. Capsules afloat in rum inside him. Not against each other but with. Back at it right away. Because no one can tell him. Except him. What he is doing. Put me in there. I made it. Him outside the wall. Shouting in the darkness. FACK'N IDIOCY UH DA W'RLD. Outside. The house he thought was his. With the rain beating down. Not enough to drown anything. Having walked there. Back of Coombs Hill. The prison. Put me in there. Everyone inside ignoring him. The prisoners hear him shouting all night. While he stumbles around the walls. FACK'N IDIOCY UH DA W'RLD. Jumping to get over. Trying to grab but sliding down. Feeling with his hands. Knowing every nook and cranny because he made it. Built it. This body. He would kill it off if it weren't already.

Chapter XIII – 1989
Valdez

(*March, 1989, 35 years old*)

Driving through Wreckhouse is always cause for concern. The winds can gust up to 165 kilometers per hour, lifting cars and tossing them off the side of the highway. Last week, Blackstrap saw a fox roll across the highway, like a tumbleweed on one of those western movies he sometimes watches on Sunday with Junior. The boy going into kindergarten in two years. Patsy can't wait to get him out of the house, to get a break. There's no end to it, she complains to Blackstrap. Junior doesn't sit still. A friggin' torment the way he's always poking at everything.

In the sort of fog that Blackstrap is barrelling through there is no telling what might appear out of the woolly grey. His nerves are on edge. He wishes he had taken a flask of rum along, but there was no time to get one. Only empty bottles in the house when he checked through everything. He is already behind schedule with a load of fourteen grey containers on his truck. They're filled with codfish in need of offloading at the plant in Badger's Tickle. Workers waiting on him because the fog has made him late. He doesn't like the thought of the looks he'll get from the workers who've been sitting around outside the plant, talking or smoking. They'll rise to their feet when they see the truck and face him like a long-overdue challenge. Not his fault. Tell them that. They'd never listen. Just wanting someone to blame for the sorry state of their lives. Fuck them. When he's done with his delivery, he'll drop by the Cozy Glow for a few shots. No hurry to get home then. He might even sleep in the back of the truck.

He's doing 100 km. If anything gets in his way, it'll just be knocked to the side. He feels the wind pushing at his right, coming from the north, gliding down over the mountains to pick up speed, nudging the rig, making the steering wheel seem jammed. He doesn't care. He won't slow up.

The wind is a wonder on this part of the island. Always its own weather report on the radio. In the Wreckhouse area, high winds. Wind warning in effect for Wreckhouse. The CN Railway used to have a man named Lockie MacDougall on the payroll. Blackstrap heard a story about him once on CBC Radio. Lockie lived with his wife in a house next to the train tracks. They called him the Human Wind Gauge. He could step outside and sniff the air and know when the wind was coming. The railway paid him to do this. There was only one time they didn't listen, and sent the train through anyway, because something on board couldn't be delayed. The wind came then, and hurled the train off the tracks. The locomotive and two cars derailed. No one injured, but it cost CN millions. They listened to Lockie after that. His word golden.

The rig takes another punch.

Blackstrap's driving for Rex Fowler who's laid up in the hospital with a bad back. Sitting behind the wheel of a rig, living on French fries and cola can pack the weight on. The weight did something to one of the discs in Rex's spine. And he was rushed off in an ambulance. No one knows when Rex will be out of the hospital. Rex's wife told Blackstrap that Rex can't move without yelping in pain, like a struck dog. She's the one who called him with the job. They needed someone quick and no one else was available. Blackstrap doesn't believe that Rex was actually yelping. He can't see Rex yelping. Always such a quiet, shy fellow.

Blackstrap stares into the grey. It's possible to imagine anything in that grey, anything that isn't there at all. It's even worse because he's tired, and he feels like he's coming apart. It's starting to get dark, the light grey deepening. He could take a pill. A pack of wake-ups in his pocket just in case. But, he won't. He's sworn that he won't. A pledge to himself and to Patsy. He checks for the package, rattling the box in his pocket. They're not like painkillers. But he won't take another. Not after the harm done to Patsy. The hand raised to her that he could not remember. The deep shame of that. Not another drink either. That's what he'd said. How long did that last though? Not long. His head almost on right after six months. Maybe he won't stop into the Cozy Glow. Maybe he'll drive right back home after. He pulls on his head-lights, but they don't show him anything, only make the grey brighter, glowing back at him. The stretching cones of his headlights make their shape in the fog.

He turns on the radio to keep his mind alert. A throb of bass from the speakers. Rex has a good system hooked up. Cassette tapes in the glove compartment if Blackstrap wants them. 'Fight the Power.' A thud of music. A beat to beat on something. 'Fight the Power.'

He catches himself in a half doze and starts awake, his skin prickling. He raises his hand and belts himself across the face as hard as he can. His head jerking to the right.

'Uh,' he says, wincing, then surprised that the sound came out of him. He slaps his face again. It's not doing the job. He reaches behind his neck, pulls at the short hairs near his collar, pulls until his eyes water and he has to curse.

He stares and, gradually, his chin dips toward his chest. He startles, his body warning himself awake, his eyes desperately searching to see where he is, what reaction is needed. The rig still on the road where it should be. No need to cut the wheels one way or the other. His hand in his pocket for the box of wake-ups, stopping, then going for the radio. 'Fight the Power' turned up until the speakers pop with bass. He rolls down his window to let the wind pound against his face and eardrum. A gust shoves him sideways, and he almost loses hold of the steering wheel, scrambles to roll up the window. The chill gone right through him. He slaps himself as hard as he can. Curses and grits his teeth. He tightens up his muscles and lets his palm come at him again in a vicious snap of movement. Tears warming his eyes with a faint blur.

He checks his speedometer: 110 km. The music is making him go faster. He turns it down.

When he looks up again, he sees a shadow. Not a show from his head but something out there. The shadow darkens to a vague outline. A moose stood on the asphalt. In the truck's path. Blackstrap tries gearing down, hits the brake. Useless. He'll lose the load if the rig jackknifes.

The moose turns its head to look into the two cones of lights. It knows nothing about what's coming. What to expect.

One thousand, four hundred and twenty-six pounds.

Like a rock carved out of stillness, until it's popped up into the air. A second of waiting for what might happen. Then a huge sound buckling the windshield. A spread of curved points rammed forward and stuck.

He only knows that he is lying down. He thinks it might be in the middle of the road. There are people moving around him talking. In the fog, he hears the words: 'Head injury.' He cannot breathe deeply. Something is wiped across his face. He draws in short breaths. It takes him a while to realize he is seeing because he is seeing double.

'You have to stay aboard,' someone says to him.

He tries to focus.

'On this board,' someone says. 'Aboard.'

He wants to say 'what.'

'Don't move,' someone says. 'Until X-rays. Please. Try not to swim. Move. Stay on this board. No, you have to lie flat. Float.'

'His ears,' says another person. Somewhere behind the top of his head. 'Gauze.'

Something is stuffed in both his ears.

He tries moving.

Dull, muddled words: 'Keep him down.'

'Get the girl clear . . . from him.'

He goes away again.

He comes to himself in a room. A child across from him. Is it Junior? His fourth birthday. Wasn't it just a few minutes ago? The boy seems

671

older. On his side with a tube in his throat. The tube is clear. But there is red draining from the boy's mouth. A bandage around his head. A great wave of emotion, a surge of pain comes over every single inch of Blackstrap's body. The pain tightens itself around his thoughts, crushes them into a misshapen ball.

He makes a sound that has nothing to do with him.

A nurse hurries over. She tosses back the sheet and stabs his leg with a needle.

'Can you tell me where you are?' she asks.

He does not know what she means. He watches her pluck the needle out. Then she swabs his leg.

'What's your name?'

Junior, he thinks. Where is Junior? There was an accident. Underground. In the earth. Where his mother is. Where Ruth is.

'It's okay,' she says.

'Junnr,' he says.

It's okay.

He drifts off. Wonders if he has spoken. If he is asleep. He thinks and speaks at once. But he is doing neither. Effortlessly. Worming through a tunnel of the blackest red.

A woman in a long white coat is outside his door. She's talking to a nurse. The beautiful nurse with the dark hair. Has the baby been born yet? He tries looking at his hands. All of his fingers there. His mouth opens. And he stares toward the doorway. The other woman has a stethoscope hanging from around her neck. The nurse has on a nurse hat. The nurse nods and walks off. The woman leans toward the doorway. Knocks.

'Hi,' she says. Smiling in a way that makes him feel better. 'Remember me?'

Blackstrap wonders if he has seen her before. In the hospital. He is confused because he does not remember exactly. He reaches for his face, not knowing why. His fingers feeling around. A bandage on his forehead. But he seems to know the woman. She is pretty. Long dark-blonde hair pulled back in a ponytail. He checks her belly. But she is not pregnant. Did he have a child with her? Part of him knows. But she is different. Part of him knows her deeper than he can ever feel. Because tears begin running from the corners of both his eyes. He is awake in what? He cannot be.

'Agnes,' says the doctor.

He stares.

'Agnes Bishop . . . From Cutland Junction.' So different from herself.

He sniffs and begins bawling. Nothing real now. Finally, his mind not his. Bawling and sobbing with his mouth open.

The doctor pulls a tissue from a box on the side table and dabs at his tears. 'Can you tell me where you are?' she asks.

He breathes through his open mouth. A wet sob. He presses his lips together and breathes through his nostrils. His eyes on the woman's face. She smiles like everything's okay. Then she looks toward the window. A woman doctor. She glances back at him and smiles again. The best she can. Who is this woman he knows? How she has been trained to know him not too dearly.

'Agnes,' he says. The way he says it, like he has teeth missing. Is that so? His lips swollen.

'Yes.'

He tries and moves his eyes over the room. There is a white curtain pulled around a bed.

'You had an accident. Do you remember?'

He looks back, not knowing where the words have come from. Or how long ago they were spoken. The woman is gone. He swallows. Startled, he checks toward the darkening window. He wonders what he is looking at. Trees. A forest. A mountain. One or all of these things. He is scared for what will not come to him.

A moment later, Agnes is back. She reaches forward and shuts his eyes. Her fingertips lightly on his lids. He is sleeping or he is awake. The swirls of her fingerprints up that close, even when they move away.

When he opens his eyes, Blackstrap sees a man in uniform. The policeman has coughed. It is that sound that has brought him back from a dream of Agnes into the room.

'He shouldn't be told,' says a voice.

He shifts his eyes toward the door. But there is no one to match the voice. Tubes going into his arms. What sort of dope? he wonders. He doesn't want the same as before. Two nurses are stood there. 'Not yet.' One of them looking in, the beautiful one. The other one turns away because there has been a sound somewhere else. A scream. A shout. Something tipped over. A clang. A rattle. A bang.

The police officer says, 'I'm Constable Fry. I'm the officer investigating your accident.'

Accident? The question not in his mouth, but somewhere on his face.

'Your semi hit a moose on the Trans Canada Highway outside Wreckhouse. Correct?'

Blackstrap remembers greyness. A head with antlers. The crashing intrusion. He takes a deep breath in pain. He cannot stop the pain from taking control of him. The pain is centred in his back, but everywhere at once.

The police officer waits until Blackstrap sees him again. Sweat runs out of every pore. Blackstrap tries licking his lips.

The pain is mute noise.

'We've done toxicology tests on your blood. Everything's in order there. Just so you know. That's out of the way. But I'll need your licence. Not right now. Later's fine.'

This is meant to be a good thing, Blackstrap thinks. But there is something else, something the constable has to say whether he wants to or not. What? Time passes through his eyes. The rest of him does not sense a thing.

'Unfortunately, your semi struck another vehicle in the oncoming lane when it swerved.'

Struck.

Blackstrap tries to remember. The bulk tumbling up over the front of the semi. Those antlers not snapping, but punching holes in steel. The glassy web of the windshield caving in.

'There was a woman in the other vehicle, and her six-year-old daughter.'

The other vehicle.

The windshield in a web at first. Then the furry stilt of a leg and a hoof coming through the hole, straight toward his head. An instant of jumbled movement. The bulk still rolling or tossing and then antlers.

'The woman was killed instantly.' The policeman takes a breath, the news seeming personal to him. Talking about it is making him uncomfortable. He glances toward the doorway, his jaw set, then toward the window.

Blackstrap makes a noise that is meant to be a question. A question about the little girl. Without moving, he feels the pain take the full of him. He has done something to his head. The little girl being wheeled past him. A slow rolling shape through the clutter on the grey pavement. The gradual and instant shift of the earth. The grey sky. The fog a trap. He tried to move but was not allowed. He twists in bed to escape or help someone, and the pain rushes at him in a blazingly silent shriek that deafens and blinds.

Only one small voice saying 'hello' as a question. Shrill ringing in his ears.

Jacob sits in the chair by the side of the hospital bed. He watches Blackstrap for a while, then reaches forward, takes hold of his hand, rubs and pats it.

'Cripes, b'y,' he says. 'Dat's no way ta bag a moose.'

Blackstrap cannot find a stain of humour in it. He thinks about Jacob, thinks there should be other people. From that house. He wonders who: a woman and a boy. Not a girl. His child. A boy, not a girl.

'Tell us wha' happened,' says Jacob, seated in the chair by the side of his bed. 'I looked fer da doctor but he's not in till later.'

She, thinks Blackstrap. She's not.

'She,' he says.

'Wha'?'

'She doctor.'

'She dev'l?'

'Agnes.'

'Who?'

'Agnes.'

Jacob checks toward the doorway. No one passes in the hallway. He turns his attention back to Blackstrap. 'Tell 's wha' went on. Wreckhouse's da wickedest of places.'

Blackstrap remembers about the moose. Larger than the entire windshield. Something about a little girl. Tiny. He sighs right away, anger from confusion mounting. He shuts his eyes. He wants out. His head muddled. He sees a little girl, but the face is entirely unfamiliar. She could be anyone.

'Best not talk den. I'll get da news from da doc.'

'Who?' he says, not knowing why.

'Yer out of it.' Jacob laughs. 'Patsy couldn't come 'cause o' Junior.'

Blackstrap tries looking for the doorway. Patsy there. No one there. A bundle in her arms wrapped in a pink blanket. A girl. Isn't that what happened? Or was it something else about a girl. They grow up, all of them. They grow up and old.

There is a small television on an arm that can be pulled out over his bed. The screen put in front of his face. The nurse shows him how this is done. She presses the button and an image beams on. A picture of water turned black. Black washing up on a beach. Dead sea birds. The woman puts the ear plug in his ear. 'Eleven million barrels of oil spilled . . .'

'Someone has been calling for you,' says the nurse.

'What?'

'A man but he won't leave his name. You should get a phone in your room.'

Agnes steps up to the foot of his bed, like she just came from somewhere else where she was busy. She stands there smiling at him. Her hands in the front pockets of her white coat.

'You know where you are today?' asks the nurse.

Blackstrap looks at the nurse, her face a mystery. He thinks: The beautiful nurse. The one from the delivery. In a different hospital. Where is he?

'Do you know where you are?'

'A . . . hospital.'

'Right.' The doctor looks at the nurse. 'Good.'

There is talk in one of his ears. Tiananmen Square. Troops opened fire on demonstrators. Hundreds dead. Orientals. Who's to do what about it. The people watching are expected to stop it.

Agnes is talking. Why is she there? Why is she looking after him? So many years after she left, here now.

Blasphemous. A five-million-dollar reward to murder a man who wrote a book. Was he British? Was he from India? A man on TV wants to know. A British man says 'yes,' another argues 'no.' 'Of course, he knew what he was getting into.' 'Even though he speaks with a British tongue, he's intimate with the Muslim faith.' The men with British accents but with dark skin.

'I can't hear.'

'Do you want me to turn it up?' asks the nurse.

'What?' He looks at her, looks back at the foot of his bed.

The space where Agnes was.

Outside, there is a smell in the air, a rotten egg stink on the wind. Cars are parked everywhere. Set up in lines. Back to back. Front to front. Colours that would startle anyone. Jacob mentions a pulp and paper mill. 'Smell dat?' He looks toward the water. The brick building with smoke billowing out. He knows a few people who work there, men whose families were from Bareneed. They moved to the west coast of the island for whatever work.

It takes them a while to find the truck. Jacob does not remember. Blackstrap does not know either, even with Jacob asking: 'Where'd I park da pickup?'

Finally, it is there before them, backed into the space the way his father always parks. The hard part first, then easy out. Straight ahead.

Blackstrap opens the passenger door. His fingers doing what they should, despite his head. Jacob stands close by, asking if Blackstrap needs a hand. Blackstrap's legs not all there. Movement hurts his eyes, makes him feel stomach sick. People and cars. Colours shifting. The size of the sky above him. It takes a second for his mind to catch up, to settle him down.

Damage of some sort. Tests were done by a man with cards asking questions. The man's face a blank. 'This is not about me,' the man kept saying, when Blackstrap wanted to know.

The honking of a horn in the parking lot. Blackstrap turns his head. A car is there, facing them with its headlights on, even though it's daylight. The car starts rolling toward them. The horn keeps making a sound. Short toots. A warning. A series of letters. A code. Then a straight long honking.

Are they in the way? Blackstrap thinks.

The car pulls right up beside them. The man jumps out from behind the wheel. He rushes toward Blackstrap. He's shouting: 'You fucking, *fucking* murderer.' He pushes by Jacob, shoves him toward the pickup where Jacob strikes the bonnet. Then he's against Blackstrap. A body pressing near his. The man shouting in Blackstrap's face. The man's face full of rage. The man's eyes in dark circles. White spit on his lips. The man's hands shoving at Blackstrap's chest. Shoving and grabbing, then letting go. All at once. A fist held back. The pain roaring up. Blackstrap cringes forward. A blade down between his eyes. He slopes forward but does not fall. There is a scuffle of movement. The man being pulled away.

Blackstrap's hand against metal. He straightens to see a police officer holding the man back, holding the man behind the arms. The policeman's talking to the man. Talking quickly into one of his ears, trying to reason with him. Buddies that know each other. On a first-name basis.

Blackstrap looks toward the man's car because there has been movement there. He sees in the back window. A baby's seat. A girl in it. Her head on an angle, staring straight at him. She just keeps staring, for all the world to see. She's too big for a baby seat. Then she smiles, a big wet smile that stays that way. Her face as happy as anything possible. Her tongue slipping out. Until her hand comes up and slaps at the window. The girl smiles and screeches.

Sweet Jesus Christ Almighty!

The man checks toward the car. He sees the girl and looks back at Blackstrap. His face a mess of anger. 'Don't you . . . you look at her.' He tries pulling away, to get at Blackstrap.

Jacob now stood in front of Blackstrap, pointing at the man. Jacob uttering oaths and nodding solid. 'Mind yerself.' Words fast and clipped so that Blackstrap has trouble making them out.

'Just get in your vehicle,' says the police officer. 'Please.'

Jacob takes a while to calm down. 'Get 'im in '*is* vehicle.'

'Just drive away. Now, please, sir.'

A crowd has gathered, slowly walking through the grey. Sad faces turned to watch in. But there is nothing to see.

Blackstrap cannot help staring at the little girl. She bangs a toy against the window. A clear hole made of something. He shifts his jaw to one side. His shoulders go weak. He opens his mouth and takes a wet breath. The image of the little girl slips out of focus.

To put his head against hers.

To shut his eyes.

To whisper to her in whatever language.

She might likely understand.

For all the love that could never be hers.

The nine-hour drive east, from Corner Brook to Cutland Junction, goes by in silence. Occasionally, with Blackstrap shifting more and more in his seat, the pickup pulls into an Irving gas station on the highway. Blackstrap gets out, aware of how he's paused in a spot in the middle of nowhere. The movements of wheels stopped. His feet on the ground, just like the others taking a break in mid-journey. He goes inside and watches people buy coffees, chips, soda pop and bars. There's a restaurant attached where people sit at tables or in booths. He's been here plenty of times over the years, but never is there a familiar face. Only now he seems to recognize everyone.

They get back in the truck. Without a word, his father hands Blackstrap a chocolate bar like he used to do when Blackstrap was a boy. His favourite type. He takes it and looks at the wrapper. Saves it for later.

Back home, Patsy gives over bits of news. Things that have happened while Blackstrap was gone. She remembers more bits of news as she is reminded by other things. Blackstrap tries to imagine what or who she is talking about, but can only put together fragments.

He is meant to rest for three weeks and then physiotherapy should be scheduled. People call from the hospital in Corner Brook. And then people call from the nearer hospital in Carbonear.

The physiotherapy causes more pain than he thought possible. Even after everything, he stops going to the appointments in Carbonear. The

679

long drive only makes his back worse. There are exercises he is meant to do. Leg lifts. One leg bent at the knee, then raise the other. Tilt the toes back. Pelvic tilts. Lie flat on the floor and angle the hips up, hold for five seconds, then down. A crushed lower vertebra.

Agnes calls to check on his progress. She asks specific questions, then waits, listens. Patsy has answered the phone and handed it to him. It might be anyone, but the voice he hears he recognizes. Patsy stands right there and watches him, mouthing: 'Who's dat?' He answers quietly; small words while he studies his feet. The missing toes behind the socks. Lumpy is how he feels. The pain not so bad in the light of her voice. He won't take the pills like he's supposed to. He sweats from the pain. And the headaches that blind him, until Agnes says that it appears he will make a full recovery. But by the sound of her voice, he knows that she is worried. Not asking about the mother and the little girl. Those two people fill the space of what's been taken away, keeping them at a distance. Every single person dead in his life. That woman and that little girl add it all up. Strangers, but once his. Once, they were more to him than now. That's how he feels. He's positively convinced.

Full recovery, he thinks after hanging up. Will she call again?

Patsy watches him, her arms folded across her chest. 'Dat doctor again,' she says. 'She was from 'round here, right? You just try it.'

Strained words: 'Try what?'

'Just try it.'

He does not understand what she is saying. Or why she is saying it.

Up and around, he cannot lift Junior into his arms. Work, he loses track of. The thought of work smothers him. His back pains if he moves his legs to the side. And, sometimes, his mind just goes. It leaves him. He finds himself again a few moments later. On a journey through a blizzard. A voyage. A fire. A hanging. A battle . . . Coming back from something he cannot rightly place himself in.

He barely breathes as an onlooker.

At night, lying in bed, the pain like metal in his blood, he can feel it in his teeth, coating the roots. He tries tilting up his hips, holds it. He is glad that he is alone, that Patsy is watching television, that she is not next to him. He does not like her. He hates her now. He has always tried not to hate any person. Something his mother used to say: Never hate a person. They can never do so much badness to deserve being hated. But he feels hatred toward her. Patsy knows nothing of what he is feeling. She doesn't care. Only complains about herself.

He tries not to, but he has to take a pill.

He struggles up to sit on the edge of the bed. Shifting his legs is the worst of it, his arms stiffening with the effort. A bottle of pills from the night table in his hand. All of the physical misery adds up to a memory of his mother. He watches into the hollow of the pill bottle. How many would he need to take, to relive Christmas?

Patsy keeps telling him there is no money coming in. No worker's compensation. Blackstrap without a rig licence in the first place. Compensation cut off. An investigation under way and talk of him being charged with something. He shouldn't have been on the road without a rig licence.

The police come by and serve him a summons.

Then, a few weeks later, another summons. A lawsuit from a man in Corner Brook. The husband of the wife. The father of the little girl. Blackstrap cannot fix cars or haul wood, and Jacob is useless. He doesn't like it when Patsy says that word. 'Useless' to describe his father.

Patsy goes to work at the fish plant in Port de Grave. She comes home stinking. She has to take off her rubber gloves, boots, hairnet and apron outside before she steps into the house. While Patsy's at work, Blackstrap or Jacob watches Junior. Most times, after kindergarten, Junior sits in front of the television, watching children's shows. *Sesame Street* or *Teenage Mutant Ninja Turtles*. Junior has only half a day of school in the mornings or afternoons. Hard to keep track of which days. Junior there one minute, gone the next. Sitting in front of the television in his space. Then his space a blank.

Blackstrap takes Junior out for slow walks. He can't drive the truck yet. It's easier to manage the car because it's lower. But his mind. One stretch of road like another. He wonders where, and watches every car that passes in the other direction. The faces of the drivers never the same. He gets lost for a while, but eventually finds his way.

The woods is easier to remember. They step along trails. It's difficult over the uneven ground. Plus carrying the chainsaw. He cuts down two trees before he begins to sweat. Almost collapses to his knees. His hand against a trunk. Junior kicks at trees, side-kicking and pretending to punch while making karate sounds. Swatting at flies, Blackstrap wants to show Junior, but the way he is now is wrong. He has to stop. He has to give up.

The reason Patsy is working is because she's pregnant. More money needed for the baby. She told Blackstrap when he came home, but she hasn't said much to him since. The pregnancy his fault again. Blackstrap knows Patsy wants her own house. Her own car. She doesn't want a sick husband. She holds his injuries against him. Blackstrap wonders why things have changed. Why Patsy is no longer nice. Why she doesn't do as he says. Why she scoffs at him whenever he speaks.

'Your hair's funny,' Junior says, pointing at Blackstrap's head. The hair on the top of his head has grown back enough to have all of it buzzed down the same length. He goes to Jocelyn's to have it done. She asks him what number he wants. He has no idea so she shows him pictures. He asks Junior which one is best and Junior picks one. Jocelyn names the number and clips one of the comb attachments to the buzzer.

He watches himself in the mirror. The top of his head hurts when the buzzer goes over it. A woman working on his head with something electrical. His reflection in the mirror. The dent in his cheek. He grips the armrests of the chair. 'Sorry,' says Jocelyn. The scar on his head throbs. He has lost weight, his eyes in a face not his. He wonders why he did not die. His hair falls to the floor. He had taken the bottle of pills and Agnes had called. The pills had put him to sleep while she spoke. He had died or he had lived. He kept hearing her. She told him he already had a crushed lower vertebra, one from before besides the new one. An older injury. He suspects it was from when he rolled the car six years ago with Patsy in the passenger seat.

Done with the haircut, he pays Jocelyn and gives Junior the change. Junior looks at it in his palm. He pokes at it. He grins and jumps up and down. Excited, he bobs his head.

Blackstrap stares for a long while at the boy. He has no memory of ever being that small.

Jocelyn gives Junior a red sucker.

The boy grabs it.

'Ha,' says Junior, leaning forward.

'Say thank you,' says Blackstrap blankly, his mother in his head.

'Thanks yooooo.' Junior runs for the door and side-kicks it, almost falls over. Then shoves it open. 'Cowabunga!'

Out in the car, Blackstrap makes sure Junior is buckled in. His hand trembling while he checks the belt. Even after it clicks, he tugs on it with his hand as hard as he can. His arm a mess of unsteadiness.

'Ninja,' shouts Junior. 'Ninja, ninja . . .' thrusting forward against the restraint.

'You goin' out?' Patsy asks.

Blackstrap nods and pulls on his boots. A job just to lace them up.

'Where?'

'Dun know.'

'Yeah right. How long?'

He doesn't answer. Dizzy when he stands up. He wants to shut his eyes but worries of the consequence.

'I'm goin' out, too, with Rayna.'

'Sure.'

She watches him while he turns without looking at her again, without seeing her eyes. Junior is upstairs playing. The boy a trouble to him. Why? He doesn't feel good. He feels burnt and wasted. Always in pain makes him not want for anything. He'll take a drive. He can drive now. A little further than before. He can make it as far as Bareneed and back. He will go and see the ocean, ride on the water in the *Floating Nut*. The water his again, with no fear of it. He thinks it might be the medication.

He drives at a crawl through Cutland Junction, passing the houses with people in them who he knows of. He crosses the highway and takes Shearstown Line down to Bareneed. The once-rocky road paved now. He passes the graveyard. His eyes staying away from there. He parks down as far as he can go. Then takes his time walking to the wharf. A few men are there who he's not familiar with. They're on boats with polished hardwood inside. The sound of them talking reminds him of hearing voices through a speaker. One of them on the deck in shorts says hello to him. He nods and watches out over the blue water. There is talk of a yacht basin being built here. More houses being bought up by people with boats. Not for fishing. Pleasure crafts. His boat, the twenty-footer he bought from Doug Bishop, is tied up at the wharf. The one from the insurance money for his crushed testicle. He hasn't been out on the water since the truck accident and the boat might be gone soon. The lawsuits against him taking everything. He can't stand to worry about it, so he doesn't.

He stops on the wharf, smelling the sea air. He can't get his mind off Agnes and the face of the little girl in the car window. His mind makes him think the girl belongs to him and Agnes. Why this screwed-up thought? Confused by sadness. Worn down by whatever is playing with his mind. A million little things he doesn't even know are there.

He wants to go back to Corner Brook, to the hospital where he'll be safe. He'll take the boat if he can't drive. Patsy pregnant. Another baby. When was that? The time of conception. When and where? He wants to remember. But can't. The sound of Agnes' voice. The way his mind is he feels he is dying.

He steps down from the wharf. Not on land anymore.

Casting off, Blackstrap heads for Port de Grave, the long finger of land extended east, across from Bareneed. His intention is to travel north. Up over the top of the island. Then his head tells him different. North would be too long a voyage. All the way up and around the Northern Peninsula, then down. He should head south first. That would be better. He recalls the map of Newfoundland. The old map up there in front of the classroom. The map pulled down on material like a blind. He's seen it countless times since then, but that's the one he remembers. Something he should already know. Its shape is gone. He thinks on it and sweats from the idea of not knowing. The island a jumble of broken-up bits. He swings the boat around. Full out. Seven knots. By his calculations, it'll take him a little more than a day to get there. A change of clothes already on the boat. Toothbrush. Deodorant. No food though. He's not hungry. He's in pain. He must have dropped ten pounds since the accident. He forgot his pills. The idea of the pills being far away makes him unsteady.

In despair, he heads the boat toward Brigus. Then out toward Bell Isle, past the towering cliffs that shape the island, like a fortress. With

Junior there somewhere in a hollow shaft of the earth. Far beneath the sea. He remembers to switch on his radio. The squawk of transmissions. Small boat chatter and warnings that trouble him even more. Down around the Avalon Peninsula, he passes St. John's harbour in four hours. The sight of ships in through the narrows where the cliffs rise from the water. Buildings and houses just barely lit up in the cup of the harbour. It reminds him of flying home from Toronto at night.

Darkness soon.

He heads out farther from shore.

No pills with the night closing in. When the pain will be worse. He licks sweat from above his lips. Shifting the pressure from leg to leg. But pressure never relieved, only rising up his spine into his head. Impossible to sit down. Agnes will have pills.

St. Shotts. Branch. St. Lawrence. The clusters of lights far off, on land. The water black and glistening. And then the slant of sunlight shows houses nearer the shore than expected. Wharfs and fishing boats, the closer ones with people waving to him in the otherwise perfect stillness.

No time for sleeping. The pain tightens and tires him out. His stomach grumbles and burns. He belches liquid. Battery acid in his throat. When he was in the hospital, they said something about an ulcer. Medication he never took for it. Lay off the fat, Agnes said. Lay off the beer. A glass of milk with the pills. Watch your diet. Sure. He could agree with her, but do nothing.

Grand Bank. Burgeo. He knows the names of places. He has been through these waters before, but not in years. Not ever, really. He thinks on it. He knows the cut of the land. He knows the places. But has he been here? Not that he recalls. Not on a boat. Only that map up in front of the classroom.

Tracing the contours, now near the place of shipwrecks where Francis Hawco lived. With the new sunlight over his shoulder, he coasts closer to shore. Eases back the throttle and carefully studies the cove. What he expects to see is the graveyard of ships' masts. The shack on the shore where Francis Hawco is stood, watching, waiting for him to strike rock. To sink.

The pain easing up at the thought of a capsule broken open. Through the wheelhouse window, he watches down into the water. The underwater hull of a ship in movement. The reflection of his own passing.

Port aux Basques. Stephenville. He refuels for the fifth time. Corner Brook by dusk. He falls asleep on his feet. How long is he gone? He has no idea, but wakes to the lop of water, his hand on the wheel. Land within sight. The sea with wind in it. Not so restive as before. Entering the Gulf of St. Lawrence. He sails frighteningly near a huge ship. The CN ferry on its way to North Sydney in Nova Scotia. He turns up the radio to listen for traffic. He checks his maps. Twenty kilometers away from the inlet. Then another forty kilometers inland.

Five more hours and he'll be there.

When the sky begins to darken, he looks for the shadow of the Long Range Mountains. A continuation of the Appalachian belt. Stretching up from Georgia in the US. Only interrupted by the Atlantic Ocean. A mass of faded blackness where he finds the inlet from the open waters of the Gulf.

The beauty of this place brings Agnes fully to mind. Why did she settle here? Because of the land. Not just for the job in the hospital. That wouldn't be like her. Not from here, but the land reminds him of her. Those mountains and the lush green. The inlet that he floats down. Maybe her family had people from here. He didn't know enough about how far back she went.

The smoke from the pulp and paper mill is barely seen, like a distant fire's signal. Life. The bow of a freighter up ahead. In time, its immense hull passes near him. The few men by the railings pay him only the slightest attention.

As light moves completely from the sky, he approaches land.

The reality of civilization when it was only him on the water for such a long stretch. Him alone with his thoughts only. And then upon this. Houses and buildings where hundreds of people would be moving around. They would be driving cars or shopping. Eating at tables. They would be on schedules, knowing little of the land occupied. The way he sees it, gliding in from miles away, up to the wharf. He shuts off the engine. Tossing out a rope, he steps up, pain slicing into his back, and slowly ties the boat, his feet on something solid, built with wood and

686

nails, attached to land. An ancient structure. The pain makes him feel like he's out of breath. A few men gathered in shadows on the wharf. Hands in pockets or leaning back on a rail. Wordlessly, they watch him pass. He notices them less than the sour smell from the mill.

The hospital is on a hill to his left. The stacked floors of lights. A boxy complex of buildings. Off the wharf, he hurries across the lot and up over a bank. Then on a road. Asphalt. Knowing the way. Not a big place at all, but big enough to be called a city. Walking, he finds his legs wobbly. The speed he travels is unnatural, too fast. He might trip or bang into something, his body too light.

He comes upon the parking lot like a puzzle solved. He wonders if Agnes is working. The inside of the hospital makes him too aware when he steps up to the information booth. Off of the sea and into this place, he will need to speak.

The woman behind the glass looks up at him. 'Can I help you?'

'Agnes Bishop,' he says right away. Agnes might be married for all he knows. But her ring finger had been bare. Were doctors allowed to wear rings? Jewellery. He thinks of this only now, his stomach knotting. Back in the hospital. Did he even leave? Travel by water an entirely different world. He checks his clothes. He might be standing there in a hospital gown. Time throbbing in reverse and forward through every inch of him. He glances toward the dark glass doors. Night outside that has brought him in here.

'Dr. Bishop?'

'Yes.'

The woman makes a call. She watches him like he's a patient who's escaped.

Blackstrap straightens. He does not listen. He looks down at his boots. Then at his pants. He's wearing jeans. His shirt is dark blue. Then he looks around the waiting area. A few people there, watching him with lazy wonder. Or watching the floor. A man leaned forward in his chair, rubbing his hands over each other. He turns back to face the woman.

'She's not in tonight.'

'Where then?'

Something small changes in the woman. She barely shows it while she studies his face. Not such a regular thing now. But her answer is just that: 'I don't know, sir.'

'Okay, thanks,' Blackstrap says, already striding toward the door, limping now for some reason. It must be his back. He goes through the door, re-enters the night, and makes his way along the streets. A telephone book is what he needs. He wanders down a street and takes a turn. The people driving by in cars make him feel unusual. Wheels rolling over earth. He will not go back into the hospital. He feels that he has shamed himself in some way. There are houses everywhere with telephones on tables or hung on walls. How far from his boat now? How far from Bareneed? Turning corners, he comes upon a street with old shops in a row, then he finds a Holiday Inn on a narrow road. A smaller version of the ones he's seen on the mainland. In the lull of the lobby, he recognizes the fact that he must be quiet. The young woman behind the desk takes a quick look at him. A bit of a smile. But she's busy with other things behind the counter. He scans the lobby to see the telephones with books beneath them. Turning the thin pages, he struggles to find Agnes' name. 'B' for 'Bishop.' The sequence. The order of letters. Something he memorized. He works hard at it. Then takes a break to look back at the young woman. Because he has been making noises. His stomach growls. He licks his lips and keeps watching her until she goes back to business. Again, he checks the letters. Muttering with his finger against the page. His eyes not the best in the lobby light. He checks toward the young woman, but she's gone. It takes a second to notice her next to him, off slightly to the side.

'Can I help you?'

'Agnes Bishop,' he blurts out.

'Dr. Agnes Bishop?'

'Yes.' He steps away from the book because she's edging near it. He points at his eyes like he can't see.

The young woman smiles and leans to check the names. The sour burn in his mouth. The spikes of pain in his stomach.

'Office or home?'

'What?'

'There're two numbers.'

'Home.'

The young woman reads off the number. But the number is of no use to him.

'What's the address?' he asks.

The woman goes back to the book. 'Forty-four Pittman Road.'

'Thanks.'

'My pleasure.'

He wanders off toward the main door, checking over his shoulder to see the young woman heading for the front desk. He forgets the address and goes back to look it up again, pretending he can do it himself. But he gives up and asks, 'What was that address again? My eyes are no good.'

'Forty-four Pittman Road.'

'Where's the way to there?' He is embarrassed by how she is watching him.

'Pittman Road?'

Blackstrap nods without knowing.

The woman gives him directions. She's used to it. She speaks without an accent and points toward the door. Bright and friendly, she explains in detail.

Blackstrap thanks her and leaves, moving forward in the direction she indicated. But after two turns, he can't remember and asks a man in a driveway just getting out of his car.

'Not far. Left. Left. Right. Just remember that.' The man's voice is from somewhere else. Plain as anything. He has a plastic bag in his hand. 'Left. Left. Right.'

Blackstrap walks in the darkness. He takes a left and another left. Then a right. He does not know where he is going. He thinks he finds the house. The number 44. Knocks on the door. An old woman comes out to answer.

'Pittman Road,' he says.

The old woman stands there, blinking. Then she smiles broadly at him. 'Who're ya look'n for?'

'Agnes Bishop.'

'Dr. Bishop.'

He nods.

'Yer just about dere, me luv.' Stooped slightly, she points with a wrinkled finger up close to her face. Then says: 'Yellow house with an old sled outside. Once pulled by a 'orse, way back when.' She chuckles. 'In my time.'

He looks where she is pointing.

Darkness and a quiet street.

'Thank you,' to the old woman.

'Okay, bye now. Yer welcome to come back if you have trouble with it.'

Blackstrap waves and walks on. A car with its headlights shining slows with his step. It might be the RCMP officer from the hospital. Would he know Blackstrap was back? Word travelling fast if the woman at the hotel desk called him. The woman seemed to know of Agnes. Maybe she knew about him. His picture probably in the newspaper about the crash. But the car is plain, the driver looking at him for a second. A fat woman with curly hair.

He finds the house.

A sled out front. An old horse's sled. A cart. A memory of some other time.

He steps up to the door and knocks. There is no answer. He waits, wondering for how long. Then he knocks again. A light is on in there. And one on over the door, shining down on him. There for everyone to see.

No answer.

He thinks of trying the knob, his hand going for it. But he backs away from the house when he realizes his intentions. He stands in the front yard and watches the windows. No movement. No sign of her drifting past. The night close and foreign around him.

He waits across the street, his eyes fixed on her house. It's an older house. The clapboard seems fine in the light from a streetlamp. He wonders about the roof, when it was last shingled. If it was daylight, he could have a look around the foundation, check for rot.

Where is she? He starts to become angry. Not at her. At himself. What is he doing? What? How many miles from home? What does she have to do with him? Nothing. He tries to find his way back to the hotel. Christ! To face Agnes after the long journey would be too much. His nerves raw. This close to tears. He takes corners. Wondering if there is a bar in the hotel. There has to be. Faster around another intersection until he finds the hotel. Inside, the quiet lobby where no one seems to exist.

But the young woman is there. 'Hello again,' she says. 'Did you find it?'

'Yes.' He tells the young woman that he needs a place to stay. She puts a card and pen in front of him. He slides it back to her. She looks at his hands, at the missing fingers and understands wrongly.

'That's okay,' she says and fills in the card for him. Name. Address. 'Sign here, please.'

That much he can manage.

'Do you have a vehicle?'

'No.'

She ticks a box. Then asks him how he would like to pay.

He gives over his last few dollars except for what he needs for fuel. The young woman counts the money, then gives him back change and a key.

'Have a nice night, Mr. Hawco.'

'Yeah. Hope so.' He looks at the key. 'Which floor?'

'Second.'

Exhausted, he takes the elevator up. He gets off and walks down the corridor, matching the numbers on the key with the numbers on the door. Then he fits the key into the lock, opens the door, and steps in. He shuts the door, treads across the room, falls onto the bed, his body and mind one solid thing, sleep easing the pain as he quickly goes under and dreams of a bottle with a ship in it.

The light warms his face through the open curtains. He should have shut them if he expected to sleep. Still in his clothes and boots, he rises stiffly from the bed. What time is it? A clock by the bed when he sits up: 6.38. At the window, there is a view of the parking lot with cars and trees around the edges. He splashes water on his face, then looks at himself in the big mirror. A shower is what he needs. He turns on the tap in the tub and takes off his clothes. His body. What is left of it. The things that doctors must see from one day to the next. He pulls back his lips and remembers he forgot his toothbrush.

The elevator is something he cannot stand. Going down. Sinking.

The smell of food in the lobby. Coming from a restaurant some-where. The clatter of dishes through an archway. A man behind the desk looks at him. Hello or goodbye. He says neither. He leaves the hotel for the fresh air outside. He knows the way to her house from memory. Only once needed. Even in darkness.

He thinks on the time when he walks by her house and keeps going. There is a rumble in the earth beneath his feet, which he takes for heavy trucks passing. They would be loaded with wood for the pulp and paper mill. He finds a small playground and watches the steel poles of the swing. He steps nearer and sits on the wooden seat. The sun on his face, on his hands holding the chains. He waits, thinking that Agnes' children might play here if she has any. He tries to notice where he is. He tries to realize the land around him, to place himself in it, to be not so detached. He watches toward his boots. An ant down there, in the dust and pebbles worn and packed tight. Another ant and more and more while he watches. His boat in his mind. The water at a distance he cannot see. He wonders if he will be charged dock fees. He checks his pocket for the keys. Good. He didn't leave them on board. They might take the boat. Hold it. They might tow his boat to a compound. Shit. He never thought of that. He gets up off the swing, the chains jangling, and heads out of the playground, striding down toward the wharf. Speeding up, he finds himself almost running, the limp getting worse. Both legs aching, but the left worse than the other. His boat is there okay. No one around it. He gets on board and brushes his teeth. That helps him feel better.

In the bit of broken mirror, he touches the scar on his cheek. Pushes his tongue against the inside of his mouth. Will she ask about it? He looks out to sea for a moment of rest before he makes his way back to her house. He knocks on the door right away. What to say? He has no idea. His heart thumping in his chest. He hears his breath and looks down. Gives his head a little shake. He checks over his shoulder. Another house right across the way. Someone up in the window. Barely seen in the slight part of the curtains.

He could run off now. Right now.

His legs make to move but the knob rattles. And she opens the door, her hair down, wet like she just got out of the shower. In her housecoat. White and silky. Bare toes without nailpolish. She watches his face.

God only knows what he looks like to see her this way. The perfumed smell off her out in the morning air. He feels like he is unrecognizable. The unbelievable expression on her face. Who are you? He does not know with her watching him that way. Until she starts to smile and says his name, not entirely in disbelief.

'I thought you were gone home.' Not talking like a doctor now, more like herself.

His eyes take in the walls. Photographs of old fishermen and houses running up the wall by the stairs. One of a house floating from shore with two boys watching it being pulled by a boat. Another of a man with a leathery face and hands, mending a net. An old woman in an apron bent over sweeping the slatted floor with the wing of a gull.

The walls are covered in old panelling, trimmed with hand-bevelled slats of wood. Fine workmanship with wide, thick mouldings and base-boards of a sort unavailable now. There are old rugs on the floor and a worn runner on the stairs. The house reminds him of the old woman in Toronto. Her apartment. He thinks what might have become of her. The tale of the black sea. He never went back to see her, after the news of the death of his mother. He imagines her at the window, watching out over the unfamiliar street. He sighs off the memory. An image of that loaf of raisin bread she gave him left in his room on Brock Street. Right beside the keychain from Boston with the lobster on it. A gift he bought for her at the bus station.

Agnes' voice coming from deeper in the house, down the hallway toward where he thinks the kitchen is. 'Sorry, but there's no one here for you to beat up.'

What does that mean? It takes a few seconds. Not her. He wouldn't harm a hair on her head. He thinks of the accident. Is that what she meant? If so, it was unkind. Then he remembers Halifax, that lifetime ago. Gone. Her boyfriend. The university. The train yard. The hookers. He was shot, wasn't he? How badly? The young hooker, whose name he never learned, with her palm pressed over where the bullet went in. His blood through her fingers. Whatever became of her? He would like to know. Him with a wife and a son. Another baby due soon. He follows after Agnes' voice. A big kitchen with a heavy table in the centre. Agnes stood at the long counter. A letter is opened in her hands. She folds it up and puts it back in the envelope.

'I could call someone if you like.' Like she knows him after all, will not forget the specifics of what was. 'Someone you can lay the boots to.'

He feels his face go hot. He might be blushing. Something he hasn't done in years. He tries to mutter 'sorry,' but it's barely heard.

'I thought you might show up. One day.' She looks at him, simply confirming her belief. 'People often come back here,' she says. 'They come searching for me.'

Blackstrap watches her. Who comes searching for her?

'If they've had a head injury particularly.' Stood there with her arms folded across her chest. Lots of light in the kitchen. 'To explain things.' Her hip against the counter and almost a smile on her lips. 'Because there are pieces missing. With head injuries, the job's never finished.'

'You're my head injury,' he says, not knowing where it came from.

She laughs a little, obviously not expecting him to say such a thing. 'That's nice. I could be worse, I guess. I could be your ruptured appendix.' She lets her arms hang at her sides. She watches him like she's in a daze. Remembering what? Then she turns and takes down a blue teapot. She raises it to him, her face turned to look over her shoulder. And he nods.

'Your father's not seeming well,' she says. 'I spoke with him when he was here.'

'He's okay.'

'Is he seeing anyone?'

'Like who?' He thinks of his mother.

'A doctor.' Two teabags from an old tin, dropped into the pot.

'No. He won't have any of that.'

The ocean at day and night.

A hotel room.

And now her in this kitchen in her bathrobe. A dressing gown, his mother used to call it. All this way, just to lay eyes on her.

Then the kettle is filled. Agnes slides it onto the burner and turns the switch. 'Have a seat.'

He glances at the chair, then at her. Her eyes on his hands, his fingers.

'You're not one for sitting.' Her arms folded again because she had wanted him to sit.

He looks at his hands to see what she might be seeing. Nothing there except his wedding ring. A gold band. That finger mercifully salvaged. He checks her hands, but they're tucked away. Back home, he heard she had been married. He knows she isn't anymore. He can tell by the way the house feels. Someone living alone. And what about children? He hadn't heard anything one way or the other.

The kettle begins to whistle. Agnes silences it and makes the tea. No ring on her finger that he can see. She sets everything down on the table. A plate of biscuits and some jam in a mason jar with a lid. 'Try my jam. It's blueberry.' She sits and her long wet hair moves in a way he admires to the point of weakness. 'You like that, right?'

He nods, hopeful because she remembers.

'It's Mom's recipe.' She sips her tea and watches how his hands hold the cup. 'Last time I saw you . . . No, make that second last time, you had blood on your hands. Knuckles to be exact. Last time you had blood all over your face. You're a real bleeder. But it couldn't be any different, could it?'

He looks at his hands now. Her eyes keep going there, almost nervous. The missing fingers. She is thinking of him in the water. The *Ocean Ranger*. The scar on his cheek. But she will not ask.

'You thought that might fix something?'

'What?' He wonders if she meant the accident.

'Beating someone up.' The memory is still strong with her. Strong enough to have darkened her voice.

He scratches his cheek. There's another flush there. He thinks on standing, on leaving. The one-nut wonder. Everything too close to him in this room. Too near. The room shifting like it's afloat. His hand almost goes for the table to steady himself. He doesn't know what she's talking about. The way she's talking now, smart as anything, out to get him with what she says.

'I talked him out of laying charges. He needed three teeth capped. You broke his nose. In a bad way. Broken nose. That's an injury forever.' She shrugs. 'Fortunately, I don't really care anymore. The way things are now, you could've done worse.'

'Not much worse.'

Agnes straightens in her chair. She puts her elbows on the table, her hands joined. 'Did you drive? I didn't see a car.'

'Boat.'

'Boat? From where?'

'Home.'

She just stares at him, thinking or not. 'That's a long way. Did you come here to do a bit more bleeding?'

A long way from home.

He snorts in amusement at the thought of his answer. Internal. Internal bleeding. Watching her face, he wants to tell her that he loves her. He knows he does. The only woman he has ever loved. If he could leave Cutland Junction, forget everything, Junior, his son, not his son, he would stay here in this house. The baby. Afraid of the baby to come. Another newborn anchoring him to Patsy, barbs curved through him. No way of ever getting free of a family.

If Agnes would have him, if she would care for him, that would be enough. To care. He would do whatever she wanted. He would walk three hundred miles in the direction she pointed. A life in this house with her, in warm hiding. He would give up his family. Wouldn't he? He sighs and looks at his cup.

'How's your back?'

'Okay.'

'Your head was never okay, so I won't ask about that.'

He laughs. Bursts out. The laugh almost made of tears. So that he has to wipe at his lips. 'Yer way funnier than I remember.'

'You don't remember much, I bet.'

And the light changes in the room. The sun coming out from behind the edge of a cloud somewhere through the window. A small stained-glass one up high. He feels the heat right away. The room filling up with it.

'You've been through a bit. The *Ocean Ranger*. That crash.' The corners of her mouth dip down. 'Hard luck.'

He does not want to talk about any of that. He finishes his tea and stands from his chair.

'That little girl,' she says right away, like she's trying to get it in, like he might storm from the house. Escape. And she needs to have him hear. Her arms on the table, her hands in fists now.

But Blackstrap's not certain because of the noise of his chair. He looks at her eyes. She might have said that. Or anything else. Something important. He might have only heard what was in his head. What he was expecting.

'What?'

'Nothing.' But the way she stares at him makes him feel that she knows more. He breaks the look. She checks into her cup and silently pours more tea. 'You have a son now.'

'Yes.' He feels ashamed standing there. Why? Ashamed of his son. And his wife. Ashamed of what is yet to be born.

'I can't have children.' The way her eyes pin him now. This confession he does not deserve to hear. 'I was married.'

Blackstrap leans against the counter, his back hurting. The pain like hot copper filling up his teeth, pouring down his legs. It gives him a headache through the left side of his face. A blade with serrated teeth, jerking through, inches at a time.

'To Peter. In Halifax.'

'Was?'

'Was, yes. He left me.' She swallows, smiles bravely, but not bravely at all. Only for him to see. 'When he found out I couldn't have children. He's married again now. Three boys.'

'Good for him.' He wants to say, Better to have you.

'You think so?'

'I don't know . . . what I meant.'

'Me neither.'

There is silence. Again, he considers leaving. If only the pain would stop. It's making him irritable. Angry at her. Just to be near her now is making him angry. The two of them in a room he has never seen before. Nothing the way it ever was. He does not like the house. It's too grand.

'When'd you get a new boat?'

'A few year ago.'

'What's it like?'

'Come see it if you want.'

'Haven't sunk it yet.'

697

'No. I'll take you for a run.'

'In a boat with you? You're kidding.'

He frowns and she sees how her words did it.

'I need to get dressed,' she says, in a voice almost shy. 'What time is it?' She looks at the clock on the stove.

There comes a knock on the front door. Right away, Agnes checks toward the sound, then back at the clock. She raises her cup, sips her tea.

They watch each other.

Blackstrap knows there's a man at the door. That a man is expected. He can tell by the way Agnes' eyes avoid it.

There is another knock.

Something moves against his leg. He flinches and darts a look down to see a cat.

'That's just Resurrection.'

He thinks he knows the story behind the cat. But that story was his. The cat, too. How old would it be?

The cat jumps up on the counter, sniffs at a plate and licks it. One paw on the envelope with the letter Agnes had been reading.

Another knock on the door.

'I better get that.' She stands and leaves the room.

Blackstrap follows after her, only a few steps, just enough to see down the long hallway. Agnes opens the door. A man is stood there, looking straight in, happy to see her, saying: 'Hi.' Then seeing past her. A face Blackstrap recognizes, but from where? Because the man stares. Disappointed at first. But then confused before he puts it all together. Not too long ago.

The hospital parking lot.

Right away, the man brushes by Agnes.

She puts up a hand as though to stop him, but he is in, hurrying toward Blackstrap.

Wind reaches him first down the long corridor.

The man raises his fist and hits him.

Blackstrap's face slams sideways, his head against the hard wall as fast as that, like a skull-echoing ricochet. A noise and an ache telling him how hard the world is. He will not raise his hands. Another punch. He falls over and strikes the wall again. Then his knees bang the floor while he's kicked in the chest.

'Stop it.' Agnes calling out. 'Gordon, stop.'

He falls over, his eyes shut. Being kicked feels right. He stays there. Does nothing to protect himself. Will not move to prove anything to her. This is what he has come for.

The boot to different parts of his body, until he can't breathe.

Agnes screaming Gordon's name.

The kicking slows to a beat, then stops.

It feels quiet because his lungs are paralyzed.

He opens his swimming eyes.

A deaf noise in his throat.

The cat rubbing against him.

She leans near.

Her face.

Her wet hair.

Her robe open at the top.

The heat of her.

Not the way she ever smelled before.

His eyes watching, dim and hopeful.

Her hands on his face.

Her saying his name.

Her eyes searching in a way that makes her worry.

He cannot breathe.

A boom. The slam of the door.

He can barely hear.

The cat.

The little girl? he wants to ask.

Who is looking after her?

Chapter XIV – 1990

The Berlin Wall

(June, 1990, 36 years old)

Blackstrap likes quieter bars where he can rest his elbows and listen in on the conversations of men. The talk about what's wrong or right in the world, what was done to them, what they were lucky enough to get away with, who they fell victim to, who they got the best of.

But there are benefits to louder bars, putting up with booming music to watch women dance. George Street is where the action always is. 'Go'n ta George Street,' someone would say to another with a laugh. An inside joke meaning it's time to get loaded and laid. It's where the women are all done up in the latest mall fashions, trying to look the same pretty way, going around in expensive sneakers with logos on them and jeans bought with rips in them. He can't figure that one out. Maybe he could get a job as a ripper in a jean factory.

To get into the Sundance Saloon, he has to wander up from Water and step through the loose crowd of people, keep heading west on George. It's a fine summer's night, so people are slow-moving, happy just to be out at night without a coat on. Girls calling to one another. Clip-clopping on heels they can barely walk on and acting a bit too foolish for his liking.

There's a line-up at the Sundance when he gets there, the conversation a mess of uselessness. Women screeching about nothing. A few of them chawing on gum. Guys in their white shirts and jeans, and perfect hairdos. Jocks by the looks of them, most of them in shirts with logos for companies. Then there's the shabby-looking guy in front of Blackstrap. A little guy in a baseball cap and grey windbreaker with his hands in his pockets. He teeters a bit, stares back at Blackstrap, squints almost meanly like Blackstrap might be responsible. He wavers his head around front, then checks back again: 'Who fuh'k're ya look'n 't?'

Blackstrap just stares. It's almost funny though. The nasty, little fellow.

Little Tuffy makes a sound with his lips. A sound that says he'd punch Blackstrap's lights out, but it'd be too much of a bother. He turns to face forward, still with his hands in his pockets, like they're glued in there. He shuffles sideways, trying to catch up with his own feet, about to fall, working to tug his hands from his pockets. But he can't.

Before Little Tuffy can tip, Blackstrap lunges sideways, grabs him and straightens him up.

Little Tuffy regains his footing, staggers around, then leans back into the line-up. He looks at Blackstrap, sloppily straightens the beak of his baseball cap. He does that for a while, using both hands, then he winks at Blackstrap, slaps him on the arm. 'S'aw'right, b'y,' says Little Tuffy. He gives Blackstrap a thumbs-up, shuts one eye, keeps it that way. Frowning for a while, he then smiles. 'S'aw'right, buddy. Yer a'right, b'y.'

By the time they reach the door, Little Tuffy has made Blackstrap his best friend. He tells Blackstrap about all the bars he's been in that night, pointing with his unsteady arm. This way. That way. He gives the specifics of the fights he could've been in, if most of the guys he threw himself up against weren't 'fuh'k'n pussies.' Always backing away from him. 'Beat the face right off 'em. 'Fraid they might get a bit of dirt on 'em. Fuh'k'n quiffs.'

The door opens and a few pissed-off girls step out. They're arguing about something one of them did to the other. A guy's name is mentioned. Little Tuffy holds his hands out by his sides. 'Nut'n on me,' he says as he goes into the Sundance. 'Wanna search?'

No reply from the muscle-bound bouncer.

'Hey,' calls Little Tuffy. 'You got nut'n on me, a'right.' He points a finger at the bouncer, tries his best to seem sober, but his eyes are looking to be made of soaked stone. They don't move that easily. Little Tuffy takes off his windbreaker, grunting and pulling his arms from it, then working a while bunching it up into a tight ball. He hands it to the coat check girl. 'Lissen, swee'eart. Tha's 'xpensive coat. Keep eye 'n 't. It used ta belong ta Sonny Bono.' He winks. Laughs. 'Sonny Boner.' He looks back at the bouncer, wheezing a laugh. 'You need a be tha' fuh'k'n big? Musta hurt. Grow'n tha' big.'

'What?' asks the bouncer, acting not interested.

'Yer mudder when ya pop'd out. Fuh'k'n muscles on ya. Jeeez. Cripes! She must'a yelped.'

'He with you?' the bouncer asks Blackstrap.

Blackstrap looks up, thinks: What a voice. Grumbly rock. Goes with the shaved head. Then he nods.

The bouncer doesn't bother replying. He just clicks his silver counter twice. Enough distraction to do him a lifetime. He watches toward the half-open door. The line-up wanting in.

Nothing getting by that bouncer, Blackstrap thinks. He studied for years to get his degree in being the most wonderful sort of prick.

Little Tuffy is gone on ahead of Blackstrap. As soon as he gets into the crowd, he claims the party as his, clapping his hands together. He goes right for the dance floor, arms above his head, stumbling around to the beat of 'Ice Ice Baby' and coolly mouthing the words, like he's Vanilla Ice himself, minus the fancy hairdo, minus the fancy clothes and fancy steps. Blackstrap can see Little Tuffy's lips moving. Little Tuffy's as happy as a pig in shit. He doesn't have a care in the world, even when his baseball cap is knocked off. He doesn't even seem to notice. He's bent forward at the hips, boogying, hands on his thighs, shaking his backside, and laughing at the craziness of it all. Hands back up over his head, he's trying to bump hips with a girl or two. His mouth twisted up, his tongue half out. 'Ice, Ice Baby.'

With Little Tuffy's hat gone, Blackstrap sees the strange clots of hair on his head, like someone's yanked out handfuls of it in patches.

'Ice Ice Baby' is replaced by Madonna's 'Vogue.' Little Tuffy starts striking poses, pushing his palms against his cheeks, so his lips puff out like a fish. Then wrapping his arms around his face, so he can't see anything. He almost trips over his own feet, banging into a few well-bred merchant boys made of good looks and money. They give Little Tuffy those sorts of sneers that say 'what's his problem, the little piece of dirt,' like they never dealt with a drunk before, were never drunk themselves. Them being the worst sort of drunks, raised spoiled, the most brutal in groups, the most cowardly alone. They act like their lives have always been perfect, up until that moment.

Enough of that, Blackstrap tells himself. He goes to the bar. He has to wait a while because the crowd around the bar is two layers deep. He reaches forward, nudging a couple of white-shirts out of his way. They give him the look they think they're entitled to, but he doesn't bother with either one of them. Not yet anyway. The night's too early. He calls out for two India, one for himself and one for Little Tuffy. He pays the barmaid a ten, waits for his change and pockets it.

He drinks his beer, and holds Little Tuffy's bottle until Little Tuffy is done with dancing. The dancing has left him even more sloppy-limbed, blowing out breath, but laughing it off. A little more sober, too. It's a strange mix. Little Tuffy wanders next to Blackstrap, not even knowing what's up, just wondering. A woman comes behind Little Tuffy and puts his baseball cap back on his head. Little Tuffy turns around, watches the woman's ass while she walks off. Tight jeans. Chunky. 'See that? Loves a big fuh'k'n piece of ass 'n my face.'

Blackstrap smiles and holds out the beer. Little Tuffy stops, his eyes on it, like it's some sort of roadblock. A trap. A trick. Something he has to pass to get through. He looks at Blackstrap. Little Tuffy's smile says he knows Blackstrap, says he knows Blackstrap better than himself. Little Tuffy points at Blackstrap, says: 'Aaaaaaaa,' in a good way. 'Is you, ain't it, buddy?'

Blackstrap straightens the baseball cap. Little Tuffy winks and takes the beer, tries putting his lips to it, barely misses, then gets it. He drinks the beer back.

'Ex's'lent,' says Little Tuffy. 'Wha' yer name again, buddy?'

'Blackstrap.'

Little Tuffy laughs. 'Dat's a'most as funny as my head.' He points to the side of his head, then reaches into his pocket, pulls out a thick wad of money. Little Tuffy has lots of money. He's proud of the fact.

'Law'r got me money,' Little Tuffy shouts in Blackstrap's ear, the sound extra loud because of the loud music. The sharp voice needles Blackstrap's ear, but what makes it worse is that Little Tuffy is swaying back and forth, so it's even harder to hear. Bits of words come clearer than others. '. . . 'cause . . . dis brain tumour . . . I got. Where'I worked . . . a bunch've 's got . : . brain . . . Fuh'k'd if . . . it ain't stupidest . . . t'ing in . . . walls.' Little Tuffy throws his fingers in front of Blackstrap's face.

Stiff fingers. 'Stuff,' says Little Tuffy, his eyes opening wider, like he's hypnotized. 'Stuff in dere.'

Blackstrap watches Little Tuffy turn his head to wink at a group of girls. Making hoo-hoo sounds while twisting his hips like he's dancing, he laughs and takes a big chug of beer.

'Women loves me,' he says. ''Cause I'm dying. Haaa.' He slaps Blackstrap's arm. 'Come on, wha're ya drink'n?' He tries focusing on the bottle in Blackstrap's hand, turning his head one way, shutting one eye. 'Wha's dat?'

'India,' says Blackstrap.

'A'most good 's Dominion.' Little Tuffy stumbles off. Blackstrap waits, but Little Tuffy doesn't come back. When he's done his beer, Blackstrap wanders to the bar and sees Little Tuffy in the corner, talking to a table of girls. He has his baseball cap off, pointing at spots on his head and nodding sincerely, oh-yeah, he's saying, that's right.

Blackstrap leaves Tuffy be. He gets himself a beer and returns to the dance floor, satisfied to have a little time to himself, to watch the dancers without Little Tuffy shouting in his ear. The bar makes him think of Halifax, watching women dance years ago. Agnes still in Corner Brook. Still there alone. No, not alone, but with Gordon. The guy's name with the little girl in the back seat. The girl he damaged. After she told him about everything. How Agnes looks after that damaged girl. Did she think she was supposed to? He drinks from his bottle. He wants to shut his eyes and keep them that way. Agnes told him that he shouldn't come back, that he should stay away, go back to his family. She wouldn't have any part in breaking up a family. Go back to Patsy. You have another baby on the way. And Junior. That's his name, right? Junior? How did she know? After your brother, I guess. He's meant to take Junior trouting tomorrow. He'll get back to Cutland Junction in time. Junior barely able to hold the pole in his small hands, but that's when he should learn. Start learning. He drinks some more. Agnes telling him not to come back. Another doctor in the hospital wrapping his chest. A broken rib or two. It still hurts when he laughs or coughs, so he doesn't. Laying off the smokes because of it. He finishes off the bottle, wishes he had had Junior with Agnes. She would be a good mother, a gentle mother, a perfect mother. A mother to that girl now. Is that what she wanted? Did that make her feel better? Him feel better?

The beer would go great with a pill washed down. Or maybe just another beer would do it. He focuses back on the dance floor. A black-haired woman catches his eye. He likes the look of her. She dances with her hands hanging delicately by her sides. She's got a bit of meat on her, the way he likes a woman now. None of that skinny model crap from magazines. He used to like that when he was younger, thinking that sort of thing was pretty, but it changed when he got older. He keeps watching her, staring at her, until she starts blushing, and leans to whisper to her girlfriend. The one she's dancing with who gawks over at Blackstrap. Blackstrap takes a swig of beer. The bottle empty. He doesn't like the looks of the friend. She's trouble. Nasty. It's easy to see, but it's good to watch women dancing together. He knows they're not lizzies like some people think. Girls just like dancing with each other, that's the thing to do now. It's like showing off.

When the song is done, the black-haired woman sits down.

The new song is 'Personal Jesus.' A song Blackstrap doesn't mind, the beat and what is being said. The song reminds him of Junior, his brother, something to do with worshipping false idols, but said in a different way. A song Junior would appreciate. He goes over, asks the woman to dance, like the memory makes him stronger.

The black-haired woman shakes her head.

'Good,' he says, not moving.

'Good?' says the black-haired woman's friend in a shocked way. She laughs and dips her head forward, shakes it, mouth open, like he's retarded or something.

Blackstrap ignores the friend. She's a nuisance. He keeps watching the black-haired woman.

'I didn't want to dance,' he says, careful of how he talks in here, in St. John's. The city. Not a stupid baywop like he's heard people saying.

'No.'

'Just wanted to say hello, anyway.'

The black-haired woman nods. She understands. She's okay.

'Blackstrap.' He puts out his hand.

'Karen,' she says, politely.

'Hey, you, hey, hey,' a voice rushes up behind Blackstrap. He turns to see Little Tuffy. 'Howya know my sisser, Blackman?'

'Fuck off, Teddy,' says Karen's friend.

Little Tuffy bends down, makes kissing sounds in front of the friend's face, 'Smooch, smooch, smooch, mmm-yum-mmm, loves ya, too, BattleAxe Witch.' Then Little Tuffy straightens, arm reaching up to go around Blackstrap's shoulders. Stood there like it's photo time.

'Dis feller's da best man ev'r. Saved my life in da line-up. Fuh'k'n dang'rous place. T'ings pull'n at ya. Fuh'k'n line-up.' Then he turns, twists his hips toward the dance floor. 'Watch out, laaaaddeeeees.'

'You know Teddy?' Karen asks.

'Yeah.'

She looks at him, carefully, deciding.

Two other girls come over from the dance floor, and glance Blackstrap up and down. Then they sit at the table, wondering about him. Not saying a word because they don't have a clue. It's too crowded now, too many bodies, too many eyes watching or not, on purpose. A stupid game.

He nods and backs away.

Karen with her eyes on him during the night. Until she finally comes over, just like he thought or hoped she might.

Blackstrap is chasing Karen around a big steel ship tied up in St. John's harbour. Kissing her up against the metal hull. The way she keeps moving away from him. Kissing but not wanting it to go any further. But it's not a ship. It's a shipwreck now. All around them. Full and broken masts stuck up out of the water. And there are big creatures that look like Ninja Turtles. They are dark, evil, with wide swords. He knows that they're from Iran. There's a wall surrounding everything. They're tearing it down with hammers, pulling at chunks of it with their hands. Throwing the pieces at cartoon characters that are like real people. The men on the ship are speaking German. The sunk ships sink deeper. All at once that feeling. He looks for Karen. She is in the corner, slapping Patsy. Then they're dancing together, rubbing up against each other. One of Patsy's legs pressed between Karen's. Then in bed on the dance floor with colourful lights. He's in there with them for the show with everyone watching. The touch of their bodies better than anything that could possibly be felt. A horn blowing, like a growl, telling them it's over. Before he has a chance to go all the way with both women. Loud blasts of a fog horn. Snores coming from another room. He sits up quickly and waits a minute, letting himself come back into the world. Catching up with himself. On a couch somewhere. A peek at a memory. A mess of clothes scattered around, and take-out trays and pizza boxes on the table. The smell of greasy food eaten. A bit of light through the window. Dawn through the open curtains. Feeling guilty already. About what? Thirsty as hell. A drink of water. Water. Junior, he remembers. Trouting. What's the time? He goes to the kitchen and runs the water. The smell coming up to him. Like freshness, but chemical. Chlorine. He drinks down a full glass with his eyes on the stove clock that's not working. He figures this out after a while. A baseball cap on the counter. Little Tuffy's place. He checks for his keys and anything he might've left behind. Then he leaves the apartment. He's in a building, but has no idea how he got there. Down the stairs. The hollow sounds of his steps.

Outside, the air is early-morning still. Not too hard on him. Not yet. The full weight of his tattered exhaustion lingering off in the distance. Not enough sleep. His mouth a mess. The sky brightening a touch more, enough to see plainly while he treads around the parking lot, scanning the area one vehicle at a time. One row at a time, until he finds his pickup. Sitting there toward the far corner, in a space where he can't remember parking.

Only an hour's run to get Junior.

He climbs in and starts the engine. His back bothering him when he twists his head to see behind. His ribs aching too. He backs out, then pulls up and stops at the lip of the parking lot. A muscle in his neck stretching tight. The apartment building is somewhere downtown, by the looks of the old row housing across the street. The steep slant of the road before him. Not a bad morning for a run on the highway. He turns left, heads uphill. The sky is brighter now. He finds LeMarchant Road. From there, he knows his way to the Trans Canada, the line cut through the wilderness that will take him home.

*

He pulls into the driveway with the morning sun gone behind the clouds. The flies will be bad where they're going. No wind. He'd prefer if it was a little damp. The flies probably even worse then, but the trout biting on the glassy surface of the pond with new ripples. That circle of the splash expanding in his mind. The trout there and gone. Sometimes a split-second view of their heads or silvery bodies. Then smaller trout, nippers, making their rings in the water.

No one up in the house. He had expected Patsy to be there, waiting with arms folded, ready to bawl him out, like she did when he went off. His father at the kitchen table, not saying a word, just watching out the window from where he usually sits.

Blackstrap cuts a slice of homemade bread. Fresh as anything. Soft to go through. The doughy smell of it. The knife bothering him as something so sharp near his nerves. The serrated teeth. Margarine easily spread and molasses poured from the carton. He drags his finger along the spout where the molasses is running on in a string. He gets a good gob on his fingertip. Eats it. More sweet than metallic. A childhood thrill to the taste of it. The scent of his mother and the house as one.

Then he looks at his father while he eats the bread. The point beyond saying hello has passed. Eating, he feels he must be quiet, so as not to disturb his father with the growth of beard on him. Whiskers still growing after death, they say. He takes his final bite of bread and goes upstairs into Junior's room. The boy's not in bed with Patsy. She won't let him sleep in there, even though he always wants to. Needs to get used to sleeping alone, she says. A boy can't sleep with his mother like that. It's not right. He cries sometimes, but most times he's okay by himself.

Blackstrap kneels by the bed, watches the boy's face. Nothing more perfect than the sleeping silence of that little face. He moves Junior's bangs over to the side, like it's been combed, like he's dressed up especially for sleep, something like going to church. It makes him smile to see that face. It sets some peace in him. He puts his palm on Junior's soft cheek and leaves it there. Then he stands up.

'Hey.' His voice sandpapery. He coughs a little to clear away last night's debris. 'Rise and shine, little buddy.' Like his mother used to say.

Junior doesn't move. Long eyelashes and plump lips open a bit while he breathes through there.

'Time fer trouting.' He nudges the bed.

Junior moves his head and wipes at his nose. Then he tucks his hands under the cheek against the pillow and goes back to sleep. Almost snoring with his lips pushed out like that.

Blackstrap picks him up in his arms and carries him down the stairs. Pain in different points of his body. One slow step at a time. He listens for Patsy, his ears straining, not wanting to hear her stirring. His father no longer sitting at the kitchen table. Gone off to a grave dug a while ago. He turns to go through the back door. His father in the shed window. That old woman from Toronto. His father turned away then, searching for something in what's been saved.

Outside, he puts Junior in the passenger seat. The boy still asleep. Leaning in that way, Blackstrap finds his back, the pain troubling. Difficulty straightening. He takes his time. Stands there dealing with it a while, then returns to the house. A plastic grocery bag filled with canned wieners, canned hash, Irish stew, a few tins of cola. He'll get chocolate bars and snack cakes along the way.

He loads the poles and rubbers in the back of the pickup. It's done before he notices half of what he's doing. Then he goes to the shed for the tackle box and wicker basket, takes them from where they're hung from his father's hands, and out into daylight.

'Bring us back a few pan fries,' his father calls lightly.

The sun trying to brighten. He smacks at a fly on his neck. A smear he doesn't care to feel. He stores the box and basket away, climbs in the pickup and looks at Junior. He checks the rearview. A woman watching back at him. Watching over him. Nothing new to see with his damaged eyes. His father's profile in the shed window, holding a kitten up to his face.

He heads for the highway again, back toward St. John's. Driving now with his son aboard. From a couch in an unknown apartment in St. John's to this, in what seemed like a span of no time. An unwelcome thought. He looks through the windshield, aware of the road. The quietness of space. Scanning the forest growth near the highway for signs of moose. His eyes wanting to check the rearview. But he looks at

Junior instead. The boy still asleep in his pajamas with cartoons from TV coloured on them. Big creatures with wings. Fierce looking. The way the day is, the boy won't need any other clothes.

An hour and a half to Horsechops, his mind sifts through thoughts from earlier that morning and the night before. What he did right and what he knows he can't change from wrong. Nothing done or said ever good enough. His mind on the club outside Horsechops. Where he likes to stop in for a beer, before tackling the narrow rocky road to the pond. Then his eyes finding it there, the white siding in need of a coat of paint. Junior wakes up to the feel of tires slowing, rolling over the gravel lot. Rising up to see out the windshield, his small hands grip the dash.

The club is wide open inside. Hollow sounding underfoot or against any small word spoken. A jukebox with a country song playing low against a far wall. That sound carrying in an almost echo. The beer and cigarette ash smell of last night or years of it. No one there on a Sunday before noon. He orders a beer at the long bar. The bartender has a plump face, one turned eye, short black hair greased back, and a black T-shirt. There's a tattoo of a mermaid on his forearm. The blue ink thick and smudged. Blackstrap checks the empty wooden tables that go toward the back. A pool table down there with one cue stick laid across the worn green cloth. Junior climbs up on a stool, having a Coke with a straw. A pickled egg soon on a napkin in front of him, the napkin with a wet stain spreading. A salt shaker nearby. Junior still half asleep with his head held up on his palm, elbow on the bar, barely tall enough to stay that way, nodding a little, catching himself.

Blackstrap wishes he had a camera. His brother on his mind for some reason lately, the camera up to his eye, so his face is hidden. One of those severed fingers on the shutter button. Sometimes his memories are perfectly still, like he's watching what someone else captured for him. That photograph he saw in the Boston pub. That was the sort of thing Junior would take. A beer with his brother at this time of the morning would have given him something worth listening to. A whiff of the egg and vinegar. He musses up his son's hair, and Junior smiles without looking. Eyes shut while he drinks more through the straw.

'Eat yer egg,' he says. And the boy does as told, shaking on salt and sleepily chewing small bites.

Nothing but suds in the bottom of the brown bottle. He eats what's left of Junior's egg in one bite.

They get back in the pickup, his eyes seeing a little more clearly after the beer. The sun brighter than before, edging out of the clouds. Humidity thickening so that he can't come all the way awake. He feels like he needs a shower and rolls down the window.

A mile ahead, he stops into the store for provisions. A half-dozen eggs in the container left there from a full dozen, and bacon and a quart of milk. A loaf of bread to toast on the bent hanger on the woodstove. Tea bags. A half-dozen India and chocolate bars for Junior. The boy walks up and down the aisles in his pajamas and black rubber boots, bare feet inside.

Blackstrap lifts Junior up on the counter at the checkout.

The chubby, curly-haired woman with glasses smiles at both of them.

'Look at you,' she says to the boy. 'Still in yer jammies.'

'Goin' trout'n,' says Junior. He raises one leg and points at his boots. 'See?'

The woman laughs, looks at Blackstrap while bagging the items. 'Fine day fer it.'

Blackstrap nods, checks toward the front window. The road with a car going by. Pays the woman.

'Ya got worms?' asks the woman.

'Right,' says Blackstrap, going back to the cooler. He opens the long glass door and bends down to lift a styrofoam container. He thumbs the lid off and pokes around in the dirt. The thick worms in a clump down toward the bottom, sleekly inching around each other. A surprise of hidden life. He takes the container back to the counter. 'Thanks.'

The road is always worse than he remembers. It depends on the amount of rain and the ruts worn away. Some of the boulders scrape the undercarriage of his truck. A cursing cringe whenever that happens. The ride bumpy. The truck swaying one way, then the other, while branches and bushes scratch the sides. He takes it slower in different places, but wants to go faster to get it over with. No matter how many times he travels down this road, he can never judge the time. It vanishes in concentration. It might take him an hour to get in. It might take half an hour. Usually, a few ginger-coloured rabbits hop across the road. Blackstrap points them out to Junior, the boy too low in the seat to see. He kneels up, but never in time. Stays kneeled up for now.

Birds flying close across the front of the truck, near the grill or up over the bonnet. That chunk of moving steel not supposed to be there. Those birds going so fast, getting out of the way is how it looks. Maybe there are nests nearby that they've been startled from.

When he reaches the fork in the road, he knows it's not much further. Take the road branching right. Only a few minutes more.

The cabin comes into sight like he expected, ten feet in off the road, the log side of it facing him, the front door set away from the road, toward the trees.

He pulls in on the grass, avoiding a few rusted tin cans on the ground. Parking the pickup, he gets out, the sound of the brook reaching him, the sound of birds. Summer heat stillness nothing like the air inside the truck. The land with its own dry, living sound. The sun muted entirely now, only the throb of it off somewhere. He knows the sound of this place. It puts him at ease. The absence of everything other than its uncomplicated self.

He gets the key from under a nearby rock and fits it into the padlock. He goes back to the truck to take the supplies into the cabin. Junior stands outside looking at the brook, then squats to pick up a rock and plunk it in. The surface changing.

'Mine,' he says to Blackstrap. 'Junior's B'ook.'

Junior's Brook. That's what they named it.

When Blackstrap used to come to the cabin as a boy, he'd wake in the mornings in the top bunk and listen, looking up at the log rafters or facing the log wall. Moss stuffed in to seal the gaps. The sound of rain pouring down outside. Every morning the same sound of rain. Disappointment at the thought of a day stuck inside.

But when he'd open the door, the sun would be hot and blinding.

What he thought to be rain was only the brook running so close, tricking him.

He lays the supplies on the single shelf by the door. Turning, he sees the two sets of bunks. The wooden table between them. Many a card game played there over the years. The uneven roar of conversation and laughter in the haze of cigarette smoke. The men who sat at that table from the time he was a boy. Some of them dead now. The small window above the table that was pure black at night. The woodstove to his right. The 410 shotgun for hunting rabbits stood up behind the stove, the barrel aimed at the ceiling. The same shotgun he almost shot his father with when he was a boy. Ten years old. The first time he used the 410. His father tossing cans up in the air, straight up above his own head, and Blackstrap aiming as they came down, waiting and following and waiting and then pulling the trigger. The shot scattering inches above his father's head. The memory of it still unsteadies him. The same feeling as when he shot at seals far out on the harbour ice in Bareneed. He was eleven, and not having learned his lesson. Shooting and walking ahead and shooting more and walking out further on the ice, hoping to see the seals stilled, until he saw the dark forms gain in size and keep moving. People as shadows, maybe facing him. He ran home on weak legs with the scare chasing straight after him inside.

Pulling on his long green rubbers, he takes up the older trouting poles from the corner, the ones with the cork bobbers he forgot were always there. He fits Junior with a vest too big for him, just in case it gets chilly, although he doubts it. They cross the road in the airless heat, the dust from the road almost rising, down over the low incline through the dry bog with its humps and watery patches and bog trees and tangles of burgundy bushes not yet dotted with blueberries. He can see the flat surface of the pond ahead, shimmering in a flash of the sun freed from a cloud. The heat gaining with the mere hint of the sun uncovered. Nearing water like that, needing to squint, he looks back to see Junior taking his time walking through the rough terrain, the boy's eyes on the ground. A sight to see, so small in the wide-open land. So small as to be almost lost.

'How ya doing?' Blackstrap calls out, a fly buzzing near him, then darting off. He smacks a black fly on the back of his hand, smears the blood in his jeans, blows another away from his lips.

'Where's da fis'?'

'There.' He points his trouting pole high toward the pond.

They keep moving.

Junior watches the ground, then has to stop. The boy worn out until Blackstrap goes back and lifts him, carries him like a sack of potatoes over his shoulder. Junior giggles with the wind jerking out of him, making a noise like blunt rhythm.

After ten minutes, there is the sound of water moving. They edge around a line of trees and the sound clarifies, becomes fuller, wetter, fresher. The wide river spotted with rocks making a sound as it runs into the pond. Blackstrap sets Junior down and looks around. Years of trouting here alone with the men back at the cabin drinking beer. The river he has stood in, balancing on two rocks. A big rock steady and flat enough to put both of Junior's feet on.

'Watch yer step.'

Blackstrap stands with his feet on two rocks, setting up Junior's rod. He adjusts the bobber and lets the line drop into the water, where it's swept away. He clicks over the bar.

'Leave it where it is.'

Junior holds the rod. 'Where da fis', Dad?'

Blackstrap casts out into the water, avoiding the rocks and shallows, toward a deeper pool where he knows the trout gather. Stood there, he does not move, only slowly reels in, faster nearer the gush of water over the closer rocks, and tosses out again. Getting a bite, a nudge in the rod, the tip arcing, he tugs to set the hook and reels in against the steady pull of the river.

A flopping in the water here and there.

'Fis',' says Junior.

Blackstrap keeps reeling until the fish is up out of the water, dangling on the near invisible line. Flicking. Straightening. Bending. Holding itself bent, like it's already dead and drying. A mud trout. Brown and black with spots and orange on its belly.

Sleek and beautiful.

The hook not set through the gill. Blackstrap flings the trout toward the riverbank, the grass and bushes and big trees. The fish flies off the line and Blackstrap steps in front of Junior, one boot in the water, to block the hook from snapping back. The line moves clear of them and he reels it in, goes for the trout, finds it wrapped in long dry strands of grass, jerking around. Armlessly, he thinks, watching it. Useless on the ground. He takes hold of the trout, the slime of it on his hands weakening his grip. He bends to smack the head against a rock, to make certain it dies, even though it never does. It still moves in his wicker basket. A slow tangle in the moss on the bottom to keep the trout fresh.

'Ya got'n, Dad.'

Blackstrap nods and winks, trying not to make too much of it.

'Nice'n.'

He takes Junior's rod. The worm has been nibbled away, more black hook showing than anything. He pulls off the torn-up worm and tosses it in the water. The new worm is warm and squirms as it's curved into the hook, gushing out brown like shit. He lays the styrofoam container back on the ground and navigates the rocks to his spot next to Junior. Tossing Junior's line toward the deep pool, he holds the rod until he feels a bite, makes certain he has one on, then he points overhead at two geese flying against the grey but soon nearer to land.

Junior watches until they are gone over the far-off trees.

Blackstrap hands the rod back to Junior. Then he flicks his own line out and waits patiently, pretending to know nothing.

'Check yer line,' he finally says in a way that admits to nothing. 'Keep 'er tight.'

Junior reels in, the tip of the rod bending. ''S heavy.'

'I think ya got one, buddy.'

Junior turns the reel, struggling, the rod arcing more.

'Reel it in, b'y. Slow 'n easy.'

When the fish flops in the water, Junior screams and lets go the rod. It falls in the water, clattering off rocks. Blackstrap makes a grab for it, one boot going fully in. He almost slips on the slimy underwater rocks, but manages to catch hold of the cork handle. The rushing water cool despite the heat. A fury of water down that low. The pull of it with his arm in the flow. One leg still up on the rock, something in his back making a pain in his head. He sweats a little more and strains to give the rod back to Junior, shakes the warming water from his hand.

The trout up out of the water again.

Junior squeals with delight.

'Hold it.' Blackstrap picks up Junior, the rod still in the boy's small hands. 'Don't let go. Hold it, hold on.'

The trout jerking at the end of the line, swinging in mid-air, snapping to get off.

He lays Junior down on the bank.

A larger pain in his head now, in his legs, in his back and arms. He tries not to let it cut too deeply, to ruin the situation. But he has to wait a few seconds.

'Take 'er off.' The trout already on the ground, the barb through the red jagged lines of gills.

Junior squats down to watch the fish flop around. He touches it. Jerks back. Frightened of its movements.

Blackstrap twists the hook from the gills, scrunching it free, doing damage. Holding tight so the trout won't flip back into the nearby water. He gives the trout to Junior. A two-pounder. The boy holds it across both his palms and stares down at it, wondering. The flap over the lines of gills opens and closes. Its tail shivering.

Then Blackstrap takes it and bashes its head against the rock. Blood sprays out, flickering across the back of his hand, one round eye loose from where it struck the rock. He puts the trout in the wicker basket. Two trout in there now, the first one not fully dead yet, its skin already beginning to dry, not fresh and slippery like the new one against it.

Then they go back to their rocks.

'Fine job,' says Blackstrap, mussing up Junior's hair.

Junior back at it again, more anxious now to catch another, having done so well on the first.

In the cabin at night with the fire going, the heads are cut from the trout before their bellies are slit down the middle in a silky flutter. Sticky strings of red and purple guts pulled out, then the orange insides washed in a pan of water from the brook. Junior watches Blackstrap roll the trout in a bit of flour, and carefully place them in the sizzling butter in the frying pan. The skin going crispy before the butter goes black. The orange meat tender and hot.

'Watch fer bones.'

They eat at the table with the darkness outside the small window, black like it always is beyond the lit propane lantern hissing low. The heat and wind of the day still in their faces. The pure darkness of the country surrounding them with nothing but faint clear sounds momentary and far away outside. Blackstrap tells Junior the story of

Patrick Hawco caught in the spray of the wicked sea while trying to save the Portuguese sailors, cast off in an open boat in a vicious storm, not able to save a single soul, his own body washing up on the shores of Bareneed five days later. A look on his face that was remembered by all until the sight of further death coupled it. The story of Ace Hawco facing the polar bear on the ice, a beast twice the size of any man, yet Ace able to drive it off with words of such a mad concentration that they became the final ones he ever spoke with no one within hearing distance. The story of Jacob Hawco on the trapline, the fox that befriended him then wrapped itself like a scarf around Jacob's face to keep him warm.

Junior listens without word, picking the thin bones from his trout, trying to get them off his fingers where they're stuck. Every now and then his eyes go to the trout heads on a plate on the counter, or shift up to watch the slow throb of shadows on the ceiling. Until Blackstrap rises from his chair and opens the cabin door to night. Tosses the trout heads far out into the trees.

'Fer da fox,' he says.

Tired from the country air and the full warming comfort of the stove, they climb into their bunks early, the hiss of the lantern going down to utter darkness. Only those sounds beyond the walls, held special in blackness.

And in the morning when Junior wakes, he hears the rain pouring down outside, then rises from his covers to open the door and face the brilliance of land lit up by pure sunshine.

Jacob has his good days, but most are difficult. He does not recognize Blackstrap, keeps asking who he is, and asks for Emily. Junior and Ruth. 'Where're me chil'ren?' he wails. Other times, he exists in his own private silence.

Occasionally, when Blackstrap comes into the room, he catches a putrid, stomach-turning smell. Jacob has shit himself. But Jacob knows enough to take care of it eventually. He still realizes it's him. If anyone tries to help him, he stares at them in dumb surprise.

Mrs. Shears comes by to look after him. Jacob watches Mrs. Shears' face, wondering or talking. A story or not. Other days, he sits there like himself, winking and speaking of a time that was, or watching the TV and commenting on what's being shown. Patsy doesn't want the burden. She thinks Jacob should be put in a home. She wants her own house, if only across the yard.

They argue about putting Jacob away in the old age home in South River. Jacob in the next room, like he can't hear. Making Blackstrap so furious he has to leave the house before he smashes something. Junior in front of the TV, turning up the volume with the remote, his parents' arguments a distraction.

Blackstrap storms off into the woods, cuts trees down for lumber, wishes the chainsaw would rip his leg off, his arm off. The teeth tearing through his throat. Another piece of him gone. Not a story but an ending. His miserable unwanted life. Those men he saw drowning. Gone for good in a mess of something that can't be cleaned up. The Yanks giving orders. Not a fucking clue. A rig in the middle of the Atlantic Ocean. Not in Louisiana. Sitting in a bayou. Those men drowning. Those seas in dreams are real. He wakes to know this. The branches swaying around him when they fall. He works blindly, felling trees, until a spot is cleared where he stands with his heavy breath raging out of him, checking over the space, the stumps, the grass. He hauls the first load of trees to the pickup. Doesn't care about his back. The worse the better. He won't let it stop him, like a challenge against whoever, whatever. His cunt-ugly, fucking life. He jumps into the truck, drives to Norbert Peach's on Shearstown Line and unloads the trees for Norbert Peach to mill into two-by-fours.

He figures the house can be done in two years if he takes his time. He's got a start on it just to shut Patsy up for once. The foundation this summer. Walls up in the fall. Leave it for the winter until he gets more money in the spring. After the court case to see what's taken, what it's going to cost for the lawyer and, maybe, a fine. Court in St. John's. Driving without a proper licence. Witnesses brought in to testify. No doubt Agnes will be there to see or explain the injuries, to give details. The man and the little girl. That's the killer of it. The sight of that little girl. Will she be there? Will he have to see her? Put him in a cage for all eternity for that, just so he didn't have to look at her. The poor crippled thing. Ruined. He would step freely into the cell, if not already.

He'll go sealing if he can, to pay for whatever that little girl needs. Sell his boat. He'll offer to do that. They can have it. The loss of his nut good for something anyway. What does that little girl need? He'll have to ask. Out on the water to the sealing grounds. Stuck in ice for days. His gut churning at the thought of it. The house afloat. A boat. A ship. And Patsy at him all the time. She'll get her goddamn house. Just to shut her up. Have it and rot in it.

But Patsy leaves, is gone after telling him: 'He had me up against da counter. In front of Junior. Groping at me.'

Jacob had been trying to hug her, trying to hold on, trying to remember. This is how Blackstrap sees it.

With Patsy gone and his father being looked after by Mrs. Shears, Blackstrap goes back and forth to St. John's. Gets a job working backhoe in the city. Up at 5 a.m. to drive in, home at seven, unless there's overtime. On the weekends, he stays in with Little Tuffy. He buys the beer and hangs around the apartment for two reasons. He likes Little Tuffy. Plus he wants to see Tuffy's sister again. Karen. She shows up sometimes, out of the blue, while they're at the table with a case cracked open, cigarettes going and talking about Tuffy's big plans to start his own bar downtown. 'No line-ups,' he says with his palms held up like he's trying to stop something. 'That'd be a rule.' His wheezing laugh while he looks from Blackstrap to Karen.

Karen not giving any sign of them kissing on that ship. Only there like she's joining in just for the sake of it. But Blackstrap catching her eyes on him every now and again, when he's explaining something.

Tuffy knows about Blackstrap's troubles from the newspaper. *Ocean Ranger* Sole Survivor Sued. Little Tuffy offering Blackstrap some money, if he needs it. No, Blackstrap says. No need of dat. Little Tuffy wanting to arm-wrestle eventually. Blackstrap putting up a good fight, but letting him win.

Little Tuffy with a 'ha-ha,' a wink and a finger pointing straight at Blackstrap's face. 'Ya can't beat the brutal likes of me. I'm near godly, sure.'

Karen sits and has a beer. Blackstrap likes the way she's quiet. The way she drinks from the bottle, her lips barely around the top.

Refined. Her eyes on him to see what he thinks, or seeming to want more of him.

On the weekend, he goes downtown to see a band or two. Mostly young people in the clubs. A few oldtimers sitting alone, out of the house so they won't be by themselves forever. He likes watching one musician in particular. A guy with a guitar sitting up on a little riser. Long curly black hair. Blackstrap hears he's a poet too. And an artist. Boyd Chubbs is the name given when he asks the bartender. A gentle man. A delicate man with a soft face. Dressed in black all the time. Blackstrap buys him beers and gets the girl with the tray to deliver them. And sometimes Boyd comes over to sit and talk. Blackstrap admires the way he speaks. Careful, almost whispering, like he's from a faultless and kind world where no harm is ever done.

Boyd tells him, 'My father was a fisherman, up on the Labrador where I come from.' He pauses to slowly smile, his eyes knowing so much, his words soft and exactly formed. 'My father used to say, the fish come to a fisherman. The fisherman knows.' He touches Blackstrap's hand. 'You know. The fish come to the fisherman, as with you.'

Boyd tells stories about Ireland, where he's been playing the guitar, where he's been reading his poetry. Just back from Dublin a week ago. Blackstrap doesn't tell him he plays guitar too. Used to. Before his fingers were lost to him. They talk about family, and discover they share memories of people they've heard of, a relative from Bareneed who went up to the Labrador and settled there. Related to Boyd Chubbs, too, from way back. They might even be related themselves. Small world. They smile at the thought of that.

Cheers. Bottles tapped together.

Boyd Chubbs the way Patrick Hawco was.

Blackstrap takes Karen to see Boyd play at the regular spot on Duckworth Street. He's secretly thrilled when Boyd comes over. A celebrity. But more than that. Hoping Karen will be impressed. Blackstrap watching her face when Boyd talks, seeing what she thinks of it. She is polite and doesn't say much. She listens like she really wants to know, not like Patsy who listens to get it done with, so she can start arguing. He sees an affection in her that is the same as love.

'This is a good man,' Boyd says to Karen, his eyes steadily on Blackstrap, then a serious, almost priestly, nod. 'A good soul.' He turns his head to face Karen: 'You take care of him.'

Chapter XV – 1991–1993
Serbia

(September, 1991, 37 years old)

The construction of the house has been delayed, just the hole dug for the basement filling up with water. Blackstrap did that himself with the backhoe borrowed from Lloyd Batten. His own machine gone. The payments too hard to keep up. After Patsy left, he would have no part of it. But with Karen living in his father's house now, he wants a place for her, something new and better.

He waits to hear about the court case against him, but word doesn't come for a while. Then he gets a call from a lawyer telling him that the man has dropped the law suit. He wonders if Agnes had anything to do with it. Her looking after him despite everything. A fine for driving without a licence. He pays that off a bit at a time. And tries to forget, but his sleeping hours won't let him.

He picks up more lengths of two-by-fours from Peach's mill, tosses them down to bang against each other on the soft spring ground. The wood is enough to crib-in the basement.

He goes back for the two-by-sixes – joists for the floor.

Karen has gone to Homeowners Trust to get money, enough to buy windows and doors. She wants it all new, not the recycled ones he has out in the shed. She wants a brand new house, like her mother's in St. John's. Blackstrap has nothing to do with it. She just brings the money home and gives it over to him. Her contribution, she says. He won't take it at first, but she comes close to crying, her eyes filling up, until he agrees.

When he's done cribbing in the foundation, he calls the cement truck from Burke's. The driver stands with his hands in the pockets of his overalls, moving the chute a little one way then the other while the cement flows. He tells about working on the mainland in Alberta. Hauling cement around. The money to be made. 'The heat's fierce though,' he says. 'I've seen big men drop from it.' Back to Newfoundland in the fall after he gets his stamps, collecting pogey plus working for cash. 'That's the way ta do it.'

Blackstrap stands over the basement and stares down into it. The hollow in the earth, all walled in. Never has he had a basement in a house. Lots of room down there for storage. He wonders what might be put down there to fill up the space. The main floor will be done tomorrow. Then the studs for the walls built on the floor and raised. The whole works eventually crowned by trusses. He's been pricing vinyl siding. Karen wants white. He looks at the hammer he's using. The small one he bought for Junior to teach him like this. How far away in Heart's Content? He should go and visit, but a clean break seems a better plan. Not the sight of anyone to torment the other. He won't show his face in Patsy's house. Not that way. Like a dog with its tail between its legs. He won't be a part of that. Junior seeing him crawling back. He hasn't heard a word about the baby being born, if at all. A boy or a girl? he wonders, hammering the floor planks in place.

Word is going around that the cod fishery will soon be shut down. People are blaming it on the seals eating all the cod. The seal population growing to alarming numbers. The Keep It Green people claiming that seals don't eat cod. There are jokes about seals eating pizza and hamburgers and fries. That's what seals eat, hanging around fast food take-outs. Some blame it on foreign overfishing. Others blame it on mismanagement by the federal government, the scientists not having a clue.

The days of going out in the boats are numbered.

In Bareneed, where Blackstrap is working doing up houses, there are only a few fishing boats tied up. Mostly expensive ones now, owned by townies. Leisure crafts.

When he gets home for lunch, a furniture truck pulls in behind him. He checks his fingers. They're full of splinters from tearing old wood out of old houses. Terrible how those splinters trouble a man. He keeps it in

722

his mind to remember his gloves, but they're only a nuisance most times. He'll see what Karen can do about it with a pair of tweezers. The driver of the furniture truck gets out and puts on his gloves. Slides the back door up. The other man pulls on his gloves while Blackstrap watches.

Karen is up in the window of his father's house.

The truck from a store in St. John's.

Blackstrap nods hello to the men and goes around back of the house to open the door. At once, there's the smell of new wood and new carpet. He leaves the door open.

The men take out a fridge, tilted to carry it properly. They bring it in. Then a stove, a couch and recliner, bureaus, headboards and mattresses. Blackstrap gives them a hand to move the stuff in. All the things Karen saw on the television ad for the store. And then in the flyer from the mail.

Blackstrap thinks of all the furniture in his father's house. Old things that Karen didn't seem to want. Furniture made by hands that knew what they were doing. The items he has been collecting over the years, for his mother's sake. Not that Karen refused. But Blackstrap told her she should get what she wanted. So Karen did just that. Laminate over pressboard.

Blackstrap has to sign for everything. The man holding the pen over the piece of paper. He calls for Karen to do it. She's on her way out from checking everything in the new house. Blackstrap watches her signing her name. There's a perfectly pleased look on her face that makes him smile.

When the men go away, Karen steps around inside the new house, checking the different pieces of furniture in boxes or covered in plastic, happy with what she sees. A new life in a new place. This much she has said to Blackstrap.

A new start.

Blackstrap strips the cardboard off the stove, the splinters in his hands bugging him. He thinks of stopping to get a tweezers or nail clipper, but, instead, finds the wire. No plug. Shit. This is something that should have been checked. His own stupidity. He has wired a female 220 plug already. He'll have to splice it in a box. Or buy a male 220 connector.

He strips the cardboard off the fridge and opens the door. Clean in there. He plugs it into the wall socket he installed just for the fridge. The unit clicking in. Blackstrap opens the door again just to make certain. The light on. The shelves bare. He likes the look of that. The clean smell. The steel shelves and plastic walls. Before everything gets cluttered up.

Karen comes up behind him. She wraps her arms around his waist, then turns him around.

'Thanks, Blacky,' she says and kisses him warmly on the lips. Her eyes going to the scar on his cheek. 'You're a keeper.'

(December)

Karen does up the new house with tiny white lights along most surfaces. They smear in the corners of his eyes if he looks at them quickly. Spruce boughs from real trees stapled around doorways. Blackstrap cut them from the trees out back on specific orders from Karen. Little houses with little lights. White teddy bears here and there with red bows around their necks.

Their first Christmas in their new home.

Karen buys boxes and boxes of coloured lights for the front of the house. It takes Blackstrap two days to put them all up. He wonders if the breaker panel will handle it. He takes the face off the panel and carefully clips onto the main line. He turns on all the lights and heaters. Does an amperage test. Plenty of juice to spare.

The house lit up like nothing else, aglow from a distance whenever he comes up over the valley and takes the turn. He thinks Junior would like it, wonders if he should go get him, just take him to show what he's done. And Ruth almost two months old now. He hasn't seen her yet, hasn't laid eyes on her. But he knows that she's named Ruth. Patsy called to tell him that much in a saucy way. He thought it might have been out of respect, naming the baby after his dead sister, but it might have been out of spite. He can't tell for certain. Patsy always angry. There's no way of figuring her out.

He should get Christmas presents for the kids. Karen has mentioned it, offered to do it for him. But she has no place in that. He told her so. No. Even though he keeps thinking of shopping, believing it might be the right thing to do. But the wrong person to do it.

Two days before Christmas, Karen invites her brothers out for dinner. Glenn and Little Tuffy. No sign of her parents. No talk of them either. He doesn't ask. Karen does up the house weeks before, worried that everything should be perfect. She vacuums twice a day, washes the windows and dusts everything. With her acting like this, he wonders about marriage. There's been no mention of it, so he leaves it that way.

Glenn and Little Tuffy arrive in the same car. Little Tuffy, already on the beer, hugging everyone and joking around with Karen. He has a big sack of presents slung over his shoulder that nearly topples him. 'My Santa sweater,' he says, tugging at the front of his red sweater with a big Santa face on it. 'Wha' ya think? Sexy or wha'?' He passes out early on the couch, after dancing a few jigs to the cassette of Christmas fiddle music he brought along. Glenn doesn't drink. Doesn't touch a drop. His face doesn't seem pleased with anything that's going on. Blackstrap hears him saying something to Karen about it being the cruellest season of the year.

Glenn gets the whole meal on video. The table. Karen bringing things out. He gets a lot of Karen. The lens aimed at her.

'Show the house,' she keeps saying.

Glenn gets a little of the living room. Zooms in on Little Tuffy on the couch. One arm hanging over the edge.

Blackstrap can't stand Glenn. Always with his video camera, looking out through the lens, thinking what he's capturing is important. It's just life. Every second comes and goes. No need to be seen again because there's always more. Another minute. Hour. Day. Blackstrap just turns his head when it's aimed at him. It makes him angry, like a weapon pointed his way. Someone trying to take something from you, to have it as their own. No way of acting natural. He'd like to punch Glenn in the face and smash the video camera.

After dinner, Blackstrap comes out of the bathroom and sees Glenn talking to Karen. Face to face. Talking low. Bodies too close for his liking. Glenn steps back when Karen's eyes go to Blackstrap.

Glenn watches the kitchen tile. 'Time to head off,' he says.

Blackstrap loads Little Tuffy on board by himself because Glenn won't lend a hand. 'Let him crawl,' says Glenn. 'Never raise a finger to help an alcoholic.'

'Is that what dey say?' Blackstrap asks hotly.

Little Tuffy sings and waves his arms, protests about leaving so soon. He kisses Karen before getting in the car. 'I loves you, sis. Dun't forget, a'right. Loves ya.' Karen tries laughing him away. Little Tuffy kisses Blackstrap. Blackstrap lets him. Then Blackstrap laughs at it. Laughs loudly. 'Loves ya, too, buddy. Yer watch'n fer my sis.'

Blackstrap glances toward his father's house. His father in the window, drawn there by what must have been noise. A shadow that refused to eat with strangers. But it's not like he's facing them. He's facing straight ahead, staring off. Only a little light behind him so his outline can be made out, but nothing else. No Christmas lights over there. No Christmas tree inside.

Karen waves goodbye. Blackstrap is already on his way up the path. Around back. Into the porch. The kitchen.

He is silent. Something about the gathering he does not like; what was left from it. Glenn. He doesn't mind Little Tuffy much. A sick man. A man destroying himself. It's a funny way of life, but sad too. He helps clear away the dishes, scrapes them off in the back porch bin. Karen loads them in the dishwasher, turns it on. The hum he hates.

She is quiet all the rest of the night.

Then in bed. Two of them silent, eyes on the ceiling, until she turns to face him.

'Turn off the light,' she says. He switches off the lamp by his bed, the one Karen picked out. Then she switches off hers. She stays still. A while later, he shifts toward her, his hand on her belly.

'No,' she says, moving his hand away.

This makes Blackstrap angry. What is she after? He waits, thinking of other lives, other lives he might have. Other women. In the dark, he sees anything. Agnes with that man in Corner Brook. He should go back there. The way that man beat him. Why did he let that happen? Stronger now. Then Karen with her hands on him, one hand down his underwear, pulling.

She climbs on top of him.

'Shut your eyes,' she says.

He can barely make her out. He shuts his eyes when she puts him in her.

726

Her movements getting faster. 'You won't tell.'

Only a noise with him not saying anything.

'Just be a good boy.' Moaning and then gasping, sniffling, moving faster. She holds down his arms, leans forward and moves faster, the heavy meat of her breasts pressed into his face. 'Suck my titty.'

A deep, long moan that stretches her body higher, then stillness for a long time.

Small weeping sounds, quiet like a girl.

Blackstrap flinches. Tears spotting his face. No idea why or what has made her, in the darkness, in the clean sheets, in the new bed, in ruins.

(February, 1992, 38 years old)

It's a hard run into St. John's in a blizzard. No definition to anything in front of you. By the time Blackstrap reaches Holyrood, he has to slow to ten kilometers. On the booze last night. Drunk with Paddy. Karen still pissed off at him. He should give up driving a plough in St. John's. It's too hard to get in there and back again. But it's a job he's held on to.

The hours are good because there's been plenty of snow. He clears parking lots in the morning and at night. Bob Buckingham has the contract to clear the university lots. Blackstrap enjoys that. Not a car in sight at night. In a parking lot, pushing snow into mounds. The lone sound of the engine over the cleared lot. The sound of his machine beeping, backing up. The snow falls so gently that it can only be seen in the lights of a nearby streetlamp.

He sits in the plough in the middle of the parking lot. With no one around to bother a man, he has a nip from his flask of rum. He could drop off to sleep, he's so content. Not a care in the world with him in the middle of that cleared lot. The snow in the lights of the streetlamps a miracle to him. Leaned back in his seat, just watching that.

(May)

A few welfare houses are left in the lower section of Bareneed they call the Gut. The townie yuppies can't drive the poor people out. Government houses that the yuppies can't buy, no matter how hard they try. Blackstrap still has a boat tied up there. The *Floating Nut*. Its real name: *Bareneed's Pride II*. There are other local people from the region who've taken to gathering there, standing on the wharf and griping about the state of the fishery. More men there now that their livelihoods have been taken away. Too much time on their hands.

'Dose bloody foreigners,' says Walt Drover.

Blackstrap smokes a cigarette, pinched between his remaining fingers, and stares out to the water.

'If any of us had a spine,' says Donny Cole, 'we'd be out dere blasting dem foreign vessels outta da water.' Donny is Johnny's younger brother. Johnny who died on the Ranger.

Blackstrap takes another draw from his cigarette, paying extra special attention to Donny's words. Still staring out to sea. The back of Bell Isle and a far-off horizon that tells him nothing.

'We're eeder being robbed from 'r tol' wha' ta do.' Words that might have been from Blackstrap's father's mouth.

'Right,' he says loudly, dropping his cigarette and crushing it out with the heel of his boot.

The faces of the men and oldtimers all look at him because of the way he's said it.

'Right, wha'?' asks Walt Drover.

'We'll go dere,' says Blackstrap.

'Where?' asks Donny Cole.

'Two-hundred-mile limit.'

Walt Drover busts out with a laugh, half amused, half disbelief. 'Naw. What?'

'Are ye at wit's end, b'y?' says Tommy Bishop.

'We'll need some guns,' says Blackstrap.

The humour wilts from the oldtimers' faces. But Donny Cole smiles, just like his brother, the exact same grin. Andrew Fowler looks interested too. But like he still thinks it might be some sort of joke.

'Guns?'

'Big ones,' says Blackstrap, watching Walt Drover. 'You were a gunsmith.'

'Were,' says Walt Drover. ''N I never made no big guns.'

'Navy guns,' says Blackstrap.

'From where?' laughs Donny Cole, liking the idea even more now, interested as anything. Stepping closer to Blackstrap. Ready to go.

Blackstrap thinks for a while, wondering if there are any navy vessels rusting away anywhere. He remembers Halifax. The naval base. The guns would have to be removed. How to make off with navy guns? They could sail from Bareneed and surprise the Canadian Navy, pull up alongside and climb aboard. A bunch of Newfoundlanders making off with navy guns. Impossible. What they'll have to do is hijack a navy boat. That's what they'll do.

'Navy boats in Halifax,' says Blackstrap, looking around at the men gathered there.

Donny Cole nodding. He slams his fist in his palm. 'Fuh'k'n right, buddy.' He nods again, confirming the deal. 'When?'

'Halifax,' says Walt Drover, seeming confused.

The men and oldtimers check Blackstrap's face. Then give attention to Donny. Men of action. Then they glance at each other, their mouths silent. A few with jaws hung open in disbelief.

But soon a glint of humour returns. Tommy Bishop laughs outright. Blackstrap just looks at him, until the whole lot of them go serious. And soon a prickle of excitement passes from one to the other.

'Da navy should be da ones out there,' Blackstrap says. 'Protecting us. If we had a Newfoundland navy, we'd be out dere chasing off dem bastards.'

'Like dey done in Iceland,' says Paddy Murphy, nodding.

'Ya t'inks we can just storm da Canadian Navy!' asks Walt.

'Dey won't be expecting it,' says Paddy, sniffing. 'Who dey ever fight? Not a friggin' clue, the lot of 'em. We could take 'em.'

There is little agreement, but the idea has been laid down. And each man holds it in his head as he travels back home that night to smile or fret over.

Blackstrap thinks it through while Shearstown Line stretches off in front of him. The more he thinks, the more he believes it's possible. He has been inside the naval compound. The security is nothing he couldn't handle. Boats passing along the water all the time. Who would ever know? Who would ever expect it? Hijack a Canadian naval boat. Wouldn't that be something.

He starts figuring out cost. Where would they get the money? How many boats to Halifax? How many men to take a destroyer? A lot of fuel required. He thinks of talking it over with Karen. But she wouldn't want him getting involved, not with the new house and all. She wouldn't want to be left alone. Any hint of bad news always puts her on edge. She'll just go to the bedroom and shut the door, lie there watching the ceiling, hiding from it.

There's a chance they might go to prison, be made an example of for trying to steal Canadian property. Federal property. Send them to a federal prison. One right here in Cutland Junction, so there's not so far to go.

Off Shearstown Line and into Cutland Junction, past Agnes' old house. He could talk to Agnes about it. He could call her and see what she thinks. An excuse to hear her voice again. She would laugh at the idea, but not in a mean way, like it was just something else he was going to do, something expected of him. What about Patsy? She'd call it a bunch of foolishness. Tell him he was nuts, then warn him, threaten him.

His mind reverses. Guns is what they need. A plan not so complicated. How to board those vessels once they reach the 200-mile limit? That'll be a problem. He thinks of where he might get big guns that will do damage. Huge guns. His mind imagining the sort required. And soon it comes to him. He drives right in front of it. There in the Cutland Junction Museum run by that little townie woman, Mrs. Foote, the one who tries saving all the old houses, and goes around picking up litter on her walks. He sees what he is after. Something of no use to anyone in this day and age.

Blackstrap stands outside his father's house. The extension to the living room that had been added on twenty years ago is being torn off. Some of the studs still there. The clapboard stripped and piled on the ground. This seems peculiar. If anything, the house needs more space. To make room for the furniture Jacob and Blackstrap have been collecting. It's like Jacob has it backwards. He needs more space, so he got rid of space.

In the kitchen, Blackstrap watches his father at the table. How to stop a man from tearing down the house? His father is interested in Blackstrap, wanting something from him.

'Where's yer mudder?' Jacob asks, his jeans and plaid shirt covered in dust and wood chips. His face grey and unshaven beneath a turned-around baseball cap.

'Out.'

Jacob stares. Then he looks down at the plate on the table. Deep-fried chicken wings and fries from Ernie Green's. 'Where's Sunday dinner?'

'It's not Sunday. It's Friday.'

'Dis,' he says, pointing his shaky finger at the chicken wings and fries. 'Dis ain't fish.' He suspiciously tips the plate up and checks the bottom, like he's looking for something hidden. Higher and higher until the food spills off. 'Dat bastard, Smallwood, were defeated. Moores booted his arse fer 'im after Smallwood broke me good leg over da head of Fidel Castro.'

Twenty years ago.

Blackstrap looks out the kitchen window. Two strips of land where the vegetable garden used to be. The grass lush and green there. His mother checking the sprouts. He wonders about Karen in the new house next door. When he left, she was repainting. Soft, pale colours: pinks and blues and greens. She paints the walls every few months. A new shade of some colour she's picked out.

'I were wrong 'bout you,' says Jacob.

Blackstrap shifts his gaze to his father.

His father shaking his head in disappointment. 'Yer mudder said you were different. She t'ought you'd turn out different. But yer jus' like Blackstrap, yer brudder. Just like 'im fer da world.' Pouring ketchup over the mess on the table.

The telephone rings. Blackstrap goes over to where it's hung on the wall and picks it up.

'Hello?'

'Blacky?' Patsy's voice.

He hangs up.

'Who were dat?' asks Jacob, a mash of food in the hole of his mouth. 'Were it da niggers?'

Blackstrap squints a questioning look at his father. The first time he has ever heard that word out of his father's mouth.

From the living room, the sound of a TV preacher.

Blackstrap turns and strides into the smaller living room with the new wall up. He grabs the TV cord and yanks the prongs from the socket. Then hoists the TV and carries it to the kitchen. It's heavy, hard to be lifted by one man.

Jacob watches him carrying the load. 'Where ye go'n widt Mudder?'

Laying down the console, Blackstrap opens the porch door. The outside door is there ahead of him. He comes back in for the TV, turns sideways to edge it out. Down the drive and heaved into the back of the pickup, the TV clunks in there. Wood against metal. He gets behind the wheel and drives away, his mind on Bareneed. Passing through the junction, he has to take a detour. The road blocked off for the Soiree dance later that night. Through old narrow roads and lanes he seldom takes, like going through a strange land that was always near. He leaves the community and crosses the highway. Heads down the long stretch of Shearstown Line until reaching Bareneed. Bumping over the rougher patches until he's near the water next to the Gut. He parks on the tall grass and drops the hatch on the pickup. Climbing up, he slides the TV toward the end of the hatch, then gets down again, picks up the console and flings it over the jagged edge. Losing his footing, he stumbles and tilts sideways. One hand going for the ground. He drops to his knees.

The TV tumbles and smashes. Sound not so clear with the white wash down there. The pieces of wood already afloat. He looks back at the land, toward the houses, to see two small shadows shifting. A boy and girl coming toward him. He rises from his knees and the children vanish. His eyes searching the open spaces.

When he gets back to the house, Jacob is not in the kitchen. He is in the living room, seated in his chair, watching toward the corner, nodding. 'Dere were adventures ta be had,' he says to the space where the TV stood. 'Dat journal were nut'n. I'll write me own one day 'n dey'd make it inta da finest kind o' movie.' He grins and laughs, slaps his knee and points toward nothing. 'Dat's right, course I would. Ya knows it. I'd even play meself if dey took it inta dere 'eads ta ask.'

It took two nights. The men bolted sheets of steel reinforcement to the insides of their boats. Blackstrap did the welding where needed. The boats were anchored offshore, behind the headland, to hide the flame of the torch. The steel supplied from Donny Cole's metal shop. They had figured out the pounds per square inch of impact. Then they had determined the thickness of the steel. Without reinforcement, all the boats would be sunk when the time came to make their noise.

Now, the five boats idle in Bareneed harbour. A warm, peaceful night. A clear, deep-blue sky with stars. Only lights showing from within the wheelhouses. Three twenty-foot skiffs and two forty-foot boats. On their decks, large objects covered with grey tarpaulins. Roped down.

Blackstrap thinks ahead to what he'll be doing out on the ocean. Far out to the 200-mile limit. Not close to shore like the trips he's taken recently. No land in sight. Paddy has said he wants to come along, but Blackstrap can't have him in the boat. He can't manage the distraction. Paddy either drunk or wanting a drink. Plus Paddy's scared of water, which won't help the situation at all. So Blackstrap knows Paddy was just asking to tag along for Blackstrap's sake. He had to come up with an excuse for Paddy to stay on land. Blackstrap's scared enough himself of water. He didn't need Paddy adding to that. It'd be a mess. He told Paddy that he could be their media spokesman. That makes Blackstrap smile more.

The wharf has a single man standing on it. Paddy with his arms loosely folded, watching the boats gear up. He shifts from one foot to the other, tapping the toe of his boot. Behind Paddy, another man comes up with the strap of a black case over his shoulder. Paddy turns when he hears the sound. The man is a townie from St. John's who bought a house in Bareneed last year. Paddy knows him from when he and Blackstrap delivered a load of wood. Blackstrap brought the man felled wood, trees that'd been sitting on the forest floor for a while. Seasoned wood, good and dry, so the man wouldn't be burning green wood, trying to light a fire for hours, the wood charring instead of burning. The man didn't know any better. And Blackstrap said nothing of it. If the man bought wood from anywhere else next year, he'd find out all about it on his own. The same man had been hanging around when they were loading the boats last night. A bit of an accent when he talks, but it's not a Newfoundland accent. Probably Irish, by the sounds of it.

Through the side window, Blackstrap sees the man raise his arm, moving his fingers in a way that means for Blackstrap to come nearer.

Paddy looks the man up and down, but Blackstrap ignores him. He checks his watch and goes out on deck to clear the line. No time for chit-chat. The man bends on the wharf to do it for him, brushing Paddy aside.

This pisses Paddy off because Paddy has been waiting.

'Where you heading?' the man calls.

'Las Vegas,' Blackstrap plainly states.

The man laughs while holding the line. 'I know what you've got there on board,' he says.

'Toss that line here,' demands Blackstrap, raising his hand.

'You're going to the two-hundred-mile limit. I heard rumours.'

Paddy stands behind the crouched man. He swings back his boot, pretending he's going to kick the man in the arse. His face is tight with the silence of a grumbling curse.

'The line,' says Blackstrap, trying to keep his tone serious, his eyes on Paddy.

The man glances back, sees Paddy whistling and watching the other ships. 'I'd like permission to board.'

'What's in the case?'

'A camera. I'm a reporter.'

'Where you from?'

'The *Independent*.'

'Dat a country?' asks Paddy.

'No, a newspaper,' the man says to Paddy, then to Blackstrap, 'I'm from Ireland originally.'

'Ireland, eh.' Blackstrap thinks on this, something he had not planned on. A man who could make a telephone call and ruin everything. No question about it.

'Get aboard.'

The announcement brings a look of shock and insult to Paddy's face.

The man tosses down the line with one hand and passes down the case with the other. Blackstrap receives the case. It's lighter than expected. The man puts one foot on the side of the boat, practically jumps onto the deck.

Paddy steps to the lip of the wharf, shrugging and trying to meet eyes with Blackstrap, but Blackstrap won't have any of it.

'Keep a watch out,' is what Blackstrap says, then turns away. Back at the wheel, he eases the throttle down, heading from behind the massive headland. The other two skiffs trail after him. When the three boats clear the headland, they face the bigger shrimp boats, waiting there, idling.

Five boats in formation under a black sky, heading toward the black horizon, over the black sea.

The lights are pinpricks in the distance. The way the lights from the houses on land had been behind him, eight hours ago. The reporter has finally stopped talking. So many questions and no answers readily at hand. The reporter sits out on the deck in a chair salvaged from Jacob's old wrecked boat, the first *Bareneed's Pride*. Occasionally, he raises his camera and takes a picture of nothing Blackstrap imagines. A flash goes off, lighting up the nearest water. In the trail of moonlight, Blackstrap expects to see a glimmer of steel rising out of the sea. A stiff length of pipe or a whip of chain.

Blackstrap senses movement behind him and checks over his shoulder. The reporter taking out another camera. Video. Those things everywhere now. He aims ahead and begins talking. The reporter gives the time.

'How far are we from land?' he calls out.

'Hundred 'n seventy miles.' Blackstrap looks over his shoulder, sees the camera pointed at him, a blinding light switched on above it. He faces forward. He'd sooner toss that reporter overboard than give him another look. No matter if he's from Ireland or not.

'Only a scrap of an accent left in ya,' says Blackstrap.

'What?'

Blackstrap sees no point in repeating himself.

'Accent? . . . Did you say "accent"? . . . Well, you learn to speak proper in this world. Reign of the great white eye. All that.'

'You speak Irish?' This question louder.

'No. You know, Irish never made it through one generation in Newfoundland. The language, I mean . . . You know that?'

Blackstrap hasn't understood the question.

'The language. Only the people who came over spoke Irish. After that, not one of their children spoke it. Any idea why that was?'

Blackstrap says nothing. Hands on the wheel, watching ahead. The pinpricks of light grow a little bigger, like coming into a city at night, from far away on the black liquid highway. The Ranger lit up like that too.

'They spoke English in Newfoundland. Learned English right away. I have a few pints with a university prof every now 'n again. He's an expert on the Irish in Newfoundland. The British wouldn't allow Irish to be spoken. Just like the missionaries with the Indians and Eskimos up north. Beat them if they didn't speak English.'

Blackstrap stood at the wheel, watching, not wanting any more part of conversation. That bright light still on over his shoulder, not helping him see. The glare in the glass. 'Shut dat light off.'

'What language do you think they speak here now?'

Blackstrap says shortly, 'Newfoundese.'

The reporter laughs. 'Most people can't understand a word from the old folks around the bay . . . I can't. Some of them. But I can understand their children. It's like that again. Irish gone. Then Newfoundese corrected out of existence. We're all just a bunch of mimics, after all, talking like in movies.'

'Shut up, will ya,' he finally says. 'And switch of dat fuh'k'n light.'

The reporter switches off the light. And everything seems calmer. He even hears the sound of the engine more clearly.

'What are you going to do when you reach the foreign vessels?' the reporter calls out.

'Socialize,' says Blackstrap, watching ahead. The dots of light. A city afloat. The bright light behind him again, reflecting in the glass.

'What was that?' The reporter's voice comes louder, clearer.

Blackstrap turns to see the light and camera hovering near the door. That light on again. 'Outta the wheelhouse,' he barks.

The light backs away.

'Turn that Christly thing off, I told ya.'

The light stays on.

'Now,' Blackstrap shouts.

The light switches off.

''N keep it off.'

Blessed silence for a while. The flush in his face as he waits, thinking what he might do next. He turns for the wheel. Every moment getting more important as they sail closer.

'It's peaceful out here,' the reporter finally says, not able to keep his mouth shut, the sound of his own voice. 'I thought it would be nastier. Violent seas and a bit of adventure. Sort of disappointing.'

Blackstrap glances back at the reporter, stares while his memory rages on its own. A man sitting in a chair on a calm sea. He hears the sound of an airplane engine, leans forward toward the glass and turns his head, strains a look up at the sky. Blinking lights from a plane. DFO, by the looks of it. He will not be stopped. He raises the radio, 'This is *Bareneed's Pride II*. DFO plane overhead.' The other vessels make their acknowledgements.

Steadily they go. Not one of five engines slacking off.

As they near the foreign vessels, the sky begins to soften. The lights from the vessels lose their strength to dawn. No longer merely lights, they take on dimension. They are big boats made of steel. Sixty-foot draggers with massive nets trailing behind them, deep down on the ocean floor. Nets three hundred feet wide, two hundred feet high, like a huge mouth tearing at the bottom, scooping up every bit of life, netting twenty-five thousand pounds of fish in one haul.

The reporter stands off at Blackstrap's side. The video camera aimed at the nearest ship. 'The *Algarve*,' he says.

'Portuguese flag,' Blackstrap comments.

The reporter turns the camera to face Blackstrap who lifts the radio in hand.

'Calling the *Algarve*,' says Blackstrap, easing up on the throttle. He waits, listens. Static. Engages the radio again. 'Calling the *Algarve*.'

There comes an answer. Foreign words.

'We are a battalion of Newfoundland fishermen. We will not leave this area until you have evacuated it.'

More foreign words.

'English,' says Blackstrap. 'English.'

Then a different voice, barely understandable. 'Hel . . . lo.'

'We are Newfoundland fishermen. We order you to move off this area.' Blackstrap waits, listens.

Static.

Nothing.

'Calling *Algarve*.'

"Oo . . . are . . . you?"

'We are fishermen. Newfoundland fishermen.'

The Bareneed vessels slow even more, halting in formation. Side by side, they make a line one hundred feet from the *Algarve*. Gradually, *Bareneed's Pride II* steams ahead, passing starboard of one of the shrimp boats, to idle at the forefront.

A voice replies through the radio, in a language unknown to Blackstrap.

'English,' he hotly mutters to himself. 'Fer fuck sakes.'

There is a silence and then a crackle of static: 'Who es deez?'

'Blackstrap Hawco.'

"Oo . . . you wunt?"

His words spoken clearly for the sake of understanding: 'The . . . fishermen . . . of . . . Newfoundland . . . are . . . ordering . . . you . . . to . . . leave . . . these . . . waters.'

"Oo are you wid ahrders?"

The DFO plane cruises overhead, dropping lower for a better look.

'This is the Canadian Department of Fisheries. Please identify yourself.'

The DFO on the radio now.

Blackstrap gives no response. They can see his call numbers by now. Enough light to make out the name too.

'This is the Canadian Department of Fisheries.'

'Calling the *Algarve*. If you do not leave these waters in five minutes, you will be attacked.'

There is no more sound.

Then another voice comes back. It is amused. 'Attacked? You will ram us?' Another different voice: 'Who are you? Are you police?'

Other larger vessels have started turning to face the confrontation. What might be happening. A ship flying a Japanese flag two hundred meters away. Starboard. No problem to see even at that distance. His eyes always with perfect vision. He looks up at the railing of the Portuguese boat. Sees two men with rifles aimed toward him. He makes a sound to himself.

'They've got guns,' says the reporter.

'Who cares.'

A gunshot goes off. A muffled ping.

Blackstrap looks up to see the rifle aimed toward the sky. Something thuds onto the deck and Blackstrap turns to see the reporter looking down. A grey bird with a black head and orange beak. A tern.

'Jesus, Mary and Joseph. Nice shot,' says the reporter. 'Can you eat them?'

'This is the Canadian Coast Guard. Please identify yourself.' A Coast Guard ship in the area.

The DFO plane is so low the engine drills at Blackstrap's ears. He sees someone up there taking pictures through an opened door.

At once, fishermen are stood on the decks of the *Atlantic Charm*, *Amanda Jane*, the *Divinity*, the *Sacred Love*. All of them watching toward *Bareneed's Pride II*, awaiting the signal.

Stepping out on his deck, Blackstrap kicks the bird aside and brushes past the reporter. He goes to the flagpole, takes the rope in hand and hoists the Newfoundland flag. It flaps in the bit of morning breeze, making a sound that charms him.

The fishermen all spring to action, raising their flags. Then they begin untying the ropes from the tarps. The shapes of the objects hidden away on each boat identical. When the ropes are loosened, they pull off the tarps. One boat at a time, starting with the boat farthest down the line. Tarps yanked off to expose the iron black cannons set on wooden pedestals with wheels.

Six cannons collected from historic sites around the island, all aimed at the *Algarve*.

The Portuguese fishermen gather near the railing. They point. A few laugh and joke with one another. But two others straighten and slowly step back, realizing something deeper than laughter. More rifles are aimed over the railing. No longer at the sky. Five in total now.

A voice comes from a megaphone, from the overhead plane. All sorts of official words spoken, not one of them understandable. The speed and the height. All the words garbled, vibrating together.

The reporter watches the sky, but Blackstrap gives the plane no attention.

The position of his boat is exact. Side on. The anchor dropped. A clear shot over the edge of the hull. Soon, he'll drift out of line. Quickly, he takes a pouch from his pocket, loosens the drawstring, pours gunpowder into the vent and pokes the pouch away. He lifts the stick with its gasoline-soaked head, flicks open the Zippo from his pocket and the fabric blazes alive. A waver of orange and black, whooshing when he holds the flaming stick straight up above his head, and stands perfectly erect.

The Portuguese watch. A few of the rifles lift away, aim harmlessly toward the blue sky.

Blackstrap carefully lowers his arm, looking down to direct the fire to the ball on the cascabel. The black powder, wad and cannonball packed against it. Breathlessly, he brings the flame nearer the touch-hole, and waits, not knowing what to expect. They had tested the cannons offshore. The guns had worked then. But what about now? Hoping not to be made into a laughing stock. Cannonballs collected from museums and houses around the community. From the crawl spaces of old houses. Souvenirs found and kept. So many men with cannonballs just sitting in their homes. Conversation pieces of no true use to anyone until now.

An explosion sounds and the carriage jolts backwards, striking the reinforced steel, soundly denting it, one of the wheels nearly running over Blackstrap's boot. The percussion of the sound crackles and bounds and rebounds endlessly over the breadth of sea.

Across the water, the ball pops a clean hole in the side of the *Algarve*, high above the waterline. The action barely making a sound. There is silence all around, and then more laughter from the deck of the *Algarve*. Other faces watching down with interest, bodies straining to lean toward a look. A few smoking cigarettes, wondering what that tiny hole might mean.

The vessel toots its horn. An almost silly sound.

'Good Christ,' says the reporter, video camera to eye.

The radio going from the wheelhouse. Warnings from official voices. Words recited about treaties. The Canadians always with something to say.

That's all there is to it. That's how it seems. The silence extended to hold the entire morning in a state of anticipation and grace. The hole high above the waterline. But then three other cannons fire in succession. The booms not so loud at varied distances, each explosion ricocheting off the other.

Two more holes ripped in the side of the *Algarve*, closer to sea level.

Blackstrap watches the smoke drift from where the cannons have been emptied. He sees the men quickly load more cannonballs, the bores packed, and he snaps from his trance to load his own.

The cannons fire once again. More holes torn open in the side of the *Algarve*. There is concern on the deck now. Much concern. Gunshots are fired directly at the smaller boats. The fishermen take cover, ducking from their decks toward wheelhouses.

The larger scattered vessels from Spain, Russia, China and Japan remain where they are, watching, but not bothered by what might be going on.

Water begins to flood into the *Algarve*'s hull. In a time shorter than what Blackstrap expected, distress signals are given.

The DFO plane flies lower, its belly near the heads of the fishermen.

In the distance, port side, a Canadian Coast Guard ship approaches. Painted red and white with a flag of the same colours.

The *Algarve* takes on water.

Blackstrap's stomach churns with nausea.

Another report of cannon fire strikes the hull toward the bow.

As suspected, the onboard pumping system cannot handle the rush of water through the scattered punctures. No more cannon fire is necessary.

It is only a matter of time before the ship begins to list. The ugly angle of it scaring Blackstrap into stillness. The heavy hull of a ship tilting toward him.

But everything is calm now. A blue sky. A tranquil sea.

Regardless, the fear rushes up in him.

The Portuguese men take to the lifeboats, but there are not enough. Never enough. Men toss pieces of wood or life preservers into the water. Then they leap from the ship, falling with arms whipping around. Others dive expertly to splash into the water, and are left floating as the boat lists on a 45-degree angle. The men in the water watch over their shoulders, and struggle to swim away. Blackstrap checks for the positions of the other Bareneed boats. They have steamed in reverse, anticipating the swell from the ship soon to be submerged. More men jump over the sides of the *Algarve*. Splashes of entry all along the ocean. Other men stay aboard, leaned back against the old steel, like they're trying to keep the boat up, until fully facing gravity and they are forced to jump, practically flung.

The ship groaning a sound that blackens the sky. The swell from its sinking pushing at the lifeboats, almost smothering the men bobbing in the water, rocking the skiffs and shrimp boats. The swell from its sinking drifts everything backwards a hundred feet.

Blackstrap in a trance for moments, eyes trained on the sailors bobbing in the loppy swell of water. What now? He looks around his boat to aptly position himself to rescue the Portuguese. And notices the video camera aimed at the men struggling to swim toward and clutch on to the lifeboats. Rushing out of the wheelhouse, Blackstrap plucks the camera from the reporter's hands and hurls it overboard. At once, the reporter dives in after it.

The Newfoundlanders on the five Bareneed boats pull Portuguese sailors from the water with gaffs. They toss lines to the lifeboats and tow them along. All of this is done before the Search and Rescue helicopter arrives or the Coast Guard ship has a chance. Blackstrap makes certain that every man has been collected, every name accounted for. He loudly questions the captain, pointing to one man, then another. 'One, two, three . . .' The captain calls out names across the water. The men reply, or others reply on behalf of the called name. The men talk crazily and point at Blackstrap. They argue as though they might kill one another, all of them stood cramped on the decks of the vessels. They call out to their shipmates, where other Portuguese are sat or stood on Bareneed boats or in lifeboats. They call out more names. People answer in reply. Some of them related, no doubt, by the way they look concerned checking for others.

Mutiny, Blackstrap thinks. What happens then? More of them than us. But where would they go? Where would they take the boats? He has already thought of this on land. They seem content to squabble among themselves or stand dripping wet, some of them shivering with blue lips, maybe thankful just to be saved. They watch up at the helicopter in the sky or at other ships. An interesting diversion. A few of them have dry cigarettes that they share with the other men.

How are the men meant to get home? Blackstrap's head begins to hurt more. He had gone there with the intention of bringing harm to them, but he had saved them instead. Wasn't that how it was? No, a statement was being made. We won't stand for it anymore. He hadn't intended to hurt anyone. A ship would come for them. A Portuguese ship would take the sailors home. There were plenty of them fishing off the coast.

Asked again for a head count of his men, the *Algarve* captain finally gives a nod and says, 'Sure.' Portuguese sailors gesture in agreement, some more emphatically than others. The Newfoundland boats then head toward the other big ships, trying to drive them off with cannons still uncovered. But the other boats will not budge, their nets too costly to cut, until the DFO plane runs near them, the Coast Guard ship sails closer and a few of them cut their nets and steam off, their load illegal.

Many of the Portuguese gesture toward Blackstrap and argue more. At one point, one of them gets too rowdy. And Blackstrap storms out of the wheelhouse to stare him down. He feels his muscles tighten to snatch hold of the sailor by the sweater front. The other Portuguese go quiet while he scalds them with his look. But he does not move ahead. There is no need to punish anyone more than this. The sailors turn one way, lower their eyes, or edge back a few inches.

The language of disbelief muttered.

The Bareneed boats make wide circles while the foreign ships back off, again and again. The draggers veer east and steam away, but idle further off. The air is filled with airplanes and helicopters. Then another Coast Guard boat.

More big ships anchored miles in the distance.

Blackstrap had expected them all to leave the area belonging to Newfoundland, but there is no dividing line here. Where can a line be drawn in boundless miles of water? Blackstrap cannot fire at them because there is no room for the cannons to fire. No room for other crews on their decks. No men lost. He will not have it, although he would like nothing more than to sink every last one of them. Leave the surface of the ocean bare.

Thirty minutes later, after refuelling from diesel carried by the shrimp boats, Blackstrap gives the order, and the five boats steam west toward unseen land.

Blackstrap thinks ahead, wondering what might happen when they arrive. He imagines Paddy there giving a few interviews already, stating the fishermen's case. Stood on the wharf in his loose grey sweater and with his big lips and missing teeth. Simple as that. Paddy the smart one. With an education at least, made to finish high school by his father putting the fear of God in him.

The Portuguese sailors talk low among themselves. A couple of them quietly inspect the cannon. They run their hands over it. A few squat and look into the barrel. Blackstrap smells smoke. Foreign cigarette smoke.

The reporter, back aboard after giving up on the video camera a while ago, won't say a word to Blackstrap. A merciful blessing, thinks Blackstrap. The reporter aims his still camera at the men and snaps photographs. Some smile or strike manly poses, and take draws from their cigarettes, while others turn their backs, their hands in the pockets of their coats which they had donned before the *Algarve* sank. And Blackstrap wonders about the cigarettes. He wouldn't mind trying one.

The sky is filling with more noise, not just two planes now, but others. Small planes. Private planes out for a look. And another helicopter. He leans to check through the glass. A helicopter flying low, straight out in front of him, swooping down to almost skim the water, then rising to tilt back. He sees one with the colours of the police. A white boat up ahead with purple stripes and the crown insignia of the RCMP racing toward them. A super-fast boat. It cuts the water nicely, with urgency. The big yellow Search and Rescue helicopter follows them in, keeping the same pace. The DFO plane cruises by overhead, not so low now, just biding time.

When the RCMP boat nears, it circles around the five Bareneed boats, racing fast as though trying to rope them in. The lights on the top of the boat are switched on which means the boats should all stop. They do not. So the RCMP boat continues to circle, then rides between Blackstrap's boat and Donny Cole's. One of the police officers has a bull horn up to his mouth.

The Portuguese sailors watch the policemen. They smoke cigarettes. They tilt their chins up at one another. Comments are passed back and forth. The sailors then watch Blackstrap. This continues for an hour.

It is a relief to see the distant shore with dusk an hour off, to be sailing back into Bareneed. Whatever waits for him is home. Miraculously, the weather has co-operated. Seas of no great consequence.

As they near land, there are more helicopters overhead. One comes low and Blackstrap sees that the side door is off. A man sits there with a video camera aimed at him.

The water is getting crowded. Twenty-five or thirty boats from the area, off to the sides, leaving a clear path in. Dories. Sailboats. Skiffs. All there to see or welcome. People stood on the decks, watching in silence. A little boy jumping up and down, waving. Others start waving too. A man cups his hands around his mouth and shouts, 'God bless ya, b'ys.'

They pass the headland in Bareneed, a bump like a nub on the head of a rocky giant. The cliffs toward the left. Houses seen along the road. People lining the shore, arms rising now, one by one, waving down the line.

The sight stirs something in Blackstrap that troubles his breath.

It was worth the effort now. He sees through the fear that it was a simple enough action. Nothing went too badly. Clean and easy. He has not slept in days, thinking it all through. His nerves are still raw and rattled, even more so by the memory of that ship going under. Who will pay for that if the ship was fishing illegally? But every one of those sailors saved.

Sailing into the bay, he sees the cars and pickups parked facing the water. The thicker clumps of people gathered there. Someone toots their horn and then another horn starts up, until the air is alive with car horns blasting. Bells ring in reply from the brigade of boats. Hundreds of people are lined along the roads. Must be from every community around. They wave, some of them with both arms. They cheer and whistle. Many of them sweep Newfoundland flags through the air. Two small children hold a Newfoundland flag, one on each end, barely big enough to keep a grip.

Blackstrap passes the towering headland, heading for the community wharf. He glances at the boat beside him. Donny Cole stood on the deck, making a muscle at the crowds and grinning. It makes Blackstrap laugh outright.

A roar of shouting and cheering. Louder and louder. Car horns blast as the five Bareneed boats return to port. Decks crowded with Portuguese sailors. Fresh from the water. The catch of the day.

(August)
Little Tuffy hangs up the telephone and stares at Blackstrap. Tuffy likes to look dramatic by holding the moment for a bit of fake suspense.

The hospital room is quiet. Glenn has just left. There for a visit with his video camera, documenting his brother's slow, miserable death. Asking questions that Tuffy laughed off. But Glenn keeping at it, trying to make Tuffy answer seriously, trying to make it all sink in and get the honest reaction.

It's 9.00 p.m. Visiting hours are almost done, but they let Blackstrap stay later. He just shuts the door and no one says anything to him. Still a bit of a celebrity with word after getting around. He's heard the nurses whispering about him, telling each other what he did out there to those foreign vessels. Sunk a whole bunch of them, they say. Using cannons just like a pirate.

'She's looking fer ya,' says Tuffy mysteriously. 'Others, too.' He grins and laughs. 'She tol' me wh' ya did widt dat backhoe.' Tuffy laughs, slowly. 'Ya needs your head examined. The way you gets on.' He grins and turns his head on the pillow to look out the big window of the Health Science Complex, seeing other things, imagining with the medication. ''N those cannons.' Tuffy squints. 'Geez, b'y, I saw all that on TV. Blackass, the hero. Don't mess with you. You're a fuh'k'n genius.' He steals a peek back at Blackstrap, grins again. 'When's da court date? Ya think you'll do time fer kidnapping them Portugee?'

Blackstrap shrugs. 'Who knows.'

'Good on ya.' Tuffy laughs quietly, then squints in pain, squints harder and harder. 'Christ!' he mutters. 'I could throw up. If I didn't want ta make waste of dat good hospital food.'

Blackstrap stands. 'You want something? A drink? I mean cola or something else.'

'I'm alright.' He watches Blackstrap's face, then scans him up and down. 'Nice ta be the hero, eh? I saw on the news how the Fishermen's Union paid yer bail. Good on dem.' He keeps watching Blackstrap like he doesn't know anything for a second or two. 'How ya manage that?'

'What? They offered.'

'Naw, I never meant the bail.' Tuffy pauses, swallows, gives his head a slow shake, his eyes somewhere else. 'I meant surviving everything.'

Blackstrap scoffs, turns away. 'I never survived nothing.' It just comes out. He isn't even thinking it.

'Wha'?'

He knows exactly what he meant, but he doesn't want to say more, not in the presence of this dying man.

It's a shame to feel alive. A mortal shame.

'You survived. Look at ya stood there.'

He gives a blunt shake of his head. Glances back at Tuffy.

'Christ, b'y. Look at the face on ya. You just need a drink, that's all.' Tuffy reaches by the bedside table. Groaning lowly, he opens the drawer and takes out a flask of rum.

Blackstrap watches Tuffy take a swig, then wince at the sting and tilt his head in agreement. 'Sum good . . . If it weren't so god-bloody bad.' He holds the flask out to Blackstrap, the sweet smell reaching him. A nice smell in place of the foul ones in the room.

Blackstrap takes a swig without wiping the rim, and hands it back.

'Dat John Crosbie's here on Friday. You see that on da news? Making an announcement on the fishery. Not gonna be good. Shut 'er down, I suspects.'

Blackstrap shifts his gaze to the other man in the other bed. He's sleeping. A shadow laid flat. This is the ward where they're put to bed forever. There's a name on it that Blackstrap can't pronounce.

'What you gonna do 'bout it?'

''Bout what?' Blackstrap's attention drawn back to Tuffy. He notices

Tuffy's face, how thin it is, how far gone. The light outside the window dimming over the landscape. A skeleton in a narrow bed. A bed that looks too big. Little Tuffy lost in it.

'Dat Crosbie feller,' says Tuffy, running out of breath. 'Wha' you gonna do . . . 'bout him, cause yer the man?'

Back in Cutland Junction, the telephone keeps ringing. Blackstrap had the number changed after the sinking of the Portuguese vessel. But it's not long before the new number circulates around the community. Men from the area won't stop calling to see how he's going to deal with this John Crosbie business. Donny Cole tells him Crosbie's on his way to St. John's with his suit pockets stuffed full of bad news. 'As is usually da case,' says Donny. Someone in the community has been talking to the media because they soon get Blackstrap's new number. They call wondering if he'll be attending the meeting. Does he have a plan of attack? A group of fishermen from Port de Grave, Cupids and all around are heading to St. John's for a show of solidarity.

Pickup trucks meet in front of Blackstrap's place for the drive in. Karen doesn't want anyone in the new house. She hides in the bedroom, more and more nervous all the time, like she fears everyone, scared of everything. The way she sees the world turning worse while Little Tuffy wastes away. She won't go visit him. He'll be dead soon and she won't even go see him. A fit of nerves. Blackstrap's even had to stop bootlegging. There's nothing he can do that doesn't worry her. The telephone ringing is the worst.

'Something's going to happen, Blacky,' she says. 'Something bad.' Like a trapped animal always backing away.

He tells the men to gather in Blackstrap's father's house. His father knowing everyone. Almost back to himself since the Portuguese incident, like it snapped him out of it. The way he talked to the media about the decades of companies raping Newfoundland of every virtue and treasure. His father with fit words for every reporter who put a microphone in his face. Then watching himself on Karen's TV. Coming over to catch the news. Unable to believe it was really him. Chuckling and shaking his head. He sits for hours in the kitchen, wanting the story from Blackstrap's mouth every minute of the day. Leaned forward and then sitting straighter and straighter as the story goes along. 'Dose Portugee showed ya da respect ye deserved.' He encourages the fishermen who come into the house. 'Dis it wha' it's all 'bout,' says Jacob. 'Yays, b'ys. Dis is it.' He smacks his fist on the table and tells the men the story. 'Out on da two-hundred-mile limit, I were. Firing cannons at dose foreign bastards.' He laughs and slaps Blackstrap on the back. 'We sunk one o' 'em. Didn't we, me son? Den captured da Portugee. Dey never gave us no worries. Dat lot.'

The fishermen crowd into the kitchen, standing or seated at the table. Cigarettes and beer bottles in hand, nodding at Jacob's words, waiting on Blackstrap. The heat of so many bodies, mingled with smoke and gruff anticipation. When Blackstrap finally stands, they all stand. Chairs scraping over the wooden floor. Cigarettes snuffed out. Beers finished off. Bottles set down on the counter.

'Right, b'ys,' says Blackstrap.

And his father stands laughing at the burst of movement. 'Go get 'im,' he calls out, tears of joy glistening in his eyes.

A string of pickup trucks head in over the highway.

Court in a week, Blackstrap thinks, hands on the wheel. The insurance company will be looking for damages, the Fishermen's Union's lawyer has told him. The cost of the vessel and equipment. A small fortune. The lawyer asks: 'You ever give any consideration to declaring personal bankruptcy?' That's what's in his mind now. Losing the house. Karen. Such a mess of considerations on such a fine, sunny day. Heat through the windshield. He struggles to pull off his coat while driving. What more harm can be done? What's there to lose? Fucking John Crosbie. The Crosbies. Another family of merchants with a bunch of big businesses in St. John's. Businesses built from the profits earned off the sweat of half-starved fishermen. Merchants turned politicians, as was always the case. Government-sanctioned slave drivers.

When Blackstrap rolls near the big hotel, some of the trucks are there ahead of the others. There's a bit of traffic. A mess of cars and trucks parked everywhere, on both sides of the road and up on the curbs. Blackstrap has to park a few minutes' walk away. Men and women already in the street, marching past him, heading for the hotel. He leans back against the bonnet of his pickup, smoking a cigarette, one boot heel up on his bumper, waiting for the men from home to join him. People wonder who he is when he approaches the hotel with a crowd behind him. Others know exactly what he's done. They call out and wave. 'Good job, Blackstrap.' Thumbs up and a wink from a man or a woman here and there. More friends and admirers pat him on the back and follow after him. An oldtimer in a baseball cap, with a hairy hand extended. 'You showed 'em, Mr. Hawco, sir. Dat's da way ta do it.'

The guy in the fancy uniform at the front of the hotel opens the door for him.

In the lobby, there's a mean buzz of conversation. People standing everywhere in groups. Nice couches and chairs. Nice tile underfoot. A fancy place to make a devastating announcement. The lives of men and women soon reduced to nothing, but everyone sitting comfortably. Men talk to other men, no end to the heated discussion. Women the loudest of them all. The sauciest, the ones who won't stand for being treated like dirt. A few chubby and scrawny ones cursing and making pledges. Not fucking likely. They'll push us too far. The government and plant owners. Mark me words. They've got their money and we're nothing to 'em. We're just a bunch of bottom feeders. There'll be blood. He won't be getting away with it, that Crosbie feller.

There is not enough room for everyone. The heat and the noise only make it worse. When John Crosbie shows up, the volume of the crowd rises at the point where he has entered. The chatter surging over the people like a wave as Crosbie is led through the crowd by two men in suits. Just the sight of his grey hair, fat neck and jowls, and him straightening his glasses while he's being moved by fast, makes the fishermen press nearer, wanting a piece of that man. Crosbie barely makes it to the conference room. Then the doors are shut with the reporters in there. No fishermen permitted access. A press conference. Men and women knock on the door to gain entry. They wait, growing angrier by the second. Snubbed is how they feel. They pound on the high doors, rattling them, and shout in anger. Enough is enough. Barred out like that. Pouring gasoline on fire. They can't hear what's being said, only muffled words, so their minds finish it for them, make it worse, add insult to injury. Treated like shit, they are. Treated like the scum of the earth. They begin beating on the doors. Kicking on them. Politicians destroying our communities, everything we worked for. The son of a merchant. They pick up a couch and try to beat down the door with it. Me fadder were a fisherman and his fadder before 'im. I won't have none of it. Rallying calls in agreement. The couch hurled ahead by twelve strong arms, ramming the shut doors, rattling the brass handles and catches.

The city police, the Royal Newfoundland Constabulary, have had enough. They are given the signal to clear the men out, arms are grabbed and twisted. A chin knocked to the side. A head banged. The throb swells worse with the ache of injury. The crowd growing more rigid, tighter and fiercer.

Blackstrap is front and centre, his back killing him, the hollow where his left testicle is gone, hands with fingers missing, a headache with the roar like waves on a beach all around him. Always a headache with noise since the accident. What accident? Which one? He can't recall. His vision clouds over. Something is suddenly pulled in his back. He notices his body when he thrusts ahead, his mind slicing up with pain. Not himself at all. His mind in the shell of someone else.

The shove of men peaks him ahead, closer, bawling his name out: 'Blackstrap.' That's all they need, his name to make them stronger. He pulls at the door, might pass out in a second, until the door is slowly opened out, the fishermen having to shuffle back or be struck. Blackstrap given credit for yanking those locks open, praised to the high heavens as the fishermen spill in, ready to fight.

But the sound of them dying low as their progression slows to a crawl.

The room is empty.

Only rows of chairs with the stray bit of paper here and there. Whoever was in there was taken out the back way.

In stillness, in inactivity, the murmur dies down up front, until a single fisherman curses the sight of a government press release laid there on a chair and kicks it over. A rattle. A bang gone off. An explosion. With the ripple of movement spreading from one man to another, the noise gains in volume, prompting the fishermen to commence wrecking the room, tossing tables and chairs, bellowing in rage, overturning anything within reach. Hands gripping and legs kicking, heartbeats speeding, the men flow toward the back doors that lead to the kitchen. No time for the constabulary to block the way. A corridor there that is filled by their teeming numbers. They pass by cooks and the clatter of dishes. They pass through the heat of cooking and washing.

But no John Crosbie to be found. The Minister of Fisheries safe in a car and gone, the driver heading directly for the airport. Crosbie in the back with his briefcase on his lap. A first-class seat back to Ottawa, to the mainland capital of Canada.

(November)

Karen denies the death of her brother, refuses to attend the funeral because Little Tuffy isn't dead. This she screams at Blackstrap, 'Why are you saying that?' Her hand to her forehead while she wanders around the living room.

One of the saddest days of Blackstrap's life, watching that casket go down. Glenn there with his video camera aimed at the broken earth. Two old people up front. The mother and the father, he suspects. Two of them back together, even though they were separated decades ago. Information he heard from Karen. All she ever mentioned of her father. But two of them reunited now, the way death can do that. Glenn near his father's side, so close their arms brush together.

Two weeks later, Blackstrap's father's death.

Karen does not attend that funeral either, stays at home, muttering something about being the cause. Nothing he can do with her except feel hurt and angry. In his head, he hears the words he knows others are saying: Just what's to be expected of a townie like her? But Patsy is there, with the children. Patsy shows that much respect because she was raised proper. Standing there by his side with Ruth in one arm and Junior by the hand.

The two funerals coming in a row like that has burned the life out of Blackstrap. Everything he breathes in turned to ash.

What were once the usual, unconsidered moments of life have greyed over and become noticeably occupied by absence. What to do when waking in the early morning without a catch to sail toward.

Then Karen disappears. Dropped off the face of the earth, people think. And an RCMP officer comes sniffing around, asking questions he has no reason to. Friend, father, lover, all gone, taken away as though to spite him.

Blackstrap thinks on Patsy. Junior and Ruth. He's already been to visit once. Couldn't stay away from seeing his daughter after his father's funeral. Ruth's sweet face in the forefront of his mind, because she looks like his father and mother. The similarity so intense it spooks him. Junior and Ruth stuck there in his head now. That little girl. His daughter not what he feared, not twisted up and sick.

At night, in the darkness, the thought of being alone starts to grieve him. The shorter November days. The empty house. With the darkness coming on, there's a dread he cannot explain. He cannot sit still. He walks fast through the community. Then back into his father's house. From the moving darkness into the brightness and stillness to check his father's room. The man just watching the ceiling, the walls around him. Whose face on his father. Whose body in that bed where Blackstrap lies down to rest.

That announcement from Crosbie. The news that did this to his father. Their failure to stop the man.

The thought of his children in his head. Failing them.

The thought of Patsy.

Agnes an impossibility that could choke him. He does not want to seem desperate, even though that's how he feels. The more he drinks, the more he feels. The smell of beer when he uncaps a bottle brings his father fully to mind. Lights on in all the rooms. The stillness of the furniture a torment to him.

Then he hears about Karen being found in St. John's. Where? And why? Something about a hospital, Mrs. Shears tells him. An accident. Run over by a car. Fell down over the stairs. Attacked by dogs. She has heard how Karen took up with the RCMP officer. The one who can't speak good English, from Quebec.

He remembers how he stopped visiting Tuffy in those last weeks. Would not watch the final ugliness taking hold. A monstrosity. A perversion. And when he died, he seemed to take Karen with him.

At least Patsy didn't hook up with another man, didn't put the children through that.

Patsy calls Blackstrap while he is thinking, fearing the early darkness, fearing the coming winter cold, seated at the kitchen table with his eyes on the black window. The receiver in his hand. Patsy mentions Christmas. The children. It would be good to be together, maybe. He doesn't say anything, but feels both relief and the quickening dread of certain mortality. A chance to gather his family together might rid him of that fear.

Two days later, he drives to Patsy's parents' house in Heart's Content with his father's pickup to start moving them. Just the basics. Clothes and toys. The TV. The rest can be collected later. The children are happy to see him. The comfort from them absolute.

Patsy tells Blackstrap she doesn't care much for the new house. He knows that she can tell it was a mistake with that St. John's woman living in it, decorating it. The smell of her in it. Patsy went in there once, her eyes going over everything, growing more vexed with every step, because that house had been meant for her. She left right away.

'Not having my children living in dat,' she told him. 'Widt da stink of dat uppity c'nt all t'roo da place.'

At night, sleeping in Blackstrap's bed, Patsy gets up to check on the children, even though she already did before turning in. Blackstrap wonders why she does this in the middle of the night. Her spot empty beside him. And he's gotten up, too, to go to the bathroom. His father's big bed in his parents' bedroom. Junior's small body lying in it. Ruth in her crib that Blackstrap set up in the corner between the dresser and the washstand.

Patsy watching Junior and Ruth sleeping. Her return to his father's house not fully right. Not natural. She stays clear of him in bed, her back toward him. Maybe there's a space between them that Karen fills up. They don't go near those unspoken words, waiting to gain distance from the way things were.

Blackstrap watches Patsy's neck, the hair that grows along there. Moving close, he slips his hand over her stomach and lets it rest in the hollow. He kisses the back of her neck, carefully rubs her belly. Patsy does not stir. He is struck by the thinness of her body, like what they once were has wasted away. His fingertips still accustomed to Karen's solid loving body.

Blackstrap rolls onto his back and stares at the ceiling, thinking of his father. The darkness he cannot see into. The funeral. Jacob's face. The white gloves on his hands that he sobbed into, right there in the front of the church, in front of everyone he ever knew. Sobbing into one of those soft white gloves.

He gets out of bed and moves into the kitchen. A vague heat from the woodstove still lingers. His father would often sleep on the daybed by the window, to keep the fire going at night, waking at all hours to put another log in.

Blackstrap finds himself staring at Jacob's daybed. He can almost hear the old man talking, yarning on about Uncle Ace and the sealing fleet. How his father was lost by that pirate of a captain, Abram Kane. The father he suspected was dead, but lived for years off the bounty from shipwrecks. Never returning when he could have returned. There were boats that might have brought him home. What prevented him? What made him want to lead another life? About Blackstrap's mother and what an angel she was. How her father was a big-time criminal from England who went loony. And how the wind had taken Emily, the wind and the cry of a cat, and about Isaac Tuttle and his lifelong attempt at romance. Da scoundrel. Jacob watching Blackstrap with uncertainty. Then laughing at the idea, laughing so hard he had to swipe the tears of pain from his eyes.

Blackstrap notices the pile of cut wood beside the stove. He sets aside the memories of his father, concentrating on the shadow of his backhoe through the window, a newer model bought from money left by Jacob. A bank account that the old man had in Bay Roberts where he deposited every one of his old-age pension cheques from the federal government. The bank manager had called to tell Blackstrap. The money sitting there for years. Not one withdrawal from the account. Blackstrap suspects that Jacob wouldn't touch a cent of it, but left it there for his son to take because times had changed. Money always from no good source.

The jobs set up for tomorrow. He will ask Junior if he wants to come along. Sunday. His father would never work on Sunday. Only church on the Lord's day. Even the wood would be chopped on Saturday. The bread baked. The vegetables peeled and cut for the cook-up. The laundry taken in off the line. Every chore completed. A day of rest.

How many years ago was that?

No rest now with the bills needing to be paid. Not enough money coming in from the backhoe alone. He should have kept some of his father's money and bought the backhoe on credit, but he doesn't trust credit, knowing it accounted for the death of many a man and many more to come. Nothing to do but hope for more work. He's heard of jobs that'll be there in the spring. A company harvesting water from icebergs. Work on a tugboat to hook or net the pieces of berg. The growlers that snap off and drift down in iceberg alley from the north. Twelve-thousand-year-old water to be sold to Saudi Arabia. An outfit from the mainland getting in the business. Making booze too. He'd heard from Paddy. 'The cleanest booze in the world' was the slogan. The idea of floating on water. Afraid again of sailing after the trip with the Portuguese. Too much attention coming from it. Too many people making you question your every move. Land is where he'd rather be. He touches the scar on his cheek and looks at the table with the pale yellow oilcloth. The chair where Karen used to sit, eating her muffins with dates and orange peels that she liked. The one thing she knew how to bake. Having a cup of Earl Grey tea, she would paw the strands of her black hair away from her lips. Her laugh and her naked body on the rumpled white sheets. In the new clean house beside his father's, the fresh carpet and smooth walls, Karen's peaceful smiling face, her shut eyes as he came into the room, with her knowing he was standing there, watching her, pretending to be asleep until he touched her and her eyes opening with that smile that never failed to weaken him.

The fresh, clean memory of things in that new house.

But it all went to shit.

There's a photograph he keeps of her in the bedroom dresser. Sometimes at night, he goes over to the new house and stares at it. Karen's underthings still in some of the drawers. He thinks he was not in love with her at all, but with who she looked like. Noticing now with that photograph in his hand. Caught by the image of his mother. In her company, if only for a few days or weeks, he would endure anything. His heart rotting inside him for the prospect of a life not possibly his.

*

756

(November, 1993) ,

'You gonna eat?' Blackstrap asks.

'I got no appetite.'

Ruth on Patsy's lap, reaching for the table, taking something, dropping it.

Blackstrap scoops up the last of his scrambled eggs, using his thumb to shift the pieces onto his fork. Eating, he glances at Junior who brashly pushes a spoonful of cereal into his mouth.

Mimicry.

'You make sure he's in sight all da time.'

Blackstrap looks at Patsy, but does not respond. He already understands about boys, having been one himself.

'Okay?' she says, like always. 'He's only six.'

'Almost seven,' Junior protests.

'A small job,' Blackstrap says. 'We won't be long at it.' He eats the last corner of toast, pushes his chair back from the table while still chewing. He wipes his mouth with the back of his hand. He knows this bothers Patsy. When he glances at her, he sees that he has succeeded, but she's half smiling and shakes her head.

'Nuisance,' she says. 'G'wan.'

He leans close to kiss her, but she turns her head, allowing him her cheek. He kisses Ruth, takes her small hand in his, her small warm fingers. 'Bye, beauty.' Straightening, he smiles for the smile that she gives back. Then turns for his lunch on the counter, his heavy boots sounding across the wooden flooring.

'Junior's not ready,' Patsy calls.

'I'm just getting things together, womb'n. Don't fret. Ya worries too much.'

She looks at her son who lifts the bowl to his mouth, to drink back the milk.

'Finish yer juice.' She nods toward his glass.

'Jus,' says Ruth.

'Where's the dozer?' Junior asks his father.

'Up on Cabin Road. No one touches it.'

Junior laughs under his breath. 'Not with Dad, right.'

Blackstrap likes the sound of that.

757

Dad.

'You be careful, ya hear.'

Junior stands from the table, leaving his bowl and glass there like his father.

Blackstrap at the counter, checking over the lunch in his tin. Extra food in there for Junior.

'I'll put yer dishes away, g'wan now.'

The boy waits a moment, then turns to face his father. Blackstrap notices him there at his side. The boy's eyes on the scars on Blackstrap's arms. His sleeves rolled up. 'Where'd you get them?'

'Nowhere.'

'Leave yer fadder alone now, Junior.' But she laughs so loud that Junior turns to look at her.

With Blackstrap's eyes now on Patsy, she says: 'I t'ought you'd be right proud ta tell 'im.'

The thought of Jacob's presence settles in the room. The empty daybed. Blackstrap's changing face because Patsy had been referring to Blackstrap's father. The willingness to always tell, to bend anyone's ear with a yarn.

Junior kisses Patsy goodbye and pokes Ruth before racing for the back door. Shoving it open with both hands, he's out before Blackstrap.

Watching him leave, Patsy's face goes sad. 'Blacky,' she whispers, looking at him, strange like.

Ruth begins crying from the poke that Junior gave her. Patsy distracted now. She gets up and goes into the other room to silence the cry.

Outside, Junior is in the pickup, bouncing on the passenger seat. There's a flat on that side that needs changing. Always something to bother a man, just like his father used to say. The truth to that stronger than ever, now that he's left to do every scrap of work himself. No one to ask advice from or complain to who would ever understand.

He calls to Junior to get out of the truck and come help.

The man from St. John's has a healthy tan. Dirty-blonde hair combed in a nice way. He's watched every move of Blackstrap's bulldozer. The man has even gone so far as to scramble up the hills of fresh clay and stare down. Not as big as he thinks he is, not realizing that those hills will all be moved again once the foundation hole is dug. Blackstrap has had to shut down the machine and climb out, tell the man to move for his own safety. The second time just sweeping his arm through the air without saying a word.

'What's he doing?' Junior asks, stood beside Blackstrap in the dozer.

'Fucked if I know,' Blackstrap snaps, not meaning to curse in front of the boy. But feeling it won't harm him. Just a word he'll hear soon enough, if not already.

The man becomes a major aggravation. People getting in his way. People telling him what to do, like they know better, like he'll make a mistake. How long you been doing this? he wants to ask the man. How long you been clearing land for a living?

When the job is done, the man wanders around the site with his hands on his hips. Then steps over to Blackstrap and the boy with a you-done-good wink and a big smile on his face.

'Not bad,' says the man. He searches Blackstrap's eyes, like he's trying to figure out something, maybe put a name on his face. He gets that a lot since being on the news.

Blackstrap nods and rolls a cigarette.

'You take a cheque?'

Blackstrap glances at the man's face. It's hard to tell if the man is sincere or not. Always hard to tell with that sort.

'You got cash?'

'No.' The man puffs out a laugh, suspiciously looks from the boy to Blackstrap. 'I don't carry cash around with me. Who uses cash anymore? Tons of plastic though.' He shows Blackstrap his wallet, all the different coloured cards, some of them flashing like metal in the sun. 'You take plastic?' He keeps the wallet open, holds the pose, his eyes a little wider than usual, like he already knows the answer.

'No.' He'd like to feed him plastic. 'You got no cash.'

'That's what I just said.' A smile like an asshole tightening.

'I guess I'll take a cheque then.' He wants to add, *So why bother asking?*

'I'll need a receipt, too. You have a receipt book?'

'Junior.' He looks down at the boy while he rolls the string of tobacco tighter in the thin paper.

'Yeah.'

'G'wan up in the backhoe and get the blue book outta the little box front of the seat.'

Junior smiles. 'Sure.' He races toward the machine parked out on the road.

Blackstrap strikes a match, puffs his cigarette to life, shakes out the match, cracks it in half between his thumb and middle finger and lets it drop.

The man keeps staring at him. 'I know you from somewhere.'

'Probaly recognize me from da movies.'

The man is confused, but still trying. 'Right.'

'Here,' Junior says, his breath straining. 'Fast, huh? You time me?'

'One second was all it took.' Blackstrap nods toward the man. 'Give it to him.'

The man takes the book reluctantly.

'Fill it in fer what you want and I'll sign 'er.'

The man studies Blackstrap, then lifts a pen from his top pocket. 'I'd prefer if it was in your handwriting.'

Blackstrap takes a long draw on his cigarette. 'You just fill it in. I'm sure you'll do a fine job of it. Educated man like yourself.'

The man keeps his eyes on Blackstrap, then starts to smirk. 'Oh, okay,' he says with an intake of breath. 'I get it.' He looks down at the boy, then back at the dozer. Snorting out a bit of amusement, he shifts his attention to Blackstrap's clay-covered boots.

'"Oh" what?' Blackstrap says, only the slight shifting of his shoulders, the straightening of his neck.

The man notices Blackstrap's arm, the row of deep scars, like notches on a wall counting time.

'Nothing. No problem.' The man fills out the receipt against the steel of the dozer and hands the book to Blackstrap to sign. Blackstrap takes the pen and leans, balancing the book on his knee and squinting the smoke away from his eyes. Slowly, he shapes his name with the wide loops and straight lines that his mother taught him.

The man is smiling when Blackstrap tears off the top copy. A smile that is better than any deed ever done.

Blackstrap hands the book to his son. 'Put it back now, Junior.'

'Sure.' The boy takes it and races off for the backhoe. 'Time me.'

'You got that cheque?'

'In the car.' The man tosses his thumb toward his Lincoln.

'Get it and be lucky I don't break yer fu'k'n neck.' His lips gone bloodless tight in an instant. 'Be lucky I let ya outta here with all yer teeth, ya fluffy-white townie.'

'What's your problem?' the man snickers. Right away, he sidesteps along the fresh clay, but his eyes go to Blackstrap, again and again.

Blackstrap watches the man move away, then bend into his car to write the cheque up. When Junior returns, Blackstrap places a hand on his son's head without glancing down, waiting for the shame-made hatred to clear from his eyes.

'What'n arsehole,' Junior says outright.

Blackstrap checks the boy who is looking up.

'He's just a townie,' he tells the boy. 'Awright?'

The boy nods, as if he's the one being chastised.

'He can't help it.'

The man comes toward them, the cheque ready in his hand. 'Here you go.'

Blackstrap sees the amount. The numbers more than what they agreed on. 'Is that okay, now?' The man nods, trying to make amends, but not really meaning it.

Blackstrap folds the cheque, pokes it into the top pocket of his flannel jacket, then spits off into the dirt he has shoved into a heap.

'That should help you get ahead,' says the man, a smile directed toward the boy before he turns and steps back to his car, humming a tune along the way. Climbing in, he toots his horn as he drives off. Nice guy in a big car.

Blackstrap holds himself still.

'Yyy yuh yuh yyer nnnot at much,' Wilf says to Blackstrap. 'T'day.' Wilf shuffles slightly to the side, his bushy beard tucked in close to the fabric of his plaid shirt, his head tilted on a permanent angle, cheek set against his shoulder. 'Haven't buh been in fffer a while.'

'No, b'y,' Blackstrap plainly responds, lifting a beer bottle to his mouth. He stares at Wilf's lame arm held in against his beer-gut stomach. He remembers the accident Wilf was involved in years ago, coming upon it on the highway. Blood all over Wilf, and the one in the passenger seat dead. Then he remembers the car that he himself had rolled, kicking open the door of the upside-down vehicle, falling out without a scratch. He wonders why the difference. Why Blackstrap walked away while Wilf didn't. Two wrecks with different outcomes. The thought sinks deep before he shifts his gaze to see the rack of cheezies on the other side of the makeshift bar he has leaned one elbow on. Behind Blackstrap, billiard balls crack. A boy named Gilbert plays a game of eight-ball with himself.

'Rrrrr . . . right on,' Wilf says, wiping the bar with the damp cloth, turning it over with his one good hand, rubbing the same space again.

Blackstrap watches Wilf, sees in his face and actions that he is wanting to tell Blackstrap something. The way Wilf peeks up at him. An expression in his sad eyes with wrinkled sacks under them, like Blackstrap can read his thoughts. They have known each other since they were boys. Wilf from Bareneed too. Forming a friendship when they both first arrived in Cutland Junction back in '62. Blackstrap wonders what news would be so bad for Wilf to hold back from him; it can only have something to do with Karen. More news of her in this place. It would be the only thing Wilf would be fearful to speak of.

Blackstrap stares the question into Wilf's eyes. Wilf blinks, shuffles to the side to toss the cloth toward the bare plywood ledge in the back. Shuffling face forward again, he sees that Blackstrap is still watching after him.

'Cuh cuh cccan't say,' Wilf mumbles, his head jerking against his shoulder with the sideways intentions of a nod. Blackstrap stares, wants to grab Wilf. Anger still taut in him from his confrontation with the man in the Lincoln. Junior brought home, back to Patsy. The ride in silence. Blackstrap not knowing what to say, to clear the air, to explain. Junior out of the pickup and gone into the house. Blackstrap just staring at the place where Junior had been sitting. He will make people answer him. The way people should answer anything that is asked, plainly. Staring through the anger, buzzing in his ears, Blackstrap barely hears the door open behind him. He glances over his shoulder to see past the pool table that occupies most of the room. Isaac Tuttle shuffles in from the daylight through the door, a cardboard carton in his arms. Back from the insane asylum.

Carefully moving toward the bar, he lays the carton there without looking at anything. Only straight ahead, like a blind man.

Wilf leans toward Tuttle, dragging his numb leg along, and nods.

The day Blackstrap went after Tuttle with his shotgun through the woods, the day they took the man away, months ago, something he wanted out of his mind. That life. A mistake. Karen. Tuttle gone. And back again, dragging the memory in with him.

Karen off with the mountie.

Tuttle's doing.

'Rrrr . . . right on,' Wilf says, then flicks his sad, nervous eyes toward Blackstrap.

'Kleezies,' Tuttle thickly says, his tongue seeming swollen. An accident, people have said, but unable to figure out the possibilities of hurting one's tongue so fiercely by accident.

'Cheezies' is what was said, Blackstrap suspects.

Isaac pokes his glasses up on his scarred knob of a nose. From another injury no one knows the cause of. 'Y'order'd, reet?' He writes up a bill from a book, tears it out, then recognizes Blackstrap for the first time. He shifts away, startled. 'I nayer,' he blurts out. 'Nayer.'

'Never what?' Blackstrap grumbles, taking another glug of his beer to finish it off.

'Nayer . . . Nayer.' Tuttle turns his seemingly misshapen head away, holding his hand forward, while Wilf, using his one good arm, counts the dollars out onto the bar.

Tuttle's fingers wait for the money despite what might come.

'Never did what?' Blackstrap asks, laying his bottle down, twisting his body to fully face Tuttle. Almost an old man now. Late sixties or older, but ageless. The invoice book has reminded him of the man from the city. A hole poked through by a trickle.

'Din't.' Money in hand, Tuttle shoves it into his pocket and hurries for the front door.

Blackstrap waits a moment, then – eyes on Wilf where Wilf is watching him – turns and strides across the room. He glares out the open door to see Isaac Tuttle pulling clear of the dirt drive in his small grey van. Faded red letters for Tuttle's wholesale company printed on the side.

The boy Gilbert comes up behind Blackstrap.

'He were say'n t'ings 'bout yer missus,' the boy professes. 'He were drunk here one night and he were saying all sort 'a ugly t'ings. Crazy religion stuff. Fuh'k'n Cat'lic.'

Blackstrap turns on the boy. A dangerous boy. Never to be believed. Never to be trusted. A fatherless boy. A mother who'd suck you off for a package of cigarettes.

Gilbert steps back, pool cue in hand.

A voice from the back of the room. Wilf now joining in. Someone having already started it, calling, 'I hhheard 'em say'n he hhh hhh ad sum of 'er. Took 'er. Pissed drunk were 'e ruhrrrrave'n.'

'Emlee,' says the boy, Gilbert, in mimicry, 'Emlee, dat's wha' he were saying.' The boy laughs. A buckled-up mouth full of brown teeth. Looks at Wilf. 'Emlee,' a childish taunting moan, then bucktoothed laughter.

His mother's name spoken like that.

'Duh-Dancin' 'round,' Wilf says. 'LL-luh-LLLike 'e were wwwwaltz-ing widt duh-da dead.'

It carries Blackstrap from the room in a rush. His wilful body hurling forward into the outside air, across the dirt and grass, the earth something he glides over, something that holds him up.

Climbing into his pickup, Blackstrap revs the engine, tears out of the drive, flinging dirt up in his wake. The sound in his head, *Emlee*. Memories of the shy Isaac Tuttle stood in their Bareneed kitchen when Blackstrap was a boy. The simple, quiet man who delivered coal and brought presents for his mother. Presents he'd seen her hide from his father. The betrayal he felt, even as a boy. Something not sitting right in his stomach. That retarded man. What would his mother want with that ugly, retarded man?

Blackstrap screeches out onto the pavement, races down the main road of Cutland Junction. It takes no time to find Tuttle's van pulled up in front of a convenience store. Blackstrap is out of the pickup before it seems to have stopped, speeding through the confusion. In through the shop's door. *Karen, Emily*. Tuttle in love with his mother right from day one. Everyone knew it. Joked about it. And now this. What he has done to Karen. How he drove her away. How did he change her? Everything after that destroyed. Everyone knowing what was done every time they looked at Blackstrap. The disgrace that Tuttle has brought upon the Hawco name.

Down an aisle, Blackstrap sights Tuttle through hot steady eyes, moves toward him, roughly grabs him by both shoulders, spins him around. Lips tight, eyes furious, Blackstrap pulls back his fist and strikes Tuttle full in the face with all the pain and hate of decades gathered in him. Tuttle's scarred knob of a nose hard against Blackstrap's fist. Not giving like a real nose. Clumped like a soft stone fitting into the spaces between his knuckles. Tuttle's glasses fly away, his naked eyes wide and seeing upward as he tilts back, striking a steel-edged shelf with the back of his neck. A crackling sound, like a small moist branch giving way. The sound that mutes everything in the store because it is uniquely internal. A sound from inside the body for all ears to hear. It is a final sound from the human catalogue of quiet disasters.

Blackstrap knows that it is only a matter of time before the RCMP arrive to knock on the front door. He sits in the old rocking chair in his father's bedroom and traces the rows of scars on the underside of his left arm. Junior had told him that the scars looked like claw marks from a man named Freddy, a man with steel blades for fingers. Junior has asked about them and Blackstrap has said nothing. One day he would tell him, when Junior is old enough to understand. Knowing that he might not be there for that time, Blackstrap calls out to Junior, waiting and watching the doorway until the boy appears, his expression expectant. Blackstrap tilts his head for the boy to enter.

'Close the door.' He stands from where he's been resting and nods toward the rocking chair. 'Sit down.'

Junior does as his father says. Then Blackstrap thinks about how he is stood there above his son looking down. He settles on the old pink bedspread, the mattress gone soft ages ago.

A strange position to be in. The smell of Blackstrap's mother still in the room. The sounds of his father. The smell of gasoline off Blackstrap. Chainsaw smoke in his clothes. He catches a whiff of it himself.

'This is yer grandfadder's room.'

'Yeah.'

'You 'member him?'

'A little.' He nods in a disappointed way.

'You knew 'm when you were jus' a baby. He thought the world of you.' Blackstrap recalls the day that Patsy left, pregnant and with Junior. And Jacob's silence for almost a month before he even said one word to Blackstrap. Blackstrap's fault to let his family go, to fall apart that way. A man's duty to keep it together. Nothing but selfishness otherwise.

Where was Jacob's family now? His duty?

How bitter would that make a man?

'You know yer great-uncle Ace were a sealer.'

'Yeah. You told me,' Junior says, his hands tucked between his knees, pushing them in deeper. 'That's cruel clubbing baby seals. I saw on TV. Blood everywhere.'

Blackstrap watches his son's face. 'It's no crueller den killing other things. You gotta eat, right? Or someone else has ta do it fer you. A butcher in a supermarket. Dat's easier for some people.'

Junior nods in agreement. He stares at his father's hard eyes. 'I'm gonna be a vegetarian when I grow up.'

Blackstrap snorts a small, futile laugh. 'Good fer you. But who's gonna strangulate all those vegetables fer yer supper?'

'They're not alive.'

'No? Well, yer grandfadder had an interesting conversation with a turnip once.'

Junior laughs, good and clean merriment of the young sort.

Blackstrap leans and reaches forward, touches the boy's head, his palm resting there in silence. Then he takes it away. He thinks of hugging the boy but does not know how Junior might respond.

'Yer Uncle Ace sailed on big ships up to da ice. He were a hero, just like me brudder, da one you were named after. He saved a man from when da roof collapsed down in da ore mines on Bell Isle. There were an explosion, too. Nut'n left of him but his fingers.' Blackstrap holds up his own fingers, a few of them nothing but stubs.

'Really?' Excited is how Junior's eyes look. 'That's gross.'

Blackstrap recalls what he has done to Isaac Tuttle. The man lying there on the shop's floor. Not breathing. Dead or maybe not. He'll find out soon enough. To harm a man in defence of a woman who was his.

Who means almost nothing to him now. He'll go to jail. The law made only to take things away from a person. He stares off, toward the dresser, the articles belonging to his mother, the perfume bottle with the little oval rubber ball he used to squeeze when he was younger, breathing in the perfume, squirting it at Ruth. She loved the smell of it. The smell would settle her right down, still her. She'd sit with her eyes closed, like something asleep, just feeling the smell. It reminds him of someone he saw on television, a woman sitting cross-legged on the floor, hands out and resting on her knees, meditating was what it was called. Black tassel with long silky threads hanging from the ball. His eyes skim over the porcelain-handled brush and comb set. The single photograph of their family together. His mother, his father, Junior, and young Blackstrap. Ruth not yet born. Junior not yet dead. That photograph taken by who? He does not remember exactly, but suspects it was Isaac Tuttle. He recalls hearing that Tuttle had a camera and used to photograph people and their houses. He thinks of the shotgun out in the shed, of going to get it and shooting whoever it is that will come for him. The gun turned on himself. But he steadies his thoughts. No use for confusion in a situation like this. No use for further complications. Nothing the boy needs to see. What would he learn from that?

When Blackstrap looks at his son again, he sees Junior's curious eyes on his scarred arm. Blackstrap has rolled up the sleeve of his green and grey plaid shirt so he can tell the story. Only now with Junior's eyes on the scars has he remembered why the boy was called here.

'You wanted ta know 'bout these scars.'

Junior nods. 'Yeah.'

Blackstrap thinks of the boat, the blinding January storm that hurled itself in front of him, grey sweeping in from all directions at once. Viciousness with him in the centre. The growl of the white wind. And then him nothing but a part of the blinding gale. Trapped in an open boat for over twenty-four hours as the snow piled up, covered him. No matter how much he moved. Snow trying to bury him. And the rocking of the boat in the swells. The engine puttering and finally choking off. Lost. Taking his hunting knife from the box and slicing lines into his arm to frighten his body, to keep it awake. Alive. Rubbing that warm blood in his eyes to melt the ice, to see, on his lips to barely feel. Even

767

drinking a little to keep up his strength. His own blood feeding him, sticky in his mouth and throat, warming his innards. Until another boat sent out to find him did just that, the men aboard suspecting he was involved in some sort of slaughter. What would Junior think of such a story?

It all seems so vivid to Blackstrap. Sitting in his father's room with those memories in his head. His own blood on his face, on his hands. But how would Junior see it? It is not what Junior expects. Blackstrap has seen flashes of the video movies that Junior watches. Filled with action, guns, screams, car chases, explosions, monsters blown apart, blood and gore. His story is not the one the boy wants to hear. It is a slow, careful story about the world trying to claim him, spoken of in a calmed voice. A trapped story that cannot be respectfully released. Not with his tongue. Not with his words.

His fingertip runs back and forth along one scar then moves to the next. He thinks about the words before he says them, wondering how they will sound: I believe I just killed a man, Junior. But they are garbled in his mouth.

Blackstrap searches the boy's face.

Junior stares down at the scars, squinting as if they might somehow be responsible for what he is about to be told. 'What about those?' he asks.

'Cut meself shaving.' Blackstrap gives a weak smile and a chuckle that makes him feel like a boy himself.

Junior laughs, uncertain tears of sadness and joy bubbling up in his eyes. He knows. 'No, you didn't.' He stands and slaps at his father's arm, sits on the bed beside him, looking up. 'It was an animal you fought.'

In realization, Blackstrap can't help but stare at his son. Something centuries old almost there in the boy's eyes.

Who are you?

Junior's eyes still trained on his father's arm.

Blackstrap undoes the top two buttons on his shirt and slides the material over, showing the two round clumps of scars beneath his shoulder.

'Wow! Were you shot?!'

I don't know, Blackstrap thinks. But this is the scar he has chosen to explain. Not the ones on his arms and not the one on his cheek. Perhaps his last words as a free man.

'I was driving a transport truck, carting salmon from the Northern Peninsula caught up on da Labrador. Run it into the plant down in Cupids.' Blackstrap watches openly into his son's face. He sighs and shifts a little nearer. Not true, he thinks. That was another time. He was coming from Cupids, on his way to the Northern Peninsula. A load of codfish. His pause confuses him. Wasn't it? he wonders. Or was he shot that time? Where was that? In Halifax? Or out at sea with the Portugee?

He is drowning. Finally, that's how he feels. Finally drowning now.

'Were you hijacked?'

'Hijacked?'

'Yeah.'

'No.'

'Who shot you then?'

'I was driving through Wreckhouse.'

'Where's that?'

'West coast. Winds run up to a hundred miles an hour. Used to toss trains from da track. Back when we had trains.'

'We had trains?'

A tiredness plummets over Blackstrap. A weighty exhaustion accumulating in his bones that might be akin to death itself. He wants to shut his eyes, lie back on the bed, and give up. In his mind, the length of train rolling through Cutland Junction. The steel-heavy rumbling in his chest as the cars surged out of the station. The pennies they used to put on the rail lines. *Flatter den piss on a plate.*

'Trains,' Blackstrap mutters, lost to the memory, carried off by a locomotive through the cut of the wilderness.

'What happened? ' Junior asks.

'What?'

'With Wreckhouse.'

He makes a low sound of uncertainty, drawing the thoughts back through a length of endless highway. 'Was foggy,' he quietly begins, 'and the wind was shoving me t'ward the side of the road . . . I had ta keep the wheel turned a bit into the wind just ta keep straight. It was dark and I had ta get this salmon home. The workers were waiting in the plant and . . .' Blackstrap's voice trails off. He is trying to keep his mind away from the death. The woman and the crippled little girl. It is a curse put on him. The man in the hospital parking lot. In Agnes' house. Agnes' eyes burning into him then and now. The years have given bits of it back to him. Images he did not want. Maybe partly dreams. Maybe not.

So much of life only.

'What happened then?' Junior says.

'I was taken by trying ta keep the truck on the road. I was barrelling ahead through the fog, the thick grey all I could see, roaring along, I t'ought of slowing for some reason, don't know why. I just had this feeling . . .' He searches his son's face as though wondering if the feeling he speaks of might be found in the boy. 'You never know go'n through da fog like that. It's always something, anything any second right in front of ya. And there it was.' His lips pressed tightly together. His nostrils flaring.

'What?'

'Just a brown bulk that hit the truck and spun in the air and all I knew next was the crashing of the windshield . . . and the antlers busting in . . . two points ramming right through there.' Blackstrap places two spread fingers on the scars.

Junior's eyes shift to the scars. 'Really!'

Two holes. Shot twice. The explosions ricocheting out over the city streets, through the wilderness, across the ocean and icefields.

'Da moose pinned me ta the seat and the wheels went over onto the soft side of the road 'n the machine tilted 'n the wind did the rest, lifting the truck and setting it atop a bunch of spruce, everything was still . . .' His voice goes lower, like the wind hushing. With lips parted and eyes shifting to the window, he listens for something. A whistle far off, a light through the woods. Steel wheels over steel lines. The shriek of a train waking him. 'I 'member blinking 'n my eyelashes could feel anudder antler point an inch from my right eye, trying ta focus.' Blackstrap breaks off from the memory to check Junior. The stunned, silent interest. 'Except for da sound of da moose's breath, its big glassy eyes looking at me up close while it snorted through its nose 'n moaned a painful sound, its head the size of all of me from da waist up, I just sat there, pinned to the seat, watching in pain, hoping he wouldn't kick or move anymore 'n drive the rest of the points inta me. He was as worse as me, dat moose.'

'Jeez. What happened?'

'He were in pain, so I stretched me fingers to reach the buck knife I kept under the seat of da truck, I lifted it up,' Blackstrap purposefully, exactly raises his right hand, 'and I stuck it inta the moose's throat.' A thrust with gritted teeth.

Junior flinches back.

Blackstrap yanks at the air. 'I tugged and tugged, cutting it across dere.'

'It wasn't dead?'

'No.'

'You had to kill it?'

'Yes. Because he were in pain, Junior, and it's best fer da moose ta be dead.' Blackstrap taps the two round clumps. 'Busted up inside like dat.' Old scars without feeling. 'These two was through the shoulder, nothing damaged, a little lower I would've been a goner, through da heart.'

'How'd you get out?'

'Rescued. They had ta saw off the antlers that were stuck through me and get da moose outta there with a crane.' Partly memory, partly what he was later told, partly invention.

Junior shakes his head in bright disbelief. 'Did it hurt?'

Blackstrap smirks, musses up his son's hair. 'Nawww. It never hurt, Junior. Stuff like that doesn't hurt. It's only da things that happen ta other people that hurts ya most. Never stuff that happens ta your own self.'

'I don't know. I bet it hurt.'

Blackstrap licks his lips, his gaze toward the window with a view of the trees. Hovering above the entire story. The crippled little girl. The dead mother. The angry father. Fighting what? He will not speak their damage into existence. Agnes always knowing this might happen, afraid of him. Away from him because of the danger he would cause. All those years ago, gone from Cutland Junction because he was part of a life not hers.

Isn't that the way it was? A life not hers. A life not his.

'Have you ever seen a ghost, Junior?'

'No. Have you?' The boy moves back to the rocking chair, rocking a little.

Blackstrap stands from the bed, facing his son, then puts his hands a little ways out by his side. To raise them any higher would make him feel foolish. 'Take a good look.'

'You're no ghost.'

'You know, they used ta be everywhere, but they jus' don't come 'round anymore. I saw the ghost of my little sister for years after she died, my brudder, too, Junior's ghost. Where're they now?'

'I don't wanna see a ghost.' Fear in the boy's face. His body tightening up to let nothing in. He wipes at his nose, hunched in that rocking chair, the armrests worn by his grandfather's hands.

Blackstrap watching into the silence, listening beyond the walls, and into the forest, until something comes to him: 'Maybe you're one too.'

Junior gives his head a nudge of a shake. 'I'm not,' he says. 'Definitely not.'

'Don't ever be 'fraid of ghosts, Junior. It's not like in da movies. Spirits used ta be welcomed everywhere. They did not a bit of harm. If you were scared, then that wouldn't make me feel too welcome when I came 'round ta say hello.'

Blackstrap has drawn the curtains in the spare room and stands in the late afternoon dimness, studying the fabric, not knowing if he's trying to see out. Dazed, he steps away and sits back against the low wooden dresser. Light edges in and he watches the door open up. Patsy staring ahead at the bed, then searching the room. She reaches for the light switch, flicks it on, but it does not work.

'Blacky?' she asks with Blackstrap's shadowed form off to the right. 'Where ya to?'

'The bulb's gone. Shut the door.'

Patsy glances up. The bulb gone. The shade also. She steps in and pulls the door closed.

'Wha' ya do'n in da dark?' She steps toward the curtains to open them.

'Leave 'em.' He moves for her, roughly taking hold of her arms, squeezing tightly and staring into her face. A woman in his hands.

Patsy makes a sound of displeasure. 'Let go 'a me.'

Blackstrap throws her back onto the bed where she bounces and settles, her elbows into the mattress, already half risen, her face ready for him, to take anything and give back worse.

'Don't ya dare,' her voice quivering. 'I'm not fond 'nough of ya ta have ya in me.'

The savage need to bust out of himself, to punish someone for what he never meant to do. He kneels to either side of her and tears open her blouse, popping the buttons while she slaps a hand against him.

Her nails in his chest. Her neck going tight.

His hands shoved beneath her bra.

Her breasts smaller than he remembers. Practically not even there. Her ribs aching out from her skin. The stretch marks along her belly, the only loose skin remaining.

He squeezes her breasts to make something of them.

Her nails digging deeper in his chest.

He quickly stands away from the pain, then leans forward right away and yanks down her elastic-waist pants. Her hips protruding like the contours of a skull, her cunt lips thicker, fleshier.

Stood there, thinking of unbuckling his belt, he watches his wife's mean eyes. He kneels there on the bed again and holds the sides of her head. He watches her face flinch, the burst of his tear against her chapped lips. Her eyes open, seeing him above her.

He leans closer to kiss. The fluid of his tears moistening her lips, making the kiss easy, warm and salty.

Patsy's eyes fully open, her lips not kissing back. But no fingernails in him now.

He drops his weight onto her. Holds on. Holding and squeezing and kissing the side of her neck. Holding on for dear life.

A shivering whisper from her: 'Wha's da matter, Blacky?' Knowing nothing like this of him through their years.

She reaches down to tug up her pants. 'Junior might come in,' she says, a heart-sick warning.

Blackstrap takes hold of her hips, rolls her over on top of him. Light as a feather. He stares up at her face. Not even bothering to wipe the wetness from his eyes and cheeks. The tears that have pooled in the scar on his cheek.

'Wha's da matter?' she asks again, her body beginning to tremble from the fright. Tears in her own eyes now.

Husband and wife.

'Wha', Blacky?'

But nothing. Not a word worth the breath of it.

The bedroom door open a crack and Junior watching through the slit.

Ten minutes later the RCMP car pulls into the paved driveway. From his father's front window, Blackstrap watches the two policemen step out of their cruiser. The sound of two car doors closing. They walk up the concrete steps that lead to Karen's bungalow. He recognizes one of the men from months ago when Karen went missing. The man from Quebec who came asking questions. The man who had found her. And kept her for himself.

Blackstrap turns away from the window, looks at Patsy sitting on the old grey couch. Her worried eyes fixed on him. Ruth right there on a blanket sleeping. Junior out in the back yard. As long as he stays there and does not see. But then he is mortally discouraged when Junior comes out from alongside the house, wandering near the sleek car that means danger.

'Call Junior in here and put'm in the room,' Blackstrap says sharply.

'Wha' fer?' Immediately, Patsy stands to look out the window.

Stepping toward Ruth, Blackstrap picks up his daughter and holds her sleeping body against his shoulder. His free hand straightens the material on the back of her pink and white top. He begins making shushing sounds, until Ruth wakes and looks at him, laughs sleepily and shoves two fingers into her mouth. Sucking and staring at him.

'Da!' Her small fingers on his face.

The knock on the front door.

Ruth laughing and making a sound with her mouth shaped like a surprised O.

Patsy at the window.

Blackstrap's eyes on Patsy, not knowing what to do. Either one of them. Run, thinks Blackstrap.

The knock louder. The door opening. Junior calling out.

'Cops're here.' The boy moving down the hallway to stand by his father's side.

Ruth in Blackstrap's arms, her perfect eyes and lips. Junior at his side. He faces the two RCMP officers.

Patsy steps up behind.

Checking over his shoulder, Blackstrap then turns and hands his daughter to his wife, carefully allowing the transfer. One look at the sweet, little face. The loss of that enough to mangle him.

Patsy not fully understanding.

'Is all,' he says. Nodding, he steps toward the men, thinking of something to pass on to Junior. Something for his son. And for Patsy. So they will not believe him to be a horrible man. But he cannot think in the midst of such shame. Cannot look at the faces behind him. Not in his memory. Not to live with them for years. Wishing his life away. That's what he has done. A life not his. Not ever his, but he in it. Not knowing any better. He walks with deliberateness, past the officers and out into the front yard, so that one of the officers makes a noise like a protest.

The woods across the dirt road. The way the light is filtered through the branches. The way it touches the evergreen boughs. He has not been seeing this, but now it comes at him in full force.

'Are you Alphonsus Hawco?' the policeman from Quebec asks, stepping up beside him.

Blackstrap thinks of saying 'That's not my name' but, instead, says nothing. With his back to them, he lets them put the handcuffs on as Patsy bursts into tears. The sound that will not draw his attention. Ruth in her arms who starts crying now too. Screeching 'Da-da' as Blackstrap is led toward the RCMP car.

No one coming near him, then the sound of rushing in his direction. His family. Patsy with Ruth in her arms. Junior. The sounds of them following after him, drawn like magnets. Footsteps over grass and the beachrock path.

He will not look.

An order from the man from Quebec: 'No, please. You go no closer now.'

*

Flat on his bed, Blackstrap sleeps the hours away. Not a muscle in his body knows how to move with the new weight upon him. He has been given a private cell for the time being. The long-haired lawyer from the government comes to see him. Blackstrap could not afford his own. The lawyer wonders what he thinks of the private cell. The lawyer says: 'It's because you're a Newfoundland hero.' A cell to himself despite the overcrowding. For now, the superintendent agrees to the luxury. 'We'll see how it goes,' the superintendent tells Blackstrap.

The trial in two weeks.

Not premeditated, says the lawyer, although there are men from Wilf's New Place, ones who might say different. Blackstrap remembers the conversations, plays them in his head, unable to change the words or sequence of events.

How to live in here without sleeping, his eyes on the seams in the cinder blocks?

The other men watch him to know who he is.

He stares.

He vanishes.

He comes back.

Not a morsel in his mouth.

A cave that he sails into.

A crack in a rock the shape of him.

In the courtroom, Blackstrap's lawyer talks death: the recent death of his client's father, the death of his friend, the accident in Wreckhouse, medical reports, injuries to the head, the hoof of a moose, and the disappearance of his common-law wife, Karen. Mental strain. Post-traumatic stress disorder. The sole survivor of the *Ocean Ranger*. Blackstrap Hawco. A man who struggled to save another man while he, in great peril himself, was being pulled toward the safety of the supply boat, risking his own salvation, jeopardizing his own survival for the life of another man, a man who slips from his grip, from his frozen fingers.

How true is any of it? To hear it spoken aloud sickens him.

Blackstrap Hawco. A man who stood up to foreign fishing in this province, in Newfoundland where the people have been downtrodden for centuries, where the island's riches have been stolen or given away for a pittance.

This man sitting here before you, a hero in countless people's eyes.

Blackstrap Hawco.

Stupidity, he thinks. All of it pure stupidity.

The courtroom is nothing like he expected, nothing fancy, a room that smells of bodies, old paper and wood. The people gathered there to watch. They sit in the pews mostly dressed in plain clothes. Some of them not even in suits. A room full of people having nothing to do with him, like they just came in off the street. Common people out for entertainment. He imagines them eating popcorn from a bag. And remembers what the lawyer said days ago. 'It would've been better if you weren't a hero. Once upon a time that would've worked to your benefit, got you off with anything. I'm not too sure about now. About today. They like to see the hero cut down to size. The media lives for that sort of thing. But it's worth a shot . . . Our only hope.'

Our only hope. Fucked.

The faces in the seats studying him. A creature on display. No longer one of them.

Blackstrap has no idea what any of this has to do with the accident or the death of Isaac Tuttle. He wonders about the funeral. Who might have attended. He does not care for the way this system works. How they must know everything about a man, but learn absolutely nothing of the cause of things. How they will judge him on what is said. He stares at the judge. The way the man is sizing him up. A life of condemning other men. His seat up higher than everyone else. Everyone told to rise when he comes and goes. Lord over everything. Bullshit perched above bullshit. A man who goes home in a car, eats dinner, goes to sleep. And that man sleeping while other men hate him because he has judged them and been paid to do it.

Blackstrap's lawyer touches his shoulder, squeezes gently to silence him. What was he doing? Making a noise? The lawyer had wanted to call Karen as a witness, after hearing rumours from people in Cutland Junction. How it was said that she had been raped by Isaac Tuttle.

Blackstrap will hear nothing of it.

'No,' Blackstrap said. 'That'd be no good.'

'For who?'

'Her.'

The lawyer then glanced at a copy of Blackstrap's statement, a full confession.

'You're illiterate, right?'

Blackstrap gave no answer.

'I don't know if that can work for or against us.'

Blackstrap's thoughts on Karen. None of his business now. His thoughts on Agnes. He looks over his shoulder for a face that might be hers. Eyes on him as he scans the crowd to find no one he knows.

The judge keeps watching him while listening to a witness, a middle-aged woman who saw the entire episode. A woman from a cabin, not from out his way. A townie capable of explaining exactly what went on. The judge thinking and staring at Blackstrap who stares back. Face giving nothing away. Which one of them knows more about the other. The judge does not like the look. What a man is made of. Blackstrap will not show him.

After the preliminary hearing, Blackstrap is taken to a room where he sits in private with his lawyer. His lawyer tells him it would be best to opt for trial by jury.

Blackstrap nods, his hands joined on the tabletop.

'You have to help me here, Mr. Hawco. You're not helping me at all. We have to introduce the fact that Karen Hawco might've been raped by Isaac Tuttle. Even if it's thrown out.'

'No.' Blackstrap slams the table with both palms, catching the attention of the guard. Loudly: 'No one needs ta know it, ya hear me.'

'Yes, people do need to know. Yes, they do, for your sake. It might be the truth, after all.' The lawyer smiles kindly, then sighs when he sees the smile carries no weight, shaking his head as he sets the papers one by one back into his case. He glances at Blackstrap as he closes the top and clicks the latches shut. 'Do you understand the gravity of the situation?'

Blackstrap looks away, pressing his lips together, his breath raspy from his nostrils. 'I'm from a family,' he says, not really knowing what that has to do with anything.

'We're all from families,' the lawyer says, standing. 'All of us. That's how it works.'

Blackstrap gazes at the lawyer.

'I've got a family,' the lawyer says, setting his fingertips against his tie.

'A family dat looks after its own.'

'My family looked after me.'

'And where're they from?' Blackstrap asks.

'West coast.'

'Corner Brook?'

'Pulp and paper people.'

'Not anymore,' Blackstrap says, sizing up the lawyer's suit. 'They're legal people now.'

'That's called change, Mr. Hawco. People change. Just because my father worked in a mill, doesn't mean I want to work there. That's nonsense. I wanted to be a lawyer.'

'Good fer you. Ya got yer wish.'

'And how exactly are you looking after your family, if you're locked away? Answer me that.'

Blackstrap stands from the table, leaning near the lawyer. One face inches away from another.

'Okay, boys,' says the guard. 'Recess time is over.'

Blackstrap is sentenced to ten years. His lawyer is disappointed. It might have been much less, if only they could have put Karen on the stand.

Bygones be bygones.

Blackstrap understood little of what was being said. The language used. The lawyers asking questions that seemed to have no true purpose, leading up to what? No answer. He couldn't get the gist of it. People inspecting him, then studying other people. Who worth what? Who to believe? He'd lower his eyes. He'd look away. The courtroom crowded. Standing room only. All sorts of people interested in what was going on, sitting there and watching. That's what they seemed to do, just there to watch and listen. Didn't they have lives to attend to?

'I did the best I could, really. Considering.'

Ten years in a cage for killing a man who raped his woman.

The judge had stood from his bench. No expression on his face. They all had to stand and keep silent until the man left the room.

The old man must be rolling over in his grave, Blackstrap's only thought.

'Less than ten years,' explains the lawyer. 'Out in three. And, of course, we'll be filing for an appeal.'

The pale-green space of the prison cell. Every muscle in Blackstrap's body useless to know what it once did.

Sitting at the foot of his narrow bed, he rubs his knuckles, two of them busted and scabbed over from the sharp and blunt edges of bone and teeth, from when he was bent over the Indian. Beating in the Indian's face. The man in his cell had been from Winnipeg, Manitoba, a big man with nothing to do to get Blackstrap off of him.

Blackstrap didn't want a bandage.

He wipes at his mouth, thinking too much and too hard now. Nothing but thought in here, with action trapped outside the walls.

In the quiet space of the cell. And in memory that takes up more space in a man in a cell, more space than in a room at home or the entire house, community and woods:

The Indian had watched him. Asked where he was from.

After a while, Blackstrap said, 'Bareneed.'

'A name like that. People there have a sense of humour.' The Indian stood staring out the cell bars. Lockdown after dinner. Lockdown on the unit. Food in the body making every man uneasy. 'That's in Newfoundland, right?' The Indian turned to look at Blackstrap where he was sat on the lower bunk.

'Yeah, here.'

'Like Indian names, these place around here.' Facing a view of the high windows across the narrow walkway, the man could see nothing but sky. 'You don't have First Nations. Not many.'

'We do now.'

The Indian glanced back at him and kept watching. 'You killed someone. I killed someone, too. Big deal, okay.'

Blackstrap said nothing to this and ignored the staring man's brown eyes.

'A white man. He was saying things about Indians. What everyone thinks. "First Nations" is what we're called now. Used to be "Natives." They keep changing our name to make us better. They say we change it, but I don't know. A conference where they pick a name. Who invented a conference? Not here in Newfoundland though. Right? The people here before killed the last Indian. When they were still called Indians.'

'Beothuks,' said Blackstrap. One too many men in this cell, he was thinking. Small enough for one man, not for two. If he had been left alone. If his body didn't want out.

The Indian was looking at Blackstrap's bare arm. The tattoo there of Karen, and the one beneath it, the island of Newfoundland.

'Newfoundland,' said the Indian so that Blackstrap shifted his eyes to him. 'I read a lot about Newfoundland. They ship me here. A prison on an island. Middle of nowhere with Newfoundlanders. What I know, they're all ignorant, like every white man. If he's a man. Women are different. Never so ignorant as men.'

Blackstrap tried harder to ignore the Indian.

'No different from other white men. Every fish scooped up . . . You got an interesting history of wiping things out, Mister Newfie.'

Scratching the back of his neck, Blackstrap's eyes fixed on the concrete floor, head growing heavier, wishing the words would just stop digging into him.

'Blaming foreign fishing vessels.' The Indian made a sound then turned to stare back through the bars. Across the corridor, a view of bright clouds now. 'They'd still be gutting the ocean, if the government didn't shut the fishery down. Even this food fishery they give you. I read in the paper about how Newfies got caught conning the government. Tags for food fishery. The ones they're supposed to put through the gills when they catch a cod. Only so many fish allowed for food. But Newfies putting the tags in a microwave to loosen them. So they can use them again. Put the tags through the fish gills but don't click them, like they're supposed to, only if a fisheries officer comes. No sense of letting nature put things back. It's only themselves they're destroying, their way of life. Maybe because of your history. Trained by the merchants to get everything out of the water. Desperate Newfies, trying to steal enough to eat. Still desperate. Slaves still trying to please the man with money, only you've become the merchant now with all your expensive toys. Learned that greed pretty good, huh? Like any dog with a trick.'

Blackstrap rubbed his hands together. The Indian's words were making his shoulders ache, making his stomach burn. But there was no way of not hearing. He would not put his hands over his ears.

'Hook every fish. So you can get another car, another snowmobile, another satellite TV. It's not about just eating anymore. Everyone's looked after in Canada, except the Indian. The ghetto dweller. The Royal Canadian Nigger.'

Blackstrap shifted on his bunk, but the Indian didn't look. He didn't care enough.

'I read about that in a history book, right here in the library. Used by the merchant and, so, now, forever and ever more they should be handed a living to make up for it. It's a bunch of bullshit, NewfieMan. Just a lazy bunch of good-for-nothings is what you are.'

Blackstrap stood. The distance between them not enough.

Still, the Indian did not bother turning. 'Just one more white breed dug itself into a hole. And blame everyone else for your own greed and ignorance. Beaten dogs, cute with big, sad eyes, but they're still beaten dogs, NewfieMan.'

Three prison guards were needed to pull Blackstrap off the man and hold him away. Then the silent Indian, bent on his side on the floor, was lifted from the cell.

No longer three years in here. More time added on. Anyone's guess what it might be. The Indian unwell forever now.

His eyes flit to the steel toilet in the cell. He leans forward, joins his hands into one fist dangling between his knees. He languidly scans the concrete floor toward the corner where the drain covering is set slightly lower. He looks toward the height of steel bars that he had lifted into place with the other men, workers paid to do a decent day's work.

Sighing, he scans the muffled room.

Slow footsteps outside.

The creaking of a bunk.

A page being turned.

A rush of not knowing. Not knowing anything. A rush of unsteadiness that means to send him drifting.

He breaks out in a sweat and thinks of his father moving through him to get in or out.

A federal institution in Cutland Junction.

The memory of a photograph he has seen of Uncle Ace makes his palms sweaty. The picture clipped from an old newspaper. Uncle Ace on the wharf in St. John's after the sealing disaster.

That look on his face.

He is that man.

The disaster of this.

Sounds beyond him travel through the expansiveness of the outer chamber. He will float through the top of his own head. If he shuts his eyes he will disappear. He thinks of hockey sticks slapping ice. Boys shouting and chasing each other on skates. The sound down a corridor. Black Duck Pond when he was a boy. Barrel staves taped around his boots. The harsh echoing sound of a cell door clanging shut.

Years to be lived in this room.

The fear again. The deathly fear without death.

A harsh clanging to his side as another door closes.

In sad or angry waiting.

Isaac Tuttle dead. And Blackstrap Hawco not sorry.

Except for this.

Never will he regret the doing, nor strike out again, *so why the fucking cage?*

Blackstrap is directed to an office. The orange-haired man who sits behind the desk is short and plump, his skin pink along his cheeks and across his forehead, his face seemingly scrubbed shiny clean.

'Good morning,' says the counsellor, his eyebrows raised.

'Morning.'

The counsellor motions toward Blackstrap with pudgy fingers. 'Please, sit down.'

Blackstrap remains standing. He wishes the counsellor would clear his throat.

The counsellor leans back in his chair and folds his arms high across his chest. 'Nice to see you.' The counsellor smiles, pokes his big glasses higher on his nose, refolds his arms.

Blackstrap almost shrugs. He doesn't understand the man.

'Well, you know, we're hoping you're up for a challenge. A man like Blackstrap Hawco enjoys a challenge, I bet.' The counsellor nods, but it seems more of a nervous habit than anything. He reaches for a cup on his desk. Then, with his arms folded, he sips from the cup. To Blackstrap's mind, it's a strange way of doing things. He sips again, eyeing Blackstrap. 'You're wondering what sort of challenge, right?' The counsellor hasn't given his name yet, his name supposedly known.

'Cough, will ya,' Blackstrap says.

'I'm sorry, what?'

Blackstrap makes the noise, clearing his own throat as an example.

'Oh.' The counsellor follows Blackstrap's example. 'Sorry, I've got a cold. What was I saying?'

'Challenge.'

'Yes, it's the challenge of literacy, Mr. Hawco. What we're wondering . . .' The counsellor holds up his arms and slowly moves his hands through the air, like he's shaping a sun. '. . . is whether you'd be willing to join us for our literacy program meetings. The program is taught by normal, everyday people. People just like yourself.' The counsellor pulls his hands back and holds them against his chest.

'Just like me,' Blackstrap says, eyeing the empty chair in front of the desk.

'Yes. Yes, that's absolutely right.'

'Prisoners?'

'No.' The plump counsellor straightens, his hands joined reasonably on the desk. He gives a fat-lipped smile and bobs his head a little.

Blackstrap thinks the counsellor might be on some sort of drugs. 'Then not like me.' He sits in the chair, his back hurting from standing there, shoots of pain stretching in his legs. No way of getting any relief, even with the pills that only mess up his stomach.

'Good point.' The counsellor chuckles, refolds his arms. 'A valid observation.'

Blackstrap watches the man. What sort of life out there? He sees the man with a floppy hat on his head, riding a bicycle, living with a little dog that wears a sweater or has bows in its ratty fur. 'I'm not interested.'

'You don't *want* to make yourself a better person?' The counsellor leaning forward, almost shocked.

Blackstrap looks away toward the window. A nice view. The back of the prison where the land slopes off. A pond there. Apartments and houses surrounding the pond where boats row and race over the still surface. Across from his cell, there are only windows up high, the sky the only view. Blue or grey. A bird is an occasion.

'You don't think people who read and write live fuller lives?' The counsellor's eyes go large behind his glasses. 'Mr. Hawco. Mr. Hawco, please.' He leans sideways, tilting to get a serious look at Blackstrap's face. 'Don't you think that being able to read and write opens up all sorts of doors to a person?'

'Sure,' he says, eyes on the lake. He has to keep checking the counsellor though, because he doesn't know what the man might do. Maybe even spring from his chair and start flapping his arms.

'Wouldn't you like to be able to read to your children? You have children, right?' The counsellor glances down at Blackstrap's open file, then looks up to see Blackstrap staring directly at him. 'Your . . . children . . .' the counsellor stammers. 'Rrruth ahnd . . .'

'Shut yer fuh'k'n face,' Blackstrap says, his eyes clear, steady and cool blue, his tanned, wind-worn face covered with blondish-white stubble, his lips tight.

'That's unnecessary, don't you think?' The counsellor jabs his glasses up on his nose, waits, like he's wondering what might be the next step. 'Really.'

'What?'

'Hostility . . . Literacy might help you get your children back,' the counsellor suggests, quickly regaining his calmness. 'When you're released. Articulation. The courts might look favourably on your efforts. If you went into the courtroom and spoke eloquently of your desire to reclaim your children.'

'Why's that?'

'They want change. Show them change.'

'Where's the need to learn anything I don't already know?'

'So you'll be able to better apply yourself.' The counsellor holds out an arm and indicates toward the window.

'Apply myself to what?' His voice a little louder, only now realizing.

'To . . . tasks. So you'll better deal with situations that arise. So you'll learn to use *words* instead of *actions*, so you won't be so frustrated, so aggressive. Like now, for instance. A perfect example.' The counsellor holds out his hand, tilts his palms up. Nods twice. Blackstrap the living proof.

Someone always preaching. 'Right.'

'Reading takes you places, lets you see things you wouldn't otherwise. It's wonderful. You'd be amazed. Truly.'

'See things.' He checks around the office. 'Like what?'

'Well, for example, I'm reading a brilliant novel about India now. It's a prize-winner. Absolutely rife with atmosphere. *You* could read about India.'

'India? What the fuh'k would I want ta read 'bout India for?'

'It's a foreign place. Different customs and traditions. It's fascinating. Foreign places are interesting.'

'I'm in the most foreign place there ever could be. It's not interesting.'

'To expand your horizons then.' The counsellor slaps a palm onto the desk, whacking Blackstrap's file. 'How about that?' He folds his arms and nods. Blinking now, too, more than usual.

'What?'

'To learn more.'

'I don't care about learning. I never did. I only want to . . .'

'Yes . . . to what?' The counsellor leans across the desk, like things might finally be going his way. The prisoner about to share.

'. . . endure.'

'Endure?'

'Yeah.'

'But isn't that what endurance is, in a way, learning? The more you know the easier it is to endure.'

'No, the less you know the easier.' Blackstrap shifts to the side, so he is facing the window and not the man. The pond. A slim boat being rowed across there. Six men going for speed. 'Just ta get up in the morning 'n chop wood, 'n go out onto the water with your fadder, and bring home a catch of fish, or a haul of spruce from the woods. Food and heat. A roof over your head.' His eyes on the houses. The streets.

The group of low apartment buildings. So much to see from this window. People out there, like they're floating or drifting. If they only knew what they had.

'You had to learn to do all those things. That was an education of sorts.'

'No.' Blackstrap goes silent as a cloud moves across the blue, propelled by sky-high wind. Then he shifts to face the counsellor, the sound of his rough voice like a bark: 'You just know from yer life. Living. That's all you need. Living. People say you need ta know other things, and you think you do. I don't need ta know because you say so.'

'Yes, exactly. You see, you're a smart man. I understand what you're saying. I do, Mr. Hawco, believe me.'

'Well, I feel privileged.' Blackstrap checks over his shoulder to see through the window in the door. The guard watching in, then looking back at the counsellor, him nodding toward the guard. Everything's okay.

'Go ahead.' The counsellor raises his hand toward Blackstrap, mannerly, like it's his fair turn. 'Please.' He folds his arms and sniffs, rubbing at his nose.

'When I were in Toronto, I'd look at all the office buildings. Hundreds 'n hundreds of windows. People in there. What they all had ta learn. I'd watch them moving around. Small and high. The higher, the smaller. And I t'ought, look at all those people in those buildings, on the street, passing by, they're all just out hunting.'

'Hunting? Searching, maybe.'

'Just hunting. Everything they're doing. All the work, all that fast walking 'round, in a hurry. Looking important. They're just hunting. What they're doing just to put a piece of meat on the table. Fancy hunting. Instead of shooting it, they go ta the supermarket. So, then there's no blood on their hands.'

'Fancy hunting, hey?' The counsellor chuckles and leans his pink cheek on his pink hand. 'That's very good. I like that, a lot.'

Staring back at the window, Blackstrap joins his hands, holds them between his knees. Then he leans forward to watch the tile flooring beneath his feet. The talk is making him tired. Those office towers in Toronto. Desks and papers and filing cabinets and telephones and machines. And pretty women all done up. There had been something exciting about it too. The buildings and the factories. The blind woman, Heather. He wonders whatever became of her. Stuck in his mind like that. Returning to him for a moment, as though she were there. He'd like to be back in Toronto to see what might have happened. Or maybe he just wants to be anywhere except here.

'I know you're a smart man from your psychological evaluation.' The counsellor flips a page over in the file folder. 'Very bright. Superior IQ.' His eyes up from the papers to see Blackstrap. 'But you're one of those stubborn men who thinks there's a certain way of doing everything and that's the only way. Right? I know. I see it every day. You think you're special. Born of tradition, from generations of sea-going hearty men. I'm a Newfoundlander, too. There's more than one kind, Mr. Hawco.'

Blackstrap still watching the floor, shaking his head. He tilts his eyes up to look at the man. 'The ones not interested in changing people are easier ta stomach.'

'It's my job, friend. I'm just trying to do some good.'

'In here.' Blackstrap shifts his eyes to the yard. 'There's no fuh'k'n good in here. And how'd you know what you're doing's good?'

The counsellor goes silent, thinking. Elbow on the desk, his fingers against his temple. 'Why so bitter, huh? Why? You're in here now, locked up, but maybe your head's already been locked away for years. How about that?'

Blackstrap's eyes go narrow. 'And maybe you're just . . .'

'What? A pompous ass who wants to force everyone else to believe in what he believes? I know the word for what I am: *pompous*. Pompous. Pompous. Pompous. Do you know how to spell it? Why don't you spell it for me?'

Blackstrap snickers. 'Right.' Smiles at the floor. 'Good for you. You win, sir.'

'No, not win. It's not about winning. If you had a little more education you could have said that yourself. That was my point.' His voice not hostile, but full of pleading. 'Defend yourself with words, instead of beating the daylights out of someone. Deal with your frustration. Articulate it.'

Blackstrap smiles a little more, shakes his head again as though he can't believe any of it. The man at the desk who knows the everything of nothing. 'You know, that sounds just like a brilliant plan.'

'Believe me, I'd like to beat the daylights out of people sometimes too. I really would. God, how I would *love* to, really and truly, *love to*. I mean it, but then we'd all be animals in cages. You get what I'm saying.'

'I don't need words to pretend I'm a better man because I don't got the *guts* to defend what should be.' A burning has risen in his face. All these words are the most he has spoken in years. No reason to ever talk, but maybe a reason now, with this man. Or maybe not.

The counsellor eases back in his chair, sighs, then frowns, seeming to be done with it. He pokes at his glasses and blinks for a while, then stands from his chair. Pausing, he shoves his hands into his pockets and moves things around in there, while watching down at Blackstrap. 'It's a shame. You could accomplish so much. I know your potential. I can see the potential *wanting* to get out of you, *trapped* in there. I've read about everything you've done. Serious accomplishments. Serious. But, that's not enough for you. Killing your own potential, you seem intent on doing that. Why?'

Blackstrap frowns.

'Don't you feel like a lost cause? Going around trying to prove yourself all the time. Haven't you already done that? Losing more and more of you in the process. That's all, just less and less of you.'

'You have any children?' Blackstrap asks.

'No, why?' The counsellor straightens, almost takes a step back.

'Sounds like ya need a few. The way you talk to people.'

'Is that so?'

'Yeah.'

'Maybe these men are my children.'

Blackstrap bursts out with a laugh. 'Jesus Christ . . . God help us.'

'You find that sort of thought amusing, right? That's part of not being comfortable with yourself, not knowing—'

'I know what I am.'

'Yes, you most certainly do, Mr. Hawco. I have to say.'

Blackstrap stands from his chair and stares the man down. 'I know what I was born into.' His finger pointed at the desk, tapping the surface. 'I'm not pretending to be something else. Trying to make myself out better.'

'Better than what, who?' More words in the counsellor's eyes that he won't speak. Instead, his attention shifting to the door. 'That's sad. For me or for you, I don't know. Let me think about it.' And he seems genuinely bothered, watching the floor.

The door opening.

The guard stepping in.

'You leaving?' asks Blackstrap. 'Because you can leave, ya know. You're just the sort. You can just walk away.'

'No, no, your time's up,' says the counsellor, coming out of deep thought, his eyes on Blackstrap. 'I'm sorry to say. There are people waiting.'

'Just walk away,' Blackstrap says, passing by.

'I've been here almost ten years, Mr. Hawco. And I'll be here when you're gone. Some people I have helped, others not, but I don't plan on ever leaving.'

Blackstrap dreams of being on water, gliding up and down over the crests of waves on the blue sea, the green sea, the grey sea, the black sea. A storm lashes salt water in his face, spray that never stops. He dreams of his snowmobile, gliding up and down over fresh snow, like floating, opening up trails through the evergreens, ducking to protect his head from the low, snow-laden, evergreen boughs. The machine straining, rattling and banging across a stretch of open brook and rocks to rise freely again, up over a snowbank. Not caring about the machine, running the machine, punishing the machine to get him through. If it breaks, he will leave it where it sits. The time he went through the ice down on Black Duck Pond and crawled his way out. Paddy's pickup that came and pulled the snowmobile out of the water. Everything freezing and popping when it resurfaced into the air. The speedometer shattering. The engine a block of ice. His dream of that machine sealed in ice. And then Paddy in his house. Being beaten by his father with a belt in the kitchen. Paddy escaping to Blackstrap's house. Spending the night until his father's rage from drink died down.

He dreams of Mrs. Foote, the woman from St. John's who moved out to Cutland Junction. The woman who picks up wrappers, tin cans, and coffee cups on her slow walks, watching around the community, stopping to study an old house, lord over everything. The woman who runs the train museum, who has taken control of the memory of the town, and is disliked by most for sticking her face where it doesn't belong. The woman who fights the council, working to stop old houses from being torn down because no one else cares. Suburban bungalows going up in place of square fishermen houses. Demolished. The woman who raised the money to restore the cannon that Blackstrap stole to sink the Portuguese trawler. The others borrowed from museums and historical sites across the island. Port aux Choix, Signal Hill, Lance Cove, all under the cover of night, all of them back in their places now. Pointed at nothing. Guarding what?

In his dream, he follows Mrs. Foote from above, like a bird tracing her wandering steps along the road. He sees where she stops to consider a house, a group of trees, a dog running loose. She is in no hurry as she crosses the train track where the rails and ties have been torn up, where all-terrain vehicles and snowmobiles now race wild. A train bed cut right across the island by men who slaved for the sake of transport. He sees Mrs. Foote stooping down, picking up an empty fast food box thrown out the window of a passing car by one of the residents of Cutland Junction.

She keeps walking and walking. She will not stop.

He floats, following her from above, mesmerized by every detail of the community.

This woman he could never understand. What does she know about anything?

The guards, all ex-fishermen from Cutland Junction, send out a warning. He has heard it from others. Everyone leave Blackstrap Hawco alone. No one lay a finger on Blackstrap Hawco. The prisoners wonder about him. Some of them have heard how he sunk that boat for overfishing, how he survived a capsized oil rig when all others died in the ocean. Then he murdered a man. Why? No one knows. Gone wild on his own power, thinking he might be immortal. Indestructible. They'd seen it happen before. Bits of speculation passed back and forth at meal time.

He walks through the corridors, unseen, untouched.

'Dis place,' one of the guards, Darren Quilty, says to Blackstrap. 'Dis fuh'k'n uniform.' The guard has a job. This is his job. Once from Bareneed by the ocean. Night watch inside now. Checking the concrete corridors, looking in each cell, what's left of everyone. One hand always held covering his own throat, a flashlight in his other hand, sweeping the beam over a bunk, making sure the men are sleeping, not trying to do away with themselves.

One night, Darren Quilty slips Blackstrap a postcard through the bars, an old photograph of Bareneed from decades ago. Blackstrap sees writing on the back. Someone sending someone news. An old postage stamp with a king on it.

'It were a message sent frum me great-gran'fadder,' says Darren Quilty. 'To 'is mudder back in Ireland.'

Blackstrap stares at the old handwriting, then flips it to look at the photograph of houses and schooners in the water. The photograph turns his breath hot. Houses and boats and water caught there in a sepia tone.

'Me mudder gave it ta me ta give ta you, when she 'erd you was in 'ere.'

Blackstrap shifts his eyes to Darren. 'Why?'

'She said t'were criminal fer a man like Blackstrap Hawco ta be locked away like an animal. She said ta give dis ta you and ta tell you dat yer in 'er prayers. She knew yer mudder 'n she always looked up ta 'er.'

Blackstrap recalls Darren's mother, an old woman who used to keep vigil at the window, searching toward the sea, like all the women in Bareneed, stood or sat there behind their windows, patiently scanning the water for the boats' return. An old woman, like all those other old women, dead so many years. He hands the postcard back to the guard.

'She wanted you ta keep it, Blacky.'

Blackstrap shakes his head.

'Not in here,' he says. 'It was nice of her though. Tell her I said that.'

'I will.' Darren takes the postcard and shifts his eyes over the words. Then he looks at Blackstrap and his eyes deepen. 'I'll go back and tell her.' That hand still up to his throat, holding it covered in a way that makes Blackstrap know.

'Darren?'

'Yeah?'

'How long you been dead now?'

'I dun't 'member.'

'How's that?'

'I dun't know. It's not like dat.'

'How'd you die?'

'Prisoner killed me widt an electric cord.'

'Take it back to your mother.'

The guard nods. 'If I had a key, I'd let you out. I cun only check on da men.'

'That's okay,' says Blackstrap.

'How long 'av you been dead? You can't tell, can you?'

'No.'

'Ya see, it's like dat, truly. 'Cause yer not proper dead.'

Blackstrap stands with his hands holding the bars.

Darren Quilty turns and walks off with the postcard in one hand, the other up to his throat. He whispers into other cells, wondering who might hear him, his voice carrying through the corridors like a sift of dust.

Book Three

No Time, No Land

The walls in Blackstrap's cell are blank. They remain blank. The cell is not his. There has been mail for him. He has sent it back. No visitors. Not after Karen years ago. He has heard of how she survived. But not her baby. The policeman from Quebec in here now too. For a while and then gone in the ground. The mystery of who removed him.

Visitors amount to nothing. Patsy seeing him in this place once. Enough to end her. Patsy gone now, as expected.

Bury them all. How to join them in their blessed repose.

The long-haired lawyer brings a small TV. Donated from some group on the outside. The lawyer still visits every so often, working on appeals.

'I know you never wanted one of these,' the lawyer says, setting the TV down next to his toiletries. 'But there's something you should watch.' The lawyer names the channel, the day, the time.

Blackstrap wonders how much longer the lawyer will hang on for. He lies with his cheek against the pillow. Stares at the black and white screen. The program the lawyer suggested. A talk show with suffering every day. This one about National Child Abuse Awareness Month. Teenagers and young women in their twenties, talking about what happened to them. What was done by relatives.

The host introducing everyone. Seated in chairs in a line up there on stage. The name. The face. One after the other. Until Ruth Tuttle. Her teenaged face alarming him. That can't be her. His daughter. Not a toddler anymore. But it is her. Her last name changed. He watches her tell her story. Ruth's voice shaky with emotion. A quiet story that hurts and leads to tears. Trying not to listen. Only to see. Trapped in that box. He does not believe it is possible. He weeps. The pillow over his

797

shaking, open-mouthed head. He reaches to slap off the volume. But slaps off the picture too. He scrambles to sit and switch the TV back on. Ruth talking with no sound. Ruth crying. Being comforted by the others. Words beneath Ruth's image on the screen. Words he can almost read. He watches until she is done talking. Faces in the audience looking horribly sad. Then another teenager. Not Ruth anymore. He waits and watches. Only a flash of Ruth's face every now and then. The show over soon enough. He thinks all night until the next day. The same show with different people. He watches every single morning at the right time. But Ruth is there no more.

He hands the TV to one of the guards.

'What?' asks the guard, eyes on the TV.

'Take it.'

'You don't want it?'

'No.'

Watching Blackstrap's face. 'I know . . . I saw her too.'

What to think of that?

One day only.

Hold to it when you wake.

Let it go when it ends.

Never add them up. Try to not make it feel like time, like one hour to the next. All the prisons on all the lands beyond the walls. The land where animals roam. Outside these walls.

Lights on.

Lights off.

Lights on.

Never make these men his brothers. Never create a society from nothingness. Like the other men do. Create a society from how you have been made less than yourself. He refuses to become this place. While in prison, he becomes a blank. A blank is what he is meant to be. He will not try to make this blank into something else because that something else will be him.

He will not speak. He will not remember.

Never attempt to create a family in here. Never attempt to claim space. Only accept what is given him. Not land, but space. He will not claim space.

He becomes the no one
They thought
And wanted
Done with

Book Four

2007

Home, a House

(53 years old)

The last thing Blackstrap Hawco sees when he steps across the prison yard is the Newfoundland flag flying on a pole near the visitors' compound. His attention is drawn by the ruffling sound of it flapping high against the blue sky that he has watched from a narrow window for fifteen years. The flagpole next to that one is empty. The Canadian flag is usually flown there, but the Tory premier, Danny Williams, ordered all the Canadian flags taken down to protest a broken promise made by the Canadian Prime Minister, a Liberal, about offshore oil revenues. It was a stroke of political genius, in Blackstrap's mind. Take down the Canadian flag, and burn the fucking thing.

Blackstrap had heard that the Newfoundland flag was designed by a man named Pratt. Karen had told him as much. The man was an artist, a famous Newfoundlander whose work sells for tens of thousands of dollars on the mainland.

As the Newfoundland flag waves lightly in the breeze, its design appears like something broken up and fitted back together. The geometry of peculiar lines that makes Blackstrap feel uneasy because it gives him the sense of symmetrical perfection. But there is something about it that he admires, too, that anchors in him. Perhaps the idea that the flag is a singular creation and theirs. The glimpses of the Union Jack, patterned after the British flag, would have pleased his mother. He knows his father hated the flag. His father's decree when it was first sighted, flying in a yard that they drove past down in Bareneed: 'Looks like someone got a turned stomach on what he already had in 'is head 'n t'rew up a bunch of snotty nonsense.'

As the steel door is opened by the guard, Darren Quilty, Blackstrap sees an RCMP cruiser parked in the empty visitors' lot.

'Looks like ya got a ride,' says Quilty, maybe joking but seeming to know more.

Blackstrap glances back and nods.

Quilty touches the bill of his hat. One thumb missing from where it had been lopped off in a winch when he was fifteen. That was years ago and here he stands now. One hand covering his throat. Just another dead man in a uniform about to shut a door.

'Take 'er easy,' says Quilty, going back inside.

He could walk home from here. It would take no more than twenty minutes. He wonders why the RCMP cruiser has come for him. If that's what it was there for.

A young officer is seated at the steering wheel, observing Blackstrap with a plain look. The officer couldn't be more than twenty-five. A young pup still on his fist dick. He probably still squats to pee.

Blackstrap walks by the car, heading for the paved road at the end of the parking lot. The cruiser follows after him. There comes a toot from the horn, the driver leaning to peer out the open passenger window.

'I'm supposed to drive you home.'

'Says who?'

The officer just smiles.

'No need.' Blackstrap keeps walking. The trees never so lushly green. The barrens awash with colours: burgundies and browns and blondes . . . The low brittle bushes with tiny leaves. The huge grey and beige boulders deposited there since the withdrawal of the ice age. They haven't been moved since then. His feet on the flat pavement, softer than cinderblock, and softer still, once warmed by the sun.

A pleasure to be walking with no end in sight. He checks over his shoulder to be certain. His body drifting away from that compound.

The cruiser, inches ahead, while the officer leans and watches Blackstrap.

'Please, get in. I'd like to drive you.'

Like to.

Blackstrap continues walking, then he stops while still staring ahead at the evergreens. He knows he shouldn't get in, knows that he does not need to, but feels that he must, because he is being asked, being told by being asked.

When Blackstrap climbs into the vehicle, the officer nods in a practically friendly way. 'Thanks. I'd like to talk to you.'

Blackstrap stares through the windshield as the car rolls off. Then he glances through the passenger window at the landscape gliding by. It is a gift to his eyes; an expansiveness that is almost frightening in its clarity. He makes a point of naming the brush and the swamp trees to himself. He remembers what he has learned about the barrens, the name reindeer moss for what he had looked at all his life but never knew exactly what it was called. The population of the island. The resources. The areas where soil is good for farming. The types of farms. The types of mines. Where the people came from. The Walshes and Powers and Taylors. The inlets and coves and bays around the island, and who settled them. From what county in Ireland or England. Poole. Limerick. Kilkenny.

The counsellor had taught him, had read to him from books when he visited his office. Blackstrap returning twice a week for the view through the window. The lake and the boats with their rowers, practicing for the annual regatta. Then the counsellor turning the book toward Blackstrap and carefully setting down a finger on the page, on a word. And because Blackstrap eventually was willing to learn, the counsellor had treated him better, had made certain that he was given particular liberties. Behind the locked door in his office, the counsellor had given Blackstrap consolation.

Blackstrap looks at the side of the officer's face, a young man with no recognizable features, who licks his lips anxiously. A plain man you can see right through. He feels the urge to reach out and touch him, to see if his hand passes beyond. Such an entirely different face from the ones he has watched for years. Not a face changed by cruelty or harsh incident. Nothing of consequence has ever happened to him, except his own death.

The cruiser glides off the asphalt and down the dirt road that will lead to Blackstrap's house.

The officer glances at Blackstrap. 'Good to be out?'

'Yes.'

A few moments later, the officer says: 'I guess you knew him, hey?'

'Who?' Blackstrap is thinking of his father, watching ahead for the sight of his house, but it is slow coming, as though the land, the trees and sky have filled themselves back in to erase the house.

'Hotel Room Pope.' The officer grins and his face changes for the worse. 'The serial killer? I saw in your file how he was one of the arresting officers.'

Blackstrap thinks it over.

'He died in there. When you were in, right?'

'Yeah.'

'Suicide, they said. Birds of a feather.'

The car takes the slow corner and to Blackstrap's relief he sees the two houses down the incline.

'They made a movie about him. You see it? The guy won an Academy Award. He was involved with your girlfriend, right?'

The cruiser pulls into the cracked paved drive with patches of grass growing up through it.

The two houses. The two doors.

'Here we are,' says the officer, his hand reaching for something between the seats. A thin case with a picture on the front. It's sealed in plastic. 'I got you a copy of the movie. DVD.'

Blackstrap scans the cover. A picture of a man in a police uniform. Not the uniform of the RCMP, but a uniform that he recognizes as traditionally American. A pregnant woman with long black hair is stood behind him in ropes. He says nothing more, merely opens the door.

'Live and learn,' says the officer, his eyes darkening to slits.

'Keep it,' Blackstrap says, then carefully closes the door, pushing it shut until it clicks.

'Okay, stay out of trouble,' the officer says, with a newly boyish smile and a laugh to please himself.

The voice in Blackstrap's head, coming from where? Before or after the door shut. When he looks back, he sees the nervous glitch in the young officer's eyes. The law, but from where and of what?

And the car is gone, just like that.

Not that man's fault, he decides.

He never knew there was so much to be learned about blame.

Blackstrap hesitates, making certain the car is gone, a lapse of time he has lost track of. Faced by these two structures, he finds his son and daughter brought to mind. They had been living with foster parents from what he heard. Patsy dead from cancer years ago. They had given him a pass to attend the funeral. A prison guard on either side of him. His two children there with their foster parents on either side of them. Grown more so that he barely knew, but never would he not.

Him on one side of the grave.

Them on the other.

His children raised by . . .

His daughter.

His son.

Not his to have.

Raised by . . .

His original sentence served. He would have been released when they were still children. He could have tried then. But that was when his sentence was shorter, before he attacked the Indian, and others, too, before the problem of Pope. His sentence extended, again and again, complicating any custody fight. His children grown now. Junior twenty-one just last month, and Ruth soon to be seventeen.

The place for his children.

Junior. He spells the name in his head: J-U-N-I-O-R.

Patsy. P-A-T-S-Y.

His daughter: R-U-T-H.

The new house has a few smashed windows. He notices how the vinyl siding is stripped in places. The big window taken out completely. A hole there that gives no reflection. Blacker than expected is why he knows.

But his father's house.

A sound to his right, a rustling and snapping of twigs. Someone coming for him through the trees to take him back. He jerks his head to see a moose lumbering out from the trees near the edge of the road. It stands there with its head dipped, eating the new sweet grass in the ditch.

M-O-O-S-E.

Blackstrap stands with his right foot on a bit of a rise, higher than his left. Finally, he swallows and the moose sways its heavy head up to look at him. Rubbing its back legs together, it shifts its rump and urinates, then stares a while longer before stepping in reverse, along the exact path it came from, into the woods.

The rustling and crackling of branches and twigs under one hoof, then another . . .

There is not a trace of the moose, except for the patch of grass that had been torn from its roots and chewed, and the urine that had gushed through the air, onto the grass and into the warming earth.

Again, Blackstrap sees movement, this time lower, closer to the ground, hearing no sound. A dog. A cat. A rust-coloured fox trotting out a few feet away from where the moose had appeared. It pays Blackstrap no mind as it scampers across the road, a limp kitten in its jaws, and into the bushes beside where Blackstrap's backhoe used to be parked to the left of his father's house. The backhoe has since been seized by the courts as partial payment to settle lawsuits brought against him by a few of Isaac Tuttle's distant cousins. The new house taken too, but who living in it now? No one by the looks of it. Everyone having moved away.

F-O-X.

K-I-T-T-E-N.

J-A-W.

The ground rumbles beneath his feet. He thinks of a missing locomotive, then turns his head in the direction of the unseen ocean. The distant sound quaking from Bareneed. The quarry company finally granted a permit. He heard from Darren Quilty. The headland being demolished and dug up, the gravel, dirt and stone transported to other places for fill. The faultline soon to split, releasing so many from its hold.

Those two houses: one old with its top storey torn off, its narrow wooden clapboarding grey in patches, in need of a few coats of paint, the other house rectangular with the bay window gone and white vinyl siding, made to last forever, masking and sealing in the rot.

Deciding, he steps up the bank, his boots along the uneven beachrock path, past the old tires and automobile debris, an engine, rusted wheels, and a transmission off further. He reaches into his pocket for the keys that the man in prison had returned to him, then checks over his shoulder, expecting to see his father behind him, following him up the path with a headful of intentions – but – instead – seeing the expanse of the evergreens and barrens gradually rising and falling off for miles in all directions.

The exact same view he had witnessed before being taken to confinement.

What do you want with any of this? he asks himself. Go.

Returning to the task at hand he finds the key and is about to fit it into the lock when he decides to try the knob.

It turns in his palm. Unlocked.

Stepping into his father's house, he discovers everything in its place. No one would think of entering his father's house. No one would be so heartless as to disturb the placement of a single artefact. For a moment, amid the articles collected, Blackstrap feels painfully out of place, and calls out to his father, 'Dad?' the sound of his own voice jarring in the emptiness.

And with the unexpected voice in return, the hope that time might not have tormented him so mercilessly.

Stood in the cluttered living room, listening for the voice that most occupies him, he finds that he is not breathing. Again, the voice sounds, and he looks toward where his hand rests against an old roll-top desk.

To be home.

To be here.

In this place.

He pulls up the dusty roll-top lid to see paper and envelopes tucked away in the slots. Resting there on the desk, an old-fashioned pen with ink still in it when he scribbles the nib against the blank parchment of a journal.

He pulls out the chair and sits, applying himself in the way he has been taught. A series of careful strokes patterned by hand. Trails of ink with each letter strung together to compose the meaning of a word.

Hunched forward in concentration, Blackstrap Hawco writes what he remembers, and vanishes in the telling, one story at a time.

Book Five

Children

I

Toronto

4 yrs, Jr hs hurd Ø bt vile fings bout hs dad. Junior's foster dad, Doug Tuttle, hs alw z dat Jr came frm murdering stock n dat wz Y d boy wz so useless, shiesty n laZ. Doug traced d Hawco kin lineage 2B drunkards n thieves hu ran frm Ireland. Doug z dat Jr xpectD evryting 2B handed 2 him on a silver platter. d boy alw n tears, a real sissy. prolly a fag, Doug uzd 2 sA. d boy needed 2B watchd @ evry chnc. u nvr knw w@ he'd do f u turnD ur bac on him. n Ruth wz no btr. Slutting arnd ll d tym. dey wr both lamo n ungrateful.

2 Jr, Bareneed wz a borin plce 2 gro ^ n. Ø 2 do, Xcpt woch tv n play gmes on d comp. No shpg malls or moV theatres. d foster parNts owned Junior's great-grand uncle's old hous n Bareneed. A mn named Ace had livD der a lng tym ago. d govt had done it ^ 4 ppl on welfare, tore ot mosta d insides n rebuilt.

wen d social wrkR found ot bout d hist of d hous, n d fact dat foster parNts livD n it, d social wrkR thort twas d perfect plce 4 Jr n Ruth 2B placed. aftr ll, d hous had Hawco hist 2 it. dis discovery had glad d social wrkR quite a bit. d social wrkR lOkd dat wA wen she tld Jr n Ruth bout it. She seemD rly glad 4 w@ she'd done.

der wr sme houses lk dat n Bareneed. Welfare houses done ^ nce n divided N2 2 diFrent units. d houses lOkd gud on d O/side, bt dey wouldn't stay done ^ nce 4 vry lng. Trash wd Nd ^ ot on d lawns n d paint wd peel off. sum1 hired frm d govt wd eventually cum arnd 2 fix ^ d houses. bt 1ly aftr a bunch of gripes frm d merikuns n mainlanders hu had bawt mosta d oder houses n Bareneed. doZe ppl wr alw tryiN 2 drV d welfare ppl outa doZe houses. dey md heaps of noyZ. dey had petitions done ^. dey rOt letAs 2 council. Junior's pal, Sean Mugford, had an uncL on twn council n so Sean knw dat ppl wr tryiN 2 gt d welfare ppl booted outa d comunity. Sean Mugford wz on welfare, 2.

He knw d names of sme of d ppl hu had bn complaining, so Jr n Sean wd sumtyms go arnd 2 doZe houses n smash a wndw or steal something – a TV or a stereo – and thrO it ovr a cliff N2 d sea, jst 4 a *L*. evry1 knw hu wz doiN d damage, bt Jr n Sean nvr got cort. bt d ppl hu had bn vandalized uzd d crime as a gr8r xQs 2 gt rid of d low-income housN n d comunity.

wen Ruth wz 15, she got prego, dropD outa skool, n kept d bb. movD 2 St. John's. She z it belonged 2 Muck Coveyduck, bt Jr knw d bb belonged 2 their foster dad, Doug Tuttle, Bcz he sumtyms came @ nyt. Jr hurd him. He hurd it ll W hs lyz opN n turnD awy, staring ot d wndw, ^ d valy @ d lyts glowing n d redone houses of Bareneed. Ruth wz %-) 2 kip d bb. She movD outa dat hous n strtd workin n St. John's @ Leo's. She wz nuts 2hv kids. He wd nvr av kids. w@ wr dey gud 4? Ø bt a pain 2 feed n put clothS on their backs n buy fings 4. dey wr useless. dey 1ly md ur lyf miserable.

Jr couldn't leev d hous 'til he wz eighteen. He wtd 2, bt hs foster dad kept sAyn dat he'd set d RCMP on Jr f he lft. av him locked awy n d boy's hom n Whitbourne. So Jr stayD n hated evry1, Xcpt hs sis. He pitied her coz she let ll dat stuf hpn 2 her. She wz a lamo bozo, d wA she got on.

On hs eighteenth BDay, Jr hits d road. He tAkz off 4t hwy n heads west, drivS ll d wA ax Newfoundland, stopiN 1ly n Terra Nova n Gander 4 sme fst f%d n gas. He stops d car n Port aux Basque n waits 4t ferry dat wl taK him 2 Nova Scotia. He waits n d line n watches d huJ ferry pul N2 dock. d crs n trucks cum off n thN d crs r waved on. He drivS hs car on2 d boat n parks it n d hollow steel belly of d boat. thN he goes ^ on deck n stares bac @ d rck. brwn cliffs n green spruce. That's ll there's 2 it. A plce 2 leev. wen d ferry pulls awy, he stares 'til d l& S gon. Ø bt d drk blu of H2O. dat nyt, n d bar on d ferry, there's a ;-o playN Newfoundland muzc. d ppl r drinkN n clapping along 2 d tunes. d ppl n d bar rly lk d muzc. itz foolsh 2 him. He wonders Y d guy isn't playN sngs frm d radio. aftr he hs a few (B), he calls ot requests. bt nun of em r plAd. Mac Babb, d guy W d grey beard n guitar, jst sEz he doesn't knw doZe tunes. n evry1 n d bar sEmz hpE bout dat. dey clap n holler. wen d ferry arrives n nth Sydney Jr can't w8 4 hs tires 2 tuch asphalt. He can't st&d d sway of d boat. d massiveness of d sea. ll dat H2O. ll dat blu. It maks him feel sick.

He follows d hwy signs n keeps drivN 'til he maks it 2 Ontario. there's NOT! he's gunA stop along d wA. Nova Scotia S lk Newfoundland, d l& l%ks d same, 1ly d trees r bigA. n thN d signs *t changiN 2 french. Quebec. He stops ina gas st8N n asks f he's goin d ryt wA. d pRsN @ d countA sEz somit n french n pts 2 a map on d countA. Jr buys 1 n unfolds it on d passenger seat, chekin 4 road #s. @ lEst d road #s Rnt n french. itz evn hrdr 2 kip trak of fings @ nyt. He begins 2 drift off, catching himself fallN |-| a few tmes, 'til he pulls ovr n sleeps. d sun wakes him. d heat. &he drivS on. hngry bt nt wantN 2 stop. finaly, hes drivN thru opN fields of farmland dat seem peculiar 2 him. Farm houses n big barns set bac frm d hwy, sittN der ll solo. Big bails of hay n d fields, lk d big boulders on d barrens bac n Newfoundland.

He drivS ryt N2 Toronto. nt a clue whr he's goin, bt he sEz d big clump of buildings n d distanC. It l%ks sml. cUd it B Toronto? It's lk he cn C d hol CT. drivN on roads W 4 or 5 lanes. evry1 speeding lk maniacs. CABs almst clipping him. thN, wen he gets nearer, hes 404. Buildings towering ovr him. Streets ll d same. He's lkn4 a parkN space. It tAkz a yl. ll d crs mak hs lyz hurt. He lastly finds a parkN space n pulls n. He notices der r signs n d windoz lkn4 employees. hlp wtd. He goes N2 d 1st plce, a donut shop n asks 2 apply. He gets d job ryt awy. d boss finds ot dat he nEdz a plce 2 stay n recommends a plce run by d manager's bro. It's a rooming hous on Brock st.

aftr he gets hs bearings, he goes 2 d subway n asks h2 gt2 d Eaton centA. He's hurd bout dat. d subway trains r fst. dey rck thru blackness. He lyks d feel of em movN lk dat. 1 plce 2 nothA qkly. He gets ot @ d Dundas stop. tAkz d stairs ^ N2 d Eting area. Keeps walkin thru 'til he finds d escalator. stors evrEwhr. He wnts a job n d comp gmes stoR, bt he duznt gt it wen he applies. nt smrt nuf. dats hw d boss l%ks @ him. d guys workin der r smrt. dey ll av glasses, bt don't lok lk jerks. dressD n rly QL clothS n sneaks. dey knw evrythin. He nos evrythin bout d gmes der bt he cnt Xpln it 2 d boss wen d boss asks him ???s.

bt dey hire him n d sneaker stoR. He lyks ll thOs sneakers. XpNsiv.

He triS 2 figure ot a wA 2 steal a few pairs, bt they're watchd prety teyet. aftr a yl, he hears frm 1of d guys n d boarding hous dat he cn B mking jst as mch $ on welfare. He duznt tel em he's gunA quit &he tAkz a pair of three-hundred $ joggers W him n sme csh frm d til wen he goes. d nxt dy, he applies 4 welfare.

sum1 tells him dat d welfare S bst n Ontario. evrytings btr on d mainland. Jr S glad 2B outa dat plce. Newfoundland S Ø bt a sht hol. d rck, dey cll it, lk it's somit specl. bt it jst sits der stuk n d midL of d sea. lamo baywops. lamo accents. He's proud wen ppl sA he doesn't sound lk a Newfoundlander. Who'd wn2 sound lk a Newfoundlander? 'Ow she goin' b'y. A big Newfie jk. 'ow's she get'n on, pal?' Retarded. He lyks d CT. It's QL. tunz of moV places. hs mum ded. hs dad n jail. jst a crim. n doZe Fkng foster parNts. He cUd nvr go bac der. nvr wd. Who'd evr wnt 2? Toronto S wA btr.

He nvr thort of it mch. bout hom. He triD nt 2 tnk of it. d wA fings shudve bn. He remembers d tale bout hs dad slicing d moose's throat. d tale hs dad tld him B4 he wz taken awy. dat wz QL. He collects knifs frm a stoR on Yonge st. Keeps em ll n hs rm. He'd lk 2 slit d throat of a moose. D throat of a dog. D throat of a fox he did once.

B4 Junior's mum died on him, deserted him, &he wz put n dat hous. hs dad on TV. d 1ly survivor of d drill rig dat sunk. On TV. d mn hu sank dat Portuguese trawler. A hero, dey cllD him. hs foster dad laffin n shaking hs hed. lamo fckr, z hs foster dad, (B) n h&, wotchN Blackstrap Hawco on TV. w@ a Fkng loser.

d 1ly reasN he's contmpl8N it nw S coz of d f@ Nvelop dat wz n hs bx dat AM. Twas addressed 2 Jr Hawco. W no addresses on it ltha n no stamp. jst Jr Hawco. dat isn't evn hs lst nme no mor. hs foster dad had Jr n Ruth's lst nme chngd 2 Tuttle. He cUd do dat coz he adopted em. d Nvelop hs d nme Blackstrap Hawco ^ whr d rt adr wz, bt it l%ks lk d nme wz prntD by a lil kid.

He wonders hw d mail gotta him. hu wd knw whr he lyfs. No 1. He nvr tld NE1.

He tears opN d padded Nvelop n pulls ot a thik bunch of folded sheets of ppr. There's also an old b%k n der. myt B wrth somit. He stands der n opens d b%k. d pp r yellO. Old. d wrds r ritN ot n old styl ryTN. He triS readN em, bt it's ll big wrds n it tAkz 2 lng. He finx bout bringiN it 2 dat b%k shop dwn on d Danforth. d 1 W ll d old bux n d wndw. mayB he cn gt sme $ 4 it.

He l%ks @ d sml TV on d seat n d crnA of hs rm. An ad cums on 4t nu moV W Jenna Darcy n it. She's Canadian. She lyfs n Toronto frm w@ he read on www bout her. He nos whr she lyfs evn. u cn gt NEfin frm d www.

wen d comercial S ovr 4t horror moV, Jr unfolds d letta pp. He reads evryting dats ritN der. d old b%k isa jnl dat Blackstrap found n uncL Ace's old hous. A jnl dat uncL Ace rOt wen evry1 thort he wz outa hs mnd. wen he wouldn't sA a wrd. dis S what's ritN on d letta. He reads thru d pp. thN he reads it ll ovr agn. stuf bout d 1880s n bout ppl he doesn't knw. sum1 named Patrick Hawco. Fishermen. n men n women frm oder countries. Ireland. England. Merchants. What's a merchant? sum1 hu owns a stoR ina mal. Merchant somit or oder. He remembers hearin dat. What's a trapline? He skips ovr big sections coz it's borin. It's suposD 2hv somit 2 do W him, bt he an't C d point. It's lk somit he had2 read n skool. borin poo bout hx. hu cares bout w@ hapnd? wuz dat hav2 do W nw? hs nme isn't NEware n it.

He triS readN d pp ovr agn. bt evn on d 3rd n 4th try it maks no senZ 2 him. Ø S rly hapNg. Xcpt 4 sum1 frezn 2 deth. That's prety QL. n d shipwreck stuf. bt mosta it's ll 2 slO. mayB it isn't frm hs dad @ ll. d stuf he wz readN sounded Ø lk hs dad. nt a wrd of it. hs stepfather tld Jr dat Blackstrap wz iliter8. dey z dat ryt on TV wen he sank dat Portuguese boat. An iliter8 fisherman st&ing ^ 2 Portugal.

Jr thort d wrds myt B bout prizN n stuf. killN ppl. mayB sum1 jst sent it 2 him as a jk. That's w@ it feels lk, a jk. Didn't he Nta dat contest 2B on a tv shO wen he bawt d nu TV lst mth? dat must B it. dey go aftr ur past lkn4 stuf u didn't knw bout. stuf that'd MbrS u, bt u win gr8 prizes. clothS n cmputAs n Ntrtainmnt systems n cell fons. He rOt hs nme dwn 4 dat. n synD it. givin em permission 2 do NEfin. fnd ot NEfin bout him. Must B w@ it's bout. wen dey gt thru havN fun W him, thN he gets 2 battle it ot W 10 oder ppl 2C hu survives. e@tiN gross fings or makin hs wA thru d jngl. d 1 hu survives gt a million $. He'd gt thru dat ez. Survive NEfin.

He can't hlp bt <s>. mayB he'd gt2 mEt Jenna Darcy. He shakes hs hed n puts hs arm ovr d bac of d seat. hs lyz go evrywhr arnd hs room,

lukin ^ @ d ceiling n @ d walls, 1dering whr d camRA S hidN. It cUd
B NEware.

He checks hs woch. tym 2 hed 4 Yonge st n ck ot a strip joint. He's
ReD, dressD, hs nu outfit, baggy pants, baggy shirt, nu sneaks, hs D:-)
hat on sideways. He lks W styl, W ata2ud 2 d door n goes dwn d
stairway ot N2 d st. ppl ll arnd him, he passes an alleyway n trns hs hed
2 ck der. Hands grab him, n there's a curse thru skrood ^ lips. A gun
n hs face. d smel of steel n oil. Pulled deeper n deeper 2wrd d
dumpster n Bhnd it. Banged against it. d bac of hs hed smacking der,
hurtin.

'ur Fkng wallet.'

'Got no wallet. Don' carry nun.'

'ur Fkng $.'

'Got nun.'

Hands n hs pockets. Ø bt a bunch of chng n subway tokens. Flung
ax d alleyway, bouncing n jangling off brick. lyz jerking frm hs face, dwn
ovr hs bod, 2 d ground.

'ur sneakers, MoFo.'

'No, Fkng wA.'

'Now.'

'No Fkng wA.'

'Now, u fckr.'

'No, fuK off.'

'fuK u.'

'fuK u, fckr.'

'FUUUUCKKK u.'

'FFFFFUUUUUUUUUUUUUCCCKKKKK!'

gunshot bang'n

wyt boy's face

red 187

footsteps runN

slap my streetment

hrd W bl%d

sEz so hom 2 d 'ho

hu suk my dik

'n she no knw
i blast a hol
n 1 mor
whip-cracker
mastA

Unidentified Man Found Dead in Alleyway

(from the Toronto Star)

(Toronto, ON) Aug. 12 – An unidentified man found dead Saturday in a burning dumpster had been shot to death, the Toronto medical examiner's office has ruled. The body was discovered in an alleyway off Brock Street West by firemen responding to the blaze.

Police do not have a motive or a suspect in the homicide. They are asking anyone with information about the crime to contact the Toronto Police or Crime Stoppers.

CityTV News Update:

City police are still trying to identify a man found Saturday morning in a burning dumpster on Brock Street.

The man, described as between 18 and 30 years old, was shot in the alleyway before being dragged to the dumpster. Investigators have no further details about the case.

Anyone with information is asked to call the nearest Toronto Police detachment.

II

Cutland Junction/Bareneed/
Corner Brook

Catherine, Amanda, Emily, Ruth, as he hopes to believe.

It is Agnes Bishop who has come, not as a doctor but as the woman he expects, a visitor he refuses to see; she has made the journey regardless. Agnes, near enough now to hear his final words: a litany of injuries she reads again and again from the autopsy report in the yellow envelope she keeps in the drawer beside her bed.

It is she who finds him in the water after the boat crash, identifies his features, sprinkled with windshield glass, unzips his drowned bloated body from the survival suit, turns her face away from the body parts left once the locomotive has passed, hears the flesh-trapped slosh of water in the lungs. It is she who is called to his cell and loosens the tightly knotted sheet, marvels at the heart-stopping gunshot wound, the antler gouged through the heart. It is she who notices the locket around his neck, the fine strand of chain cut into his skin, and gently plucks the progression of tiny links from the flesh etching, exposing the trail of strangulation, her fingers lifting the locket to slide her thumbnail into the crack. The split not so easily opened. She must use both thumbnails, prying them into the silver crevice, forcing them deeper until the pressure pops the clasp. And in the confined space, so small that they might barely be contained, two photographs are fitted. On the right, there is Ruth. On the left, Junior. A sight Agnes cannot bear for its duplicity, the reflection of features in each of her eyes melding to imprint a single image of Blackstrap. The pale ovals of two children's faces watching each other for all eternity across the quarter-inch chasm once the locket is shut. With Agnes' fingers fastening the catch behind her neck, the length of chain dangles, the locket slipping down to settle in the divide of her barren breasts.

III

St. John's

Ruth Tuttle is wheeling the stroller up Long's Hill when she looks back to see a man behind her. He's the same man she's seen for the past few days or weeks. She's not exactly certain of the time frame. The trouble is she can't tell if the man is really there or not, because she thinks she might have seen him in a dream first, or once when she was half drunk downtown. Her mind is hazy and sharp at the same time, burnt out from lack of sleep. There hasn't been much rest for almost two years, since the baby was born. The place she's walking around in feels like something not exactly her life, her body just a bunch of flesh and bones she's taking up space in.

The man has blonde hair with grey in it and a rough face. Hands in his pockets, he slows down when she looks at him, his eyes dead set on hers. He's following her. Not just behind her. The energy of want coming off him, almost reaching her, like a weird touching sensation.

She pushes the stroller faster, leaning into it because the hill is sort of steep. When everything levels off up on Freshwater Road, she waits for a clear space in traffic, then crosses the street. The man behind her is a worry, and it's even worse because she's already feeling horrible after coming from the welfare office. She decided to quit her job at Leo's Take-Out to stay with Jacob. Every time she dropped him off at that daycare, she had a sick feeling in the pit of her stomach. He would cry and toddle after her. The women there would have to hold him back, saying reassuring words to him. They'd always try to make it look like Jacob would be okay, but they'd be restraining him all the same, holding on tightly while trying to smile her away. And every time, he would manage to get loose and be at the big window, with his hands pressed against the glass, bawling and screeching out 'Mommy,' his little face a mess of tears. There was only so much of that she could take, her mind always going to that memory when she was dishing out orders of chips, dressing and gravy. The smell of cooked food making her wonder what they were feeding her baby at that place. She'd rather be at home with him, playing games or reading books, than having strangers doing whatever they wanted to him. Why did everyone tell her she had to work anyway? People saying she had to get a job because she had to make something of herself. And, besides, she should take advantage of the work programs because there were plenty of daycare programs that would look after her child. The government funded those places, so the mother could go out and feel worthwhile by making money of her own. But that didn't make her feel worthwhile. It made her feel worthless.

Ruth takes another peek back when she gets to the turn for Field Street. The man is still there, coming straight toward her, steady but holding back, like he's walking through water. He's probably in his fifties. One of those guys who still wears jeans and a jean jacket. He's got a black T-shirt on underneath. Even though he's familiar, it's like there's only a part of him she recognizes. That's why she thinks of the dream. But she doesn't know if it's because of his face or the way he dresses.

She turns around the corner and walks up Field Street, hurrying for the row house where she's renting the bottom floor. One of the stroller wheels gets caught on a rock and she has to stop to kick it loose.

'Ruth.'

She's right outside her door now, her name echoing in her head, but she won't look back. Just because the man knows her name doesn't mean he knows her. In fact, because he knows her name it might mean that he's dangerous. Not knowing her, but knowing her name. That means he knows something about her, went out of his way to find it without her having any idea what he was up to. She checks Jacob, sees that he's sleeping, and digs in the pocket of her tight jeans for her key. There are a few guys in their twenties up the road. Drug dealers, she knows, but they're okay. They'll help her out if this guy gives her any trouble.

She senses the man drifting nearer, and has to stop the little movement of her head trying to look back because she feels that he's stopped about ten feet away.

The man's voice quieter now, 'Ruth?'

'Yeah?' she asks, finally giving in to curiosity and turning to see him. 'What?'

'Ruth Hawco?'

'No.' She lowers her eyes.

'Ruth.' The man watches her, then moves his gaze to the stroller. He can't see the baby from where he's standing. His voice even quieter now, 'Ruth.'

'I said "no." I'm no Ruth.' Her eyes with the gleam of a threat in them, she stares the man down. But the man seems so familiar that she feels sad, wrong, misplaced. It's not like she knows him from seeing him around. It's more than that. The way she gradually recognizes him is doing something to every part of her body. Excited and scared and loving and hating . . . She thinks she recognizes him from TV. Someone she saw on TV before, but not famous, not like an actor or anything. It's so confusing to try and remember that her heartbeat speeds up and she starts sweating. The man is like a blind spot in her eyes, scaring her, filling her with panic.

An arguing boy and a girl slapping at each other in the street come over to look at Jacob. The boy smacks the girl hard on the top of her head and runs off.

'Oww,' says the girl, 'you frigger,' shouting after the boy who calls out: 'Ahhhh-ha-ha,' and joins the drug dealers, bumming a smoke off the oldest one stood there like a statue.

The tough girl whispers sweet things to the baby, the way her body moves turning soft as butter. 'He's sleep'n,' she says, smiling so kindly and natural that every bit of harshness is erased from her.

Ruth gives the girl a bit of a smile, then checks for the man, because she thinks he might have left, the vacancy there in the corners of her eyes.

'Who're you?' she snaps, finally seeing him, even closer now and more disturbing in daylight than in darkness.

The man does not seem to know what to say. He gives his head a forgetful shake and looks down the length of the street where someone has just smashed a bottle.

Ruth sees the marks on his face. The button-shaped scar on his cheek. The other welts and scrapes. The lines along his throat.

The tough girl looks up at the man, then at Ruth, her face confused and changing.

'These are for you.' The man pulls a bunch of small envelopes out of his jacket pocket. They're held together by an elastic band, resting there in his opened palm.

Ruth sees the name Annie Gull written on the front of one of the envelopes. There's an old stamp on it. A picture of a king on the stamp. Up in the return address is the name Amanda Duncan. The envelope reminds her of the cover of a book she once read. It was a book from the library and it was about life in Newfoundland ages ago. The way women and men used to live. The work they did. Never a moment's rest in that world. But they were happy, content to be together, she suspects.

The man steps toward her, making a move like a nudge in the air for her to take the bunch of envelopes.

'Please,' he says.

'What's that?'

'Letters.'

'From who?'

He doesn't seem to have the courage to answer, but soon says, 'It's important. About your great-grandmother.'

The tough girl makes a quiet noise, a sound resembling distress. She rubs her hands in her jeans and squints in wonder, straightens from where she's crouched by the baby.

Ruth looks at the girl, and the girl checks the blank space in front of Ruth. 'Who ya talk'n to?'

Ruth stares back at the envelopes.

A photograph in the man's hand.

Not envelopes, but a photograph of the man.

Again, there is movement in the corners of her eyes. This time, to the other side. Jacob has woken. The girl too near him, drawing him from sleep, because the girl's voice is unknown to Jacob.

'I'm not taking that,' she says.

'It's from me,' says the man, his voice so low, with a hint of hurt in it. Pained. Because he is almost feeling.

Junior's voice.

His.

Ruth's.

'You alright?' asks the tough girl, pawing some hair away from her face.

'What?' Ruth asks the girl, the question only now sinking in. 'Yes.' She looks back at the man.

What man ever? Who?

The man stood there.

'Can I pick him up?' the girl wants to know.

'Sure.' Ruth sees only the man's face, thinking she might know who it is for certain now, the man on television who killed someone. It *is* him. The man who died. Was it in the water or in prison? A hero, a killer, then dead himself. How? She cannot recall exactly. If he is dead at all, if he is here. How can he be? She does not want to know. One way or the other.

Not a father. Not another father.

The real one maybe worse than the other.

Maybe the one she wanted all along.

The truer pain of that.

The photograph now in her hand.

She drops it in the white plastic bag with her carton of milk and her novel that smells old from the second-hand store. The photograph discovered in the book when she bought it earlier that day.

The man takes another step closer, his eyes shut, facing the baby in the tough girl's arms.

Ruth watches his eyes open, staring at the baby, but watching into her, while she remembers something else from television, how the man went out in a boat and did battle with big fishing boats. Draggers, she remembers they were called, the ones that were tearing up the ocean bottom, destroying every bit of life down there. She had learned that in school. Social studies. He was a hero, but then he was some sort of criminal. Nothing to her that she remembers. So, why does she feel?

Thinking this, she begins to cry. What has he ever done for her?

'Hey?' asks the tough girl. 'Jeeze, you okay?'

The man squats next to the baby in the tough girl's arms. Then he looks up at Ruth, his eyes that pretty cool blue, just like Jacob's.

The baby watching her.

She shakes her head to never know him, sniffs, and wipes at her eyes.

'What's his name?' asks the man.

Acknowledgements

Numerous individuals and publications aided the author over the fifteen years required to collect, research and transcribe the various life experiences and periods depicted in this book. The sources are too extensive to list.

The journal entries of Bishop Flax (contained in these pages) are based on the actual journals of Bishop Wix and Bishop Field (the Bishop of Newfoundland). They are interwoven with complete sections reprinted verbatim and interspersed with the author's own intentions to create a single voice of no exact religious affiliation.

The renowned and actual Bishop Flax, who hailed from Limerick, Ireland, and is a distant relative of the author, is not the one represented here. Only his name has been used for the sake of highlighting lineage.

The journal entries of Flax are not meant to reflect truth nor are they intended to ape or, subsequently, diminish the fine character of either Wix or Field, who remain two stellar gentlemen.

The stories contained within this book have been transcribed from recordings of stories told to the author by people throughout Newfoundland. They were collected and then transcomposed to create the life of one family – the Lamblys/Hawcos.

This procedure of melding the written words of true-to-life individuals, to create a single voice, mimics the style of the transcomposite narrative which was first introduced by the Newfoundland writer Kenneth J. Harvey in his novel *Skin Hound* (The Mercury Press, 2000).

In the spirit of the transcomposite narrative, various descriptions in this book have been taken (word for word) from short stories previously published by the author of this work. All of this to finger the notion that fiction is the braggart whore's child, fathered by a burglar with an insatiable itch for stolen facts.

While the author's short stories, when originally published, were exclusively in the domain of fiction, by copying them from a book that now exists in reality and in the past, they become more a consequence of fact, as the passages have been lifted from an actual book that exists on its own and in the actual or non-fictive world as a concrete product. These once fictional sections then, reused, might now be labelled non-fiction, as might a large chunk of the material in this project.

The letters written by Amanda Duncan to Annie Gull are those written (with alterations) by Lady Hope Simpson in *White Tie and Decorations* (University of Toronto Press, 1996), its author, Peter Neary, being the author's first cousin (once removed). Lady Hope Simpson, too, is a relative of the author, although farther removed.

The newspaper article detailing the death of Junior Hawco is reprinted with permission of the *Toronto Star*. Although it details an actual event, the article, once copied in this book, becomes an incident of supposed fabrication, thus erasing it from the confines of reality and reinstating Junior Hawco's fictional life.

The words spoken by the man on the soapbox at the hanging of Mary Snow were lifted, practically word for word, from a newspaper commentary printed in the *Royal Gazette and Newfoundland Advertiser*. Only one word has been changed, where the author substituted 'ideal' for 'exemplary.'

Patrick Lambly/Hawco's poems, while partially the design of the author, have lines inserted here and there, where fitting, from the long-dead master poets of Ireland along with snippets from Patrick Lambly/Hawco's writings which were discovered in original documents collected at the Centre for Newfoundland Studies at Memorial University.

Within the book, there is a plethora of such transcomposite meldings. To describe each one would mean to impinge unnecessarily upon the reader's time and thus tax his or her patience.

A slew of academics and scholars aided the author in the re-creation of various periods and settings. They will remain unnamed, as the author does not wish to embarrass them by misrepresenting a lifetime of facts collected and provided. The author hopes they will forgive him for mending the truth to suit his needs.

The above method of writing has been employed so that, as the years rise toward the actual year (2042) when the author is committing these words to paper, more and more of what has been recorded in this book will align with plausibility. In fact, there is only one day in which the underlying premise of this book becomes sound – January 22, 2042. On any other day, this book simply is not.

Jacob Hawco IV
New Bareneed
January 22, 2042

Kenneth J. Harvey's novels have met with international critical acclaim, and have won the Rogers Writers' Trust Fiction Prize, the Winterset Award, the Thomas Raddall Atlantic Fiction Award and Italy's Libro del Mare. His works have also been nominated for the Books in Canada First Novel Award and the Commonwealth Writers' Prize, and longlisted for the IMPAC Dublin Literary Award and the Scotiabank Giller Prize. *Blackstrap Hawco* is Harvey's eighteenth book. He lives with his family in a Newfoundland outport.